WELCOME

TO

BRIDGEBORO

A NOVEL BY

E.J.B.B. BARDSLEY

First printing.

United States Copyright Office Registration Number
TXu 1-294-748 – April 18, 2006

ISBN : 978-0-6151-9247-5

In MEMORY of my PARENTS

Edna Marie (Cliver) Binder and William **Friedrich Binder**

also
William Frederick Bindrim, Jr.
father of Tacy, Mark, Kimberly and Scott

and
Treasurer of The Fischer & Porter Company

ALSO
Kermit Fischer, President of The Fischer & Porter Company
in Hatborough, PA

IN RECOGNITION of

Nathan Roberts, my ancestor born and raised in Bucks County, PA, who assisted in the establishment of American Independence during the American Revolution War, serving from 1776 to 1783. Nathan joined the Bucks County Battalion Flying Camp, under Captain John Jamison and Colonel John Lacey. He was among the 11,000 patriots encamped at the 18th century **Moland House** and its neighboring fields along the Old York Road and the Neshamini Creek where General George Washington and his officers headquartered from August 10 to 23 in 1777, one month prior to the Battle of Brandywine. Here Lafayette and Pulaski joined the Continental Army.

Nathan fought in the Battle of the Billet (north of Hatborough) and in the Battle of Trenton.

And a salute to my home town

ACKNOWLEDGEMENTS

-*Mahalo* to Dr. James Bardsley, my patient and enduring husband, for his support and encouragement.

Jon Michael Miller.
thanks muchly for caring and sharing your time and energy to show me the way down the road of success, which you already have traveled.
Covers designed by Jon Michael Miller

Photo of the author by James Bardsley

Credit for the cover picture to – COVERED BRIDGES in PA, for the picture of Bartram Covered Bridge, 85 feet long and built in 1869 by builder Ferdinand Wood. The bridge in claimed by both Chester and Delaware Counties in PA. as it spans the stream named Crum Creek, west of Newton Square, near Goshen Road in Chester County, Pa. It is privately owned.

AUTHOR'S NOTE

-I first began to write this story 50 years ago! I wrote it in long hand while my children were taking naps. During the next 47 years I carried the damn thing around with me in a metal box, while moving 20 times. Now I have it in my computer and on a disc. BUT I got sidetracked with writing *Vision Quests* and *Pseudonyms* and my memoirs, *Looking in the Rear View Mirror.*

-Finally I took another look at the manuscript and realized unless my name had changed to James Michener, no one would be interested in a 900 page novel! I began the task of cutting 300 pages, and still having it make sense.

-So, if anyone likes the story enough to want more, the first person who calls may have 300 pages of outtakes, free of charge.

OUTWITTED

He drew a circle that shut me out –
Heretic, rebel, a thing to flout.
But Love and I had the wit to win:
We drew a circle that took him in!

Edwin Markham

FACTS from *Bucks County Town & Country Living* magazine –

Spring 2004 issue -
"At one time, thirty-six covered bridges stood in Bucks County. As of 2004, twelve remained. In the old days, most covered bridges were left unpainted. Or were simply whitewashed. No doubt the early Pennsylvania German residents added a splash of color "just fer nice."

So why were wooden bridges covered in the first place? Discount any tall tales and fanciful stories you may have heard. Bridges weren't covered to keep off the snow. In fact, officials would sometimes pay a local farmer to "snow the bridge", that is, plow snow across the bridge to accommodate sleds and sleighs. Covered bridges were built for a completely practical reason. A roof over a bridge protects the supporting timbers from rot as they are exposed to the cycle of rain, snow and sun. The pragmatic forefathers covered the bridges because they would last longer.

In this increasingly anxious world, covered bridges offer a timely, reassuring reminder of the value of craftsmanship, honest labor and integrity."

Note from the author – In this novel, the covered bridge referred to is a tribute to the South Perkasie Bridge which enjoys the distinction of being the oldest covered bridge in Bucks County, built in 1832. Rather than lose a part of their history, Perkasie residents began a campaign to save the bridge and relocated it to dry land in Lenape Park, about a mile north of its original site.

Also by Elaine J. Bardsley

VISION QUESTS
PSEUDONYMS revised as NAMES
LOOKING IN THE REAR VIEW MIRROR - A Memoir by EJBBB

And look for   CHEATED   which will be published in 2017   -

INTRODUCTION

WELCOME TO BRIDGEBOROUGH - Founded 1720
Here was fought the famous battle of Neshaminy Creek in 1776. Captain Nathan Taylor, who led the troops of the Continental Army to victory, was mortally wounded. He is buried in the cemetery of the Warwick Presbyterian Church in Hartsville.
Sponsored by the BUCKS COUNTY HISTORICAL SOCIETY

Approaching Bridgeboro from any of the four directions one would pass such a sign. The Battle of Neshaminy Creek had been an important event in local history. Now, more people paid attention to the principal stream in Bucks County which passed through or formed boundaries of eleven Townships, one being the southern boundary of the Borough. It flowed, narrow and deep or wide and shallow, through open fields, county parks, the campus of a Community College and between housing developments and industrial parks, until it emptied into the Delaware River.

The original name of the creek was *Neshaminehanne,* translated meant the creek of the *Neshamine* Indians who had drank from the spring water and lived along its banks for hundreds of years. First the Dutch and Swedes settled along the Delaware River, followed by the English, all of whom claimed the land for their own use. Even William Penn helped to "grant" the land away from the First People of Pennsylvania. It was a bitter lesson for the Indians to learn that one must never trust a "friendship" handshake. Not even with a Quaker!

The Delaware Nation began to experience dramatic changes in their cultural traditions and lifestyle from the time of the very first contact with the Europeans. The tradition of owning land directly impacted where the Lenape Indians had been living for over 400 years! It caused many moves from their homes in Pennsylvania, New Jersey, New York and Virginia. The Delaware (Lenape) Indians worked diligently to restore traditions, within their own communities, while saving and sharing their history with the local encroaching communities.

Bridgeborough had been named for a covered bridge which took Bridge Pike across the creek. General George Washington and his

1

Continental Army had used the Neshaminy Bridge when he led the troops north, following the unpaved Bridge Pike. They were on their way to *The Moland House* where the General would meet with the Marquis de Lafayette who had brought financial aid from France. Also, the Polish Count, Casimir Pulaski who would later be known as the "Father of the American Cavalry".

It was a known fact when the post office opened, the original name used was Bridgeborough. But in 1880, Postmaster Howard Paist changed the name to the shortened version to save space on cancellation marks.

Tools, hunting and fishing equipment and shards of pottery left behind by the Delaware Indian Nation and the Lenape sub Tribes, were still being unearthed. Muskets, cannon balls, clay pipes, buttons and even scrapes of clothing still wrapped around human bones were artifacts of the Revolutionary and the country's first Civil Wars. Because of the large collections of artifacts, a Bridgeborough Historical Society had been founded.

The Public Library was founded in 1752 but not erected until 1850. The first shipment of books had arrived from England in 1756 but housed in the private home of an acting librarian.

A large wing had been added to the original Bridgeborough Public Library itself. An auditorium, smaller meeting rooms, restrooms, cloak rooms, a children's wing, and the museum resulted in an impressive building which made the citizens of Bridgeborough pleased and proud. Peering through display cases, studying the pictures and maps on the walls and listening to volunteer docents, one could be impressed with the role Bridgeborough had played in the history of, not only picturesque Bucks County, but also in the history of one of the original thirteen colonies before it became the Commonwealth of Pennsylvania.

Next to the library was another feature of historical significance: the original wooden covered bridge, reverently relocated after it had been replaced by a four lane concrete bridge to span the creek. Any culprits who dared to carve or spray paint the aged lumber and were caught, saw their name in *The Bridgeborough Courier* and paid a hefty fine.

ONE

THE BEGINNING

RICHARD LIVINGSTON was ecstatic! His cup of happiness was running over. He had something Bill Fischer did not have. *He* had a son!

He was in his office of *Courier Newspapers* in Pennsylvania when his father-in-law called from the private hospital in Virginia.

"Congratulations, Pop. You can pass out cigars. A nurse just told us Bernice had a boy."

As usual his father-in-law's southern accent annoyed him but he forgot it as he heard the mother and child were fine and Richard must assign somebody to take care of his little paper business and "hurry on down". And oh yes, thanks for letting the first grandbaby be born in the land of his southern ancestors.

Richard did remember to say, "Give Bernice a kiss for me. And I'll call her tomorrow."

If only he had *not* called Bill and Julie Fischer to brag. If only he had not gone to *The Pub* to spread the news.

The following morning, he still was in bed when the next call came. It took him many seconds to find the telephone. Too many toasts. It was Doctor Valentine calling from the hospital. Mr. and Mrs. Rolfe asked him to call.

"Yes, I'm afraid something is wrong. ...No, your wife is all right. She's still sleeping off the pain med I prescribed. But, I'm afraid she's going to be upset when I have to tell her the sad news. It has been confirmed that your son has Down's Syndrome."

Richard asked, *"What* is that!?"

He was told it was a congenital chromosomal abnormality referred to as Trisomy 21. The syndrome also was referred to as Down Syndrome so named after the English physician, John Langdon Down, who had discovered the abnormality.

Richard demanded, *How about more tests?* The answer was that it was quite apparent, by just looking at the baby. He had the broad flat face, thick tongue, slanting eyes, short neck and short fifth fingers. Other signs would become apparent as the baby developed. After a distraught Richard heard it could not be *cured,* he wanted to know

3

whose fault it was? He was certain that no relative in his family looked like that!

The doctor explained Bernice's parents wanted him to suggest the baby be "put away". Because there also would be some mental disabilities and they did not think that Bernice and Richard would want the child to be a visible member of their family. Perhaps he could remember the Germans had an euthanasia program for these kinds of babies? And the adults who had lived past childhood.

The doctor would take the baby from the hospital to a private home for "special" children. He promised the baby would be well cared for. The home did require a flat entrance fee. Up front. To cover the child's expenses. The current fee was one hundred thousand dollars. And, if the child lived beyond twenty-one years, there would be an additional fee.

Richard asked for Bernice's room. The private duty nurse promised to tell Bernice her husband had called. He was glad he would not be with her when she learned she had given birth to a defective baby. He was concerned about Bernice but he was more upset about what they were going to tell everybody in Bridgeboro? Of course they could decide to announce the baby had died! He would put a notice in the Obituary section of his daily newspaper, *The Bridgeboro Courier.* And where was he going to get the money for the private home? To hide their family secret!

Bernice would not discuss the idea the baby had died! He hadn't told anybody, had he? He must let everybody, especially Bill and Julie, believe the baby was just fine. And she must have a baby boy in her arms, to show everybody in Bridgeboro!

"Or I won't come back!" she yelled into the phone. Immediately before she hung up.

After several days of receiving cards and gifts Richard was beside himself. Over the phone, Bernice insisted she was going to have the baby christened Richard Arthur Livingston, the Fourth. Before he was placed in the home. He insisted he did not know why she needed a baby. It was as though he was on a scavenger hunt. Finally his thoughts fell into the theme of *the hell with her and her parents.* Let her father pay to have little Richie, as she was calling their son, put in the private home. Let Bernice stay in Virginia! With her damn Confederate family.

Next he received a phone call from Doctor Poole. He was a psychiatrist. He claimed Bernice was on the verge of an emotional breakdown. Surely Richard could locate a baby. Hadn't he called any Adoption Agencies? Maybe their family doctor knew about the "gray market"?

Richard went to The Pub where he had several martinis. He decided instead of returning to an empty house and more phone calls, he would go for a drive. Maybe smash into a tree? Maybe he should collect some clothes and cash and begin life anew? Anything sounded better than what he was experiencing. He felt as though *he* was having an emotional breakdown. Being pushed and pulled by all of those crazies in Virginia.

Suddenly, several miles north of town, through the mist of his subconscious, he saw the sign. THE HOME FOR LOST LAMBS - ORPHANAGE of THE CHURCH of THE GOOD SAMARITAN. Good god! It was like an omen. He would be a fool to ignore it. He stopped in front of the several large two story buildings and observed a large fenced in playground and a baseball diamond.

If only he had a crystal ball. He almost wished his mother, Bertha Rebecca Livingston were alive. Maybe her spirit was reaching out to him? She had attended that church. How could he forget everything that ever happened in her life was "the will of God".

Some of the kids had to be babies. Baby boys!

The next morning Richard called Brother Conrad. The Director remembered Richard's mother and that she had been a faithful God fearing member who spent many hours as a staunch volunteer, cleaning the Church. And especially the kitchen. They met and Richard poured out the entire story. Occasionally his eyes filled with tears. Brother Conrad promised, in recognition of his mother's service, Richard could depend on him to keep the request a private one.

The Home was licensed for fifty children but the only infants available were two girls. However the medical staff was waiting for two teenage girls to give The Home their illegitimate babies. For adoption. They lived in Taylor Park, the government housing project. The unknowns were the overall health and sex of the babies. Richard was certain he should gamble. It was the will of God. And he could tell Bernice he was trying to find her a baby.

Richard was not ready for Bernice's reaction to his good news. First she cried. Then she wailed. Didn't he realize *that* was Earle

Phipps' church? Brother what's-his- name would tell Earle who would tell his sister, Julie and brother-in-law, Bill Fischer. Next she became hysterical. Richard hung up. After several more drinks, he decided he would call her again, to tell her to stay the hell in Virginia. And that he wanted a divorce. But he became glad he didn't. Call her.

Just as he remembered December 7th, 1941, he remembered the day Earle Phipps called him.

Bill Fischer *was dead!* He had died in a fire trying to save Earle and Julie's sister, Vicki Lynn Phipps, at Deer Lake Manor. He did ask about Julie. Earle said she was in shock. And she had been medicated.

Richard wanted to be the one to tell the news to Bernice. To make her sob again. Just as many other women in Bridgeboro, married or single, he knew Bernice had been attracted to Bill. He always referred to Bill as his best friend, ever since they had met in their sophomore year in *Bridgeboro High School*. But the truth was he was more than jealous of Bill's good looks, being a star in any sport he played, his being a hero during World War Two and especially the fact he had inherited and was the president of the international multi-million dollar Fischer Company. All Richard's father had left him was a newspaper business. He knew he could never be as popular as Bill but why couldn't he be as financially successful!

He made contact with Doctor Poole. Bernice was not permitted to talk to Richard. Richard smiled as he explained Bernice should know their dear friend was dead. The psychiatrist said he would decide what was best for her.

For hours Richard pondered. An idea gained momentum until he made a decision. He would become solicitous to Julie. He must convince her how much compassion he had for her. He must court the widow of Bill Fischer and take the place of her brother, Earle Phipps. He would make her emotionally dependent on him.

Without giving any consideration to the consequences, Richard wrote a letter. The letter of sympathy became a love letter. Richard went to Earle's house, where Julie was grieving from the death of her husband and sister. He gave the letter to Julie's sister-in-law, Alice Phipps.

Richard tried, too many times, to contact Julie. Each time either Earle, Alice or Doctor Philip Rexinger told him calls and visits were forbidden. Finally he asked if Julie had read his letter of condolence? "Yes. And Julie said it did not require a response."

How could she make light of his sincerity? How dare she spoil his plans!

It was during the hours of emotional turmoil with his thoughts flipping back and forth between Bernice and Julie that Brother Conrad called him. A baby boy had been left on the porch of the church and one of the promiscuous teenagers had moved from Taylor Park. The baby was healthy and their name was next on the list. The baby could be theirs!

He agonized over what to do. Was this a sign he should remain with Bernice? Give up trying to make contact to console Julie? What was more important? Raising an unwanted child or trying to overcome obviously being ignored? He decided that it must be *the will of God!*

Finally he called Bernice. Yes! Bernice wanted the baby!

He told Brother Conrad in addition to paying the required expenses, he would make a contribution to The Home. In exchange for consideration and cooperation that the records of the adoption be buried…deep. Bernice should not learn what a "common" background their baby had.

He drove to Virginia to visit *his son*, Richard Arthur Livingston, in the private institution. They returned to Bridgeboro where he and Bernice would receive their welcomed baby from *The Home for Lost Lambs*. Then Bernice would show off her baby boy.

RICHARD lived in continual fear that somehow, someone would learn about "their secret". Even though Doctor Valentine had issued a birth certificate recording Bradford Ratcliff Livingston was born in Virginia. And even though a lovely announcement documented he had been christened in the same Episcopal Church where all members of the wealthy and well known Rolfe family had worshipped. Still Richard believed they should tell Brad the truth. He had a retarded brother. And he had been adopted!

They both had been unwanted by their biological parents!

TWO

DON'T YOU DARE tell anybody the baby is dead! I won't come back if I can't have a baby boy in my arms!"

Bernice appeared to be sleeping while Richard drove her back to Bridgeboro, but she was reviewing the last ten months of her life. She had turned her head toward the window to keep Richard out of her sight. She had developed a knack for recovering from unpleasant situations because she could escape from reality.

She remembered yelling those threats to Richard. She knew her parents were aghast at her outbursts and the doctors had found it difficult to communicate with her. But there was no one to tell why she insisted she needed a baby boy.   And there no one who would understand why she had to recover from cancelling from Plan A and immediately go to Plan B. And why a baby boy would help her to survive.

Again . . . she began to review why she had married Richard in the first place. Yes, she was impressed by his expensive gifts and promises for a rosy future. He was more experienced in sex and after allowing him to go *all the way* she believed she was *in love* with him. Over the objections of her parents, Bernice insisted she was going to marry Richard Arthur Livingston, the Third. Had it been rebellion or that she wanted so desperately to spread her wings, as her sisters had done, that she would dare to marry a damn Yankee!

She was the oldest daughter. Her father actually had told her he was annoyed when he learned his first child was not a boy. Trying to please him she became a private school and college tennis champion, a swimming champion and an accomplished equestrienne. While she was busy upholding the family's name at the *Ten Oaks Country Club* of Richmond, her two sisters became charming popular southern belles. Eunice, the middle sister, became engaged to a handsome officer in the Marine Corps. Elizabeth, the baby sister would answer only to Eliza with their family and to Signora or Viscontess de Manzoni to her servants and trades people. She had defied their parents by marrying a recorded   Italian nobleman who was a *Catholic.*

After several months of marriage Bernice became disappointed. Bridgeboro was extremely different than her beloved South. Revolutionary War be damned! Continental Army be damned! No one in the godforsaken town cared there had been a Civil War. No one cared her relatives had been officers in the Confederate Army. And they had made their fortunes from tobacco and brood mares and stallions.

The citizens were unrefined. Richard's promises were not materializing. Except she did convince him to buy her a lovely colonial house, built in 1799. Still she had to do the cooking. And the black cleaning lady came only three days during a week. And to help them entertain.

Their lovemaking was a disappointment. Richard was too demanding. Everything was wrong! She was going to insist he sell his little newspaper business and move to Virginia. Or she would go home, without him. Her family would have to accept the first divorce.

Then one glorious unforgettable evening, Bernice met Bill Fischer. She had heard about him. His success in business was respected and envied. His reputation was exciting. He was mentioned in many conversations. And as Richard introduced Bill as his best friend, he held her hand and bowed. She remembered his dangerous smile and the all-knowing look in his eyes.

She had never felt so excited. So overheated. So giddy. She began to plot and plan. She lost many pounds and changed her hair color and style. She had as many dinner parties as possible, hoping Richard would not become suspicious and put an end to her game. In between parties and seeing Bill in town, she fed her emotions and her longings by pretending. She would attract Bill's attention. She would divorce Richard And *she* would become Mrs. William Fischer.

After Bill introduced Julie Phipps, his secretary, to the dinner group, Bernice graciously included her. Then Julie became Mrs. William Fischer. And Bill bought her Deer Lake Manor as a wedding present. Damn! Damn! Damn!

IT was during an early afternoon when Bernice's life was changed. A still nagging daydream became a reality. After the doorbell rang and she opened the door, there was Bill Fischer!

She was happy she looked so attractive because she still was dressed in the outfit she had worn to a morning meeting. He had some letters for Richard to read and gave no explanation why he had not taken them to Richard's office. Why shouldn't she believe he wanted to see *her*?

She invited him to sit down. She told him she never drank alone but would he have a glass of sherry with her? She told him he looked tired. He blamed it on the overload of business. Also he was worried about his father's failing health.

She would always believe he was depressed. And maybe as unhappy as she was?

They discussed the problems within the *Chamber of Commerce* and the upcoming benefit dance for the *Bucks County Historical Society*. They refilled their glasses several times, as they commiserated while sitting on her red velvet Queen Ann couch.

She lied about her father's poor health and confessed how she missed being near her parents. She sounded sad as she told him she missed her beloved South.

He admitted he still had nightmares about the naval battles he had survived. And he became sentimental telling her how many of his friends had been killed. He hoped he wouldn't have to use the cane forever. He laughed after she told him using it made him look distinguished.

Whenever Bernice relived that day she never could recall who made the first move. But as soon as she was in his arms she did cling to him. And poured out more despair and need for sympathy Maybe at first he was just stroking her and using kind words and healing kisses.

Finally they realized the couch would limit their positioning, so they lowered themselves to the Oriental rug. Bernice yielded immediately. She had not allowed him to make advances without completing her dream. And he would know she loved him.

THE only thing Bernice could hope for was there would have been more than one time. His expertise combined with her lust resulted in Bernice tapping into unexplored emotions and by-passing her self-control. She moaned and gasped and laughed and had her first orgasm.

But attached to the thrilling experience was the unfortunate location. It had been a struggle to remove her girdle and she did get runners in her panty hose. Also she had been uncomfortable on the carpet as Bill thrust his impressive male organ in and out of her. But she had been able to envision their *lovemaking,* as she called it, took place in her bedroom. And she had kept the panty hose and stained clothes in a small suitcase, hidden in the back of her closet. If only she had asked Bill for the handkerchief he used to pat dry both of them. Something she could cherish.

After the afternoon of bliss, she became concerned about becoming pregnant. That evening she even included some foreplay for Richard to remember, before a round of torrid sex.

Several weeks later, Richard returned from The Pub and confided that Bill had indicated he was attracted to another woman. No matter what Richard said, it was *not* Julie's sister, the well-known author. Perhaps Bill hinted it was Vicki Phipps, as a cover up. But Bernice Livingston knew she was the woman Bill Fischer loved.

She did become pregnant. After two miscarriages, did she want to be pregnant? Why not? Before she told Richard, she called Bill and asked him to meet her for lunch. At a restaurant where they would not be recognized.

Never would she forget the look on his face when she told him she was going to have *his* baby! He seemed disbelieving. Even annoyed. She emphasized only the two of them would know. He pulled a pink rose from the centerpiece and gave it to her. He squeezed her hand. "I dread to think what Richard or Julie might do if they ever find out. It must be our special, deeper than deep, secret. I hope all goes well for you." He kissed her hand. "I'll stay tuned in."

During the following months Bernice pretended to herself she was carrying Bill Fischer's child in her womb. Even Richard's proud remarks of "our baby" and "my son" did not disturb her. And after she went to her beloved Virginia to wait out the last two months, she found it easy and comforting to live in her make-believe world. She even convinced herself that as soon as Bill saw the baby, he would want to marry her.

Then she learned she had been carrying what some still called a Mongoloid! Of course it was *Richard's* child. How she hated him. Not only for helping to create a reject but for telling everyone, especially Bill, she had given birth to a boy. She never would confess to Richard she also had given thought to the idea the baby had died. It could be easier to return to Bridgeboro with empty arms.

That was before Bill called her. He wanted to congratulate her and he wanted her to know how pleased he was she had a son. If only she had replied, "The baby died. And it never was your baby." End the make-believe. But Bill immediately responded he was looking forward to seeing her and the baby.

After he hung up, she began to cry. And lament. And insist she had to have a baby boy. She confessed the story to Dr. Poole. He actually told her having a baby to hold and love would be better than medication or therapy.

NOW, eighteen years later, Bernice and Richard had two sons. Richard Arthur, the one she thought of as Richard's retarded son. And Bradford Ratcliff Livingston, her pride and joy. Claiming Brad as her son, she was doing Bill a loving favor in remembrance of that unforgettable afternoon when he taught her she *was* a passionate woman. And oh how she dreamed she would be . . . again!

Of course, sometimes Bernice dared to wonder if Brother Conrad may had committed a sin and told Earle Phipps? Or Bill would have told Julie?

She tormented herself wondering *why* he had come to their house. Had he decided ahead of time, to add her to his *hit on* list? He knew she would succumb.

What she thought as lovemaking was just another conquest for Bill Fischer?

THREE

ELIZABETH RHODES stepped off the bus and watched it round a bend in Bridge Pike until it was no longer in sight.

She shifted the school books in her arms and turned to face the opposite direction. Her destination was a house on the other side of the road. Hidden from view. She began to shiver. And not because of the cold damp weather. She was scared! Because she had been gutsy enough to send her a query letter she was going to interview the famous recluse, Mrs. William Fischer.

Beth walked along the side of the two lane highway and arrived at a familiar Historical Marker. She had read the **WELCOME TO BRIDGEBOROUGH** sign dozens of times but decided to read it again. To stall for time.

She stepped away from the sign and peered across Bridge Pike. The house was behind untrimmed bushes and thick evergreens. Newcomers to Bridgeboro generally ignored the driveway of the field stone ranch house. Old timers may drive slower and think, "Haven't heard she's died, so I guess she's still doing a *hole up* act in there."

Bridgeboro's mystery woman was referred to as Flaky Fischer and even Old Sot Julie. It was rumored no one could remember having seen her in person since her brother, Earle Phipps had died. Two years ago.

BETH knew entering the annual Essay Contest sponsored by the Women's Club would be a challenge. She even had been daring enough to choose *Victoria Lynn Phipps, Noted American Writer of the Twentieth Century* as the subject for her essay. And more daring, actually write to *the* Mrs. Fischer.

Her favorite English teacher, Mr. Stookey, had tried to discourage her because his letters had been unanswered. And she had read that numerous biographers and screen writers had received no response. Mrs. William Fischer would talk to no one about her famous sister, who had died in a fire approximately eighteen years previously.

In a pocket of her wool skirt Beth fingered the letter written on Mrs. Fischer's embossed stationary. After reading the letter in her living room, she had sank to the floor and cried. Making the event sound dramatic, she told several friends she had *almost* fainted!

Now she had the opportunity to win money to begin her college education. Even if she had to attend a state college, her dream could come true. All she had to do was cross Bridge Pike, and . . . she jumped as the sound of a car horn penetrated her thoughts.

It was Dan Friedman in his antique Ford convertible. He and three classmates yelled as Beth waved. Now he had seen her that close to Julie's house he would ask questions on their Saturday date. "Oh, I changed my mind. After you saw me, I got on the uptown bus and went home. Then I wrote a letter to her saying *thanks* but *no thanks.* "

Dan wouldn't believe her. And Mr. Stookey? He'd tell her he was disappointed. Besides thinking she was d u m b. It was easy for them to pass judgment. They didn't have to go inside that sinister looking house and be alone with Julie Fischer.

ALMOST everybody in Bucks County knew where the *Fischer Company* was located. And since the death of her husband, William Frederick Fischer Jr., Julie was the owner and president. The company was one of the largest manufacturers of industrial measuring and recording instruments and glass tubing in the United States. Government contracts during World War 11 and the Korean Conflict had given employment to more than three thousand people from Bridgeboro and the surrounding areas. Approximately eight thousand more employees worked in the twelve branch offices throughout the United States and in the six subsidiary companies throughout Europe, Great Britain, and Mexico. The big rumor was there was going to be an initial public offering of stock! Many were waiting and ready to buy.

Beth also had read that Julie was a member of a Mideast Real Estate Partnership which invested in shopping malls, apartment complexes and a new Ivyland Industrial Park outside of Bridgeboro. Only her estate planner and attorneys knew of her investments in addition to what she had inherited. It was rumored the Fischer estate was worth multi millions of dollars.

BETH forced herself to cross Bridge Pike. As she paused for another deep breath she observed how the drive disappeared behind a stucco wall of the garage. Bordering the wall was a flower bed; a grave for dead rose bushes. Her heartbeats pounded behind her eardrums. *Daddy. Help! I'm being a scaredy- cat. She's just another human being. And you want me to go to college and . . . here I go!*

She almost missed the flagstone path, hidden by weeds. Branches of large wet yew bushes slapped her face and a wild vine grabbed at her wool skirt. She could not see Bridge Pike. Pausing on a large cracked cement patio she thought she saw a blind move in the bay window. Should she use the brass knocker or the bell button? She banged the knocker. Forcefully. The impact opened the door.

Beth heard someone coughing. "Mrs. Fischer? It's Beth Rhodes."

A barely audible voice commanded, "You're supposed to come in."

Beth entered a large foyer. To her right was a mirror over a dark wood table. She was so nervous her own reflection startled her. She closed and leaned against the door and squinted down a long hallway. Four closed doors were on her left and closed louvered doors at the end.

She wanted to leave.

"Wherever you are, I'm in the living room. Just keep walking until . . . oh, there you are."

She saw the woman slouched in a wing back chair. "You shouldn't leave your door unlocked."

"I knew it was you. Come over here. So I can see you."

Beth stepped closer. She knew she was being critiqued.

"So. You're the young lady who wants to know *all* about my sister?" Leaning forward, Julie extended her right arm. "How do you do."

Beth grasped the cold limp hand. Just as a camera, she made an instantaneous picture of Julie Fischer and thought, *so thin and pale. Mr. Stookey says she's in her forties. Reminds me of somebody on TV. Or a picture of a bag lady. Hard to believe she's so rich and looks so awful.*

She smiled and said, "How do you do, Mrs. Fischer. I'm happy to meet you. Thank you for inviting . . . letting me come to interview you."

"I'm sure you *are* happy to meet me, Elizabeth." Julie pointed. "Put your jacket on the back of that chair."

Beth put her books and drawstring bag on the seat and slid out of her vinyl jacket. She forced another smile. "I'm really known as Beth."

Julie pointed to another wing back chair. "Sit down. Relax."

Beth remembered she needed a pen and a notebook. Her hands were shaking as she searched in her drawstring bag. She hoped Mrs. Fischer couldn't detect how nervous she was.

Beth appeared to be taller than she really was because she had such good posture and held her chin so high. At first impression she appeared too thin, although her legs were shapely and her bosom appeared to be oversized. The eighteen year old could not be termed beautiful but she could be considered attractive. Her full lips made Julie think *sexy* while the sparkle in her eyes suggested *spirited.* Julie also noticed the sprinkling of freckles on the perfect nose and the dark mole on the left side of Beth's upper lip. She was trying to decide what the teenager's appealing feature was, until she realized it was Beth's hair. The color was shiny black and there was an obvious natural wave which was highlighted because the teenager wore it shoulder length with heavy bangs. The shine was so apparent it truly was Beth's crowning glory.

After the girl settled in the chair, Julie Fischer sighed. Loudly. Now they were facing each other from opposite sides of a field stone fireplace.

Next to her chair Beth observed the dark wood round table with a brass lamp. There also was a brass frame, with two serious people looking at her, dried flowers in a brass vase and a brass key, a reminder of old doors with large brass locks. Julie had a matching table next to her. Another brass lamp, a box of tissues and an empty glass.

Beth looked directly into Julie's eyes. And smiled. "Okay. My first question is…"

Julie coughed before she said, "Some people call your mother Lizzie."

"I call her, Liz." She wanted to change the subject. "Don't you have any cough drops?"

"You could get me some water." Julie pointed a long thin finger to a wide archway. "The dining room is that way and then you'll see the kitchen."

Beth stepped to Julie's table and picked up the glass. Besides the tissues, she observed metal rimmed glasses. She gave a quick smile to Julie before she turned to the wide archway between the impressively spacious living room and a large dining room. She quickly observed a large oval table with chairs pushed around it and a breakfront against the hall wall. She noticed the silver service and candlesticks all

16

reflected in a large framed mirror. A large china closet was filled with dishes and glasses. Beth decided if the blinds were opened the room could be radiant. Instead of dismal and gloomy.

After Julie coughed again Beth suspected she was being watched. She stepped into the long hallway. Opposite the dining room was a partially opened door. She looked inside to what appeared to be an office. At the end of the hallway were louvered swinging doors opening into a large kitchen, brighter than the living room and dining room because the shades at the casement windows over the double sink were rolled up to the cornice boards. And four windows in a bay area surrounded a table and four chairs. Beth was used to a cluttered house because Liz was not a housekeeper. Not even a homemaker. However, as Beth observed the kitchen in the impressive ranch house, she wondered if her mom would be able to work in it?

Newspapers covered the table, chairs and window seat. Jars, cans and boxes cluttered the counters. Soiled dishes, glasses and silverware filled the double sinks. She looked into a laundry room and saw clothing piled on top of the washing machine.

As she rinsed the glass she peered through the casement windows and noticed a variety of birds flying close to the house because . . . oh there it was. A bird feeder. Who fed them? Julie? Probably the legendary black handyman, Sam Carpenter. She wished she had a bird feeder and then warned herself, *Hey, I'm supposed to be getting water.* She took ice cubes out of the freezer and filled the glass with water. Reluctantly she returned to the living room.

After several sips Julie leaned back in her chair. "Thank you, my dear."

Beth surprised herself blurting out, "I hope you're seeing a doctor. I mean, shouldn't you be taking some medicine?"

Julie shook her head. "It's just a chest cold. It'll go away. But thank you for your concern. I get lots of colds. And I still live. I got this one because of all the damp weather we've been having. Don't you think we've been having a lot of damp chilly weather?"

Beth stepped back to sit in her chair. "It's still winter. In fact, we may get snow later this week. And, it is chilly in here. Besides being . . . kinda dark."

"If you're cold put that afghan around you. And you *can* turn on the table lamp." Julie gave a deep sigh. "As soon as you leave I'm going back to bed. I have a down filled comforter and it keeps me very warm."

"You mean you got out of bed just because I was coming?"

"Yes I did, my dear."

"I really appreciate being here but you should have called the school and left a message for me to come after you feel better."

"I decided we might as well begin today. I want to get these visits over with as soon as possible. No matter how awful I feel."

Beth knew she could become unnerved. Rumors were Julie was strictly off limits. Except to Sam Carpenter and his family. No amount of cajoling nor bribery could persuade Sam, nor his relatives, to tell anyone what they had seen or heard in Mrs. Fischer's house. Beth had tried to coax some information from her only *colored* classmate, Sam's granddaughter. Besides being beautiful, Ann had a lovely contralto voice which was helping her become recognized for gospel singing. And she refused to discuss Julie Fischer.

As Julie blew her nose Beth tried to analyze the woman's attitude. Was she wielding her power? Was she attempting to seek gratification? Beth sat tall and reached into her skirt pocket. "I have your letter so I can confirm the dates you gave me." Her own forwardness was out of character but she was going to make Mrs. Fischer live up to her written agreement. She was going to write the winning essay.

Don't let her throw you off balance. Just smile back. Daddy, I always remember you said to be humble but courageous, for a faint heart never saw its dream come true. Beth thought of her father whenever she had a problem. He had died from cancer two years ago but Beth felt as though she had been with him just days before. Even the night before. In her dreams.

Beth picked up her pen. "At what age did your sister...." Julie began to cough.

Trying to sound concerned Beth asked, "Do you want more water?"

Julie held out the glass. "Just fill it halfway. I'm going to put some of my own medicine in it." She reached behind the chair and held a bottle of Scotch. "You won't care if I have a little drink, will you?"

Beth took the glass. "I hope it will make you feel better."

Hurrying through the dining room she felt frustration kicking in. She had heard of Julie's drinking reputation. All Beth could picture was Julie using her cold as an excuse and becoming a mush mouth, or passing out. She began to feel bitterness toward Vicki Lynn's sister. *Daddy, I remember Never judge others until you've walked in their moccasins for two weeks.*

After Beth returned and handed Julie the glass, Julie poured Scotch over the ice. "I'm sure you're used to people who drink."

Beth knew Julie was referring to her daddy. No one could criticize him. Not even another alcoholic. He always would be the tall, thin man who had loved and needed her as much as she loved and needed him. Holding her pen and notebook she remained silent. She could imagine the outcome if she didn't. Julie's sarcasm plus her resentment could mean no interview.

"Just about everybody heard about Norman Rhodes, the Bridgeboro lush. And Liz must come home three sheets to the wind. Working at *Lou's Bar and Grille.*"

"You know quite a bit about my family."

"Uh huh. I even know about your sister, Evan. How's she doing?"

"She's okay."

"I suppose you hear from her? Or is she too busy with her sailor boy?"

"She keeps in touch," Beth lied. "Could we begin with the interview now?"

"Aren't you just a little curious that I know so much about you?"

"Maybe you asked Mr. Jones? Or my English teacher?"

"The principal assured me that you *had* entered the contest. I also decided to ask Geoff Greer. For his input."

Beth almost gasped. Of all people to talk about the Rhodes. That tall lean good looking man who always reminded her of JFK, even though his hair was a darker shade of auburn and he had as many freckles as she did. Inside she smiled as she visualized Geoff's ice blue eyes and his charming boyish smile.

He too had been raised in Taylor Park, two blocks away from the Rhodes. His mom worked in the school cafeteria and his dad had two jobs so that Geoff and his sister could attend college. Geoff had studied law and successfully passed his bar exams. First time. Now he was a Junior Partner in a respected legal firm in Bridgeboro. And a lawyer for the *Fischer Company.* Beth always looked up to Geoff as an example of success and the nicest young man whoever had dated Evan. Because of her stupid sister who had jilted Geoff when she ran away with her "sailor boy" now she might have to fear him.

Julie grinned. "Don't look so worried, my dear. I think he's a damn fool but he says he's forgiven your sister. And he said lots of complimentary things about you. "

"That was nice of him." Beth wiped her nose with a finger.

"Oh dear. I think I've upset you. I always have lacked finesse. I wanted to tell you I know all about you. In spite of your unfortunate background, the fact that you do babysitting and keep house while your mother has to work and so forth, I know you're a conscientious student."

"Why does my background matter? Other than I need to win a contest?"

Julie sipped. "I had to decide if I wanted you to interview me."

"The only person I need to know about is your sister."

Julie nodded. "I thought, *why* should I subject myself to personal questions from some scatterbrain teenager who could be ungrateful enough to blab all over Bridgeboro. And maybe even let busy body Dickie Livingston pump her for some information to put in *The B.C.* about . . . well, about what I look like. And how I live. Especially since nobody has seen me . . . for a long time." She waited.

"I don't even know Mr. Livingston. Besides . . . " Beth pulled a tissue from her pocket.

"Don't get upset. Geoff trusts you."

Even though she felt wary, Beth also felt relieved. "That was nice of him." She pointed the pen to the top of the empty page. "At what age . . . "

Julie took a long drink from the glass.

FOUR

Sorry, Daddy. The first interview went down the drain. So I lied about lots of homework. But who needs that woman to criticize our family? While she gets sloshed. I don't care who she is. I know. I have to try not to dislike her.

As she cursed and lamented about her poor essay, Beth was walking to the bus stop, for the uptown bus. She was going home to Taylor Park.

During the WW11, a privately owned aircraft factory had been built two miles north of the Borough. The United States Government purchased the factory and many surrounding farms. After replacing the office buildings and hangers and extending the runways, it had become *Johnsville Naval Aircraft Station.* Named after the nearest Post Office.

Hundreds of naval personnel arrived and hundreds of local residents became federal employees. Because it had created a housing problem the government constructed Taylor Park. It was originally for married couples who did not mind living in the ticky-tacky one and two bedroom houses. In 1950 the government sold the housing project to a private real estate company. The rent remained low and the standard of living went even lower.

Captain Nathan Taylor, hero in the Revolutionary War, most likely would not have been honored that the community was named after him.

LIZ and Norman Rhodes moved into a two story unit when Beth was one and Evan was almost five. Now Beth and Liz were trying to maintain their *Home Sweet Home,* as a faded picture in the living room reminded them.

Beth got off the bus and walked the two blocks to her house. It had begun to rain so her hair was dripping and her shoes and socks were soggy. But she was happy because Peg Mawhorter, her next door neighbor, had asked her to baby sit while she and a girlfriend went to see the late show of a Marlon Brando movie. That meant more money in her college fund.

And, even better than earning money, Brad Livingston was going to call her.

Beth reached into her handbag to find a folded note. Brad had pushed the typed note through the air vent at the top of her locker. She paused under a street light and reread. *Completely I love you. Forever, it will be that way. Your love is my guiding light, which I must follow night and day. If ever we part, never leave me. Keep me in your heart. Throughout Eternity!*

P.S. My parents are attending a meeting so I'll call around seven.

Bradford Ratcliffe Livingston told her he used to be annoyed because his parents attended so many meetings. Just as Beth felt sorry for herself because she was practically living alone. Now they looked forward to when they could use their phones without being caught. Because Brad was going steady with Jeanne Barnes!

Brad, with his parents, Bernice and Richard Livingston, lived on an acre of choice property on Willow Drive, one of the oldest cobblestone streets in the original village.

Richard Livingston was the publisher and editor of *The Bridgeborough Courier,* one of the most widely read daily newspapers in the County. He had inherited *The B.C.* from his father. *Courier Newspapers Company* also printed other community newspapers, periodicals and maintained a commercial printing department at its plant on Monument Street.

Richard was a member of the Bridgeboro Planning and Development Association, the Bridgeboro Business Men's Association, the Rotary Club, a Mason, a vestryman of the Episcopal Church of The Big Fisherman and a member of the Board of Directors of the Bridgeboro School District.

Bernice Rolfe Livingston was as active as her husband. With a Southern accent, she explained she got her athletic build from horseback riding, and tennis and swimming at the private *Ten Oaks Country Club,* near Richmond, Virginia. And her daddy was a charter member of the club!

She was the current President of the Bridgeborough Historical Society, a member of the Eastern Star, a Rotary Ann and the Newcomer's Club which she helped to found to bridge the gap between the old and the new residents of the rapidly growing community. Another smile and she'd quickly add she was a member of The Board of Directors of the Bucks County Association for Retarded Children, The Bridgeborough Library, a member of the Women's Auxiliary of The Church of The Big Fisherman and a volunteer in the Bucks County Hospital.

Bradford Ratcliffe Livingston was more popular than his parents. Most girls in Bridgeboro High, and even some who had graduated, envied his girlfriend, Jeanne Barnes, the older child of Louise and Charles Barnes who belonged to the same organizations as did Bernice and Richard. They also held the same offices in either the preceding or the following years.

Charles Barnes had played defensive back for Penn State University. Ruggedly good looking he was the president of *Barnes and Associates Incorporated, Reality Executives and Property Managers.* "One Call Does It All" had been his slogan for the fifteen years he had been a Real Estate champion. Business had been so good, that the year before, Lou had convinced him to add "Every Time We Sell a Home, a Child at *Bucks County Hospital* Benefits".

Charlie had become a powerful and wealthy man in the community and he and Lou and Jeanne and her brother, Chuck, lived on one of the most valuable estates in the county. After he and Lou had been married, he had purchased a rundown ninety-five acre farm, with a stone house which had been built in 1770. After fencing off ten acres around the abandoned house and farm buildings, he sold the remaining ground in acre parcels, bedecked with custom built homes. The original house was restored and enlarged, a cabana and pool added. It had become an estate where lively parties and important meetings took place.

Richard and Charles kept busy gloating over their successes and overriding their failures. Their wives were occupied with the popularity of their children and planning their guest lists. When could they listen for anyone in the family who might be crying out ... in silent anguish?

BETH climbed the three steps to the kitchen door. On the top step she turned to observe the shabby condition of the houses and the litter scattered around the small lots. She wished she and Liz could move but, not together.

She opened the mail box and pulled out three envelopes, all addressed to Mrs. Norman Rhodes. Beth smiled. So who would write to her? In the small kitchen she plopped her books on the closest chair and put the mail on the table. She turned on a wall light and observed the jar of instant coffee, sugar bowl and teaspoon beside a used mug. And a movie magazine. Beth found these things daily, a result of Liz's habit of having coffee, smoking cigarettes and devouring the dirt from Hollywood. Beth pulled down the shade. She hung her jacket around the back of a chair and dried her hair on a dish towel.

Next to the sink, on top of a wringer washing machine was a pile of clothes Liz expected her to wash. Beth snickered and thought, *Oh well. It doesn't look as bad as Julie Fischer's kitchen.*

She walked into the pantry, opened a mason jar and shook four sunflower seeds and a peanut into her hand. She found a lettuce leaf in the refrigerator and walked into the living room. After turning on a table lamp she removed a screen cover from a glass aquarium on top of the book case. "Hi, Gerry," she said to her pet gerbil. "Wake up sleepy head. Here's your afternoon snack." She put everything into a metal jar lid and stroked Gerry while he nibbled on his treat.

Beth's bedroom was the smaller one on the second floor. The view was grass plots and clothes lines or beyond to a field, generally planted in corn. Liz's bedroom was larger with two windows overlooking the street and parking areas. A closet size bathroom was at the top of the stairs.

Beth turned on a desk lamp and removed her shoes, socks and skirt. In her handbag she found a key chain with a small silver key. Sitting at a second hand desk, she unlocked the middle drawer and reached into the back. Under a pile of papers, she felt the book.

The diary was a Christmas gift from Peg with a box of stationery she would use, if her sister wrote to her. She decided to keep an account of her last year in high school. And her romance with Brad. The allotted spaces were too small therefore she had taped in so many extra pages the lock no longer could hold it shut.

Beth removed a thick rubber band and found the last page she had used. She began to print. *Met Mrs. Fischer. Told me to call her Julie. Isn't too scary. Has a cold but suspect she forced the coughs. Hope she feels better because I didn't learn anything about V.L. Must write the best essay! Found some aspirin and cough medicine. Heated soup, made tea and washed dishes. Said she agrees with Geoff. I'm nice. Should call Geoff to thank him. I've always liked Geoff... but now, I love Brad.!!*

Beth reached into the desk drawer and took out a senior class picture of Bradford Livingston. She grinned as she read, *Keeps getting more and more handsome. And manly. Even has hair on his chest and has to shave every day!! Love his eyes. His nose is a little wide but okay. Only imperfection is that scar on his lower jaw where he got spiked in that football game he won all by himself. His lips are downright dangerous! And I love to muss his thick brown hair. Looks great in sweaters and tee shirts and anything!*

She propped the picture against the lamp and leafed through her diary until she found a page in the beginning of January. *Brad is everything to me. I want to sound mature 'cause I know what an important thing LOVE is. I don't want to sound like a giddy teenager who thinks she's madly in love with a guy because he's a handsome hunk. Or because she enjoys necking with him. Have to convince myself physical feelings do NOT influence my love. Since Daddy left me, Brad is everything to me. He talks to me, he listens to me, and he needs me as much as I need him. I want to know him all of my life!*

Beth and Brad were in the Drama Club. For the senior play Brad had been given the leading male part and Jeanne Barnes the female lead. Beth was the script girl and female stand-in. At least she was near Brad during rehearsals, even though it was agonizing to watch him give Jeanne the kiss at the end of the play.

The morning of the first performance, Lou Barnes called the drama teacher to report Jeanne was in the hospital with a compound fracture of her right ankle. She had fallen off her horse. In front of their classmates and a full house Beth Rhodes received Brad's kiss. For three nights!

Beth felt lightheaded when Brad whispered in her ear, "Hey, girl. I've wanted to do this for a long time." Later he told her he thought she was going to faint and she said she thought he was teasing. During the cast party, Beth believed what his glances and smiles were telling her.

Brad was first to push a note into her locker. She saved his poems and notes. Not only were they the proof but she enjoyed reading them during her lonely evenings and spells of depression. Her constant reminder was the gold watch he had given her the preceding month. For her eighteenth birthday. On the back of the watch he had the words, Yours 'till the end of time engraved. Of course he had not purchased it from Friedman's Jewelers, which was owned by Dan's father. Brad also liked to tease her that he was dating "an older woman" because his birthday would not be until later in the summer.

Beth was hungry. She locked her secrets in the desk drawer, put on a dry skirt and socks and took shoes downstairs. Walking through the living room she heard Andy Williams singing in Peg's living room. Taylor Park, quickly constructed as inexpensive housing, had two thicknesses of wall board and many coats of paint between each unit. Neighbors had no difficulty hearing what was going on next door. Except in the kitchens, with a walk-in pantry and a heater room between them. Beth heard Peg and Alan Mawhorter argue. And during their parties she could sit next to the inside wall and enjoy the gaiety. Especially the jokes.

Of course she could go to her bedroom that was next to Millie and Di's room. Melissa was almost five and Diane was three, and Beth had suffered with the girls through the measles and bronchial croup. She also had memorized their Sesame Street records.

She tuned into Andy. She was thankful she enjoyed most of Peg's favorite recording artists. After four weeks alone Peg played her records too loudly, wore her bottle blonde hair in outlandish hair styles and used too much eye make-up. Also she went to the movies frequently and shopping with her friend, Gert Connery.

Alan was on a trip. With a degree in Business Administration, he currently was a Systems and Procedures Analyst for The Fischer Company. During the past year he was installing new inventory processing in all of the Sales and Service Offices in the United States and European Divisions.

Peg had told Beth the reward for Alan's extensive traveling had been an impressive salary increase. Several times Beth had told Peg she paid her too much for babysitting. But Peg said she was thankful Beth gave Millie and Di such loving care. Peg also said Alan had told her to begin to look for a new house. It was time for the family to move. Before Millie was ready for kindergarten.

Beth hoped she might be lucky enough to move to a college campus before her neighbors moved. It would be like losing family.

She had finished her tomato soup and grilled cheese sandwich and was reading an English-Lit assignment when the telephone rang.

FIVE

BETH HURRIED INTO the living room. The telephone was on the desk against the inside wall. She was glad the music was at a high volume. She was certain if she listened on her side of the wall, Peg listened on the other side. "Hello?"

"Is this the Rhodes' residence?" Brad asked in a deep sexy voice.

"Sorry. It's *Huber's Gas Station*." Removing the phone from the desk, she slid to the floor to lean against a faded green upholstered couch. She was facing two matching tan chairs placed against the stair wall. A maple end table with a gold glass lamp was placed between them. A yellow glass ash tray filled with butts, waited for her to empty it.

"How did you make out with your first interview?"

"Wellll," Beth dragged out. "We didn't even talk about Vicki Lynn. Mrs. Fischer has a bad cold. She coughed and I fetched water."

"Water?" Brad laughed. "She didn't drink any boooze?" Brad dragged out the last word.

Beth did confide in Brad but for some reason she was going to lie. "No. She said she got out of bed just to talk with me." Why was she defending Julie Fischer? "I'm sure she'll feel better next time."

"Your essay *has* to be the best piece of writing you've ever done! So you don't have time to fool around with that . . . misfit."

"Let's remember she *is* Vicki Lynn's sister. Subject of my essay. And not only did Mr. Jones and Mr. Stookey put in a good word for me but Geoff Greer said nice things about me."

"I told my dad, since he's one of the judges, that she gave you the okay and man, he was really surprised."

"*He* was surprised!" A vision of Dickie Livingston as Julie had called him, passed before her eyes. Thinning black hair, a noticeable five o'clock shadow, a long, pointed nose and black horn rimmed glasses. "You know I've been in shock ever since I received her letter."

"I told my mom too. They used to be close friends with the Fischer's."

Beth tuned in. "How come they're not friendly with her now?"

"Mom said they were, until the fire. And since her brother died, she's just holed up in the house and only Sam and his relatives are allowed in. Mom was in Virginia to have me when the fire happened.

Dad tried to see her but her brother said she couldn't talk with anybody. After Mom came back home, she sent notes and made phone calls but Julie ignored Mom too."

"So you were born in Virginia. When did you move to Bridgeboro?"

"When I was about a month old. Mom just went back to Virginia to have me."

"What's the difference between not being born in but growing up in Bridgeboro?"

"Ah got a *much* better start in life havin' had pure Southern air for ma first breath of life."

"Don't tell me your mother is still fighting the Civil War?"

"Oh, she admits Lee did surrender. Her background is filled with the FFV, that stands for *First Families of Virginia*, plantation owners, meaning lots of money from tobacco, and Army officers, meaning Confederate Army." He paused to sigh. "I just *had* to be born there!" After Beth remained silent he continued in a southern accent. "I'm the first grandchild with Ratcliff blood in me. I was named Bradford Ratcliff after my mother's side of the family.

"In case you might care, my grandmother's ancestor, Bradford Ratcliff was among the first to sail from England to Jamestown. I think on the *Constant*. He was given enough land to develop a tobacco empire in Virginia and with two wives started half of my family."

Brad laughed. "As if you care about any of this hog wash. But just one more tidbit. I really think my mother's father wanted to make up a story about why his name is Rolfe, but he was afraid to lie about being related to John Rolfe, husband of Pocahontas. Too many people could check his story. That's why my name is such a mouthful. Bradford Ratcliffe Livingston. Sorry, but sometimes I just have to tell somebody."

"I'm really impressed. My father was named after his father, Norman Rhodes who had to go to work when he was fifteen. Did you ever know any of your grandparents?"

"My mom took me down to visit my grandfather Ratcliff until he died, about four years ago. My great-grandmother Rolfe died when I was about eleven. So I remember both of them. My mom still makes a couple of trips a year. I guess to see the old neighborhood. And to visit my Aunt Eunice."

"I never knew any of my grandparents. I've always felt sort of cheated. My father talked about his family, especially his mother, but I don't know a thing about my mother's family."

"My dad's mother and father have been dead a long time. They're buried in the Old Trinity Cemetery and my mom goes to the graves. After all she helped to found the Bridgeborough Historical Society and those old Livingston's helped to found Bridgeboro."

"I thought your dad was from a big city. Like, Philadelphia."

"Wrong. My dad lived in that little yellow house on the corner of Montgomery and Church Streets. Jeanne's mother lived down the street and they went to school together from first to twelfth grades. Mrs. B and Dad first met Mr. Fischer in tenth grade but Dad said they weren't as buddy buddy in school as they were later."

"Then Mr. Fischer wasn't from Bridgeboro?"

"His father moved from Philadelphia. And his grandfather lived in Germany."

"But according to what I've read his father started the Fischer Company."

Brad smiled. According to what I've read and according to what I've heard, were Beth's favorite expressions. "Right. From a little machine shop in a garage. And, according to what I heard from Dad last night, the company is clearing millions a year."

Beth remembered Julie in her soiled bathrobe. "Did your parents ever tell you what kind of a person Julie was, before the fire?"

"Sometimes when they're with the Barnes, they get to talking about the good old days and the big bashes they had at the Fischer's estate, Deer Lake Manor. Mr. B. would love to buy it. Even though Julie won't live there, she won't sell it. The old crowd took turns having dinner parties and cocktail parties at each other's houses. And then, the fire."

"Sounds like Julie must have been just like the rest of the crowd. In the good old days."

"Except she was never completely accepted because she was Mr. Fischer's secretary. Like he could have done better. Mrs. B said he won many a game for Bridgeboro High."

"A real jock, huh?" She remembered Julie sipping her drinks.

"Rugged. Handsome. Mom said even the limp and the cane made him more charming."

"He was a cripple?"

"He was badly wounded when his aircraft carrier went down in the Pacific. He was in and out of hospitals and had to use crutches and then a cane. He always limped."

Suddenly Beth asked, "What was your father in? Army? Navy?"

"He worked in the Navy Department. He was 4F because of his eyes and a heart murmur. He couldn't even, ah, go out for sports in school."

Beth longed to tell him *her* father had been a hero in the Army. In Italy. And she had his medals. But she knew it wasn't the time to mention that. Because she wanted their relationship to develop into a comfortable one, she decided to change the subject. "So what about Vicki Lynn? You did remember to ask about my heroine?"

"During dinner Saturday night. Mr. B said she was sexy."

Beth laughed. "And how about your father?"

"He bragged that he had a couple of good talks with her. About philosophy and writing. He said she was, these are his exact words, 'she was a charming and interesting woman'."

"No comments from the women? Or should I assume Vicki Lynn was a man's woman?"

"Mom and Mrs. B. said she was nice. Evidently a little more sophisticated than Julie and it was hard to get to really know her. Whenever she was staying at the Fischer's house she always was surrounded by fans so it was difficult to talk to her alone." Brad laughed. "Of course, I don't know what she and Mom would have had in common. Hey, I'll bet you've gotten more information out of me than you did out of Julie? Right?"

"You are cor-rect. And you know what? It's been more fun, talking with you."

"It's more fun talking with you than anybody else, but Mom did ask me *if* I saw you in school would I casually ask you what Julie Fischer looks like now. Hint. Hint."

For some reason, she did not want the Livingston's to know about Julie. "If you want a handy answer, tell her I think Julie Fischer is a handsome woman. She reminds me of Barbara Stanwyck, in some movie I saw. And I made her some soup and tea and straightened up her kitchen." That should satisfy him.

"You went to interview her. Dad says she's one of the wealthiest people in the whole county. She should have a maid. And a cook."

"I don't think she likes people," Beth butted in.

"That's too bad. Maybe she could get a trained chimpanzee."

"She does like birds. There. That's one thing I found out. She has bags of bird seed in what she calls her mud room. And suet in her refrigerator. She even told me she spends lots of time watching the birds at her feeders."

"So you two have something in common. Birds and a gerbil. That's great."

Beth forced a giggle but she knew having Gerry meant something needed her. Her father had needed her. After he died she struggled to hide her fear and pain. Her mother didn't need her and she never was close with her sister. One day she felt lonely enough to use some babysitting money to buy a gerbil and a glass aquarium. An unexpected purchase that had helped with her recovery. She was needed by something in the Universe.

"How about Betty Wright quitting school?" Brad suddenly asked.

"Because she's getting married."

"Because she's you know what. You had to notice how plump she's been getting?"

"So, she made a mistake."

"Did you get my note?"

"How else would I have known you were going to call?"

"Welllll?" Brad dragged out. "There was more in it than just that I was going to call."

"I hope it wasn't anything important. I think I left it on the bus. Or, at Julie's house?"

"Notice I am not laughing."

"Oh please, Brad. Don't hate me. Pity me," Beth teased. "And, love me. Throughout eternity," Beth repeated dramatically from Brad's note. "Of course I read the poem. It's the only thing that's going to get me through Saturday night. Without a scar."

"I really have to go to the dance. *Bucks County Association for Retarded Children* is Mom's favorite charity. You don't think I really want to go. Do you?"

"Suffer. Suffer. Hey, we'll both have fun. You with Jeanne and me on a date with Danny. You know, if it weren't for him I'd be..."

"Going out with Fred Hoetzel," Brad butted in. He waited. "Well?"

"Well what?" What do you want? An apology?"

"I'm the one who should apologize. For being such a coward. You know I want to take you to the prom…but I just don't think it's the right time to tell anybody yet."

"And I agreed to meet under cover. Or, do you have to cancel Sunday?"

"No. Same place. Around one. Got any ideas about what we should do?" He laughed. "I mean besides making out. Or run away?"

"That would be stupid. We'll find a way. If it's meant to be."

"*If* it's meant to be? Hey, girl, I love you. As Mom would say, ya heah?"

"And I love you. After my daddy died, my grades were awful. Mr. Stookey says they could affect any scholarship money. But last report period he said, 'I don't know what has come over you but I hope it doesn't leave you.'."

"Don't you wish you could tell him? I want to tell someone, I love Beth Rhodes."

"I could have trusted my daddy but Liz wouldn't even believe me. She calls me a dreamer, as it is. While Evan was still living here I almost told her. It was after a football game and you won the game and I thought you were the greatest, and I had this stupid smile on my face and she asked me what was bothering me and I told her I was in love. And I almost told her."

She glanced at her watch. "Damn it. I have to get ready to sit for Peg."

"I have to finish studying for the History test. Eddie and maybe Jim are going to stop in, after they're finished working."

"Where do they work?"

"At the *Stop and Shop Food Market*." They started a couple of weeks ago, as check-out clerks or baggers. I don't think Jim is going to last. Because…under torture, I shall never tell?"

Beth laughed and repeated. "Under torture I shall never tell."

"The other guys think it's a howl but he's messing around with married women."

"Oh, sure. Who told you that fable?"

"He did. He's bragging all over the place. And the other guys claim it's true. I don't think it's more than just flirting as they go through his line. Or if he takes their groceries to their car, but evidently he's pushing it as far as he can. And Jim doesn't need any extra credits to build up his reputation. Believe me anything you've heard about Jim most likely is true."

Immediately Beth visualized Jim Bender. With a physic of long lean straight lines and angles, their classmate was over six feet tall. He had ice blue eyes, thick unruly blonde hair, and a distracting smile. Few females could not be thrilled when Jim winked at them. "How old are the women? If they're just out of high school, even college, then you could...."

"Wrong," Brad interrupted. "Ken says they're old. In their twenties. Maybe thirties. Jim has them *acting* like high school kids."

"According to what I've read, in one of the Liz's magazines, at nineteen a young man is at the height of his sexual desire. As if you didn't know *and* at thirty, a woman is at hers."

"I don't know if I can swallow that. According to what I know about some of our classmates, that's an outdated article. Probably pre *Peyton Place*."

Beth thought about Peg Mawhorter. "I believe it! A woman in her thirties can be bored and restless. She needs personal satisfaction. This article said that a club or charity work can be the answer, but sometimes," Beth paused to snicker, "they find it in a super market."

"What has a super market got to do with a woman's sexual desire?"

"Plenty! But I don't have time to explain now. Have to hang it up."

"Wait a minute, babe. How about doing me a favor?"

Beth smiled. "By when do you need the favor?"

"Next weekend?"

"Well, okay. Since it's you."

"Now, that's what I call real communication. We haven't even mentioned what I want."

"It's something you need for this month's *Bridge*. I told you not to put three editorials in the paper last month. You should have saved one in case you got stuck. As you *are*. Oh well, I'm only the assistant editor."

Brad was the editor of the school paper, *Bridge*. Beth called him an impulsive writer because he wrote in spurts lasting from one hour to one week.

"There wasn't much news last month. And I can't write an editorial about how much I love you."

"Because I'll write your editorial." Beth referred to herself as the plodder type who wrote to convey a message or for a purpose. After some research and an outline, she could write an article on almost any subject.

"I love you, because you *are* you. And I just happen to love your kind of you."

Please Daddy, don't let him be going out with me just because . . . I'll write his editorials!

SIX

TWO DAYS LATER Beth returned to Julie Fischer's house.

In the beginning of the day she felt annoyed having to make another visit to the dreary house, to meet with the trying woman. On the bus she wondered if she was feeling guilty? *Daddy. I guess I should have called her to inquire how she felt? Ask if she wanted me to bring anything? But I didn't and I do have an empty notebook.*

She took quick strides to Julie's driveway and through the overgrown shrubbery. The door was ajar. She pushed it open and called out, "Hello, Mrs. Fischer. It's Beth Rhodes."

She heard a voice tell her, "When the door is unlocked you're supposed to come in."

Beth closed the door and walked into the living room. It appeared as though Julie had not moved since they said good-bye. She was in the same chair. Unkempt. Uncombed hair. Soiled robe. An award winning performance of a recluse.

What concerns Beth had were swept away by annoyance. How could an intelligent woman allow herself to look so appalling? She believed Julie wanted to be miserable.

"I'm sorry I'm not dressed. But I still don't feel too well."

Beth busied herself putting her books on a chair and taking off her jacket. Immediately she felt the dampness in the house.

"I'm sorry to hear that. Maybe if you opened the blinds and let the sun shine in it would help to warm up the house." She felt daring. "Or, you could turn up the thermostat."

"You could build a fire. Sam Carpenter, the dear man who does my shopping and odd jobs around here, has stacked kindling and logs on the breezeway. And there's a pile of papers in the laundry room, right off the kitchen. Sam made me a fire yesterday and it helped a lot. Today, I just stayed in bed to keep warm." Julie sighed and rubbed her hands together. "I just got up a little while ago. Just to look for you."

Without a comment of gratitude Beth walked out of the room. In the kitchen there were glasses and dishes in the sink, an empty soup can and a cracker box on a counter. If Julie wanted to live on soup and crackers, it was none of her business. All she cared about was her essay. She would build a fire and put a pitcher of water by her chair, but she also would squeeze and wring Julie Fisher to talk about Vicki Lynn. Her essay was *all* she cared about.

Beth placed logs and papers on the slate hearth. Julie got up to peer at them. "I forgot to tell you which papers to bring. I'm not finished clipping things out of the other pile." She plopped back into her chair.

Beth wadded sheets of newspaper into paper balls. While Julie coughed Beth worked in silence, but thoughts were screaming inside her head. She quickly scanned the pages hoping to discover what *things* interested Julie Fisher. Julie subscribed to New York and Philadelphia newspapers but only a few had holes where articles had been "clipped out". Mostly from the Business and Marketing sections. Beth concluded if Julie read all of the papers, she at least knew what was going on in the world. But why not? If she was an active president or CEO, or whatever she was, of the Fischer Company, she better know what was happening.

Beth realized the papers with the most holes in them were copies of *The Bridgeborough Courier*. She quickly scanned copies from the previous week and tried to remember what picture or which article might be missing. Liz subscribed to *The B.C.* and Beth read it every evening.

Suddenly, Beth solved the puzzle. Julie was cutting out pictures and articles which included information about the Livingston's. She also was cutting out the same pictures of Brad as Beth was. Several had shown Brad making a basketball shot. One was of the proud Honor Roll students in the Junior and Senior Classes.

Help Daddy. Is Julie Fischer trying to tell me something? Did Geoff Greer or Sam Carpenter see Brad and me together? Julie asked me to make a fire because she's sending me a message?

Beth lit the newspapers and replaced the screen. "I have to wash my hands. Do you want any water?"

"Not yet. Use the bathroom in the hall. I just haven't gotten around to putting the dishes in the dishwasher. And Sam is due tomorrow."

Beth decided to go for broke. "Why don't you have a housekeeper?"

Julie gave a sweet smile. "I *have* a trustworthy cleaning lady. Now go wash your hands."

Besides being in the laundry room and the mud room, while she had gone outside for the logs, she had walked across the breezeway to a door on the side of a three bay garage. Peering through the window in the locked door she had seen a big car parked inside.

ACROSS from the living room, were two closed doors. Beth assumed that since the living room was so large two sizeable bedrooms could fit opposite to it. But Julie would be able to see her open those doors. The third door opened into a large bathroom where she was supposed to wash her hands. But she wanted to see if the next two doors were opened. The first door was closed so Beth hurried to the second one and stepped into a room which was getting daylight from open blinds in large windows. It appeared to be an office. Cluttered book shelves covered two walls while a large desk was positioned in front of a double window. In the middle of the left wall was an opened door. She stepped into the room to view the unbelievable disarray. It wasn't disorderly. It was a disaster. She wondered if the cleaning lady was permitted in that room? She quickly observed the heavy dark furniture, the unmade bed, tossed clothing and scattered mail and catalogues on the long triple bureau and the bench in front of the dressing table.

Both the master bedroom and the office had access to a large bathroom which reminded her she was supposed to be washing her hands. Quickly she returned to the hall bathroom, washed her hands, flushed the toilet as though she had used it and returned to the living room. She walked to the fireplace and poked the fire. Finally she settled in her chair, picked up the notebook and pen and smiled. "I'm ready to begin the interview."

"I hope I can answer your questions," Julie whispered.

Beth knew she should ignore the reaction of the woman and begin the interview. But she remembered some of the things Brad had told her. Especially about the fire. "Mrs. Fischer, I'm sorry talking about your sister seems to upsets you. I think I can understand."

"You wouldn't understand," Julie interrupted, "even if I did try to explain."

"Sometimes it helps to get things out into the open."

Julie shook her head. "Only one thing can help me."

"At least I'm willing to listen."

"That's nice of you but . . . oh, I might as well be honest with you. It's because you admire my sister and I despised her. See, my dear. Already you don't understand."

"I don't know what you know. I admire your sister because to me she was talented and successful. Lots of people have said she wrote some of the most beautiful poetry and powerful novels which have ever been written. But as you said, you knew her as a person. So you're entitled to have opinions which differ from mine."

Julie nodded. "You express yourself well, my dear. Geoff said you were a logical thinker. Yes, I will tell you about the life and career of Vicki Lynn. My famous and award winning sister. As *I* knew her. Then, perhaps you too will understand."

"I'll try," Beth whispered. She pointed the pen to an empty page.

"Even I can't deny that Vicki was a talented writer. But, talented people are not ordinary people. She was the center of attention in our family. First, with her temper tantrums, then with her talents and then of course with her accomplishments.

"There were five of us. Three boys. Edward, Earle and Ellwood. In case you didn't know, this was *Earle's* house. But then came Victoria, followed by July. That is my real name." Julie paused before she continued. "As soon as my parents discovered how well Vicki could read…even before she started first grade, they devoted all of their extra time to her.

"My brothers were older. Ed was thirteen. Earle was ten. And Woody was eight when Vicki was born. So they didn't need as much attention. But, I was the baby. The unwanted baby. My parents made no bones about admitting they were thrilled when Vicki was born. At last, they had a daughter. Her name even meant their victory, so to speak, over nature.

"Then one evening, after too much to drink at somebody's party, my father raped my mother, in the upstairs hall. Imagine, your father doing that? Unfortunately, I was the result. Mother labored long and hard in the heat of a summer day to have me, and named me after the month which had brought her so much pain and bitterness." Julie paused to sigh.

"They should have put me up for adoption. They spent all of their time encouraging Victoria to be the *best* in everything she did. Beyond being jealous, I hated her. She always was in the top ten of her classes. She made every team she tried out for. She was popular in school, in the community and with everybody related to us. And, she was beautiful.

"This was Earle's house, or did I tell you that?" Julie paused and dabbed her nose with a tissue. "After the fire, Earle insisted I come here to live. He always looked out for me. You may have heard that the middle child of a family has the toughest time to develop a position within a family structure. That was true of Earle, although he never complained, he probably felt the lack of attention. I loved Earle the most. And I never loved my parents." Another dab.

Beth watched Julie rest her head against the back of the chair. She watched her whisper, "He's been dead for two years . . . and I still miss him." Then Julie leaned forward and frowned at Beth, as though she was checking on her attention. "Of course I miss Alice too. Earle's wife. She's been dead for...almost eighteen years. She was very kind to me. She may have had the heart attack because she was so upset over what I had to go through." Julie shook her head from side to side. "The fire was an awful experience."

Beth had an urge to scream. She had one page of notes. Could Julie Fischer be so desperate for a sympathetic ear she'd bare her soul to a stranger? Or was there an underlying motive? *Help. Daddy. She's clipping out Brad's pictures!*

Beth tuned into Julie's demanding question, "Did you hear what I said?"

"Oh, I'm sorry. I was thinking about how awful the...ex...perience must have been."

"Please get me a glass and a pitcher of cold water. I need it now. I'm upset. I knew I'd become upset. But I want to help you win that contest. So, I'm going to put a little of my medicine in the water. You won't mind, will you, my dear?"

Beth stood and looked down into Julie's pale upturned face. "I guess not." Walking through the dining room, she thought, *It might get me through this interview. Maybe a few drinks will loosen her tongue and numb her brain enough that I can get her started to talk about Victoria Lynn Phipps. Just don't let her see how frustrated I am.*

She put the glass and pitcher on the table next to Julie. She added a log and poked it into place. From the corner of her eye she observed Julie pour several inches of her *medicine* into the glass. After she added water she swirled the contents with a pointer finger and took a long gulp.

From her chair Beth watched Julie wipe her finger on her robe, smile, lick her lips and seem to relax. She held her notebook and pen to an empty page. "According to what I've read, you have all of your sister's manuscripts. And papers. Is that true?"

"So you've read." Julie took several sips.

"I was kind of hoping you'd give me permission to look through what you have? Not only for the sake of my essay, but because it would be a wonderful opportunity for me to . . . "

"I'm afraid not, my dear," Julie interrupted. "Everything is just stuffed in boxes in one of those rooms across the hall. And it's an awful mess. Really."

"I could help file everything."

"I said, 'I'm afraid not.' It's a lovely offer and I'm sure you're just itching to get your . . . to look at Vicki's manuscripts, but it really isn't necessary. All of her . . . "

"But it *is* necessary," Beth interrupted. "Don't you understand?" Damn, that word again. "You shouldn't just keep such valuable papers in boxes. In this house. According to what I've read, everything Ernest Hemingway ever wrote, is in a vault. In a bank."

"I did put all of her First Editions in a safe place. And her manuscripts and whatever were left in my care. For your information, I *am* the Executrix of her estate."

"If you think I'm not qualified, I know my English teacher would be happy to take an inventory and catalogue everything and then . . . you could give everything to the Bridgeborough Library. Or some college. Even sell it."

Julie laughed. "I don't need money, my dear."

"I didn't mean you needed money. I was thinking of what a crime it is not to share..." she stopped. Julie continued to laugh at her.

"Don't get so excited." Julie emptied the glass. "If I remember, you said I was entitled to have opinions which might differ from yours."

Beth watched her fill half the glass with Scotch before she added water. Again she stirred with her finger and licked it before she took a quick gulp. "My sister's manuscripts *and* love letters don't mean a thing to me."

"Her love letters!"

"Oh, come on now. If you've read so much about your precious Vicki Lynn, then surely you must have read about her *affaire des coeur*?"

"Well," Beth said strongly, "even though she never did marry . . . ah, I'm sure that, well, according to what I've read, she did have a lot of admirers.   I mean, I did read about the actor and the senator and I think there was an English Lord but . . . after all . . . "

"After all," Julie butted in, "the many admirers she never did marry. There's one thing I did. I was married." She raised her glass. "To the man whom every available woman wanted to marry and every married woman wished was her husband. Bill Fischer."

Julie sat taller. Her eyes began to sparkle and she appeared several years younger. "Bill was handsome, well liked and successful. Vicki might have had it all over me as far as her accomplishments but..." she smiled, "he was *my* husband."

Beth could hear the pleasure and the pride oozing from Julie's words.   She thought, *Interesting.   I'm observing a different Julie. Obviously she really loved him but there's something else mixed up in that display of joy.   Smugness?   I'd love to ask her more questions about Vicki's* affaire des coeur, *But why give her more opportunity to ridicule her sister. She's waiting for me to say some- thing.*

Beth decided to ask, "When did you meet Mr. Fischer?"

Julie laughed. "Earle introduced me to Bill. I always teased Earle, that if it had not been for his religion, lots of things would not have turned out the way they did."

Before Beth could interrupt, Julie quickly went on, and on, with the coverage of her family's history. "For some reason, maybe because he was lonely, Earle became involved in attending church. He joined some little break-away group. I think from the Baptists. The papers about it are in that room too. That's the middle room, next to the bath. I've thrown everything that pertains to the Phipps in that room. That was my maiden name...but then you know Vicki's full name was Victoria Lynn Phipps."   She watched Beth nod and quickly added, "And there's some Fischer stuff in there also.

"Earle attended R.P.I. meaning Rensselaer Polytechnic Institute. In Troy.   He received a degree in Mechanical Engineering.   Woody did too. I mean he went to college. He's a school teacher in Albany. We Phipps were born and raised near Poughkeepsie."

Beth had an urge to moan. *Help, Daddy! If only she'd stick to one subject.   No, if only she would shut up so I could ask her some of my questions.   I'm learning something about the family but her thoughts are running wild.   Probably hasn't talked to anyone for so long now that she's started she can't stop. But I want to ask her more about those love letters.*

Again, Beth tuned into Julie's story. She heard Woody had a nice family. His wife was a teacher. They always sent Julie a newsy letter with their Christmas card. And they remembered her birthday. Then Julie stopped talking and reached for the bottle.

As Beth watched Julie mix another drink she warned herself to be careful. She forced a smile before she quickly asked, "Could you tell me more about…" she paused as she noticed the expression on Julie's face. She was being challenged so she decided to finish the sentence by asking, "about your brother, Earle's religion?"

"He attended that church on Bridge Pike, above Warminister. The one that has the home for the old folks and the home for orphans."

Besides a pain in her gut Beth was developing a headache and thinking *Help. I'm still waiting to ask my questions and all I'm doing is watching Fischer get a load on. My poor essay.* "The Church of the Good Samaritan, Mrs. Fischer." If she could keep Julie talking she still might be able to steer her back to Vicki.

"I told you to call me, Julie. I remember telling you that. You better remember."

Before Beth could stop herself, she blurted, "I will. And would you please stop saying, my dear? "Remember my name is Beth."

Julie sounded "Hmmmm." before she began to laugh. Then she began to cough. "See my dear. Beth. I can't even laugh."

"Oh, after your cold goes away you'll be able to laugh. If you want to."

"If I want to! Do you think I enjoy living like this?"

Beth lowered her eyes to the tablet. In her mind she responded, *Then why do you? You have enough money to have a blast.*

She raised her head and asked, "Do you have any more to add . . . about the church? Because if you don't I'd like to ask you about…"

"*You* asked me about the church. I was saying if Earle had not joined that religious group and traveled to Philadelphia for conferences, he wouldn't have met Alice. *She* belonged to that church. So he fell in love, got married and settled in Bridgeboro. Then he got an excellent position with the Fischer Company."

BETH decided to give up trying to change the subject to the story of July Phipps Fischer. Trying to sound interested she asked, "And why did you move to Bridgeboro?"

"To be near Earle. Even though our parents were in poor health, they didn't give me any indication they needed me. While Vicki was away all they talked about was their daughter, the writer. And while she was hanging around the house, they devoted every waking hour to wait on her." Julie studied Beth over the top of the rim. Even though the glass was not empty, she added several inches of Scotch into it and took another drink. "Vicki made slaves of all who knew her. Her personality was as dynamic or, should I say overpowering, as her writings?"

Beth felt elation. "She was a, an . . . an assertive person?"

"Huh!" Julie grunted followed by a cough. "With a strong will and unyielding ambition." She took another deep drink, wiped her chin and declared, "To know my sister was either to love her or to detest her. I found it very difficult to love her.

"Earle understood what I was up against and insisted I move to Bridgeboro. I got a job in a dress shop. I didn't like the job but I was happier than if I had stayed in Poughkeepsie."

Quickly Beth asked, "Where was Vicki living at this time?"

Julie gave Beth a deep dark frown. "Maybe in her apartment in New York City? After she began to make money and meet important people she left mommy and daddy high and dry. She had to have new experiences and make more memories. She became a citizen of the world."

Yeah! Beth felt excitement. At last! She was taking some notes. "I've read all of her poems. I think it's wonderful the way she could describe people. Or a scene. She was a wiz . . . with words. My daddy also read all of her books and he believed Vicki Lynn was the greatest American poet. Of course, we both admired Frost and Sandburg and I just love to read Edna St. Vincent Millay. But of all of them, Vicki Lynn is . . . was the greatest."

Beth became aware she had been rambling. She also was aware her excitement had caused a negative effect. Instead of drawing out Julie, she had caused her to recoil. Her smile faded and the excitement was swept away by frustration, as soon as she heard Julie's response.

"It was nineteen hundred and forty-two when I decided to take a job with the Fischer Company. Earle was climbing the ladder of success helping Dad Fischer run the company and all of a sudden there was Bill, Junior. The company really went to town. Besides making recording and measuring instruments, we branched out into plastics and glass tubing. With subsidiary companies all over the world." She paused and chuckled. "But not in Japan. Or China."

Beth watched Julie empty the glass. She knew she had lost. Julie Fischer did not want to talk about Vicki Lynn. Beth glanced at her watch. She could use the time for having to leave.

"Don't leave yet. Stay and have dinner with me. I have TV dinners in the freezer."

Beth filled her lungs with a deep breath, hoping to keep from fainting. She had been so unprepared, caught off guard, taken aback, by Julie's invitation she was at a loss for a reply. Realizing Julie was waiting for an answer, she said, "Thank you. For asking me. But I have lots of homework. Maybe the next time I'm here?" She closed the notebook and covered the pen point.

Julie leaned forward. "You still need to eat and after all, my dear, I mean Beth, you eat alone and I eat alone meaning, we're both in the same boat."

Beth squinted into Julie's puffy eyes. "In the same boat?"

"Oh, you know what I mean. You and I are alone in this big wonderful world. Haven't you been listening to me? I've been telling you I was unwanted from the moment of my conception. And now, I've got nobody and you've got nobody."

"I don't know about you, Mrs . . . Julie, but I have lots of people in my life."

Julie laughed. Sarcastically. She coughed and laughed again.

Beth felt annoyance. Then fear. Then panic! The name Brad shot through her mind. Had she played right into Julie's hands?

Julie cleared her throat before she slowly and distinctly stated, "You are so naïve. It sounds as though you might believe in Jesus Christ and the Golden Rule. And all of that other crap." Julie put the glass to her lips and tilted her head back.

Beth stood. She must weigh her words.

Julie banged the glass down on the table. "Let me tell you about people. My dear young innocent . . . why, I bet you're even a virgin. Now that's more than we can say about your sister."

"My sister is living in Norfolk, with her husband and anyway, what has Evan got to . . . ?"

"Ha! You mean you believe that too? My god! You'll swallow anything." Julie laughed. Coughed. And tried to laugh again.

Beth wanted to throw the notebook at the woman. And yell, *Shut Up!* Instead, she walked to the chair where her books and jacket were waiting for her.

"Poor you. You even believe Vicki Lynn was some kind of a goddess, when all she was . . . was a god damn bitch!"

Beth took a deep breath. She had to calm herself. Even though she felt unnerved, she softly replied, "I believe she's worthy of my essay."

"She was a bitch! She was a dirty, sneaky, lying whore."

Beth locked her eyes on Julie's. "You can say anything you want to but you'll never change my mind." She picked up her jacket. She had to escape.

"I can't believe you would still admire a miserable bitch."

Beth held her jacket in front of her. "*Who* is miserable? You're so resentful and jealous of your sister, you're the miserable one."

Julie couldn't open her eyes any wider. "Jealous, am I? Of what? Her reputation? Ha!"

"You're jealous of her success. And because she was so admired." And before she weighed her words, she actually added, "And that she got love letters."

"You're walking on eggs, my dear. I won't be talked to that way. Especially by a drunk's . . . " Julie paused and frowned.

Beth was beyond being afraid. Even though she knew she was shattering her dream she remarked, "By a drunk's kid. That's what you're thinking. Right?" She put on her jacket. Looking across the gap between her and Julie Fischer, Beth wished the floor would open up. What could she say next? I hope you feel better. Thanks again for inviting me for dinner. How about, I changed my mind, I will stay for dinner? How about, I'll see you in a couple of . . .

Julie's next remark gave Beth her answer. "Good luck with your essay, my dear. I just decided I don't give a damn what I wrote in my letter. This is the end of the interviews."

Oh my god! Help. Daddy. I really did push her too far. She watched Julie pour scotch into the glass and without adding any water, empty the glass. "I'm really sorry. It's just that…"

"That we have different opinions about my wonderful sister." Julie wiggled out of the chair and stood. She wrapped the soiled bathrobe around her thin body. "And because we have such different opinions, it will be impossible for us to continue. I'm just too sick and tired to..." She appeared to run out of words, or energy to continue.

Beth hated to beg but she knew she had to. "I really believe we can discuss your sister, without arguing. If I can come back I promise I .."

Julie slowly scuffed toward the archway into the dining room. She turned and held onto to the frame. "I do not wish to have any further conversations with you. Make sure the door is closed tightly and goodbye. Beth dear."

SEVEN

AS BETH WALKED down the driveway to Bridge Pike her mind was racing. *Oh, Daddy. How stupid, can I be? Why did I think I could dare to have an argument with the Mrs. Fischer? She hates her sister and now she hates me. I'll just have to use the notes I have and do more reading and...should I dare to go back? Try to apologize again. I'd even kneel on the floor and kiss her dirty bedroom slippers if she'd just say I could continue to... Hey, what time is it? Oh, wow, better hurry to the bus stop. Maybe I'll call her!*

She sat behind the bus driver and studied the wrinkles in his fat neck above his frayed collar. How was she going to explain what she had done to Mr. Stookey? And to Geoff Greer, after he had praised her to Julie. Would she dare tell Brad? Who would sympathize with her when she told them she had been so brazen as to...to what? Blow it. She had really messed up her chance to write the winning essay. Because she had antagonized Julie Fischer. She began to berate herself. By the time she reached the door of her house she was crying tears of hatred toward Beth Rhodes.

She threw her books on a living room chair, her jacket on another and took off her shoes. She turned on the wall lamp in the kitchen and cursed loudly when she saw the mess Liz had left on the table. She pulled down the shade before she went outside to look in the mailbox. Only an envelope addressed to Mrs. Elizabeth Rhodes. Why did she keep looking for something with a Virginia postmark? Evan was never going to write to her. And Evan and Liz said they hated each other.

Beth remembered she had promised Peg she would sit with the girls. She looked at her watch. She wouldn't have been able to have a gourmet TV dinner with Julie after all. Could that be a reason to call her? She could force herself to explain to Julie, *It was a good thing I didn't stay for dinner because I promised my neighbor I'd baby sit. And her husband works for your company. And I'd like to apologize again for saying the things I did. I hope I can come down again. Pretty please?*

As Beth drank a glass of milk and ate stale sugar cookies, she continued thinking, *The fire must have been a rotten experience. But, having to tell me she was unwanted from the moment of her conception. There're millions of kids who are unwanted.*

She gave Gerry some nuts and lettuce and went to the second floor. She washed her face, brushed her hair, applied fresh lipstick and grabbed a sweater. She didn't have time to write in the diary. She decided to take her Literature book instead of the Social Science one, in case she could ignore the television and do some reading. She locked the door before she paused on the large cement step and closed her eyes. Breathe in deeply and try to relax. She had to have an upbeat attitude before she knocked on Peg's door.

Peg was washing dishes. Beth looked at the wall clock and knew Gert Connery would arrive momentarily. They were going food shopping.

She put her sweater on the back of a chair and bumped her hip against Peg's. "I'll finish cleaning up." They both laughed.

Peg glanced at the clock. "Thanks. I was so sure that I'd be on time tonight, but late again. I'll probably be late for my own funeral."

Beth liked Peg. She considered her a good mother and a dependable neighbor. She actually wished they were closer in age and they were girlfriends. She believed Peg would listen to her and besides advice she would teach Beth how to use more make-up so maybe she could look sexy? As if Beth Rhodes could look sexy.

Peg was not beautiful but her upbeat personality was expressed through her eyes. She had the prettiest hazel eyes that any twenty some woman could want to have. She also was a great teaser who emphasized her remarks with a wink. Besides her fun personality, Beth envied Peg because of her bright colored sports clothes which accentuated her shapely figure. That evening she was wearing a hot pink turtle neck sweater, short black skirt and black boots.

"Okay, girls. I'm leaving in a few minutes," Peg said to her daughters who were watching a television program. "See you later and I love ya. You two behave for Beth." She turned to Beth and winked. "Because she knows where the fly swatter is."

Peg and Beth heard a car horn. Peg quickly put on a white ski jacket, grabbed her tapestry handbag and hurried out to Gert's automobile.

As usual, Millie and Di were good. After their favorite puppet show was finished, they played a new block game on the living room floor. Beth knew the girls would be happy if she sat on the floor to play with them but she pretended she was reading. Her book was opened but she wasn't reading the words. She was actually wondering what Julie Fischer was doing? Maybe having a reaction to their argument? Maybe she was sound asleep? Or she had passed out? Maybe she wouldn't remember what they had said to each other and she should call her tomorrow to ask how she was feeling? But, she knew she wouldn't.

Almost two hours had ticked by, when Peg called in the back door. "Hey, Beth. Would you help me with some bags? I'll bring them up to the steps."

Beth put two heavy bags of groceries on the table. Peg carried in two more. She wiggled her arms out of her jacket as she asked, "Can you stay a little longer? "

"You're going out again?" Now why did she ask that way? It wasn't any of her business. And Peg would pay her. And she knew Brad could not call her. Maybe Danny would? Maybe Jill Kennedy, her best girlfriend since first grade. She didn't want to talk to anybody because she might slip and tell them she had had a disagreement with Julie Fischer. "I can stay."

"Gert is coming back. After she puts her groceries away. I'd really appreciate it, if you'd give the girls a bath and put them to bed. They love the way you read to them. Then I can put my stuff away and be ready when Gert gets here. You probably know it can get to be a real drag, being alone night after night so Gert said that she'd have a drink with me. I'd really appreciate it and you can earn a few more dollars."

"Come on, Peg. I don't want any more money, just because I can stay. In fact, I shouldn't take anything for tonight."

"If you're talking about those slacks I gave you, just forget it." Peg began to fold a paper bag. "They were too tight and taking up room in my little closet. At least Liz can use both closets in her bedroom." Peg made a face. "I'm sorry. It's better to share closets with a husband. You know I've gained six pounds since Alan has been on this last trip? All I do is eat junk food, and pout. It's not fair that his boss decided to send him to Mexico. Without me."

"Sounds mean," Beth remarked watching Peg shove a bottle of dish detergent and a box of scouring pads under the sink. "But, who would have taken care of the girls?"

"I'd have taken them with me. Or, maybe Alan's mother would have come to stay with them. She thinks her son's job isn't good for our marriage."

"Really? Okay, I'll take the girls upstairs and put them to bed."

While the girls were in the bath tub Beth heard music. Peg had selected a Sinatra record.

Finally Peg called up the stairs, "Are my cuties ready for a kiss?"

"Come on up, Mommy," Di hollered.

"You can kiss us goodnight, but Beth isn't finished with our story," Millie added.

BETH finished the book which the girls had selected and insisted she had to read *every* page. Since she was sitting on Di's bed, if she were home she could have heard herself reading to them. Through the walls. And, as soon as she returned home, she was going to hear Frank Sinatra singing through the living room wall. For a little while anyway, until she thought she could stop thinking about what had happened at Julie's house and get to sleep. Beth kissed Millie and Di good-night and turned off the table lamp.

Walking into the kitchen she observed Peg mixing a drink. "Want a soda?"

"Thanks, but I have tons of homework. Oh yeah, I almost forgot my book." Beth walked into the living room. As soon as she returned to the kitchen Peg handed her some paper money. "Thanks a lot, Peg." She decided not to unfold the bills because she knew the amount was more than she had earned and she was too tired to argue.

Peg raised the glass in Beth's direction. "It's either vodka or a tranquilizer."

Beth forced a smile then carried her sweater and book to the kitchen door. With her hand on the knob, she said, "Tell Alan I said Hi. See you around."

"Wait a minute." Peg took a sip. "I know it's none of my business, but after all, I did know her. Do you ever hear from Evan?" She watched Beth shake her head. "You know I hardly ever see Liz."

"Neither do I."

Peg stepped up to Beth and put her hand on her shoulder. "You're a good kiddo. Everybody says so. You have to know how we all watch each other and just the other day, Yvonne Wiley and Mrs. Smithers and I were talking," she paused to laugh, "about our neighbors. What else? And Mrs. Smithers mentioned you and we all agreed how good you are."

She paused as if to give Beth an opportunity to say something, then continued, "A teenager living in your situation, has every chance in the world to have other kids in. I'll tell you," she took a sip, "I don't know if I could have been as good when I was your age. I mean, not that I was wild or anything, it's just that everybody is different and you're lucky you like to read so much and..." Peg sighed deeply, "maybe I should get some books from the library? Or knit. It gets to be a drag watching that boob tube night after night. But, Alan called me yesterday to tell me he got a call from his boss. He just got another raise. Old Julie's not too bad after all."

Peg swirled the ice cubes around with a finger. "Hey, I know Julie doesn't have anything to do with raises. She doesn't even know who Alan is. It was his boss, Howard Whiteside, who got the raise for him." She looked into her glass. "Alan is so upset right now. Howard has been the Executive Vice President, for something like ten years. Julie's brother brought him into the company and Howard more or less took over. After Earle Phipps died. Howard knows that company inside out and sideways and Julie just slapped him in the face by bringing in another man and giving him the title of Assistant Executive Vice President!"

Beth stepped away from the door. "Could I have a soda after all?"

"Help yourself." Peg watched Beth open a can and take a long drink. "Alan says the company rumors are that Julie thought Howard and the V.P. of Finance weren't doing a good enough job in getting a loan. The V.P. of Finance up and quit. The company is growing so fast the Executive Committee recommended they build an office building. Then move all of the office people into the new building and some people in the shops could move into the old office space. Mr. Whiteside and the V.P. of Finance suggested they should have a stock issue."

Peg wrinkled her nose. "Whatever that is. Alan says if only Julie would stay out of things. She has good men who are perfectly capable of managing that company. Howard Whiteside has been a slave for that place. She let him and the rest of the V.P.'s run it after her brother died, and now all of a sudden, she butts in and screws up everything. About four months ago she got her nose in the Sales Department and the V.P. of Sales quit." Peg emptied her glass and filled it halfway with vodka.

As she opened the door to the refrigerator she stated, "I better put some tomato juice in the glass. You know Alan says losing V.P.'s not only lowers moral but it makes a bad reputation for the company. They're having trouble getting a replacement for the V.P. of Finance and," she laughed, stirred the drink and took a sip. "He tells me not to repeat what he tells me because there're so many people around here who work at the company. But you don't know Howard Whiteside. Do you?"

Beth shook her head NO. "Remember my daddy worked at the plant. Until his back started to cause him too much pain and he had to quit." She paused and wondered what else should she say? *But I know Julie Fischer! Maybe even better than Alan does.*

Out loud she added, "I'm glad Alan is doing so well." She drank fast from the soda can. It was time to leave.

"Of course, he's a brain. But you know that. He's really too smart for me. I was over at Southampton Estates, just this afternoon." Peg wrinkled her nose. "I didn't like their first floor layout. Gert and I are having fun, looking at samples. Of course, we'll miss you. We've all been through a lot together. Your dad and Evan...and," Peg shrugged. "I told the girls that if you don't get a car I'll come get you, so that you can still baby sit for them."

Beth put the empty can in the trash bag, under the washing machine. "I'm hoping to go to college." She watched Peg smile at her and added, "I guess it does sound like I'm kinda dreaming out loud because I'll have to take out a loan, but Daddy wanted me to go so I'm going to give it my best shot." She picked up her book and sweater. She had to leave.

Peg swirled her glass making noise with the ice. "I'll bet you still miss him. I mean, I know how close you two were. Just the other day, Bert Smithers and I were talking and we said he was such a polite guy. I know you really loved him. And he loved you too."

"I think of him every single day," Beth whispered. She grasped the door knob as she thought, And I talk to him because I believe he's tuned in to what I say. And do. Her eyes filled tears.

"I'm sorry. I didn't mean to upset you. Just remember, we all liked him."

"It's okay. After all, remembering and talking about someone . . . makes them immortal."

"Well, if I can ever do anything for you, just let me know. Like go through my jewelry box to find something for a date. Maybe borrow one of my evening bags. Isn't it almost prom time? Do you have a date?" She watched Beth nod. "If you want me to do your hair or your make-up, let me know."

Beth snickered.. "Thanks. As if you can make me look sexy."

"I did with Evan. Tell me if you hear from her."

So you can tell Yvonne and Mrs. Smithers. She forced a big smile. "And you remember to tell Alan I'm proud to know him."

EIGHT

BETH HATED TO return to her house. She threw her sweater around a chair and turned on the wall light in the kitchen. She washed the dishes and wiped the table. What did she feel like doing? Instead of homework. Was she hungry? Maybe call somebody? Turning the clock back to when she got up that morning? Then she'd know what she knew now. All the day, words to weigh. *Right, Daddy? Translated, do not argue with Julie Fischer. Damn. Shit. And every curse word I might not know.*

She wandered into the living room. She didn't feel like reading about "*Famous English Authors of the 19th Century*". She looked at her watch. She could start working on her essay. Maybe if she read a few of Vicki's poems she might get in the mood. She got her notebook and a pen.

Searching through the book case she tuned into hearing music. Why did Peg have to put the record player next to the wall? She remind herself to, Look for a book. There, that one. Now turn on the new garage sale floor lamp and read. Read!

Beth did force herself to read several sonnets. Out loud. She rested her head against the faded upholstery as she thought of words to express how she would describe Vicki's works. She picked up her pen and wrote, "Unique. Unmatched power. A form of original blending of words. An expression of true genius and … spirit." If only she didn't have to do more research and make up stuff about Vicki, all because she couldn't go back to interview Julie.

Eyes closed and tears trickling down her cheeks Beth slowly allowed her thoughts to travel through the wall to the words Andy Williams was singing. She whispered, "Sing to me, Andy. I'll tune out all my miseries while you sing love songs to me. Oh good. Gert must have arrived. Peg's lowered the volume and . . . she's laughing. Peg's happy now. Vodka happy."

After Beth heard Gert laugh she sat on the floor and leaned against the wall. She wanted to hear as much of the conversation as she could. She longed to be with them.

She heard Peg laugh. She must be sitting on the couch. "Oh my god, I'll have to tell Alan. She won't French kiss with her husband, but she'll kiss the dog and everybody knows what a dog licks." Peg laughed again. "Do you French kiss?"

". . . sometimes . . . doing anything and . . . sometimes you don't." Beth knew she was missing what Gert was saying because she was sitting next to the stairs.

"The same with me," Beth could hear Peg said. "Alan did that kind of kissing. Before we were married. Not it's the old routine."

"Maybe . . . think I'm crazy, but . . . have to ask. Do . . .get the urge to kiss other men? . . . see a guy . . . store and think . . . be like with you?"

Peg's voice became louder. "Sure. Women look at men, like men look at women."

Gert laughed and spoke louder. "Just . . . at him, Peg. But . . . not touch him."

Beth waited for someone to say something! *Who* are they talking about?

"I'm missing something. Fill me in." Louder Peg added, "After I fill up our glasses."

Beth waited against the wall. Andy's voice faded and Gert remarked, "I hope this one isn't as strong. I turned down the volume. And, you know damn good and well I'm talking about the hunk in the *Stop and Shop Food Market.* You could end up with a real mess on your hands."

"For god's sake. All I do is talk to him. And tease a little. I'm going to get some pretzels."

"It has to be Jim Bender." Beth whispered to herself.

"Hey, Peg," Gert called out. Obviously she wanted Peg to hear her in the kitchen. "I honest to god know how you feel. Oh good. I like the mini pretzels. Thanks."

"Ok? This is crazy but how do I feel?"

"Frisky. Even if his line is longer, you wait. How am I doing?"

"Making me hate you."

"And all the time you're looking him over and thinking how you can casually get to know more about him. I know from his tag, his first name is Jim, but what's his last name?"

"Bender."

Oh my god! Brad was right. Should I tell him?

"Jim Bender. And how old is our Adonis?"

"So okay . . . he's a senior at Bridgeboro High."

"Hmmm. An eighteen year old keg of dynamite. Hey, I'd be lying if I didn't admit I've looked him over. More than twice. He's got the cutest buns of any guy in Bridgeboro."

Peg laughed. "And how about those legs and how they fill out those tight pants?"

"You mean you just stopped at his legs?"

"Shut up. Remember, you can go home to Chuck but I have to go to bed alone."

"So. It's all physical. You don't have a damn thing in common with that boy and that's all he is, he's a boy and . . . "

"Wait a minute." Peg's voice was strong. "There're lots of eighteen year old boys who are married. Some of them are even . . . fathers."

"But would you want a toy boy? After being married to Alan almost ten years, you must know the advantages of being married to a mature male?"

"Besides two degrees and a damn good job." Peg laughed. "What if you found out I had gone all the way with you know who?"

"I'd feel sorry for you. A casual affair isn't worth feeling guilty afterwards. Oh, don't look so surprised. Did I ever indicate I was Saint Gertrude? In fact, after two drinks I feel brazen enough to admit I'm included in that group of married women who have had relations with other men. And, if I weren't guilty of that, I'd be guilty of what I think. One of those Commandments mentions that to lust after another man isn't kosher either."

"Who's going to admit they've got the hots for their best friend's husband? Or maybe their brother-in-law?"

"Agreed. Just don't get tangled up with an eighteen year old checkout employee. Who'll most likely tell all of his boyfriends of his conquest."

Peg laughed. "But a real affair would be worth the . . . thrill?"

"I'll even add it's worth every tear, lie, pang of guilt . . . and every year of remembering. It can mean a lot more than just having sex with a smart aleck teenager."

"You have to agree that over six feet, about a hundred and seventy pounds of hunk, with those sexy blue eyes, unruly blonde hair and beautiful white teeth, has not gone all the way!"

"Agreed. I'm sure he has quite a hit list. But damn it, Peg, you'd be no different than the rest of them."

"In other words, you really think he's . . . getting ideas about me?"

"Is the Pope Catholic? Ask Alan sometime what he used to think about when he was eighteen. But sweetie pie, I'm sure it would be a big disappointment for you. Even though you're attracted to him . . . physically that is, it would be a wham! bam! thank you ma'm! and you'd want to scream in the pillow."

Peg laughed. Heartily. "You do know you're a riot. And making me need a drink."

"I have to get home. Chuck doesn't mind how late I stay out but I can't be cranky with the kids the next day."

"I'm so tired of doing cross word puzzles and watching television. Look at my hands. I'm back to biting my nails."

"Why don't you change food markets?" Gert laughed before her voice faded out of range of the living room wall.

Beth stood and turned off the lamp. She was going to bed. And do a lot of thinking.

About sex.

And Brad.

NINE

FOR A WINTER day in March, Saturday morning was sunny and warmer than predicted.

Beth was happy to see the sun after she raised the shade in her bedroom window. She watched a flock of birds searching through the field of corn stalks that bordered their little lawn. Birds. Bird feeder. Julie Fischer.

Daddy, help me. Should I call her? Just to ask her how she's feeling? Or maybe I could ask if I can do anything for her? She'll remind me that Sam Carpenter does her errands, thank you, my dear.

Another *damn* because it was Saturday, the day Beth was expected to clean the house. But that didn't annoy her as much as knowing she and Liz would cross paths. After Liz would finally arouse herself and before she would become the hostess at Lou's Bar and Grille, Beth and Liz would have to acknowledge they lived in the same house.

She also had to get psyched up for her date with Dan. She did like Dan but during the movie he'd put his arm around her. And he'd expect her to sit close in his automobile and shift gears. And the worse thing, she'd have to kiss him goodnight.

Maybe he'd ask if she wanted to go to his house for some ice cream and cookies . . . or whatever goodies the housekeeper might have made. She would appreciate the offer because it gave her an opportunity to see how other people lived. And she did like his parents, although they should be attending the same dinner dance as Brad's parents were attending. Where Brad and Jeanne would be dancing. Close to each other.

SHE wondered why Dan's parents had not insisted he go to the dance? But then who would he have asked? And she wouldn't have a date because he wouldn't have asked her to a community fund raising event. It was almost as though they were doing each other a favor. He wasn't a looker and she was one of the girls who lived on the "other side" of Township Line Road.

Beth drank some orange juice, ate a stale muffin and decided to wait and have her coffee after Liz was ready to join her. She sat at the kitchen table, and watched Mrs. Smithers wash her kitchen window.

Which room should she clean first? Not the bathroom. Before Liz was finished in it. Beth had learned that every Saturday morning Liz took a minimum of forty-five minutes to shower, shave her legs and underarms. Next she would lotion and powder her body, leaving the bathroom messier than it was before Beth cleaned it.

The same procedure applied to the living room. Many times before Liz left to go to work she dropped ashes or spilled something, somewhere. And newspapers and magazines ended up on the floor, even if she had not read them.

Liz could care less about the appearance of the house but about herself she was immaculate. She used disposable cigarette holders to keep her fingers stain free. She had lovely dainty hands which she literally treated with kid gloves. Beth always remembered the day, while she was still innocent, someone asked her, "Does your mom like to cook?" And Beth blurted out, "No. She likes to paint her nails."

Another of Liz's attractions was her hair. She didn't have a beautiful face and with her natural "mousy brown hair" as she called it, she did not cause second glances, until she dyed it silver gray. Overnight, Liz became an attractive sensation. Even Beth had to admit the color and a new style made her mother a look-twice woman. Although Beth knew some people referred to Liz as a "broad".

Beth was not as impressed as her older sister, who decided to do the same thing. That meant Evan took after Liz for two reasons. Her hair and her bust. They both had large busts. That attribute helped Evan with her popularity in school and at the Navy Base, where she went to work after she graduated from Bridgeboro High School. As for Liz, she took advantage of her voluptuousness by wearing low cut blouses and tight sweaters. Beth already planned to have Liz "laid out" in a sweater, so she'd look natural.

Beth decided to clean her bedroom. She changed her sheets and pillow cases and was dusting her bureau when she heard Liz begin to wake up. She knew the routine of Liz trying to get up. She and Evan used to sneak a look. And laugh. It was always an ordeal because with loud yawns, deep sighs and groans, she fought every inch of the way having to get out of bed. Next, she would sit on the side of the bed and squint and search for her peignoir which matched her sheer nightgown. Then she would begin the search for her fancy mules and *clip clop* into the bathroom.

As usual Beth wished she could hide. She knew she didn't hate the woman but she knew she didn't love her. Admitting that Beth felt guilt. After all, they were relatives. Liz was the woman who had allowed her to use her body to become an Earthling. That was what her daddy used to call her and himself. Earthlings. And she loved him. But, every girl wants a mother to love also. Sadly, Beth knew she didn't want Elizabeth Rhodes to be *her* mother.

Beth realized Liz was a frustrated woman. She accepted Liz's faults and failures and even felt sorry for her, until . . . Liz had gone to work at Lou's Bar and Grille about six months after her husband had died. She had been working as a waitress at the Pike Diner but one day she left Beth a note to explain she had changed jobs. Lou King had offered her the job of hostess and cashier at his popular business which was located on Bridge Pike. In the heart of downtown Bridgeborough. Liz was thrilled because the new job offered more money and more prestige. Her hours were from four to midnight, therefore Beth never saw Liz, when she got up in the afternoon and left for work. Except on Saturdays.

On Sundays, their paths might cross until one of them declared she was going out. Monday was another black day when they might see each other again *if* Beth went home after her last class or *if* Liz could make herself stay home on her day off. They kept in touch via notes. For both of them this manner of communicating was the most acceptable, in more ways than either would admit verbally.

With her husband's insurance money Liz bought another used car. Beth swallowed Liz's story the first time, the second time and even the third time that the junker had had a flat or else it wouldn't start and Liz had to ask one of the men in the bar to bring her home. Beth even accepted Liz's reason that she should invite the man in for a drink after he had done her a favor.

Until the night Liz allowed some loud mouth bull bring her home. He wouldn't pay any attention to Liz's *shhh's.* He laughed too loudly and his boots made loud noises. Until the house became quiet and Beth believed the noisy man had left. But she was so annoyed she had to tell Liz she should not invite any more men in for a drink. Peg and Alan might hear them. And what would they think?

Liz was not on the second floor. Beth began to go down the stairs when she heard moaning and grunting. She descended until she could see the couch. Liz was straddling the man. Her skirt was up to her hips and she was slowly moving her buttocks up and down as the man thrust his hips in time with her. The moaning was coming from Liz while the man grunted, "Yeah, yeah, oh yeah," over and over.

Beth backed up the stairs, went into the bathroom and threw up.

Other mornings Beth found a disheveled Liz on the couch. Beth would help her up the stairs, help her flop on her bed and throw a cover over her. Then skip breakfast before she went to school.

BETH began to wash her bedroom window while Liz was running water. Then the bathroom door opened, Liz *clip clopped* into the hall and yelled, "Beth."

"I'm in my room."

"I can't find that stuff for an upset stomach."

Beth stepped into the hall. "You left it in the kitchen. Next to the toaster."

"I need it. I feel like hell."

"Maybe you have a virus?" She tried to look concerned. "Some of the kids have been out of school because of running at both ends."

"This is a shitty hangover. Too much celebrating last night. For Lou's birthday."

Beth quickly envisioned Lou King. Each time she had seen him she imagined him as the tough, rough Chief Petty Officer she heard he had been during World War 11. He even looked pugnacious because of his crooked nose and short thick neck. The mean looking scar on his right temple gave people ideas about his past. And Beth suspected Lou was more than just Liz's boss.

Lou was so different in appearance from her taller and thinner daddy. Norman Rhodes had been a handsome man. And Peg and other neighbors considered him to be a gentleman.

"Go back to bed and I'll bring the stuff to your room"

"I don't know why you have to clean so early." She *clip clopped* into her room.

Beth pretended not to notice the mess in Liz's bedroom. They had decided that room was Liz's responsibility. Liz was lying across the rumpled covers but struggled to prop herself up to reach for the glass. She drank the bubbly liquid and flopped again.

Beth finished cleaning her bedroom and decided to clean the kitchen. Surely Liz would not want anything to ea. Meaning the room would remain tidy until Liz got to it on Sunday. While Beth was cleaning the electric stove she heard the annoying *clip clop* on the stairs and thought, Shit! Here she comes. Oh well, I guess it's better than her sneaking around in her bare feet.

Liz settled into a chair and lit a cigarette. "I think I'll try some coffee."

Beth put water in a pan and turned on a burner. She took two cups, saucers and spoons from the dish rack and put them on the clean table. "Feeling better?"

"A little. But who wants to stare at a ceiling? I think we should bring each other up to date."

Beth added more water to the pan. This could be a two cup morning. It could be a long wait before she would hear what Liz wanted her to know.

Liz exhaled a cloud of smoke then studied it as she casually inquired, "What have you been doing with yourself lately?"

Inside Beth coiled. She was becoming ready to be stepped on. "Nothing much. Lots of homework and babysitting for Peg. And Gert."

Liz reached for the clean ash tray. "How many more weeks of school?"

"Until the end of May. Minus a few holidays. Then we'll have finals . . . " Beth paused. She hated to talk about the end of her senior year. She didn't want to leave high school. Have to face the future. Everything was so uncertain.

Liz tapped her cigarette against the ash tray. Some of the ashes fell onto the table so she picked up the ash tray and blew across the table. "Think you'll graduate?"

Beth checked the water. She frowned to the stove as she replied, "Of course."

"And then what?"

Beth turned to look at Liz. She might as well say it. "I'm hoping to go to college."

Liz's eyebrows went up. "You're hoping to do *what*?"

"I'm hoping to get a part time job and go to college."

Liz laughed. Loudly. She shook her head. "Good god! You think up the damnedest things. So you're old man put the idea in your head and you took him seriously."

"Daddy said I should try to go and I'm going to . . . ."she stopped talking as she realized Liz was not interested in what she was saying.

Liz lifted her cup. "I need my coffee. Now more than before." She watched Beth pour hot water in two cups. She leveled out a teaspoon of instant coffee and proceeded to stir.

"Look kid, that was a couple of years ago. When you and him used to dream together. Even though the Ladies' Aid was feeding us and the neighbors were giving clothes to you girls, he still used to think big. Now you have to stop dreaming. The cold hard facts are you have to get a full time job." She put her wet spoon in the sugar bowl.

Beth raised her chin and stood tall. "I can have a job and still go to college. And I entered an essay contest so I may win some money." She measured instant coffee into her cup.

"Oh sure. Remember I've been signing your lousy report cards. I thought you were supposed to have good marks or be good in sports to win money?"

"I had good grades in my college exams and . . . " Beth suddenly remembered that Liz did not know she had taken any exams for college, "and my marks have improved."

"You're still dreaming." She sipped from her cup. "What about this essay contest?"

"The Bridgeborough Women's Club sponsors one each year. Want a piece of toast?"

"Yeah. A piece of dry toast. So what's your essay going to be about?"

Holding two pieces of bread Beth leaned against the counter. She needed support as she said to her reflection in the toaster, "Vicki Lynn."

"Oh shit. That's another great thing your father did for you. Vicki Lynn. Vicki Lynn. You might have thought that he . . . "

"It wasn't only daddy who thought she was great. After all, she won the Pulitzer Prize." She put two knives and a jar of jelly on the table.

"So you're going to turn in an essay about the great Vicki Lynn and then sit back and wait for the money to come rolling in." She took a deep drag and crushed her cigarette in the ash tray.

Beth thought fast while she waited for the bread to pop up. Should she say anything about interviewing Julie Fischer? If Liz found out from somebody else, she could really be annoyed. But if *she* did mention Julie, then *help.* Liz wouldn't let her up for air.

Beth put a slice of toast on a plate and a paper napkin in front of Liz. "I'm interviewing Mrs. Fischer." She enjoyed watching Liz's reaction as the words sank in.

Beth concentrated putting jelly on her bread as Liz declared, "*The* Mrs. Fischer?"

She nodded and chewed slowly. "I wrote to her and she told me which days we could meet. I've already met with her two times this week."

"You've been in her house?" She watched Beth nod. "Is she nice?" After Beth replied, "Yes." Liz blurted out, "Wait until I tell Lou. And the girls. My kid visiting old Julie. They'll flip." She finished her coffee. "What if you don't win?"

Just like that. The fun of gloating was gone. Beth shrugged.

"Just like your old man. So full of daydreams you never stop to think. You better move your butt and fill out some job applications. Before other kids beat you to it. Instead of asking Julie about her sister ask her about a job. Haven't you been taking shorthand and typing?"

"Just typing. For extra credit."

"Maybe you can get a Civil Service classification for a job at the Navy Base. One of our waitresses has a kid sister who just started up there and I can ask her where you go to take the test, unless you remember where your sister went? How much money do you have saved up?"

Looking into her cup Beth deliberately lied, "A . . . couple hundred." What if Liz asked to see her bank book? She had started the account with her daddy.

Instead Liz yawned loudly. "I'm glad one of the Rhodes can save money." She pushed back her chair. "I guess I'll straighten up my room. Got a date tonight?" After Beth nodded she asked, "Who's the lucky guy?"

Beth quickly stood to clear the table. "Danny Friedman."

"Jeez. He looks like a squirrel with those big teeth. And you can't see his eyes behind the thick glasses. I imagine you don't have the pick of the litter but can't you get anybody better looking?"

Beth faced Liz. "For your information Dan is fun to be with. He dresses nicely, he's polite and . . . and I have a good time with him."

"And his parents are loaded. Where's he take you?" She laughed. "Out for dinner?"

"He has. Before we went to a play or a concert."

"Ever meet his parents?" After Beth nodded she added, "You have?"

"I went to his sister's birthday dinner. And I went with them for dinner and a play."

"You really are full of surprises. Meeting Julie Fischer. Out with the Friedman's." The smile turned into a frown. "But don't get your hopes up. Dan might be polite and his folks might overlook where you live but Jews stick together. He'll never marry you."

"I'm going to college."

"Getting married might be the easy way out. Even marrying a Jew could be better than working although I've heard they're lousy lovers but they're good to their women. Nice clothes, maids, vacations." Liz shook her head. "If Dan doesn't meet a nice Jew girl I'm sure his parents will find one for him and..."

Beth couldn't stop from blurting out, "His brother married a Catholic!"

Liz stood. "Okay. Okay. But I still say you should start dating some

other guys. Maybe you can meet somebody while you're working."

Beth stood tall. She would be five inches taller if Liz were not wearing her high heel mules. "If I go to work it'll be to pay for college. Or to travel. But I'm not going to rot away in some office or . . . " she noticed the amused look on Liz's face but she had to finish. "Or get married until I know enough about life that I can write about it."

"Why don't you join the Navy?" Liz laughed as she walked out of the kitchen.

Beth wanted to scream out, "Go to hell."

Inside, she cried out, *Couldn't you even pretend? Just once? Couldn't you really listen to me? And hear what I'm saying?*

TEN

ON SATURDAY MORNING, Brad Livingston was eating an omelet, bacon and toast in the breakfast cove. The three Livingston's usually ate their breakfasts and lunches in that cozy area.

Brad enjoyed eating in the large bay window because he could watch the birds and squirrels. Sometimes, rabbits and infrequently a groundhog ambled across their manicured lawn, to brazenly nibble on forbidden plantings. Mostly there were song birds using the bird feeders which Brad kept filled from Labor Day until Memorial Day.

The sun was shining on him and his yellow place mat and yellow napkin, both the exact shade of the bouquet in the center of the antique pine harvest table. His mother had cut branches from the large forsythia bush by the garage and brought them inside to force them into blooming early. The yellows looked pretty with the brown pottery dishes they used in the breakfast room.

At dinner time, if the Livingston's were all together, they ate in the dining room. Then they used ironstone dishes and the silver service, a wedding gift from Bernice's parents. When the Livingston's entertained, Bernice used her Grandmother Rolfe's *French Limoges* china and her mother's antique crystal and silver.

When Brad ate alone, which was often, he ate on a tray in front of the television in the library and was happy to use a paper plate and his favorite mug which Beth had given him. They both liked the saying, *Life is a bitch. And then you die.*

Brad's mother had prepared his breakfast, although occasionally she missed a Saturday morning. Especially if she had an early meeting. Only a fractured ankle and pneumonia had kept her from fulfilling her motherly duties on a school day.

"More bacon, dear?"

"No thank you, ma'am." Brad wiped his mouth. He really wanted to leave the table but knew his mother would be disappointed if he did not stay to talk with her.

After Bernice put a plate covered with four strips of bacon and scrambled eggs into the warming oven to wait for Richard she carried her plate around the room divider and sat on a deacon's bench opposite to Brad. "What are your plans for today?"

"Since it's warmed up I thought I'd wash my car. Yours too, if you're not going to use it."

"That would be nice but I have to help decorate the Club, for the dance tonight." She glanced at her watch the face of which was encircled with diamonds. "In fact, I better hurry." She put a large forkful of eggs in her mouth and chewed rapidly. "I told Lou I'd meet her around tenish. I ordered a corsage for Jeanne. It'll be delivered here with mine. This afternoon."

Brad nodded. "I appreciate that."

"Lou told me Jeanne's new dress is purple. Because she just made her hair silver." Bernice shook her head. "I'm glad I'm not her mom. Anyway, I ordered white carnations. I think it's mighty extravagant her buying a new dress for every dance but then she does look lovely." Bernice smiled at Brad. "You always look so attractive together. But I was hoping tonight you could be a little more dignified and not dance those vulgar dances."

Brad forced a laughed as he refolded his napkin. "Jeanne likes to do them. But I could ask Ken if he'll dance…"

Bernice placed a fleshy hand on top of Brad's. "Oh no, dear. I want
you to dance with her. It's just that I prefer to watch you dancing the slower ones. Did you hear that Lillian Hobensack was accepted by Vassar?" After Brad said, "Yeah", she added, "It's so far away. She'll only get home during holidays."

Brad pushed back his chair. "Mom, forget it. I'm not coming home from Princeton every week-end. I've told you before if I have to go into the service I won't be coming home. May I be excused, please?" After his mother nodded, he stood and collected his soiled dishes.

Bernice followed his every move. She never tired of watching him.
"Heaven forbid. Having you away in college will be hard enough on me but I could never stand it if you went into the . . . oh, good morning Richard."

"Good morning," Wearing casual clothes, Richard Livingston
walked to the back door and peered between the curtains. "I wish we could discourage those damn Blue Jays from coming to the feeder. Their shrieking woke me up."

Brad decided to put on a big smile. "It's a great day out there. When I got the paper it even smells like spring."

"My bulbs are peeping through already," Bernice added proudly. "I'm hoping they'll be in bloom for the luncheon at the library." She removed Richard's plate from the warming oven and placed it where she wanted him to sit.

Richard unfolded his napkin. "Where are we going tonight?"

Bernice tried not to sound annoyed. "The dinner dance for the Bucks County Association for Retarded Children and I ..."

Richard put up his hand. "Okay. Now I remember. I'm still pushing for them to change the name to Citizens, instead of Children. After all, the people in the workshops are . . . well, some of them are in their forties and fifties."

"Are you going to be home this afternoon?" Brad asked.

"If everything is under control at the office. Why?"

"I thought I'd wash your car."

"Oh? Spring fever, huh?"

Brad smiled and walked to the doorway leading into the center hall. "I guess you could call it that. First I'm going to finish typing some English notes." He had decided when he woke up he would finish all of his homework before Sunday. He smiled as he thought about being with Beth the next day. He stepped out of the room.

"Just a minute," Richard called out. "Have you had a chance to talk to that girl? The one who's interviewing Julie."

Brad backed up and grabbed the door jam. "You mean Beth Rhodes?"

Bernice spoke. "If that's her name. Have you had a chance to ask her about Julie. You know, how she looks? And how the girl is making out with the interview?"

"As a matter of fact I had a chance to ask her, ah, one day this week, and she said that Julie is being very nice. And helpful. And she thinks Julie is a handsome woman."

Richard smiled, smugly. "She sounds like a smart young lady to me."

"And that's all she said?" Bernice asked, softly.

"Yep. But remember she's on the Yearbook Committee so if I get a chance you want me to ask her anything else?"

"Not really," Richard replied. "We were just wondering. After all, we used to be very good friends. And we wonder how she is. Since her brother died."

"You go do your typing, dear. I'll let you know when I'm leaving." Bernice watched Brad walk out of sight and turned to Richard. "I wonder how she really is?" She moved the butter dish closer to Richard. "How many pieces of toast do you want?"

Richard shrugged. "Who cares?" He held up two fingers.

"Well, evidently she isn't as incommunicado as we heard she is, if she's meeting with that girl. Imagine the girl saying she looks *handsome*." She put two slices of wheat bread into the toaster and turned to face Richard. "Can I read the girl's essay?"

"If you can keep your mouth shut? I don't want anybody to think you influenced me."

"As if you need any influencing. Just remember to be fair. I'm sure she needs the money. Living in Taylor Park and all."

"I'm always fair," Richard remarked as he broke his bacon into bite size pieces to become finger food. "Where are you going this morning?"

"To help decorate. For tonight."

"Besides checking on the new receptionist, I'm going over bank Statements. So leave your check book home."

The toaster popped. Bernice put the bread on a plate and placed it on the table. "Will it take long?"

"Now what's on your mind?"

Bernice filled Richard's cup with coffee and put more in her own cup. "I thought it would be nice if you could wash the cars with Brad."

Richard began to butter his toast. He pressed so hard the slice broke into three pieces.

He wiped his fingers on his napkin and declared, "He's only washing them to keep busy. Besides checking up on everybody on a Saturday morning, you know how much work I have to do, just to keep up with all of my commitments. I have to finish the report for the church Vestry and by Tuesday night I have to…"

Bernice held up her hand, "I know how busy you are. I am too. But before not too long, Brad will be gone and then . . . " She stood and began to take dishes to the sink.

"For god's sake. Are you on that kick again? You know he's not going to stay with us forever. And furthermore, I do a helluva lot more than other men do for their kids. Only meetings kept me away from football games and track meets . . . or whatever. And I give a great deal of my time to be active in, well, I've given speeches on writing in several high schools. And, I'm on the School Board." He picked up his coffee cup and added, "I'm a damn good father, considering everything I have to do."

"Of course you are." She began to rinse the dishes. She always did that before she put them in the new dish washer. "I'm going to leave Ellie a note to tell Tony I want to see him. About cleaning out the garage. And then the basement."

"Good idea. And remind him about the branch that fell down last week. Or maybe Brad would like to saw it up? It would be good exercise for him."

"He might get hurt. Let Tony do it."

A picture flashed behind Richard's eyes. He saw Tony Miles sawing

the branch into firewood. He would enjoy watching the big man work for him. He smiled. Smugly.

He began to think about all of the blacks who lived in Bridgeboro.

MOST of the black families lived in small identical ranch houses, across the street from the train station. All took great pride in keeping their houses in excellent condition surrounded by trimmed lawns and flower beds.

Ellie Perkins, a young widow, was working hard to raise her two daughters. She worked for the Livingston's every Monday and Friday. If they were entertaining she stayed until the clean-up was finished. Tony Miles worked with her, tending bar while she served the hot and cold hors d'oeuvres. She and Tony enjoyed listening to the small talk of the influential citizens of Bridgeboro. Sometimes they heard conversations they were not meant to hear and even hesitated to repeat. The amount of money Bernice paid them compensated for the orders which Richard gave them.

Sam Carpenter also lived on Station Street. Since he had become a widower, he lived with his son, Lukas Carpenter, and his wife and three children. One of the children was Ann Carpenter, a classmate of Brad's.

Richard Livingston remembered the girl for her great figure. And light skin. He wondered if Brad was among the white boys who wished they could date her. Or do more than just date her?

Emma Carpenter used to live on Station Street. Now she had a lovely apartment on the third floor of the Barnes' house. She was Sam's youngest sister and had never married. Her fiancée had been a cook and killed when his battleship went down in the Pacific and she never allowed herself to love another man. Barnes also had an apartment over their six car garage in which their white and witty caretaker, Dick Slight, lived with his prize winning Siamese cats.

Sam Carpenter was the prophet and philosopher of the old and the young residents on Station Street. As the caring handyman for Mrs. William Fischer, he made more money, worked fewer hours and received more fringe benefits than any of the other blacks. Everybody knew he was devoted to Mrs. Fischer.

With a deep sigh Richard allowed his thoughts to return to the tree. "Tell Tony I want him to do it when I'm going to be home. I want to supervise him and show him where to stack the wood."

Bernice wiped her hands on a terry towel. "If you don't have any thing else to tell me I'm going upstairs and finish getting dressed. I'm going to wear my black two piece evening gown tonight. Is that all right with you?"

"I don't care. Wear whatever you want to." He was unmindful his wife left the room.

AS Richard sat alone, sipping his second cup of coffee he remembered saying, "I don't care." When had he begun to say that? Five years ago? Ten years ago? And why had he said, 'I'm a damn good father'? He pushed up his glasses, a habit he was performing more frequently. He should get them fixed. Richard wiped his mouth with the yellow napkin, looked at the dirty dishes and decided to leave them on the table. He was going to collect what he needed and drive to the office to do his financial calculating. He had to be alone.

It was time to plot. And plan.

ELEVEN

ON THE WAY to his office building, Richard drove past the *Jiffy Car Wash*. Five cars and one pick-up were backed up. Even if it still was backed up on his way home he'd have his car washed there. To hurt Brad? To annoy Bernice? Of course not. He was driving it to the Club that evening.

Richard pulled into the parking space reserved for CEO-EDITOR. Not even Bernice parked there. The newly paved parking lot was on the side of the one story building which housed his printing business. Crossing the parking lot the familiar feeling of discontentment weighed him down. Three years previously Richard had the front of the building modernized. The oldness and the dinginess of the rest of the building were hidden behind a new facade and fresh paint. The lobby had been enlarged and wall to wall carpet, central heating and large plate glass double doors were installed. The business appeared to be successful. He reminded himself to just remember his business was in a prime location in Bridgeboro.

Richard unlocked the double doors with the shiny brass trim and walked inside. He glanced at the large planter, the modern lounge chairs and tables and the impressive new desk where his receptionist smiled her greeting five days and Saturday morning. Everyone had been thrilled when the old switch board had been replaced by an updated telephone system. He had allowed his secretary, Florence Mann, to select the decorations. He would sell his soul to have a commercial building as attractive as the one Charlie Barnes owned. Having to visit Charlie in his huge office which included a fireplace and a wet bar, annoyed him. Sometimes he would drive past the Fischer Company and feel the bile churning in his stomach. Richard walked through the lobby and main office and re-entered his past.

Richard Arthur Livingston the Third, hated his past. After years of perspiration and pretentiousness it was still the same. None of his relatives had done anything nor said anything worth bragging about, let alone remembering. His name was recorded in the earliest records of the Borough since his great-great-grandfather had been among the first settlers along the Neshaminy Creek. Maybe the old man had even met General George Washington when he had ridden through

Bridgeborough. So what? Joshua William Livingston owned nothing more than the local livery stable and blacksmith shop.

His grandfather's name was in the town's records as having started the first newspaper in the County. His father, Richard Arthur Livingston, Junior, had been the first Mayor of the Borough. He hated his father's strict code of ethics which oozed from his editorials and restricted his family's life style.

While Richard was in the Boy Scout's it had been okay to have such an honest father. Later it became damn annoying. He was embarrassed when his older sister became a missionary and took the Bible to Africa. After his younger sister received her college degree, she married an ass hole High School teacher and moved to a little dusty town in Arizona. Her disappointment of not having children of her own was compensated by working in a day care program and wiping the noses and butts of poor Indian children.

His mother, Bertha Rebecca Livingston, a frail, thin woman, did not
tolerate a curse word nor an off color joke in her presence. The Holy Bible was the only book she had read. She was unbearable for her cleanliness. Richard remembered her as a religious fanatic who found her happiness, or was it her escape, through countless hours of volunteer work and worship at *The Church of the Good Samaritan.* No wonder he had begun to cheat and lie when he was barely ten years old. No wonder he began to smoke and tell dirty jokes and quit Boy Scouts when he was fourteen. It was revenge for such strict upbringing.

He thanked God his mother's parents had left enough money for him
to go to Princeton University. No matter if God had helped with his inheritance, Richard insisted he would not get a degree in Theology. At least his mother agreed her only son should graduate from an impressive college to compensate for his inability to participate in sports. Damn his poor eyesight and his heart murmur, which his mother did admit he had inherited from her side of the family.

His college days were unimpressive. He was in the third level of the
popularity groups. All except for John Brockway whose popularity with the opposite sex and his success in making *deals* and walking away unscathed was something Richard always envied. The note on

John's last Christmas card had indicated he had just married wife number three. And his wedding present was a new Cessna, 180.

Richard's girlfriend in high school was a skinny daughter of one of his mother's friends from church. But she was allowed to go to dances and parties. The one time he tried to kiss her his mother knew before he had gotten up the next morning.

John had introduced him to Anna Mae Kirk, the first girl who let him screw her. He didn't think the experience was as great as it was supposed to be. Because she liked oral sex, Anna Mae never got pregnant, like one of John's girls did. They found a doctor who would perform an abortion and saved John. Again.

What a blow when he couldn't get into the Military and he had to settle for a job in the Navy Procurement Department, in Washington, D.C. He would have died from embarrassment if he had been assigned a job in the *Johnsville Naval Air Station*. And be only five miles from home. Bill Fischer's aircraft carrier had been sent to the South Pacific and Charlie Barnes's Division had been sent to Europe. After he graduated from college he almost decided not to return to Bridgeboro, even though he knew his father assumed he would "take over the paper".

Then he met Bernice Rodden. She was chunky but a curvaceous Southern Belle from Virginia. At first he disliked her. The other girls in the office called her a snob. Especially when she made it known she didn't *have* to work. She was coming to the aid of her country while her boyfriend was fighting in the Pacific. She had so many of his own traits he was afraid of her. Then she invited him to the family estate in Virginia. To meet her Mama and Daddy.

He began to court Bernice, the oldest daughter of Mr. and Mrs. Theodore Rodden. Within several months Mr. Rodden offered Richard a place in the family's tobacco business. Richard saw a future of subservience. He decided he would return to Bridgeboro to carry on *his* family's business. He could not let down his hometown. By not returning to his proper place.

Bernice wanted to get married and declared she would move above the Mason and Dixon Line! The move would be an adventure. Richard had qualms about Bernice meeting his parents, although his mother was gracious enough to die before Bernice met her. Neither his father or sisters attended the wedding. But Bernice had met them at his mother's funeral. It was obvious there would not be any family admiration.

Richard was concerned about Bernice's adjustment to living in Bridgeboro. There was no Ten Oaks Country Club. That was one reason why he was listed in the records of The Bridge Valley Country Club as a charter member. He helped form the Club after he returned to Bridgeboro. With his thoroughbred Southern Belle.

After they became engaged Bernice admitted she had subtracted five years from her age, making her thirty to his twenty-five. But she was a virgin. And Richard found himself remembering Anna Mae Kirk whenever he was having sex with Bernice. She let him use her body whenever she thought she could become pregnant. She did want a baby. Desperately. The first grandchild. At least there was a lot of trying to get her pregnant.

Bernice Livingston definitely was a helpmate to him. She had become round and shapeless but her weekly trips to a beauty parlor and expensive clothes made her attractive. After twenty years, Richard summed Bernice up as a frigid fizzle or Freudian fodder who gave their child and charities more time and concern than she ever gave him.

HE would always remember knowing Audrey McNeil. She had been a waitress at the Pike Diner. He had pursued her during one of the times when Bernice took several weeks and several thousand dollars to *go home.* She wanted to help her sisters give Momma and Daddy an extravagant fiftieth anniversary party at The Club. He was too busy to attend.

He had developed the habit of stopping at the Pike Diner on his way to or from the office. He noticed Audrey's pretty smile and her attractive bust and her wedding ring. He settled for a pleasant greeting and good service, wishing for more.

One night, he had to go to the *Beef and Ale Club*, to discuss political problems. The Pub was the hang out where he met with Charlie Barnes and Bill Fischer. Much to his surprise, he noticed Audrey McNeil in a dark corner, alone. Richard took his drink to her table and whispered, "You look as though you need a shoulder."

She told Richard her sad story of how she had just divorced her abusive husband and had to move into Taylor Park. With her two sons.

She hoped her girlfriend could keep taking care of her boys because she was going to have to get a second job. So she could pay the rent. Richard told the bar tender to tell his friends he could not wait for them.

They found a country road. He overlooked the fact Audrey was a waitress and cringed when she used poor grammar. He hid his disappointment when he discovered she wore "falsies". After she gave him a blow job and let him use his finger to please her, he wanted to be with her, again.

Richard offered to pay her rent. She let him take her to a motel. Audrey made Anna Mae seem like a novice. He learned how much he could pleasure a woman with his tongue. He became addicted to sexual gratification. After several hours he was exhausted and exhilarated. He wanted to shout from the rooftops he had come three times in two hours!

He paid for shoes and clothes for her kids. He paid for her baby sitting. During his first unforgettable experience of being in the sixty-nine position he thought about Bernice. Would he dare to suggest this position to her!

One night Audrey refused to accept money and to meet him again. She made him feel *macho*. Several times, when he remembered what he had done with Audrey he masturbated in the guest bathroom, while Bernice was knitting in the den. He hated himself, because he knew that Charlie and Lou still had a passionate marriage and he remembered how Bill used to brag about Julie's willingness to please him.

Audrey told him she would meet him, one more time. He stuffed his wallet with large bills. They did have sex, but lying in a motel bed, hoping she would use her tongue to arouse him again he heard her say this *definitely* would be the last time they would meet.

"I've been seeing someone else. And he wants to marry me. We're going to move to California and I'll have a blessed chance to start over." She got off the bed and quickly dressed.

She refused to take his money. She made no threats. Their affair was not even worth enough that she wanted to take advantage of it. He watched the door close behind her.

YES, Richard Livingston hated his past. There was *nothing* and there was *no one* . . . except Bill Fischer. Richard used the word friend whenever he spoke of Bill. Sometimes, since Bill's tragic death and after too many martinis, he'd even get tears in his eyes.

But how much had he really liked Bill? How much of their friendship was marred by his own envy of Bill's good looks, his charm, his manliness and his success with his company. And with women! How many times did he feel like throwing his drink in Bill's face as he listened to Bill mention his affairs in college and the beautiful Navy nurses who took care of him. Especially the one who dressed his wounds with such tender, loving care!

It was a known fact how many females in the *Fischer Company* would gladly lie down for Bill. Julie Fischer had and even though Bill admitted he doubted her pregnancy, he married her because he knew she adored him and she would make him a good helpmate. It was obvious Lou Barnes and Bernice were smitten by Bill's good looks and dashing personality.

How many times had he driven past the Company and watched a new addition being built. How many times had he realized Bill was gaining on him in wealth and power.

THAT Saturday morning Richard Livingston sat at his desk and carefully arranged the contents of his brief case on his new desk. After an hour of reviewing his assets a smug smile appeared. The old feeling of hope was filling his heart. He could control his future! Who had said, *A wise man will desire no more than he may get justly; use soberly, distribute cheerfully, and leave contentedly?* What a damn fool that would be! He had been slowed, even stopped in the past, but he was ready to try again.

Richard reached into his briefcase to find the Prospectus. Included was a picture of a three story Dutch Colonial farm house. Other photographs showed out buildings and a large barn. He absorbed the details describing how many acres, location, features and price. Charles Barnes had given the Prospectus to him.

"Here's some bedtime reading, Unless you talk in your sleep. Bottom line is, I'm looking for a partner. For an idea I have. Let me know if you're interested."

Richard reached for the telephone. As he waited for someone to answer in the Barnes' Real Estate office, he was grinning. He had enough money and more than enough determination, and he would have Charlie working with him.

He would beat Julie at her game. This time!

TWELVE

SUNDAY MORNING brought cloudy and windy weather.

Beth didn't care. She was going to be with Brad Livingston. Sneaking another secret date.

Liz still was in bed so she left a note about going to the movies. She didn't mention with whom but she better check what was playing.

As she already had done previously she would take the bus to Doylestown, one of larger towns in Bucks County, where no one should know them. She would get off the bus a half block from the movie theater. Where she would blend in with the ticket lines.

Her heartbeats began to pound out of synch as soon as she saw the familiar car. She felt excited as she quickly opened the door and slid into the front seat. "Hello."

"Hi." Brad leaned over and kissed Beth's cheek.

Beth inhaled his after shave cologne. "I don't remember seeing that sweater before."

"Mom bought it for me." He patted the seat next to him. "Hey girl, I need you closer to me. Any particular place you want to go?"

"Not really. I don't know the highways and byways in and out of Bucks County like you do."

"Then I'm in charge. I'm going to take us to a place I want to see. A big farm. On Quarry Road. Outside of Buckingham. Okay?"

"How come you want to see a big farm?"

"Under torture I shall never tell?" Brad laughed.

"Again? You have more secrets than the Easter bunny has jelly beans. Okay, under torture, I shall never tell."

"I just found out my dad and Mr. Barnes are going to buy it."

"Oh? Am I allowed to ask why?"

"Sure. But you'll have to cut your finger and let me suck the blood before I can tell you."

"Forget it. I'm anemic and I can't waste my blood."

"Okay, see if I tell you."

They drove in silence for at least a minute, testing each other's perseverance, until Beth kissed Ray's cheek and whispered, "Why?" into his ear.

"I've decided not to tell you. Until you tell me what you and Dan did last night."

"Wellll. We saw that Elvis Presley movie. Had a milk shake and talked about his trip to Israel. And we necked until we were both worn out. P.S. Joke. But he does kiss me goodnight. How was your date last night?"

"As a matter of fact your date sounds much better than mine. Jeanne
was in another bitchy mood. It was obvious she's as bored with me as I am with her. Even though the band was good I couldn't wait to get her home. I was in bed before mid-night."

"Sorry to hear that." Of course she wasn't. She decided to let Brad do the talking.

"Is that music okay or is something wrong?"

Beth put her hand on his thigh. "I feel kinda nervous. It's been a couple of weeks since we've been alone."

"Hey, it's me, babe. You can't feel nervous with me." He took her left hand to his mouth and kissed the palm. "I'm the guy who loves ya." He kissed a finger and put it on her mole. "And your beauty mark."

Sissy bit his finger. "I still feel as though I'm dreaming and I'm going to wake up and . . . you know one of Liz's favorite words for me *is* dreamer. She says my father was a dreamer and he passed the trait on. Hey, why are you pinching me?"

"To wake you up. I want you wide awake so you can hear me. And
watch me say I l-o-v-e y-o-u. Now, do you think you can remember that?"

"I have to believe you because you take big chances. I try not to think about what might happen if somebody found out about us."

"Pretty soon, I'm going to tell everybody. My folks first and then, you know who."

"Oh god, no! They just might get mad enough they won't pay for you to go to college. Or do something else to punish you."

"How long do you think we can go on like this?"

Beth shrugged and then watched Brad turn off the main highway. "Hey, that sign says Norris Road. Where is this place?"

"We're almost there."

"Why do your father and Mr. Barnes want to buy this farm?"

"I'm going to tell you because I trust you. I just happened to hear a telephone conversation, between my dad and Mr. B. Something about an Industrial Park."

Beth remembered Julie calling Brad's father, Dickie Living-ston. Wouldn't Julie love to know what Dickie and Charlie Barnes were up to? "So you can take Business Administration and Marketing at Princeton and take over managing the park."

"Sounds like a plan. I could give you a good job. And we could be Mr. and Mrs. Industrial Park. I even heard Dad say something about a Mall. Eventually."

"I really think I'd rather be Mrs. Mall, if you don't mind."

"Here's the big **FOR SALE** sign I've been looking for. See the sign says this place is being offered by the BARNES REALITY COMPANY."

"What a lane. This is . . . was a big farm. Who lived here?"

Brad turned the car into the lane and began to drive very slowly around ruts and rocks. "I think a family named Hunsburger. The old folks died and the kids don't want to be farmers. So, here it is. The end of family tradition and ripe for development."

Beth peered through the windshield and frowned at a forlorn scene. Unused, no longer needed out buildings. A large barn with a solid stone foundation with wooden sides covered with faded red paint. And a tired looking three story house.

Beth felt a wave of sadness. "You mean ready to be raped."

"I'm going to park behind the corn crib. Out of sight from the road."

After Brad parked the car Beth opened her door and stood next to the car. She noticed a Spring House and hoped she could take a look inside. Then she observed the gambrel roof of the Dutch Colonial farmhouse and stared at the porch. She envisioned rocking chairs there. "Sorry, Brad. I wasn't listening. Repeat, please."

"I was asking if you want to walk around?"

"Love to. I don't get to see any old houses and I already love this one." Beth walked across a cement patio and looked through the window of a door. She immediately thought *mud room* and smiled. Thank you, Julie. Otherwise I would not know what I'm looking into.

She felt Brad behind her. He put his arms around her waist. "What's
so interesting?"

"A mud room."

"How about a shed?" Brad nestled his face in her neck and kissed
her.

"You call it what you want to and I'll call it what Julie Fischer told
me."

Brad pulled back. "Hey, do me a favor and don't mention her any
more today."

Beth snickered. "Okay. If you let me get off this step. *Por favor,
amigo.*"

"Not until you tell me the pass word."

"*Yo le amor.*"

"That'll do for now." He backed down the steps.

Beth walked past a bay window and stepped onto the porch. There
were two doors in the front of the house which faced in the direction of
the driveway. Beth peered into the first window and saw a large room
with a fireplace. The wide mantle went from one end of a walk-in
fireplace to the other. She walked across the porch to a double window
which gave a view of a larger room   Along the outside wall was
another fireplace with a more ornate mantle. A large archway led to a
landing and she could see up the stairs for about half the height of the
high ceiling. She felt sadness when she thought of the words
destruction and then *progress.*

She walked to the edge of the porch and peered across the lawn.
"What a pity . . . to destroy all of this. Can't you just imagine what
could have happened here? First the Indians. Hunting in those woods
over there and probably fishing and trapping in Poquessing Creek,
because I saw a sign at the last intersection that named the creek. Then
the damn settlers showed up.

"Those Dutch and English brought their ambitions and their goals
about creating a new country for their children. What were dreams for
some meant nightmares for others.   But, that's past history. End of
speech."

"But you like this house and the Indians could never have built it."

"I'll bet your dad and Mr. Barnes aren't planning on letting it be
part

of the Industrial Park? Right? I believe your shrug means a *no*. So, in just a few months all of these buildings will be past history. Just like the Indians."

Beth walked to a large oak tree. It was surrounded by a bed of ivy. "Just try to imagine how old this tree is. Most likely over two hundred years old and in fifteen minutes a saw can rip through it, or a bull dozer will knock it down. And for what? A stupid parking lot. I know, you think I'm . . . " Beth paused as Brad wrapped his arms around her. " . . . crazy."

"No. Sentimental." He kissed her nose. "Tell you what I'm going to do. I'm going to ask my dad to save this tree. Just for you."

Beth looked into Brad's dark brown eyes. She always admired his long lashes. She traced a finger along the scar on his jaw as she remarked, "You do that. And, while you're at it, tell him I want a brass plaque put on the trunk. I want it to say, *In Memory of Beth Rhodes - Who Once Stood Here.* Then all of the thousands of people who come here to work, or hopefully to shop, 'cause I want you to also tell him that I want a mall instead of a business park, will know that once upon a time, there was an Earthling named Beth Rhodes." She wrapped her arms around Brad's waist, "Then I'll be remembered. Before the next group of developers come along and saw down the tree. For the next project."

"Isn't it enough that I'll remember you. Here with me."

Beth shook her head. "You're also going to be past history. And when you go, that will be the end of me too. Just like my daddy. Oh sure, he has a marker on his grave and Liz and I talk about him. . . but not too many people really knew him."

Brad pushed Beth away from him. "Man, you *are* sentimental today.
Or, in a mood. Just remember that *our* children will remember us."

"Huh. Now, who's a dreamer? How many times do you ever talk about *your* great-grandfather? And you even knew some of your relatives. That's more than I ever did. Who remembers the Indians who hunted here and, okay even the settlers, who lived here? They most likely were forgotten, a few months after they returned to the happy hunting land."

"Know what? You won't be happy with just a plaque."

Beth grinned. "I know. I want more than just a piece of metal. I'm going to do something . . .special. I want to be remembered, long after I'm gone."

Brad kissed her forehead. "Yeah, for Beth Rhodes. As famous as Vicki Lynn."

"At least I know what I want to be." She held his hand. "Let's walk
to the Spring House.

"What do you want to do? That will make a lasting impression on the world?"

Brad looked up at the gray sky, as if searching for his answer. He shrugged. "I guess I've never thought past college, followed by a good job hopefully *not* in *The B.C.,* getting married, no, wait a minute," Brad pulled Beth closer and whispered into her hair, "The way I feel right now, I think I want to get married before I leave Princeton and then worry about a job. Think you can handle that?"

Beth nodded. "Sounds great but according to what I've read, that would not be a good idea. Sometimes so many other things interfere, that the person doesn't finish college. I think you should get your degree first. At least one of them."

"How ambitious do you think I am? And how do you think I can concentrate on getting any degree with you on my mind?   And not having you to study with.   Or to write my papers?"

Beth felt tears welling around her eyes. She squeezed her eyes shut but still they slid down her cheeks. She quickly wiped them away, hoping Brad did not notice them.

But he did. "What did I say wrong?"

Beth snuggled against his new sweater. "Just hold me. Real tight."

Pressing her against his chest Brad ran his fingers through her hair and rubbed the back of her neck. "Okay. Okay. Tell me what's been bugging you. I knew from when you got into the car, that something was on your mind."

"Just hold me.   So I can smell your after shave and even the detergent
smell in your clothes. I need to remember. Being with you." She tilted her face up to his and kissed his cheek. "You know my daddy was my confidant and now . . . I don't have anybody. Except you. I love you, Brad.   Too much for my own good."

"You can never love another person too much.   And I love you back.

You know that. Want to go sit on the porch, so you can tell me what's wrong?"

"No, let's keep walking. I'll be okay."

"Good. And now, Mrs. Livingston, besides the lovely old house, which probably needs a new heater, a new pump, maybe new plumbing and wiring and lots of paint, let me show you the other great feature of this property. Ta da. The barn!" Brad steered Beth to the ramp which led to double doors, wide enough for a tractor and a divided door which led to the hay loft.

After they closed it behind them, Beth let her eyes wander around. "Wow. It doesn't look this big from the outside."

"These are just the hay lofts. The box stalls, feed room, tack room, and whatever else opens into the barn yard, are below us. Do you plan on having horses, Mrs. Livingston?"

Beth shrugged. "Later. First, I plan to have the house restored and get advice from an interior decorator on colors and furniture. But right now, I'm just thinking about . . . right now."

Brad lifted her face. He leaned down and rubbed his tongue across her lips. "And right now, I'm thinking about how I can make you know . . . how much I love you."

Beth noticed she was beginning to feel warm. "Just being here with you tells me that you do. And the poems you write for me. And my watch . . . and," Beth's eyes filled to overflowing again. "Because you're my . . . everything."

"I won't let you down. I promise. I need you too."

"I guess I'm also feeling guilty. Cheating on other people. Even our
selves."

Brad led Beth to a small pile of hay which had accumulated under the ladder to the loft above. "Are you allergic to dust?"

"Not that I know of."

Sitting on the hay and leaning against a wall he pulled her to lean against him. "You have to know I want to throw up every time I have to be with Jeanne. And when I know you have dates with other guys and you're going to the prom with Dan. Tonight, Mrs. B. is having a big family dinner for Jeanne's birthday. It isn't until Tuesday and already Mom bought two presents for me to give to her. With a smile on my face."

"Do you ever tell her that you love her?"

"I used to. Hey, I'd be lying if I didn't admit I used to think she was

a trophy steady. Of all the guys in Bucks County I was the lucky one dating Jeanne Barnes. And I told her I loved her. But now I don't even like her. She can be a stubborn bitch and I'm getting to be such a habit with her that as soon as we get any place, she ignores me.

"I've never really loved any girl, until you came into my life. This morning I even hinted that Jeanne and I might be getting tired of each other and Mom exclaimed, 'Don't be so silly. Why you and Jeanne are havin' so much fun. And you looked so cute dancin' together last night. Now go get ready for church and you'll feel better.'." Brad shrugged. "Beth, please believe me. Even though I haven't proved it to you yet."

"Don't be dumb. Don't tell anybody yet. It could be worse than walking across glowing coals." She lifted his hand to her lips. "Lying and cheating are enough for now. Let me dream that after we get into college we can write and call. .And maybe even meet some place."

"Hot damn. That sounds exciting. I can hardly wait."

"But you'll still have the same problem you have now. Even if you've broken up with Jeanne, I can imagine what your folks will say when you tell them you're dating Beth Rhodes. From Taylor Park."

Brad looked into Beth's eyes. "That I'm in love with Beth Rhodes. And I'm happy to hear you're planning on going to college. Because you are going to write the best essay." He kissed her forehead. "I'm going to talk you up at home, because Dad is one of the judges and I'm going to remind him how many excellent articles you've written for the school newspaper and how hard you've worked on the Senior Yearbook and how Mr. Stookey is always posting your poems in Lit class. After you win, it'll be a lot easier for me to tell them about us."

"Then I'll try even harder."

Brad rubbed his tongue along her lips until she let him put his tongue into her mouth and explore. After he pulled back he murmured, "I want to show you how much I love you."

Beth allowed Brad to push her down to the pile of straw. She put her arms around his neck and pulled him next to her. She clung to him while he covered her face and throat with moist kisses. A strong desire began to flow through her like a rushing river. She knew she could succumb . . . and drown. While she still was in control, what did she want to do?

86

Brad unbuttoned her jacket and pushed it away from her turtle neck sweater. "Now."

She let him push her sweater above the top of her bra. They had gone this far before. So she wasn't afraid. Yet. Next he would begin to kiss the bulge of her breasts above her bra. And then he'd rest his head on her breasts and whisper tender . . . *oh oh, what was he going to do now?*

Brad was pushing up her skirt. Was she going to stop him? "Brad? Let's not get carried away. I really don't want you to . . ."

"I just want to make you feel good." He watched her roll her head. "Okay, then you feel me." He took her right hand and laid it on top of the bulge in his chinos. "I just want you to feel how pumped up I am. You have to know what you do to me. Sometimes, I even get a hard on. In bed. When I'm just thinking about you."

Beth became aware of her pounding heart. Her moist skin. The building desire beginning to consume her. This was the most excited she had ever felt. Brad had never tried to do anything like this before. She moved her hand away from the bulge in his slacks. Was getting her to go all the way one of the reasons he was dating her?

"I just want to kiss you," she whispered. She pushed his head down to the floor, leaned her face closer and began to caress his face. What were his eyes telling her? She kissed them closed so she didn't have to look into them. She kissed his eyelids, his cheeks, his chin and his mouth. Again, she felt his hand slide up her thigh. She stopped kissing him. And waited.

"I won't hurt you." He rolled to his side and covered her mouth with his.

She had to believe he was hoping she wouldn't tell him to stop. She felt his hand slide across her underwear.. Slowly, Brad circled a finger around her sensitive area. Then he stopped as though waiting for her to say something. Of course he knew she was perspiring and her breathing had changed so he must know she was getting aroused. She grabbed his hand.

Beth had to take several gasps before she exclaimed, "Stop. Now. I don't want you to do anything to me. I mean, I want to stay a virgin."

"I just want to . . . to make you feel good." He gave her a long kiss. "This is the first time anybody has touched you down there, isn't it?"

"Yes and I don't want to do anything because I don't want to believe that's why you're dating me," she said into his sweater. And you know what to do, because I'm sure you and Jeanne have…"

Brad covered her mouth with a hand. "Don't ask me what Jeanne and I do and I won't ask you what you and Dan do. And this isn't why I'm dating you. I love you. And I honest to god promise, I will not hurt you. If you would just let me keep kissing you . . . you could enjoy what I'm doing."

Beth pushed his hand away. She pulled down her skirt.

Brad pulled down his fly. "I have to . . . pull out my dick." he breathed into her ear. "He needs more room." He waited.

Beth struggled to sit up.

"What are you doing?"

"I want to look at it. I've never seen a . . . one . . .before. I've only seen a picture in a book. In Health Class."

Brad laughed. He wrapped Beth's hand around what she was looking at. "So what do you think?"

Beth pulled her hand away. "I think we should stop teasing and testing each other . . . before we go any farther." She began to rearrange her sweater.

"Just lie back and relax. I'm not going to do anything that will get you in trouble."

"I can't. I'm just not ready. I know you have a right to be mad at me but . . ." She felt hot tears rolling down her cheeks. "Maybe even hate me. Maybe I'll hate myself. She looked at what he had called his *dick*. She remembered what Evan had told her that *doing it* can make you feel as though you're riding a roller coaster. And you can't wait until you get to the top so you can feel the thrill and excitement. And even beg for another ride.

"I promise I won't hate you. And I won't touch you anymore. But I have a small problem. He won't fit in my pants until he calms down. Or you could help him get smaller?"

Beth stared into his eyes. "Ahh. You have to be kidding."

"Nope. Or I'll do it myself." He reached into his pants pocket and pulled out a handkerchief. He studied Beth's face. "When you say you love me you're supposed to mean all of me. And . . . whatever you want to call it, is part of me."

"And if I do it . . . I'll be making you feel good. Right?"

"Right. And this is not why I am dating you and I am n.o.t. going to tell anybody that you held my member. While it moved up and down in your hand. What's so scary or..."

She gently wrapped her right hand around what he was holding. "I'm doing this because I love you."

"I love you too. Don't squeeze so hard. Just a firm hold and . . . slowly . . . and yeah, that's good." He handed her the handkerchief and whispered, "I'll tell you when you'll need to use that. Keep doing it and . . . " He began to move in her hand and then gasped and finally called out, "Cover it up. Now."

Beth wrapped the handkerchief around Brad's member and continued to hold it. As Brad moaned she watched the cloth become wet. Then what she still was holding became soft and bent. It was almost unbelievable she had actually witnessed what she had read about. And whispered about. And snickered about. And dreamed about . . . doing with Brad.

Brad whispered, "Someday I want to make you feel good."

"Now I feel closer to you. I mean now that we've been more personal with each other and . . . what are you going to do with the handkerchief?"

Brad held it up and asked, "Toss it in a trash can."

Beth nodded. "I'll rinse it out at the pump. And put it under my pillow."

Brad tucked his male parts into his shorts. "Since you just saw what I'm calling my member, for the first time . . . I should tell you that mine is bigger than lover boy Jim Bender's. He sat up and kissed her.

"Thank you for telling me. I appreciate knowing the first member I ever held, is bigger than Jim Bender's. No other girl can say she's had more than I've had. Except those who have had Jim's member inside of her."

Why, out of a clear blue sky, did she think .. .*And Peg I hope you never find out.* Then she heard herself actually say, "Brad, honest to god, I really want to . . . go all the way. Someday."

"I know we will, babe. But we do have something to remember what we did in the barn."

He looked at his watch. "Yo. We have to leave. I can't be late for the damn birthday party."

THERE she was, staring at the bedroom ceiling, hoping to get to sleep. She had to go to school tomorrow. How could she forget Julie Fischer did not want to see her again! How could she forget how much work she had to do to write the best essay?

And how could she forget what she and Brad had done in the barn. He said he wasn't mad so maybe he wasn't dating her to go "all the way". After all he didn't have a condom. Only a handkerchief. But she could keep it under her pillow. Maybe she could go to a drug store where nobody knew her? After all, she was lying when she said she didn't want to *do it!*

Maybe next time?

THIRTEEN

ON TUESDAY AFTERNOON of the following week the secretary of the principal of Bridgeboro High School hurried to the door of the senior typing class. Looking through the glass she observed the students engrossed in their typing exercise. She hated to interrupt them but she had to tell Mrs. Beach that Elizabeth Rhodes had a phone call.

"Mrs. Fischer wants to talk to you." She began to lead the way to the office.

Beth's mind was racing. *Daddy. Tune in. I hope she didn't tell Mr. Jones I had the nerve to argue with her. Of course I'll apologize. Oh god, here we are.*

They entered the large office where Mr. Jones was standing behind the waist high counter which divided the waiting area from the general office. He was smiling! In fact, the usually stern looking principal appeared elated.

"What a surprise to have Julie Fischer call one of our students. How are you making out with the interviews?"

Beth nodded. "Okay." *Liar.*

"Come on into my office. And use my phone." He led Beth into his inner sanctum. She forced a smile as she took the receiver. She thought fast about what she should say, for Mr. Jones to repeat. Did he notice her hand was trembling? "Julie? It's Beth. How are you feeling?"

Grinning, Mr. Jones quietly closed the door behind him.

HOLDING the receiver Julie smiled. She was certain her idea was a good one. After all this was one of the days she had scheduled the girl. For another interview.

"I'm feeling much better, thank you."

"That's good news. Did Dr. Rexinger give you some medicine?"

"Yes. Philip gave me some foul tasting medicine. I'm calling to tell you we're going to continue with the interviews."

"Oh. Thank you. Very much. And I really do want to apologize for . . ."

"Never mind what you said. I really haven't been fair to you because I haven't told you enough about my sister. And why I say the things I do. So, come on down this afternoon as you were supposed to do. And I'm going to tell you the entire story. So you *will* understand."

"Okay. I can be there."

"You'll be glad you did. But before you come down, I want you to go to *Joe's Meat Market* and buy us a Porterhouse steak."

"I really can't stay. I have an awful lot of homework and..."

"You don't have to stay late. I do have enough vegetables and salad stuff. Philip had dinner with me Sunday so I have things left over. Just buy a steak or chops if you'd prefer them. Tell Joe to charge it to my bill."

"Maybe the next time?"

"You have to stay. Maybe every night. I have so much to tell you. I can make your essay a sure winner. I know how important that is for you." She waited.

"Okay. I'll see you . . .soon."

Beth hung up the receiver and stood by Mr. Jones' desk. She closed her eyes and thought, "*Daddy. Help. I think I'm making a big mistake. To make our dream come true.*" If only she could discuss her fear with her father. Impossible. With Brad? Another impossible. She looked at her watch. She was going to see Julie again. In about an hour!

She walked out of Mr. Jones' office and saw the principal and his secretary standing behind the counter. Four eyes looked at her as she asked, "Should I shut the door?"

"It can stay open. Everything all right? You know I did put in a good word for you."

Beth felt frustrated. Mr. Jones sounded just like anybody else would. But then why shouldn't he be curious? After all, Julie was almost like a shaman. She had contact with the high priestess of Bridgeboro. But didn't anybody know it wasn't easy? Thank goodness she had avoided a conversation with Mr. Stookey so that she had not told him she had been dismissed by Julie. Another thank goodness, she had not confessed to Brad!

"Thanks for whatever you did. Julie wants me to go to *Joe's Meat Market* to buy something for our dinner tonight."

Mr. Jones raised his thick eyebrows and nodded to his secretary. "I always said that Julie isn't as difficult as some people want you to believe she is. You be nice to her and she'll be nice to you." He nodded several times and added, "I'll excuse you from returning to your typing class. Just go to your locker if you have to and then do your shopping."

ABOUT an hour later Beth played those words back in her mind. As she walked up the driveway. Slowly. *Daddy, I remembered. You be nice to her and she'll be nice to you. Messy house, uncombed hair, I'll just keep smiling. And asking her questions and hey, the shrubbery's been trimmed.*

Before Beth was able to knock, the front door opened. Julie stood in the doorway, grinning. "I got Sam's son-in-law, Tony, to trim the bushes. So I could watch for your bus."

Beth had to smile. What a surprise. Julie still looked pale and tired but attractive. Her hair was arranged in a becoming style. She was wearing a red woolen skirt with a white blouse and red flats. Beth was no judge of the difference between costume and expensive jewelry but she had to believe she was admiring a real gold bracelet and hoop earrings. And she noticed the wide gold wedding band and a diamond that had to be several carets on Julie's third finger, left hand.

She quickly decided *not* to ask, "Am I in the right house?" But she did remark, enthusiastically, "You sure do look as though you're feeling better"

Julie ignored Beth's remark. She took the bag. "What did you buy?"

"After I told Joe I was buying it for you, he insisted I buy two fillets. Said you'll love them"

Julie closed the door and headed down the long hallway. "And he loves my tips."

Beth followed Julie into the kitchen. It was ready for a picture in *House Beautiful.* Beth watched Julie put the meat into the refrigerator. "We could never afford fillets."

Julie turned and gave Beth a sly smile. "Surely you've heard the saying, 'You can't buy happiness with money?' At least I can spend my money on the best of whatever I do buy."

Beth nodded. "I imagine you can be happier, if you do have money."

Julie sighed. "You're so young. And being poor has influenced your way of thinking. "Of course," she added, as she walked into the laundry room, "money can be a curse."

From the doorway Beth observed the washer, dryer under an outside window and a laundry tub next to the chest freezer. Watching Julie peer into the freezer, she whispered, "I guess I'll never have to worry about that."

Julie selected a package of green beans and one of peas. She showed them to Beth as she announced, "I'm trying to explain, it's all according to the way the money is given to you."

Beth pointed to the green beans. She would have agreed to squash!

Julie put the beans into the refrigerator. "See. I've already made two salads for us. For heaven's sake, take off that awful jacket. And let's go into the living room."

Julie began to lead the way. In the dining room she opened draperies to reveal the bay window. It was obvious the furniture had been polished, the silver cleaned and the papers and typewriter removed from the beautiful table. It was a room to be admired.

The living room looked friendly because several of the table lamps had been lighted. And there was a welcoming fire. Beth put her books on the same chair she had used before. Then her jacket. She quickly took out her note book and watched Julie poke at the fire.

Julie settled in her chair and folded her hands. "I'm sure you can understand what a difference it would be if you were given happy money. Instead of begrudge money."

Beth studied Julie's face. She couldn't take a reading. "I think so."

"Sit down and relax. Now let me ask you, my dear . . . sorry, I remember you want me to call you Beth, how would you want money left to you?"

Beth forced herself to laugh. "In cash."

Julie also laughed. "I mean under what conditions?"

Beth shrugged. "That the person really wanted me to have it."

"I'm sure caring about, even loving others is important to you."

Facing Julie from the opposite side of the fireplace Beth said, "You're right. Loving others does mean a lot to me."

"I told you over the phone I'm going to tell you something which will make your essay a sure winner. The judges won't even consider the other essays." Julie smiled. "I'm going to tell you the story behind Vicki's love letters."

Suddenly Beth felt tense. Holding the notebook and the pen she murmured, "I'm ready."

94

Julie settled into the wing back chair. She crossed her shapely legs. "Vicki was not a beautiful woman. By that, I mean as far as having movie star features and a rose petal complexion. I have to admit she was pretty but she had a tanned weathered complexion. She loved the outdoors. I like to stay indoors."

She reached under the chair and held out a frame. She indicated Beth was to take it. "I thought you might like to see what I consider a good picture of Vicki." Julie watched Beth study the picture. She felt pleased. Confident. After Beth finally looked up, she stated, "I'm certain you've seen that picture before. It's the one which was used on many of the book jackets. And in newspapers and magazines. But as you can see, that one is autographed. Maybe you would like to have it?"

"I'd love to have it. Thank you. Thank you very much." How could she feel so elated, and hesitant?

Julie sighed. "Unfortunately that picture doesn't show the Vicki I knew." Julie smiled at the girl's frown. "You see my famous sister had a dual personality."

Beth squinted. "You're not trying to tell me that she had a . . . a mental problem? Because if you are, I just . . . "

Julie held up a hand. "Vicki was quite sane. Perhaps eccentric would be a good word. She could be a vibrant and unforgettable women. To strangers she was charming and gracious. To her family she was a bitch. Yes, I know I used that word before and you cringed, but I'll use it again."

"Did Earle and his wife think Vicki was a bitch?"

Julie grinned. "In other words am I speaking for the family? Yes, my dear, I am."

"Why would your brothers dislike her? What did she ever do to them that was so awful?"

Julie coughed before she replied. "It's what she didn't do. She never bothered with them. She never remembered anybody's birthdays. Maybe cards at Christmas time? But she completely shut herself off from her own flesh and blood."

"But wait a minute," Beth blurted out. "She never actually hurt them or pulled off any dirty deals on them? I mean, like borrowing money and never paying them…"

Julie put a hand up again. "Vicki didn't have to borrow money. From the time she sold her first novel she was on her way up. She had a good financial advisor who invested her money wisely. She backed several plays which turned out to be hits. She was filthy rich."

"But your brothers still hated her?"

Julie held a long fixed stare at Beth. "You still believe it's personal."

"As you said, I don't understand." She looked at the picture.

"See that smile?" Julie used a strong voice. "That glow in her eyes and the sexy but sweet look. It's all an act. A joke. She didn't live her life the way her books and her poems would make you believe she would." She coughed several times before she exclaimed, "She didn't really like people. She liked to hurt. She didn't know how . . . Julie continued to cough.

Beth put the picture on the table. "I'll get you some water."

"Fill up a pitcher. And bring me one of the bottles under the sink."

Beth hurried into the kitchen. She had a mental picture of Julie getting a load on and leaving both of the fillets for her to eat. She smiled and whispered, "Damn. It's not funny. It could end up being another dud of an interview. How do I get her to talk about the letters?"

In the living room Julie gave Beth a sheepish smile. "Even a glass of ice. Thank you for waiting on me. Now, let's get . . ." Julie stopped as the phone rang. "Be a dear and answer that for me." She pointed to an end table alongside a three cushion couch. "Just say Mrs. Fischer's residence."

Beth followed Julie's instructions.

"Ask who it is." Julie said loudly.

"Mrs. Fischer would like to know who's calling please?" After she heard the man identify himself she covered the mouth piece and said, "It's Matt Fox. From the *Cribb Real Estate Company.*"

Beth was surprised at how quickly Julie moved. "Do you want me to leave?"

"No need to," Julie responded. She took the receiver and sat on the couch. "Matt. What did you find out?" While she listened she nodded, she smiled and she frowned.

"I don't care if it is both of them. Get it." She paused as though thinking, before she added, "God knows what I'll do with it, but I'll figure out something. And I might have to sell something to buy it. But if they think it would be a good location for an Industrial Park then you start looking into that possibility for me."

Beth walked to the fireplace to use the poker. She wanted to appear as though she was concentrating on rearranging the logs. While she looked busy her mind was racing. *Could Julie be talking about the farm Brad took me to on Sunday? She wants to buy, our barn. Should I tell Brad? Of course not. He'll tell his dad and I really want Julie to buy the place. I can't believe that I'd actually hear about a real conflict between Dickie Livingston and Julie Fisher.* She poked more glowing coals and decided to add another log.

Julie laughed. "No. I don't want to move the plant. I still have five acres where we are now. In fact, I have the blueprints for a three story office complex... What?.. They're all rumors. Howard is still the CEO. I just got a new man to be his assistant." She listened, shrugged and replied, "Yes, the V.P of Finance left. His choice. I'm still looking for a man to fill his place... Yes, Howard is good. His problem is that sometimes he forgets who the president still is."

Julie laughed, then coughed. "Oh, I'm still recovering from a cold. Now, about the farm," Suddenly she had firmness in her voice. "How much did they bid?... Okay. Stay higher.... All right.... Fine.... Just keep in touch. I'm counting on you. Goodbye."

Holding the receiver, Julie did not move.

Holding the poker, Beth did not move.

Finally Julie hung up the receiver and laughed. It sounded forced. "I'm buying a farm."

Beth turned to face Julie. "Just like that?"

Julie stood. "Just like that. Now, I really do need a drink." She took long strides to her chair. She opened the bottle and poured some of its contents into the glass. She pushed the cubes around and then sipped.

Beth decided to gamble. "Why are you buying a farm? I mean, you said you don't know what to do with it?"

Julie's smugness was apparent. "It'll be a good investment. That's something else money is for. To make more money." She drank until there were only ice cubes in the glass.

While Julie was pouring in more Scotch and water on top of the ice, Beth decided to be even braver. "Where is the farm?"

"I think it's somewhere near Buckingham."

"I guess somebody doesn't want to farm anymore?" Beth softly suggested. "It's amazing there still are some large farms left in the County."

"I think Matt said this one is around one hundred and eighty acres. He mentioned the Poquessing Creek runs through part of the property. Supposed to have some historical significance that I don't really care about. But Matt did say it's a lovely location."

Beth did not think before she said, "I think I may know where it is."

Julie's eyebrows went high. "Oh? How come?"

Beth wanted to disappear from the scene. How stupid could she be? "Well, maybe I do." She quickly looked at her watch and was about to suggest they think about dinner when she heard Julie ask her a question which she did not want to have to answer.

Julie concentrated on Beth's face. "You go for drives with a boyfriend?"

Beth felt the signs of a familiar pain in her guts. If Julie could find out what Mr. Livingston was doing why couldn't she find out about Brad? "I really don't have a boyfriend."

"Don't you have dates?"

"Danny Friedman. He and I . . . pal around together."

"That doesn't surprise me. Who else?" Several quick sips.

"Fred Harding."

"His father works at the plant. In Production Planning. Good man."

Beth looked at her watch again. She *had* to change the subject. Or she wouldn't be able to breathe. "It's after five o'clock. Shouldn't we start dinner?"

Julie shook her head. "Not yet. I still have more to show you." She reached behind the chair and produced two large manila envelopes. They were bulging from their contents. The larger envelope had been reinforced with tape. Julie made it appear she was having difficulty holding them before she leaned them against the front of her chair.

Beth watched Julie's dramatic presentation of the envelopes. Now what was going to happen? What was she in for?

"Come over here and take this stuff Before I change my mind."

Beth stood in front of Julie. "What . . . are they?"

Julie reached into one of the envelopes and pulled out a bulging notebook. And loose tablet paper. "This notebook contains an outline and even several chapters for Vicki's next novel. The one nobody knows about." Julie held up two loose pages, "Vicki also was an artist. Without instruction too. Whenever she was inspired by something or someone she would either write a poem or draw a sketch. Or both." Julie offered Beth the notebook and the loose papers. "Just think about it, my dear. You're holding something that Vicki Lynn actually held in her hands. Doesn't it do something for you?" She laughed, sarcastically.

Holding more loose pages, Julie declared, "My beloved sister was making a collection of her favorite quotations and philosophical sayings which she had found along the way. Plus things she had written. She told me she was going to combine everything in one book and use the title *Vicki's Vignettes.*"

Beth was thrilled. Overwhelmed. She held the book, almost reverently. "Oh, wow. This is un*real.*" Why did she feel she should be careful?

"I'm not finished." Julie picked up the envelope that still was on the floor. "I won't take it out, because you're not ready to read it yet but this envelope has another notebook in it. This one contains the original scribbles for what would have been her fifth book of poetry. If it had been published." Julie held the envelope out to Beth. "Here. Take them. Have fun."

Beth backed into her chair. She laid the envelope with the unpublished poetry on the floor. Slowly she began to look through *Vicki's Vignettes.* She was actually looking at Vicki's handwriting. And sketches. She wanted to close her eyes and call her daddy. Finally, she become aware Julie was coughing.

Beth looked up. "I'm so excited I feel like crying. It's so nice of you to let me read these notebooks. But I am kinda puzzled. I thought you told me that everything had been published?"

"I did say that, didn't I? Well, now there are two of us who know the truth."

"You mean no one else knows?"

"Earle did. But he wasn't interested. Remember I told you Earle was a religious man and he disapproved of Vicki's writings."

"I can't believe he'd feel that way. Her poems and stories are filled with beauty and . . . and love! Vicki Lynn was…"

"No good!" Julie poured more scotch into her glass and after a long sip declared, "Our sister was no damn good!"

Beth heard the words which Julie yelled at her and translated them to mean, I will not allow you to admire my sister! Beth held the notebook against her chest.

Seconds ticked by as the teenager and the widow stared at each other, each thinking her own thoughts and daring the other to try to contradict them.

Finally Julie lifted her glass to her mouth. She tilted it so fast she spilled some of the contents on her skirt. She brushed off the drops and said, "I'm sorry you're so excited over the unpublished books, my dear. I think you've misunderstood my intentions of letting you see them." She paused to smile as she watched Beth's expression change. "I've given them to you, only to read. Here, in my house."

"You mean I can't write about them? In my essay?"

"Not even in your essay."

"These would make my essay the best one. Everybody would be so excited. And you even told me you want me to win. And not only that, but you can't keep these…"

"Oh yes, I can," Julie snapped out. "Just consider yourself an exception. If you tell anyone about these unpublished books, I'll call you a liar. Right after her death, Earle went to her apartment in New York and packed all of her belongings. He had a moving van bring it down here and we put most of it in the middle bedroom. And some things are in the loft over the garage. And that's where it's all going to stay. Until I decide what to do with it. After all I am the Executrix of her estate."

"But after you die. Then what will . . . "

"After I die," Julie butted in, "the vultures might find bare bones." She watched Beth over the rim as she emptied the glass. "I may destroy everything. Just as my life was destroyed."

Beth was afraid whatever she might say would be misconstrued. Except sympathy. "I imagine the fire was the most awful thing that ever happened to you. I'm sorry you had to have such a sad experience." She waited. Nothing. Wisely, Beth decided not to dwell on the subject of the fire. In a lighter voice she blurted out, "Maybe it's time we do start dinner?"

Julie grinned. "You think I'm drinking too much."

Beth shrugged. "I don't know how much you can drink."

"Lots. Before I get really tight. Right now I have a desire to get loaded."

"You really shouldn't drink so much. It isn't good for you. Especially your liver."

"Ha! Then I should be dead by now because I've been drinking for years and years. And I haven't had the good fortune of dying."

"But you are," Beth said with as much concern as she could show. "Every time you drink, you die a little."

"That's the best news yet." Julie coughed before she added, "It isn't good for me, huh? Do you have any other reasons why I should stop?" She filled the glass half way from the bottle.

"You should remember who you are. I mean, you're an important person in this community." She watched Julie smile and shrug. "You must be proud to be Mrs. William Fischer. So maybe you should try to cut back and . . . " She knew she was rambling.

"Of course. Like you father did."

"My father cared very much." She could barely breathe watching Julie grin at her. "He really did. It's just that he was a dreamer instead of a doer." Why couldn't she stop talking? "He wanted to be things and do things he couldn't do. He couldn't accept his physical limitations. So he drank to lessen his frustrations."

"I drink to drown my despair."

"My father experienced despair. And he had bouts of depression."

"Really? I imagine living with your mother would depress any man."

"My mother is frustrated also."

"Hmmm. And besides that she has hot pants."

"Did Geoff Greer tell you that!"

"Why does it matter who told me?"

"I just can't believe that Geoff would say anything like that." Beth felt hot tears building up around her eyeballs.

"Geoff did not tell me. In fact, he never has said a nasty thing about your family."

"He was always nice to my father. And Liz."

"All Geoff has ever said about your family is that he thought it was a shame your father was so gentle. Personally I think he was too much of a wimp for his own good."

"My daddy was brave enough to get the Purple Heart. I have it now."

"Too bad he didn't pretend your mother was a German and knock her around a little." Julie sipped. "Didn't it bother him to know his wife was running around?"

"He blamed himself. Just in case you don't know, my daddy was wounded in Italy. He and some other soldiers got caught in a mine field and there were lots of explosions and daddy's back was broken. The operations only made him stiffer. And he stayed thin and pale and always moved very slowly. He was in the Vets Hospital for many months. But, even while he was overseas, Liz started to waitress. And she got restless. But daddy loved her and he . . . " she shrugged, "just stuck it out."

"He was a damn fool."

"He told me he couldn't complain because he couldn't offer her any more. He never even finished high school because his father died when he was sixteen and he had to help his mother feed his brother and two younger sisters. And pay the rent."

She clutched the manila envelope with Vicki's poetry to her chest. "Inside, he was very frustrated. And when he drank he was bigger and better . . . than he really was."

Beth sat tall and lifted her chin. "He could write while he was drinking. Oh sure nothing too super but I have all of the poems and stories he wrote for me." Hugging the envelope she began to rock. "They're very special to me."

Julie felt sad watching Beth struggle. But now the girl was ready. "I can tell how much you loved him. Even though he was a flop as a husband and a dud as a provider"

"He *always* loved us. We always had enough food to eat. It's just that no one tried to understand how he was suffering."

"Except you. You understood what he was going through." She smiled and added, softly, "So you loved him." She watched Beth nod before she brought forth a larger manila envelope. She plopped it on her lap, knowing she had Beth's attention. "Do you know what's in this envelope?"

"Of course not."

"It contains the reason why *I* drink."

Beth heard the intake of her breath. She suspected Julie was carrying out a plan. And the plan included *her.*

"You just told me why your daddy had to drink. Didn't you?"

"I guess so."

Julie offered the envelope to Beth. "This is my reason."

Beth moved the tablet from her lap and took the bulging envelope. She unfastened the metal clasp and peered inside. She was looking at envelopes. Twenty? Thirty? Finally she pulled out one of the business size envelopes and studied the address. To herself she read, *Mr. M.H. Chesterfield, Box 114, Pineville Post Office, Pennsylvania.* She knew if she wanted an explanation she would have to ask so she forced herself to look up. She hated the smug expression on Julie's face.

"Pull out another one."

Beth searched until she saw an address which grabbed at her. *Miss Victoria Lynn Phipps, 1700 Delancy Place, Apartment C, New York, New York,* She pulled out more envelopes. They had been addressed to either Mr. M. H. Chesterfield or Miss Victoria Lynn Phipps.

She felt Julie watching and waiting. She might as well ask. "These are the love letters?" She watched Julie nod. "Who is Mr. Chesterfield?"

Julie reached for the pitcher to pour more water in her glass. She made the girl wait while she added Scotch. "Don't you want to guess?"

Beth cleared her throat. "It's someone I know?"

Julie grinned. "If you're thinking of Dickie Livingston or Charlie Barnes, the answer is n-o. They were never macho enough or charming enough for my dear sister." Julie lifted her glass as though proposing a toast. "Here's to Victoria Lynn Phipps, the great. The genius who had everything. Except a husband. My dear sister, the lying sneaking no good bitch!"

After a long drink she announced, "Mr. Chesterfield, my dear, was William Fischer, Junior." She waited for the girl to respond. "I think you're speechless. You can't believe what I'm telling you. But those letters will reveal everything that was going on behind my back."

Beth *had* become speechless. Why couldn't she be thrilled? Just think how much she was being told. Instead she felt despair. Anger. "What do you call your husband?"

"You think I'm condoning his behavior? He was a dog. But what dog wouldn't fuck a bitch if she stuck her tail in his face?" Julie stopped talking. "What are you looking for?"

"I'm just checking postdates. How long this affair lasted."

"Their affair lasted the longest. Bill and I were very much in love. But business was booming. Meaning we couldn't take time off and I agreed we'd have a big wedding, later. So we had a small wedding. At Earle's church. Only Dad Fischer and Alice and Earle attended."

Julie paused to gloat. "In fact, we just took business trips and called them honeymoons." She paused to study the puzzled look on Beth's face. "But I was happy, no matter what. With my wonderful husband and my beautiful wedding present, Deer Lake Manor."

"When did your sister meet Mr. Fischer?"

Julie took a long drink before she sounded, "Hmmm. About a year after we were married. She had just returned from an overseas book signing tour."

Julie stood. "I am going to start dinner. And set the table while you read some of the letters. I know you'll enjoy them."

"I kinda feel like I'm prying."

"Nonsense. Think of your essay."

Beth felt apprehension. How could she pit herself against such a clever woman? She nodded. "Yes, I do want to . . . " Julie interrupted her.

"If you can't finish reading the letters tonight you can come back tomorrow and as many days as it takes to read all of them."

"And the manuscripts? I want to write about the poems and her unpublished book."

"You don't have to take time to read those. I already told you, you can't mention them in your essay."

Beth sat tall as she looked up at Julie. "But I can use the letters?"

Julie held onto the back and leaned against the arm of the chair. "They'll make your essay the winner."

Beth returned some of the white envelopes into the manila one. "My daddy and I read some biographies that mentioned Vicki's love life. But I never read about an affair between her and your husband. Why do you want to expose their affair?"

"It can't hurt Bill now. Nor the company. And the media can't hurt me. Not even Dickie Livingston."

Beth wanted to creep into the safety zone. "But after all of these years?" She checked a date. "Nineteen, twenty years? Why don't you just destroy this evidence? And allow yourself to forget about it all?"

Julie focused on Beth's face. "I want to help you win the contest. And those letters will . . ." her voice trailed off as she paid attention to what Beth was doing.

Beth returned all of the letters and stood. She placed the manila envelopes on the seat of the chair and picked up her pen and notebook.

Julie watched the girl put her notebook and pen in her stupid looking drawstring handbag. Now she was picking up her cheap vinyl jacket. "What are you doing?"

Beth held her jacket against her chest. Her posture made a statement. "I'm leaving. Before you tell me to get out. And I will be the one to say I'm not returning."

Even though she was trembling inside, Beth was proud of her composure. Her voice was loud and clear even though it seemed as though someone else was saying, "Since I won't use the letters I guess this will be my last interview."

Julie held tight to the chair. "Are you crazy? You put that jacket down and listen to me." Her face was flushed. She had a wild look in her eyes.

"No. I'm not crazy. Just innocent and naïve. That's what you called me the last time I was here. And how you hoped I'd stay that way. So you could get me to fall into your nifty trap. Well, I'm sorry but I've caught on and I want nothing to . . ."

"What are you talking about?" Julie demanded loudly. "*What* have you caught on to. I don't understand what..."

"Oh boy, there's that word again. That's the word you used over the telephone. 'Perhaps I am jealous but after I tell you my story you'll understand.' Well, I've heard your story and suddenly I do understand."

"So why are you leaving?"

"Because you're not telling me about Vicki Lynn. All along you've been telling me about Julie Fischer. I know I'm an alcoholic but it's not my fault."

"You *are* crazy," Julie said loudly. "Because you won't try to understand."

"But I do. You were real clever helping me remember my father. You hoped I still had compassion for drunks. I loved him because he was my father. But that doesn't mean I forgave him for being so weak. And I can't excuse you either."

"I'm not asking you to excuse me. I'm merely asking you to . . . " Julie paused, knowing she wanted to say *help,* but instead she said, "realize what I've . . . gone through."

"It must have been a great shock to discover your sister, who always was more successful than you, had also succeeded in wooing away your husband. It must have been a terrible blow to your pride.

But you still were young. And attractive. You could have found love again. You still could. You don't have to wallow in self-pity and alcohol forever.

"Ever since I got your letter I wondered why I was so lucky. But after you learned about my background, you decided I would be a good one to help you. A sympathetic and gullible drunk's kid who wanted to go to college so badly you might be able to trick me into doing you a big fat favor. Well, I don't know what's going on between you and Mr. Livingston or anybody else in Bridgeboro but I do know that nobody is going to read about that love affair in *my* essay." Beth began to put on her jacket.

Julie's eyes filled with scorn. For both of them. She hated the girl for being so clever, and herself for being so foolish. "You may leave now," she breathed. "We have nothing more to discuss except . . ." she scowled, "except if you mention anything I've told you I'll have you punished. Somehow."

Beth picked up her handbag. She lifted her chin high. "I still intend to write my essay."

"You won't win," Julie snapped out.

"You can't keep me from winning."

"You don't have enough information."

"I still can try."

"Spunky, aren't you?" She really admired the girl.

"Because I won't give up or because I won't let you use me? I figure you can't hurt me. I'm at the bottom already. But I can still have my own opinions and live up to my own beliefs."

Beth picked up her books. She already felt defeat but she had to put on a good show. "I really have enjoyed meeting you. Thank you for the interviews." She walked toward the foyer. "Take care of yourself."

Julie was too dumbfounded to make a comment. Too spent to move.

Beth did glance back. She actually felt compassion for Julie Fischer. The woman who could afford to buy the best her money could buy. Hoping Julie could not hear her, she whispered, "And good luck." She closed the door quietly behind her.

Beth tried not to stumble as she walked to the road. *Daddy. I need you. Bad. Do whatever you can do to help me. And guess what? I don't have the picture of Vicki Lynn.*

JULIE looked out the bay window. She watched Beth walk out of sight. She had to admit she not only admired the girl, but she liked her.

"Damn" she said out loud. "Now I have to think up another way to influence her. And call her for another interview."

FOURTEEN

SINCE NINTH GRADE Dorothy Kennedy and Jill Gillion were Beth's closest friends. Jill also lived in Taylor Park. Therefore she and Beth went to school together, almost every day. On nasty days they took the school bus. On nicer days they walked the two plus miles, both ways. Then they could walk with Dot who lived only three blocks from the high school. Walking also meant Beth and Jill could stay away from Taylor Park that much longer.

They had joined the hockey team and chorus for four years giving them more time together. They went their separate ways only when Dot practiced with the band front, Beth and Jill met with the Drama Club or Beth worked with the staff of the school newspaper and the senior Yearbook. Sometimes they went to the Girls' Room together.

Friday was a lovely day. The teachers had opened the windows to invite the smell of spring into the classrooms. Waiting for the last bell, students and teachers were in an upbeat mood and looking forward to the beautiful week-end which the weather men had promised.

Everyone except Beth Rhodes.

Dot and Jill waited for Beth outside the largest Girls' Room on the first floor of the school. It was time to primp before they walked uptown. In case one of them might meet a certain male whom she was hoping to attract. They entered a large room with a row of doors along one side and sinks, shelves and mirrors on the opposite wall.

Dot put her books on a shelf over a sink and was the first to speak. "Did you read the ice skating rink on Almshouse Road is ready to open? My dad said he's going to pay for a family membership."

Jill responded to her reflection in the mirror. "I can't ice skate. You and Fred have gone skating, right Beth?"

"Yeah, but I'm generally down more than I'm up."

Dot frowned at Beth in the mirror. "I notice you're still in your shitty mood. 'Cause you don't have a date over the week-end?"

Beth began to concentrate on a search in her drawstring handbag. She could not cry.

"Hey. If you tell us, we can help make it all better."

"I'm mad at myself." She wished Brad were with her. She needed a hug. "I did something very stupid. On Wednesday."

Eyebrows raised, Dot turned to Jill. "What happened on Wednesday?"

Jill shrugged. "She had dinner with Julie Fischer."

Beth leaned down to look under the closed doors. "I didn't even eat with her. I was stupid enough to tell her off." Tears overflowed.

"You had the *guts* to have an argument with Julie Fischer?" Jill asked. She looked horrified.

Beth pulled a paper towel from the nearest holder. She blotted her cheeks as she nodded. "Besides that was the second time I had an argument with her. Don't tell anybody. Please?"

Jill looked puzzled. "What do you argue about?

Beth wiped her nose. "Stuff. Nasty things she says about her sister."

Jill spoke up. "Did she say you can't write your essay about her sister?"

"She said she wouldn't stop me. I tried to work on it last night but I can't even concentrate on what I want to write. I know it won't be worth turning in."

Dot blotted her lips and asked, "How about Mr. Stookey? Have you told him?"

"I've been avoiding him." Beth stared in the mirror and talked to the reflections, "I *am* going to tell him. And Mr. Jones. I know I have to.""

"Mrs. Fischer is a crack pot anyway," Dot announced. "Maybe you're lucky you don't have to see her anymore."

Beth shook her head. "That's not true. She's still upset over the death of Mr. Fischer. You go on ahead. I know Mr. Stookey's still in his room marking papers. And even though I don't think Julie will call him, I have to tell him."

"Shall we meet at Powell's?"

"Yeah. After Mr. Stookey hears what I did he won't keep me."

Powell's Drug Store and Ice Cream Parlor was the popular hangout. Dozens of students congregated there to discuss the day, future plans and gossip. For the price of a soft drink or a soda, over the noise of the juke box.

After Dot and Jill walked out of the Girl's Room Beth looked in another mirror. She knew she had to perk up. She need more lipstick and . . . use a toilet. Carrying her books, handbag and jacket Beth walked to the last booth. She hung the jacket and handbag on a hook on the locked door and pulled down a shelf for her books. Sitting, she began to review the last few days.

What a fool she had been not to read the letters. Bill Fischer had an affair with his sister-in law! Brad's parents would like to know. Even the Barnes. What had he looked like? She imagined handsome. Macho? At least a great lover.

Next she remembered what she and Brad did in the barn. She knew she wanted to do it again. But a note in her locker told her he wasn't certain when he could meet her. *Just remember how much I love you - until the next time.*

BETH heard loud laughter. Damn. The voices were familiar. One was Jeanne Barnes. With her ladies-in-waiting, Mary Jane and Shirley. What should she do? Cough. Sneeze. Anything to let them know someone else was in the room. Then blot her eyes, walk out, say HI and leave fast. Not even wash her hands? Because the three girls were not Beth's close friends they would not expect her to linger. *That's Shirl talking.* She decided to listen and heard Shirl comment strongly,

"Cripes! Wasn't that Shorthand test a lulu? I didn't think the bitch was going to cover so much. I only looked at the last two chapters."

"She told us on Tuesday she was going back to Chapter Ten." Mary Jane began to brush her long brown hair.

"I never heard her say that."

Jeanne laughed. "That's because you were too busy thinking about your date with Irv."

"Drop *mort*," Shirl said.

"Yeah, I saw them together, Sunday." Mary Jane teased.

Jeanne stared at Shirl in the mirror. "After you called to tell me he was pretty lovely dovey after the movie and you had to fight to keep your pants on. So how about Sunday?"

Shirl smiled at Jeanne in the mirror. "I decided not to fight."

Beth knew it was too late to leave her prison. She put her feet up on the seat so that she was completely concealed in her little torture chamber. Thank goodness she had put her books on the shelf and not the floor.

"He's okay," Mary Jane stated. "You've been out with him, haven't you Jeanne?" After Jeanne nodded, she added, "I'll bet you noticed a difference necking with Brad. Right?"

Jeanne raised her eyebrows at Mary Jane. "In what way?"

"Well, I never went out with Brad but he seems to me as though he'd be..." she shrugged, "ah . . . you know."

"Since you're prying, Brad does say 'excuse me' when he burps. And he's never farted yet. But . . . he's just like the rest of the guys. Hot to trot."

"You're saying Brad's a lover boy?" Shirl blurted out.

Jeanne smiled. "Now he is. Since I taught him what to do."

Mary Jane laughed. "You girls are crazy. Someday you're going to get a guy so worked up . . . that you're not going to be able to stop him. And it won't be so easy to laugh afterwards."

"Who says we want to stop them?" Shirl coughed out. "As long as we have a Coke. You do know how to use a bottle of Coke, don't you Mary Jane?"

"Yeah. I've heard you shake it up and . . .but I still think you're crazy."

Shirl waved her comb. "My sister told me they use plastic wrap at her college. Of course, it's best if the guy has rubbers. I really wish I had a diaphragm."

"But where can you get them?" Jeanne sighed. "I'm certainly not asking *our* doctor."

Shirl laughed. "How about old Doctor Rexinger? He's the one Betty Wright went to. For the exam." She giggled, then added, "That was bad enough but then he insisted she had to tell her mother or he wouldn't take care of her."

Mary Jane closed her handbag and picked up her books. "I still say petting is one thing but going all the way is not for me. Even with a condom or a diaphragm. And besides it *is* against my religion. I have to get going. My mom wants to go shopping."

"Is anybody taking you home?" Shirl asked.

"Dick. If he's still waiting for me."

"Hey. He keeps a bottle of Coke in the glove compartment."

"Well I'll never have to use it," Mary Jane replied. "See you on Monday."

Beth heard the door close. Hopefully Shirl and Jeanne were getting ready to leave also. It was so maddening, wondering and waiting. Suddenly she heard someone cough and Jeanne ask, "Do you like my hair this color?"

"Welllll," Shirl said. "Since you asked, I really like it blonde better."

Jeanne laughed. "My father hates it."

"How about Brad?"

"He could care. My dad says I have to change the color before graduation. And one thing I've learned from my mother. Give in and get more. I've got to buzz too. Brad probably is having ten fits. He hates to wait."

"He'd probably have more than ten fits if he saw what I saw last night."

Beth's heartbeats began to boom boom in her ears. They were so loud she feared Jeanne and Shirl could hear them. Why had she been so dumb to remain hidden?

Shirl waited for Jeanne to respond. "What were you doing out with Jim?"

"You think you saw me with Jim? Where?"

"On Creek Road. Parked."

"Who were you with?"

"I have nothing to hide. I was with Dick."

"How about if I told Mary Jane?"

"Go ahead. He hasn't asked her to go steady. We decided to go to Creek Road, to do a little feeling. But we saw a car parked in the best spot so Dick decided to try Meeting House Road and while he was turning around, with the lights off, I figured out that it was your mother's car. And I could see Jim. And you were so busy doing something you didn't even know another car had pulled in." Shirl waited. "Well? I've given you your cue."

Jeanne reached into her hand bag and pulled out a pack of cigarettes. She lit one and took a deep drag. She held the pack out to Shirl. After Shirl shook her head from side to side she returned the pack to her hand bag. "So? I was out with Jim?"

"So I think it's a dirty deal. You and Brad have been an item for months."

Jeanne coughed. "This room should have a window. The ventilating system sucks."

"You can't be afraid of getting caught. Not with the guts you have. That wasn't the first time was it?" After Jeanne shrugged she asked, "How long has this *so what* been going on?"

"What's it your business?" After another drag she held the cigarette under the spigot.

"I can make it my business. Days? Weeks? Months?"

"A couple of months. You make it sound like some kind of a crime."

"Brad doesn't deserve to have another guy laughing behind his back."

Jeanne jammed the wet cigarette deep into the trash can. "It won't be much longer. I'm giving Brad the heave ho as soon as school is finished."

"I heard that Brad was going to give you a ring for a graduation present."

"If you remember who told you, tell them they're nuts. I'm not getting engaged to Bradford Livingston. I wish I could break off with him right now, but I can't. Because of our parents. You might think that the Prom was my coming out party. They have dinners and parties and all kinds of shitty things for Brad and me to do." She sighed. "We're having a big dinner party next Sunday. For the great white father's birthday. And Mom already is making plans for a wing ding on graduation night. I can't louse up their plans. Yet. God, I wish I had a joint."

Beth smiled. Even though she felt shooting pains in her legs and back and her fanny was stuck to the seat she felt elation. Brad had been telling her the truth about his relationship with Jeanne. And best of all, he would soon be free. Forget about Mrs. Stookey and Julie Fischer. Bradford Livingston was the most important person in her life.

"Couldn't you at least have waited to go out with Jim?"

"No. Sure, Brad's one of the best looking guys in the County, has a neat car and he's loads of fun, but I can't stand his parents. His mother is a fat snob and the way his father looks at me makes me want to puke. And he bores me."

"Just a few minutes ago you said he's a lover boy and…"

Jeanne began to laugh. "Have you ever been out with Jim?" She shook out another cigarette.

Shirl watched what Jeanne was doing. "Hey, don't light up another one. I want to go home. Not to Mr. Jones' office. And yes, I was out with Jim a couple of times. Last year."

"Were you bored with him?"

"All we did was French kiss and touch a little. From the look on your face you went for broke. Good, huh?" She watched Jeanne nod and grin. "I had a feeling he would be. Once it was the wrong time of the month and the other time I had to get home. I don't like to hurry. I like to fool around and take it slow and easy. Don't you?"

"As soon as Jim kisses me I'm ready."

"You've done it with Brad?"

"You sound as surprised as I was. Oh, we've had some oral sex but last Sunday I couldn't stop him. And get this, he apologized afterward."

"I can't believe Brad would force you."

"Hey, he didn't rape me. We were in our pool cabana and he was so damned scared our folks would wonder why we were gone so long, it was lousy. I'm tired of him and my parents can't stand his parents."

"Is Jim as good as I've heard?"

"He's a ten and a half."

"How's he built?"

"You're too innocent to want to know things like how a guy is built."

"You're too chicken, to tell me."

"Yo, Shirl. When have you known me to be chicken?"

"Compare him to Irv."

"If I can remember about Irv, I guess about the same. And I don't know about Dick."

"You mean you've done it with only three guys in our class?"

"In our class, yeah. If I counted a couple of summer camps and a trip I took with the Ski Club from church, I could add a few more." Jeanne pulled out a change purse. "Do you have a dime? I need one for the Kotex machine."

Shirl found her wallet and handed Jeanne a dime. "Another lucky month, huh? I'll blackmail you unless you tell me about Jim."

Jeanne replied from the stall, "He's great. And I'm as frustrated as hell 'cause I'm going to have my period over the week-end."

"Poor Brad."

"Hey, Brad will find somebody. During the summer. Or at Princeton. He'll make out just fine, 'cause he's built even better than Jim." She flushed the toilet.

Jeanne walked out of the booth as Shirl announced, "In-ter-est-ing to know."

114

Jeanne washed her hands. "Listen. I trust you to keep your mouth shut. I can't imagine what would happen if my parents found out."

Shirl hugged her books. "I'm insulted. You have to tell *me* to keep quiet?"

"Just so you understand I'm going to stick it out with Brad until graduation. After all," she crooned, "Daddy promised me a convertible and I'd be nuts to make him mad."

"I think I'm getting a new typewriter." Shirl walked to the door. "If I wanted to be a creep, I'd have said something in front of Mary Jane. But a favor for a favor? Just remember to tell me as soon as you break off with Brad." Shirl laughed and pushed the door with her hip. "If I can catch him on the rebound he might be fun for the summer. Hey, don't walk so fast."

SUDDENLY the room was like a theater, after a show. Large and empty and quiet. Except for the corner stall. Soft sniffing could be heard coming from a girl who was experiencing what a broken heart felt like. Beth felt as though she had just been dragged down from a whipping post and been tied to a torture rack.

Slowly she moved her stiff body to a standing position. She flushed the toilet. Then rearranged her clothes, picked up her books and opened the door. She lifted her jacket and handbag from the hook and walked to a mirror. She felt as wretched as she looked.

"I know she's lying," Beth whispered to the face in the mirror. "He's going to wait for when we do it. She just wanted Shirl to think they really had done it. If Jill and Dot ask if I've been crying I'll tell them, Mr. Stookey said I was a jerk."

FIFTEEN

AT NINE O'CLOCK on Saturday morning Beth Rhodes convinced herself she might as well get out of bed. She yearned to hide under the covers. Forever. She had spent most of the night, tossing and thinking. And cursing and crying. Should she pretend she was sick?

Whenever she thought about Julie Fischer, she hated herself. And it certainly did not help her moral remembering the look on Mr. Stookey's face when she told him the interviews had come to an abrupt end. He did say he was sorry. But he was disappointed she had not thought of the consequences before she argued with Mrs. Fischer. And what a shame she had forgotten the autographed picture of Vicki Lynn. What would he have said if he knew Julie had told her Vicki Lynn and William Fischer had an affair! And she had ruined her chance to read their love letters.

During her soul searching Beth thought about Brad. Was she just angry with him? No! She was furious. Did she still love him? No! She hated him. He had lied to her! He didn't really love her. She had to erase him from her life. At least avoid him. Maybe just a nod when she saw him? And if he asked why, she'd tell him what she heard in the girl's room.

If only she could die. Then Julie and Brad would be sorry. *Wouldn't* they? They should blame themselves. No, she didn't want to die. Just stay in bed. Not have to face another day of *This Is Your Life*. She'd have to lie to Liz. But then her mother didn't pay much attention to what she said anyway. She probably could even tell her *I had an argument with Julie Fischer,* or *I hate Brad Livingston* and Liz wouldn't even hear her. But it was Saturday and she did have to talk with her. Damn. Damn. Damn.

Beth got out of bed and removed the sheets and pillow cases. It was laundry day. She put on a pair of slacks and a faded sweat shirt. In the kitchen she added the laundry to a pile of clothes which Liz had put on top of the washing machine. She forced herself to eat a stale donut and drink some orange juice.

She really wanted to make some noise to get Liz out of bed. It was a warmer than usual spring day and she wanted to hang the laundry outside. She returned upstairs and selected clean sheets and pillow cases for her bed. The closet door closed with a bang.

It worked. She heard Liz yawning and coughing. "Good morning," Beth sang out.

"Good morning yourself," Liz replied sarcastically. "It would be a better one if I have a cup of coffee waiting for me."

"You will. Want some toast? And jelly?"

"Just coffee." *Clip Clop* into the bathroom. "I'm going to take a shower."

Good. She had enough time to make her bed. Beth hurried downstairs and got the dust cloth and vacuum cleaner. She decided if Liz asked her about Julie, she would fake her way through the conversation. After she quickly dusted the furniture and vacuumed the rug she returned to the kitchen. While a pan of water began to steam, she waited.

LIZ looked stunning Of course, her platinum hair was always a plus in her favor. She was wearing black slacks and a pink sweater. Her nail polish and lipstick matched her sweater. She had added large gold earrings, a wide gold belt and gold flats on her small feet.

"Hey. Look at you. Going somewhere?" Beth poured hot water over the instant coffee.

"Shopping. With Marge. Looks like a nice day." A dramatic yawn followed.

"Nice enough to hang the sheets and pillow cases outside. They should dry fast."

Liz began to stir the usual two teaspoons of sugar. "Got a date tonight?" She lighted a cigarette and watched her daughter shake her head. "How come? Even a date with a Jew is better than no date at all."

"Will you please lay off about Danny. He's a nice guy and one of my best friends."

"And don't forget his parents are loaded. Babysitting for Peg?"

"I'm just staying here. I have to start reviewing. We're up for some big tests next week."

"By the way, last night I was talking to a sailor from the base. In case you're interested he heard Les was shipped out of Norfolk." She watched Beth load the washing machine. "The guy didn't know where to but I hope Evan went with him. We don't need her wandering back here." She reached to the over flowing ashtray. "I haven't had a chance to tell you but everybody was more than surprised when I told them you were interviewing Julie. How are you coming along with the story?"

"I plan on working on it this week-end."

"Have you seen her this week?"

"Yes. But I'm finished interviewing her." *Daddy, I'm not really lying. I am finished.*

"I told the girls and Lou you said that she was really nice. You shouldn't stop seeing her. Call her, now and then. I'll bet she gets lonely, living all alone, and she must have liked you to let you see her and..."

"And," Beth butted in, "maybe I can get something out of her?" Beth stared into Liz's face. "Isn't that what you really mean?"

Liz hunched her shoulders. She knocked her cigarette against the side of the ash tray, spilling ashes on the table. "So? I'm not going to support you forever. I got a job and moved out when I was sixteen. Does

she have a housekeeper?"

"Yes. And a gardener. I'm going upstairs and get your sheets."

"Whoa, just a minute. So, if you don't ask Julie if you can clean her house then maybe you could be her social secretary? Why the look? You *are* taking typing. With no kids of her own, ahh, maybe you can get to college, after all?"

"I got your message," Beth said strongly.

"You'll never get ahead, if you're not clever."

"And what makes you think Julie isn't more clever? She'd see right through the plan.

"Well, in my mind, a plan is better than a dream. And you do want to go to college."

"I will. My way."

"Okay. And while you're figuring out how you're going to pay your way I'd suggest you get a job." Liz took a deep drag and crushed out the cigarette. She lifted the ash tray and blew the ashes off the table.

Beth measured detergent into the washing machine and began to fill the machine. She wanted the conversation to be over. She took several steps toward the living room and then turned to face Liz. "How about getting me a job at Lou's place? I could waitress."

"You're not the waitress type. And anyway you're under age where drinks are served."

"Well, then I could hide in the kitchen. After all, I've had lots of experience cooking my own meals. Even washing dishes."

"Don't be a smart ass. Lou doesn't hire teenagers. Your best bet is to butter up Julie Fischer." Liz laughed, "Or get married."

RICHARD Livingston was using the telephone when Bernice hurried into the den. She was wearing a pink silk sheath dress and pearl jewelry which had belonged to her mother. The color was flattering to her complexion but the sleeveless style revealed she was becoming shapelessly round, with flabby under arms. She chose a chair to toss her mink stole and evening bag. She and Richard were going to the Bridge Valley Country Club for cocktails and dinner.

Bernice had heard the telephone ring in the master bedroom, while she was using her cosmetics in the master bathroom. Richard already had gone downstairs so she made no attempt to answer the phone. Now she was curious to know who the caller was. She backed up to him, indicating she wanted him to pull up the zipper and fasten the hook and eye at the neckline.

As Richard silently obliged he decided he did not like the dress. Of course, he wouldn't tell Bernice. She never would wear it again and it would go into the attic or be given to the Thrift Shop for the *Bucks County Association for Retarded Children*.

"Like I said, Charlie, if you've heard she hasn't signed anything maybe she isn't sure yet. Right... Right...I think we should just sit tight . I'll bet she wants us to bid again. Listen, Charlie, Bernice is ready to go... Okay... Right... Bye." Richard hung up the receiver. He wiped his brow and pushed up his glasses. "God-damn bitch," he hissed.

"Was that Charlie Barnes?"

"How many Charlie's do I know? He wanted to talk about the farm we're interested in buying. He doesn't want to mention it at the Club. Especially near Dave and Joe. He's fuming because Julie just bid higher."

"Oh, no. Not again." Bernice's pink glow began to fade.

Richard pounded his fist on the desk. "Why can't she leave us alone!"

Bernice looked distressed. "When you told me I remember saying, 'It never will work.' And see. I was right."

"But she doesn't have anything on Charlie and Lou."

"And the distressing thing is we really don't know if she has anything on us." She sat on the arm of a new cranberry leather chair next to the desk. Suddenly she looked tired.

"If only we knew. I'd bid her up to the sky. Even if I had to go into debt, again. Just to show her we're not afraid of her. Charlie will think I'm crazy. Or a god damn coward. He claims she doesn't really want any more real estate. And she's making plans to enlarge the office building. Or build a new one."

Bernice stood. "So what are you going to do?"

Richard walked to the wet bar, in a corner of the den and opened a cabinet below the sink. He reached for a bottle of bourbon. "Right now I'm going to get a drink." After selecting a glass he left the room.

Bernice followed him. "We'll be having cocktails at the Club. If we leave now you can have an extra drink at the bar."

"I need one now." Richard strode into the large kitchen. Right up to the double door refrigerator. He put ice cubes in the glass, covered them with bourbon, stirred the contents with his forefinger and took a long drink.

"You know what baffles me is how in the hell she found out this time? Last time I blasted my intentions all over town that I was going to buy that property north of the church but this time I deliberately kept quiet. I even asked Charlie to keep mum." He took several more sips and then covered the ice with more bourbon.

Bernice nodded in agreement. "Even though everybody says she's out of touch with what's going on, she still finds out." She watched Richard take a deep drink and had to add, "Don't you want some water?"

"No. I don't want water. Look, I'm upset enough. I don't need you nagging me."

"Not so loud. Brad is still upstairs."

"You have to be kidding. His radio is so loud he couldn't hear a fire siren. And anyway," Richard paused to sip again, "I want Brad to know about this." He opened the freezer door and reached for more cubes. He covered them with bourbon. "She's a bitch."

Bernice pulled out one of the Captain's chairs from under the table in the bay. She decided she should continue to talk with Richard and observe his drinking. She smoothed the dress over her thick thighs before she said, "If you make too big of an issue about this farm, Brad might begin to wonder why she seems to give us such a hard time."

"Seems to! That woman has had her claws in me for eighteen years and there's nothing I can do about it." He emptied the glass and stared at the cubes.

Bernice watched him reach for the bottle. "Richard, please. No more to drink. We're going to meet new couples tonight."

"Who's bringing couples?"

"Lou and Charlie. He's looking for a house for them. Their name is Early, or something like that. I think they're from Long Island. I know Lou said New York."

"And why would somebody from Long Island move to Bridgeboro?"

"He's the new Executive Vice President. At the Company. The other couple lives in Warrington Estates. They're new neighbors of Jean and Dave's."

"Hmmm. Early, huh? Good news. Everybody says Whiteside is a pain in the ass the way he runs such a tight ship and is true blue to Julie."

THE sound of thumping on the uncarpeted hardwood stairs came into the kitchen. Brad was descending into the center hall. He appeared at the doorway. "I thought I heard voices."

"We're getting ready to leave. You'll be with Jeanne?" Richard gave Brad a sly smile.

Bernice frowned. "Why are you wearing *that* sweater? You're certainly not very dressed up for a Saturday night date."

"Jeanne cancelled tonight. She has a headache. So I'm only going to the movies," He pulled on the bottom of the pullover. A nervous gesture. "With Dick."

"Want to come with us? You could eat in the snack bar and maybe find someone to play pool or ping pong with in the game room?"

"Come on, Bernice. Brad doesn't want to be with the old folks." Richard dumped the cubes into the sink and put the glass on the drain board. "I'm certain he and Dick can find some fun. But remember, one o'clock."

"Yes, sir." Brad smiled as he began to back out of the room, hoping to escape without having to kiss his mother. He had to stop as his father put up his hand.

"Before you go. Remember my telling you about that farm. Up on Quarry Road?"

Brad tugged at his sweater again. "Ahh, I think so."

"Charlie Barnes just told me Julie Fischer wants to buy it."

Brad frowned. Had Beth told Julie?

Bernice rubbed her hands over the arms of the chair. Back and forth as she asked, "How about that girl who's interviewing Julie? Remember we asked you to…ah, casually talk to her? Maybe you just might have…" Bernice watched Brad shake his head.

"I already told you, I hardly ever talk to her. So why would I tell her about a farm?"

"Do you know if she's still interviewing Julie?"

Brad shrugged. He had to appear as calm as he knew his parents were trying to be.

Finally Richard said, "Just remember whenever we discuss any kind of business, it stays in this house. Because somehow Julie gets wind of it."

Brad nodded and erased the look of concern with a charming smile and cheerfully declared, "Well, she is giving you an opportunity to get rich. I mean, by keeping your money." He backed out of the kitchen, into the laundry room. After he opened the back door he waved and called out, "Hope you have a good time tonight."

"You too, dear. Drive carefully." Oh, how she wanted to remind him she would like to have a kiss. Bernice stood. "Let's go. I'll get my handbag and stole and . . . what's wrong?"

"WHY don't we tell him?" He picked up the glass, although he knew he would not fill it. Just holding it would upset Bernice. He leaned against the double sink.

"The answer is still *no*." She stared at Richard and repeated louder, "I've told you before and I'll say it again, it's too late."

"Damn it, Bernice. I'm sick and tired of your using 'it's too late' as an excuse. I'm sick and tired of cowering every time Julie Fischer makes a move. Because she might be warning us Earle told her and Bill about Brad but she'll keep quiet if we keep quiet. About her lousy marriage. You know damn well, it's possible while she's swilling the booze, she'll tell *somebody*. So we should be the ones to tell Brad."

Staring at Richard, Bernice felt hatred. Damn him. Why? Again? Now? Tears would show on the pink dress. She used a dish towel to blot her eyes.

Richard rolled the glass between his hands. "He has a right to know. Before he goes to college. We don't know who might have talked about the Mongoloid, down in Virginia."

Richard paused and waited for Bernice's usual reaction. First the gasp, a hand to her mouth and then tears. How come he could not feel any remorse? After all, the baby *was* his son. "I'm sorry. I did promise I would say Down's Syndrome. But," he said, loudly, "it's because of your parents he's in a little home, in a little town. Because they didn't want anyone to know. Hell, they weren't any more embarrassed than I was! He might as well have died!"

"Please. Not now. You know we didn't want him to live with us. We're getting ourselves upset and we should be getting ready to…"

"Damn it, Bernice. I'm not allowed to drink. I'm not allowed to talk. Every time I bring up the subject, it's always 'not now, Richard.'"

"Just because I don't want to discuss the subject, doesn't mean it isn't important to me. I think about it every day." She blotted her eyes again. "You know damn well that's why I have to keep so involved. To keep from…thinking."

Some of the anger in Richard's voice had been replaced by eagerness. "I know it'll be a bitch to tell him. And God only knows what we'll tell him as a reason why we never told him before now? Stupidity? Pride?"

"I've already told you, if he ever does find out, I'll take the blame. I just never wanted him, or anybody, to know. But Richard, don't tell him. Please?"

"You'd rather live this way? And take the chance that someday, someone else is going to tell him?" Richard pushed up his glasses.

"Yes, because I believe Earle Phipps and Brother Conrad and the doctor at the orphanage were honest with us. There are no records available and we have all of the legal papers. In our safe. And if Julie does know, why hasn't she told anyone else by now?"

"Because, she just isn't sure how much Bill told me. Do we know she screwed around with him and then tricked him into marriage by claiming she was pregnant? Or he told me he wanted a divorce because he was in love with another woman. And I still say it was Vicki. Someday, I'm going to ruin that woman." He watched Bernice leave the kitchen. "And you don't want to talk about it anymore."

"I have to repair my make-up."

Richard followed Bernice to the stairs. "Okay. I know we have to leave but soon, and I mean very soon, we *are* going to decide how to tell Brad.

"And do it!"

He pushed up his glasses.

SIXTEEN

BRAD DROVE OUT of the driveway and headed north. His destination was a gas station where a classmate was working that evening.

"Hi, Ralph. Fill it up and take a look under the hood." He hurried to a phone booth. He lined up coins on the shelf before he dialed the numbers he knew by heart.

Beth was sitting on the couch, trying to concentrate on a TV movie when the telephone rang. She also was forcing herself to eat canned spaghetti and meatballs, out of the pan. Who could be calling? Jill and Dot had dates and Peg told her she had to balance the checkbook before Alan returned from Texas.

"Hello?"

"Hi, babe. Whatcha doin'?"

"Oh. It's you."

"So who were you expecting? Dan? Or Fred?"

"Well, I certainly wasn't expecting you. Don't you have a date?"

"Yeah. With you. I'll pick you up wherever you say. Just make it soon."

"Forget it. What's wrong with your lover girl, Jeanne?"

"She has a headache." He began to rearrange the coins. "Listen babe before I forget, did you ever say anything to Julie about that farm you and I went to?"

"Of course not. Why are you asking me such a stupid question?"

"Just tell me where to meet you. And I'll tell you."

"Didn't you hear me say, forget it! I'm not going out with you anymore."

Brad leaned against the side of the phone booth. "I must have a lousy connection."

"You heard me. Lover boy." She began to stab her fork in and out of a meatball.

He watched Ralph slam down the hood and give him the thumbs up sign. Brad waved. "I wish I knew what the hell is bugging you."

"*You* are bugging me. Thinking I'd go out with you – after what you did." She slid off the chair down to the floor and moved to the front of the couch hoping it would help block her voice. No one else in the world should hear this conversation.

"I still love you as much as I always have. And I want us to be together. Tonight."

"You didn't remember how much you love me last Sunday. At the birthday party."

Brad searched his mind for words. Shit! Damn! "Who told you?"

"I'm not going to tell you how I found out."

"I know it wasn't Jeanne."

"You got that right."

"She's the only other person who knows."

"That's what you think. Lover boy. Just your tough luck, huh?"

"I guess so. Just as it was my tough luck we had pink champagne and I drank too much."

"I can't believe your parents would let you drink that much. If that's your excuse."

"It's my reason. Evidently you don't remember what happened in the barn. I mean..."

"Just because I wouldn't go all the way you had to do it with somebody else. Well, you know what? I think you're going out with me for kicks. Either you bet one of your buddies you'd stoop so low as to date someone from Taylor Park or you're doing research or..."

"Will you shut up and listen to me." Brad yelled into the receiver. "Nobody else knows about us. And I didn't say it was your fault. I still felt sexed up and the champagne made it worse. We went to the pool house and before I knew it we were going all the way."

"Oh, how sad."

"For god's sake, Beth. Try to understand. I mean, after all you've told me, how you get worked up. How you think you'll explode."

"I keep my emotions under control."

"You're so perfect." Suddenly he changed his tone and blurted out, "Look babe, let's not be nasty with each other. I'm sorry. S.o.r.r.y. Please forgive me and . . . " his voice trailed off.

"And what? You asked me to understand. *You* understand. I love . . . loved you. I wanted to be the first girl you made love to. Not did it with. It's all spoiled now."

"I'm hurting too. And I was telling you the truth. I don't know how you found out, but that was the first time. And I promise, honest to god Beth, it will be the last time. You know I love you. And I need you."

"Sure you do."

"I said I'm sorry. We could be together . . . and make up. Please?"

"I'm just going to say goodbye." Beth used the napkin to blot tears.

"For now? Or forever?" Brad closed his eyes waiting for the answer.

"Forever. Do you want the watch back?" She held her breath, waiting.

"Hell, no. If you don't want to wear it, save it for laughs. Or throw it away. Burn the notes. And the poems. Whatever will make you happy." Brad waited. He needed air. He opened the booth door. "Did you hear me?"

"Goodbye, Brad."

Brad wanted to kick the booth. Pound the wall. "Okay. I'll say it one more time. I'm sorry and . . . I love you. Even though you won't believe me. I really have to go. You're sure you won't . . . oh what the hell, goodbye. See you around." He waited a few more seconds, until he heard her phone click.

Brad hurried inside the station to pay Ralph. He was grateful another customer was talking to him because he certainly didn't want to have to linger. Brad got into his automobile and slammed the door. Who would have some beer available? Who might have some joints for sale? Anything to help him forget. Damn Jeanne for blabbing. And telling him he lacked technique. Damn Beth for hearing the story Damn himself. For screwing.

He drove out onto Bridge Pike and with no reason began to drive north. Did he hate Beth? No. He despised Jeanne. He detested himself.

As the mileage indicator rolled over and over, he began to feel despondent. Desperate. Speeding to nowhere, Bradford Livingston realized he had never before felt so suicidal.

BETH could not finish her dinner. She turned off the television and sat in the dark on the floor and cried into the paper napkin. She suffered until she heard laughter coming through the inside wall. Damn. How could other people be happy when she was so miserable.

Wiping her eyes, Beth leaned closer to the wall.

GERT Connery was talking. "So Chuck went bowling and I got Betty Powers to sit because Beth's line was busy and I wanted to see you. In living color. Happy Birthday!"

Gert handed Peg a paper bag which she had carried under her jacket. "Here's a little something to celebrate with. You told me you liked this. So I even chilled it. So we can have some now."

"Oh, wow. Dry Sack. I love it. Two glasses coming up."

Within minutes Gert raised her full glass. "Here's to being twenty-nine." She took a sip.

Peg took a longer sip. "You are a dear. I thought maybe after I didn't get a card or even a phone call, you forgot."

"I did call. First your line was busy, then no answer."

"I accepted a dinner invitation from Alan's mother. And you know how I hate to drive into the city. Then after I put the girls to bed I worked on my check book. I was going to call to find out if you could come over for a drink. But I always feel funny asking you to leave Chuck. Especially on a Saturday night."

"Does Alan have any idea when he'll be back?"

"He thought next week. But when he called this morning he told me he better stay a few more days. I thought the people in Texas were supposed to be smart. And learn fast."

Gert watched Peg stand and held out her empty glass. "Hey, you've been holding up so far. Don't let Alan down. Or yourself."

"It's just that I get so lonely. I'm going to bring the bottle in. And Beth gave me a new Johnny Mathis record."

BETH turned on a lamp and pulled down the shades. No matter how depressed she felt she was happy Peg had company. She could relate to how lonely she must be.

Beth settled in a chair on the opposite side of the living room. She was hoping she could concentrate on studying some French. Johnny Mathis certainly could be distracting. Especially when he sang *Twelfth of Never*.

Beth convinced herself she *was* studying. Until, she heard Peg's favorite drum music seep through the walls. Damn Herb Albert! She should go into the kitchen or try to study in bed.

Beth stared at the inside wall. Why did Peg have to play the music so loudly! Didn't she ever stop to think just maybe that kind of music bothered Beth? Bothered her to the extent that she couldn't keep her feet still. She slammed the book closed.

She could hear Peg and Gert laughing. She wondered what they might be doing until she heard Gert remark, "More, girl. Wiggle that fanny. Move those hips."

Beth knew Peg must be feeling the music the same as she was. And she wasn't drinking whatever they were drinking.. Maybe she *should* have a drink? She knew where there was a bottle of gin. Maybe the music could help her release the disturbing sensuous feeling which was building up inside her. She stood and began to gyrate her hips.

She caught her reflection in the mirror behind the desk and began to go through the motions of taking off long gloves. Next she pretended she was stepping out of a dress followed by a bra. She swung each piece of imaginary clothing overhead then tossed it to her appreciative audience. She strutted up and down a runway to the cheers of her fans. She noticed how much she was perspiring. And she really was thirsty.

Within several minutes she had filled a glass with ice and was drinking an Orange Blossom. There had been other times when she had also felt the need. The time when she learned her father had cancer. The time she finally believed he was going to die. The time she realized he had left her. Forever.

And here she was alone again. Liz was trying to push her out of the nest. Evan had gone away. And now she had lost Brad. But *she* had pushed him away. So why shouldn't she? After all she always suspected the Livingston's could not be trusted. Even Julie had been hurt. By her own husband. And sister. It just went to prove you shouldn't trust anybody. Beth mixed herself another drink and went back to her dancing. Until the music stopped.

She plopped into a chair and tuned into Peg's voice.

"That's enough of that kind of music. It irritates my itch."

Gert laughed.. "Oh? Where's your itch?"

"Between my big toes."

After a moment of silence in Peg's living room, Gert began to laugh.

IN her living room Beth sat still and pondered. She frowned as she whispered, "Her big toes? There's nothing that could itch there..."and finally Beth began to laugh. Holding her drink, she slid down to lean against the inside wall.

GERT reached for her glass as she said, "You're a riot. Here's Chuck's joke for the day. Did you hear about the sultan who had ten girls in his harem and nine of them had it pretty soft."

Peg laughed merrily. "God love 'em. At least that's better than nothing at all."

"I'd call that frustrating and..." Gert paused to drink deep from her glass. "and speaking of being frustrated did you go to the *Stop and Shop* this week?"

"Yeah. Why?"

"Since we didn't go together I thought *maybe* you went to another store?"

Peg stuck out her tongue.

"I was there last night. He was so damned handsome that I felt a little giddy myself. He was outside talking to a group of other virile young men and he smiled at me. God, when he smiles with those perfect white teeth and those blue eyes with that look of the devil in them. He shouldn't be allowed out. He's dangerous."

"For god's sake Gert, make up your mind. Last week you were advising me to shop elsewhere and now you're telling me he's the devil's gift to virgins and married women."

"And how about that dark complexioned one who works at a register? He may be Italian. Or Spanish. Anyway, he has the sexiest eyes. He's about six even and..."

"His name is Eddie Gotzi. And yes, he does have pretty eyes." Peg took another drink before she went on. "And you know another really good looking hunk in town? Brad Livingston. His old man is editor of *The Bridgeborough Courier*. For years I've seen his picture in the paper but last week I saw him in person. Dynamite."

BETH laid her head against the wall as she felt a surge of emotion hit her. *She's right. Brad is a dream boat. Even better looking than Jim. At least to me. But I hate him!* She lifted her glass and whispered, "Here's to that handsome shit head." She took a long drink as she tuned into the conversation in Peg's living room.

". . . he's definitely off limits." Gert said. "You know the Livingston's are pretty high and mighty in Bridgeboro."

"Hey, Gert. I'm only allowing myself to look around and up and down. Just for kicks."

"Then have your kicks with the small potatoes." Gert lifted her glass and declared, "May we never be around after they grow up or God help us restless housewives."

"Restless *and* desperate. God help us now. It's all I can do not to give him my address and ask him to deliver my groceries."

"If you had seen him last night, you would have. He must have finished work 'cause he didn't have his green apron on. I bet he spends most of his money on clothes and I'll bet at the *Squire and Statesman Shop* too. Have you ever been in that shop?"

"No. Where is it?" Peg reached for the bottle of Dry Sack.

"Down near the Firehouse. I bought Chuck a shirt so I could look around. It's the *in* place for the latest in men's wear. And from the way Jim Bender was dressed last night..."

Beth pressed her left ear against the inside wall. Jim was beginning to sound appealing. And not only that but it was amusing to hear about Jeanne Barnes' lover boy. Jim. Jeanne. Brad. Sexy. Beth. Sexless. She took a drink.

"When you get right down to it, it wasn't what he had on it was the way it fit. A brown jacket shirt with the collar turned up and khaki colored jeans which he must have painted on."

Beth turned her thoughts inward again. *Daddy. How can I hate and love Brad at the same time? How can I be so hurt and yet want to be with him too? Damn it. I want someone. Not just sit here and listen to other people have fun. I want someone to hold me. The gin must be working.* Beth tuned into Peg.

PEG laughed and asked loudly, "Am I getting a present?"

"Yep. But before I give it to you I have to make a little speech." Gert quickly emptied her glass, then stood and faced Peg.

"I'm both glad and sad that you still shop at the *Stop and Shop*. It's obvious you still are suffering and wondering what a romp with that Romeo would be like. And it's not good for a woman to have to suffer so much. Just to buy food."

Gert and Peg laughed. Hard and long.

Finally Gert was able to continue. "On the other hand I'm glad that handsome stud still bothers you. Otherwise we, whose husbands are beginning to fight the battle of the bulge, couldn't possibly have a reason to shop in The Squire and Statesmen Shop, unless it was for socks or ties for our dear ones. So because you are smitten with that hunk I could buy an article of wearing apparel.

"I present you this little gift with my very best wishes that by your next birthday, you will have gotten up enough guts to change food markets or he'll be in college." Gert paused to laugh. "But if during the coming year you still continue to suffer," she finally handed the red gift box to Peg, "I hope this gift will . . . will help you."

Peg let out a scream. "Oh my god. Black jockeys. And look at them." She held them up and exclaimed, "What size are they?"

"Thirty-two," Gert replied. "I measured him, with my eyes."

"But they look so . . . small." Peg almost caressed the briefs.

"Because they're jockeys. They're made to wear under jeans and pants cut very slim."

"I'll have to hide them from Alan."

"That's a small problem compared to your staying out of trouble. I just thought you'd get a kick out of owning these. Maybe they'll help reduce your itch."

BEFORE Beth realized what she was doing, she reached for the phone. She dialed Livingston's number and listened to the ringing in her ear. In her mind she pleaded, Come on Brad, answer it. I don't know what I'll say except I still love you. And want to be with you.

No one answered the telephone in Livingston's house.

Slowly Beth replaced the receiver.

She began to cry.

She felt so alone she was afraid.

SEVENTEEN

IT WAS THE ringing of the telephone that awakened Beth the following morning. It took many seconds for her to identify the ringing and decide what she had to do to stop it. She almost tripped while hurrying down the stairs and across the living room to reach the desk. *Please Daddy. I want it to be Brad. I want to make up. I want to tell him, I love him.*

With eagerness in her voice Beth said, "Hello?"

"Beth?" The voice was faint and quivering.

Trying not to sound annoyed she asked, "Who is this?"

"Julie." A loud cough followed the identification.

"Julie?" Beth repeated. She knew she was disappointed but she felt a surge of interest. She glanced at the watch which she had not removed. Why was Julie calling her at eight o-clock on a Sunday morning? "What can I do for you?"

"I don't feel well. I want you to come down and be with me."

"Ahh. You really should call Doctor Rexinger. Maybe you need different medicine?" She wondered if Julie was drunk? Or for real?

"I'll call him. But I don't want to be alone."

My god, what to do? "Ah, o-kay. You call your doctor while I get dressed and get a bus. I'll come down for...a little while. Beth hung up the receiver and looked in the mirror behind the desk. Yep. She was awake. Yep, she was going to Julie's house.

Beth's thoughts were colliding as she pulled on a sweat shirt which had been her daddy's. Before Beth went downstairs she carefully opened the door to Liz's bedroom. Her mother was puffing between pursed lips. As Liz slept Beth could almost like her. She had to tell Liz where she was going.

In the kitchen she propped a note against the sugar bowl. If you need me I'm at Mrs. Fischer's house. She gave Gerry carrot slices and some gerbil pellets. Besides doing the laundry Beth had planned on giving Gerry fresh litter. Hopefully Liz would not complain she had not cleaned her pet's habitat after she found out *where* Beth was! Beth slipped into her daddy's flannel jacket. She put her notebook in the quilted drawstring bag and left the house. She waved at Mrs. Smithers to let her know she saw her watching behind her kitchen curtain.

Beth continued to ponder on the noisy, bumpy bus. Julie's words, *I need you,* kept echoing in her head. As she repeated them the more pleased she became. It was nice to be needed by *someone.* Even Julie Fischer. Her daddy used to tell her he needed her. She closed her eyes and remembered how much she missed him. Her special person. Always would be. Brad was special also but . . . *Daddy, please help me. I have to tell him I forgive him.*

What if Julie was intoxicated? Like in loaded? No, she really sounded sober. But wouldn't it be something to go all the way down there and have her say, "What in the hell are you doing here?"

Maybe Julie would have had enough to drink that Beth could talk her into giving her the letters again? And the picture? Or best of all she'd let her go into *that* room? Look at some of Vicki Lynn's personal belongings and furniture. How she wanted to include some poems and mention the unfinished manuscript.

If only she could persuade Julie to give everything to the Bridgeborough Library? Then she could be the heroine of Bridgeboro. Mrs. Livingston had helped raise the funds for the new wing and the museum. Beth Rhodes could be responsible for a special room just for the personal belongings and original manuscripts of the famous Vicki Lynn.

As the bus rumbled down Bridge Pike, Beth looked out the window and sighed deeply. *I know, Daddy. I better stop thinking about helping the Library or the Historical Society and start thinking about helping Beth Rhodes. I need to write the winning essay. But imagine her calling me.*

BEFORE Beth knocked she saw the door was slightly opened. Julie wasn't so sick that she couldn't get out of bed. "Julie. It's Beth. Where are you?"

She heard a faint, "On the couch." She locked the door and hurried into the living room.

Julie was in a fetal position with a crocheted afghan heaped over her bathrobe. Her hair was mussed and her complexion was sallow. Next to the couch was a wastepaper basket filled with paper handkerchiefs and newspapers. Then she noticed the empty bottle.

Beth slid out of the shirt and draped it over the arm of a friendly looking rocking chair. Next she opened all of the blinds. It pleased her to welcome the sunshine into the room. On the coffee table she took account of Julie's reading glasses and a box of tissues. There also was a spoon, a soggy tea bag in a mug, a box of crackers and an empty glass.

"You know you should be in bed."

"I'm tired of being in my bedroom."

"What do you want me to do for you?"

Julie rolled onto her back. Looking forlorn she murmured, "Call Philip."

Beth frowned. "You know it *is* Sunday?"

Julie coughed. "He'll come down. No matter what day it is. His number is in that address book. Under the phone."

BETH told Doctor Rexinger who she was and why she was calling from Julie Fischer's house. She felt relief when he said, "I'll be right down. As soon as I get dressed."

Beth helped Julie shuffle through the hall. As she walked into her bedroom Julie said she had to go into the master bathroom. Beth folded back the comforter and top sheet and shook the pillows. She opened the blinds and looked outside. There was a robin! The first harbinger of spring. She hoped it was sign of . . . a good day.

Beth helped Julie remove her robe and settle into her large bed before she asked if she could get anything from the kitchen. Julie consented to drink a small glass of orange juice. After she walked into the kitchen she wondered if Mr. Carpenter ever grew weary of cleaning up after Julie? Should she do it today? Maybe. If she could read the love letters?

After Beth watched Julie drink the juice she told her she was going to clean up the living room. While she was filling a trash bag with tissues and newspapers she heard a noise at the front door. Before she could reach the door it opened and a man stepped into the foyer. He was holding a leather key case in one hand a black bag in the other.

"Somebody locked the door so I finally got to use my key," he commented putting the keys in a coat pocket and putting the bag at his feet. He handed his coat to Beth. "And you are?"

Beth had to smile. "I'm Beth Rhodes, Doctor Rexinger. I called you. And locked the door." She reached out to shake his hand.

Even though he had forgotten who she was and expected her to wait on him, she immediately liked the man. He was shorter than she, rounder and wider in the belt area than anywhere else and kind of reminded her of a balding Santa Claus, without a beard but with a pure white bushy moustache.

He hiked up his trousers over his protruding stomach. "You can call me Doc. Everybody else does." He picked up his black bag. "She's in her room?" After Beth nodded he added, "I never know where I'm going to find her."

He stepped farther into the living room, took several deep whiffs and declared, "Hmmm. Now I have to decide if she's really sick or just hung over. Have you found a bottle of what she calls her sleeping medicine?"

"There's one next to the couch."

"Give it to me." Holding the bottle he asked, "Why did Julie call *you*, young lady?"

Beth shrugged. "I guess because I've been interviewing her."

"Ohhh. You're *that* girl. The one who's making her talk about Vicki." He watched Beth nod. "I tried to talk her out of letting you come down. Just *thinking* about Vicki makes her thirsty." He picked up his black bag. "I might as well go see her."

He walked through the hall until he reached Julie's bedroom. Standing by the bed he said loudly, "Look at you. You lied to me when I called to ask how you were doing. I should know better than to trust you. You always wait until you fall completely apart and then expect me to put the pieces together again."

Beth stepped into the room. She was surprised at how gruff Doc sounded. She felt nervous. Maybe Julie would tell her to leave?

Julie murmured, "I really felt better after I took your damn pills."

"How many times do I have to warn you that prescription medicine and Scotch do not go together. Also I told you not to let the girl interview you." Doc held up the empty bottle. "You just have to let Vicki stay dead. Or else she's going to be the death of you."

"Just be quiet, Philip." She looked beyond the man and noticed Beth's concerned look. "The interviews are not to blame, my dear. I'm upset because of the company."

Doc handed Beth the bottle. "I heard you got involved in the company again and forced two good men to resign." He opened his black bag and took out a stethoscope.

"Well you heard wrong. The treasurer resigned because his wife just inherited a bundle and she wants to travel. And," Julie said in a stronger voice, "it is *my* company."

"You're lucky Howard is still putting up with you. He's a damn fool. Too dedicated for his own good." Doc casually reached inside Julie's nightgown with the stethoscope. "I also heard you can't borrow any more money. You have a lousy reputation hiring and firing . . . and your damn drinking habit. Now you can't build the new office building."

"Liar. Why do you keep making up lies and blaming me?"

Beth remained in the doorway. She wanted to be available in case she was asked to "fetch" anything. Also the conversation was very interesting. She might end up knowing more about the Fischer Company than Alan Mawhorter.

After Doc was finished tuning in to Julie's chest and back she leaned against the head board. "I have serious decisions to make." She looked at Beth. "The problem is the company is growing too damn fast. I'm negotiating with two banks for a loan. If I can't borrow I might have to sell some real estate. And I have been researching selling private equity stock." She looked at Philip. "You know Bill's will states the Fischer's are to always be the majority shareholders." She sniffed and wiped her eyes on the sleeve of her nightgown.

Beth stepped forward to hand Julie a box of tissues.

Doc found a plastic box inside the bag. He removed a thermometer, shook it vigorously and put it in her mouth. "Think big. Bill would decide to expand. Doesn't Howard agree?"

Julie removed the thermometer and declared, "It's his idea that I consider a private sale of stock. It's a low-cost source for growth capital without getting involved with investment bankers. He even wants to buy some and says he has a few friends who would be interested."

"I will and..." he snickered, "and I'll bet even Dick Livingston will want to buy some."

"And I'm afraid he might. Now you know why I'm drinking."

"I know how much you miss Earle. I wish you could change the will and sell the company. It's not the Mom and Pop business it once was."

Julie blew her nose. "And you know I can't sell it."

"You could at least let Howard run the show."

"Not until I cut the ribbon for a new office building."

Suddenly they all heard the knocker on the front door. Beth looked at Doc who nodded. "Close the door behind you," he said.

She watched Doc gently put the thermometer back into Julie's mouth. She also saw him take Julie's hand and pat it. As she pulled the door closed she thought that Doc really cared about Julie. Could they be more than good friends?

The doorbell rang. What impatient person was she going to face?

AFTER opening the door Beth felt a thrill surge along every nerve. She knew she looked surprised. Astounded. But how could she not feel emotional when she was facing Geoff Greer?

"Well, well. Look who it is!" Geoff exclaimed. "Hello, Beth Rhodes. Now I am glad I decided to stop."

She was feeling giddy, but managed to say, "What a surprise! I never expected to see you. When I opened the door." How dumb could she sound?

Geoff smiled. "I just happened to be driving by and saw Doc's car in the driveway. I wanted to make sure Julie is okay."

Beth became an eighteen year old mature young lady. She lifted her chin and replied, "As a matter of fact she isn't feeling well. She has a bad cold." As Geoff stepped into the foyer she observed he was wearing a white turtle neck sweater and perfect fitting slacks. He always did look good in whatever he wore. She also inhaled his after shave cologne.

Geoff closed the door behind him. He noticed Beth's hair was still as shiny and thick as he remembered. Following her into the living room he eyed her shapely fanny.

"You have been able to interview her?" He sounded concerned as he was noticing how pretty her eyes were and how long her lashes were and how many freckles she had on her narrow nose. But didn't remember the mole on her upper lip.

"Only three times. I need a lot more info to write a good essay. But Doc says the interviews are upsetting her so maybe he'll tell her no more."

"I really talked you up when she called me." Why was he being so tense? This was Beth. The little girl who used to live two blocks away. All he had to do was to be friendly.

Beth smiled. "She told me you gave me a good recommendation. I knew I should call to thank you but . . . even after I heard your mother died I wanted to call you. But . . . " she shrugged.

"So why didn't you?"

"I thought maybe you wouldn't want to talk with me. I mean because of what Evan did . . . " she paused. Was he going to move closer?

He decided to wrap his hands around her upper arms. He felt her become rigid. Even though Beth was taller than Liz and Evan he had to look down to peer into her eyes. "Time out," he whispered. "We'll talk about the interviews and the essay and whatever else has happened later.

Right now I want to tell you how great you look. It's good to see you all grown up." Either he pulled her into his arms or she just kind of slid into them. But there they were hugging and laughing and hugging and whispering what a happy surprise it was being together.

Geoff did kiss Beth's forehead before he murmured in her hair, "How lucky I am that I saw Doc's car and decided to stop."

Beth giggled. "Next to Daddy I've always considered you one of my best friends. No matter what happened between you and Evan and how old you are."

Geoff scowled. "Gee, thanks. Here I was thinking you've caught up with me." He gave her a sexy smile. "Almost out of high school and going to college and looking mighty good in that sweat shirt." He gave her another gentle hug before he released her.

Beth laughed and whispered, "And you still have those piercing blue eyes." After she regained her composure she added, "How *is* your father?"

"Great. He's living with Ellen in San Diego. She married a Lieutenant Commander from the Naval Air Station and that's where he's stationed.

"I read about the wedding in *The B.C.* And you were best man."

"Dad's sister in Delaware wanted him to move in with her because she's lonely since my uncle died and she refuses to live with my cousin and his family. But he decided to live with Ellen. She'll need him too. She's expecting twins in about four to six weeks. According to Dad she's the size of an elephant." Geoff was beaming with pride as he always did whenever he talked about his family.

Beth felt happy for him. If Geoff was so pleased because his sister was expecting what would he be like when *his* wife was expecting? Imagine having his baby? She became annoyed with herself. There still was a Brad in her life. Right?

"What did Julie say when she called you about my letter?"

"Welll, besides remembering you're Evan's sister and you still live in Taylor Park she wondered if I knew anything about your character." He smiled. "I told her you were definitely a big one."

Beth snickered. "So maybe my letter helped her decide to rejoin the world of the living?"

"Between you and me she told me she was unhappy being a recluse. So after she got your letter she decided to take advantage of an opportunity to let an outsider into her home. Hopefully your visits could help her work her way out of, I think she used the word, doldrums. She sounded so sincere and enthusiastic that I'm really surprised she's still drinking. I guess making a change wasn't as easy as she thought it was going to be. I'm sorry. For both of you." He gently touched Beth's cheek. "Especially for you."

Beth forced a weak smile as she thought, Especially when I'm not as understanding nor as cooperative as she hoped I'd be. To Geoff she commented, "It hasn't been easy."

"Maybe after she feels better?"

"I hope so. You know I'm up against some pretty stiff competition. Mary Ann Powers is another Pearl Buck. And Art Slight has picked old Mr. Parry to write about and you know what an exciting life he's had. Some kids already have been accepted to colleges. Dan Friedman is going to M.I.T."

"I've seen you with him several times. Is he your steady? "

As Beth replied, "We're just friends," they both heard Doc clearing his throat.

Geoff put out his right hand. "I saw your car in the driveway and I decided to find out if Julie was okay."

Doc shook Geoff's hand. "Good to see you, Geoff." He turned to Beth. "Can you stay here, young lady?"

"I guess so. For a couple of hours."

"I mean longer. I mentioned getting a nurse to Julie and she almost injured me. But she does need the pills I'm going to prescribe, round the clock. I'm going to Jamison's Drug Store and pick up the prescriptions. The fewer people involved the better." He looked at Geoff. "She needs tranquilizers. Again." To Beth he said, "She'll need you for a couple of days."

"You could stay couldn't you?" Geoff quickly asked. He smiled and added, "You take care of her during the evening. And prepare her breakfast - before you go to school. Mr. Carpenter could be here during the day." He watched Beth frown at him. "And I can take turns with Doc, to stop in and check on her. Liz shouldn't mind if you stayed a few days."

"Especially if I tell her Doctor Rexinger asked me to."

"It's Julie's idea. She never cares how much trouble people have to go to, just so she gets her bossy way. If I got a nurse she'd most likely shoot her. And then me."

"Can I go see her?"

"Sure. You too, Geoff. Give her hell. She's not that sick that you can't give her both barrels. I'm going to drive up to Jamison's and get the medicine. And we all have to make sure she takes the pills because with what I prescribed before she should be feeling better by now. She probably flushed them down the toilet."

As soon as Doc left Geoff stepped closer to Beth and whispered, "I know I put you on the spot but I won't desert you."

She nodded. She felt his closeness. Did he know he was throwing her off balance?

They walked into Julie's bedroom and stood by the side of her bed.

Geoff smiled and remarked, "Hello, Julie. I saw Doc's car and decided to stop in. What a surprise to see Beth and find out I better stop thinking about her as the little girl who lived down the street." He observed Julie with the look of a concerned friend and added, "I'm sure as soon as you begin to take Doc's medicine and get some T.L.C. you'll feel better."

Julie reached out for Beth's hand. "Philip says I shouldn't be alone. So I've decided you should stay with me."

All Beth could do was move her head up and down. If only she had a crystal ball.

Julie squeezed Beth's hand as she smiled at Geoff. "She is a nice girl, Geoff."

Geoff winked at Beth. "You mean you didn't trust your Corporate Counselor's judgment?"

"Has she told you how mean I've been?" Julie paused to sigh and look forlorn. "But then I haven't felt well. This cold just won't go away."

She looked into Beth's face and smiled. Sweetly. "As soon as I feel better I'm going to help you write the best essay. Of course I'll get better faster with you taking care of me."

Beth felt apprehension but smiled. She looked at Geoff. He looked convinced. Pleased. Easy for him. Beth looked back at Julie. She pulled her hand free. "I'll stay with you because Geoff is going to check on you and I know Mr. Carpenter will be here." She felt better letting Julie know she expected help.

Julie reached for Geoff's hand. "You be a dear and take her to her house so she can get some clothes. And whatever she'll need - for maybe a week?" She smiled at both of them. "Now I must rest. I'll see you both later."

Geoff and Beth made convincing comments. They both knew even though she appeared forlorn, Julie was in control.

As they walked to the hall door Julie added, "It would be nice if you would get to know each other better." She chuckled and added, "Freckles together. Friends forever.

" In case I'm asleep when you return, Beth, just put your things in the front bedroom. That will be *your* bedroom. So use the bureau and the closet. Make yourself at home. Okay?"

Beth nodded to Julie. "Thank you."

Inside she yelled out, *Help! I've been hooked.*

EIGHTEEN

AS SOON AS Geoff drove his red sports car out of Julie's driveway he whistled. "What an exciting Sunday this has been for you. And it's not over yet."

"I can't believe what's happening."

"You'll be hot news when your friends find out you're staying with Julie Fischer."

Beth shrugged. "And I can't wait to tell Mr. Stookey." She leaned her head against the window and thought the words, *Essay. Love letters. College. Brad. Geoff. Ye gads, why is he turning into Willow Drive? Does he know about Brad and me? Is he telling me . . ."*

"Hey. There's Brad Livingston. Polishing his car." Geoff sounded his car horn and waved to Brad.

Beth wanted to slide down in the seat and hide. But Geoff would wonder why. So she looked. There he was. Waving and grinning. He was wearing a sweat suit and sneakers. Beth waved back. *A good looking shit head. How can I hate him when I love him so much?*

"Nice guy. Do you know if he and Jeanne Barnes are still an item?"

"Last time I heard."

"I never could see them as a twosome. She seems a little . . . well, too fast for Brad."

"Really?" Beth swallowed hard. She longed to say "For your information he's not so slow. He's been writing love letters and poems to me. But I hate him" She hoped the tears would go away before they ran down her cheeks.

Geoff turned on to Jacksonville Road. "And there it is. The company that causes Julie so much grief." They drove past the two story office building which had been built behind a parking area. Black names painted on white signs designated who was permitted to park near the front door. Beth noticed the sign **President/Chrm of the Board.** Spreading out behind the office building was the manufacturing plant consisting of the original building and three additions all of which were surrounded by parking areas. This was Bill Fischer's legacy and Julie Fischer's nightmare.

Geoff laughed as he drove into Taylor Park. "Seems like an eon since I was in here."

"You haven't missed anything. I'm sure it still looks the same."

"Hey, you'll be getting out of here in a couple of months. I never did ask you where do you want to go to college?" He sounded enthusiastic.

"*Penn State.* Hopefully, Main Campus." Beth forced a chuckle. "Although I would settle for Kutztown or Shippensburg. Who knows? And I have read there's going to be a *Bucks County Community College* so I may still be living here?"

"You know a Community College is an okay place to start."

Beth smiled as she noticed Mrs. Smithers peeking out her kitchen curtain. If her neighbor recognized Geoff seeing them together would make interesting gossip. Oops. There was Peg's car in her parking area. She would remember Geoff!

"Come on in. Maybe Liz will still be asleep."

"I'm not afraid of Liz. I see her once in a while. When I stop in Lou's for a quick meal." Geoff got out of the car and walked around to open Beth's door.

Beth thanked him and imagined Mrs. Smithers might be on the phone already.

Inside Beth immediately walked to Gerry's habitat. "I have to take you with me," Beth whispered. She carried the large terrarium and bag of gerbil food to the kitchen table. She noticed the pile of clothes on the top of the washing machine. She got a bag from under the sink and separated what belonged to her. She'd wash them in Julie's laundry room. And even use the dryer. Sorry Liz.

Geoff sat on a chair and picked up Beth's note. "Just add, 'I'm going to stay for a week'."

"I wish I could be here when she reads it. I'll get my books and you can take Gerry and my laundry and books out to the car. While I get some clothes." She smiled. "Please?"

Beth was as quiet as she could be while she stuffed clothes into a shabby suitcase. *Hey, Daddy. I'm using your suitcase because I'm going to stay at Julie Fischer's house. How about tuning in? I'll need you. If only Liz knew who's downstairs.*

Beth and Geoff did leave the house before Liz did find out.

IN Julie's house, Geoff helped Beth carry her suitcase and clothes bag into the front bedroom. When Beth put her books on a kitchen counter he put Gerry's habitat next to them. They found a note from Doc giving Beth directions to give Julie the red pill every eight hours and give Julie the blue and white pills every four hours even during the night. She must insist Julie drink lots of juice. Beth sighed and Geoff shrugged. They smiled at each other.

Without Beth asking him Geoff dried the dishes and pans which Beth could not fit into the dish washer. He emptied the trash and filled the bird feeders.

Beth was thrilled to have Geoff with her. She always had been pleased whenever he was in their house although she had never gotten to know him too well. After all he was eight years her senior and Evan's boyfriend.

Geoff had graduated among the top ten of his class from Bridgeboro High School. Next he earned a degree in Law and passed his bar exams. He was invited to join the *Law Firm of Gillon and Gerber* one of the oldest firms in Bridgeboro. It was Harold Gillon, who urged him to further his knowledge to become qualified in Corporate, Business, Contracts and Securities Law. After Paul Gerber retired, Earl Phipps named Geoff as the Fischer Company legal counselor.

As they drank a soda and ate some crackers Geoff inquired, "I guess I shouldn't ask but capital I and F, you don't win the contest and can't go to college right away what is Plan B?"

"Work. And save enough money to carry out Plan A."

"Doing what?"

She sipped from her soda. She would have enjoyed a cup of tea but they couldn't find any tea bags. She'd have to tell Julie her daddy had taught her to drive and she had a license. Then maybe she could use the car in the garage to go shopping? She laughed. "Do you need a girl in your office? I can type."

Geoff raised his eyebrows. "We do need another paralegal in our office. But that requires two years minimum of college. I was just wondering if you'll leave Bridgeboro. Like Evan did."

Finally! She had wondered when he was going to mention Evan. She had been waiting for him to ask., "How is she? Does she write?" After all, hadn't he loved Evan. Once? Had he ever believed Evan loved him?

"I like Bridgeboro. I feel secure here." She laid a hand on top of his freckled one. "And I'm sorry but I don't know where she is."

Geoff nodded. "I guess I was hoping you might be in touch."

Beth removed her hand. "You are kidding, aren't you? Before she left we had a twelve megaton explosion in our house. Liz was screaming, 'Get out you bum. And stay away.' Evan was yelling, 'Who taught me how to be a bum?' And I was crying, 'I hate both of you!' And we haven't heard from her since she walked out the kitchen door. She said she was moving to Norfolk, with Les. But another sailor told Liz that Les shipped out of Norfolk. So we don't know where she is."

Suddenly she wanted to know how does a person feel after they've been hurt by a person they loved? For Geoff's sake. And also for her own sake. "How do you feel about her now?"

Geoff's blue eyes penetrated into Beth's brown eyes. "Just an occasional relapse. When I remember how much I loved her."

Damn. That was not what she wanted to hear. "If only she knew."

Geoff winked before he stood. He stretched his long lean body. "Listen dear one, you cannot live on crackers and cereal which according to what I put in the trash seem to be Julie's favorite foods. How about if we make up a list and I'll do some shopping for you?"

Beth immediately forgot about Evan. And Brad. "I would appreciate that. And I know you'll buy lots of juice and milk because you don't want me to have to drink Scotch."

"Fear not. I shall buy only nutritious foods for your mind and body."

She had forgotten how charming he could be. How boyish he could look. Now, who could she tell she had been with Geoff Greer on Sunday and she was going to see him every day. As long as Julie was sick. Maybe after Julie got well? Then she reminded herself he probably thought of her as a teenager.

BETH watched Geoff drive out the driveway. What a predicament to be in. She wanted Julie to get well so she could ask for the love letters and continue to interview her. But as long as Julie needed T.L.C., Beth would continue to see Geoff.

Beth felt the watch. There still was a Brad Livingston and she was going to see him the next day. Was she going to acknowledge him?

She would pretend she was Scarlett O'Hara and worry about seeing Brad, tomorrow. Right now, she was going to tidy up the living room.

She studied a picture whom she believed to be Earle and Alice Phipps. Who else would Julie have in the house, except her favorite brother and his devout wife? Beth studied Earle's face. She finally decided Julie and Vicki looked more alike than Earle resembled either sister. What had William Fischer looked like? Maybe someday she would be brave enough to ask Julie if she could see a picture of her beloved husband. And lover of Vicki Lynn? Did Doc know about the affair?

And thinking about pictures she must remember that Julie was saving Brad's. She sure had learned a lot about Julie Fischer. More than she had bargained for.

Too bad she wasn't writing an essay about *her*!

NINETEEN

THE RINGING OF the telephone made Beth jump. She quickly picked up the receiver and almost whispered, "Mrs. Fischer's residence."

"It really is?"

As soon as Beth recognized Liz's voice she felt annoyance. "Yes. It is." She hoped she had answered fast enough that the phone in Julie's bedroom did not disturb her.

"Well, hi. I just read your note."

"I thought you should know where I am." She decided to sit on the couch.

"I thought you were finished with the interviews? With Julie."

"Mrs. Fischer has a bad cold. Doctor Rexinger asked me to help take care of her. And while I'm in school, either Doc or Geoff will stop in." There, she said his name.

"Geoff Greer?"

"Uh huh. He drove me to the house to get my clothes and books. In case you didn't notice. Gerry is with *me*."

"I don't give a damn about your rat. I just can't believe that Geoff . . . honest to god, kid, you are the one. Wouldn't Evan love to know you'll be seeing Geoff. Wait a minute, I need a cigarette." She inhaled and exhaled loudly. "Okay. Why not try to get to know him better?" She laughed into Beth's ear." If he had a soft spot for one Rhodes' girl he just might get interested in the other one. And you're a damn lot smarter than Evan."

"Marrying me off seems to be your big push."

"At least I want you to do more than your sister did. Has Geoff asked about Evan? I mean, whenever he meets somebody in Lou's, we just say hello and goodbye."

"He asked how she is."

"I hope you told him she's probably the mascot of the Norfolk Navy Base." A deep inhale. "Don't you think it's a good sign that Julie wants you to stay with her?"

"She doesn't like nurses."

"She must like you. And I know I've said this before, but I'm going to say it again . . . "

"Don't bother. I know what you have in mind." Suddenly Beth had a desire to hang up.

"If you don't win that contest, working for Julie Fischer wouldn't be too bad. Just be nice. Maybe she'll ask you to live with her. And she'll send you to college? But even if she doesn't, just working for her could be fun."

"Why do I suspect you want me out of the house?"

"I'm going to move."

Beth remained silent, eyeing everything on the coffee table but perceiving nothing. She was waiting for Liz to fire the other barrel. Maybe one of the bullets would ricochet?

"Did you hear me?"

"Uh huh. You're going to move. And you're waiting for me ask why? Or when?"

"Lou asked me to marry him." She laughed. "I guess you're surprised?"

"I guess I am." Why should she have tears in her eyes?

"I've got to, kid. I don't mean that I'm pregnant. I just mean, well, we have been getting kinda serious and it's too good of an opportunity to . . . to turn down."

Beth blotted tears on her shirt sleeve. "Congratulations."

"I never thought I'd get married again. But Lou is crazy about me. And he's loaded. So, I figure, why not?"

Beth knew that Liz was seeking her approval but she could not give it. "Did he give you a ring?" Did she really care?

"Last night. I wanted to show it to you this morning. But, you'll get to see it. Everybody at the restaurant is happy for us. So you'll have to think up where to go. Lou has an apartment over the restaurant but it isn't very big. Only one bedroom and not only that but Lou doesn't like kids. He says he's glad his first wife never got pregnant. And being around a bar ain't the nicest atmosphere for a girl your age. There's rough talk and dirty jokes and, you know what I mean."

More tears rolled down her cheeks. This was unreal. One minute she was considered an annoying kid who would be underfoot and the next minute she was old enough to understand dirty jokes and rough talk. She saw the tissue box, next to Julie's chair. She sniffed but still had to wipe her nose on her sleeve.

149

"We haven't definitely decided when we'll get married but I did tell him I want to be a June bride. So he's going to pay the rent on our mansion, *he ha* until the end of June."

"I'll . . . plan accordingly."

"It's kinda up to Lou's brother 'cause Lou wants him to be at the restaurant while we're away. He's going to take me to Florida for our honeymoon. Nice, huh?"

"Sounds that way." Beth wiped her nose again. *Help Daddy. Are you hearing this* crap? *Julie. Call me. Geoff. Save me.*

"So . . . whenever his brother can take off, then Lou and me will go away those two weeks. When you have your own business, you really have to do a lot of planning." Another loud drag. "Why not let Julie know you have to move? She might ask you to . . . is she real sick?"

"I told you, she has a bad cold."

"You stay with her as long as you have to. It's okay with me."

"I thought it would be. Listen, do me a favor? Tell Peg I won't be able to baby sit this week. And I'll call her later."

"Wait 'til I tell her why. I'll bet she'll call Alan."

"Thanks for calling," Beth murmured. "Gotta go. Goodbye."

"Okay. But keep in touch. And oh yeah, hello to Geoff."

AFTER Beth hung up the receiver, she took several deep in and out, breaths. She had to dislodge the pain. She closed her eyes as she yelled inside, *Why don't people get warned before they get that kind of a phone call?*

She used a finger to wipe her nose which convinced her to get the tissue box. She looked around the living room. With the blinds open, it was warm and homey looking. In fact, it *would* be a nice place to stay. She blew her nose.

Beth walked slowly through the dining room. She paused in front of the breakfront and studied the silver service. *Nice. Right, Daddy? Lucky anybody who lives here. Or works here.* The old thought of why was she ever born dashed through her mind. *I'm certainly not enjoying being an Earthling. I'm tired of being alone. And scared. Daddy, that's what I am. Since you left me. I'm scared.* She began to cry.

A knock sounded on the outside door. Beth walked into the mud room and saw Geoff grinning through the glass. He was holding two paper bags with the red logo *Stop and Shop Foods Market* on them. Beth opened the door and returned to the sink. She did not want him to see her face.

As he followed her, Geoff commented, "There's four more bags in the . . . hey, what's the matter? Is Julie okay?" He put the bags on the closest counter.

Beth quickly wiped her cheeks. "She's okay."

"Did you two have an argument?"

"She's still asleep. I'm just tired."

"A good fibber you will never be." He put his hands on Beth's shoulders and turned her around. "What's happened to make you have to cry?"

Beth walked into Geoff's arms. She leaned against his sweater and whispered, "Hold me."

Geoff wrapped his arms around her and held her close. He let her sob in his sweater while he stroked her hair. "Tell me what's wrong. Then we can take care of it." He tucked his handkerchief into Beth's right hand.

Beth wiped her face. She even wiped Geoff's sweater as she whispered, "Sorry."

"No, you cannot pull away from me. Until you tell me what's wrong."

Beth held the handkerchief against her face before she put her face against Geoff's chest. "I'm scared. Liz just called to tell me she's marrying Lou. I have to move out of Taylor Park by the end of June. So I have to find a place to live. And get a job. And . . . "

Geoff put a finger over her mouth. "Wait a minute. Just hush up."

Beth pushed his hand away. "I can't hush up. I know there are lots of other kids who have to be on their own. Some guys go into the service and maybe get sent overseas. I know all of that. There's one thing in cutting the umbilical cord but I feel as though mine was just yanked out... and nobody cares if I bleed to death."

Geoff smoothed her hair. "I'll try to help you."

Beth stared into Geoff's blue eyes. She never noticed there was a circle of dark blue around each pupil. She peered into the irises and wished she could reach his soul.

Suddenly more anger filled her mind. "And Liz had the nerve to keep suggesting that I butter up Julie. To give me a job and take me off the streets. It would make it real easy for her, wouldn't it? That's if she could possibly care what happens to me."

"Liz cares and Julie probably would be glad to . . ."

Beth pulled away. "I'm going to college," she declared. Strongly. "Daddy wanted me to go. And I'm going!"

"Just remember Vicki Lynn never went to college."

"Maybe I'll never be a writer." Beth responded. Strongly. "But with a degree, at least I can get a decent job. Make a career for myself." She stared at him. "That's what you did."

"True. But," Geoff put a twinkle in his eyes, "we just met again and here you are, talking about moving away already."

Beth had to smile. She felt flattered. After all. Here was a good looking man, eight years older saying nice things to her. At least teasing her. "I'm too young for you. You have a good job and your own apartment and . . . I'm just a teenager."

Geoff raised his eyebrows. "I could wait for you to grow up."

Beth frowned. She felt a quick thrill vibrate throughout her body. How serious should she become? With Geoff Greer. Or should she get serious at all because somewhere in the back of her mind she remembered *Brad Livingston.*

Coyly she whispered, "Ah do declare, Geoffrey Greer, Esquire. You certainly can make a distressed female feel better. In a hurry. Now let's remember the groceries."

TWENTY

MONDAY MORNING cancelled Spring. Many residents did not bother to check the temperature and discovered that just a suit jacket or a sweater was not enough to stop the cold gusty wind. The nasty weather was the topic of conversation as the students and morning work force waited for their busses. With chattering teeth and much cursing.

Beth Rhodes was waiting for the bus to take her uptown. She was wearing her vinyl jacket but she had not brought gloves or a scarf from home. She was aware of how cold she was but she really was not suffering. She felt too elated to care about the weather.

She was remembering that Geoff had stayed to have dinner with her. Julie had tea and soup in her room. After Geoff loaded the dish washer he informed Julie he would return the next afternoon. He gave Beth a friendly goodbye hug. And best of all, a kiss on her forehead.

When Beth went to check on Julie, she complained the medicine was making her sleepy so would Beth please leave her alone. Beth had been hoping Julie would offer her the letters to read. She was afraid to ask for them. Maybe the next day? She needed to write her most important literary composition. She must impress the judges. Especially Richard Livingston!

Sitting on the bus, she smiled. She was looking forward to telling Mr. Jones' secretary the address and phone number she would be using for the coming week. And updating Mr. Stookey. Then Beth reminded herself she also would see Brad. Face to face.

BRAD Livingston had just finished his scrambled eggs when his father hurried into the kitchen.

"I'm just going to have juice," Richard declared as he threw his overcoat over a chair. "I'll get something at the Diner later."

Bernice frowned at her husband. "Why are you in such a hurry? It will take me only a minute to cook you an egg and the bacon already is . . ."

"I only want juice. I remembered something I have to get out in the early mail." His Adam's apple went up and down with each gulp of orange juice.

Brad observed his parents as he finished his hot chocolate. It was obvious that whatever love they may have had for each other had gone down the drain. They were not doing much more than tolerating each other, for the sake of the commitment to their vows. He remembered how much he loved Beth and hoped when they got married they would continue to care for each other. Always!

She had to forgive him. For being such a jerk. He would just have to wait. And hope.

"Will you pick me up for the meeting?" Bernice inquired.

"Oh, damn it," Richard exclaimed as he pushed up his glasses. "Is that the meeting about saving the *Odd Fellows Lodge* from being torn down?"

"Yes it is. And we have to be there."

"I'll call you later. Or Florence will. I seem to remember I have a luncheon date."

"You're working too hard. You didn't even relax this week-end, except on Saturday night at The Club."

Bernice smiled at Brad. "We had a lovely time. We met two new couples. One of the men . . . what was the last name of the couple I liked, Richard?"

"O-e-h-r-l-e," Richard spelled as he put on his coat.

"Oh yes. Hank Oehrle. He's the new Executive Vice President at the *Fischer Company*. Quite impressive. His wife is nice too. I'm going to invite them for dinner."

"He's the assistant to Howard. And we just met them. Let Lou entertain them first. You've done that before and we found out we didn't like them."

Richard picked up his briefcase. He pecked at Bernice's cheek and murmured, "Don't talk too much at the meeting. I still don't trust that Clara Norton." He looked at Brad. "You better push your Yearbook Committee. I want all of the pictures by next week. And I don't like your hair that long. I would advise you to get a haircut."

Without waiting for Brad to defend himself, Richard walked out of the mud room door.

RICHARD Livingston had an idea. It had been conceived while Earle Phipps had taken the helm of the Fischer Company. After Bill's death. Now it had been resurrected after talking with Hank Oehrle, During dinner at the Club.

Included in the renovations to *The B.C.* office building, Richard had his office redesigned to have an outside door installed directly opposite his designated parking area. Now he could avoid walking through the outer lobby and past the offices and desks of his editors and secretarial personnel. Richard threw his coat over the back of a chair and settled behind his desk. He punched a familiar number into his telephone.

"Good morning. Charles Barnes. How may I help you?"

"How the heck are you this chilly Monday morning?"

"Life is great. We missed you at the Club yesterday. Are you and Bernice okay?"

"We're fine. I just had too much paper work piling up so I decided to skip playing golf. How did you make out?"

"As a matter of fact, I did quite well. But you were smart. I should have been in here. That's why I came in early. I can't let myself get too snowed. Business is booming right now."

Richard pushed up his glasses. He really wanted a cigarette but he could not reach the window or the switch to the fan. He had promised his secretary he would not smoke inside his office. Damn women. Not only did he have to keep Bernice happy by not smoking in the house or the car, but his secretary was just as demanding. "You alone?"

"Uh huh. That's why I answered the phone. The rest of the gang begins to wander in between eight and nine. This is the best time of the day to get the little things out of the way. What's on your mind?"

Richard messaged his forehead. "The farm on Quarry Road." Damn. Was he going to get a tension headache? "As much as I hate to tell you I've decided you better deal me out. I don't know how Julie got wind of our idea but evidently she's going to do the same thing she did before. Only this time it's you and me she's going to outbid. And there's no reason why you should lose out on the chance to purchase the farm just because she has a grudge fight with me. I'm even going to print my decision in *The B.C.*" He heard Charlie scraping the bowl of one of his pipes.

"Then what? You'll sneak in the back door?"

"As much as I would want to I better just stay away from this investment." He had to make Charlie believe he was willing to make a sacrifice. "It'll make it easier for you."

"I've been wanting to say this for many years. There is no reason why she should be able to keep you off balance. It just doesn't make sense to me." When it became obvious Richard was not going to respond Charlie added, "I know it's none of my business, but maybe there's something that could be bothering her?"

Richard could almost smell the pipe tobacco over the telephone. And damn because he wasn't as prepared as he thought he was. "She doesn't like Bernice, or me."

"And you still haven't spoken with her since the fire?"

"You know we both tried to see her. After Bill was killed." He had to say that slowly and dramatically because he wanted Charlie to know that was what he believed. That Bill had been killed.

"Just as Lou and I did. After Bill died. From the explosion. Of course she did back out of circulation. And socializing. I'm sure you haven't said anything but it seems as though . . . ahhh, Julie seems to be sparring with just you. Maybe you've forgotten you said something personal that got back to her?"

Richard was glad he was alone. He knew his face was becoming flushed. He hoped blotches wouldn't appear. If only his secretary would knock on his door. Of course, he could pretend he had to hang up, because . . . why? Why chicken out now? Keep on the subject. Julie could not defend herself. And the dead could not talk.

He kept his voice low and even. "I don't think we've said anymore that anybody else has said." He could blame Bernice. "After Julie and Bill got married Bernice must have told the wrong person she suspected Julie wasn't really pregnant but was lucky enough to trick Bill into marrying her because he really was in love with another woman."

"And how did Bernice know that?"

"I guess I must have told her. Bill insinuated more than once, their marriage wasn't exactly made in heaven. I had to believe he was telling me he and Julie were having some problems. And I told you she used to get damned annoyed if she found out Bill and I stopped at *The Pub*. She must have worried he might be telling me too much."

"So Julie was jealous of you. So what? For god's sake, if that's all this friction is about. It's ridiculous. All marriages have their ups and downs."

"Welllll, Bill almost told me he . . . ahhh, that there was *another* woman in his life. He kind of made it sound like maybe she was even in his plans."

"What you're indicating doesn't shock me. Even after he got married I don't think there was a woman in Bridgeboro, and let's admit it our wives included, who wouldn't have given up her reputation just for a week-end with him."

"In fact, Lou used to brag that she went all the way with Bill." He paused to chuckle. "Attending high school. Why make Bill sound so guilty? I'm sure some of us have been risqué, in our day. Just how long can Julie hang on to being a hurt wife."

Obviously Charlie was not impressed with his explanations. Or could it be possible Charlie was either bragging about his own affairs or was hinting he knew something about Richard's past? He had to change the subject. "We all know Julie *is* an eccentric woman."

"Why not try to have a nice friendly talk with her. Editors have a way with words and I know you could be gentle and convincing. I'll just bet you two could solve this misunderstanding."

Richard knew that Charlie was testing him. "I don't think a talk would solve anything. We just said she's eccentric."

"*You* just said that. Right now she may be too sick anyway."

"She's sick?" Richard asked too eagerly. "Who told you that?"

"Well, yesterday, on my way to meet a client in Willow Grove, I noticed Doc's car parked in her driveway. On my way back Geoff Greer's sports car was in the drive. And while I was in *Jamison's Drugs*, to get some pipe tobacco, Wally told me Doc had picked up several prescriptions for her. Wally said she may have pneumonia."

Richard did not say *good,* but he could not stop himself from remarking, "Evidently something which cannot be cured with Scotch."

"I know it sounds damn ungentlemanly, but we could close the sale while she's down and almost out?"

Finally, Richard heard some activity in the main office. "She can be besotted and she still knows what's going on in town. I'd love to know how she found out about our bid. Anyway, that's my decision and as much as I hate to back out it will give me a chance to get solid for Brad in college. God help the bank account. And I hope Jeanne is feeling better."

"She felt better yesterday. Lou is insisting that she starts to take some vitamins."

"Bernice and I thought Brad might be getting whatever Jeanne had. But he went to school this morning. Okay Charlie, Flo just looked in so I have to go."

"I'm still going to think about what we can do, to keep you in on the bid. When I come up with something I'll give you a call"

Richard closed his eyes and shook his head. "Ahhh, okay. Bye."

After he heard Charlie hang up he banged down his receiver. Damn!

RICHARD looked at his watch. He had not intended to talk so long with Charlie. He wanted to make one more phone call before he had to open his door and discuss the day's schedule with Flo Mann, his overly efficient secretary. He had nodded and smiled after she opened his door on a wide crack. For him to see she had arrived.

Richard knew she would hang up her coat and go into the outer lobby to check on the readiness of the receptionist. Next, she would go into the supply room to make sure coffee was being made for the office personnel and anyone who might come in from the outside. The ancient employee who worked in Advertising always made coffee for the gals and guys who worked in what was termed *the shop.*

Richard knew Flo would bring him a mug of coffee, flavored with the right amount of sugar and skim milk. But she would not linger if he were talking on the telephone. So Richard checked the phone number one more time before he proceeded to dial.

A female voice responded. "Good morning. This is the *Fischer Company*. How may I help you?"

"Good morning. This is Richard Livingston, editor of *The Bridgeborough Courier*. You may help me by connecting me with Mr. Oehrle's telephone."

After three rings another female voice. "Mr. Oehrle's office. How may I help you?"

"By telling him that Richard Livingston would like to speak with him."

Finally he heard, "Oehrle here."

"Good morning. Richard Livingston. How are you on this chilly morning?"

"Fine. And you?"

"Great. It certainly was our pleasure to meet you and your lovely wife. Bernice plans on giving her a call soon to invite her to a luncheon or for Bridge . . ." he forced a pleasant chuckle, "or for something. You know how women can think of things to do."

"I hope she won't be disappointed. Audrey doesn't join anything."

"Oh? A homebody, huh?" Richard pushed up his glasses.

"Not exactly. She writes. She's had several short stories published and now she's knee deep in a novel. She's very disciplined. So many hours writing per day. Six days a week."

"How about *that?* I had no idea or I would have had a talk with her on Saturday evening. She and I have a lot in common. After all, writing is my forte also and . . . well," he chuckled. "I guess she knows Bridgeboro is where Vicki Lynn wrote several of her best novels. And I happen to have known Vicki. In fact, I was a close friend of hers and . . . " his voice trailed off as he realized he was rambling. Besides lying. He better be careful. He had not called to talk about Vicki Lynn anyway.

"Then you knew Bill Fischer?"

"He was my best friend. We were buddies in high school. So I've always had an interest in the company. I watched it grow from a machine shop in a garage, to what it is today. And since talking with you on Saturday, I got a brain storm. I'm going to begin a series of articles covering all of our local industries. And small businesses. I know our readers will be interested in the successful employers who contribute to our local economy." He paused to chuckle. "Of course, I'll have to include the Navy Base.

"I imagine you would turn one of my feature editors over to your Public Relations Department but I wanted to check out the idea with you first." Finally he was on the real subject.

Hank cleared his throat. "It sounds like an interesting idea. Of course I will have to discuss it with Howard Whiteside. Do you also have pictures in mind?"

"Sure do. Inside and out. I thought I'd begin with the larger companies. Didn't you say on Saturday evening the Fischer Company is considered one of the top ten instrument companies in the United States?"

"I don't remember saying that, but it is true."

"And . . . what was the name of that book you said you were in?" Richard asked.

"I might have mentioned the *Fortune* magazine."

Richard pushed up his glasses. He sat tall almost pretending he was interviewing Hank. "And your profit last year? Didn't you tell me that, at the bar?"

"I don't believe I did because I'd have to ask the controller for the exact figures. I wouldn't want to give an inaccurate amount."

"Someone told me a guesstimate was around fifty million. I thought it was you."

"Sorry. I'm not one to guess."

Richard knew he better change his direction. "By the way. Any nibbles for the V.P. of Finance opening yet?"

"We're still interviewing. But our controller is well qualified so we don't have to make a hurried decision."

"I see. Well, I won't take any more of your time right now. But I would like to make an appointment with you, for a walk around the company." Richard realized how badly he wanted to see Bill Fischer's memorial. "Maybe sometime this week?"

"Just a minute while I check what my week looks like." After many seconds Hank asked, "How about Wednesday? Nine AM."

"Ahh, nine AM on Wednesday." He was hoping Hank would believe he was considering if he was available. "I can make that." He quickly wrote in H.O. at 9 AM in an empty block for the coming Wednesday.

"I know this will bring the company to the attention of the new residents of this fine town. Also to those who don't know how successful The *Fischer Company* has become. Please remember me to your lovely wife. Tell her I'm looking forward to having a . . . well, a chance to talk shop with her."

"I'll do that. See you Wednesday. Goodbye."

"At nine," Richard said. "Goodbye."

After he hung up the receiver he folded his moist hands on the top of his desk. He appeared to be praying but he was reviewing the telephone conversations.

Even though he felt drained and anxious, he sensed elation. The plan had to be full of potential. Even though Hank would not quote him a figure, Richard knew the Fischer Company was worth at least twenty-five million dollars. Maybe more. He'd find out. Somehow.

He reached for a tablet and printed, *Read* FORTUNE. *Tell Stan Connery to contact Bridgeboro Landscaping* **re.** *new series.*

Richard Livingston smiled. Smugly As he thought, *I hope Howard tells Julie. I want her to wonder what in the hell I'm doin*g.

TWENTY ONE

BASIC TYPING CLASS was every Monday and Thursday. It was an elective for Beth and Brad. On the first day of the class they had unintentionally sat next to each other. During September, they were only classmates, laughing at the mistakes they made. On their IBM keyboards. After they had discovered each other in Drama Class they enjoyed having only an aisle separate them.

That particular Monday Beth dreaded having Brad close to her.

Beth made too many mistakes as she wondered what to do about their relationship? She was suffering from a mix of emotions. How could she convince herself she was angry with him when she liked him so much? How could she be saying the word *hate* when she knew the word *love* described her feelings?

Two times they glanced at each other at the same time. Beth smiled, weakly. Brad winked. Immediately, she was certain she wanted to make up with him. She began to write a note to meet her someplace. But it ended up in little pieces when she remembered he had hurt her. She still did not want to rush back into his arms. Maybe it would do him good. If he was suffering? Such as she surely was.

Maybe, just maybe, she could encourage Geoff Greer?

After the last class, while students were either rushing to somewhere or ambling through the halls, Beth realized which one of them was going to suffer. Walking through the main hallway she had to pass a group of other seniors clowning around outside of Mr. Stookey's classroom. Among the group was a laughing Brad leaning next to a grinning Jeanne. She had an arm wrapped Brad's waist.

Beth hoped to stroll by as nonchalantly as she could. However Mary Jane Conrad asked loudly, "Hey, Beth. Are you still going to interview the Mystery Woman of Bridgeboro?"

Beth forced a smile. "I'm still going to interview Mrs. Fischer, if that's what you're asking?"

Jeanne took the stage. "I heard she has three eyes and green hair."

Beth avoided looking at Brad as she replied, "She hasn't scared me yet. In fact, I'm enjoying interviewing her."

Brad moved away from Jeanne. Just inches, but it was obvious to Beth. He smiled before he asked, "How's your essay coming along?"

She nodded. "Okay. I'm getting pages of interesting information."

"In fact," a deep male voice said from the doorway of the classroom, "the famous recluse of Bridgeboro likes Beth so much, she has invited her to live with her."

All Beth could do was shrug and feel embarrassed as several of her classmates responded with "Wow, no kidding", and "Man, you're sure to win now."

Beth was pleased that Mr. Stookey was making a fuss over her and her classmates were making her feel important. Still she had to blurt out, "I'm really staying with her because she has a bad cold. And Doc, Doctor Rexinger wants me to stay with her. Until she's better. "

BECAUSE she had not seen Geoff's car parked in the driveway, Beth was surprised to find him sitting in the living room. She felt a tingle of excitement travel from her head to knees. How could she be so foolish? He said he would stop by to see Julie. He had not made a special trip, to see *her*. All she could manage to murmur was "Hi, Geoff."

"And good afternoon to you."

Beth thought Geoff looked dignified in a light blue dress shirt with a tie that complimented his charcoal gray suit. Could he tell how happy she was to see him?

"If I looked surprised it was because I didn't see your car."

"Julie asked us to park behind the garage. She doesn't want my car or Doc's car to be on display. Too many people will make too many guesses why." Putting a paper clip over the papers he had been reading he added, "So from now on, if you don't want to be surprised, use the back door and see our cars."

"How's Julie?" Why did she feel so nervous? He was only Geoff Greer.

"As far as I know she's doing okay. Doc didn't tell me otherwise before he left." He reached for his briefcase next to the chair. He watched Beth throw her jacket on a chair. She's been asleep since I arrived."

They both smiled after they heard the sound of coughing.

"I guess I better let her know I'm here." *I almost said home.* She gave Geoff a quick grin and began to walk out of the living room.

Geoff followed Beth. "I'll say hello and goodbye."

As Beth entered the bedroom, Julie held out her hand. "I've been waiting for you."

Beth decided to take Julie's hand. "Hey, you put on lipstick. Does that mean you're feeling better or you wanted to look pretty for your male nurses?"

"I did it to let you know I'm feeling better." She focused on Geoff. "She's taking good care of me. I feel so lucky that you helped me find her." Julie smiled a happy smile. "Instead of being a writer, she really should be a nurse."

"Hmmm," Geoff sounded. "Maybe I should get sick so I can get some special attention."

While Beth was blushing and without asking Julie, she heard herself ask Geoff if he could stay for dinner. He thanked her but had a dinner meeting in Philadelphia. She was surprised how dejected she felt as she watched his sports car pull out of the driveway.

Could Julie sense she was moping the rest of the evening? What would she have explained if Julie asked why she was so quiet? She could say she just miss talking to Brad Livingston. Or she had been hoping she could get Geoff Greer's attention. *Okay, Daddy, so I'd tell her a fib and tell her it's because I have bunches of homework.*

ON the following day Beth again hurried back to Julie's house. She felt disappointed that Doc's car was parked behind the garage. She put her books on the kitchen table and her jacket around a chair. Then convinced herself to walk to the doorway. Into Julie's bedroom.

"Hi, to you two," she said cheerfully as she noticed that Doc was taking Julie's blood pressure. "Oh, wow, look at the lovely flowers." She had caught sight of a picture perfect bouquet on the triple bureau. Beth found a card which read Gillon and Greer, Attorneys-at-Law.

"Aren't they lovely?" Julie remarked "And Geoff put another arrangement on the dining room table. While I was talking with Howard Whiteside this morning I got a coughing spell and had to hang up. So I guess he decided I should have flowers while I'm still alive." She paused to laugh. "Even though the arrangement must have cost enough for a dinner for four."

Beth returned from the dining room and declared, "I never saw such a beautiful arrangement. Proves how important you are. You're sure looking better this afternoon."

"Because I'm feeling much better."

Doc remained seated on the side of the bed. "She's feeling like a worn out dish rag," he said gruffly. "And she knows it. Her blood pressure is too low and she still has a fever."

Julie snickered. "He wants me to be sick because he likes taking care of me. And I help pay for his fishing trips."

"You're always sassy, no matter how bad you feel. You know damn well you still feel like hell." He looked at Beth. "She had a nasty sore throat and chest cold. I really expected to have to put her in the hospital."

"You'll never get me in a hospital." Julie snapped out. Then she coughed. Hard.

"If I want you in a hospital I'll give you a needle and ship you out cold. For a person in your condition, you have too damn much to say." Again he spoke to Beth. "I just laid down the law. There is to be *no more drinking.*"

"Just . . . shut up," Julie mumbled as she turned to face away from both of them.

"I want this young lady to hear what I have to say because she must be a caring friend. To be able to put up with you. Maybe she can help me put some sense in your thick head."

Julie rolled back and glared at Doc. "You leave Beth out of this. It's not her problem."

"If she's a friend then she should know. I'm going to lay it right on the line, in front of her." Doc looked into Beth's eyes and continued, "I'm sure she hasn't told you about the warning she got last year." He watched Beth shake her head. "She had a needle biopsy which showed she already has liver damage. She was warned she's heading for severe cirrhosis. She *has* to stop drinking. Or else."

He turned back to Julie. "I can get you back in pretty good shape. Maybe just one more time. But you are asking for real trouble if you start bingeing again. I called Sam to tell him the rules. You have to break the habit of reaching for a bottle every time *some*thing bothers you.

"The company is too damn big of a responsibility for you and besides, women aren't supposed to be running companies. Oh go ahead, cry. I don't give a hoot. But damn it, if you have to keep the company. Although I don't understand why in the hell you can't break the will, and then for God's sake let the men run it. And . . . and you stick to knitting."

"I…hate…to…knit," Julie said, through clenched teeth. And sniffed.

"Then write a book. You could write a best seller about you and your sister. And how you drove each other crazy." He shook his head from side to side as he began to replace and rearrange the contents in his black bag, "You better be taking what I'm saying seriously. You're a rundown hunk of junk. Only you can decide if you want to be restored. Or scrapped."

Doc stood and hiked up his baggy trousers. He looked tired just holding up a bottle of pills to show Beth. "She's to keep taking these tranquilizers until I say she can stop. They just might keep her calm enough she won't need a drink. Every time something upsets her."

To Julie he said, "Don't just sit in this house day after day. And suffer. Call me. Call Geoff. Call this young lady. For God's sake, at least try."

Julie reached out. "Okay, my dear doctor. And friend. I will try."

Holding her hand, he patted it, over and over. "That's what I want to hear."

He released Julie's hand and backed up to Beth. He put an arm around her shoulders. "Now let's let the patient rest. I gave her her medicine and some juice and you can bring her some dinner. Later."

"Before you go, I want Beth to go into her room. There's a surprise for her."

Beth froze. "A surprise?"

Doc urged Beth to walk out of the room. "Okay. Let's go see what the hell she's been up to. When I told her to stay in bed."

In the hall they both heard Julie snap back, "You just *told* me to use the phone."

The "surprise" was a television set on a heavy brass stand next to the dressing table.

"Well, look at that," Doc declared. He examined the set. "Now. Wasn't that nice of her."

"I guess so," Beth replied. "I mean, I certainly didn't expect . . . a surprise." As Beth walked through the long hallway she wondered why she wasn't feeling as pleased as she was feeling suspicious.

Julie was waiting for her. Smiling.

"That's quite a surprise. Especially when I didn't even know I needed a TV set." Beth knew that wasn't what she should say. How come she couldn't say *thank you*?

166

"Nonsense. Every young person should have their own TV. Even Joe Palmer agreed with me when I called the *Pike Appliance Store* to order it. He said his kids have their own sets. So now we can each watch our own programs. And it's a color set too."

WEDNESDAY afternoon Beth became depressed. She missed walking uptown with Dot and Jill. To stop in *Powell's* for a soda and gossip. They coaxed her to call Julie and tell her that Mr. Stookey wanted to talk with her.

Or just tell her she was missing out on the fun of being with her friends. After all, Julie wasn't dying. Beth could not be led astray. She knew her daddy would want her to live up to her commitment. And what her friends did not know she was hoping, that Geoff Greer might be at Julie's house.

Beth got her first surprise before she got off the bus. Looking out a window as the bus drove past Julie's house, she realized she actually could see the house! After she got off the bus she almost ran up Bridge Pike. Yep, the grounds had been landscaped. And a new storm door had been hung at the front entrance. She was beginning to take an interest in Julie's house. Even feel at home.

Beth walked into the living room. The drapes were pulled back and
the blinds were opened. It looked cheerful. And friendly.

"Beth?" Julie called out. "Is that you?"

"I'll be right there. I'm taking off my jacket."

Beth was ready to mention the "new look" to the front of the house but as soon as she saw Julie sitting up in bed she blurted out, "Does Doc know you're working?"

Julie was leaning on a bed table, surrounded with mail and newspapers. "Phooey with what Philip says. I feel the best I've felt in days. How can I help but with you taking care of me? Delicious meals, so much forced rest and so much damn medicine?

"So I told Sam to gather up all of my mail. In fact, I'm going to get out of this bed tomorrow. Philip says *no,* but I'm going to get dressed and work in the office. And I'll have some typing for you to do."

Beth began to rearrange the newspapers. Had Julie been cutting out anybody's picture? She tried to quickly scan the papers. "Doc says you shouldn't do too much too soon."

"Don't you preach to me too. He doesn't have a multinational business to run and so many damn decisions to make. Besides reading everything everybody is sending me about stock issues. That's what needs my immediate attention and I'd be worse off if I, "she paused to snicker, "took it lying down."

Before Beth knew she was going to she blurted out, "I agree with Doc. Why don't you let your CEO and Vice Presidents worry about things like that? They must know enough about the business they should be able to make decisions."

Julie squinted. "You mean if I allowed them to? Sounds as though people are talking about me again. Although I don't know whom you'd know who would be complaining?"

"I'm the one who's telling you. Because I'm worried about you."

Julie sat higher against the pillows. "Beth. Don't try to play games with me. I know how people talk about crazy Julie Fischer. But let me tell you, no matter what you hear about me just remember, nobody knows what they're talking about."

Julie laughed, coughed and laughed again. "Only I know what I'm doing and why I'm doing it. That's what I tell Phillip. As long as I take his evil tasting medicine and those damn tranquilizers, stop criticizing what I do. He's really surprised I feel so well, so fast. I told him having you here is better than taking any of his awful medicine."

Beth grinned but still felt wary. "I was surprised when I saw the house from the bus."

"You gave me enough hints. So I finally called the *Holweger Lands-* caping Company and told them to trim everything alive. And pull out the dead stuff. Did they do a good job?"

Beth shrugged. "Mr. Carpenter would know better than I do. But you have to remember to lock the doors. Are Doc and Geoff and I getting new keys with a new door?"

"I don't think anybody will kidnap me. And yes, you'll all get new keys. Sam and Ellie got theirs today. Did you notice how shiny and clean the house is?" After Beth nodded, she added, "Now that the house shows from The Pike the next improvement will be to get it painted. But, I thought I'd wait until July. And go away to avoid the smell and the mess." She looked directly into Beth's eyes. "I haven't visited the companies in Europe for too long and I think it will be nice for us to take a trip. Before you start college. How's that sound to you?"

What should she say? Julie Fischer was inviting her to go away with her and she didn't like the idea. "I'm . . . speechless. I've never been any farther than New Jersey. With my girlfriend's family."

"You've never been to New York City?"

Beth shook her head. "You probably read that we can't go on a class trip. Because last year's class got kicked out of a hotel. They behaved like a bunch of country bumpkins who had never been out of Bridgeboro. I don't know where I would have gotten the money but I was hoping we would be allowed to go someplace."

"For heaven's sake. I'll get Tony Miles to drive us so we can have lunch in Central Park. And go shopping. I thought every young lady would have somebody take her to New York."

Beth forced a laugh. "None of my friends can afford it."

"Not even Dan Friedman?"

Beth looked down at the floor and pretended to be shy. "I would never expect Dan to do that."

"We'll just have to see that you get better dates. From what I've read in *The B.C.* I know you're a busy student. I've seen your name mentioned with the hockey team, the debating team and the drama club. You've noticed, I do read a lot. I'll bet people don't realize how much I know about what's going on."

Julie reached for a copy of *The Bridgeborough Courier.* "I follow all of the happenings in your high school. And what's going on at the Bridge Valley Country Club and . . . "she paused to give a sarcastic laugh, "and just about everything the Barnes and Livingston's are up to."

"How did you find out Mr. Livingston and Mr. Barnes were going to buy that farm?"

Julie appeared smug. "Spies. That's another reason why money comes in handy. You can hire people to do all kinds of jobs for you."

Beth decided to play it cool. "I don't believe you have spies working for you."

"You asked me a question. I gave you an answer." Julie yawned deeply.

"You *really* know all about the Livingstons?"

Julie raised her eyebrows. "Everything I need to know. So I can keep one step ahead of tricky Dickie. And now you're going to ask why I have to do that?"

Beth shrugged. "It doesn't mean you'll tell me."

Julie patted the side of her bed. As soon as Beth sat down she began. "Okay, I *will* tell you. Even though you won't really understand what it all means. I have to keep one step ahead of Richard Livingston for my own protection. And satisfaction. And because I loathe him."

Beth decided to remain silent. And look as non-committal as she could.

"I know that Dick and Bill confided in each other. The Pub was their favorite hangout. For an after work drink. And confession time.

"After Bill and I were married we began to socialize with the Livingston's and the Barnes. And now and then, we'd include other couples. We became a tight group and were the back bone of the community.

"We attended all of the community fund raisers and activities. People would almost kill to be invited to our dinner parties and galas." Julie paused to smile. She appeared to be enjoying reminiscing. "Bill and I were treated like royalty when we entertained at Deer Lake Manor."

Julie almost gloated. "Have you ever seen my manor house?" After Beth shook her head she added, "Captain Bittner is leasing it but I can make arrangements with his wife for us to visit. He's in command of the *Johnsville Naval Air Station.* They're renting it furnished with the understanding their two college kids cannot entertain in it. My caretaker and his wife live in the carriage house so they make certain the house and grounds are the way I want them to be."

"I'd be honored to see your estate."

Julie sighed. She looked tired but continued talking. "Our good times lasted for quite a while. Then Victoria came into the picture. I tried to keep up a good front and I think I succeeded in fooling most of our friends.

"But meanwhile, back at The Pub, Bill and Dick were having their drinks. So I have a feeling Dick has even told Bernice that if he doesn't *actually* know about the affair, he thinks he knows. Do you follow me?"

Beth felt her heartbeats begin to pound behind her ears. She nodded *yes* and remembered she wanted to read the love letters. "You dislike Mr. Livingston because of something he might know. I remember reading he was joining the investors in the development of the Northampton Shopping Mall. Then I read in *The B.C.* that *Colman Real Estate* bought the land and you were among the investors. So you two are playing an investment game?"

"You're right. And now he wants to go in with Chuck Barnes to build an Industrial Park." She gave Beth a quick grin. "I do know his business is doing extremely well since he's been doing offset printing and his advertising department got a new *gung ho* department manager. Also, they got a nice sock full after Bernice's father died. I just like to block him as much as I can. And I certainly do *not* want him investing in the *Fischer Company*."

"Can you stop him?"

"I can keep trying." Before Beth could reply Julie said, "I'm tired. Please take this table away. You must have some homework to do."

Inside Beth screamed, *The letters. The manuscripts. You said I could read them. Please remember.*

AFTER Beth and Julie had dinner Julie said she had more reading to do. The dishwasher was doing its job while Beth sat at the kitchen table. Reading an assignment in Social Science.

She looked at her watch and wondered, *Brad. What are you doing? I miss our telephone conversations. Your notes. Why don't I just write you. . . was that a knock? Yeah. On the mud room door.*

Beth hurried to the door and turned on the patio light. There was Geoff, holding two large boxes. She opened the door. And grinned. "Hi, Geoff. Surprise."

"Didn't Julie tell you to expect me?" After he saw Beth shake her head *no,* he added, "I'm the delivery man." He handed her the boxes so that he could wiggle out of his leather jacket and throw it over a chair. He was wearing khaki chinos and a navy cable stitch sweater. Also intoxicating after shave cologne.

Damn him. And damn her to allow herself to have such a reaction just because he was standing close to her. And looking too damn sexy. It wasn't fair he could make her become so uncomfortable.

Geoff took the boxes from Beth's arms and said loudly, "I hope she's awake."

"I've been waiting for you," Julie's called from her bedroom. "Only Geoff can come in. Beth has to wait until we call her."

Beth observed how form fitting Geoff's slacks were as he walked out of the kitchen. She heard Julie's bedroom door click closed. How dare they have a secret without her? And why had she been wishing Geoff would hug her?

JULIE quickly sat up. She had an eager look on her face and her eyes were sparkling. She patted the bed. "Put them here."

Geoff opened the top box. He folded back several layers of tissue paper until he came to something black. It was a dress. One that would be tight and short. With long sleeves.

Julie examined the dress. "I like it. I knew Mae Fleck has good taste. As soon as I called her shop and described what I had in mind she picked right up on it. Let me see the other one."

It was a red dress with a fuller longer skirt. And a matching jacket. Julie examined it and then asked, "Which one do you like?"

"Both of them. But I hope she picks the black one."

"Okay, call her in here."

Julie looked happy and Geoff looked smug as Beth walked into the room. Then she looked at the bed. Dresses? That's what they wanted her to see. She forced herself to smile. What should she say? "Why do I need a new dress?"

"To go with our surprise." Julie looked like a pleased mother.

Beth looked at Geoff. She watched him shrug before she asked him, "What surprise?"

Julie explained. "After our talk this afternoon, while you thought I was reading, I made a few phone calls. Now, be a dear and try them on. Geoff and I want to . . . "

"I don't need any new dresses. Especially ones that come from *Flecks Apparel Shoppe*. They had to cost a lot of money and I won't ever have a need to . . . "

"Oh, but you will, my dear." Julie frowned at Geoff. "She sure is making it difficult for us." She smiled at Beth and declared, "One for the prom and one to go to New York City. With Geoff."

Beth looked at Geoff and raised her eyebrows. "Oh?" she managed to breath and then added a stupid, "Really?"

"Yes. Really," Julie repeated. "I told you that every young lady has to go to New York. You can do some sightseeing before you have dinner at the *Tower Club* and see *Don't Stop Now.* You'll have a wonderful time."

"But how about poor Geoff having to take a teenager around New York?"

He winked at her. "Don't worry about poor Geoff. As soon as Julie called I volunteered Greer's Escort Service to take the assignment. We're going to have a blast and I'll have you home before you turn into a pumpkin."

AS Beth lay awake, staring at the ceiling, she wondered how she could be so thrilled and so worried, at the same time. *Daddy. Here I am, in one of the most comfortable beds I've ever slept in. In one of the largest bedrooms of what any of my girlfriends have. In one of the nicest houses in Bridgeboro and . . . I'm not happy. And besides all of the above, I have a dream date with a dream guy for Saturday night. The black dress makes me feel like a movie star and why can't I just relax and let it happen?*

Why do I have this feeling of suspicion?
That it ain't for free!

TWENTY TWO

ON THURSDAY AFTERNOON, Beth was not as anxious to go to Julie's house, even though she admitted it certainly was more enjoyable than going to Taylor Park. Also, it was satisfying to know how many other people she was making happy. Including Geoff Greer. Julie was recovering, looking much better, and insisting she was feeling great. And praising her over and over. Even Doc told her, what a great "young lady" she was. Still, Beth did not feel like hurrying away from Bridgeboro High School. She knew why but she didn't want to admit it to herself.

She had a strong yearning to see Brad! Alone.

As she ambled through the main hall, she looked in each classroom. She knew she would talk to anybody who might delay her from going to Julie's house. Suddenly, she heard a familiar voice call out, "Hey, Beth. Are you going to Julie's?"

Dot, Jill and Mary were walking toward her. "We're going to stop for a soda."

Inside, Beth could feel the conflict. Commitment was winning. "I'd love to, but . . . "

"Damn it, Beth," Jill spoke up. "Can't you call tell her you're going to be late? I heard you tell Mr. Stookey she's much better. So why do you have to hurry down there?"

Mary spoke up. "Beth better not get her fairy godmother mad at her. After all she bought Beth her very own color TV set. For her very own bedroom."

"Who told you that!"

"Eddie Palmer's father told the whole family at the dinner table the day Julie called him. And she bought you a stereo for another surprise."

Dot spoke up. "Julie just wants Beth to be happy. While she's staying with her."

"Sure." Mary said. "And Beth is going to have *her* bedroom done over too. Julie called my uncle and asked him to bring down color samples. All shades of lavender because that's Beth's *favorite* color." It was obvious Mary was enjoying her contribution to the conversation.

Beth forced herself to laugh. But she was annoyed. She was saved by another classmate.

"Okay, that's enough laughing," Walter Smith remarked. "Can't you giggling girls remember? *These* are hallowed halls? Although now that French exam is over I guess you are allowed to laugh. From unadulterated relief. What's so bleep bleep funny?"

Dot gave her explanation. "We're teasing Cinderella. About how she has it made with her new fairy godmother."

Suddenly Beth blurted out, "It's *not* my bedroom. And, I'm *not* living with her. I told you I'm only staying with her as long as she's sick."

Mary shook head, "You're crazy. I'd stay as long as I could."

Walter nodded in agreement. "You betcha. Or at least until you get the car she's going to buy for you." His pimply face took on a smug look.

Beth felt lightheaded. She stared a fierce look at Walter. "What car?"

"The car she ordered from my dad. She called yesterday and ordered an Impala. She said it was for you." He looked from girl to girl. Everyone knew his dad was one of the successful automobile dealers in Bridgeboro. But here he was taking advantage of an opportunity that did not happen too often for him. To brag to an audience of girls.

"You *are* crazy." Beth stated.

"I'm not *crazee*. I'm jealous. Here my father owns the Chevy agency and what am I driving around in? A ten year old Rambler. And all you're doing is babysitting Julie Fischer." Walter paused for a reaction. "And oh yes, she also said to my dad you are making her very happy. So for being so lucky and plucky, you are getting a new car with everything in it but a built in toilet." He put much emphasis on the last word and waited for laughs.

Finally Beth talked her way out of the conversation and hurried away from her friends. Although maybe she really didn't like them anymore? Except for Jill. She had noticed that Jill hadn't teased her. Her friend since kindergarten even looked sorry for her.

As soon as Beth walked out the double front door of the high school she decided to walk to Julie's house. She had only two books to carry. Even if she had had to carry every book in her desk and her locker, she still would have decided she needed the walk in order to sort out her frustrations. By the time Beth reached the driveway to

Julie's house she had made a serious decision. She would tell Julie she was going to leave!

She held the new screen/storm door against her hip, unlocked the new front door and walked into the living room. Looking through the archway she had to smile. The lovely chandelier in the dining room was brightly beaming down on Julie sitting at the dining room table. She was dressed in a skirt and sweater with combed hair and makeup on her attractive face. Beth had to make a complimentary comment. Why shouldn't she let Julie know how happy she was to see her dressed and busy?

Beth put her books and jacket on a dining room chair and stood by the table. Julie had been reading a thick book and marking sentences with a highlighter. There also were two other books with titles indicating they contained information about Stock Issues.

Julie closed the book. "You look as though you had a tough day in the salt mines." She removed her reading glasses and smiled. Even her eyes were sparkling.

Beth smiled back and thought, *Maybe she looks like Kathryn Hepburn?* "But I'm better than I was since I see you have to read books as dull as some of the ones I have to read. And it hasn't even affected how good you look." Ha Ha. Make her believe she looks great. Recovered. Make yourself believe it's okay to leave her.

Beth lingered to make small talk before she remarked she should let Julie get back to her reading. And she would do her own homework at her favorite place, the kitchen table. After she fed the birds and Gerry.

For almost two hours they left each other alone with their dull reading, until Julie appeared in the kitchen and insisted she was going to prepare dinner.

Standing by the refrigerator, Julie remarked, "We're having something really yummy tonight." While tying the apron strings behind her back she smiled. "Lamb chops. I called *Joe's Meat Market* and had him deliver a supply of choice cuts of meat. I thought we could ask Geoff and Phillip to join us for dinner on Sunday. So I ordered a standing rib roast. Then you and Geoff can tell us all about . . ."

It was now or never so Beth blurted out, "I won't be here on Sunday."

Julie never missed a beat. She continued to take things out of the refrigerator while she said, "Nonsense. You're supposed to be taking care of me. And what else do you have to do?"

Beth had to think fast to present a reasonable reason. When, in effect, she really would be lying. "I have lots of things to do. At home. After all Liz works and I've always been in charge of the washing and the ironing. And all of the cleaning. We don't have an Ellie or a Mr. Carpenter."

Julie stared at Beth. "Let Liz do her own damn washing and cleaning. I need you here."

"But you're better. You look great. In fact, I really was planning on leaving tomorrow."

Julie coughed. "I won't hear of it. Whatever put such a . . . a notion in your head?"

"You knew I just came to help you. Well, I have to help at my house too."

"Beth dear. You are needed in this house much more than you are in Taylor Park. And what's more I've decided you *should* be here. Taylor Park is not a good atmosphere for a teenager. Especially one who practically lives alone. You're much better off here with me. We can help each other. I can't remember having such a happy week for as you say, many moons. I think it would be good for both of us if you just moved in."

Beth stood and leaned against the table. Her legs felt shaky. She shook her head from side to side. "You knew I was going to leave as soon as you got better."

Julie smiled and said gently, "Well, let's not put any definite date on our plans. I mean let's let this week-end come and go. We'll just plan on your fun trip to New York with Geoff. And then dinner here on Sunday. How's your essay coming along?"

Inside Beth felt herself flinch. Her chin went higher as she whispered, "Okay."

"You are still working on it, aren't you? I mean you haven't mentioned it this week?" She opened a drawer and picked up knives, forks and spoons.

"I didn't want to talk about it. While you were sick."

"Don't you want to read the manuscripts? And the letters?"

"I don't think so. Thanks, anyway."

"How come?" Julie put two place mats on the table before she began to arrange the eating utensils in their correct location.

"I've decided I don't want to mention the letters."

Julie walked to the sink. She began to wash some lettuce. "Not even if I let you tell the world about the manuscripts also?"

"I've decided to write the essay without them."

Julie frowned. "I know I told you you're spunky. Now you're being just plain stupid."

"I think I'm being pretty smart. You just won't give up trying to use me. Please. Just let me finish. Whatever you say won't do you any good anyway. Because I know what your motives are. I began to figure them out when you bought the television. You wanted to impress people. How thoughtful and generous you are. Because I'm being so nice to you. And you had to convince me you can make life real nice and cozy for me, if I'll cooperate with your plan."

Julie shook her head. "You're wrong. You are so wrong."

"I was wrong to hope I was wrong." Beth said emphatically.

Julie walked to a chair. "You think I made myself sick to get you down here?"

"I guess not. And I'm happy you're feeling better. What I do think is that you never gave up hoping you could use me. I might be poor but I do have pride. Today I was embarrassed in front of my friends. I wanted to...to die when Walter Smith told my girlfriends you've ordered a car. For me."

"That's not true. It's for me. The one in the garage is too big for me to drive. And I thought you'd enjoy driving me around in a sports car. Although it's not as sporty as Geoff's. Julie wiped away several tears that had to overflow.

Beth felt no pity. "Oh sure," she laughed out. "Well, if you want to look like a fairy godmother then pay for some new equipment for the Child Care Center in Taylor Park. Instead of trying to bribe me into writing how mean and hurtful Vicki was. Even your husband. Why can't you just forget about their affair? Let them rest in peace."

Julie wiped her eyes on the apron. "That's more than they left me."

"I'm sorry, Julie." As she watched how forlorn Julie looked she did feel compassion for the woman. She could relate to her loneliness. Even her anger and her desire to hurt. Maybe, perhaps . . . they could help each other?

Julie saw the look of concern in Beth's eyes. "Help me. Please?"

"Not with the essay. By going home tomorrow so we can stop antagonizing each other. I want to be your friend but all we're doing is hurting each other."

FRIDAY morning when Beth Rhodes left Julie Fischer's house she had her suitcase with her. Unfortunately, she could not pack the new dresses and all of her clothes in the suitcase. She had books to carry and no help from Geoff as she had the Sunday before. But she wanted to take the suitcase for several reasons.

First, she wanted Julie to understand she was serious about going *home*. She did not belong at Julie's house. She belonged in Taylor Park. And she wanted her friends in Bridgeboro High School to realize she was finished with her obligation. She had helped Mrs. Fischer become well again. She especially wanted Mr. Stookey to know.

Obviously, Julie was upset. She refused Beth's offer to prepare her breakfast. She would get whatever she wanted, later. If she felt like eating.

After Beth heard Julie's curt reply she began to feel guilty. After all, she really had not done anything to hurt Beth. Except louse up her dream of writing a winning essay!

Beth went back into Julie's bedroom a second time to say goodbye. She wanted to thank her for . . . for what? For letting her get a taste of what life could be like outside of Taylor Park. For making arrangements for a date with Geoff? Yeah, that was something she could say.

"Ahhh, Julie. I'm going to ask Geoff if he'll pick up Gerry tomorrow. And the dresses. I mean, if I can still have them." She felt sad as she saw how forlorn Julie looked. Still in her nightgown, hair uncombed and no make-up. Was Julie's sudden decline her fault? Inside she worried, *Dear God, please do not let her have some Scotch hidden somewhere.*

"Of course you can have them. No matter what you're doing to hurt me, do you think I'd deny you the trip to New York. Why ruin Geoff's plans?"

Should she kiss Julie goodbye! At least pat her shoulder. "I'll call you."

After Beth walked out of Julie's bedroom, she wanted to scream. She had known this women for only a few weeks and already her life had taken a turn down a different path. How could she have known merely wanting information about Vicki Lynn would cause her such grief!

IN SCHOOL, Beth made an issue of asking Mr. Stookey if she could leave the suitcase in his classroom because it would not fit in her locker. Of course she could have left it in her homeroom but then Mr. Stookey wouldn't have seen it. She quickly explained why she had it with her. She was disappointed in Mr. Stookey's reaction.

While Beth was eating lunch with Jill, Dot and Mary, she asked if any of them wanted to stop at Powell's with her after school.

Jill had to go right home because she was going to her aunt's house for dinner. Dot had to baby sit for neighbors and Mary had to get home. And what was more disappointing was that her classmates didn't seem to care she was returning to Taylor Park. Beth began to feel depressed. Just remembering the emptiness of her house and the bleakness of the neighborhood was a downer. Julie might feel depressed also. But she had tranquilizers.

She must call Julie as soon as she arrived home. But what if Julie was angry enough that she wouldn't talk with her? Then what would she do? Would she confess to Liz what she had done? And what was Doc going to think of her? It really mattered because she had grown fond of the dear man. And Geoff? What was he going to say? That mattered very much.

IN Chemistry class Beth sat behind Brad. She remembered holding his head in her lap and kissing him. Then her thoughts zeroed in to a man named Geoff. The man who was going to take her to New York City! She wanted him to kiss her again.

After the last class Beth hurried to Mr. Stookey's room to get the suitcase.

"How's your essay coming along?" Mr. Stookey asked.

"I really should have more info but because Julie has been sick I haven't been able to . . . " she shrugged but yelled inside, *Get out of here. Before you tell him you may withdraw from the competition.*

"Well now that she's better I hope . . . oh, hi, Brad." Mr. Stookey's eyes darted from Beth to a place behind her.

WELCOME to BRIDGEBORO

TWENTY THREE

BETH QUICKLY TURNED to see Brad standing behind her. "Oh! Hi, Brad," she blurted out.

Brad nodded to Mr. Stookey and then peered into her eyes. All the way to her soul. "I have a message for you."

Beth frowned. "Who from?"

"Geoff Greer. He's parked out in the driveway. Waiting for you."

"I wonder what he wants?" Inside she thought, *How can I be so lucky? Of course, I want to see Geoff. But did Brad have to see him too?*

"Obviously he wants to see you."

"Well thanks for the message." She felt sheepish. Even frustrated. "I'll see you on Monday, Mr. Stookey. Have a nice week-end." With suitcase in one hand and books and a handbag balanced in her other arm, Beth walked out of the room.

She heard Brad say good-bye to Mr. Stookey and knew he was going to follow her. As soon as he stepped beside her she remarked, "He knows I can take a bus."

"Stop acting so damn innocent." Brad declared as they began to walk through the hall to the parking lot. "I saw you in his car last Sunday."

Beth turned and remarked sharply, "He *did* blow his horn at you."

"So he's Julie's lawyer and he probably has to go to her house. But you two could be paying attention to each other. After all . . . "

Beth stopped and shook her head. She was going to tell a lie. "Just shut up. It's nothing. . . like what you're thinking."

Brad laughed. "Sure. Maybe that's what you keep telling yourself."

She was not going to be challenged. "Sure yourself. You don't have any room to talk."

Brad sighed, deeply. "Okay. You win. I can't blame you if you go out with him. After all he is a nice guy, but . . . " he hunched his shoulders. And looked sad. "But I have a right not to be happy about it. I still love you. And I don't like you to go out with other guys. Oh, Danny and Fred. But Geoff Greer is a . . . man."

"I should just sit home? While you're screwing around with Jeanne?"

Brad watched tears roll down Beth's cheeks. "I need you in my life." he whispered.

Beth put down the suitcase and quickly smeared the tears with a fist. "How do you think I feel? Watching you two day after day. And then finding out . . . what you did."

"And I hate myself for what I did. But I love you and only you."

"Hey, Beth," a girl's voice said loudly, farther down the hall.

As soon as they heard their classmate, Mary Gero, Brad picked up the suitcase and they began to walk toward her. Their hands bumped. To Beth it felt as though she had touched a live wire. She had only seconds to decide what to do.

She looked down and whispered, "I still hate you. But I love you back."

"I'll find a way. Just remember I need you." Brad lifted his head and smiled broadly at Mary. Brad's smile could charm any of his female classmates. Even female teachers!

Beth forced a laugh as she looked into Mary's face. "If you're going to tell me Geoff Greer is looking for me Brad is guiding me to the parking lot."

"Well, Geoff didn't really ask me to find you. But as soon as I saw him I knew no other girl in Bridgeboro High was going out with him so it had to be you he was looking for."

"Thank you very much, Mary," Beth remarked.

Brad had picked up his stride so that Beth had to hurry to keep up with him. And Mary was hurrying with them, although she did stop at the top of the steps which led into the parking lot. It was obvious she wanted to observe what was going to happen.

Geoff quickly got out of his car. While he smiled at Brad Beth realized Brad was the taller of the two. One with short dark brown hair and a football players' physic and the other with wavy chestnut colored hair and a tennis players' build. How could she ever have imagined she would be standing with two important people in her life. Smiling at each other. While she was dying inside.

"Here she is," Brad handed the suitcase to Geoff.

"Thanks Brad," To Beth he added, "Hi, girl."

"Hi." Then she looked into Brad's eyes and muttered, "See ya."

Brad did smile. "See ya. Have a nice week-end." He walked away.

Beth Rhodes did not look after Brad Livingston although she imagined he was walking across the driveway to his car. And maybe saying "Hi, babe," to Jeanne who was waiting for him.

"Why didn't you come in to find me?" Beth asked. Trying to sound friendly. She was finding it extremely difficult to switch from one hat to another. "They allow ex-cons to return to the prison." She forced a laugh.

Geoff sensed that Beth was nervous. "I was going to. In fact, I had already gotten out of my car when I saw Brad. And he said he'd find you." Geoff opened the trunk and put Beth's suitcase inside. He saw that Beth was waiting for him to open her door. Before she got into his car, he gave her a slow hug. It was only after he closed the door to the passenger's side that he noticed Mary watching from the top step. He was glad he did what he knew Beth wanted him to do.

Geoff sat behind the steering wheel, turned and asked, "Just what have you been up to?"

"Ahh. Nothing. Why?"

"Then where are you going with the suitcase?"

"Home. I said I'd stay until Julie was better. She's out of bed and working."

"Doc says she's not fully recovered. She's pretending. And pushing herself." He patted Beth's hand. "Julie said she begged you to stay with her."

"Yeah. She did."

"She said she even offered you a job. And a salary. To live with her."

How could Geoff be making her so uncomfortable? "She mentioned that."

"Doesn't it sound like a good idea?"

"Not really."

Geoff remembered they were still in the parking lot of Bridgeboro High School and most likely being observed so he turned the key and listened to his sports car come to life. "Okay. But you will be going back. Don't you still need to do more interviewing?"

"I've decided to withdraw from the contest."

"I hope you're kidding. Why do such a dumb thing like that?"

"Because I don't have enough information to write anything but a half ass essay. And because I will not ask Julie for any more information. That's why."

Geoff began to slowly drive out of the parking lot. "What happened between you two?" He stopped at the STOP sign to the entrance onto Bridge Pike. He turned north. The way to Taylor Park. "Last time I was down at Julie's I thought you two were getting along just fine. Were you
pretending?"

"I was. And I suppose you thought how generous and how thoughtful she was to buy me surprises. Just like Doc. Well, did you ever think I could be embarrassed? Being teased in school." Beth paused to take a deep breath as she stared out the side window. "I wish I had listened to Mr. Stookey and never written the letter. All I wanted to do was to ask her some questions about Vicki Lynn. And all I've had are more gut pains and more arguments than since the Rhodes bunch lived together." She turned to look at Geoff and forced herself to laugh. "Of course, Julie did help me to have a date with you."

"Meaning you still want to go to New York?"

"Don't you?"

"Hmmm. I don't know. After all, Julie is footing the bill. Which could embarrass you. Or are some gifts okay?" He laughed. "If you won't chauffeur her around in her new Impala, then I guess I'll have to."

"Have fun. I just want to go home. I'm tired and I have a headache."

"And here I was going to invite you out for dinner. There's a new restaurant in New Hope. Or we could go to the Old Mill Inn. Wherever. We could have a nice leisurely dinner and get psyched up for our date tomorrow."

Before she could change her mind Beth blurted out, "I don't think so. Even though it sounds like fun, I don't think I'd be good company. I'm tired. From giving out medicine every night and. . . " she laughed. "I'm going to bed early. To get psyched up for our date."

"Okay for you. I'll try to believe what you say. But you're too young to be tired."

After driving in silence for many minutes, Geoff finally turned into Taylor Park. Slowly and carefully. He had to avoid dogs and children and toys.

He parked in front of Beth's house and declared, "And here you are, nurse Rhodes. Home from your private duty case." Geoff quickly got out of the car to open Beth's door.

Beth was happy that Geoff opened her door. She knew her neighbors could be watching. After all, a red sports car attracts attention. And she wanted to be treated like a lady. While he got her suitcase out of the trunk she unlocked the door.

As soon as Beth stepped into the small kitchen the familiar feeling of frustration seeped in and around the depression. She forced herself to smile at Geoff. "Well, it doesn't look any worse than when I left." She took the suitcase and put it in the living room. "Thanks a lot, Geoff. I sure do appreciate the pickup and delivery service."

"A hot shower and different clothes and you'd forget you're tired." Standing in the kitchen he waited, smiling his charming smile. "In fact, I'll even wait for you to get ready."

Beth thought fast. She had to convince him and herself why she could not go out with him. She gestured toward the top of the washing machine. "Tired or not. You can see what I have to do. Since I'm going out tomorrow, I better do it tonight. I can hang it in the shower."

"Let Liz do her own wash."

"That's what Julie said. But you've never had Liz mad at you." She had to change the subject. She didn't want to talk about Liz. "I thought you'd have the dresses in the trunk. Didn't Julie mention the dresses? And Gerry?"

"She never mentioned them to me."

"Somehow I do not believe you. You know I'm supposed to wear one of those dresses to New York."

"Really?"

"She told you to leave the dresses there, didn't she? She wants you to persuade me to change my mind. She wanted you to take me out for dinner and . . . talk to me. Right?"

Geoff shrugged. "So? Why can't you?"

"I told you. I was there until she got better. I had no intention of staying."

"Beth, Julie likes you. She wants to help you."

Beth raised her eyebrows. "You sound just like a lawyer. Well for your information, she wanted . . . wants, more than that. And she's really not easy to live with. She likes to be in charge. She enjoys bossing people not only in the company, but people in Bridgeboro. She's mixed up, from some personal frustrations. In fact, I really think instead of Doc, she needs a psychiatrist."

"That would be a damn shame if she had to pay to have someone listen to her when all she might need is a friend. Someone who knows that life and the people in it are not as . . . well, not as perfect as we wish they would be. You know that, Beth."

Beth repeated she appreciated what Geoff was suggesting but would not change her mind. To return to Julie's house or go out for dinner. He pecked a quick kiss on her forehead and stated, "I might call you tonight." He paused to chuckle. "Just to make sure you're home and doing all this work you're using as an excuse."

WHILE Beth was sorting clothes for a load of under garments there was a knock on the door. It was Peg Mawhorter. Beth was not in the mood to answer a barrage of questions. Still she smiled broadly as she unlocked the screen door.

"Hello, stranger," Peg said as she stepped into the kitchen. "I just wanted to say Hi. Are you here to stay?"

"Yes. I'm back."

"So Julie is okay now? I mean, Liz said Julie was sick."

"Doctor Rexinger said she almost had the flu."

"You know Liz never comes over to tell me anything about Evan. But she came over to tell me about you. I didn't even know you knew Julie."

Beth had to laugh. She felt embarrassed. Sheepish. "I met her about three weeks ago. After she agreed I could interview her. I'm writing about her sister. For an essay contest."

"That's what Liz said. She was real wound up about you staying at her house and I just had to call Alan. He got a kick out of the story."

"I'll bet he did. How is he?"

"Last phone call he admitted he's gained some weight so I won't be surprised when I see him." Peg held up crossed fingers. "He says he'll be home next week. I was just kinda wondering. Do you know anything about the company?"

"Not really. Mrs. Fischer and I talked mostly about her sister. Why?"

"Well, Alan says they have to hire a new Vice President of Finance. That makes three new Executives in about five or six months." Peg shrugged. "Alan says he's worried about so many changes. It's real bad for moral you know." She watched Beth hunch her shoulders.

"Alan says he thinks, this is his idea and it's kinda weird, but he thinks Julie either has an urge to ruin the company or she has a desire to ruin the name of Fischer."

Beth raised her eyebrows. "That's interesting." The idea didn't sound weird to her.

Peg chuckled. "Oh well, maybe if we had as much money as she has we'd do strange things too. She has to be sitting on millions."

Beth nodded. "I've heard that too. However we never discussed her wealth either." Beth began to do more sorting. She wanted to end the conversation.

"Who brought you home? Her chauffeur?"

Beth forced a laugh. "Come on, Peg. That was Geoff Greer."

"You're kidding. I thought he kinda looked familiar but I didn't remember him having such a good build. And so good looking. Did he want to know anything about Evan?" She watched Beth nod and added, "Because he was just curious? Or because he isn't married yet?"

"Both."

The two women studied each other's faces, each knowing what the other was thinking.

Finally Peg grinned and sounded. "Hmmm."

Beth shook her head. "Hey Peg, he's too old for me." She began to stuff under garments and blouses into the washing machine. Just enough to hang on the shower curtain rod. The towels and sheets would have to wait until she could hang them outside.

"What's age got to do with it?" Peg stepped to the screen door and appeared to be listening. "I've got to get back but can you sit with the girls tonight? I have to go shopping."

"Food shopping?"

"Yeah. Why?"

"Ah, because you won't be too late. I want to work on my essay."

"Around six-thirty. Okay?"

"Sure. That's great that Alan is coming home next week. I'll bet the girls are happy."

"Yeah. Because this time I told them he really is. With the trouble in the company, they want him back in the office."

"That's good news. For both of you. Have you found a house yet?"

"No. Now Alan can take charge and find something."

"I'll see you in a couple of hours." And in her mind she added, *I hope if Alan does find a house you have to change food markets.*

While the washing machine was doing its job, Beth forced herself to eat a peanut butter sandwich with a can of soda. The milk was sour. Should she ask Peg to buy her a quart?

As she sat at the kitchen table, looking outside but not seeing the children fighting in the street, Beth thought of Julie. *Earth to Daddy. I wish I knew what Julie is doing, right now? Eating? Drinking? I really should call her. Just say, Hi, Julie. And then just talk. I will, after I come back from babysitting. And should I call Geoff? To let him know I'm going next door.*

I wish I knew who he's dating?

TWENTY FOUR

AFTER SHE RETURNED from Peg's house, Beth did not call Julie. Nor Geoff. She did review her notes for the essay. She even added some ideas before she allowed her thoughts to stray. *Should she really write an essay? Was she still determined enough*? She could hear Daddy whispering, *Do it, Beth. For you. And for me.*

Of course she wished she had more notes. But wasn't it guilt that was causing her to consider withdrawing from the contest. She began to realize she almost believed that Vicki Lynn *had* been a bitch! She had been an evil woman who created chaos in Julie's life. Vicki Lynn and Bill Fischer. And now Beth Rhodes.

Beth closed the notebook. She put it under her school books. Like hiding it. *Daddy. I don't want to think about the essay. I don't want to think about the money I need to go to college. I don't want to think about anything. I would like to have a nervous breakdown. So I'd have to go into an institution and . . . hide. Even if I have to have shock treatments.*

Beth wandered into the kitchen. She decided to have another soda. Hey, how about an Orange Blossom? Maybe just one would relax her? She decided not to. She might need more than one. She looked at her watch and thought *Brad. What are you doing?*

Why hadn't she gone out for dinner with Geoff? She really wanted to be with him. So why couldn't she? Not because of dirty clothes. Was she punishing herself? She and Julie. Both on a self-destruct course.

Beth wandered back into the living room and studied the list of television programs. Nothing looked interesting. She turned off the floor lamp and sat on the couch. In the dimness from a low watt bulb in a table lamp she concentrated on the overstuffed chair on the opposite wall. Her father used to sit there. He always had a glass or a can on the table next to the chair. It was a wide chair and many times she'd squeeze in next to him. Then they'd share the same book, or magazine, or watch the same show on their little black and white television screen. Sometimes, they'd just talk. For hours.

"Daddy," Beth whispered into the stillness of the room. She squinted. She almost believed she saw a pearly, translucent wisp of something that shimmered and settled into the chair. There was no form. No face. Just a presence of something. Familiar and waiting. "I know you're really not here. I just wish you were. I wish I had you with me, again. Even though I used to get mad at you. Even ashamed. But I was glad I had you. Sometimes you couldn't talk too much because you were so fuzzy. But you did try to listen to me." She sighed, deeply before she continued to whisper, "I need somebody to talk to. I'm so mixed up. Especially about Julie. Sometimes I think I hate her because she hated Vicki Lynn. And you know how you and I used to feel about Vicki Lynn. I still do, except she took Mr. Fischer away from Julie. In fact, she really made Julie's life miserable. Or so Julie says.

"Daddy. I do feel sorry for Julie. But sometimes . . . I'm afraid of her. She's powerful. I think even Mr. Livingston is afraid of her. Although I don't care about him. But if he ever gets hurt, then Brad could too. And I have to worry about him. Because I love him. But I think I could love Geoff too. Daddy, I get so sad when I think about getting married. You'll never be able to walk me down the aisle or see my first baby. I wish I had you to talk to. I need somebody to help me and . . . " Beth began to cry, "And I don't even have a mother who will listen to me."

Beth cried hard for many minutes. She had to find a box of tissues. After she plopped back into the couch she believed she felt less frustrated. She had brought the accumulated concerns out of the attic of her mind. Now, if only she could find the answers.

She peered into the chair again. The feeling of a presence was gone. Beth felt utterly alone. She recalled the advice Doc had given Julie. Why didn't she call Julie? She probably was lonely too. But she really was tired. She probably should go to bed. She needed a good night's sleep. She stood and stretched. There had to be hundreds of people all around her, laughing, on dates, talking or eating, maybe making out? And here she was. Feeling sorry for herself. Even sharing the house with Liz she was almost living alone. If she wanted to be honest it was more enjoyable, more satisfying, being with Julie.

She frowned as soon as felt her senses kick in. Voices? No, music. Someone was singing. Oh damn, Peg was playing her records again. Very softly. Beth moved to the chair, closer to the wall. Maybe she should go next door and visit with Peg? They could talk about Jim Bender. Sexy Jim. Jock Jim. Was Jeanne with him right then? Or was she with Brad?

Beth whispered, "Please, Alan. Come home soon. So that your lonely, frustrated wife won't be so . . . " Beth paused to listen more intently. She knew she was hearing a male voice. *Please, have it be Gert's husband. Or Peg's neighbor on the other side. Listen to that voice . . . oh my God . . . it couldn't be!*

Beth settled on the floor with her head against the wall. So she was a busybody? So she was a shit head. Who cared what she was. If it *was* Jim, she wanted to hear him. In action.

She heard the male voice say, "I thought maybe you'd call the store and...... had changed your....." Then he laughed.

Peg replied, "I thought maybe ...... yours too. Do you like....Beatles?"

"I .....slow stuff too. Mrs. Mawhorter." He laughed again. "Can ...call Peg? Then....me, Jim." Laugh Laugh

"Hi, Jim." Laugh Laugh

Laugh, Laugh "Hello, Peg."

Beth shivered. Maybe she should call Peg and ask her if she could borrow a handbag for Saturday? That surely would sound logical.

"...something to drink?"

The conversation faded and Beth envisioned Peg and Jim going into the kitchen.

Then voices again. Louder. "Want to dance, Peg? Good. No shoes."

Silence for several minutes.

"Where .... your car?"

"On Perkins Street."

Another record. Andy Williams. No talking.

"Where's your husband?"

"In Texas. .....next week."

Beth cursed out loud. "He should be home. Julie, your damn company is lousing up my neighbors' lives."

"Hey, Peg, how about .... drink?"

"Won't .... mother or .... where you are?"

"Naw. She knows after work us guys go ...."

Silence. Beth shuddered as she pictured Peg and Jim mixing more drinks. Or whatever they were doing in the kitchen. Maybe she should mix herself a drink? No, she didn't want to leave the wall. She wanted to listen to Jeanne's lover boy. No, she really wanted to be available, in case her neighbor might need her. Ha! If anybody needed somebody, it was Beth.

The voices became louder. "I like the way you dance, Peg."

"Thanks. Hey. You shouldn't do that." Laugh. Laugh. "But I did like it."

Silence for several minutes. Followed by Jim declaring, "Wow. You kiss better than I thought you would. When you first started coming into the store, I almost …"

"I've been shopping … store before you … to work there."

Jim's voice became louder. "Okay, so I saw you and I knew you saw me and I got your name from a coupon you filled out. One night after I found out which car was yours, I was going to let the air out of your tires. So you'd have to ask me to help you."

Peg laughed. "I would have called *Crouthamel's Gas Station*."

Beth snickered to herself as she thought about calling Peg and telling her it was her friendly towing service, to the rescue. *Get him out, Peg. Make him leave. He's trouble.*

"One more record and then …hey, stop that."

"Come on, you need some kissin'. I'm going to mix us another drink."

"No more. You could have an accident or your Mom could …."

"I'll be careful. Relax."

"I'm going to make some coffee."

During the silence on the other side of the wall Beth thought, *Yeah, Peg. Be smart. Sit at the kitchen table and drink coffee. Oh damn, they're back in the living room.*

"Now do you feel better? I'm having a cup of coffee. You're as much of a worry wart as my mom is?"

"She sounds smart to me …but I hope I never meet her. I'd …'

"You have if you shop in *Flecks Dress Shoppe*. She . . . there."

"Thank goodness, I don't shop ……," Peg blurted out. "And, tonight ….. last time ….shop in *Stop and Shop Market*."

Yeah, Peg, Way to go. Goodbye, Jim. You're past history.

"You mean, you just asked me to ………to say goodbye?"

"Yes. I just wanted to talk to you a little bit and…stop it! Just drink your coffee and…"

"You know what? ……scared. You were pretty sure of yourself as long as …in the store. And played the game to get …. But now that we're all alone, you're scared."

Keep fighting, Peg. Let him know he's not so great. Alan is much better. Jim is only a sexy, macho, desirable, hot teen-ager. Damn it, I wish I were with Brad.

Jim's voice stayed loud enough that Beth heard every word. "How long since you've had a good kiss, before tonight?"

"A week." Peg laughed. "My father-in-law is a good kisser."

"Oh wow. Big thrill."

"I'm not looking for …a thrill. If I was, I've changed my mind. So you can dance and you can kiss, and …please…don't… where did you learn to kiss like that?"

"In Biology. And let me show you what I learned in Physics. You'll love …"

"No. Don't. You're a crazy …kid. Save your energy for ….. a…"

"I don't want a girl. I want a woman. A sexy woman to teach me how to make love better than ….I know..."

Silence.

Beth wanted to pound on the wall. She didn't have the guts. But she had to do something to save Peg. The mixed up, crazy, sex hungry woman, who was degrading herself. Why? For s-e-x. Peg wanted some of what Beth would like to have. *Two lonely females, hungry for attention, for comfort, followed by trouble. Help! Save us! I guess I'm glad that I'm safe. safe. But poor Peg! Listen, somebody's talking.*

"When did you first …do it", Beth just about heard Peg ask.

"When I … fifteen."

Silence. Beth felt like screaming. What was Peg allowing Jim to do?

She finally heard Jim. "Let me … I've dreamed of …ever since I first saw you."

Beth pulled her head from the wall and leaned against the side of the couch. *Why in the hell am I crying? 'Cause I know I'm an eavesdropper? 'Cause I know what is happening in Peg's living room. 'Cause I feel sorry for Peg? And Alan. Certainly not Jeanne Barnes. Help, Daddy. Will I ever be able to look Peg in the eye again? I hate myself. I'm the one who should be embarrassed. My god, why am I trembling? Why am I perspiring? Move. Now!*

Beth moved away from the wall. Staring at her jacket still on a chair, an idea kicked in. Why didn't she call Brad? Maybe he could meet her? If one of his parents answered, she'd hang up.

Except if Jim was with Peg, then Jeanne could be with Brad.

AFTER she heard one or maybe two people moaning through the walls she knew she had to get out of the house. Without attempting to understand what she was doing Beth put on her jacket, picked up her books and handbag.

She turned off the lamp and without wondering why, picked up her suitcase opened the kitchen door, and put the suitcase on the top step, while she locked the door.

She was going to pretend she had not even come home.

TWENTY FIVE

DURING DINNER, THE Livingston's discovered it was going to be an unusual Friday evening. All three had planned to stay at home.

After he helped clear the table Brad went to his room. He said he had a book report to finish. Richard went into the den. He had been unusually quiet during dinner so Bernice was not surprised when he said he needed some alone time to finish a report for the Church Vestry. After Bernice put away left-overs and stacked the dishwasher she sat at the kitchen table to search through cook books.

She was going to plan a buffet dinner. No matter what Richard said she was going to have a "Welcome to Bridgeboro" party for Audrey and Hank Oehrle. Plus she wanted to show off the new Oriental rug in the foyer. Bernice methodized the menu for Ellie to prepare and serve. Of course Tony would tend bar and help clean up. Plans complete she returned the books to the shelf above the dishwasher.

With her knitting bag Bernice "wandered" into the den. She walked to the leather chair next to the desk where Richard was sitting. .

"Okay if I sit in here?" she asked softly.

Without diverting his attention from the desk, Richard mumbled, "If you want to."

Bernice positioned herself in the chair and took out the dark blue lap robe she was knitting. She had one more to knit before she would have a dozen to deliver to the Women's Guild at the church. They would be delivered to inner city nursing homes. Before she began to measure how many inches she already had knitted Bernice decided to remark, "That doesn't look like a report for the church."

"I'm reviewing some figures," Richard stated. "I should have stayed and finished them in the office, but I thought you said you were going out tonight . . . " his voice faded away.

"Will you be finished soon?"

"Not if you keep interrupting me. Why?"

Bernice continued to knit. "I want to talk about our plans for this summer."

Richard released a deep sigh of exasperation. "Good god, Bernice. Can't we talk about summer, later? I still have to finish writing my report for the Church Vestry."

"I want to write to Libby. She's waiting for me to tell her when we're going to Europe."

"Well, you can tell her I've changed my mind. We can't go to Europe this year."

Bernice dropped her hands to her lap. She pouted. "You said we could and I've already told Libby and . . . "she watched Richard shake his head.

"I said it sounded like a nice idea. And we *might*. Now I'm saying we *can't*." Richard turned back to the desk. He began to rearrange some papers. "That was several weeks ago. Since then I've made some changes in my plans."

"Such as what?"

"Such as an important business venture I'm working on. I'm not going into any details, because there's nothing definite . . . yet. But as you know it takes money to make money and . . . "

"I don't like your important business deals. You could end up in another mess. The least you can do is to let me know the details. In fact, I deserve to know. After all it is my money too. That you tend to lose."

"I'm not going to be losing any money." He pushed up his glasses. "I just need what we have in our accounts right now. After all, we decided we tucked aside more than enough to send Brad to college and that . . . " He wished she'd leave him alone.

"Then I'm going to use *my* money for the trip." Bernice blurted out.

"I thought we decided there is no your money and my money. But if there still is, then I'll need to borrow your money. I may need it to invest, in my...." Richard paused as he noticed the hostile look on Bernice's face. "Look, Bernice," he said with a softer tone, "you can stay home this year. Make a sacrifice. So I can try to . . .", he paused. But why repeat to Bernice what she already knew? "I just want to get ready to buy . . . "

Richard paused. They both heard Brad pounding down the stairs. He took several steps into the den holding a copy of that day's issue of *The Bridgeborough Courier*. "Sorry to interrupt but I wanted to ask Dad something."

"It's okay, dear. Bernice smiled as she noticed how handsome he looked in his new jeans and black tee shirt. When had he become so mature? So adult looking. His arms were covered with course dark hair and his beard was becoming quite heavy. But then so was Richard's.

Bernice caressed Brad's face with her eyes. She had almost convinced herself that his birth mother had been the bank teller who was rumored to have an affair with the bank president and supposedly got pregnant. But no one ever knew what happened to the baby? That was better than believing what Richard used to tell her. That Brad's mother was some teenager who kept the sailors happy.

Richard smiled at Brad because he had saved him from an unpleasant conversation. Although he knew Bernice would mention the summer plans, again. However, when Brad held up the copy of *The B.C.* and pointed to an article on the Editorial page, Richard felt despair.

"Hey, Dad, do you think Julie will take some action?"

"I was kind of hoping she's too sick to be reading the paper." He forced a laugh.

"Let me see what you're talking about." Bernice stretched out an arm. "I didn't read all of today's paper." She scowled at Richard. "Why didn't you tell me about this?"

"Why don't you read the paper?"

Brad decided to add his comments. "Man. Mr. B. really let Julie have it."

Richard shrugged at Brad and commented, "I told him I thought some of the comments were unnecessary. In fact, too damn strong. All she wanted to do was to buy a farm which he wanted. But Charlie wants everyone to know what a tyrannical tycoon she is. He wanted to use monopolizing monster but I did talk him out of that." Richard forced a laugh to Brad.

"She'll probably use the farm for what Mr. B. says Bridgeboro needs. A mall or an industrial park. Just for spite."

"She could do a lot of things. Just for spite," Bernice said softly.

Richard decided to defend himself. He looked from his wife to his son as he explained, "I couldn't change Charlie's mind. And I couldn't refuse to print it. After all, he *is* a friend. And the newspaper is a public service."

"And his agency is one of your larger advertisers," Brad added.

"You could have told me so I could have called Lou," Bernice said.

"Why? He's mad."

"Maybe you should write to Julie?" Bernice suggested. "To explain it's strictly Charles' opinion and that you . . . "

"*I* should write to Julie!"

Bernice put her knitting away. When she was annoyed she lost the desire to do anything charitable. "So what are you going to do?"

"Wait. Julie will make the next move." He frowned at Brad. "How about that girl? That Betty or whatever her name is?"

"You mean Beth?"

"If that's her name. Is she still down at Julie's?"

Brad forced a frown. "I think she should be finished interviewing Julie. The essays have to be turned in soon."

"I wasn't referring to her essay. Joe Palmer said she's staying with Julie because she's sick. When he brought his ad in for Saturday's copy he told me that Julie had bought the girl a television set. And a stereo. He delivered them."

"Oh come to think of it, I did see her with a suitcase. And I heard her tell somebody Julie was all better."

"Hmmm," Bernice hummed. "Maybe she'll invite her back. From time to time."

Mother and son waited. For Richard's latest idea.

"I'm sure she's not in your group of friends but are you in any classes together?"

"Typing. And she's on the Yearbook Committee."

"Well, if the time seems right ask her if she's still seeing Julie. And if she happens to know what Julie plans on doing with the farm?"

Bernice immediately added, "Only if the time is right." Bernice looked at husband "The girl might wonder why Brad is being so inquisitive. Even tell Julie."

Brad nodded and gave his mother a smile he knew would please her. To his father he blurted out, "What's the latest on the boat we looked at last month? Any decision yet?"

Richard pushed up his glasses. "The decision is, not this year. Your mother wants to go to Europe to visit your Aunt Libby and . . . "

"Richard! You just told me..."

Richard put up his hand as he spoke louder than Bernice. "So I better put off buying a boat until next year." He smiled smugly at Brad. "Maybe I can afford a bigger one by then."

Brad nodded. He indicated he accepted his father's explanation although he knew he was not being told the truth. Parents who lied made it difficult for kids to believe in them. Brad was positive his parents had always lied to him about their friendship with Julie and Bill Fischer.

Maybe their entire past was one big lie. And their future. He could not believe they were going to Europe or that his father was going to buy a boat. Any size. Any time. If they could lie to him then he could lie to them.

"I'm going out. After I finished my book report I wrote to Dick Mann. He's the guy whose dad was transferred last month. I'm going to mail the letter and walk around town."

Bernice smiled. "Do you and Jeanne have plans for this weekend?"

Brad shrugged. "I don't know. If Shirl's mom is letting her have some girls stay over Saturday night then Jeanne will go there."

"I've been meaning to ask if you want me to plan a party before or after graduation?"

Brad smiled. "That's really nice of you but there's going to be enough parties. The Barnes' are having a big one. For Jeanne."

"Lou told me. I still think the School Board was just awful, not letting you all go on a class trip of some kind. All because of the way some parents raise their children nowadays. And we have to take children from Taylor Park in Bridgeboro High. They should be going to Southampton High. I've heard the living conditions there are awful. So how can the children help but be destructive and have low morals. They don't know any better."

BRAD needed to escape. To breathe deeply in the fresh air. He stepped closer to the doorway and remarked, "Adults do things even if they know they shouldn't. See ya later." He hurried out of the room.

"Don't be too late." Bernice had to call out.

Brad began to jog. He was glad to be away from his parents and the tension between them. But he was not happy he was alone. He wanted to be with Beth. He'd at least try to get her to talk with him. He jogged three blocks until he reached a phone booth outside of *Burdick's News Stand.* He closed the door, turned his back to the sidewalk and laid out the large amount of change he had brought with him.

As the telephone rang, Brad thought of the many things he wanted to tell her. How much he loved her. How much he needed her. And how much he wanted to see her. If she'd meet him, he'd run home and get his car. He would make up otherwise known as lying, some kind of a tale to tell his parents. Beth was worth any disapproval he might receive. Beth was his life line.

After the telephone rang fifteen times, Brad hung up. Determined, he dialed again. He counted eighteen rings. Finally, he realized Beth was not going to answer the telephone. Where in the hell could she be? Maybe she had a date. With Danny? Fred? Geoff Greer?

He decided to go to *Powell's* and have a soda. See if any if his buddies were hanging around. Maybe one of them might have a joint. He sure could use one. Even a beer.

No such luck so he took the long way home. How forlorn could he feel?

Oh yes, he must remember to mail the letter to Dick.

TWENTY SIX

BETH DID NOT remember walking to a bus stop so she was surprised when a bus stopped at the corner. From habit she boarded it, found the necessary change and sat down. She was on the bus that was going to take her to Bridgeboro. She decided to return to Julie's house.

Beth sat behind the driver. She noticed the deep crevices in his long
neck. He needed a haircut. Suddenly Beth realized the bus had stopped. On Hilltop Drive. Two more blocks and the driver would turn onto Bridge Pike. *Hilltop Apartments.* Geoff Greer. Beth got off the bus.

Carrying the suitcase, school books and handbag, she walked into the vestibule of the middle apartment building. She scanned the names on the mail boxes. There it was. **G. A. Greer**. Beth pressed a button and waited.

GEOFF was talking on the telephone when the buzzer sounded in his apartment. "Just a minute, Terry. Somebody pushed my buzzer. I hope they pushed the wrong button."

Geoff's voice came through a speaker into the lobby. "Greer here."

Beth responded loudly, "Rhodes here."

"As in Beth Rhodes?"

"Yep. Are you alone?"

"What are you doing . . .? Never mind, I'll push the button so you can open the vestibule door." As he pushed the button Geoff whispered, "Now what does she want? I'm sure Terry heard me." He quickly picked up the receiver. "Sorry, but I have unexpected company. It's the teenager I'm going to take to New York. I have a feeling she has a problem. I'll call you as soon as I can." He listened and frowned. "I promise. Sunday for sure. I want to be with you too. I love you too. Bye."

Riding the elevator to the fourth floor Beth decided she would tell Geoff she really was going to Julie's. Yeah, but what if Julie refused to welcome her. She'd have to go back to Taylor Park. Since she was here why not talk to Geoff?

Geoff stood in the hall as Beth got off the elevator. She looked worried. He reached for her suitcase. "Sorry, but I just rented out my last room. Or are you lost?"

"I think I'm running away." Beth whispered.

"Well, let's talk about it inside." In a pair of jeans, a faded rugby shirt and bare feet Geoff stepped back and allowed Beth to enter his apartment. He shut the door and automatically locked it. He put the suitcase next to the door, faced Beth and waited.

Unmoving, Beth stared into Geoff's eyes. "I thought I was going back to Julie's house. But then I heard the bus driver call out Hilltop Drive and, here I am." She noticed a basketball game on mute, on the television. "I'm really sorry to bother you." She looked back at his face. "Honestly, I hadn't planned on coming here. I just had to get away from the house."

"Not to fret." Geoff stepped up to her and placed his hands on her shoulders. "But if you had gone out for dinner we could still be in New Hope and you wouldn't have to run away."

Beth forced a smile. She studied the expression on Geoff's face. "I really feel stupid." She slid out of his hold and picked up her suitcase. "I'm not going to stay."

"I'm glad I was here. Let me have your jacket and offer you something to drink. Then I'll drive you to wherever you want to go."

Beth allowed Geoff to help her slide out of her jacket. She took several steps into the room and stopped behind a long black leather couch. She was facing a glass and chrome coffee table. While Geoff was hanging her jacket around the back of one of the ebony wooden chairs which were at each end of an ebony wooden table she swept her eyes around the living room and dining area. The contemporary decor surprised her. Why had she thought Geoff would decorate in Early American with golds and greens and rusts and dark wood furniture? Instead, she was seeing black and white leather furniture and chrome and glass tables. She noticed the large red pillows, a red shag area rug under the coffee table on which was a large arrangement of scarlet poppies. She smiled as the splashes of bright purple in interesting places caught her attention.

Beth liked what she was observing until she remembered she was in Geoff Greer's apartment! She actually was alone with him in a place she never dared dream she would be. And he was watching her. Did she look as nervous as she had suddenly become?

"So? What do you think? You like the way I furnished my abode?"

"It's like, wow. I'm really impressed. I mean, it's real nice."

"I never believed I could go modern, but . . . well, I'm glad you like it." He smiled a charming smile as he wondered if he should tell her a friend had helped him. Decorate? A special friend. Who stayed with him? And didn't need to bring a suitcase. "Now, how about something to drink?"

Beth shook her head. "Thank you but I'm not going to stay."

"Nonsense. If we can't be dining in some elegant, expensive restaurant in New Hope, we might as well be here, watching a basketball game and having a soda and pretzels." Geoff moved toward the kitchen, turned, smiled and asked, "Or would you prefer milk and cookies?"

Beth looked at the table next to a recliner. "Looks as though you were having a beer. I don't really like the stuff but can I have one?"

Geoff put up a hand. "Whoa. What you feel like drinking and what I serve you can be different drinks. You wouldn't want me to be arrested for corrupting the morals of a minor?"

"I *am* eighteen," she declared. A quick rerun of what she had heard through the wall of her living room played again in her mind. And the conversations she had heard in the Girls' Room and what she and Brad had done in the barn. And Geoff was afraid a beer would corrupt her? "I need to relax. It's been a rough week. In fact, could I have an Orange Blossom?"

"Against my better judgment I will mix you a weak one."

BETH wandered around the living room, studying the abstract paintings and prints. Had Evan seen all of these things? Should she ask him? Did she care?

She was peering at a print of Harlequins engaged in a sword fight when Geoff handed her a tall black glass filled with ice cubes and orange juice. He watched her take a deep drink. "Okay?" he asked.

"You mean what's on the wall or what's in the glass? The drink is too weak and the picture is . . . weird."

"Well here she is, without being invited and passing judgment on my art!"

"It's too modern," Beth blurted out. "You seem more like the landscapes or really seascapes type. Something more . . . " she shrugged.

204

"Something more conventional?" Geoff raised his eyebrows. "Perhaps more dullish? Such as what your sister used to call me?"

Beth shook her head from side to side. "Evan never told me anything about you."

"Thank god! Then it's you who thinks I'm Grandpa Moses?"

"I must think you're nice. Or I wouldn't be here."

He pointed to the couch. "Let's talk about why you *are* here?" They each turned sideways to lean against an arm. "I certainly don't want you wandering around. With a suitcase." He paused to smile. "I'm a good listener, Beth. Not just because I'm a lawyer." He offered her a bowl of pretzels sticks. "Have you had dinner?"

Beth nodded. She did remember having a peanut butter sandwich. An eon ago. She took several pretzel sticks. "Before I sat with Millie and Di while Peg went food shopping."

"Did you have a fuss with Peg?"

"No*." But I am furious with her. And I want to make up with Brad. And I'm nervous about being with handsome, mature you.* "I guess I'm mixed up. Because Julie wants me to work for her."

"So you're allowed . . . to be mixed up."

Beth took a long drink from her glass. "I do know it's a good opportunity. Especially, since I have to move out of Taylor Park. And she'll pay me in tuition money."

Geoff sipped from his bottle of beer. "Therefore I shall ask you *why* not?"

"I'm scared to say okay."

"Do you know why you're scared?"

Beth hunched her shoulders. She finished her weak drink and jiggled the ice cubes. "Because it may not work out. And I'll get hurt again. I know you miss your mom and dad, although you know where he is living, but I was mad at my dad. For dying. I was really mad at everybody. Because I was hoping we could be a family. But it never turned out that way. Then when daddy told me he wasn't going to get better I was going to lose the person who meant the most to me. I really sound sorry for myself."

"Hey, you're a sensitive young lady and some things are very important to you. Things such as caring and missing special people, and . . ." He waited.

"And love," Beth whispered. The names Evan and Brad slid to the forefront of her mind. Don't you think that love is important?"

"Very. It's the energy of the Universe."

"And even though we get hurt from losing special people we set ourselves up, to get hurt again. And . . . can I have another drink?" She reached the glass toward him.

Geoff took the glass. "Dear Beth. Life is filled with making choices and taking chances. You wanted someone to talk to so you took a chance. But what if I hadn't been here?"

"I think I would have gone home again."

Geoff frowned. "I was hoping you would have gone down to Julie's. In fact, would you want to call her and . . . " He stopped talking when Beth shook her head from side to side.

"I'm scared for more than just one reason. If you let me have another drink I'll tell you why." She giggled, made a face and put two pretzel sticks in her mouth.

"What time does Liz get home?"

Beth shrugged. "Whenever. Maybe she won't even come home? I haven't been home since she told me she's engaged so I don't know what she's doing."

Geoff looked at his watch. "You won't tell her you were in my apartment. Right?"

"I won't if I get another drink." Holding her glass Geoff walked into the kitchen. She followed him and said, "I want more gin and less Vitamin C."

"Only if I can make you testify why you're afraid of Julie Fischer."

"Put me on the witness stand and grill me. Come on, Geoff. More gin."

"I beg your pardon. I'm a lawyer. Not a cop. I do not *grill* my clients. But I know that gin can loosen one's tongue which could be illegal and thirdly, remember we are going to New York tomorrow."

"My dress is at Julie's. But heck, I can wear some school clothes." She reached for the filled glass and took a long, thirsty drink.

"I will pick up your dresses *if* you answer my question. Has she threatened you?"

Beth returned to the couch. She kicked her shoes off, sat on her left leg and stuffed a red pillow under her left arm. She watched Geoff reposition himself against the opposite end.

"I'm waiting for an answer."

Beth sighed. This was not going to be easy. "She tried to convince me her drinking is Vicki Lynn's fault. She was hoping I would make Vicki out to be a villainess in my essay. Thus exonerating Julie's behavior."

"And you refused to cooperate." Geoff took a drink from a glass of Turkey Hill which he had poured for himself.

Beth nodded. "No way am I going to blame my favorite writer."

"Did she tell you anything about anybody else?"

"You mean like how she hates the Livingston's? And the Barnes. Maybe everybody except you and Doc." She laughed. "And *maybe* me?"

Geoff gave one of his charming or disarming smiles. "Did she?"

They both laughed before Beth declared, "You sneaky lawyer. I plead the fifth."

"I may be sneaky but I am honest. I do not know. Except she and tricky Dickie would experience great satisfaction from destroying the other." Geoff studied Beth's face over his glass. "Me thinks your eyes are telling me you wish you did not know what I do not know."

"I almost wish I had listened to Mr. Stookey and hadn't asked for the interviews. Julie had planned to set me up by making so much available to me. A television, a stereo, almost a car, clothes. I'm not so moralistic that I wouldn't dearly love to have all she can give me. And do for me. Talk about being tempted by Satan!"

Beth reached for a handful of pretzel sticks. She studied Geoff's face and realized how much she was enjoying being with him. In his apartment. Alone. With no one knowing except the two of them. Everybody thought she had gone home. "Have you reached a verdict yet?"

He cleared his throat. "I've come to the conclusion your case is quite interesting."

"That's it?" Beth laughed. "Just interesting? I want to know if it can be solved."

"Oh, I think so. And I would be willing to handle it."

"I don't know if I can afford the services of such a successful lawyer."

"I have a special fee. For special friends."

Beth tilted her head. "Oh?" She finished her drink.

"I'll even throw in some advice." He hoped she knew he was teasing. Flirting. He should be careful and not mislead her. After all, she was vulnerable.

"Wow. What more could I want?"

Geoff removed the twinkle from his eyes and took on a serious look. "You have to know how much you and Julie can help each other. Why not tell her you're willing to discuss a compromise? Don't shake your head *no,* before you think about it. Now what are your other concerns."

Beth felt alarm. Damn. He could read her mind, better than she could read his. "What makes you ask that?"

Geoff shrugged. "Because, *I'm getting to know you,*" he sang, "*know all about you.*"

While she was laughing, Beth thought of an answer. "Well, I am concerned about having to move. Liz getting married. If I can write a good enough essay to submit and... even Evan." She decided to put the ball in Geoff's court. "What would you do, if she came back?"

"Give her a hug."

"You still care about her?"

"Is that also one of your concerns?"

"It might be. I'm wondering how long a person can love another person?"

"Maybe forever. Or, maybe just for today. With no regards about tomorrow."

Beth studied his mouth. Nice kissable lips. "Don't you ever get lonely?"

"I'm too busy. But in case you do," he smiled, "Julie's house is big enough for two people and it certainly would be a nice place to live. Don't take her offer too lightly."

"She blames Vicki for her drinking but I'll bet a lot of the reason is because she's lonely." Beth held out her glass. "I'll have another one, please."

Geoff laughed. "Sorry, the bar's closed. If you're still thirsty I have cherry soda."

"But soda won't help me."

"I thought you were here for *me* to help you?"

Beth giggled. "Then do it. Give me another drink."

"No way, kiddo. You've had enough. And anyway it's time to take you home."

Beth shook her head. "I don't want to go home."

Geoff frowned. Somewhere in the back of his mind those words sounded familiar. How many times Evan had said that to him. He almost could hear her whisper in his ear, "Please don't take me home yet." She hated to go back to Taylor Park. She complained about the family fights. The atmosphere. The unhappiness. The loneliness. She'd do anything just to stay away, a little longer. And here was another Rhodes girl saying the same thing. He decided to make Beth tell him more. "When did you start drinking?"

"Before my daddy died."

"How often do you drink?"

"When I'm depressed. That's how come I started. Daddy was in the hospital and I wanted to die. With him. And there's always gin and whiskey under the sink, so I made an Orange Blossom. And it relaxed me and . . . well, I never take a drink when I'm out. Oh. Once Mr. Friedman offered me a small glass of sherry. To make a toast. Or celebrate something. But you're really the first person I ever drank with." She giggled. "With whom I have drunk."

"I'm honored."

"No you're not." Beth licked her lips and smiled. "You're nervous."

Geoff raised his eyebrows. "I'm concerned."

"For whom? You or me?"

He looked at his watch. "You. It's getting late and you should be home in bed."

Beth managed to stand. "Okay. I can take a hint. You want to get rid of me."

Geoff remained seated. "Not if you have something else you want to discuss."

"I've bored you long enough." She looked around the living room. "Oh, there's my jacket. And you don't have to take me home. I can take a bus."

Geoff stood. "You have to be kidding." He watched her struggle with her jacket. "Chief Zeigler would have a fit if he knew I let you go home alone."

"Especially if he knew I had been drinking in your apartment. Huh?" She felt clumsy.

Geoff sighed. He decided to let her struggle with her jacket while he went into the bedroom to get his car keys, shoes and wallet. He reached around the corner and flipped a wall switch, lighting the lamps on the bedside tables. He did not know Beth was following him.

Beth decided she wanted to, no, *had* to look into his bedroom. She leaned against the door frame as she looked at the triple dresser, the highboy, two chairs, two night tables and the queen size bed. She knew what she wanted to do.

Geoff saw Beth holding her jacket and watching him. The light from the lamps allowed them to look into each other's eyes. Slowly he spread open his arms. She walked into them and leaned against him.

Beth tilted her head back and whispered, "Kiss me."

Geoff did. Tenderly. Brotherly. Quickly.

"Do it again. Like. . . I'm a woman." She pressed against him.

"What kind of a game are we playing, Beth?"

"A -I-want-to-stay-here game."

"I think that last drink . . . "

Beth put a finger over his mouth. "Gave me enough nerve to ask you." She giggled. "Nobody has to know. Liz thinks I'm at Julie's. Julie and Doc think I'm in Taylor Park." Beth pulled Geoff's face down to hers. She kissed him, passionately. "I need you to love me."

"I've always loved you." He forced a laugh. "Ever since I saw you in your stroller."

"You know what I mean."

"I know you'll be sorry in the morning." He watched her throw her jacket into the living room and sit on the side of the bed. She patted the spread and smiled into his face.

GEOFF studied her coaxing him to join her on the bed. "I refuse to do something we'll regret later. You came here because you felt down. And like a stooge I gave you the wrong stuff to drink. I'm going to make some coffee and no crying. You're going to feel . . ."

She wiped away her tears on his sweater and whispered, "Please let me stay with you."

"We'll talk about it while we drink some coffee." He took her hand and led her to the kitchen. Of course she should stay. She was depressed and mixed up. And a lonely teenager. And he could sleep on the couch. And not tell Terry that Beth stayed overnight.

His sleeping on the couch was what Geoff explained. "And then tomorrow morning I'll pretend I picked you up and we'll get your dresses and . . . " He gave her a mug of coffee from his instant coffee maker. And waited.

"Damn you, Geoff Greer. You want me to tell Julie I've changed my mind. I know why you *and* Doc are hoping I'll move in with her.

You guys want me to baby sit her. Remember I'm the one who has to sell my soul."

Geoff grinned as he stirred sugar in his mug. "Oh, I don't think it'll be quite that bad. And speaking of Doc and me, we'll always be hanging around. I won't make a pest of myself, because I know you have other guys in your life. But I'll keep in touch."

Beth began to weep. "I'm afraid I'll hate her. It'll be worse than living with Liz."

Geoff reached for a box of tissues. He moved his chair closer to her and patted her shoulder. He knew if she didn't live with Julie she'd have to get a job. And live alone. Somewhere. He lied to her about being alone. After Evan had left him he joined the Racket Ball Club. And met Terry. He didn't want anybody to know he was moving. Into a house. Where he and Terence, nickname Terry, Haines could spend more together time. He shouldn't have to worry about Beth. But he would give her a hug. He pulled her head to his shoulder. He had been seven years old when he first saw this unhappy teenage. Pushed in a stroller by her proud four year old sister. With their tall thin father walking with them. Now she was alone and afraid. What would her father have done to help her?

"I know you're in the Drama Club so why don't you try to pretend you're the lead, in a play about an eighteen year old who is wise enough to realize she should live with a person who needs her as much as she needs the other person. Until she goes to college in September." He squeezed Beth's hand. "How's that for a plot?" He blotted her tears.

Beth blew her nose. "Okay, you win. The jury just voted in your favor. But the judge said I have to stay here tonight."

Searching into her dark brown eyes, Geoff sounded, "Hmmm. Well, truthfully, I did think it was kinda late to be calling Julie. As you said, Julie thinks you're in Taylor Park and Liz thinks you're at Julie's". He watched her nod.

He gave her a quick hug and slid away from her. What was his next move? She would sleep in his bed and he would sleep on the couch. He had to remember where the sleeping bag was. Calm down. It most likely was in the hall closet. He had to take charge because he had to be responsible for whatever they did.

"Okay, now listen up. You must be as exhausted as I am from making such an important decision. And we have to be peppy for New

York tomorrow." He walked to the hall door to make certain it was locked. He picked up the suitcase. "I'll take this into the bedroom so you can find what you need. You're going to sleep in my bed and I'll sleep on the couch."

Beth swallowed a yawn. She put the mugs in the sink. And filled them each with water. When she did walk into the bedroom Geoff was collecting underwear, a sweat shirt and shoes.

"If you have a Bible, I'll swear I'll never tell." She waited until he turned to look at her. "That we slept in the same bed."

"And what makes you think we would sleep?"

Beth snickered. "You just said we're both exhausted."

"Of course. Okay. You do whatever you do in the bathroom." Geoff laughed. "While I figure out how we're going to keep this a safe and sane p.j. party."

TWENTY SEVEN

TOO EARLY ON Saturday morning the telephone awakened Geoff and Beth.

Geoff became alert immediately. The telephone was on the table next to him but he was having difficulty reaching it because he had become encased in the sheet which he insisted would keep Beth and him separated. The arrangement had not hindered them from doing some necking but it had saved them from, as he had insisted, doing anything they would regret later.

Wearing the bottoms of his only set of pajamas he finally managed to sit on the edge of the bed and pick up the receiver. "Hello, Greer here." He stopped Beth from tugging at the sheet. "Oh, damn. I'm sorry to hear that."

He covered the mouthpiece and turned to Beth. "Julie called Sam to go to *Bartle's State Store* to buy a case of Scotch. So Sam called Doc." He hoped the message was sinking in.

Beth was disregarding the conversation Geoff was having with Doc. She was remembering the thrill of being held in his muscular, hairy arms and enjoying his kisses on her mouth and neck. Down to the swells of her breasts, above her bra, which he had forbid her to remove.

He also had restricted her to just rub her hands over his chest and kiss his ears and trace her tongue around his nipples. That was when he had told her, "Time out! You eighteen year old vixen. I don't want to short out or I won't be fit for our trip to New York." Reluctantly, she consented to "go to sleep".

While Geoff held the receiver, she knelt behind him. She wrapped her arms around his waist and pulled him down to the bed. He cooperated by rolling onto his back and reaching with his free hand to hold her head on his chest. She wished she could tell Jill, or better yet let Jeanne Barnes know that Beth Rhodes had slept with a real man. Would she ever tell Brad? Suddenly, she felt her heart skip several beats as she paid attention to what Geoff was saying.

"When I picked Beth up at school yesterday she was very upset. Trying to decide what to do. She realized she shouldn't leave Julie alone but she hadn't planned on staying with Julie indefinitely. And she does keep house for Liz." He stroked her back.

"Yes, she is a considerate and caring young lady." He flinched as Beth pulled some hairs on his chest. "I know. Another thing that upset her was the way Julie tried to use her. She not only didn't appreciate her classmates teasing her about the gifts but Julie was attempting to influence her with the way she wanted Beth to write her essay. About Vicki."

As he listened to Doc, he suddenly realized Beth's free hand was sliding down to the tie on his pajama bottom. He grabbed it and held it tight.

"What do you want us to do, Doc? Beth and I are going to Julie's to get her new dresses. I guess you heard Julie is treating us to dinner and a show? In New York. So after I grab a bite to eat and take a shower and pick up Beth we'll meet you down there?" Again he listened. "I think I can talk Beth into moving down there. As I said, she was very upset when I picked her up at school. She does realize Julie should not be alone."

Geoff smiled as he watched Beth sit up and stick her tongue out. Next, she got out of bed and hurried into the bathroom. In her pants and bra.

After Geoff replaced the receiver he stood and walked to the closed door. "You can take your shower and use the shampoo now. While I make coffee. There's a hair dryer under the sink Shift into high gear because Doc is going to Julie's. And wait for us."

After Geoff took a quick shower he appeared in the kitchen in khaki trousers and a yellow oxford shirt. Beth was sipping coffee from a mug. "And a good morning to you, Beth Rhodes. You can set the table while I scramble some eggs and toast some bread. We'll put your suitcase in the trunk because we'll be leaving from Julie's house. My jacket and tie are already in the living room." From the refrigerator he took out eggs, bacon, bread and butter.

"And *why* is the sleeping bag open on the couch?"

Geoff put a frying pan on the stove. "In case one of us snored?"

"Or because you really didn't want to sleep with me?"

"It was an unexpected pleasure. But I did have to be prepared in case I had to open the door for an emergency. It had to appear I was sleeping on the couch."

"Thanks for thinking about my reputation." She sighed. "So now it's time to face reality. Just don't desert me."

He turned away from the stove. "Dear one. Doc and I will be as close as . . ."

She couldn't stop herself. She had to wrap her arms around his waist and hug him. "I don't want Doc. I want you to save me." Beth tilted her head back and whispered, "I love you. No, hear me out. I know we're just having fun. But I believe you've been sent by my Guardian Angel. According to what I've read, everybody has one. And mine sent you back into my life. To...to. . . ."

"To keep you safe and sound." Geoff kissed her forehead and turned back to the stove. "Just think of me as your brother."

She hugged him from behind. "I...I kinda guess you do have a special somebody. Like a girlfriend," she paused to force a laugh, "maybe even a mistress in your life. But I'll never forget being with you. Just stay in my life also. . . while I have to live with Julie."

"Until Doc and I get you in a college where you can live on campus." He unwrapped her arms and put her scrambled eggs on a plate. "Eat up. So we can get the show on the road."

DOC had arrived before them and called out, "It's unlocked," after Geoff knocked on the mud room door. Julie was visibly surprised when they walked into the kitchen.

Beth was disappointed to see Julie in her soiled bathrobe. She had not combed her hair and again, was without make-up. In the one night Beth had been away, Julie had a relapse. And become pathetic.

"Good morning. Julie. Doc." Geoff remarked. He gave Julie a broad smile and nodded to Doc. "Hmmm. Smells like there's coffee somewhere."

Now it was time for Beth to smile. "Hi, you two. Can we join you?"

Julie slowly studied Geoff and Beth. Sarcasm was dripping off each word as she said, "What a surprise. First, Philip and now you two. I've either done something right. Or something wrong."

Julie's three guests ignored her comment. Geoff walked to the coffee pot and picked it up. "Ahh, feels as though there's still enough for two mugs."

Beth walked to a cabinet to select two mugs.

"And how are you two kids today?" Doc asked. He sounded perfectly innocent.

"Fine and dandy," Geoff remarked as he filled the mugs. "We stopped by for a couple of reasons." He spooned sugar into his mug and glanced at Beth. He gave her a look of reassurance. Driving to Julie's house, they had reviewed what each one of them should say.

Geoff would begin the conversation about leaving for New York from Julie's. That way, after Beth put on the new dress, Julie could see how sharp they looked. Then Beth would jump in, feet first, and tell Julie she would accept her invitation to live with her.

But then Beth had laid a hand on his thigh and asked, "Can I stay with you tonight? After all, it will be late when we get home."

Why should he feel nervous? All he had to do was to tell her he had a date, with that special somebody. "My mind tells my heart not to. I'm going to take you home to Taylor Park. After all," he paused to force a laugh, "we are two good looking, appealing, impressive, sexy and vulnerable human beings. How much goodness can you expect of us? Especially after a taste of the big time in . . . Sin City. Or is that Las Vegas?"

"It'll be hell trying to sleep in Taylor Park, when I want to be in your apartment."

"Think of it this way. We have a secret that no one else. . . hey, stop hitting my leg. I know you must be disappointed but how am I going to explain the bruises to my tennis buddy?"

IN Julie's kitchen, Beth was trying to appear nonchalant as Geoff explained she had asked him to bring her down for the sexy dress she was going to wear to New York.

Beth took a long drink from her mug and added, "And I want to ask you, if the offer to stay here is still open, then I'd like to . . . to live with you."

Julie raised her eyebrows as she mouthed an "Oh? How about that?"

Her three guests waited. For the rest of her comment. They all knew she had the winning card and she was prolonging the game.

Finally, Doc could not keep quiet any longer. "For god's sake, Julie, tell the young lady how happy you are she's going to be a live-in companion."

Beth and Julie peered into each other's souls before Julie smiled and nodded. "Beth knows how I feel. I wouldn't have asked her to move in if I hadn't given it a lot of thought. After all, it'll take some adjusting for both of us. Even some sacrificing."

Beth knew it was her turn. Wishing she could reach for Geoff's hand, she smiled and added, "Well, that's why I decided I shouldn't move in, all at once. I mean, I'll just stay a few nights every week, so we can make the adjustment slowly. We can decide which nights and . . ."

Beth paused as she realized she wanted to change the subject, "and we can invite Geoff and Doc for dinner tomorrow. So Geoff and I can tell you about our trip to New York."

Now it was Geoff's turn. After making an issue of comparing the time on the kitchen clock to his watch, Geoff remarked, "Which reminds me, you need to finish getting ready so we can leave. New York is not around the corner. I'll give Gerry some lettuce and seeds."

Beth began to leave the kitchen but stopped when she heard Julie call out, "I put a black woolen stole which I bought in Scotland, on top of the dress. I refuse to let you wear that ugly jacket. And use that red purse I laid out. You need some color with that outfit." Beth hurried through the hall, to *her* bedroom. To see what Julie wanted her to wear.

Geoff decided he had to say, "I'll take a rain check for dinner. I already have plans."

Julie tried to clear her mind so she could comprehend what was happening. She knew she was in the middle of a game, but not as a player. "I'll think about dinner later. You all caught me off guard and I have to catch up."

Doc decided he would enter into the conversation. "Well, I'll call tomorrow, in case you want me to get anything. And I'll even come down early to help you get dinner."

Julie laughed. "So much attention. You do know my birthday is not until July."

Many minutes later Beth walked into the kitchen, wearing the black dress with the stole over an arm. Geoff whistled and Julie and Doc clapped their hands.

Beth slowly twirled around. "And Julie, I heard you mention your birthday. Just know we are going to have a big party." Suddenly she got a brain storm and added "And maybe it could be a ground breaking celebration? By then, it might be time to start building the new office building."

Doc lifted his mug and said, "Hear hear. Now Julie, there's a goal. To keep you busy."

"You do know, Philip . . . there are more State Stores. Than the one in Bridgeboro. And Beth, you look very nice." She snickered. "Or as Geoff puts it, sexy." She turned to Geoff, "Take her to *Binder's Shoe Store,* to buy something more attractive than what she's wearing."

Beth nodded and whispered, "Thank you."

Doc stood and walked to Julie. "I also know you are killing yourself. All we can do is try to be your friends. How long you want to know us, is up to you." He hiked up his baggy corduroy trousers and said to Geoff and Beth, "You both look great. Not get out of here. Drive carefully and have a great time. The sky's the limit and bring the receipts back to Julie."

Beth left the kitchen to get the handbag. Just like that, the old gut pain hit hard. What Doc had said was sinking in. What had she just done? Signed herself on to be Julie's keeper. Geoff and Doc would have to remember she tried with her daddy, and failed. If Julie wanted to self-destruct, she would find a way. And blame whomever she chose.

After Beth returned to the kitchen, Julie held out a hand. She knew to reach out to take it.

"Don't pay any attention to Philip. You and I are going to have a great time. We're going to move to Deer Lake Manor, go on trips and . . . have a ball."

Beth smiled and nodded and took Geoff's outstretched hand.

After Geoff said, "Goodbye," for both of them they hurried to his car. "You can do it, kiddo," he said firmly. "It's only until August."

TWENTY EIGHT

SUNDAY MORNING ARRIVED before Beth was ready. She had reluctantly said "goodnight" to Geoff around midnight because Liz's car was already parked in their designated parking place. If she couldn't go to Geoff's apartment she wanted him to come into her house. But Geoff had told her a neighbor most likely would notice his sport's car and watch the clock. He had given her several quick kisses, waited for her to enter the house. Then drove away.

Why had she cried? Because Geoff had told her he had other plans for dinner? She had enjoyed one of the most wonderful experiences with the most wonderful man, she could ever hope to have. But wasn't he just being nice to her . . . because of Julie? She had to be smart and just be happy to have him back in your life. As a friend.

Carrying her new shoes and Julie's stole and purse, she went to her room. After she got into bed she realized she still was wearing the watch which Brad had given to her. She remembered she had also kept it on the night before, in Geoff's bed. Did she still love Brad?

Much too early in the morning, Beth had been disturbed by Di and Millie arguing with each other, in their bedroom. She was too tired to wonder if Peg was still in bed. She managed to fall back to sleep until the sound of Liz, *clip clopping* from her room to the bathroom, awakened her. Beth squinted at her watch and was surprised to see that it was ten A. M.

Even though she wished she could go into the bathroom before she went downstairs, Beth put on a pair of slacks and an oversized sweat shirt, which Evan had left behind, and hurried into the kitchen. The reason for leaving her bedroom was she did not want to give Liz the opportunity to enter her bedroom. She detested having "talks" with Liz in what she considered her only private place on Planet Earth. She always hoped if she did not give Liz a reason to enter her bedroom Liz would not be as likely to enter it while she was away. After Liz told Beth she would be responsible for cleaning her bedroom, Beth agreed she would respect Liz's wishes and be responsible for cleaning her own bedroom and the bathroom. Beth could count on one hand the times that Liz had cleaned the downstairs.

"Beth," Liz called down the stairs. "Are you down there?"

Beth hurried to the bottom of the stairs. "Want some coffee?"

"Yeah. I'll be down in about twenty minutes."

Beth smiled. What Liz called twenty minutes, others would refer to as forty-five. She knew she would have time to use the bathroom, make her bed and check that her school clothes were ready for Monday. She would take them when Doc came to deliver her to Julie's house. He had insisted she should not ride on the bus. She hoped that Liz was going to leave the house soon, so she could call to give Jill a news update.

Beth returned to the kitchen and put a pan of water on the stove. She remembered making coffee in Geoff's apartment. How much better it tasted than what she and Liz drank. She had to admit the coffee she drank at Julie's tasted the best, with an added treat of watching the birds outside the bay window. She willed herself to believe she and Julie were going to be friends and enjoy many cups of coffee or tea together.

Beth was seated at the kitchen table, eating a slice of toast covered with peanut butter, when Liz appeared. She immediately noticed how attractive Liz looked. Besides her usual becoming hair style and bright red nail polish, she was wearing a very short black wool skirt and a frilly long sleeved white blouse. Across the top of the washing machine, she laid a black jacket which matched the skirt and a red handbag which she must have purchased at the same store as her matching shoes. She also was wearing perfume and a wide friendly smile.

She sat opposite Beth. "Good morning stranger. Are you just visiting or here to stay?"

Beth poured hot water into Liz's cup. She wondered if Peg had told Liz she had seen her on Friday night?

"Julie and I made an arrangement." She decided to look right into Liz's hazel eyes, heavily lined with thick black lashes. "I'm going to stay with her a couple of nights every week and stay here the rest. And after I have to move, I'll move in with Julie. Until I go to college."

Liz smiled a broad smile. "Hey, didn't I tell you to be smart and . . ."

Beth held up a hand. "I remember. But I am going to *work* for her. And *if* you hear any rumors around town like she's giving me a car, it isn't true. She's buying a new car for herself. And I'm just going to drive her. She and Doc are calling me her com-pan-ion." She said the word slowly.

220

"I take it she's well enough to show up at the company. Peg says that Alan is worried about the morale and . . . "

"If she wants me to take her there," Beth interrupted, "she'll tell me."

"I hope you get to that place up in the country. Peg said that Alan took her up there, but you can't see much from the main road. And you need permission to get any closer."

"The house in Bridgeboro is nice enough for me. I have my own bedroom. And in case you heard, she did buy me a television and a stereo. *And* a dress to wear to New York." Beth nodded after Liz's eyes open wide. "She asked Geoff to take me up there. Yesterday."

"You are hard to keep up with. Lou can't believe you were even able to see her. Now I can tell the gang you're going to live with her." Liz lighted a cigarette. "Need I ask, but did you have a good time? With Geoff?"

Beth grinned. "Of course. New York is a different world. Just remember. Geoff and I are just good friends."

"Okay. Okay. But so you know, I think it was last week, a sailor from the base was in for a couple of beers and we got to talking and I forget how we got around to it, but he said he met Les while he was stationed in San Diego. Les was living in the enlisted men's housing with his wife and kids." Another long drag followed by a cloud of smoke. "As far as this guy knows, Les didn't have any girlfriend named Evan, out in California."

Liz finished her coffee and stood. "I gotta get going. Lou hates it when I'm late." She ground out the cigarette in the overflowing ashtray.

"Did you tell the guy Evan is your daughter?"

"Hell, no. I wouldn't tell anybody she's related to me. I hope I never see her again."

"Come on, Liz. You are her mother and . . . "

"I never want to see that bum again. And I've given you some good advice. Like working for Julie and getting to college. So make a play for Geoff. In case she does come back."

Beth decided to bypass any more references to Geoff and return to the subject of her living with Julie. "Please do not tell people Julie is paying my way to college. I'm going to borrow money from her. With the agreement of working . . . to pay her back."

"At least you don't have to write that essay."

"I'm still going to," Beth heard herself say.

"Why? Why do all that writing? When you don't have to?" Liz walked to a small mirror hung on the wall next to the pantry. It had been hung there for last minute checks on her face and hair.

"Because I have pride. And I need to." She watched Liz pat her hair and tighten a large earring. *And you know Daddy, I'm also going to convince Julie I should mention Vicki's unpublished manuscripts and the love letters.* "Are you going shopping?"

"No. One of Lou's buddies, from the service, and his wife, have invited us for dinner. So they can meet me." Liz snickered. "Lou is telling everybody he knows, that he's getting married."

"So, why doesn't he pick you up here? Geoff picked me up in lovely Taylor Park."

"Lou refuses to return to this place. I guess you didn't know he used to live here. Him and his first wife. Before she left him. She really missed out 'cause then he fixed up the apartment above the restaurant and moved in there. It's really nice. It's got a big living room and a nice modern kitchen and two bedrooms and ..."

"I thought you said it had one bedroom?" Beth said loudly.

Liz lighted another cigarette. "Lou has the other room fixed up like an office. That's where he does his paper work and has his collection of bowling trophies and his guns and junk from WW Two. He wouldn't let anybody stay in there." She took a deep drag. "One more thing. You don't have to keep writing notes. Just let me know when you decide to move out."

"I'm not moving out . . . until after graduation."

"How come?"

Beth's mind raced in high gear as she tried to catch up with a logical answer. "I'll have lots of studying to do for our finals. And, I sort of have to get used to living with someone . . . full time. After all, you said you'll pay the rent until June. So I might as well use this place." Surprised, she watched Liz sit down again.

"Well I'll be here too, 'cause Lou doesn't want me living with him until after we get married. I've stayed at his place a couple of nights but he thinks it would look better, since he belongs to Rotary and the Chamber of Commerce, if we don't shack up. And we can't get married until June." She took a quick drag.

Beth decided to just watch and wait.

"I was hoping I could get out of here before then. But if I want a honeymoon, I've got to wait. Christ, I haven't been any farther than Wildwood and New York City since I've been born. So I ain't about to turn down a trip to Florida." She seemed to perk up as she declared, "I guess I haven't seen you since Lou said he'll take me to Daytona for two weeks. And maybe a little side trip to some islands out in the Atlantic Ocean, somewhere."

Beth had to sound pleased. After all she'd like to go to Florida. "Sounds great. When are you getting married in June?"

"The first Saturday. Lou's brother can't get his two weeks' vacation until the first two weeks in June and Lou wants him in the restaurant while we're gone.

"Tony is real nice. You can meet him at the wedding. I'm not crazy about his wife but Tony and me have hit it off real good and he says he'll give up his two weeks' vacation this year. Just for his baby brother and Sexy." Liz giggled. "That's what he calls me. Sexy." Liz took a deep drag before she crushed out the cigarette. She made a move to put on her jacket.

"You'll be away the first two weeks in June?"

"Yeah. I'll move out all of my stuff before the wedding. And now that you won't need any of the furniture we'll have to decide what we're going to do with it."

"I wasn't thinking about the furniture. I was thinking that Baccalaureate Night and Class Night and Graduation are all in the first week in June."

"Oh shit. Well, you know I didn't do it on purpose. I mean Tony and Lou made the plans and I have to go along with . . . hey, I'll bet Geoff would go. And you won't miss me if *the* Mrs. William Fischer shows up."

Beth longed to say, *She's not my mother*, but instead she shrugged. "Sure. Julie Fischer with Geoff Greer on one arm and Doctor Rexinger on the other. What more could I ask for?"

She stood and yawned. "You have a good time today. I'll give you a call now and then. Or maybe stop in to see you. Even though Lou thinks I'm too young to be near a bar."

Liz opened her handbag and took out a wallet. "Listen, kid, I'm really sorry. I know graduation is a big night. And you really wish your old man could be there." She pulled out some bills and counted. "Maybe I can be there when you graduate from college. Here's some money for a dress and shoes. For the prom or another date with Geoff." She laughed as she handed Beth five ten dollar bills. "And I'll pay for the dress you wear to my wedding." She quickly put the handbag under her arm and walked to the back door

Beth held out the money. "I really appreciate this."

Liz made a half turn back to Beth. "Tell Julie I said thanks. It's real nice what she's doing for you. And for me too. 'cause I won't have to worry about you being here. Alone."

She opened the door. Then she stepped up to where Beth stood and gave her a peck on the cheek. She gave a quick smile. "Good luck, kiddo. I know your old man would be proud of you." Liz closed the door and hurried toward her car.

Beth opened the door and called out, "Goodbye. Have fun." She watched Liz drive away.

She looked at the money "My God. If it weren't for money how would I ever know how much people like me? And instead of a peck on the cheek, why couldn't she say *she's* proud of me?" She closed the door and leaned against it.

Tears were wetting her cheeks

TWENTY NINE

ON MONDAY MORNING Beth shut off her alarm clock and squirmed and stretched. So much had happened since Friday, it was difficult to believe she still was Beth Rhodes and not Cinderella. But Cinderella did not have to go to school.

She smiled at the ceiling remembering Geoff and the magical hours of being with him, in his bed, his car and the trip to New York. She knew she was thinking about him too much. He could not become an important person in her life because there was someone else in his life. Someone he still wouldn't tell her about. Probably a beautiful impressive female lawyer, whom she didn't want to know about. So she had dinner with Doc and Julie on Sunday. And Doc had brought her home. She promised to stay with Julie on Monday, Tuesday and Wednesday of the coming week.

She had called Jill before she went Julie's. To tell her about her date with Geoff. She also told her best girlfriend she had to take the school bus because she would have extra stuff to carry.

She hurried in and out of the bathroom so she could pack the last minute stuff she was going to take with her. Maybe she should buy more cosmetics and whatever, to keep some in each house? Ha. Ha

After they settled on the hard bus seats, Jill remarked, "I'm sure working for Mrs. Fischer is going to work out okay for you. But what about college?"

Beth forced a laugh. "You mean, am I going to use the money I win, to go to college?"

"I like your attitude. But just in case you don't win?"

Beth shrugged. "I guess I'll take Julie up on her offer to loan me what I'll need. I might as well work for her, to pay her back."

"Good. You wouldn't be happy if you don't go to some kind of college."

Beth peered into Jill's eyes. "Have you been able to make any plans?"

"Dad says he can afford to send me to Business School."

"Good," Beth said cheerfully while inside she felt sadness. She knew Jill wanted to go to college. She wanted to be a teacher. Not a secretary. Beth wished she could distribute some of Julie's money to special friends. They should be as happy as she was.

Beth's happiness lasted until she walked into Bridgeboro High School. As soon as Jim Bender passed her in the locker room her elation become a heavy dose of guilt. Even though she had a desire to whisper, "Hi, sexy," she felt remorse for intruding into his private life. Next she passed Jeanne Barnes on the way to their first classes. She felt smug. But when she sat next to Brad in typing class, she felt distress. Or was it downright deceit?

Beth realized that no matter what had happened during the past week-end, Brad still was part of her life. How big of a part she was not certain. Maybe he was just part of her past? Maybe she wished Geoff would be part of her future?

But she did know there would come a time she would have to make a decision. She could not see Brad day after day, sit near him, hear his voice, let him walk near her, smell his after shave cologne she had come to enjoy, and watch him walk away. With Jeanne next to him. She was studying his profile when he turned to look directly into her eyes. His soul touched her soul. He winked at her! Beth felt her throat become so constricted she thought she might suffocate.

After the last class Beth decided she had to know how she still felt about Brad Livingston. And talking with him would be one way of finding out. Beth wrote two words, ***Let's talk*** and waited until it was safe to push the paper into his locker. The next move was his.

JULIE was sitting in the living room when Beth unlocked the front door.

"Hello, Julie. Wherever you are?" She heard Julie respond, "I'm in the living room." She shut the door with a hip and carried her overnight case, books and handbag into the living room. "Hey, look at you. What a pretty dress."

"And I even feel pretty," Julie said cheerfully. There was a sparkle in her eyes and a big smile on her face. She still looked pale and too thin but she was wearing another attractive dress. As she had done on Sunday. Her hair was shiny and becomingly arranged to show off another pair of earrings.

Daddy, do you think she looks like Rita Hayworth? At least, she could pass for a movie star.

"Put your stuff in your room and then I have something to discuss with you."

Beth put her books on a chair and took her overnight case and jacket into her room. She paused in front of the mirror behind the triple dresser to brush her hair and freshen her lipstick. All too soon it was time to return to the living room and learn what Julie had planned.

Julie indicated that Beth should sit in the rocking chair. She had remembered the night before that Beth had commented the rocking chair was her favorite piece of furniture. And Julie had laughed and declared, "It's yours. You may take it wherever you go."

Julie frowned. "You look tired."

Beth forced a smile. "I stayed up to begin typing my essay."

"I hope you're not too tired for what I have in mind. Do you have much homework?"

"It's according to how long it takes to write a haiku and study for an English test. Why?"

"I was just wondering. In any case, I am in charge of dinner. I'll call you when our gourmet meal is ready. Although after what Philip made yesterday, Fettuccine Florentine Carbonara will be a letdown. But I have made a nice salad and . . . oh I'm not letting you do your homework. But one more question. Has Geoff told you who he's dating?"

Beth shook her head from side to side.. "Why don't *you* ask him? Then tell me."

WHEN Julie called Beth for dinner, she had finished writing three haikus. She decided to read them to Julie and ask for her critique? It would give them something to discuss. After they agreed on which haiku was best, Julie announced, "Before I can really decide I want to read them myself. Now I have something to share with you." She took a long drink of iced tea and began.

Beth found it difficult to believe what she was hearing. She was so excited she had to force herself to look sympathetic as Julie explained her problem was having to make a decision. About Deer Lake Manor. Captain Bittner had informed her that very morning he had received orders to take command of a Naval Air Station in Hawaii. He and his wife would be moving within a month.

"I think I want to move back. It was thoughtful of Earle to leave me this place because he knew how painful it was for me to stay at the Manor. Someday soon you and I are going to drive up there and have a look around. I'm sure the place will need some touch up, maybe even some repairs." Julie paused to grin. "I've heard those Navy people can give some ambitious parties but then," her eyes took on a faraway look, "Bill and I were Mr. and Mrs. Protocol of Bucks County. People used to make damn fools of themselves to be on our guests lists."

Beth put more food in her mouth and concentrated on chewing. She did not want to distract Julie. She wanted to test her with some reminiscing.

Julie's eyes focused on Beth's face. "You can have parties there too and be one of the most popular young people in Bridgeboro." Without pausing for Beth to respond Julie quickly added, "What do you know about Manorial history?"

"Not much. Except it's a big house with lots of land. I guess, like a plantation?"

Julie laughed a merry laugh. "Not exactly. There are only four such places in Bucks County worthy of being called Manors. Pennsbury Manor and Deer Lake Manor are two of those. Several have been destroyed by fire and others were broken up into such small parcels of land that . . . " she paused to sip from her glass. "I want to scream when I think of how things become corrupted. Real Estate men and money hungry farmers have made history of Manors simply meaningless. Practically every other new development is named Buckingham Manor or Warrington Manor or some bastardly name. And hundreds of dummies buy those ticky tacky boxes all in a row and don't even know the meaning of the word. Deer Lake Manor was one of the grants from William Penn. From the original deed, it consisted of thirty thousand acres. But it's lost a few thousand acres. Along the way."

Beth whistled. Deer Lake Manor sounded like power. "Now what do you own?"

"I'm guessing. About twenty thousand. And over a thousand are covered with virgin woods. Great place for the deer. But the land is not the important feature. To be termed a Manor a homestead must possess essential features. A stone mansion house and I have a magnificent twenty room house, a spring house, with a stream or a pond, and I have a lake, a smokehouse and a carriage house which has been made into a darling cottage where my caretaker and his wife live.

"There should be a barn and a barnyard with a wall, both of which I have and tenant houses. One of mine is used by a dairy farmer, one

I'm renting to my caretaker's son and the smallest one I'm renting to a farmer who is using about two hundred acres to raise soy beans.

"Also a Manor is supposed to have a graveyard, which I also have." She understood the look on Beth's face and shook her head. "No, they're not buried there. I thought you'd know we buried Vicki in the family plot, in New York. Earle and Alice are there too. Bill is buried in Memorial Park, right here in Bridgeboro. With his mother and father. And the baby girl, who died, almost after she was born."

"That's where my father is. Is that where you'll be buried too?"

"Of course. Next to my husband."

"I'm really anxious to visit the place. Especially now that I know more about Manors."

"I have a book on *New World Manor Homesteads* which you might find interesting. But I also wanted to tell you that Mr. Smith called. My new car is ready. He wanted to deliver it this afternoon but I said absolutely not. I want you to be the first to drive it. With me by your side.

"I took a slow walk outside the house today to test my legs, for walking around town. I noticed the daffodils are peeking through and there are clumps of snow drops blooming on the south side of the garage. Alice planted everything that blooms." She patted Beth's hand. "As soon as you get here after school, Philip will drive us to Smith's to pick up the car. This is going to be like a maiden voyage." Julie's enthusiasm was becoming apparent. I haven't been in Bridgeboro since Earle died. And Philip says he thinks the last time I left this house, was to go with him to downtown Philly." She paused to snicker. "But we can't remember where we went.

"Philip wants to stay with us. He's so afraid I'm going to get too ambitious. But I do want to drive up and down the Pike. And maybe visit some stores where I used to shop. Of course a lot of people won't even recognize me. But the old timers will."

Beth was surprised how excited she felt. "Julie, you look ten years younger and ready to stir up the town. I'm going to have a ball being with you. Want me to call Mr. Livingston? Maybe he'll send a photographer and reporter for a feature story, in *The B.C.?*"

Julie's smile vanished. "If he knew I was scouting in downtown Bridgeboro, he'd piss in his pants." Julie's voice took on an urgency. "Did you read *The B. C.* on Friday?

Beth shook her head. "Liz canceled the newspaper."

"Go into the dining room and find it. It's on top of a pile I'm saving."

BETH immediately saw the red circle around a letter to *The Editor*. She returned to the kitchen and began to read the letter which Charles Barnes had written. Beth kept her eyes on the paper as she was thinking how to respond. Could this criticism goad Julie into action? Would she and Brad ever be forced to take sides? Beth looked at Julie. "What are you going to do?"

"Whatever you want me to do."

Beth frowned. Confusion clouded her mind until the name Brad came into focus. Inside she yelled out, *Oh my god no! Please don't let her know anything about us. Even though she cuts out his pictures.* Beth almost whispered, "What do you mean?"

"Give me your advice. How should the born again Julie Fischer, respond to such a nasty letter?"

Beth felt as though she had been the "saved" one. Since Brad's name had not been mentioned she could even smile. "Wellll," she dragged out. "I suppose you should decide just *what* you are going to do with that farm?"

"How in the hell do I know? I didn't even plan on buying it but," Julie paused to grin. "I know you don't understand why."

"It doesn't matter if I understand. What matters is that Mr. Barnes is trying to ruin your image. And reputation."

Julie's laughter filled the kitchen. Followed by a bout of severe coughing. She drank half a glass of iced tea which Beth poured for her, before she was able to remark, "My god, you're funny. Kind but funny. *What* image? There's nothing to ruin?"

"Wrong. Your name is Fischer and that name represents . . . well, even I know it represents contributions to the Library and the building fund for the hospital and all kinds of charities and . . . the company is the biggest thing. You have to be proud of the company."

Tears filled Julie's eyes. She wiped them away with her napkin. "Of course I'm proud of it," she said hoarsely. "But if it isn't the death of me, then I may be the death of it."

Beth patted Julie's thin, cold hand. She was hearing an instant replay of the conversation between Julie and Doc. She had to sound enthusiastic. "You've been responsible for its continued success and the employment of thousands of people and . . . "

"Making it into a monster which is going to destroy me." Julie slid her hand out from under Beth's and put hers on top. She clutched Beth's hand as she added, "And I need growth money for the company. Success may smell sweet but it can cause problems. And I must keep control. I need a tissue."

Beth looked for a tissue box. What was Julie telling her? Was it possible for a Fischer to lose control of the company? Then who would be president? She wished she knew how to respond. She handed Julie the box and sat down again.

"If I do decide to go public, I'll be doing something Bill never wanted to do. That's why I've been so upset. Only I can decide. Because I have to weigh growth against . . . damn Bill and damn Earle . . . for leaving me with such a predicament. And success be damned."

"I have to believe with all of the expert advice available to you, you'll come out, safe and sound." Beth finished her salad, trying to ignore Julie blowing her nose.

"I just might go with an initial public offering."

Beth nodded and laughed, "Sounds like a plan to me. Even though I don't really know what you're talking about." She stood. She wanted to end the conversation. Besides being unable to comprehend the value of the company just talking about multimillions of dollars frustrated her. Never would she have to be so concerned. She almost felt sorry for Julie. Because money had to affect her life. Of course, owning a multimillion dollar manufacturing plant named the *Fischer Company* did matter.

Julie watched Beth clear the table. "I certainly don't need a farm right now. I may sell it." She grimaced at Beth. "I really am everything Charlie Barnes put in his letter. Greedy. Materialistic. Ruthless. And out to destroy whoever gets in my way."

"You could make him eat his words." Beth pulled her chair closer to Julie and sat down again. "Of course doing so would cost you what you're paying for the farm. But I have to believe you could write it off."

She knew she had Julie's attention. "Give the farm to the County. Designated as a County Park. Or if the County doesn't move fast enough, give it to the Commonwealth of Pennsylvania for a State Park. Maybe they'll name it Fischer Park?"

"Wouldn't that grab them? I'll call Geoff tomorrow. Why not draft the letter which I'll request be printed, in response to the one from Charles Barnes. There's a tablet and pens on the desk in my office."

Taking a pen from Beth, Julie commented, "I wish I could see Dickie's face when he gets this. You know the Livingstons and the Barnes think they're the elite of Bridgeboro. After I move back to Deer Lake I'm going to show them who's the hostess with the . . . " Julie began to cough. She finished the iced tea and watched Beth refill the glass.

"Dickie probably has been constipated ever since he printed Chuckie's blast against me. Because he's afraid of what I might do. When he gets this letter he won't have to take a laxative."

She laughed again and began to whisper what she was beginning to write. *"Dear Editor. Julie Fischer, President of the Fisher Company, is pleased to announce plans to deed the farm, located on blah blah Road to the Bucks County Park Commission, with the express purpose that it will be designated as a County Park. Since Charles Barnes, President of . . . "* She stopped as Beth held up her right hand.

BETH shook her head. She gently took the pen and slid the tablet to face her. She turned to a clean page. Looking into Julie's eyes, she said, "To begin with, *you* are Mrs. William Fischer. Only your dear friends may call you Julie. And, don't give Mr. Barnes the satisfaction of even mentioning his name in this important announcement." Beth could not stop grinning. What fun. She was trying to hurt Jeanne by belittling her father. But she must not hurt Brad.

She looked into Julie's eyes. "What could Mr. Barnes do to the Livingston's?"

Julie shrugged. "Maybe snub them. Stop inviting them to their wing dings. Or any important political and social gatherings. But, Dick would know he has only himself to blame. He shouldn't have tried to buy the farm. With or without Charlie. I've decided as soon as we write this letter, you have to contact Geoff. Meaning, my personal secretary, Miss Rhodes, will tell him that first thing tomorrow morning he is to contact the right person in the Court House, regarding my gift of a County Park. Hell, I'll even pay for the maintenance."

Beth nodded, enthusiastically. "You might consider approaching the idea from another angle. Since you know so much about Manors and you are so proud of yours, you have made this decision because you believe there is a shortage of County Parks for the enjoyment of the families in the County. And how about if you've made this decision because you also believe in preserving as much of the past as possible. All for the benefit of Bucks County where so much history of our Country was made.

"The buildings must be saved and I'll bet the *Lenni Lenape* Indians lived along the Poquessing Creek." Beth paused to sigh. "You mentioned how builders corrupt terms and I feel just as strongly about how they destroy precious old historical buildings and plow under acres of beautiful farmland for more ticky tacky boxes. Somebody should rattle the members of the Bridgeborough Historical Society and propose some legislation to permit local municipalities to cooperate with non-profit organizations for the purpose of preserving historic sites and properties."

Julie nodded and Beth continued. "Okay. So I have to admit that isn't really my idea. I read it somewhere. Obviously, I'm trying to express my own opinions through your letter."

Watching Julie laugh, Beth quickly thought, *My god. Daddy I accused Julie of using me and here I am, doing the same thing. I'm using her power and her money to get back at my enemies.* "Forget it. I just had to get it off my chest."

"I'm not smiling because I'm amused. Why shouldn't Julie, I mean, Mrs. William Fischer, be interested in the history of Bucks County? Maybe you and I can make some history of our own? At least do some shouting. We could do some research and even write a book! At least some articles. Who knows? Maybe I can make Vicki and me comparable to the Bronte sisters? I can tell from the look on you face, you like the idea."

Beth was excited. Imagine Julie writing a book? Imagine Mrs. Livingston and her Bridgeborough Historical Society being goaded to invite Julie to join the group? At least give a book report and have a book signing. Beth lowered her eyes to concentrate on the words before her. "How about quoting Santayana? *'The beauty of the earth is the eternal solace of mankind'*? I read that somewhere also."

"Geoff was right. You are smart."

"And how about closing by using another quote? 'We hold open space and natural beauty as a trust. If we do not do something to preserve it, it will not be here for our descendants.'" Beth pushed the tablet in front of Julie.

"You type the draft and we'll run it by Geoff. For now I was wondering if you might want to reconsider and read the manuscripts and letters. Before you finish writing your essay?"

"I guess so." Beth whispered. The time had actually arrived.

"They'll make your essay be the winner. And . . . "

"And what might you have up your sleeve?" Beth was bold enough to ask.

Julie forced a broad smile. "I know I don't have to come out smelling like a rose and make Vicki and Bill come across . . . like culprits."

"Well for the sake of my essay, I would love to tell people about the manuscripts. But what would I tell the world about where they've been all these years?"

"As clever as you are? You can make up something. Tell them I let you go through Vicki's belongings and you found them. In fact I will let you go into that room to get the manila envelopes. I've decided you deserve to read them and I know what a thrill it will be for you to have a quick look at some of Vicki's furniture. I think I told you Earle and I had the responsibility of emptying out her New York brownstone."

BETH almost ran into Julie's bedroom. She brought out the ebony box which Julie had described. After Julie gave her a key, she hurried into the hall. She paused in front of the door because she felt lightheaded. Her heart was beating out of synch and her lungs needed oxygen.

She felt as though she was going to enter the Land of Oz. She was actually going to see and touch personal belongings of Vicki Lynn's! And read private valuable, irreplaceable pieces of paper which could provoke a minor earthquake among the masses of romanticists and mild hysteria among the biographers. Julie Fischer was allowing Beth Rhodes to read private letters which Vicki had written!

She clicked on the overhead light and gasped. The room was jammed with furniture. Wherever there was a chair or a space on a chest or a table, boxes and folders had been stacked. Beth saw the desk which Julie had described. She picked up the manila envelopes, clutched them to her chest and then couldn't move. She had to look around the room. A table and two chairs and lamps, a head board, mattress, book cases and file cabinets and . . .

"Did you find what you came for?" a voice asked from the doorway.

Beth was so startled she couldn't speak. She nodded and held out the envelopes.

"Staying in here is not on your schedule for tonight. I promise another time. When I feel up to it we'll come in here and you can look around." Julie gave a soft laugh. "Even lie on her couch." Julie put her hand on the light switch. "Lights out."

Rocking chair, couch, a big basket, Beth continued thinking, as she backed out of Oz.

"You can read in the living room," Julie announced in the hall. "I'm going into my office. To do some important reading of my own. Although new contracts won't be as interesting as what you're going to read."

She shut the door and made an issue out of locking it.

THIRTY

"I WALKED ALONG the street tonight, As though I did not care, . . . But I could smell the fragrant mist, Of Autumn in the air . . . And that reminded me of you, And of the fall we met, . . . And all the seasons in my heart, That I cannot forget . . . The thrill of every meeting, And the roses on your lips, . . . The wistful skies that matched your eyes, With dreams of phantom ships . . . The joy of gazing at your smile, And knowing you were near, . . . Of being with the one I love, So wonderful and dear . . . The snows that fell upon the fields, The warmth of your embrace . . . Our toast to life and love and then, The tears upon your face . . . Yes, I remembered all those things, As I remembered you . . . And I remembered all the dreams, I wish could still come true."

That was the first poem Beth read in Vicki Lynn's notebook of unpublished poetry. On the cover of the book, Vicki had also printed, **Rough Drafts. Need revision.**

Beth reverently touched the words. As she sat in the corner of the couch holding the book she suddenly thought of her father. He would be as excited as she was. And wouldn't Mr. Stookey be green with envy? In fact, hundreds of people would gladly trade places with her.

Holding the notebook on her lap she closed her eyes and leaned her head against the back of the couch. Her mind was filled with dozens of questions.

What was Vicki feeling when she composed these poems? The desire of an impatient lover? *When I write a poem for Brad, I feel desire. Hey, Bradford Livingston, I'm reading love poems, and whamo, I think of you.*

Think about yourself, Elizabeth Mary Rhodes. She hardly ever thought about the name Mary, Liz's mother's name. And Liz wouldn't even be impressed that her daughter was reading unpublished poems. In Vicki Lynn's own handwriting. Who would care besides her daddy and Mr. Stookey? Richard Livingston! Beth grinned. Wouldn't he just love to see what she was reading? *Hey, Dickie, your old buddy, Bill Fischer, really did have an affair with Vicki Lynn.*

Beth felt a surge of excitement. She repositioned herself in the corner of the couch and tried to relax. She began to read the next poem.

"Yes, I could do without you, dear, Tomorrow and today, . . . And maybe I could get along, In my accustomed way . . . And I could live for years and years, And never see your face, . . . And still fulfill some part in life, Whatever time or space . . . But I could do a million more, If you belonged to me, . . . A million more of everything, As much as love can be . . . If I could take you in my arms, And give my promise true, . . . There would be nothing on this earth, I would not do for you . . . But if God thinks it best that we, . . . Should spend our lives apart, . . . Remember dear, you'll always be,. . . The angel in my heart.

There were only jottings on the next page. *I love you, Bill. You are I. I am you. We are and always will be one.* Beth imagined Vicki on a plane. A train. During a luncheon, while the guest speaker rattled on and on. Just having to write, *I love you, Bill.* How many times had she found herself writing, *I love Brad Livingston.* Would she ever write, *I love Geoff Greer?* Would she ever send Geoff a note or write him a love poem? She had too much to read to compare Geoff and Brad.

SHE put the note book aside and reached into a manila folder to pull out several letters.

She checked the dates and decided to read one with a May postmark. It was a hand written message, *When it came I had the same feeling I used to have overseas, when after a month or more with no mail, finally a letter would get through. I guess it's not right that I should make your letter so important - but I can't seem to stop doing so. It was the same while you were staying at Deer Lake Manor - seeing you in the evening (and in the morning, if you could drag yourself out of bed before I left for the office) was the high point of my day. And all the time I knew it shouldn't be, but there was no controlling the feeling.*

I'm wondering, Vicki, if I'm ever going to get you out of my system. Completely? Two months apart has not helped a bit. I still miss you every day and want to see you so badly, and believe me, that missing and wanting are not diminishing as the days go by. Who was the so naïve sage who originated the rhetorical but erroneous, 'Out of sight, out of mind'?

Well, hey, how are you? Whatcha been doin'? Tradition demands that one starts a personal letter in a light, airy and friendly mood - so here it is, a paragraph late. It really was wonderful to receive your letter. So nice to get a friendly letter from my sister-in-law. Ha Ha.

Beth read to the last paragraph *"I have decided I must put an addition out to the east side. Will tell you more about my plans, next time I write. Will be waiting to hear from you, every day, Love, Bill*

"How about that," Beth whispered as she replaced the letter in the envelope. In her mind she thought, just a simple beginning between a man and a woman who allowed themselves to become infatuated with each other. It seems as though they had decided it was dangerous. Or their decency got the better of them and they decided to part company. Or, perhaps a book deal took her back to New York. Let's see, New York seems to be the postmark on most of her letters, although here are some from London. And this one is from Hawaii and wow, Rome and Paris.

Beth selected another letter with a Pineville, Pennsylvania postmark, handwritten by Bill Fisher, alias M. H. Chesterfield. It had a June postmark. Out loud she hummed. "Now let's see how hard he's trying to forget her."

Vicki darling, What a wonderful letter. Just received the one you wrote on Monday and it is more than I could hope for. I love every word and punctuation mark in it. And, as if all that was not enough - you end it by saying you will write again, as soon as you get my letter. I should say, please don't take so much time away from your novel, to write to me but I just can't write those words. How can life be so wonderful? Please, do not answer that, as I know the answer only too well. There's only one more thing I want and need in my life - YOU!

I'm in a real rosy mood this morning. I know your letter did it for me plus the fact, darling, that we just got a huge contract from good old Uncle Sam. I have the papers in front of me and I'm supposed to be reviewing the details, but instead I'm thinking of YOU.

I keep remembering the last time we were together and well, I'm driving myself crazy. I can remember your hair brushing against my bare chest and how your eyes looked into my soul.

And your skin, such a rich pale tan (although since your week on the Riviera, it probably is a deep brown now) but to touch that skin was to sign my surrender. One careless caress and my former self-restraint and poise were dissipated. And oh god, how I miss you!

Beth read through the letter to the last paragraph.

Until we decide what to do, please love me - always, as I will always love YOU. Help me to make sure that nothing will ever happen to our love. Let's protect it and keep it forever.

And here I must add, I agree it would not be a good idea for you to call me. Of course I can call you in your apartment . . . so we will make plans accordingly.

Must close for now. Write SOON. I need your letters. And join me in hoping, EVEN praying, for a chance for a little time together, REAL SOON. How much I want that! Need that! Meanwhile, remember I LOVE YOU. ALL WAYS and ALWAYS, Bill.

BETH stared at the coffee table in front of her legs as she thought, Wow. What a man. It sounds as though, they went all the way. And he can't get enough of her. And here I sit, Miss Goody Goody. Who still doesn't know what it's like, to do it. I stopped Brad and Geoff wouldn't let us get started. I wonder when I'll do it? And with whom?

Beth chose another letter, which had been mailed in October. Bill Fischer described how wonderful it had been being with Vicki again. He felt guilty saying so, but hadn't they been clever convincing everyone she should hole up in the "guest house" to write the first draft of her new novel? Not even her agent, let alone the press, knew where she was. And he did mention his dislike for the deceit and hurt in which they were involved.

Beth nodded as she reviewed the lies which she and Brad told, just to be together. *Although, it sounds as though Vicki and Bill could tell us a few we haven't thought of yet. Hmmm. I wonder how Julie did find out?*

The next letter gave her the answer. She glanced over several paragraphs in which Bill told Vicki how much he regretted what he had to tell her, and then came to the words,

I'll probably mess this up completely, but please bear with me and try to get the real essence of what I going to try to convey to you.

First of all, I admit I am a coward, or I would have brought this subject up myself, many months ago. I should have told you then, while I was telling you I loved you, not waited until now, after you decided to ask me, what is to become of us? But your last letter has made me realize that I am still the same procrastinator, especially on this subject, the most important one. I knew it wasn't right to go on being so open about my love for you and at the same time not to explain to you why that love was only being expressed in words and love making, but not in any concrete action. You couldn't help but wonder why I didn't ask you to stay with me and to be mine, instead of just complaining that it could not be. I suppose in the beginning I used the excuse to myself that you probably would not want it any other way. You would still want to be foot loose and fancy free. But now that you have actually expressed a desire to marry me . . . I am searching for how to respond!!!

Vicki, please, if nothing else, please believe every word as you read this. I LOVE YOU. I want you, with my heart and with my soul. But the most important thing right now, is my father and his dreams. I cannot do anything which will hurt my father. He always has been a good father to me and now, he needs me to be a good son to him.

Vicki, darling, our love no longer is a secret! No, I should reword that. I have not told anyone about my love for you but I have admitted to Dick Livingston that Julie and I are not enjoying a marriage made in heaven. And he admitted to me, he and Bernice are putting on a good front for a shaky marriage.

I had to tell Dick, because Julie and I have not been accepting invitations for quite a few weeks. And she is beginning to look ill. Every time I look at her, I die a little. I feel so guilty even though I know she has caused some of her condition. She could end the torture, the anger and the hatred, if only she would forget her pride. I suppose it's even more than pride. She's frightened and confused. I've tried to talk with her but I cannot have a rational conversation with her. I have tried to explain that I will make certain she has a roof over her head and financial security. But these things do not seem important to her.

Please try to understand, Vicki. I feel sorry for her. Of course, I am sorry for the two of us. I want you so bad.. But darling I just cannot take the chance that Julie will do the things which she threatens to do, if I push her too far. She says she will tell Dad about our affair and she'll make it sound as crummy as she can. She said she will make as big a stink within the company as she can. She has invested quite a bit of money in the company, as has Earle, so who knows what they might do together? She says she will make me sound like a bum and you a whore, as far as she can spread the news.

I doubt Julie has told anybody yet but the other night, while Dick and I were having a drink at The Pub, he seemed to be pumping me. He seemed to suspect there was another woman in my life. I'm always afraid that when you and I are with other people, that my feelings show in my eyes. I have so much love for you, that it's bound to ooze out from some place. Anyway, I figured I would never actually tell Dick there was another woman, but I did not deny his insinuations. After three martinis, I felt just bold enough that I responded to his question, with a wink...and decided he could chew on that. But, how I long to tell somebody, about us!

I am hoping you will write again. But if you do not, I will understand. In case I receive no more letters, and you decide not to return to Pennsylvania, then I must tell you now, I LOVE YOU. I WILL LOVE YOU AS LONG AS I LIVE. I SHALL NEVER FORGET HAVING YOU IN MY LIFE. And, if it is so that I cannot have you in fact, then you will always be mine in fancy, for I shall go on remembering and dreaming, till the day I die. Forever yours, Bill.

BETH was unable to find any letters from either Vicki or Bill with December or January postmarks on them. She considered the possibility that Vicki either had been bold enough to spend the holidays in Bridgeboro or she had gone to visit. Where she could not receive mail from Bill. Beth did find several post cards from southern states which Bill had sent during business trips. But nothing from Vicki. Maybe Julie had been traveling with Bill?

Bill wrote Vicki a lovely letter in April. He must have relocated into a larger office. He began by saying, *Oh, that wonderful letter. All that love and sweetness and longing and passion and everything. It is one of the most wonderful and beautiful letters I have received from you.*

Beth decided no matter that that big impenetrable wall still was in the way, these two lovers were still going strong. Julie, Dad, the company, the neighbors, the community, the county, the government, nothing was going to stop them from . . . dreaming for their day.

Life goes on, about the same. We have been going to a few parties. Julie does look better and expressed a desire to socialize. But whatever we do isn't much fun. I drove down to Washington, D.C. by myself, and stayed for several days. It was an unexpected meeting with the Department of Defense, so I could not make arrangements for you to join me.

Business, known as orders, just keep pouring in. Dad is feeling a little stronger. In fact, he has been coming to his office for several hours every day. He just has to keep his hand in. This company means everything to him. Besides me. Ha Ha. From a little hole in the wall, with one machine, to something this big, is enough to make any man proud!

BETH had always wished she could have met Vicki Lynn but now she was reading something very personal. In fact, she really was snooping. Into two private lives. Into the innermost secrecy between a man and a woman. Maybe, she'd read just one more page and then put them away. At least for tonight.

You ended your wonderful letter with 'Yours now and forever'. They are the dearest words to me. How those words seemed to nestle up to me and put arms about me and a head upon my shoulder. You ARE mine, Vicki. And as long as you are mine, I am deeply thankful and grateful, beyond all power of speech and expression. I only pray to God, that you will remain mine ALWAYS. And I promise to you, on everything that is sacred to me, that I ALWAYS shall be yours. Always and everlastingly, YOUR Bill.

Maybe because she was drained and frustrated, Beth began to weep. She felt sadness. How could two people be so completely in love and care so deeply for each other and have to keep it hidden? Beth knew she was crying for Vicki but she realized she was also crying for herself. How about her own life? Her own predicament?

BETH began sorting through the unread letters. She was checking postmarks and dates. Finally she had found the last letter which Bill had sent to Vicki. It was dated the sixteenth of June and in it reference was made to Vicki having stayed in *the shack.* That was the term used by Vicki. Julie referred to the same location as the *guest house.* Bill Fischer referred to the building as our *love nest.* They all meant the small cottage which had been located about half a mile behind the main house, at Deer Lake Manor. It was the building which the newspapers and magazines referred to as Vicki and Bill's funeral bier, for it was there, approximately ten months after that June, Vicki Lynn and William Fischer had died.

Darling Vicki. What am I doing at the office tonight? Oh sure, business is booming and I could be working. But truthfully I am dreaming of you. I feel very close to you tonight. Almost as if you are here. Hey, maybe you are in the next room? Nope, you weren't there. When will I see you again? Not just for a visit. Forever!

Vicki, why must we be so many miles apart? Thousands of miles, in the eyes of society. Millions of miles apart, in the eyes of decency. You and your wonderful talent and fame and me with my business and a wife and . . . yet, I can't feel we are any distance at all, in the eyes of love. Are we sinners, Vicki? Is love a sin? Why can't we just turn it off? Why can't we just declare, 'This is not right. Therefore, I shall stop it?'

If I never heard from you again, never saw you again, I know on my death bed, you would be my last thought. As I leave this world, I will be wondering, 'Now, will I finally have her?'

I told you there isn't much news. And, even if there was, I don't feel like writing a newsy letter. I only want you to understand, no matter what price I have to pay, I am going to make you mine. Tell me of your love for me. So I can go on living until . . . you and I can be together FOREVER! Yours, always, Bill.

Before Beth could wipe her cheeks, several tears dripped onto Bill Fischer's hand writing causing a few words to blur. Beth murmured, "I'm sorry. I didn't mean to . . . mess up your letter. It's just you write such beautiful letters . . . they make me cry."

Beth put everything on the coffee table and stood up. She dried her face. So now she had actually held papers and read words, which had belonged to Vicki.

NOW what was she going to say to Julie? Could she say, "I cried. For Vicki and for Bill, because they truly experienced something very few people ever shall. An ultimate relationship. I also cried for you, Julie. You've lived a longer life, but your sister's life was richer and. . . more meaningful."

Yes, but what would she *really* say to Julie Fischer?

THIRTY ONE

BETH REPLACED EVERYTHING into the larger envelopes and covered them with a pillow. Looking at them made her sad.

She walked to the front windows and watched the lights of the automobiles traveling on Bridge Pike. She was responsible for the trimmed shrubbery and the freshly painted exterior and her friends and teachers were complimenting her for the new look of the house. The sound of coughing came from Julie's office. Was she ever going to stop that annoying coughing?

Beth returned to the couch and plopped in the corner. She sighed loudly. She was going to force herself to leaf through a thick blue binder.

Written on the first page in bold print, was ***Vicki's Vignettes*** She did read the first three pages before her mind began to wander again.

Daddy, I need you. A couple of hours ago I liked Julie. I wanted to save her from the humiliation of having anyone know about the affair and snicker because she lost her husband to her sister. Now I'm blaming her. I really should put these letters in my essay. She was wrong when she thought she'd come out on top. Mr. Fischer would sound charming and desirable and Vicki would sound exciting and sexy, as Mr. Barnes called her. Even including the poems might stir up some suspicions. Especially for Dickie Livingston. He just might be looking for something in my essay which could prove what he thinks he knows. It could be as controversial as did General Eisenhower have a mistress in England? And is JFK playing around with movie stars in Hollywood?

Beth stood again and wandered into the kitchen. She gave Gerry some sunflower seeds and drank a glass of cold water at the sink. She turned off the light, walked into the dining room and slowed down. Sitting on the couch was Julie.

"I came to say good-night."

Beth looked at her watch. "Oh, wow. It's that late already."

"Have you been crying?"

"No. I'm just tired." She noticed the paleness of Julie's skin. And wasn't she losing weight? Her face looked drawn and her cheek bones were more prominent.

"Since we won't have time to talk during breakfast, have you decided what you're going to use in your essay?"

"Parts of **Vicki's Vignettes.** And tell the world there's a draft for another book of poems. Beth struggled to appear relaxed. "Is that all right with you?"

"The offer still stands. The choice is yours."

"Thank you for giving me everything to read. It's really nice of you."

"Look at me. You *have* been crying. The letters upset you." After Beth whispered, "A little." Julie remarked, "So now you hate me."

"I understand more than I did before."

Julie shook her head. "You don't understand. Of course I envied Vicki. No man has loved me that completely. And I hated her for it being *my* husband. But I know they didn't deliberately plan it to happen." Julie's hand went to her chest. "And I drink because of me. I hate myself more than I ever hated my sister."

Beth took several steps closer to the hall. "Julie, I vote we discuss it tomorrow."

"Sit in your rocking chair. I want to tell you something."

"Tomorrow, please? We're both tired. You take a tranquilizer and let's go to bed."

"You said you're my friend. If you are, then sit down. And listen to me."

Beth sat, leaned back and began to rock. "I'm listening."

"I want to tell you the real story. To begin with I did trick Bill Fischer into marrying me." Because Beth continued to rock in silence Julie added, "I've already told you about my home life and how it hurt to be ignored. I told you Earle convinced me to live near him and Alice. I lied. I begged him to let me move down here. He said I should strike out on my own. In New York City or even Philadelphia, and just visit. I loved him . . . because he was the only male who gave me any attention and compassion. I resented Alice tremendously but my feelings did fall into place. I really did work in a dress shop before Earle got me a job in the *Fischer Company.* Everything was okay, until I got ambitious.

"Dad Fischer was the president of the company. God bless his soul, I loved him like the father I never had. Bill had just graduated from college but before he could join the company he was swallowed up in the war." Julie paused to smile. "The Second World War, that is.

To you, it must seem like ancient history but it wasn't that many years ago. God, whoever would have thought we'd have that damn conflict in Korea and now maybe in Vietnam.

"Anyway, I decided I wanted to do more than be in the typing pool in the Sales Department. Dad's secretary was leaving to be married so I asked him for the position. I had taken shorthand and typing in high school and a business course in the evenings. Of course I hoped as the father's secretary I would see more of the son. It was a known fact Bill was going to eventually take over. He showed up in between semesters and when he was on leave, sort of learning the ropes. I was included in meetings and discussions between Dad and Bill. I was even invited to their house for dinner."

I knew Bill did date one particular girl in the office but generally speaking, he didn't pay much attention to the females as much as he did to his father. I'm sure he knew he had a fan club. He was charming, handsome, irresistible and the girls in the office did all kinds of dumb things to attract his attention."

Julie's laugh sounded like a giddy girlish giggle. "He did pay attention to me. Because I was Vicki Lynn's sister. You have my permission to laugh. He was one of her biggest fans. Vicki never visited Earle or me and I decided she was not going to!

"When Bill went into the Navy, Dad Fischer was very upset. He thought he could keep Bill out of the war since the company had so many government contracts. Dad's anxiety was to my advantage because he leaned on me. Business picked up. We all worked overtime. Then Dad's heart began to give him problems. He grew old overnight. We became very close. I know I'm bragging,"

Julie paused to smile, "and I am, because I developed a completely new personality. Earle and Alice told me how different I was. I became poised, assertive, confident. I could talk company business with anybody." She watched Beth continue to rock. Waiting for her to continue.

"It was in the end of 1942, we received a telegram that Bill had been wounded. Dad Fischer had a heart attack. In the office. What a day that was. The father in the hospital and trying to get more details about the son. Uncle Sam decided that since Dad was not going to be able to run the company and Bill had come to the aid of his country, they would release him from active duty. Dad did come around but his doctor said he should be spared any excitement and aggravation.

"I told you Bill paid attention to me because I was Vicki's sister. But when he arrived to manage the company I was the one who helped him because of the boom in business. He still mentioned Vicki. I believe she may have had her third or fourth novel published and Bill was trying to read it between meetings and the hectic pace.

"In case you didn't know, Bill had to use crutches for many months, because his right leg was badly mangled and had plates and pins in it and caused him to limp. His slow recovery was to my advantage. I was able to say 'Now just take it easy.' Or 'You shouldn't be walking around so much.' or 'Why don't you rest and prop up that leg.'"

She paused and raised her eyebrows. "I wish I could have just one drink."

"We should go to bed. Why don't you finish the story tomorrow?"

"No. I have to tell you. Now."

"Then let me get you a tranquilizer and some milk. Or, I'll make you some tea."

"Just one of those hateful pills and a small glass of milk."

BETH had to talk herself out of taking one of the hateful pills. She had to remain calm while Julie rambled. There might be a big climax. Giving Julie the glass and pill, Beth decided to say, "I think I know how you convinced Mr. Fischer to marry you. While he was most vulnerable you convinced him he needed you to help manage the company."

Julie handed Beth the glass. "He *did* need me. Physically, he had been weakened and emotionally he was exhausted. The experience in the Pacific influenced him greatly. He talked about his friends who had been killed, when their ship was torpedoed. He was upset about his father's health. They had only each other. There were a few aunts and cousins but Mrs. Fischer had died during childbirth and the baby girl died a few days later.

"The company was Dad's lifeblood and Bill was determined to live up to his father's expectations. And the volume of business was becoming unreal." Julie nodded and smiled. "I began to read books about etiquette and how to be an executive's wife. You've heard about the wiles of a woman? I could have won first prize. Bill began to take me to social affairs. I met the Barnes and the Livingstons and the Flecks and other elite of the County. Even biggies from Washington,

D.C. I convinced him I could be a helpmate. *And* I let him know I loved him."

"Oh?" Beth blurted out. "You actually told him?"

"We began to embrace and kiss in the office. At first I suspected his kisses were signs of gratitude. But I knew when the tenderness was replaced by passion and one night after everyone had gone home, in his office on the leather couch…" Julie lowered her head and stared at her shoes. Finally, she lifted her head, tears dripping off her chin. "It seems as though it could have been last week."

She took a box of tissues from Beth and continued. "I made sure we went all the way. I worried he might put our relationship in its proper perspective and realize I was pushing him. But after that night, I knew I had to have Bill Fischer for my husband. A couple of weeks later, I told him I was pregnant." She saw the truth in Beth's eyes. "He could have insisted I see a doctor but being a man of honor, he said we should be married. A.s.a.p. That's why we did not make our wedding a big social event. For everyone to remember the date."

"Did he ever learn the truth?"

"I always suspected he knew I lied. A few months later I told him I had a miscarriage. But we'd try again. My number one priority was to keep him happy in bed."

Beth had to ask, "So? What kind of a marriage was it?"

"A short one. Bill bought me Deer Lake Manor for a wedding present. Or so the story goes, but I knew he had wanted to buy it before we were married. We settled in and began to entertain.

"Then I received a note from Vicki explaining she was scheduled for some interviews and book signings on the east coast and she wanted to make plans to finally meet our spouses. Earle was not as upset as I was. I was furious. No, I was frightened out of my mind. Here I was with a shaky marriage to a man who had always wanted to meet my sister and oh hell, I wanted to believe if I had had just another year with a baby in my arms, I would have been able to keep him. I even tried to finagle a business trip. To Mexico. To Europe.

"Bill wouldn't even discuss such an idea. He was thrilled he finally was going to meet Vicki. And he decided she must stay at our house! I didn't know how hard they fell for each other but anybody can tell from the letters and poems. I thought I had been clever in getting him to marry me, but he was far smarter than I. Finally, they told me. Vicki told me first. I keep calling her a bitch and I keep referring to Bill as a . . . a culprit, but . . . " she blew her nose and managed to continue. "I was the bitch. 'Julie,' she said. 'I wish with all my heart I didn't have to tell you, but I'm in love with Bill.' "

"And . . . what did you say?" Beth whispered.

"I didn't *say* anything. I yelled everything. I called her every name in the book. I ranted and I raved. She took all the blame. She said she was everything I called her. All she would say in her defense was she loved him. I called the office and demanded Bill come home. That was the first of our big three meetings." Julie blotted her cheeks. "I'll never forget our last one."

"What did Mr. Fischer say?"

"He took all of the blame. He had admired her for her writing. Then after he met her she was the woman he had dreamed of meeting. He never indicated I had tricked him. He was very kind."

After Beth asked her if he had asked for a divorce she added, "I think he assumed I would suggest we should get one. But, I didn't. I stopped working at the company and I began to drink. I didn't wait for cocktail time. Sometimes I had a Manhattan before lunch, with lunch . . . and the rest of the day. At least, I had one friend. Alcohol.

"Of course, my world began to tumble down around me. But the alcohol turned me into a fighter. A dirty one. I've told you how much Dad Fischer meant to me. Even though I loved him, I threatened to tell him. I threatened to cause as big a scandal as possible and drag the divorce through the mud. I was going to make their affair sound as awful as I could. God, I wish I could have a drink." She watched Beth shake her head and then whispered, "I even threatened to kill myself. Bill decided to back off. Because of Dad.

"So, during the lull in the storm, I begged and pleaded for him to stay with me. I can't imagine how many times I cried *I love you.* Of course if I had really loved him I would have let him go. If I had been rational I would have realized the only thing I would be losing would be his physical presence, although when he did come to the house he slept in another bedroom."

She wiped her cheeks and blew her nose. "One day after months of just existing, I made a decision. I finally decided to give him a divorce. I was going to ask for a large amount of money and Deer Lake Manor. Plus, some of the company. Maybe I could buy my way into another man's life?

"The *love nest* was originally built to be a hunting lodge. After we bought the estate, Bill had it enlarged and let friends use it during deer season. We had to keep our deer population under control. He also had week-end poker parties. It was well hidden in the woods and only those who were invited knew of its existence. And our caretaker and his family. At first, I liked the idea for Vicki to use it. Ha! After I discovered many of Bill's meetings were no more than excuses to be with Vicki, in my own back yard, I threatened to . . . burn it. But I realized even if I did, I never could separate them.

"Earle had confronted me before I married Bill that he saw through my plan. He even told me I was more wicked than Vicki ever was. He called me . . . a Jezebel. With all of his religion that was the strongest word he could use. After Earle and Alice learned about the affair I begged for their sympathy. And even though they did not believe in divorce, they advised me to end my false marriage.

"I wrote my terms and decided to walk to the lodge. Since I rarely got dressed I was in my nightgown and bathrobe. I walked out of the mud room to the cabin. And let me add I was cold sober.

"I was glad I had put on a coat over my robe because the crisp evening air was invigorating. I remember walking to a window and watching them while they talked and drank their cocktails. Vicki began drinking after she became a celebrity. With agents and publishers and the fast set. And Bill had begun to use alcohol as a crutch. Neither of them had reached the stage I had. I enjoyed spying on them. Envying them like hell. Finally I knocked on the door."

Beth leaned forward in the rocking chair. "You know I don't have to hear this story."

"Yes you do." Julie said sharply. "I have to tell someone. And I decided it has to be you. Bill answered the door. I told him I wanted him to go back to the big house for him to read some papers my attorney had prepared.

"He agreed after he got an afghan to wrap around Vicki because it was cool in the lodge and she had not been feeling well. In fact I even thought about telling her to take care of herself, but I didn't. He told Vicki as soon as he returned he would build a fire. Since it was cold outside I began to hurry. She must have decided to make a fire. The noise from the explosion was awful."

Beth stopped rocking and leaned toward Julie. "And the fire marshal or whoever investigated the fire decided it was because of a leak in a gas line which led into a heater in the . . . lodge?"

"That's what was decided. Bill ran back to the lodge. I ran after him. Al was running from their house and later testified he saw Bill and me running from the house *to* the lodge."

"And my daddy told me the caretaker said that Mr. Fisher could not rescue her."

Julie closed her eyes and whispered, "He tried. His clothes were smoldering when he collapsed on the ground. I wrapped him in the coat. And held him in my arms."

She stared into Beth's eyes. I told him "*I will always love you.*"

Before he died."

THIRTY TWO

RICHARD LIVINGSTON met Elmer Hoxie for lunch on Tuesday. Elmer was one of the partners of *Hoxie, Parry and Lacey, Investment Management* and Research Company.

Even though Elmer had been Richard's Financial Advisor and Stock Broker for several years, they had never become more than business acquaintances. After Rodden's estate had been settled, Richard had convinced Bernice that Brad's share of the inheritance should be invested in annuities. Bernice had been too distraught over the death of her beloved father, to disagree. After David Friedman, the successful Jewish jeweler, had shared the name of his stockbroker, Richard took Ray's inheritance and dealt with Elmer Hoxie. Upon their initial meeting, neither was impressed with the other. Richard had always been annoyed with men who allowed themselves to become overweight. And smoked cigars. Also Elmer had the distracting habit of pushing up his glasses.

Driving to the meeting Richard felt upbeat. His friendship with Henry Oehrle was developing favorably. In fact during lunch at the Club, Hank had slipped him some inside information about the Fischer Company. Julie Fischer was going to go public! She was going to sell shares in the company.

Richard shook hands with Elmer and asked the host they be seated in a corner booth. They ordered their first drink and broke the ice discussing unimportant current events.

After they ordered their second drink Richard decided to ask, "I guess you're wondering why I want to meet with you?"

Elmer smiled. "I was hoping it's because you have some money that's burning a hole in your check book."

"That's pretty close. Only this time I'm going to tell you what I want you to buy. As soon as it's on the market."

Elmer removed a small notebook and pen from the inside pocket of his sport's jacket. "I'm ready."

"The *Fischer Company.*"

Elmer raised his eyebrows. He studied Richard's face for a few seconds and then remarked, "Been hearing some local scuttlebutt, huh?"

Richard took a sip and nodded, "The word is out that Julie Fischer is going to go public. To pay for expansion."

"How much do you want to invest?"

Richard pushed up his glasses. "Well . . . as custodian of my son's inheritance I want to transfer it to Fischer stock. And all of what I have."

"Hmmmm. Must have been a good piece of scuttlebutt."

"I'd like to use a street name."

Elmer smiled at Richard before he asked, "Want to give me a name?"

"Ahhh. How about Henry Jones?"

Elmer hastily scribbled a few more words, looked up and frowned. "Have I heard correctly that they're looking for a Vice President of Finance? Last one left the scene."

"I heard that too. My source of information said they are down to two impressive candidates. Should know by the end of this week." Wasn't he lucky he knew Hank Oerhle?

Suddenly, he wished they could skip the lunch. He had a strong desire to leave Elmer Hoxie. And return to the safety of his office.

Elmer nodded. "Those government contracts come in handy."

"Yep and the way this damn mess in Vietnam is going, who knows how many more they'll get?" Suddenly Richard thought of Brad being drafted and felt a nervous shiver inside.

"Of course, Mrs. Fischer will own the controlling stock and majority voting interest?"

Richard nodded. "Sounds logical."

"Damn shame about the way her husband and sister died."

Richard managed to look forlorn. "Those of us who knew them couldn't believe it. It took my wife and me a long time to get over it." Richard drained his glass, ate the olive and said, "Send the statements and keep in touch with me, at my office."

AS soon as Beth arrived in Bridgeboro High School on Tuesday morning, she hurried to a pay phone. After eight rings she became worried before she heard Doc's voice.

"Doc Rexinger here."

"It's Beth Rhodes. I'm calling from school."

"Damn. What the hell has happened now?"

"Not to worry. I just don't want Julie to know I'm calling you. She and I had a long talk last night. About the fire. And she may be upset today."

"Why in the hell did you let her talk about such a dangerous subject?"

"I couldn't stop her. I got her to take two tranquilizers and she was still sleeping when I left. But I am kind of worried."

"Okay. Okay. I'll go down and check on her."

"I'm sorry. I really tried to convince her not to tell me the story. But she said she had to tell someone."

"I'm glad you called. She sure seemed happy during Sunday dinner. Talking about Deer Lake Manor and your upcoming trip."

"Remember you're supposed to take us uptown to pick up her new car this afternoon. She even wants to walk around Bridgeboro and . . . "

"I'll make sure she's okay. Thanks for calling me."

Beth turned away from the phone and looked right at Jim Bender.

As their eyes met Jim smiled and said, "Hi."

"Hi, Jim", Beth responded. Was she feeling tingles inside? She watched him walk away. She noticed the blue shirt looked great with his khakis and loafers. She caught herself thinking, *You virile villain. I wonder what it's like . . . doing it with you? Peg! Is Alan home yet?*

Beth hurried to her locker before the second bell rang. Since there was no note from Brad she assumed he had rejected her offer to talk. Okay, so she'd avoid looking at him.

By the time the last bell rang, ending another day of lectures and assignments, Beth felt like screaming. She wished she could get on a smelly and noisy bus, hide in the back seat and . . . never get off. Then she remembered the new car. That was going to be fun. Wasn't it? Driving Julie wherever she wanted to go. Yeah, but didn't she hate Julie? For what she had done to Vicki and Bill? Or because she did not want to be burdened with Julie's nightmarish story?

BETH decided to call Geoff Greer before she went to Julie's house. She had an urge to talk to him. He had a way of making her feel better. And with no note from Brad maybe she would tell him she missed seeing him on Sunday. Maybe he could meet them uptown?

As Beth searched for change a male voice said, "Hi," behind her. She kept a serious look on her face before she turned.

"Are you back at Julie's?" Brad watched her nod. "I've tried and tried to get you at home. Even before I got your note."

"I did sit for Peg. Then I stayed at Julie's. Tonight we're going to get her new car."

"Julie's going uptown? That'll stir up the troops."

"You can even tell your parents I'm going to live with her."

"The hell with my parents. *I* want to know where you'll be."

"I'm going to be her personal secretary. And traveling companion."

"How about your essay?"

"Almost finished. I'm going to wrap it up this week-end."

"And college? Just in case you don't win?"

"I can borrow money from Julie."

Brad smiled. "When can I call you?"

Beth frowned. "I'm planning to go home tomorrow night. To finish typing the essay."

"Good. My folks have a dinner meeting so we can have a good catch up talk." Brad looked around the hall. "Does your note mean just on the telephone, or going out?"

"Sunday afternoon?" Beth heard herself whisper.

"It's a date. We'll firm it up tomorrow night. Beth. You're the only person I love."

Beth nodded. "I hear voices. See you." And Brad hurried away from her.

DOC drove Julie and Beth to the car agency. After Julie announced she wanted to do some shops he laughed and left them.

Many salespeople who remembered Mrs. William Fischer complimented her regarding her offering the farm for a County Park. Mr. Reig, owner of the *Five and Ten Cent Variety Store*, declared, "We sure can use another park. There just isn't enough public land available. And the way people are selling their farms, it's bound to get worse trying to find some breathing room. Even for a picnic."

Mrs. Fleck remarked, after Julie had purchased two blouses in her dress shop, "Mighty nice of you to buy that farm, Julie. Somebody has to care enough to save the farms and old houses."

Beth was enjoying the attention. She would be remembered for being with Julie. They decided to have dinner in a new restaurant next to the movie theater. After they were seated the owner walked to their table and said, "Pardon me, but one of the waitresses informed me you're Mrs. Fischer. I want you to know how pleased I am for you to be here."

Julie put down her menu and extended her right hand. Beth had made a mental note that it was Julie's practice to shake hands with everybody. She hoped someday she would be important enough to have people want to shake hands with her. Beth also noticed that again Julie was wearing three rings, on the third finger of her left hand. A plain gold band, a gold band of sparkling diamonds and the attention getter was the solitaire diamond. When Beth had complimented Julie about the rings, she laughed. "I might as well play the part of the rich widow. The plain gold one is my original wedding ring. Then Bill surprised me with the diamond band and on our first anniversary he gave me the solitaire."

BETH had to believe the most exciting event happened after they had made a purchase in *The Squire Shoppe*. Beth had asked Julie if they could make a stop because she decided to buy Geoff a tie. She took her time, wandering around and looking where the briefs were sold. She longed to buy something for Brad. She could pretend it was a gift for Danny Friedman.

As they paused in front of the Fire House, to discuss what they should do next, Beth saw Richard Livingston's car approach them. She decided not to tell Julie but Julie did notice the car had obviously slowed down, as it was passing them. Julie leaned down and looked directly into the front window. She smiled and waved and Beth was certain she saw Mr. Livingston's mouth drop open as he drove past them.

"Well," Julie exclaimed, as though she was upset. "He never even waved back."

"I'll bet he'll have lots to say when he gets home." She joined Julie in laughing.

"I'm having so much fun. Being in my rightful place. It's great to be Mrs. William Fischer again."

THE following day Beth sneaked a note to Brad in Typing Class. She was not returning to Taylor Park that night. Her common sense told her to stay with Julie another night. She also wanted to copy more from **Vicki's Vignettes.** She explained to Brad she would be at the Bus

Stop in front of the Naval Air Station at two P.M. on Sunday afternoon. He pouted, then winked and gave a nod of agreement.

Saturday afternoon Beth returned to Taylor Park. After she knew Liz would be at work. She told Julie she still had more typing to do. The essay was to be delivered to the home of the President of the Women's Club on Monday afternoon. Julie accepted her reason that she wanted to use her own typewriter and pack a few more clothes. And since Liz said she didn't have to write notes, Beth did not inform her she was in the house. Saturday evening Geoff surprised her with a phone call. He wanted to know how she was doing. With Julie. And with her essay. As they talked she played reruns of being in his bed and the unforgettable day in New York. He made her feel mature and special. If Brad ever saw them together she would tell him she and Geoff were just good friends who reminisced about growing up in Taylor Park.

Why did she have to be so lucky to be mixed up?

Couldn't she love both of them?

SUNDAY morning Millie and Di Mawhorter made so much noise in their bedroom they awakened Beth. She looked at her clock and felt anger. Where was Peg?

Beth yawned and rolled over, hoping to go back to sleep. She was tired. It had been a busy week. Even emotional. Geoff's phone call and another date with Brad. If he asked her where she wanted to go would she dare say the farm? Because she wanted to go all the way? Did he have any condoms? Why did she have so many decisions to ponder? What she better do was to get her ass out of bed. She still had the entire essay to proof.

Suddenly penetrating her daydreaming, Beth heard one of the girls exclaim, "Daddy. Watch what I can do." Beth strained to hear Alan's voice. She did catch a few words before it became quiet so Beth guessed Alan had taken the girls out of the room.

She thought about knocking on the wall and yelling, "It's too late, Alan. I'm already awake." Or, "Hi, Alan," but that could disturb Liz. Unless Liz had stayed at Lou's. She thought of Liz and Lou in bed together. Did she let her hair get mused? Did she scratch him with her manicured nails?

On her way to the bathroom she noticed Liz's bedroom door was open. She must be at Lou's. Sex did make some people bolder. Good, they would not have to have a mother-daughter conversation.

ALAN Mawhorter and Beth greeted each other after Peg invited her for brunch. So she could tell Alan "all about" getting to know Julie Fischer.

Alan was pounds heavier. "I almost flipped when Peggy told me you were going to Julie's house. Of course I'm pleased. Not only for you because what a great break, but for the sake of the company." Alan sipped his coffee. "Does she ever mention the company to you?"

"Of course. She's proud of it. And it has grown even since Bill, Mr Fischer, died."

Alan smiled. "Bill, huh? Well, I give kudos to Earle Phipps and Howard Whiteside for the success of the company." Alan shook his head. "And now, Howard had his hands tied so that all he can do is watch and wait, until he has to clean up another blunder. As he always does, after the new men screw it up."

"Do you know Howard?" Beth asked, watching Alan take another helping of pancakes.

"I sure do. He and I started about the same time. I was in Accounting and he was in the Engineering Department. He was a real asset and Phipps was wise enough to recognize his potential. Within two years he made Howard head of the Engineering Department. Then about a year before Phipps died, he had Howard on the Executive Committee and made up the position of Assistant to the Executive Vice President. Phipps must have told Julie if anything happened to him Howard should be promoted to Executive Vice President, immediately."

"And then Earle did die . . . about two years ago?" Beth asked before she accepted another pancake.

"Right. And diluting Howard's authority is the biggest mistake she's made."

Beth shrugged as her mind was racing. "Because she needs money for expansion and she grew impatient with Mr. Whiteside's searching for the best way to go. So she decided to bring in somebody who would move faster."

"The word is she's agreed to a stock issue. As soon as the new Assistant to the Executive Vice President and another Treasurer get settled in, they'll get the show on the road with the Securities and Exchange Commission. Maybe you could slip her an idea?"

Beth could not keep a grin off her face. How about the County Park? How about Julie confiding to her about the explosion? How about Julie sharing the love letters with her? How about their moving to Deer Lake Manor as soon as it was refurbished? She just asked, "Such as?"

"She has to let Howard have the punch that goes with his title."

"How about the new assistant?"

"What's bad is that he's new. It's difficult to explain, especially since you've never worked for a family oriented company, but the *Fischer Company* is . . . well, it's unique. It runs on its own business philosophy and principals. You know we have our own Union which is unusual. And our own Credit Union. Bill Fischer was shrewd when it came to . . . well, he established certain procedures that would be unusual, even extreme, to someone on the outside looking in, but if they were changed it could put us months behind. Especially in Sales and Production."

"Did you know Mr. Fischer?"

"I missed meeting him. I've been with the company only five years. Five exciting and nerve wracking years. Exciting for me and nerve wracking for Peg." Alan smiled at his wife and patted her shoulder. "Especially since I've been doing my road show. Right, honey?"

Beth watched Peg return Alan's smile. "You know what Alan asked me last night? If I'd move to Europe?" I'm still in shock. And I've even picked out a house I like in Southampton Manor but . . . "

"But now," Alan butted in. "We might move to Amsterdam."

"To the Netherlands!" Beth declared. "Julie likes that company best in Europe."

"Listen to her," Alan said. "You're the first person who hasn't said Holland."

"It's only because I had a good Social Science teacher. When will you move?"

"Can't plan yet. Right now we're having problems in our EED."

"Serious problems?" Beth asked.

Peg snickered. "Do you know what he's talking about?"

"European Export Division," Beth replied.

"Me thinks you know more about the *Fischer Company* than you're letting on."

"I've read some company catalogues and I did learn the names of the presidents or managers of the plants in Europe and England. So I know who Julie is talking about."

"That's smart of you. That's more than Peg has bothered to do."

Before Peg could respond to her husband's complaint, Beth spoke up. "Julie and I are planning to visit some of the European companies."

"That's good. For you and that Julie is making a comeback. I sure hope she sees that something has to be done between the France and Germany companies and . . . " he paused as Beth began laughing.

"What is funny?"

"You. You're such a company man."

"He's hopeless," Peg said strongly. "He eats and sleeps the company."

"I'm going to tell Julie she has a guy working for her that is so loyal and dedicated that . . . it's *over* kill."

Beth pushed back her chair. "Julie is going to take a tour of the company next week. And she wants me with her. In what department should I look for you?"

"In the Accounting Department. A few kinks have developed since I've been traveling. The controller asked me to help them get back on track."

Beth stood. She decided to thank Peg for the brunch and get going. She didn't want to be late for her date with Brad.

THIRTY THREE

SUNDAY AFTERNOON WAS picture perfect. Beth decided to walk the eight blocks to the bus stop in front of the *Johnsville Naval Air Station*. Where she would meet Brad.

She had been waiting only five minutes when Brad arrived. Before he shifted into first gear he gave Beth a quick cheek kiss. "I love you."

Beth smiled a happy smile. "Ditto. Let's move it out so nobody sees us."

"To the farm? We might as well use it before it gets turned into a County Park." Brad squeezed her knee. "It was your idea, wasn't it?"

Beth squeezed Brad's knee. "I only made a suggestion."

"Just to save that special tree. And our barn. I gave an Academy Award performance as Dad read her letter to Mom and me." He took Beth's hand and kissed the palm. "You and Julie sure are hitting it off."

Beth coiled. Why did she feel tense? "Yep. And she's very good to me."

"Well, when you get right down to it you've been pretty good to her too."

"We need each other," Beth whispered.

"Hey, don't forget I need you too. I was about to freak out until I got your note. I prayed like hell you'd forgive me. And you know I don't even believe in prayer."

She laughed with Brad. "I had to be with you again. I had to be sure."

"Sure? Like you still need me even though you have Geoff in your

life now?"

"I've been waiting for you to mention him."

"Well. You two *are* getting rather chummy."

"I need him in my life right now. He helps me when I get upset with Julie." After Brad asked, "That's all?" she added, "He'll always be a good friend."

"You . . . haven't told him about us, have you?"

"Hell, no! Have you told Jeanne?"

"*Touché*. I still wish we could tell somebody. I still don't know when I can break off with her. I guess you couldn't tell Julie?"

"Julie! You are kidding, aren't you?"

"Like father like son, huh? And now you're helping her. I hope it never gets to be you and Julie on one side and the Livingston's on the other." Brad kissed her hand again. "Sometimes I get a strong feeling you sort of cringe whenever I mention my parents."

"I don't even know them except it's obvious they're ambitious. If I ever have to meet them I'm going to be scared to death. Especially of your father."

"Because Julie told you how awful he is?" Brad drove into the long lane to the farm.

"Right now because he's one of the judges for the contest."

Brad drove around a thick clump of forsythia bushes, bursting into a cascade of brilliant yellow. "I'm going to park behind the barn." After he turned off the ignition he leaned across the stick shift and gave Beth a long deep kiss. "Do you have to hurry back?"

"Nope. This morning Liz and I said hello and goodbye to each other and I just want to reread my essay one more time. Before I give it a good luck kiss and tuck it into the manila envelope. Tomorrow afternoon it gets delivered to Mrs. Fetzer."

Brad kissed Beth again. "And I'll be rooting for you. Now let's decide what to inspect. So you can make a personal report to the County Park Department."

He laughed and raised his eyebrows at Beth, "They may be interested in your opinion of the barn."

Beth decided she had to make her announcement. "Brad, you know how much I love you. And I know that many of our friends are going all the way, but I . . . I want to wait. I guess what I'm trying to say is, if going in the barn is going to . . . "

Brad pulled Beth into his arms and put a hand over her mouth. "Hey babe. You mean too much to me to louse up our relationship," he paused to laugh. "I was going to say, screw up our relationship. Let's sit on the back porch."

Beth gave Brad a long, open mouth kiss. "I don't know how I can love you anymore. I wish I could tell Jill." She quickly thought, *And tell you about Jim Bender.* "Are your parents having dinner at the Club? With the Barnes?"

"No. The Barnes are pissed at the Livingston's because Julie squashed Mr. B's big plans for an Industrial Park here."

"Too bad. He shouldn't have criticized Julie. Publicly ."

"Believe it or not, my dad did try to discourage Mr. B. But he was mad."

Beth wished she could share the joke with Julie. "How about Jeanne?"

"She's been kinda cool the last couple of weeks." Brad paused to snicker. "Okay, so she wasn't the night of her party. I don't know who to tell first. Jeanne? Or my folks?"

Beth thought fast. If Brad were the first to break up the relationship then he would have to take the blame. Since Jeanne had told her girlfriends she was going to break off with Brad why not let Jeanne take the blame? She could even tell him about Jim. "Don't tell anybody."

She put her fingers over Brad's mouth. "It's female intuition. If I'm lucky enough to be in college, then in August we can make calls and maybe sneak visits. Like your dorm or mine? Let's just play it cool . . . and walk to that little bridge we saw last time we were here."

Holding hands they ambled to a one lane wooden bridge built for farm machinery to be driven across gurgling Poquessing Creek. They sat on the bridge and dangled their legs over the side.

"Don't you want to take to take off your shoes and socks and put your feet in. And splash?" Beth laughed.

"It'll be damn cold." Brad moved closer to her.

"Okay, wimp. Haven't you ever had cold feet before?"

"Oh, what a lead in. If you tell Julie . . . I'll tell my folks."

"No way. I don't want to miss out living in Deer Lake Manor."

"You'll be having so much fun you won't want to go to college."

"Then my daddy will haunt me."

"How do you feel about your essay? After all, we writers," Brad paused to clear his throat, "can sort of tell if something is just good, or great."

Beth sighed. "On a scale of one to ten I guess it might be an eight. I know I could have done better. But Julie gave me so much to sort out, I ran out of time."

"Well, let's sin-cere-ly pray the judges vote it's the winner."

"I might give praying another try. I used to. But my father still died."

Brad kissed her long but tenderly. "I know you still miss him but my prayers were answered. You know, you're the most important person in my entire life."

"As much as I love to hear you tell me that, you have a mother and father who love you."

"As long as I perform and please them. I have a lot to live up to. And sometimes it ain't easy. Oh yeah, my mom tells me how great I am. And handsome." Brad paused and waited.

"And humble," Beth whispered. "Bradford Livingston, you are the most handsome, personable, sexy male I know. That okay? For your ego?"

"For the time being." He gently pushed her down to lie on the rough boards and leaned over her. He slid a hand under her sweater and cupped a breast. Next he put his tongue inside of Beth's mouth and slid it in and out.

Beth held Brad's face in her hands and stared into his eyes. Slowly she pushed his face away from hers and smiled. "And you're a great kisser."

Brad took one of Beth's hands and slid it down to his fly. "Guess who's with us?"

"Did you invite him?"

"He knows I have a condom hiding in my wallet."

"I . . . I never saw one," Beth whispered.

Brad rolled away from Beth and pulled out his wallet. "And I was even going to let you put it on him."

"Instead of using a handkerchief?"

"You mean . . . you'll do it again?"

Beth peered into Brad's eyes. "I know it makes you feel good."

"How about you? Do you know how to . . . feel good?"

She put her face into his shoulder. "I did it to myself."

"Don't be embarrassed. Only liars say they've never done it . . . alone. But no one else has done anything to you?"

"Never." She knew he wanted to be the first one. What was she going to do? She thought, then decided. Slowly she took one of his hands and guided it up her inner thigh. "I want you to be the first one. Just to touch me." She tried to relax as his hand went between her thighs. "Just on the outside. I want to stay a virgin."

"It's okay with me. Because I'm going to be the guy who marries you." He began to feel her sensitive area. "Beth. Just relax. This is just between you and me."

She closed her eyes as she began to feel sharp tingling jolts spreading throughout her groin. She was aware she was beginning to move in time with Brad's hand. Finally she felt an electrifying sensation travel throughout her body. She opened her eyes and looked into his. "Now I love you even more."

"And now, I think it's my turn."

She sat up and leaned against a large beam. She unzipped Brad's slacks. "And this time we're going to let the sperm . . . drown. As the condom floats down the stream."

Feeling smug, they both laughed.

THIRTY FOUR

EASTER SUNDAY WAS one of the nastiest Easters anyone could remember. Besides being cold and windy, the rain was beyond a downpour. It was a deluge causing the Neshaminy Creek to overflow its banks and many roads to become flooded.

As soon as Bernice Livingston looked out the bedroom window she began to cry.

"Now what's wrong?" Richard asked, covers to his chin as he remained in his twin bed.

"It's pouring. My new clothes are going to get soaked."

"Wear old clothes."

"Don't be ridiculous. I bought that new hat to go with my suit and I'm going to wear it *today*. My raincoat should cover my suit and you can hold the umbrella over my head."

Richard yawned. "Probably would be a smart idea to watch a church service on television but I have to go to the nine thirty service anyway. You'll have to ask Brad to carry the umbrella. It's my turn to take collection. And count it."

One of his duties as a Vestryman for *The Church of The Big Fisherman* was to take turns with eleven other men on the Vestry, every third Sunday. Easter Sunday was his day.

FIVE hours later, Richard bade farewell to the other Vestrymen who had counted the large collection with him. Richard picked up his raincoat and hat to leave the church office when he realized he did not want to go home.

Lately he had the desire to stay away as long as possible. He knew the house would be filled with the delicious smell of the ham Bernice had started to bake before they left for church. He knew he was proud and pleased with his show place house, inside and outside but he couldn't think when he was home. Bernice was always finding him. To talk. No, that was not the truth. He really was having problems thinking anywhere. His mind had become cluttered with too many concerns. Concerns that blocked his thinking in a constructive and ingenious manner.

Richard was amazed he wandered into the sanctuary. He actually felt sacrilegious as he sat in the last pew of the beautiful holy place, filled with the overpowering scent of the many lily plants. Would he dare to contemplate his hatred for a woman named Julie Fischer. And curse at his dependency on the friendship of Charles Barnes? And confess how much he disliked Bernice? Weren't churches a haven of tranquility for troubled people? Why couldn't he swear at himself for letting Bernice upset him when she began her bitching about their social life?

The Saturday before Palm Sunday she became furious when she heard the Barnes were having another party. And they had not been invited. This would be the second time since the park episode. Richard tried to calm her by reminding her the two couples had not always been together since they had met. And besides that they had gone to the Club with the Ohrele's and the Friedman's without including Lou and Charlie.

"Because of you," Bernice snapped back. "I wanted you to include Lou and Charles. Then they would have invited us to their house. It's just going to get worse, until we won't even be speaking to each other. And what's it going to be like at club and committee meetings? Lou and I not speaking. And everybody wondering why? People will start taking sides. I can't possibly live where I don't feel comfortable. I was raised in a friendly community where everybody knew and respected my family. If I'm going to have enemies in Bridgeboro, then we'll just have to move."

AS Richard sat in the last pew, he let his thoughts wander to the Thursday before Good Friday. Henry Oehrle called to inform him he had met Julie Fischer. He sounded pleased. Beth Rhodes, introduced as Julie's companion and Howard's prim and proper secretary, had made the arrangements for the tour and dinner meeting with the Executive Committee. Hank said it was obvious Julie Fischer still ran the show.

"What was her reason for the meeting?"

"To meet those of us she didn't know. And to update herself. Of course, the idea of researching a computer system and budgeting were a big topic. And we did discuss the need for more office space - and some things the company lawyer thought we should review."

"Harold Gillon?"

"Geoff Greer. A good looking young man. And quite impressive."

"And the Rhodes girl attended the meeting also?"

"Yes. I've heard she's always with Mrs. Fischer."

Richard could not refrain from asking, "How did Julie come across?"

"I was impressed. I don't know what I really expected but she's a classy lady. And very knowledgeable about little details. Of course, her concern for the continued success of the company is quite apparent. She's very proud of it and besides her late brother, Earle Phipps, she gives Howard Whiteside much of the credit for its continued success."

Richard's anxiety begin to cause mild palpitations of his heart. He also felt a dull ache in his stomach. Damn, not another ulcer. "Did it sound as though she's going to stay involved?   Or do you think this was just a . . ."

"Howard knows her better than I do but I have to believe she plans on keeping updated. Audrey is hoping she can meet her. She wants me to ask Howard if we would be too presumptuous to invite her to a cocktail party or a sit down dinner. Oh. Sorry. I have another call. Goodbye."

ON Good Friday Bernice had almost crucified Richard.. He told her he wanted to plan a party.

Bernice stared at Richard in disbelief. "And you're inviting Lou and Charles?

"I have to make amends with Charles. He's too big of a voice in Bridgeboro for us not to be friends."

"You *are* kidding! Don't you remember they didn't invite us last Saturday?"

"I'm taking your advice. You said I should bury the hatchet."

"You need Charlie's ads. And listings. And the support from all the other business owners in town."

"There's more to it than the newspaper. You want to feel comfortable living here. And you know damn well I'm not moving away from Bridgeboro. So, I'm offering an alternative. Swallow your damn pride and . . . "

"*My* pride!"

"Yes. *Your* pride. Try to be humble for a change and start making a guest list. What's one night? Get Ellie and Tony lined up. You told me you liked Hank Oehrle. And you thought Audrey was a class act. Even though she refuses to join any of your clubs."

Bernice gave a big sigh. "Well, I still don't like your idea. And not only that but . . . " Richard held up his hand and was successful in making her pause.

"Keep telling yourself you're doing it because you're a Christian."

AS RICHARD sat in the last pew, he remembered all of those conversations. He made a rerun of his apprehensions. His submissions. He had to keep in touch with Hank. He had to stay updated. He had to dissolve the rift between Charles and himself. Even if he had to kiss ass.

He, Richard Livingston, who was so intelligent. And ambitious. He, who should be more than a glorified printer. It wasn't his fault he had to be humble. Then who was to blame? Julie Fischer was the person who had kept him fearful and mediocre. If only he had not written that letter. If only he could hurt her. He wanted to, had to, do it sooner than by the slow, clever, game of taking over the *Fischer Company*. What could he do? Very soon?

He was preoccupied with unchristian like thoughts so he failed to notice Reverend Fox approaching him. "Dick. I didn't know you still were here. Until I noticed your car in the parking lot. I was going to lock up, until evening."

"I felt like doing some . . . thinking," Richard managed to say.

"And there's no better place. I receive many of my answers in here. Please don't leave. Stay as long as you want to. I'll come back later."

Richard stood and stepped into the aisle. "Thank you. But I better be getting home. Bernice is cooking another delicious dinner for us."

"I do hope you found the comfort and the answers you were seeking."

Richard nodded. "I did. I found just what I was looking for."

ON his way home, Richard stopped at his office to call Chester Jones. He not only was the principal of *Bridgeboro High School* but also one of the judges in the Essay Contest.

SIX days later, on a sunny and - open up and let the fresh air come in the screen door - day, Liz still was sleeping while Beth had positioned the ironing board in the kitchen doorway to face the living room. She wanted to watch a movie on television. The movie was entertaining, she was getting her chores finished and she felt happy.

Until there was a knock on the kitchen door.

She turned toward the door and panicked. Why was Mr. Livingston standing on the other side? Was she really going to have to talk to *him*? Maybe he wanted to see Liz? She stepped to the door. "If you want to see my mother, she's sleeping."

"Beth Rhodes. Right?" He watched her nod. "I thought that was the name Brad said they call you." He smiled. "I want to see you."

As soon as Beth heard the name Brad she felt lightheaded. She knew why Mr. Livingston had come to see her. He knew about their meetings. Worse yet, he had found her notes. She frowned through the screen, at the detestable man.

"If I promise to be quiet may I invite myself in? To discuss something."

Beth unlocked the door and pushed it opened. As Brad's father entered the small kitchen she walked back to the board. "I'm ironing."

"What I have to discuss won't take too long."

She unplugged the iron but decided to let the television on. It could cover up their voices.

She moved a kitchen chair, indicating he could sit. She decided to stand. Maybe she *should* talk loudly to disturb Liz? "What do you want to discuss?"

"Your essay. You know I am one of the judges?" He watched Beth nod. "I read it last night. And I reread it this morning. It's a fine piece of writing."

He looked at the ash tray. "You've used good vocabulary, good coherence and clear and effective language. I also was impressed with your excellent unity. All in all, as a man who has been in the writing business for many years," he paused to force a laugh, "in fact, longer than I want to admit, I would say your essay about Victoria Lynn is a good composition."

Beth stood motionless. "Thank you."

"Of course the other essays are also fine compositions. It's so gratifying to realize we have such talented young people in our town."

As Richard repositioned his long thin legs he allowed his eyes to wander around her tee shirt before he concentrated on the mole on her lip. "I want to discuss a possibility with you. Okay?"

Beth forced a laugh. "Is it some kind of a deal?"

"I consider it as an opportunity for us to take advantage of a mutual understanding." Already his shirt was sticking to his moist body. "Winning the contest could help pay for college. Right?"

How many more times would she have to nod, as if she was agreeing with this hateful man.

"I also have a lot of things that mean much to me. My family and my business are dependent on my financial success. After all, Brad is ready for college, and since his mother and I want only the best for him, an Ivy League University is mighty expensive." Richard cleared his throat and pushed up his glasses. "I do consider myself a successful person in my chosen profession, but there's always room for improvement. I'm in a very competitive field. The delivery service, the impact of the editorials, the layout of the paper, the service or space which one gives to local organizations and the plugs I have to give to schools and businesses are one thing. But the news, the real honest to goodness exclusive coverage means the most. It's just natural for people to be . . . shall we say, snoopy?

"People like to know what's going on in so and so's house more than what is happening in their own. That's why those soap operas are so popular. The bottom line is I can almost guarantee you will win if we have a meeting of the minds. You and I."

"I don't understand what you're talking about."

"I'll help you win the contest and you'll help me give my newspaper a little adrenaline."

Beth wished she could ask Brad's father to leave her house. She did not want to hear any more of their *meeting of the minds.*

"I really believe you haven't included all that you know. About Vicki Lynn." He paused to smile, a wicked smile. "Have you?"

Beth was surprised she able to smile back. Innocently. She shrugged. "Well, there may be a few little things I didn't mention. Some bad habits, idiosyncrasies, but then…" she was able to force a laugh… "she is my idol."

He studied Beth's face to find a clue as to what game she was playing. "I hear you've been living with Julie." Another nod. "I've also heard she's become quite fond of you."

"Mrs. Fischer and I have become friends. If that's what you mean."

"I mean she must have told you *much.* About her sister."

"According to what I've read, I realized some of the information has been mentioned before, but you must admit my essay does include," Beth paused to smile a knowing smile, "what you editors would call *exclusive* information. I'm sure you were as surprised as I was . . . to learn about the unpublished book."

Richard nodded. "I was surprised."

"I was thrilled the day I found it. She was nice enough to let me go through her sister's personal possessions. And then she agreed I could reveal its existence."

"In other words, Julie claims she did not know about the manuscript?"

"She and her brother were very upset when they had to pack up their sister's belongings. So without examining everything they put it all into a bedroom. In Earle's house. And the garage. So I was the one who found it."

"I'm to believe you've included everything Julie told you?"

Beth frowned. "I said I may have left out a few things but . . . "

Richard put up a hand. "Young lady. I am not here to play a guessing game. You know what I'm referring to. The explosion."

"I did mention the ac-c-ident."

"Julie has been trying to fool everybody long enough. There are some of us who just can't swallow her story. Now that she doesn't have Earle to protect her, we can bring the case into the open and . . . "

Beth put her hand up. "I never heard the accident was a case. From what you printed in your newspaper, it was determined there was a leak in the gas heater and Vicki made a fire and . . . it caused an explosion."

"The caretaker saw Julie at the cabin."

"With Mr. Fischer. As soon as they heard the explosion they ran *to* the cabin."

"So you're willing to protect her because she'll send you to college and . . . "

"I'm not protecting her. Mrs. Fischer had *nothing* to do with the explosion. And for your information she is *loaning* me the money. That I might need."

"Well. I have to believe while she had a high fever or was in a drunken stupor, she confided in you. So I'll trade you an education for sharing what she has told you."

Beth walked to the screen door. "Mr. Livingston. It's time for you leave."

Richard stood. "You know if I ever discover there is more to what happened at the cabin, you could be letting yourself in for legal prosecution. Especially if it's discovered you deliberately protected a criminal."

Beth's eyes opened wide. "Mrs. Fischer is not a criminal! And I could tell people you were trying to bribe me. If you don't leave I'm going to call Liz." Beth opened the screen door.

Richard paused on the top step. He had to add one more remark. "Julie Fischer is a wicked woman. It grieves me to think you have allowed her to influence you. Just remember it's me against you and that's not even a fair match."

"It will be after I tell Julie you were here."

THIRTY FIVE

BETH WATCHED RICHARD walk down the street. Inside, she cursed, *Damn! He is clever. He walked from somewhere so no one would see his car on our street.*

She began to tremble. Next she heard a moan followed by a loud guttural sound. A scream began to fill her head, the room, the house, and her world. It was she who was wailing. Because of Mr. Livingston. Because of Julie. Because of Brad. Because of herself.

Liz yelled from the top of the stairs. "Jesus Christ. What's the matter?"

Beth was lamenting because of Liz also.

Liz hurried around the ironing board, into the kitchen. She saw Beth was sitting in a chair with her face in her hands. "What in the hell happened?"

Beth lowered her hands and stared at the woman. After Liz grabbed her shoulders and shook her, she began to rock and whimper.

Liz was wearing only a pink shortie nightgown. And in her bare feet. "For Christ's sake, stop staring at me and say something."

Beth stood. "I wish I could die." She tried to walk past Liz. Her mother was too quick for her. While she was being held in a strong hold, she yelled, "I want to go to my room."

"No way. You're not going anywhere, until you tell me what the hell is . . . " Liz stopped talking after they heard a loud knock on the screen door.

"Yeah, Peg. What do you want?"

"We want to know what happened to Beth."

"Well come on in and she'll tell both of us. Oh no you don't, kiddo." She held tightly to Beth's wrist. "You're going to stay here and tell us what happened."

Beth stared at Peg in the doorway. She had been screaming because of Peg also.

"Alan and I thought maybe you were . . . having a fight."

"I was sound to sleep," Liz said. "Until I heard some god awful screaming. And I never came down those stairs so fast in my life. It's a wonder I didn't . . ." She stopped talking as Alan knocked at the screen door. "Come on in, Alan. I'm really not presentable."

"I just wanted to make sure Beth is okay. We thought maybe she had been . . . hurt."

"Look, all of you," Beth said strongly. "I'm okay. I . . .I just freaked out."

"I know it's none of my business, but we saw Richard Livingston. Leaving your house."

LIZ'S eyes could not open any wider as she exclaimed, "What in the hell was he doing here?" She let go of Beth's arm and sat in a chair. She wanted to put a dish towel in front of her chest but decided Alan did not really care about her breasts.

Beth looked at Alan, then Peg and finally Liz before she almost whispered, "He wanted to tell me he didn't like my essay."

Liz laughed. "That's all he wanted to tell you?"

Beth began to cry. "Is that all? Can't you even imagine how awful that is?"

"Okay. Okay. I know winning means a lot to you but why in the hell did he have to come *here?* Just to tell you that?" She looked at Peg. "Hey, do me a favor and go upstairs and get my robe and cigarettes."

As Peg left the kitchen, Alan saw the roll of paper towels and handed one to Beth. "Wipe your face and try to relax, Beth. We know how disappointed you are. But I agree with Liz. I don't understand why he . . . did he say he's giving all of the contestants a personal report?"

Beth forced herself to cry again. "All I remember is I wanted to scream when he told me I wasn't going to win. But, I waited until after he left."

"Okay. So you got upset." Liz looked at Alan. "Damn. I've wanted to scream dozens of times, haven't you? Oh, thanks Peg," she remarked as she reached for a robe and cigarettes. She found some matches on a counter. After a deep drag she asked Beth, "How about heating some water? You two want some coffee?"

"We can't stay. We have to get back with the girls. Listen, Beth, it's okay if you don't feel up to babysitting. We can change our plans."

"I'm alright, Peg. I'll sit for you."

"Then we'll look for you, around seven."

Peg followed Alan and slowly closed the door behind her.

LIZ stood.. "Don't you go away, kiddo. I want to talk with you. But I have to pee first."

Beth decided to finish the ironing. There still were three blouses and four pillow cases. She really wanted to leave the house and walk. For miles. Or maybe jump off a bridge? Or call Brad and tell him. No, she should call Geoff and ask him what would happen to her if she had kicked Mr. Livingston in the balls?

After Liz returned to the kitchen wearing the *peignoir* which matched her nightgown she poured herself a glass of orange juice and sat at the table.

She lighted a cigarette. "You know I don't believe your cock and bull story." She watched Beth carefully iron one of her blouses. "I guess you forget I *am* your mother. I know when you're happy, when you're scared, *and* when you're lying. And right now you're trying to make me swallow a whopper." She sipped her orange juice. "Why was Dickie Livingston here?" She finished her juice and waited.

"To tell me my essay isn't good enough to win."

Liz realized Beth was not going to pour the hot water into her cup. She walked to the stove and remarked," "I know your old man would have this figured out by now."

"Daddy may have figured it out, but he couldn't have done anything about it."

"It was more than not liking your essay." Liz stirred the instant coffee.

Beth took her time putting the blouse on a hanger. "Let's just forget the whole thing."

"Not so soon. I'm trying to figure out why you were almost hysterical."

"I'm okay now."

"I don't know much about contests. But I can't understand it's kosher for one of the judges to make a special trip to talk to one of the contestants. Un . . . less he has something . . . up his sleeve." Liz took a deep drag and talked as she exhaled. "He thinks you know something about Vicki Lynn, doesn't he?"

Beth shrugged as she began to fold an ironed pillow case. "Why shouldn't I? I listened for hours and hours while Julie told me about her."

"But you didn't include all of the information in your essay?"

"I would have ended up writing a book. I told Mr. Livingston the same thing."

Liz forced a laugh. "I've heard Julie's sister did lead a full life. Right?"

"Of course. After all, she traveled around the world. And had lots of friends."

"Look, kiddo. Even though it might surprise you, I do read the newspaper. And listen to the news. And I remember when Bridgeboro was big time news. Sure, Bill Fischer was a big man in the business world, meaning there were lots of people who were shook up over his death. But Vicki Lynn's death really caused a . . . why your old man was a wreck. I can still hear him moaning, 'No more books. No more poems.'" She sipped from her cup.

"Daddy was one of the thousands who knew she was a great writer."

"And a lot of other men thought she was great. What did you do? Try to make her pure and holy? No wonder Dickie said you left something out."

"I did not make her sound holy. But neither did I include a list of the men in her life."

"I'll bet Julie was sure to tell you. Do you think she told you all of them?"

"How do I know?"

"Name the ones she told you."

"Sylvester Knolt, the publisher. Malcom Turner, the millionaire. And Paul Brando, the actor. But Julie says they were just friends. And oh yeah, Kevin Forbes."

"Well, either Julie is pulling your leg or the wise ass who spread the gossip around town after the fire was . . . oh, or maybe Dickie's deal wasn't big enough to spill the beans."

"What beans? And I haven't made a deal with anyone."

Liz crushed out her cigarette. "Good god, I can't believe you're involved with the big potatoes." Liz examined her nails. "How about if I pretend I overheard everything? She watched Beth iron. Slowly. "Then you'll have a witness."

"What for?"

"Because he had one helluva nerve coming here. I'm going to put him in his place. I've wanted to squeeze his balls, for a long time. He and that fat wife of his. They think their shit don't stink and . . . "

"Just forget it," Beth said firmly. "Please."

Liz picked up her cigarettes, matches and coffee cup. She walked around Beth, into the living room. "If you don't want me to call Dickie, I'm going to call Julie." She sat on the chair, next to the desk.

Beth did have presence of mind to turn off the iron, before she hurried to stand in front of Liz. "Don't you dare. She hasn't been well and it isn't important enough to upset her."

"You've got to be kidding. That shit head came into my house and threatened my kid. And got her so upset I thought she had cracked up. And the neighbors will back me up. If we can't, then she can give him the shaft. If you don't want me to call her, you call her."

Beth shook her head. "No!"

Liz laid her hand on the receiver. "Okay, if we're going to let Julie out of it then I *am* going to call Dickie Livingston. He can't push us Rhodes around. I know something about him that will fix his little red wagon. Working in a diner isn't the greatest job in the world but it pays off. It just so happens I know he was using his dickie in a chickie who worked with me at the Pike Diner. Audry McNeil. She lived on Penn Street and sometimes we'd come home together. When Dickie didn't pick her up and take her to a motel. He even paid for her rent and food."

Beth had to back up and sit down. "Was she married?" she whispered.

"She was getting a divorce. She had three kids and she was willing to fool around with Mr. High and Mighty, to keep the wolf from her door. I ain't blaming her. I just couldn't have done it with him. I even told her so. She told me he was really upset when she told him she was getting married. Where's our phone book? I want to look up their number."

Beth could not move. The telephone number bumped around in her mind and then got caught in a word spelling B-R-A-D. Beth shook her head.

"My God! Still the Salvation Army girl." She searched on the top of the desk then opened the top drawer and found the directory.

Beth began to tremble. "Please . . . don't call him."

"Oh, for Christ's sake, if you don't want to hear me, go in another room."

BETH watched Liz leaf through the book until she found the L section. She watched her run her long red finger nail down a column.

How many times had she dialed the numbers. How many times had she heard Brad say, "Hi babe. Perfect timing. They just left."

She watched Liz dial the number. She even heard Liz say, "Hello."

Without thinking, Beth threw herself at Liz's feet and reached for the receiver. "No. Please hang up, Mom."

Liz's eyes and mouth opened wide. She hung up the receiver and laid a hand on Beth's shoulder. "My god. After all these years. You called me Mom." She stroked Beth's shiny hair. "We won't talk about all of those years. It's a little late to do anything about them anyway. And when I can help you, why won't you let me?"

Beth shook her head from side to side. She accepted a tissue which Liz found in the pocket of her *peignoir*.

"If you really want to do something, just forget about what happened."

Liz's eyes filled with tears. "I should forget that asshole upset my kid."

Beth reached for Liz's hand. "Just forget about everything. And let's start over." She handed box of paper tissues to Liz.

"Hey. Look at me. I just want to tell you something I should have told you sooner. I know you think I'm just put together with make-up and nail polish. But I do have a heart. And a mind. I know I don't use my mind too well but sometimes my heart works overtime." She stroked Beth's hair. "I'm sorry for what I've done to you. You're a good kid."

"You don't have to apologize. I'm not so great."

Liz smiled. "So you lie a little."

Beth smiled back. "And cheat." She backed away from Liz and sat crossed legged in front of her. Why not stay there on the floor and let her mother talk to her.

"So? Who's perfect? What I'm trying to tell you is I know you're nice. And it kills me because I've had to hurt you." Liz wiped her eyes before she blew her nose. "I really don't want to make you have to move. And miss your graduation."

Beth blotted her face. "It's okay."

"No, it ain't. You know I always thought you and your father were missing the boat. But I'm jealous of what you two had together. And now you have the same thing with Julie. So, now I'm jealous of her." Liz wiped her nose again and lighted another cigarette.

"I never really knew my mom. She had to go to work when I think I was in second grade. Maybe it was third. My old man left her with four kids. For another woman. My oldest sister, Peg, was supposed to look after the rest of us. Oh, she stayed home but most of the time she was in her bedroom with her latest boyfriend. I almost told my mom when I caught her with the man next door."

Beth felt her antenna go up. Never had Liz volunteered information about her family. Beth was surprised as much as she was interested even though the information was not exactly what she was hoping to hear. She put an ash tray on the desk and watched her mother take a long drag. She wanted to know more. "I have an Aunt Peg and who else?

"An Uncle Billy and an Uncle Jack. Although I don't know where in the hell they are. Could be dead. I was sort of keeping tabs on Peg. Until about two years ago. She had gone through three husbands in twenty years. Last time I heard, her name was Hughes."

In her mind Beth repeated, *Hughes. I have an Aunt Peggy Hughes.*

Liz sighed. "It's nice to be close to somebody. If I really want to get serious about why I'm getting married, maybe it's because I don't want to die alone." Liz smiled. A sad smile.

She snickered. "Besides it may be the last chance I get. Look at me, kid. What do you see? A loser. A goddamn loser. I got married when I was sixteen. To some wife abuser who loved to drink and then use me as a punching bag. One night he knocked me around so much I lost my first baby. I finally got up enough nerve to run away. Then I met your dad. I loused up what probably could have been a good marriage. I've had two kids and I never even bothered to get to know them. I'm glad you at least had your father. Oh, you think Evan and me were close. We never had anything in common except we're both losers. Everything is a damn shame. What has happened to all of us. You. And Evan. Just to think your father wasted such a pretty name on a bum."

"Don't call her that, Mom."

"My dear little nice girl. The one who believed in *Santa Claus* and the *Tooth Fairy*. I'll bet you still say your prayers. You're the only hope left for the Rhodes family. Your father did a good job with you. When Evan was little, they were real close too." Liz gave a nervous laugh. "I was the one who was disappointed she wasn't a boy. I loved him enough I wanted to give him a son for his first born. But being the easy going and, what was your father?" After Beth replied, "Sensible?" she went on. "Yeah. He was sensible enough to make me understand the sex of our children didn't matter. We should be happy we could have them and they were healthy. He wanted her named Evangeline."

Liz's eyes drifted up over Beth's head. She was looking into nothingness as she softly said, "I remember him one night, whispering over her crib. He was saying the poem to her and as I listened to him, I got chills all over. He loved our first child."

Beth was trying to embrace everything she was hearing. How could an unpleasant visit from Brad's father give her such an unexpected experience with her mother. The words of the poem she had learned with her father, flowed from her. *"Fair was she to behold, that maiden of seventeen summers. Black were her eyes as the berry that grows on the thorn by the wayside, Black, yet how softly they gleamed beneath the brown shade of her tresses, Sweet was her breath as the...."*

"That's it!," Liz blurted out. With joy in her voice. "That's it. I remember he used to say that to her. Who wrote it?"

"Henry Wadsworth Longfellow." As Beth watched her mother blow her nose she recalled the hurt and the disappointment on her father's face as he watched his older daughter, with the bleached blonde hair and the heavy eye make-up throw a kiss to them and say, "Goodnight, you kooks. Have fun with your books."

Their father would ask, "Are you going out with Geoff?" and Evan would answer, "Not tonight. I'm meeting a tall, dark, handsome sailor. We're going to a party."

And their father would ask, "Can't he pick you up here?"

And Evan would laugh and reply, "If I like him, I'll bring him around.'

And then their father would reach for his glass. And she remembered the time her father had tears in his eyes as he repeated the words of the poem. Knowing how much the poem meant to her father, she memorized the words.

She began to whisper them to Liz. *"Then would Evangeline answer, serenely, but sadly, 'I cannot. . . . Whether my heart has gone, there follows my hand and not elsewhere.... For when the heart goes before, like a lamp, and illumines the pathway, . . . Many things are made clear, that else lie hidden in darkness!'*

. . .

Thereupon the priest, her friend and father-confessor, said, with a smile, 'Oh, daughter! The God thus speaketh within thee! . . . Talk not of wasted affection, affection never was wasted; . . . If it enrich not the heart of another, its water, returning . . . Back to their springs, like the rain, shall fill them full of refreshment, . . . That which the fountain sends forth returns again to the fountain."

Tears were sliding down Beth's cheeks.   It was sad to remember.

Her dear father.

Her foolish sister.

And the woman crying with her.

Her mother!

THIRTY SIX

RICHARD LIVINGSTON was tired. Sitting behind his desk in the office of *The B.C.* he realized just how tired he was. In fact, he was having difficulty concentrating on the pile of mail which Flo had placed in front of him. He managed to read two letters before he yawned. Loudly.

He leaned back in his chair and thought how lucky Bernice was. She had done something which was rare for her on a Monday morning. She had stayed in bed.

"You and Brad will have to get your own breakfast. I didn't sleep well last night. Giving the party and being with Lou and Charlie again . . . was very stressful for me."

He couldn't complain. He always enjoyed stopping in the Pike Diner for breakfast. And Bernice had made all of the arrangements for the dinner party. Which had been a way to successfully bury the hatchet with Lou and Charlie.

Of course Ellie Perkins, their part time housekeeper and cook, had prepared the house, set the table and made the necessary preparations for a sumptuous prime rib dinner. At five o'clock , Ellie's nephew had arrived to set up a bar for the seven o'clock arrival of the Oehrle's, the Friedman's and the Barnes.

Richard tried to remain relaxed seeing Charles and Lou. Although he did feel great relief their separation was over. Because the party had gone so well and everybody was in high spirits, Lou declared that everybody was invited to their house the next Sunday. For brunch!. Damn Lou and her audacity. She was just trying to outdo them. And show off their estate.

RICHARD was deep in reminiscing, so the ringing of a buzzer on his new phone, made him jump. He fumbled with the buttons before he said, "Yes?" to his secretary.

"It's Mr. Oehrle from the Fischer Company. Do you want to talk with him?"

"Yes. I'll take it." He cleared his throat before he said, "Hank. Hello. How are you?" Richard pushed up his glasses.

"Still recuperating from the week-end. Your dinner was delicious and your house is lovely. You and Bernice out did yourselves."

"Well thank you. We're going to have to get together again because Audrey and I didn't have any time to talk about Vicki Lynn."

"I thought you'd like to know Mrs. Fischer called for another Executive Committee meeting this afternoon. Rumors have it she may be ready to make a big announcement. About getting the money for expansion. Through Corporate Bonds. I guess you know Charlie is going to take Audrey up to Deer Lake Manor. He said he's sure the caretaker will allow him to drive up the driveway so she can have a closer look."

"Oh? How about that? It is a lovely place. Of course, Bernice and I have been there. Many times."

"Rumors also have it that after Mrs. Fischer and her companion return from Europe they're going to move in. We heard she's planning a reception for company officers and wives. Oh oh, have to go. Forgot I have a lunch meeting. 'Bye."

Richard had to use his closet size private bathroom before he took his morning walk around the shop. Hopefully, the noise and the heat from the machinery would keep him from thinking.

Damn Julie. Why did just talking about her cause him so much stress?

Damn him! Why had he been so stupid to write that letter? Could he dare to believe it had been destroyed?

And damn that girl. For not being afraid of him.

And now he had to research Corporate Bonds.

THIRTY SEVEN

BETH RHODES WATCHED Liz drive away from their house. Then, damn it! She began to cry!

She had convinced herself she was prepared for Liz to move first. But this was D-Day. And H-Hour.

Reputation be damned. Liz had decided she didn't want to wait until *the last minute,* to move her personal belongings into Lou's apartment. She explained she wanted to be moved in before the first Saturday in June when she would become Mrs. Louis King.

Even though the rent was paid until the tenth of June, Doc and Geoff insisted Beth should move in with Julie. While Geoff was in California to see his new twin nephews, Doc had helped her move her clothes to Julie's house. Upon his return, Geoff called to tell her he would help her finish packing her books and favorite things. This meant only the unwanted furniture would be left and Doc had suggested she donate it to the *Salvation Army.* She couldn't tell him that she and Brad had decided to put it in storage.

Beth was sorting magazines in the kitchen when there was a knock on the screen door.

"Greer's packing service, reporting for duty."

"Please come in, sir. I have been anxiously awaiting your arrival." Beth forced a laugh. She still got a thrill when he kissed her cheek.

"I hope there isn't much left. I tried to extend my trip so I could get out of carrying the heavy stuff. Only kidding. I think."

"Ha ha, yourself. Doc and I were too smart for you. All we took were my clothes and necessary things. He left the heavy stuff for you. Glad you had a safe trip. I know you have pictures to show Julie and the rest of your fan club."

"You betcha that Uncle Geoff has pictures. Hey, I forgot to tell you. I had to take some papers for Julie's signature and she showed me your bedroom. Sex…ee. I like lavender." He hugged her and asked, "Did you miss me?"

Beth shrugged. "Ahh. I guess you hope I'll say yes? So I won't tell you." She grinned. "How about the wallpaper and paint colors we picked out for the rest of the house?"

"It won't look like the same house. And Julie insisted she feels great, even though I think she's too thin. How's Liz holding up?"

"Hanging in, but I think she's getting nervous. Not cold feet nervous, just excited."

"Julie told me you were invited for dinner at Lou's apartment. How do you like your future step-father?"

Beth shrugged. "He'll be okay. I think he looks like a prize fighter . . . but he has a good sense of humor. And he lets Liz do the talking."

"And how is Beth?" Geoff asked as he helped her wrap tape around a box of books.

"Scared." Suddenly, tears began to overflow. She quickly wiped her cheeks on the shoulders of her tee shirt.

"Maybe you're just excited. Like Julie is. Doc says he has never seen her so happy."

"That makes me even more scared." With tears glistening she looked into Geoff's eyes. "So much depends on me."

"And you can do it, baby," Geoff said with a twinkle in his eyes. "Just think, a trip to Europe, then moving into Deer Lake Manor, followed by living on campus at Penn State and . . . " Geoff reached out with a forefinger and caught two tears. "I'm proud of you. It couldn't happen to a nicer girl."

"And . . . if I tell you I missed you? Will you come to my rescue?"

He winked before he whispered, "You have my number. "

DURING the following week Beth made great progress in becoming use to living with Julie. One of the most thrilling happenings was Julie suggesting she invite Mr. and Mrs. Stookey for dinner. Doc and Geoff were also present. Julie even allowed Mr. Stookey to ask her questions about Vicki. She also allowed him to look through the unpublished **Vicki's Vignettes**. And decided to actually give him an autographed copy of one of Vicki's books of poetry!

Another exciting event was a bigger dinner party. Beth invited Dot Kennedy, Jill Gillion, Fred Harding, Dan Friedman, Mr. Carpenter's granddaughter, Ann, plus four other excited classmates. Julie and Doc cooked and served the dinner. The flaming Alaska was a big hit.

Julie also informed her she had included a note inside of Liz's wedding card that she was going to invite her and Lou for dinner. After they returned from their honeymoon.　Should she suggest Peg and Alan also be included?

NOW exams were over, and the final week for the Senior class to attend Bridgeboro High School was arriving.　Too soon.　The end of a chapter in the lives of one hundred and ten teenagers in a small town in a big world had arrived.

Before she had left for the day, Beth and Brad had the opportunity to talk.　Right in Mr. Stookey's room!　They were pretending they were discussing the final edition of the school paper, when they really were bringing each other up to date.

"The Barnes are having a big bash next Saturday.　The guest list includes some biggies from the Fischer Company."

Looking down at the pages before her, Beth whispered, "Julie will find out.　How about you and Jeanne?"

"I try not to think about it.　All I do think about is after next Thursday we might never get a chance to talk to each other.　Let alone see each other."

"And then Julie and I go to Europe and I won't even be able to send you a card."

"You know I'm really happy you're going on the trip but it's going to be hell, wondering where you are and what you're doing.　Isn't there somebody we can trust?"

Beth watched Mr. Stookey sorting and stacking books. She nodded in his direction. "He and I are buddy buddy since he met Julie. I think he might do us a favor."

"Yeah.　But would he approve?"

"You mean is he a romanticist?　All the world loves a lover.　He appreciates Vicki Lynn's novels and poems."　Suddenly Beth remembered Vicki Lynn sent her mail to Bill Fischer's private post box. "Maybe you could rent a box in another town?"

Brad nodded. "Good idea.　I can do that.　I'll let you know the address as soon as I do."　He sighed.　"I guess we better get to work finishing this paper.　He moved his shoe to touch Beth's shoe.　"Also, don't forget to tell me how much you need for the storage bill."

Under the table Beth rubbed Brad's thigh. "Just remember,　I l-o-v-e　y-o-u."

"It's the most important thing in my life.　It keeps me from wanting to run away."

AS she had done a few times, Beth entered Julie's house through the mud room. As soon as she walked into the kitchen she said, "Hi. What do I smell? Thyme or oregano?"

"Thyme. I put it in the meat loaf. Philip likes it to flavor beef. How was your day?"

"We had a blast practicing for Class Night. Mr. Stookey says our skits are the funniest he's ever seen. I helped write them you know. With Brad Livingston."

Julie ignored what Beth had said. "And anything Mr. Stookey says is the gospel truth."

"Oh oh." Beth laughed. "Does it show that much?"

"I'm sure his wife is used to high school girls having a crush on her good looking husband. You're going to miss being with him."

"Maybe I can find a college professor to take his place." She began to walk out of the kitchen.

"Wait a minute. The *Safeway Moving and Storage Company* called this afternoon. They want to know when somebody can meet them in Taylor Park to pick up some furniture."

Beth felt her heart do a back flip in her chest. "Oh? Okay. I'll call them right now."

"Wait a minute, young lady. At first I thought they were indicating Liz was storing the stuff. But you are, aren't you?"

"Uh huh. I might need it. Sometime."

"In case you can't stand living with me?"

Now what should she say? She certainly couldn't say, "Brad and I have decided we want to keep it, in case we can't wait four years." so she commented, "I'm just sentimental. I'm not ready to part with all of my past yet."

"You're not sentimental, you're scared." Julie stepped close to Beth and put her hands on her shoulders. "If it'll make you feel any better I'll even put in writing, if we have a problem and you want to move, I'll give you an apartment in Hilltop Manor. Rent free and furnished. How's that sound? Especially since that's where Geoff lives?"

"It sounds very nice. But I still want to hang on to the furniture."

Julie put anger in the word, "Why?"

"In case I have to move. I …I have a boyfriend."

Julie backed up to lean against the sink. "You mean you're not interested in Geoff?"

"And Geoff isn't interested in me. He also has somebody special."

"Whom I have to believe must be a married woman because he won't tell me any details. And now you have a secret relationship?" Julie asked, strongly. "Why?"

"I can't tell you right now. But I will as soon as we decide it's okay for other people to know. I mean, you've told me some secrets and now I'm sharing my secret with you."

"You're not sharing anything with me. Except you have a boyfriend. How long have you been in love with this boy? Or man? Is he married?"

"He's not married and I've been in love with him ever since I met him. But we've been dating for only a couple of months."

"If it's such a big secret, how in the hell do you go out with him at all?"

"We go places where nobody knows us." Beth studied Julie's face. "Please, Julie. Don't try to make it something . . . bad. It's a good clean love."

"Oh really? You're as blind as Vicki was. Love makes everything perfect" She sat on a chair and declared, "You seem so sensible. You should be encouraging Geoff Greer. A decent man who has a sound future. Which you could share with him."

"Geoff will always be a special person for me. But even before he let us know he has someone else in his life, I fell in love with this other person."

"Don't be asinine. By the time I finish polishing you, with a college degree and some world travel and education about the business world, you will be a perfect wife for Geoff. I'll help him change his mind. I can do big things for both of you."

"Give him the big future he deserves but don't spoil it, by forcing us together. Not even for Geoff could I deny my love for this other person."

Julie squinted. "Use your smarts, girl. There's no future in hiding and cheating."

"We feel badly enough over what we're doing."

"That's what Vicki had the guts to say to me. 'Bill and I feel so awful over what we're doing.' Damn you! I never thought I'd have to live through anything like this again. I never ….." Tears trickled down Julie's cheeks.

"I'm sorry. I'll move," Beth heard herself blurt out.

"You mean you'd leave me. Because of this . . . other person?"

"Because I've upset you."

Julie wiped her cheeks on her apron. "I'm disappointed it isn't Geoff. Why can't you invite this person . . . here?"

Beth leaned against the door jamb between the kitchen and the hallway. "Maybe. But could I call him from here?"

"Does he drive a car?" She watched Beth nod. "Then he can hide his car behind the garage. Your eyes are telling me you still don't trust me. I promise your secret will be safe with me. I just want to keep you off the streets. Like a common streetwalker."

"Julie, I really am grateful for your offer. But I have to talk it over with him."

"Go call that moving company and cancel the pick-up" Julie ordered. "We'll ask Sam if any of his relatives need any furniture or give it to the Salvation Army."

THE following Saturday, Beth drove to Taylor Park to meet Sam's nephews with their pick-up trucks.

Beth parked Julie's car in Liz's empty parking space. She had planned on visiting with the Mawhorter family, so she was disappointed when no one came to their door. As she unlocked the kitchen door, she decided she did not feel like seeing Mrs. Smithers. Or any others who had been neighbors for so many years. She was not in the right frame of mind to answer any questions about Julie or what her plans might be.

Beth noticed mail in the mail box. Liz and she had forgotten to notify the post office. She pulled out three business size envelopes addressed to Liz. And what could be a greeting card. Addressed to her! She glanced at the handwriting and then the return address.

Her heart beats began to skip out of synch. *1120 East Park Street, Norfolk, Virginia* Beth ripped open the flap. She held a graduation card. *Just wanted you to know I'm thinking of you. Hope you can go to college. I have an apartment and am okay. But don't tell Liz. Love, Evan.*

Of all days for her to receive a card from Evan. The day their mother was going to be married and the day she would be with Geoff

Greer. She knew she was not going to tell anyone she knew where Evan was.

LIZ was married at four o'clock. In *Lou's Bar and Grille.* Before the ceremony, Beth was embarrassed to tell anyone where the wedding would be. Only a few knew she was going to be her mother's maid-of-honor. But inside she was excited. Lou had paid for a stunning blue dress which Liz wanted her to wear. And matching shoes.

Beth was astonished at how attractive the restaurant looked. Lou had hired a local florist to decorate everything. Even the restrooms were filled with flowers. The result was beyond her expectation. Obviously, Lou had said, "Go all out."

Julie had been invited to attend the reception but declined. In front of Geoff and Doc she laughingly announced, "You're looking at the only Rhodes I'm going to see get married." She winked at Philip. "And why torture myself with so much booze available."

As soon as Geoff picked her up she thought of the graduation card. She did enjoy Geoff's compliments on how lovely she looked. She also had accepted Julie's offer to wear some jewelry which had belonged to Vicki Lynn. Beth found herself touching the necklace and earrings frequently. How lucky could she be?

Beth and Geoff, Lou's brother and his wife, all of the waitresses, bar tenders and kitchen staff had been invited to the wedding ceremony. And, a photographer.

At five o'clock, additional guests arrived for the impressive reception. As the hired musicians played and the drinking began, the restaurant became filled with swaying and sputtering guests.

Peg and Alan attended. They stayed for most of the reception before they announced they had to take the babysitter home. Inside, Beth smiled as she envisioned them giving a detailed report to the rest of the neighbors on Ludlow Street.

BETH was holding a glass of tonic water with a slice of lemon while sipping from Geoff's gin and tonic. After she had helped Geoff empty the third glass, he insisted they make platters from the sumptuous buffet. It also was Geoff's suggestion they try to avoid getting involved in small talk by dancing every dance.

Holding Beth close to him he whispered, "Of course I really want the musicians to know that someone appreciates them and not that I want to hold you close to me."

Beth snuggled against him, unconcerned as to how many eyes were watching them. She knew they made an attractive couple. She also knew she was thinking thoughts she should not be thinking. Maybe since Brad hadn't *waited* for her she shouldn't wait for him? Maybe she could entice Geoff to take her back to his apartment?

"Oh oh! Here comes your new stepfather."

"You two having fun?" Lou asked. "Did you get enough to eat?"

Geoff put out his hand to shake Lou's and remarked, "Congratulations and I'm stuffed. I'm really surprised I can dance, except I'm trying to shake it down. The food is delicious and the music is great."

Beth added, "It's a very nice reception, Lou. Everyone is having a ball."

Lou laughed a jolly laugh. "I hope so. I want everyone to be as happy as I am." He frowned at Geoff. "I'm sorry Mr. Gillon couldn't make it. How's he feeling?"

"Well enough to take Doc's advice and visit his brother in Arizona. He called the office yesterday to tell all of us he's feeling better, being with his family."

"Well," Lou patted Geoff on the back, "I'm happy you could come and thanks for the clock. It looks real nice in our living room. And thanks for being such a good friend of . . . " he paused to place a heavy hand on Beth's shoulder, "of Sis, here."

Almost like a magician he held an envelope. "I'm real sorry about your mom and me not being able to attend your graduation." Lou turned to Geoff and raised his thick eyebrows. "You'll be there, won't you?"

Geoff smiled at Beth. "I wouldn't miss it."

"And I imagine Julie Fischer will be. With her and Beth being such good friends. It's too bad I had to plan things around my brother's vacation 'cause I sure as hell wasn't going to close up this place. For two weeks! And I promised Liz a trip to Florida." He laughed. "To get her off my back."

Lou handed the envelope to Beth. "This is a combination graduation and I'm real proud to know you gift." He looked embarrassed. Quickly, he planted a wet kiss on Beth's closest cheek. Then he took long strides, to hurry away.

Beth knew her mouth was opened as she watched Lou disappear into the crowd. She did yell out, "Thank you, Lou." To Geoff she said, "I don't think he heard me." She held up the envelope. "Betcha it's a card and money. At least fifty."

She carefully unsealed the envelope and pulled out a *Congratulations* card. She looked inside and breathed, "It's a new hundred dollar bill. Oh, my god. There's five of them. This is more than a gift. It's a payment."

Since the envelope would not fit into her evening bag, Geoff gently took the money and card, put them back into the envelope and tucked it into the inside pocket of his jacket. He put his arms around Beth and forced her to resume dancing. He whispered, "I wouldn't be surprised if Lou sends you spending money. Now and then. He's loaded. Disability from being wounded in the war and this place is a gold mine. You and Liz have finally lucked out."

Into Geoff's left ear Beth whispered, "Are you rich?"

"Not as rich as your step-father."

"Don't call him that. I have to get used to the word." She grinned into Geoff's face. "Do you have enough money to get married?"

"I think so. Why?"

"A girl who should be graduating with us quit school to marry a sailor from the Base. I saw her last week with a baby and you know I got this funny feeling that I don't want to spend the next four, or maybe six years in college. I want to get married. And have a baby." She looked into Geoff's eyes. "I want to go to college . . . but maybe I might change my plans."

"I think the minister is still here."

Beth giggled. She liked flirting with Geoff. She was enjoying being so close to him. It felt good. Even exciting. Maybe she cared for him more than she realized? Or wanted to admit. She giggled again "I'm afraid I'm going to have to turn you down. Maybe I'd have to share you with a memory?"

"I don't think so."

"Then because you have someone else in your life?"

"Yes I do. And so do you."

"What do you mean?"

"I got vibes the night you came to my apartment wasn't because of being upset over Julie. You and Mr. Wonderful had a fight and you wanted to get back at him. But you couldn't stop wearing the watch he gave you. Am I right?"

Beth felt herself coil. Damn him. He was too clever. No, he knew her too well. "Maybe?" Beth murmured. She looked into Groff's eyes and whispered, "Promise not to tell?" She watched him nod.

She wanted to tell him. But knew she shouldn't. She put a twinkle in her eyes and remarked, "I also have a serious crush on Elvis Presley."

"Oh? Really. Beth, this is Geoff Greer. The guy who watched you grow up. And I've had just enough to drink to tell *you* a secret. Ready?" He watched her smile. And slowly nod. "The name of the special person in my life is Terance Haines."

Beth raised her eyebrows. "Is that . . . a man's name?"

Geoff nodded. "I'm gay, Beth. Terry is my lover. And in defense of Evan, she knew. And covered for me. Oh . . . oh, to be continued. Here comes Liz."

Geoff began to sing, "*Here comes the bride. Please step aside. And hello, Mrs. King. You look ravishing.*"

"Hi you two. Having fun?"

Geoff answered the question. "You bet we are."

"I want to show Beth the clothes I bought for my honeymoon. Did you know Lou is taking me to Florida?" Liz looked as though she were going to Paris.

"Lou just told us. And I hope you have a safe and wonderful trip."

"Oh, I'm going to. Even if it rains the whole time." As Liz laughed she reached for Beth's hand. "I won't keep her too long."

LIZ led the way up the stairs. To the second floor apartment. "You look beautiful today, kiddo. I'm real proud of you. And I have a feeling that Geoff is getting pretty soft on you." She opened the door to the apartment. "Lou and me have been watching you two. And you look real nice together."

Beth followed Liz into the living room. "Don't get any ideas. We're just good friends."

Liz closed and leaned against the door. "I've heard people say that before. Well, you don't have to rush into anything now. I take it all back about calling you a dreamer. You've got it made.   Now you're going to college . . . and all the way to Europe.

"And I know you're real smart but I've given you good advice before.   Try real hard to keep Julie happy.   Maybe someday you just might own the Fischer Company.   And half of Bridgeboro."   Liz forced a loud laugh.

Beth snorted a laugh.   "Now who's the dreamer?"

"You can never tell.   Who would have thought you and me would have made out so good."   She looked around the room as she declared, "I mean I ain't done too bad either."

"That is true.   A honeymoon in Florida, this nice apartment and a nice guy for a husband."

"What do you think of that gift he gave you?"

"I have a sneaky feeling you had something to do with it.   So thank you very much.   I'll be sure to tell Lou again how much I appreciate it." She wished she could stop saying *much.*

"Lou thinks you're a good kid.   I mean living with Julie and dating Geoff.   And all of what you're doing.   And if you write to us while you're in Europe and college and stop in whenever you're in town, I mean Julie probably will let you stay there during your vacations and whenever . . . don't you think?"   After Beth nodded she added, "But you better come see us 'cause I know that Lou will give you some spending money. We want Julie to know we care about you also."

"I'll visit. And write.   But not because of spending money.   I think we should keep in touch.   Which means I hope you write to me also." She almost reached out to take Liz's hand.

"You know I ain't much for writing but I'll keep in touch."   She turned to the door after they heard a knock.   "Who is it?" Liz yelled out.

"Marie and Helen," a voice responded.

Liz smiled at Beth.   "Two of our waitresses.   They want to see my new clothes."

For several minutes compliments and remarks were shared in Liz and Lou's bedroom.   It was obvious Liz was enjoying spending Lou's money from the designer labels on her new outfits.   Beth made appropriate compliments.   Then she decided to leave.

Holding the door knob she said, "Don't get too sunburned."

Looking at Beth in the mirror behind her dressing table, Liz cocked her head. "Do you have to leave? Oh I know, you don't want to be away from Geoff any longer than you have to,"

"I really thought I had seen everything."

Liz turned to her friends. "I told you Beth's dating Geoff Greer, didn't I?"

Helen laughed. "I seen them dancing real close. Maybe there'll be another wedding?"

Beth shook her head. "I'm going to college in August."

"And to Europe in a couple of weeks." Liz added.

"The trip to Europe is company business," Beth had to explain. "And Mrs. Fischer is loaning me the money for college."

"So what?" Marie exclaimed. "From what I've heard about her I'm sure she wouldn't do any of that for everybody."

"Damn right," Helen agreed. "Old Julie's never helped anybody else in Bridgeboro." She snickered before she added, "Except the State Store."

Beth remained calm. "I wish you all knew her as I do. She's very thoughtful and she *has* donated a lot of money to the library and to the hospital. Even before the county park."

"And she invited Lou and me for dinner. And gave us a real expensive . . . what kind of pitcher is it, Beth?"

"Waterford," Beth replied as she opened the door. She had to leave.

"Hey. Wait a minute. Don't you dare leave without giving me a good-bye kiss."

Beth forced a big smile and walked back to where Liz sat. She felt her heartbeats picking up speed. This was the moment she had been dreading.

She had told herself it would not be, should not be, too difficult. After all, she and Liz had not been bound together with cords of love nor understanding. Even after Sentimental Saturday as Beth called the day they had cried together, they still were not half as close as most of her girlfriends and their mothers were. Or were her friends exaggerating?

Looking into Liz's massacred eyes, Beth knew what never could be denied. Liz *was* her mother. Even though it wasn't as sad when she watched her daddy's coffin rolled into the crematorium or offering his ashes to the wind which blew around *Bowman's Tower*, she was saying goodbye to . . . her remaining parent.

A feeling of panic bolted through her and she felt hot tears stinging her eyes. She could not cry! She smiled broadly and said as matter-of-factly as she could, "I guess this is sort of the beginning of the end."

"Sort of," Liz whispered as she reached out and took one of Beth's hands. "Thank you for being my maid-of-honor."

"I would have been sad if you hadn't invited me. It was a lovely wedding and I'm very happy for you." Quickly Beth leaned down and kissed Liz's mouth. Before she could pull away, Liz grabbed her shoulders and held her down.

Into Beth's ear she whispered, "Stay good. And keep in touch with me."

Beth nodded and breathed, "Good-bye, Mom. Good luck. I hope you'll be real happy. Being Mrs. Louis King." She watched a tear drop onto her mother's dress. Was it hers? Or Liz's?

Liz released Beth's shoulders and reached for the tissue box.

Beth gave a weak smile to Helen and Marie before she looked back at Liz and waved. "Have a great time in Florida. And send me a card."

"I will. And you show it to Geoff. And Julie."

"See you later, Mrs. King." Beth hurried out of the apartment. As she walked down the stairs she realized neither she nor her mother had been able to say *I love you.*

Would they ever?

THIRTY EIGHT

JULIE INVITED DOC and Geoff for dinner before they attended the Baccalaureate Service. Beth forced herself to laugh at Doc's corny jokes But it was easy to tease with Geoff.

During the Baccalaureate Service she even prayed. And talked to her daddy.

It was obvious that everyone who attended was surprised to see Julie looking so attractive. Even impressive.

On Tuesday evening Beth again enjoyed having dinner with the three special people in her life. And she and Brad had been able to meet in an unlocked classroom. After Brad shut the door they stepped into each other's arms and kissed. They tried to stay unwrinkled because they were dressed for their parts in the Class Night skits.

"I want to give you your gift." Beth whispered. She watched him quickly remove wrapping paper from a small square box.

He stared at a gold signet ring. The date and their initials were engraved inside. He told her would wear it at college in place Jeanne's class ring which he was looking forward to return to her. He handed the ring to Beth and stuck out his left ring finger. "Put it on, so I can wear it for a few minutes. I'm calling it my engagement ring."

Beth kissed the ring. "Now it's been blessed." She kissed the palm of his left hand. "And so are you. With my love."

Brad whispered, "I love you and my ring." He handed her a long narrow box. "And now for you."

"Brad. I have my watch."

"Shut up and open it. We have to get out of here." He heard Beth gasp when she saw the gold chain bracelet. With a gold heart with her birthstone in it. "It's the beginning of a charm bracelet. Every time something big happens, I'll give you another charm. You know, a wedding bell, baby shoes, they even have a little gold house. It'll be fun to add to it."

Beth kissed Brad on the mouth. "I'm speechless." She fingered the heart and handed the bracelet to Brad. "Put it on my wrist. I know it's good gold so I can keep it on."

Brad looked proud. "It's going to be worth a lot of money. After I fill it up."

She watched Brad fumble with the safety chain. "I . . . tried to tell Julie about us."

"Are you kidding me?" Brad asked loudly.

"Shhh. I told her I have a special boyfriend. I thought if she knew that much I might be able to see you once in a while this summer."

"What did she say?"

"She got mad. She wants me to encourage Geoff. And even though Geoff told us he's dating she keeps talking about him and having him for dinner. Like she can change my mind. But guess what she did say? She wants to meet him."

"Oh my god. And what did you say?"

"I'd talk it over with him."

"So? What do you think?"

Beth sighed. "I still can't decide what to do. Leave well enough alone or take a chance. I want to die whenever I think about this summer. And of course you know I'm not getting any money from the Essay Contest. Not even second prize."

"Dad told me. You know I'm sorry."

"I cried when Mr. Stookey told me. Julie is blaming your father and it just doesn't seem like a good time to mention your name."

Brad wrapped his arms around Beth. "I thought more about telling Mr. Stookey but I don't think so. He's understanding but I think he'd be afraid of Dad. With him being on the School Board. And I know Dad is capable of dirty work." He shrugged. "I couldn't trust any of the guys. If we don't think of anybody by Thursday when will I be able to talk with you?"

"We've got to think of something. Like a certain place to meet on a certain day at a certain time. And we better get out of here. You go first."

Brad held out his left hand. "Take off my ring."

"Shall I keep it?"

"No. I can hide it. I want it near me. Even though I can't wear it, I'm still engaged."

Beth let him gently kiss her mouth before he walked away. She felt forlorn after he left her alone. Is this the way it would always be? Was the sneaking and lying worth taking the chances? What *if* they were caught? Just how terrible could the outcome be? Beth fingered her bracelet. If only a genie of the bracelet would appear and grant her wishes.

Beth peered up and down the hall. She left the room and joined the unsuspecting crowd. All of whom once again were impressed and almost standing in line . . . to speak to Julie.

BERNICE and Richard Livingston also attended the Class Night program. Bernice had bought two new dresses which would conceal her gain in weight. She was wearing one on Tuesday evening and the other was for Thursday. And she had talked Richard into buying a new tan suit in the Squire Shoppe. After all he was a member of the School Board and would be sitting on the stage.

She had smiled when Richard sounded like so many of the other fathers. "Where has the time gone? It seems like only yesterday that we were teaching him to ride a bike."

But Richard did remind himself he didn't always feel like most of the other fathers. He remembered his "other son" who had been given his name and had grown up in a private Home for Special Residents in the countryside of Virginia. How many other parents in the audience had a proverbial "skeleton in the closet"?

Brad truly was a credit to the family name he allowed the boy to use. He would have blamed Bernice if Brad had not made them proud parents. And since Brad was so good looking, he loved it when someone would remark he looked like Richard. Except his sister, Mary, who insisted Brad looked like their mother's father.

Richard knew how unkind he was when he reminded Bernice that Brad could be the child of a promiscuous hussy from Taylor Park, who had become impregnated by some roughneck gob from the Navy Base. Why did he enjoy hurting her by referring to Brad as a bastard?

She continued to refer to Brad as a love child whose father had been an officer and a gentleman, from the Navy Base. And the mother had been a local career girl. Or an unwise married woman. But Richard would add, then perhaps the mother knew where her son was living and was just waiting to make contact. He almost enjoyed watching Bernice's reaction. And her tears.

Already the Livingston's knew Brad was going to receive many awards and honors on Graduation Night. Richard felt himself gloating inside. He knew Jeanne Barnes was not going to receive as many awards. Unfortunately Brad had not received the football scholarship he had wanted. Because his right knee had been so injured he was advised not to play the game anymore. Of course the injury just might keep him from having to serve in the Military. At least not become involved physically in the Indochinese conflict.

Richard smiled because Beth Rhodes was not going to win the Essay Contest. He had convinced the other judges, except Mr. Stookey and Mr. Jones, Mary Ann Powers had written a more commendable essay. Of course Julie was going to help the girl go to college. But he had the satisfaction he had spoiled the aspiration of the insolent girl. When he brought Julie Fischer to her knees he would make sure the girl sat in the mud also.

TRAGIC Thursday arrived! That was the term Beth called graduation night.

Again, Doc and Geoff were having dinner with Julie and Beth. While the three were busy talking, Beth was busy mulling over in her mind, *I wish I didn't have to eat this. It looks good and Doc and Geoff enjoyed cooking it but why can't I just tell everybody I'm too nervous to eat? I don't want to graduate. I liked being a teenager and. . . . listen!*

"Beth," Julie said strongly. "I asked where Liz's card was mailed from?"

"Oh. Sorry. Daytona Beach." She smiled at Geoff and added, "They're going to Nassau for a few days. She must be having a ball from what she wrote. 'This is the life. Sleep outside all day and play inside all night.'"

She filled her mouth with green beans. She didn't want to talk anymore. Especially about Liz. She was annoyed because her mother had not even mentioned her graduation. Even after their sentimental farewell.

As she chewed Beth reviewed her annoyance. *Daddy, help. Liz thought saying she was proud of me and all that other crap should last forever. You wouldn't have missed tonight. You would be proud of me. Even if I didn't win the contest. But Evan sent me a card. I should show it to Geoff. He looks so sharp in that blue Ivy League shirt and charcoal gray trousers. And I love that red, white and blue nautical tie. And he smelled good when he kissed me. I hope he believes me that I don't care if he's gay. And how about Evan covering for him? Why do I keep thinking I'd like to see her?*

"BETH! Where are you tonight? You should know Mr. Clarke called again today."

"Oh. What's new in the County Park Department?"

Julie smiled at Doc. "Sam Clarke is the chairman of the Bucks County Park and Recreation Board." She gave a wider smile to Geoff. "He called to tell me before Richard has to print it in *The B.C.* that the Commissioners have accepted our idea to name the park *Lenni Lenape Park.* After the Indian Tribe. Which lived in this area. How about that?"

Julie Fischer looked radiant. Even though her complexion needed make-up to give it color. She had confessed to Beth that because she had lost so much weight she was wearing padded bras. But her legs still were shapely. Beth had complimented her and teased her looking sexy. She also had been bold enough to add, "No wonder you got Bill Fischer's attention. And it's obvious Doc is enjoying escorting you. Thanks to me. For graduating. Ha Ha." They had laughed together.

And Beth would always remember that Julie had added, "It's all because of you, Elizabeth Rhodes, that I am once again enjoying my proper place of ruling as Mrs. William Fischer."

Now Julie was praising her again. "The name was Beth's idea. And I submitted it to the Park Board because as Beth said, I did give them the farm and my name does carry a little weight. And why not let them know we did some research and that is an appropriate name."

Geoff looked at Beth and winked. "You and your soft spot for the Indians. Tell me the name of the closest Indian village again. So I can impress the gals in the office tomorrow."

"H-o-l-i-c-o-n-g. That really is not the correct spelling. But close enough. The *Leni- Lenape* were under the umbrella of the Delaware Nation. A lot of them were dwelling along the Neshaminy and Pennypack Creeks. In other words locally, when the settlers arrived. Their chieftain, Tamanend, was famous in these parts. I think he met with William Penn.

She paused to chuckle and decided to add a few more facts. "They stayed until around seventeen forties or so. Although stories have it that a few remained until the late, even early ninties. Most or many of them migrated into the western part of the state. I prepared a short history of the area and the information about the tribe. For the Board. They must have liked the suggestion."

"And tell them what else we're working on," Julie urged.

"The zoning idea?" She watched Julie nod. "Julie and I have thought up an idea to create a historic zoning ordinance to help preserve historical areas and buildings in the county. What do you think of that?" She smiled at Geoff, hoping for approval.

"I have to hear more."

"Well, we really don't know whether to take the idea to the County Commissioners or to begin with the Bridgeboro Council. But we do think a Review Board should be set up to evaluate and review the historical significance of buildings. Even privately owned ones. And then pass judgment before the owners can make any changes on the exterior of the buildings. In that way we could preserve our past and keep the towns pretty and quaint."

Doc nodded. "Very good idea. You two are really thinking."

"Give Beth the credit again. She's full of ideas. I'm aiming to have her invited to give a presentation at the Bridgeborough Historical Society. And maybe we'll apply to become members? So that Bernice will wet her pants." Julie laughed.

Beth gave a weak smile and filled her mouth with salad. She certainly did not want to talk about Bernice Livingston. Not any Livingston. Oh damn. Doc was eyeing her bracelet. Maybe she should have taken it off. Not have to tell any more lies. But she wanted Brad to see she was wearing it. She wanted him to know she was taking chances for him. But he wasn't wearing the ring. And she had spent a lot of Lou's money for that ring. He'd probably wear it when they were together. Whenever that would be. And he said he was going to wear it to college. Kinda a stupid way to be love.

Oh oh Daddy. Listen to Julie. Chattering away about the Evening Grosbeaks she saw at the feeder today. And her new flower beds. Why is she making this place look so lovely if we're going to move to Deer Lake Manor? Poor Sam. He has a list of instructions to follow while we're on the trip. I'm sure Tony will help him water and weed the flower beds and feed Gerry and the birds and . . . look at Doc. He's so pleased with the new Julie. He almost embarrasses me the way he keeps raving over how much good I've done. Geoff too. Well, it is true. You'd have to be deaf, dumb and blind, not to notice she's a different woman. I certainly am recognized uptown now. And Daddy, how about me naming a park. But if I ever make her mad like telling her about Brad, I'll bet she'd kick me out. Listen!

"We're meeting with investors next week." Julie sighed deeply.

"Well, don't let it get you down," Doc declared. "A Fischer will have the controlling shares. And didn't Earle and Vicki invest in the company?"

"Vicki enjoyed investing in plays. And all of them were smash successes. Of course her estate's assets keep piling up with royalties. Especially from her last novel." Julie looked at Beth and smiled, "Did you tell Geoff and Philip what I gave you for graduation?"

Beth grinned. "A complete set of first editions of Vicki's published writings. Her poetry and novels. I can't wait to show them to Mr. Stookey."

Geoff and Doc made the appropriate comments before they were interrupted by Julie returning to the subject of the much needed office building. "I've gone over the details and figures so many times I see them in my sleep. I still hate to have a stock issue. I keep thinking I should sell something to pay for the damn office building."

Doc smiled at Julie. "Be thankful you have such capable lawyers."

"In behalf of Mr. Gillon, thank you." Geoff nodded to everyone around the table. "And I must add we are fortunate to be working with capable and devoted officers and staff. Who will take care of the company while you two are traveling."

He stared into Beth's eyes, "And don't you forget, Beth Rhodes. I want a card from every country."

Doc spoke up. "Aren't you still meeting them in Paris?"

"Yep. I'm even taking a quickie course in French." Geoff winked at Beth.

"Honestly?" She still couldn't believe Geoff had accepted Julie's invitation to join them for a week and fly home together.

"Did you think I was going to let you lead me astray or order something I don't like?"

Everybody laughed and then Beth decided to change the direction of the conversation by asking Doc, "Have you ever been to Europe?"

"At least six times. I love Italy. Now I'm at the age where I just like to take it easy. Like going to the Poconos with my buddy, Jim. We just loll around in the peace and quiet. Up there in the mountains. You all remember? I am taking off tomorrow morning, bright and early?"

You will be back before we leave?" Beth quickly asked.

"I should be. Unless the fish keep biting."

Suddenly Beth felt tense. "Call us as soon as you get back. And thank you again for my present. I need a camera. To take pictures around Europe."

"And Great Britain." Julie looked at Geoff. "We may go to Mexico next. You two could have a great time in Mexico City." She looked at Doc and said with a twinkle in her eyes, "I'm going to behave so I can plan ahead. And if *you* behave I might even invite you."

Beth pushed back her hair to put her new gold hoop earrings in view. She fingered the gold rope necklace and looked at Geoff. "I love my gift. And I know they were expensive."

Geoff winked and mouthed, "You're worth every dollar."

She announced Peg and Alan Mawhorter had surprised her with a red carry-on case and two pieces of matching luggage. On the card they indicated they were going to attend her graduation that evening.

Dan Friedman had caught her off guard by giving her a lovely silk scarf and a sentimental card he had signed with "*Lots of love, let's keep in touch.*" Since they had exchanged pictures earlier she had not expected a gift. She quickly told him she planned to buy him something special, in Europe.

But of all the gifts Julie's meant the most. The books had been covered in rich burgundy hand tooled leather and lettered in gold. When Beth opened the box and realized the importance of the gift she cried. Then Julie cried with her. And they had hugged each other with compassion. And caring.

ELIZABETH Rhodes received a Certificate of Merit from the National Honor Society, a good Citizenship Award from the DAR, a Chorus Letter, A Drama Club Letter, a Debating Team Letter, a certificate for being on the Assistant Editor of THE BRIDGE, a Varsity Hockey Team Letter, and her diploma.

Bradford Livingston received a letter of Commendation from the National Merit Scholarship Program, the Faculty Award for Service to Bridgeboro High School, The American Legion Award for outstanding male athlete, the outstanding personality and compatibility Award from the faculty and classmates, five Service Letters, a certificate for being the Editor of THE BRIDGE, and his diploma.

Beth forced herself to appear pleased as Mary Ann Powers received the check for twenty-five hundred dollars as the winner of the Essay Contest. Beth shut out the words which the stout and overly dressed President of the Bridgeborough Women's Club was spraying out in praise of Mary Ann's essay. Brad was sitting two rows in front of her. She wished he could hug her.

He got a haircut. Doesn't he look handsome Daddy? And here I am, wearing the watch and the bracelet he gave me. And there he is, afraid to wear the ring. But I love him. Geoff is nice and I might not see Brad all summer? And Geoff and I have fun together and we're going to be in Paris together. And I haven't had the guts to tell Brad. Daddy. I wish you were here. I still need you.

After the ceremony was over Beth hurried into the main hall. She had a sudden desire to run. Out of the building. She knew Doc, Geoff and Julie, and Peg and Alan, would be waiting for her but she did not want to find them. And she didn't want them to find her.

She wanted to find Brad. Maybe she was a little confused about her feelings but she did know she wanted to see him. At least be near him. Maybe touch him? One more time. By the time she did find him, he was surrounded by family and friends. If one of the group had not been his hateful father she may have pushed closer to yell out, "Congratulation, Brad. Way to go."

For many seconds she watched his mother and maybe his Aunt Eunice and her rich husband praising him. Then she walked away. Feeling dejection, even depression, she began to unbutton her sky blue gown. She felt a hand on her left shoulder. When she saw who it was she smiled. And felt joy.

"I've been looking for you," Mr. Stookey said. "I want to tell you how much I've enjoyed being with you. Tthe past four years. And again I'm sorry you weren't the winner."

"Thank you. I've enjoyed being with you. I know Mary Ann needs the money more than I do. But it would have been nice to win." *Please god, no tears.*

He gently pushed Beth out of the traffic. "I read it three times. So did Mr. Jones. It may not mean much to you now, but he and I are damn mad that you didn't win. Dick Livingston influenced the other judges that you didn't need the money. We think highly of your writing and this contest was based on quality writing."

Beth felt hot tears welling around her eyes. She forced a weak grin.

Mr. Stookey handed her a folded white cotton handkerchief. "It's obvious your friendship with Mrs. Fischer had a lot to do with his attitude."

Beth nodded. She looked into Mr. Stookey's eyes. "Thank you. Because I know you worked behind the scenes with Geoff and Doc, so that I can go to Penn State University."

Mr. Stookey grinned. "My Alma Mater. Besides your writing, there is something else I wanted to talk about. Do you remember the name Professor Williams?"

"Didn't you ask Julie if you could invite him to meet with her? To talk about Vicki?"

"Right. He's the Department Head of Lit. He wants to meet you. To talk over your doing some typing and odds and ends for him."

Beth's eyes opened wide. God, she loved this teacher! "Wow. How come?"

"You've impressed him." He enjoyed Beth's surprised look. "Okay. Confession time. I've given him copies of your poems and short stories. *And* editorials to read. Even the ones you wrote for Brad."

"You knew." She was beginning to feel adoration for the man standing in front of her.

"This is to be kept m-u-m. But remember those books written by S.A. Smyth which I loaned you?" He watched her nod. "S. A. Smyth, alias Samuel Alexander Williams."

"In other words, he's been published." Beth breathed. "I really *do* want to meet him."

"And he's working on another novel. He can be a great help to you."

Beth wanted to kiss her favorite teacher. Logic convinced her to just gaze into his eyes and whisper, "I have to tell you, Mr. Stookey. You're wonderful."

"Shhh. My wife might hear you." He grinned and looked past her. "And maybe Geoff Greer can read lips," he quickly added as he saw Geoff approach them. "Remember, mum is the word. Until I can give you more details." He looked down and saw the handkerchief in Beth's hand. He wanted her to keep it.

He spoke to Geoff. "Are you looking for this lovely lady?"

Geoff wrapped an arm around Beth's waist. "I've been looking for her . . . for a long time." He looked down at Beth and remarked, "You should see Julie. She's having a ball, being recognized and shaking hands. She's causing more commotion than you graduates."

Beth and Geoff said good-bye to Mr. Stookey. She was glad he forgot about his handkerchief. As she and Geoff walked through the hall she reached inside her gown and tucked it in the pocket of her dress.

WALKING with Geoff, she felt important. And thrilled. Not only was she still excited from her conversation with Mr. Stookey but Geoff Greer was holding her hand. She was more than pleased when Jill and Dot walked toward them. She introduced Geoff and deliberately leaned against him. Then she saw Dan approaching them and she felt relief. Perhaps seeing her with Geoff would help Dan realize there was nothing special between them. She let Dan peck at her cheek and hold her hand while he flattered her.

Out of the crowd, Alan Mawhorter appeared. He kissed Beth on a cheek and hugged her, roughly. "Congratulations, Beth. I'm really proud to know you."

"Thanks, Alan. She looked around them. "Where's Peg?"

"She couldn't make it. She's . . . well, she hasn't been feeling too sharp for the past couple of weeks." Alan stepped closer to Beth. "She's pregnant."

"Oh? That's too bad," Beth blurted out. "I mean that she doesn't feel well."

"And that she's pregnant. She wasn't mentally prepared." Alan winked. "Those damn home comings can really catch you off guard. Anyway she's anxious to move to Europe."

"You truly are going to move? To the Netherlands?"

"I hope so. That's Plan A."

I hope so too, Beth quickly thought, but all she could say was "Wow."

"It could be fun because the baby could have a dual citizenship."

Beth looked past Alan to the back of Jim Bender. He was at least six inches taller than Alan. His thick blonde hair made such a contrast against the thin brown hair of the older man.

Beth thought, *You better move. In case your son becomes a six foot plus Adonis.*

"But if we don't move to Europe, "Alan continued, "at least we're moving out of Taylor Park. I imagine you two were happy to move away from there?"

Beth and Geoff nodded. Geoff spoke first. "Enough is enough."

Alan smiled. "We feel that way too. Peg wants to move. Anywhere."

Beth squinted and quickly thought, *And change food markets.* "Remember me to Peg. And my little girlfriends." She reached for one of Alan's hands. "And thanks again for the lovely luggage. I love it. Now I can start packing for our trip."

"Send us some cards. When are you two leaving?"

"One week from Saturday."

After they bid farewell to Alan, Geoff decided they had to find Julie and Doc. Julie gave Beth a demonstrative hug and a kiss. Doc kissed Beth also. With meaning.

How could she not feel important! She knew many prominent people from Bridgeboro were paying attention to Julie. She even caught a glimpse of Lou and Charles Barnes watching. Jeanne was nowhere in sight. Had she invited Jim Bender to her party? Brad was going. Would he have the nerve to tell Jeanne, tonight? Suddenly Beth felt hot tears welling up around her eyes. She swallowed several times. Still tears trickled down each cheek.

Geoff noticed and whispered, "What's the matter? You okay?"

"I don't know. I guess I'm feeling sentimental." She clutched the handkerchief and blotted her cheeks.

"Julie Fischer," a deep masculine voice boomed out from the crowd. "What a surprise."

Julie turned and gave a broad smile. "Harvey Schneider. How nice to see you." She reached out to shake the hand of the president of a local bank. Again Julie was wearing her wedding bands and the lovely solitaire diamond ring. She had worn them to the Fischer Company and on Sunday and Tuesday evenings.

Beth enjoyed observing Julie in action. She reminded herself Julie knew most of the key people in Bridgeboro would be in attendance for the graduation ceremony and she would be one of the star performers. She must always remember Julie was a woman with power and purpose. It was interesting to hear the assertiveness in her voice and observe her body language. Beth was proud she knew her. She looked at Doc and watched him glow. She returned Geoff's knowing smile in spite of the tears.

"Beth, I'd like you to meet Harvey Schneider, president of the *Bridgeboro National Bank.* Harvey, this is my companion, Beth Rhodes. You know Geoff. And of course Philip. We came to watch Beth graduate."

After everybody shook hands Harvey said, "We came to watch my granddaughter, Shirley Chappel, graduate. And I see you're weepy eyed also. Shirley is crying her eyes out. She said she can't bear the thought of not coming back here anymore"

Beth nodded. "I know what she means. It's a very sad night."

THIRTY NINE

AFTER THEY RETURNED to Julie's house, Geoff put two semi-classical records on the new stereo in the living room. He had brought them with him. Julie wanted to hear them to decide if she wanted to buy the same collection. Geoff and Doc removed their jackets and ties and Julie asked Geoff to open a bottle of champagne which she had put in the refrigerator.

Holding up her crystal flute Julie proposed a toast to Beth followed by drinking and talking while the music played in the background.

After Julie filled her flute for the third time Doc commented, "I'm watching you." He turned to Beth. "She is telling me the truth about behaving, isn't she?"

Beth nodded. "As far as I know."

"The sherry before dinner was the first drink I've had in ages," Julie said. "And we're celebrating." She held up her flute. "Beth is now a citizen of the world. And I'm happy."

Phillip nodded. "I'm happy you're happy but let's give Geoff what's left in the bottle." He picked up the bottle and returned to the couch to sit beside Geoff.

"You're not going to spoil my party," Julie declared. Tonight is a big night."

Beth was rocking and watching Julie. She was happy also. Because Doc and Geoff were with her. Geoff emptied the contents of the bottle into his flute. Julie rearranged herself in the wing back chair and began to talk about everyone she had seen at the high school.

Finally Doc blurted out, "For god's sake say it. You won't be able to sleep if you don't tell us what you think about the way Bernice looks and how much you still dislike Dick."

After Julie replied, "She's fat and he's a bastard." Doc continued. "Is that enough? I want you to get it all out or you'll be thirsty all night. I know how you and Dick can irritate each other and . . . "

Julie interrupted Philip. "It's more than irritation. I loathe him. But there's the one who's suffering." She pointed a finger at Beth. "As soon as she decided to write about Vicki and interview me she didn't have a chance of winning."

"Oh Julie," Beth blurted out. "That isn't true. I *am* a winner."

She knew the champagne was causing her to be emotional. She lowered her voice and added, "I don't want to sound dramatic but that's the way I feel." She looked at Geoff and Doc before she continued. "Hey, I'd be lying if I tried to convince you or myself I don't care that I didn't win." She forced a grin. "I had to bite my tongue - to keep from crying. But having all of you in my life and . . . " she hunched her shoulders, "makes me feel very lucky."

"I'm sure I speak for Geoff when I say we men have been having some enjoyable times." Doc patted his protruding abdomen. "And fulfilling. So we're all lucky to know each other."

After everyone agreed and added comments as they smiled at each other, Doc stood. "Now. I am going to depart this happy scene. My buddy Jim is going to pick me up at five. And I know that old son of a gun will finagle me into driving up to the cabin. Always seems to have something wrong with his car." He walked to the rocking chair. "Young lady. Thank you for including me in your special events."

Beth quickly stood. "I'm happy you wanted to attend. And thank you again for the camera." She put her arms around him and kissed him on a cheek. "Have a great time. But call as soon as you get back."

Geoff stood and extended his hand to Doc. "I'll be out of town also. A friend from college invited me to spend the week-end at his house at the shore." He looked at Beth and smiled. "But I will be back to pack for Paris."

Doc nodded at Geoff. "I hope we both have good weather." He looked down at Julie. "You go to bed. You look tired from your grand appearances this past week. But behave yourself. For your sake and," he smiled at Beth and Geoff, "everybody's sake."

Julie stood. She reached for one of Philip's hands. "God only knows why I keep you as my doctor. Your bedside manner is sadly lacking in T.L.C."

Philip laid a hand on Julie's shoulder. "It's because of my T.L.C I'm still your doctor."

Beth and Geoff watched as Julie and Philip looked tenderly at each other. Beth yearned to say, "Go ahead and kiss." She gave Geoff a quick look and saw him wink at her.

Finally Doc backed away from Julie and announced, "God help Paris after you three get done with her. And let's think up something to do together before Beth goes to college. It'll be my treat." Doc picked up his suit jacket and let Beth walk with him to the front door. He had parked his car in the driveway.

When Beth returned Julie yawned loudly. "I wouldn't let Philip know he's right but I really can't wait to get into bed. I'm pooped." After Beth added, "You certainly were popular this evening." Julie laughed. "I was, wasn't I? And I loved it. I'm going to have to attend more events. It's good for my moral."

Geoff added, "If you keep it up you might receive more invitations than you can handle."

"What everybody will be hoping for is that I'll have a big wing ding after we move to Deer Lake Manor." She raised her eyebrows. "Maybe my social secretary and I will have to plan an open house."

Beth pretended she was overwhelmed. "Ye gads. At least give us a chance to unpack and do the laundry, after we get back from Paris. Before I have to send out invitations."

Geoff stood. "I'm going home too." He covered a yawn.

"Oh no. I was hoping to listen to the music floating into my room as I drift off to sleep."

"I'll leave the records on the machine. I can pick them up later."

"You stay with them. I'm sure you and Beth can talk about Paris. Or something."

As Julie walked into the hall Beth called out, "Thanks again, Julie. For everything." She knew it sounded like a matter-of-fact statement but she felt compelled to say it.

Geoff put his hands around Beth's upper arms and kissed her forehead. "It's been a big night for you."

"It's been a big emotional week. And it's going to be a big emotional summer."

Geoff decided to stay. He sensed she needed a listening ear. And he wanted to ask her something important. After he sat at the opposite end of the couch he said, "The trip is going to be a ball. Especially after I join you. And living in Deer Lake Manor will be a nice experience. And what else?"

"I'm traveling in new territory. I've never been to so many meetings and made so many phone calls and typed so many letters. And now we're going to get involved in the financing and building the office building which," she added in a whisper, "might make her thirsty? It's scary."

"Beth, I know you still miss your dad but remember Doc and I are as close as the telephone. I'm not going to desert you even though you have a special person in your life. Just so it isn't Mr. Stookey. He's even older than I am!"

He reached out and took one of her hands. "You know we haven't had a chance to have a heart to heart talk since I told you my secret. At the reception. At the restaurant. I'd like to know how you feel about me. Now that you know about my other life?"

Beth squeezed his hand. "First of all, do your dad and Ellen know?" She watched him nod. "And I know they still love you. I fell in love with you when you were our cute paper boy. And I was jealous when Evan got your attention. I even hated her because I thought she hurt you."

Geoff sighed deeply. "She wanted us to get married and she'd play the game. She even gave herself to me, because she wanted me to be the first one. And I haven't told anybody until now, that she left me because *I* pushed *her* away. Now you know what kind of a heel I am."

Beth shrugged. "I don't know what to say. Except she must have cared about you to take the blame and follow Les. And I have to tell you she sent me a graduation card. With a return address on the envelope. She lives in Norfolk. She wrote that she's okay. And please do not tell Liz. That's all I know. But if I write to her, is it okay if I tell her . . . we see each other? Because of Julie."

She smiled. "I won't mention that we slept together." After he smiled and winked, she added, "If you're happy. I'm happy. But I am sad also. For Evan and for me. And all of the rest of the females in Bridgeboro who think you're a hunk. When are you going to tell Julie?"

"When I tell her I'm going to move. Into a house. With a man. Terry. And for your info. Mr. Gillon does know."

He grinned. "But we'll have fun in Paris."

Beth nodded and grinned back. Inside she screamed, *What kind of game am I playing? I don't even want to go on the trip.*

"*Oui Oui.* And ya betcha" He stood and smiled at Beth. "Welcome to the great big world of reality. Just remember. I love you. And am as close as the telephone. And now, goodnight."

She walked with him to the back door. She felt happy after he kissed her goodnight. Especially because he had kissed her mouth!

BETH turned off the outside light. The moon was bright enough that the lawn was covered with shadows. It looked inviting. She wondered if she should go outside and just wander around in the refreshing night air. Check out the heavens above Bridgeboro. She decided to let someone else do the star gazing. She really was tired.

She locked the screen door. But left the mud room door open. Julie had closed her bedroom door. Here she was alone while her friends were enjoying visits with relatives. Brad with his aunt and uncle. From Richmond. And Dan was excited having an aunt and uncle who lived in Israel attend his graduation. But she did have Julie and Doc and Geoff. Then she envisioned the frolic perhaps even frenzy that was going on at Jeanne's party.

She checked the plants on the window sill. They didn't needed water because Julie was taking care of them. But Gerry needed a peanut and a few sunflower seeds. She walked into the living room.

She'd wait for the last record to finish playing. How dumb could she be? Julie most likely was unconscious by now. Still why take a chance? She turned off all but one of the lamps. She cuddled in the corner of the couch where Geoff had sat. She remembered his kiss. She reminded herself how much she enjoyed being with him. What might happen in Paris? What might happen if he visited her at Penn State? Could they forget their special friends? Named Brad and Terry?

Daddy. So I graduated and I'm going to college. Julie is unhappy because she wanted me to apply to more prestigious college. But I wanted to go where Mr. Stookey went. But I am mixed up. Evan sent me a graduation card and I've been wondering if I should visit her? Before I go to Europe? Damn. I miss you.

Beth laid her head against the back of the couch and tried to concentrate on the pleasant music. Geoff. Brad. Brad. Geoff. Help! Why not just let . . .*what* was she hearing? A car?

Beth hurried into the kitchen. Was Geoff returning? Surely he wouldn't slam his door. Beth surprised herself when she admitted she really did not want it to be Geoff.

Finally she heard what sounded like someone shuffling across the parking lot.

The screen door was locked. Still she felt alarm. Somewhere out there. Was someone! Waiting? Now she could hear loud, labored breathing. And what sounded like – gagging!

Through the screen Beth decided to demand, "Who's out there?" She waited. Tense.

Finally, she heard a loud whisper. "Beth?"

Then she knew who it was.

FORTY

"BRAD!"

Beth stepped outside. She felt alarm as soon as she observed him. He was holding his abdomen and kneeling at the edge of the patio. Was he injured?

Suddenly she didn't care what might be wrong with him. What if Julie heard him? So he had a problem. What did he think *she* should do?

She stepped closer and leaned down to him. "What's wrong with you?"

"I want to die." He crawled to the grass.

Beth knelt next to him. Immediately she smelled the familiar odor of alcohol. You're supposed to be at Jeanne's house." After he moaned, "I was. That's where I got loaded." she demanded, "Where are Mr. and Mrs. Barnes?"

"I think at our house." Brad lay on the grass. "Can you help me?"

"Help you do what? And you could have had an accident!" Beth realized she was being unkind but he had to know she was not happy to see him.

"I need you."

"What can *I* do? Julie can't know you're here."

"Then dig a hole and bury me. As soon as I'm lucky enough to die."

Beth had to laugh. He was so pathetic he was funny. "Are you sick?"

"I'm everything spelled a-w-f-u-l. I feel the worst I've ever felt in my entire life."

"If you stick your fingers down your throat and upchuck you might feel better?"

"Shit. I hate to do that. Could you make me some coffee?"

"I guess so."

"I know you're mad. Because Julie could hear us."

"Or smell you." Beth stroked his wet forehead. He needed her. "I'll make the coffee."

"With lots of sugar. I'll stay out here. The cold grass feels good." He stretched out on his back. "Wake me up if I fall asleep. Or bury me if I die."

"Dead or alive, you can't stay here all night. I'll be back in a few minutes."

Beth closed the louvered doors to the hall. As quietly as she could she put a pan of water on the stove, put instant coffee in a mug and waited. As she thought about Brad in Julie's back yard she marveled he had been able to drive. Because he wanted her to help him. She was that important to him. She put some ice in a dish towel to put on the top of his head.

BETH sat on the ground while Brad leaned against her. He sipped from the mug with the compress on his head. "How much did you have to drink?"

"Too damn much. I wanted to drown my sorrows." He hiccupped. "And get back at my old man by getting drunk." Another hiccup.

"And now you want to die because you wanted to embarrass your father. Nice going. We knew I wasn't going to win the contest."

"I almost turned around to look at you when that fat broad gave the check to Mary Ann."

He laid his wet head on her shoulder and mumbled, "You know I love you. I don't want you to be hurt. Especially by my father. And all I could do was to give you a crummy bracelet. And get drunk." He began to cry. And hiccup.

She held up her arm. "I love my bracelet. But you were s.t.u.p.i.d to get drunk. You could have had an accident."

"I had to be with you." He wiped his eyes on a sleeve.

"Were the other kids getting drunk?"

"Yeah. And smoking pot. You could get high just from the smoke." He hiccupped.

"If Mr. Jones finds out . . . he's going to be furious. Especially after sending out a letter practically pleading with the parents not to have any unsupervised parties. Look what happened at Jerry's house. After the Senior Prom."

"I guess Jeanne's folks thought we'd keep it a pool party. But Jeanne and Jim wanted to make a toast and she knew where her folks

318

hide the hard stuff. While I still could count I counted four empty bottles of the best gin and vodka. Jeanne was loaded. There's going to be a bunch of sick kids who'll need a ride home."

"I'm glad you decided to leave. Drink some more coffee."

"It's so hot it's making me sweat."

"And you smell awful. If you can be real quiet I'll let you come inside and wash your face and arms in the wash tub."

"Okay. Help me up."

Beth put the mug and compress on a bench by the door. She took Brad's hands and pulled.

"I have to do it . . . slowly. I feel so dizzy I'm afraid I'll fall."

FINALLY, Beth was successful in getting Brad to a chair next to the kitchen table. As soon as he sat down he laid his arms on the table and his head on his arms. Beth went outside to get the mug and compress.

After Beth used the dish towel to wipe Brad's face, neck and arms, she sat next to him. "Lift your head. I'm going to spoon the coffee into your mouth."

Brad opened his mouth every time Beth put the spoon to his lips. "I love you." After Beth held a finger to her lips he still asked, "Do I hear music?"

"It's Geoff's records. Julie really thinks he's here."

"I saw you together tonight."

"Uh huh." Another spoonful of coffee.

"Just like you wanted me and everybody else. You like him, don't you?" Hiccup.

"Julie wants us to be twosome."

"Oh sure. It's not that he's nice looking and older . . . and rich. I'll bet you've even gone all the way with him. Right?" Hiccup.

"Why don't you just open your mouth for coffee?" She put the spoon to his mouth.

Brad shook his head from side to side and gagged. "I...think...I'm going to be...sick."

Beth put the dish towel in front of Brad's mouth helped him stand and steered him into the laundry room. She managed to pull the door half way closed behind them. She held Brad's head while he upchucked into the laundry tub. She used the spray to clean out the tub. Once. Twice. Then she washed his mouth and face. "You have to stay in here because you might have to do it again." She used the towel.

"There's going to be a lot of other sick kids. From alcohol or getting pregnant."

"That was going on too?"

"In cars. On the deck. And in some of the bedrooms."

Beth felt a shiver of something jolt through her. Excitement? Disbelief? Panic? "Are you trying to tell me something? Like you and Jeanne did it again?"

"I was in her room. But after she took off her clothes and tried to take off mine, I left. She was on her bed, naked. Begging me to. But I swear to God, I left. All I remember is the moaning and groaning and giggles and . . .oh..." Brad gagged and upchucked again.

Again she wiped his mouth. Should she believe him? Why not? She knew she had wanted to do it with Geoff.

Brad turned his head and looked into Beth's eyes. He was crying again. "She said she'd give me another chance because I had been so pathetic the first time . . . but..."

"I believe you. Just stop talking about it, or *I'm* going to upchuck." She kissed Brad's wet neck. "I think you'll start to feel better now that you ..."

BETH turned her head and looked toward the doorway. There, stood Julie!

At least seven feet tall and looking as wicked as Lucifer must have appeared to the Arch Angel stood Julie! Beth was so frightened she felt as though she might faint. She stared back at the frightening woman and breathed, "Oh, I'm sorry. We tried not to disturb you."

Julie was wearing a pink chiffon robe over a lacey pink nightgown. Still she looked menacing. In a demanding voice she asked, "What is *he* doing in my house?"

"He's sick. I'm helping him feel better."

Brad gagged before he turned to Julie. A string of slobber was hanging from his lips.

Quickly Beth wiped his mouth.

"He's sick because he's drunk!"

"He isn't used to drinking."

"I'm sorry we disturbed you," Brad mumbled.

Julie ignored Brad. She glared at Beth. "As soon as he's finished using my laundry tub I want him out of here."

"If he could just stay . . . until he feels better."

"I do not want *him* in my house!"

"I'll clean up everything," was all that Beth could think to say.

"How did *he* get here?"

"I drove."

"From Barnes'?" Julie asked loudly.

Beth nodded as she wondered how Julie knew Barnes were having a party? Her spies?

"And *why* did he come here?" Julie demanded!

Beth's mouth went dry and her tongue become thick. All within a few seconds. But now *was* the time. She *had* to tell Julie! "Because he's my boyfriend."

"*He's* . . . your boyfriend!" Julie put a hand over her heart.

"Uh huh. It's Brad Livingston."

"I happen to know who he is. I just can't believe you'd be so stupid."

Julie turned and hurried to the sink. She opened the cabinet underneath and reached for a can of air freshener. She sprayed it around the kitchen. Then she walked to the door of the laundry room and aimed it directly at Beth and Brad.

Beth couldn't move. Almost in a trance she felt the spray cover her. She knew she would not be surprised if Julie decided to spray her and Brad with insect killer. From the look on Julie's face she seemed to consider them venomous creatures.

"I want him to leave!"

"Julie," Beth said as gently as she could, "Don't you remember that you said my boyfriend should come here? So you could meet him?"

"I remember. But now I know you tried to make an ass out of me."

"That's not true. I was only asking you to help us. And you said you would."

Brad stood next to Beth. He stood tall. Convincingly. Determined.

Julie backed out of the laundry room. "Obviously," she said loudly, "If you had told me who it was I could have saved you a lot of trouble. And myself a lot of anguish."

"Please, Julie." Beth stepped to the doorway. Julie had to listen to her. "Brad has never done anything to you. Just because you don't like his father doesn't mean you have to dislike him too." She stepped into the kitchen. "Julie. I love him."

Julie stood taller. She frowned as she said sarcastically, "Really? Well for your information that means absolutely nothing to me. I'd be out of my mind to help you see *him*. He's supposed to be going steady with Jeanne Barnes." She waited.

"He's going to break off with her. As soon as he thinks he can tell his parents."

"Meanwhile you're both lying and cheating. Even if you don't have any shame, *I'm* ashamed of you!"

"We wouldn't have to sneak if you'd help us."

Julie banged the can of air freshener on a counter top. "Positively not." She glared at Beth. "I'm going back to bed."

Brad stepped to the doorway. "Mrs. Fischer. I'm very sorry to meet you this way. If Beth and I could talk with you under different circumstances we could ..." He paused as it became obvious Julie was studying him.

She slid her eyes from his hair to his shoes. Then back to his face where her eyes roamed around every feature. "There can never be different circumstances." She turned to Beth. "And in your best interest young lady, I do not want him in my house. Again."

Suddenly Beth felt anger. It was strong enough to overpower her judgment. Before she could stop herself she yelled out, "All right, Julie Fischer. If you won't help us . . . you'll be sorry."

Julie snorted. Before she laughed. Before she coughed. "Give him some ginger ale and soda crackers," she said before she stalked out of the kitchen. And slammed her bedroom door.

THEY were sitting in Brad's car in Julie's driveway when Brad asked "Do you think she'll tell anybody?"

Beth shrugged. "I don't know what she might do. Except not call your parents."

"I'm sorry. I really wasn't thinking too clearly or I wouldn't have come here."

"I know you're sorry. But the more I think about it the happier I am you did. Now I don't have to figure out what to do. And I know you need me."

"I sure do. But I know how much you have going for you living with Julie. I hope I haven't loused it up."

Beth managed to laugh. "You two could have met under more ideal circumstances. But tonight just might force the issue. The seed has been planted and…"

"And I hope, "Brad interrupted, "it doesn't grow into a weed. I know you're looking forward to the trip. But it isn't as important as going to college. And having a roof over your head. We'll find a way. Because we love each other." He kissed her forehead. "I better go."

"What're you going to tell your parents? If they find out you left the party?"

"I drove down to Julie's house. To see Beth."

"And that could make two of us out on the sidewalk. With our suitcases."

"How about I started to drive home and got sick and pulled up a side road somewhere between Barnes and our house? And fell asleep."

Beth held Brad's face and kissed him. "Good luck and I love you. No matter what happens."

"I love you back . . . more," Brad added. "And I know we'll find a way."

FORTY ONE

THE MORNING AFTER the night before Beth finally forced herself to make an appearance in the kitchen. She put on a happy face and a lilt in her voice and almost sang, "Good morning."

Julie was sitting in the bay. Her "Good morning" was flat and weak. Even though she was dressed in a colorful flower print cotton skirt and a bright pink blouse she looked forlorn.

Beth had decided to play the conversation, *by ear.* She looked at the wall clock. "Sorry, I slept so late." She really had lingered in her bedroom before she was ready to confront Julie.

Julie walked to the stove. "Do you want bacon or ham with you eggs?"

"Bacon, please. But isn't it my turn to cook breakfast?"

Julie returned to where she had been sitting.

As Beth watched the sizzling bacon her mind was racing. What should she talk about? The birds? The night before? Gerry? The night before? How should she talk about the night before? She really didn't want breakfast.

Julie cleared her throat. "What shall we do today?"

Beth shrugged. "Anything you want to." She really wanted to go back to bed.

"Some shopping? We might find some odds and ends for the trip."

"That's a good idea. But I do have to do some laundry."

"Would you like to have lunch or dinner out?"

"Whatever you want to do." Beth turned the bacon.

"I'm trying to please you," Julie snapped out. "And keep you busy."

"I'm just trying to let you know I'm willing to do anything."

"Ha." Julie put the mug down with force. "Anything to keep peace between us. Why be so thoughtful now? The damage already has been done."

"Please believe me when I tell you Brad does not drink. It was unfortunate you had to meet him like he was." Beth covered the bacon with paper towels. She saw that Julie had put out the "grease can" in which they stored drippings from bacon, ground meat or whatever. After she poured some of the bacon grease into the can she broke two eggs into the pan. She turned and looked into Julie's puffy eyes. "Just let him park his car behind the garage. We'll sit in his car and talk."

"And take your clothes off like that hussy Jeanne, and…"

"You were listening!"

"I heard that much. And it sounded as though it wasn't the first time either. How can you love a person who goes to bed with another girl?" She put two slices of bread in a toaster.

"You wanted Bill Fischer even though he went all the way with your sister."

Julie looked at Beth and smiled. "And are you Vicki or me?"

"Neither." Beth flipped the eggs. "I love Brad because I believe in him."

"And how long have you two been hiding your love? From the cruel world?"

"Since December."

"Now I know why you didn't tell me trickie Dickie was at your house. I'm sure to try to bribe you. You were afraid of what I might do."

Beth put the eggs and bacon on plates and took them to the table. "You knew that too?"

"I *told* you. I have spies."

Beth stared at her plate. Was she going to be able to eat? She watched Julie put the bread plates on the table. "Do they follow Mr. and Mrs. Livingston around?"

"Not really, but I do have a snitch, here and there."

Beth spread butter on her toast. She was going to force herself to eat. Before she took a bite she looked into Julie's face. "You know, Mr. Livingston hates you too. He told me he's almost sure he knows something more about the fire."

"Are you trying to scare me? He did put an article in *The B.C.* referring to it as a suspicious explosion. Evidently you defended Bill and me. That we tried to save Vicki?" She watched Beth nod. "I still do not owe you a favor by letting that young man come down here."

"And I don't owe you anything." Why did she say that? Julie had once said she could be walking on eggs! "You've done some lovely things for me, but I can't let you run my life."

"I'm not trying to run your life. I can't believe you would say such a thing."

"Then stop trying to push Geoff and me together. And I'm going to keep seeing Brad."

"Why are you doing this to me? Knowing what I can do for you."

"And I'm grateful. You have to know how much I care for you. Not because of what you've given me or can give me, because I have grown close to you and . . ."

Julie looked into Beth's eyes. "I think it's time for me to tell you something."

Beth felt dread. She had an intense desire to whisper, "I don't want to hear something."

"Brad Livingston is a bastard."

"Don't you dare call Brad that!"

"I'm telling you what he is. I didn't intend to. But I've just decided you might as well know. Okay, maybe he isn't a bastard, but he is adopted."

Beth pushed her chair back. She might upchuck. She stared at Julie's face looking for a sign she was playing games with her. Finally she whispered, "You're lying."

"Unfortunately it's the God's honest truth. The only biological Livingston son is a Mongoloid, who is hidden away in an institution in Virginia."

"How do you know all this stuff? Your spies?"

"This time it was Earle who told me what I shouldn't know. The pastor of his church found the baby on the porch of the church." Julie held out her mug. "I'd like more coffee."

In between sips, Julie told Beth the story Bernice and Richard feared she knew.

"He doesn't have to be illegitimate. Maybe his parents couldn't afford to keep him."

Putting spitefulness in her voice, Julie said, "Sure. And another idea might be he has nigger blood in him"

"Since you hate the Livingston's so much how come you've never told anybody?"

"I just told you. Even though you'll believe I told you because you hurt me."

Beth began to clear the table. She scraped all of the uneaten food on one plate and began to rinse the dishes. All the while she was mulling over what to say. No, really, how to say it? "I think it will be a good idea if I go away. For a few days."

Calmly, Julie asked, "What nonsense are you talking about?"

"I think if we take a little break maybe you won't hate me."

"I'll hate you if you go. Where?"

"To visit my sister." Beth reached for the hand towel and wiped her hands

"You know where she is?"

"She sent me a graduation card. She'd like me to visit her. She's been sick and . . ." She was searching for more words when she heard Julie laugh and say, "Did she tell you if she has a dose of clap?"

Suddenly Beth disliked Julie. "I want to see her while I still have a few free days. Before we go on the trip. And when we come back we can decide if I should move into the apartment. So we don't keep picking at each other. I'll still work for you."

Julie stood. "Well, aren't you clever? You'll keep yourself on my payroll but keep seeing your lover boy. At least you know you need me." Beth kept drying her hands and agreed, "I know I do." before Julie added, "I thought we were getting along just fine. Until last night." Julie breathed deeply. "How long will you be gone?"

"Over night? Or maybe two nights? I just want to see her. Again."

"Beth, how stupid do you think I am? Evan doesn't have anything to do with this. Oh, go see her. And I'm not even going to ask where she is. But now I know why you were storing the furniture. For a little love nest. Just like Vicki."

"That's not true. I want Brad to stay with his parents and not have to suffer."

"Ohhhh. You know if you leave here you might suffer?"

"I really don't want to . . . have to leave."

"And it's my fault you are." Julie leaned back in the chair. "Okay. Go see your sister. Although I can't believe you want to get mixed up in her life. Can you go by bus?" She watched Beth nod. "I'll even give you some travel money. Make a quick visit and just maybe you'll realize what you're missing."

"And . . . maybe you'll let me see Brad?"

"I'm not going to make any promises. What I will tell you is that I'll be hoping you'll come to your senses and get over this teenage crush. And grow up while we're in Europe." She hoped she had planted a seed that might germinate to her advantage. And salvation.

Beth sniffed and blew her nose while packing. Over and over she told herself she really did not want to go. Ideas and fears collided. What if Julie had some bottles hidden? Of course she could drive to an out of town State Store or maybe bribe Sam?

Maybe Brad was an orphan? His parents had been in a bad accident, or murdered, and he didn't have any aunts or uncles. Maybe his mom had been an unwed teenager and lived in Taylor Park? Ha! They would have something in common.

What if she couldn't find Evan? But if she did find her Evan would tell her to get lost? What if Julie told Geoff where she was going? She had to call him. Except he was going away. He and Doc should know . . . Julie would be alone.

BETH Rhodes struggled to keep her composure as she said goodbye to Julie Fischer. Tears of frustration continued to trickle down her cheeks during the ride to Philadelphia. She had called ahead to make a reservation for the trip to Norfolk. She had to take two busses before she arrived at the Greyhound Terminal. And found a phone booth.

"Mr. Greer's office." his secretary informed Beth.

"Hello, Betty It's Beth Rhodes. I was hoping to get Geoff before he left for the shore."

"He left right from home."

Should she ask if Geoff had left a phone number?

While Beth thought, Betty suggested, "Just in case he does call, do you want me to tell him to call you at Mrs. Fischer's?"

"I would appreciate that. Thank you, Betty. Goodbye."

Why not let Geoff call Julie? That way he would know she was alone. In fact, why not call Julie, herself? Now. She might urge Beth to change her mind? Should she?

Beth did board the bus. She was going to Norfolk. Looking at her reflection in a dirty bus window she confessed to herself she was afraid.

FORTY TWO

WHILE BETH RHODES was traveling to Norfolk, Richard Livingston was riding high.

Brad had done him proud not being at Barnes' house when Lou and Charles returned. Brad admitted he had been drinking. And had pulled off the road. But he had not been at the scene of the outrageous party. It was another gold star on the Livingston record of smart thinking.

Richard was trying to concentrate on letters and memos before him. They all pertained to the present. And to a business which was boring him. He forced himself to pay attention to the most important correspondence, before he pushed everything aside. Except one letter. He smiled as he reviewed the notes he had written when he had returned Hank Orhle's call.

It had been a good move to cultivate Hank's friendship. Hank was keeping him updated on Executive Committee meetings and Julie's frequent and unexpected visits. Hank's latest inside information was that Julie indicated she *was* going to have a public stock offering.

Number One on his Attention! note pad was – *BUY FISCHER STOCK* !! Of course it would be up to the investor response as to what the share price would be. Number Two was to polish the letter he would mail to the new shareholders. It had to be a subtle yet an undermining letter that would examine how mismanaged the *Fischer Company* might become.

He probably should decide which lawyer to contact. As much as he detested having to include another person in his plan he must keep his plans legal. He had to have all of his ducks in a row because his time in the sun was approaching reality. He rolled back his desk chair and stood. He chuckled before he whispered, "Hallelujah."

He decided to have lunch at *The Pub*. He deserved a toast to his genius.

AT the same time Richard was sipping a martini, Julie was sitting at her kitchen table. She had called Sam not to come. She too was drinking the first drink from a full bottle of Scotch. Sam had not found her hiding place among the boxes of new shoes in her closet. She smiled as she remembered there still was another bottle. Waiting.

Julie studied the label on the bottle as intently as Richard peered into his glass. With miles separating them, they both seemed to be looking for something. Julie, an answer to an old and tormenting enigma. Richard, a vision of himself as a major stock holder and member of the Board of Directors of the *Fischer Company*.

Julie wrinkled her nose. She did not like what she saw in front of her. She pushed the bottle away. She hated feeling so alone. Even afraid. She thought of dialing Geoff's office number. Even talking to his secretary might pull her out of her depression. That's what Phillip said to do. She was supposed to talk to someone. Damn Philip! Why did he have to be away when she needed him? Damn everybody.

GLASS in one hand and the bottle in the other Julie walked out of the kitchen, through the dining room, to a table in the living room To another phone. If she did call Betty what would she say to her? Want to meet me for lunch? *I need you.* She had said that to Beth, once upon a time and look what had happened. She put the bottle and glass on the coffee table. She knew she should call somebody. How about Howard? To talk company business? How about Sam? He'd come right over. How about Ellie? To change the beds and do some laundry.

Julie walked to the picture of Earle and Alice. She whispered, "My prissy prude sister-in-law. With your holier than thou smile. And my beloved brother. And your damn religion. And your damn orphanage. I hate both of you. I hate Beth. I hate that boy. Hate! Hate!" She put the picture face down on the table.

She picked up the glass and slowly shuffled to the doorway of Beth's bedroom. She peered at the unwrinkled bedspread. The precise position of the fancy white lace covered pillows which she insisted Beth must have. The stuffed purple bear Geoff had bought the day they were in New York. She ran her eyes over the lavender walls and the crispness of the white tie backs at the windows. She observed how neatly Beth had placed the brush and mirror and jewelry box and everything else on the dressing table and bureau. There was the television set Beth insisted she didn't need. And the new red luggage, waiting for the trip to Europe. At least she had taken an old suitcase to visit her trashy sister.

Suddenly the tortured woman cried out, "You damn fool you. You and your love. You were supposed to teach me how to love. You were supposed to help me. Not . . . Brad Livingston."

Julie began to cough. Hard. She leaned against the door jamb to recover. She made certain the front door was locked before she returned to the living room. She picked up the bottle and with the glass walked through the hall. In the mud room she locked the door. She'd told Sam she'd call him when she needed him. Maybe she'd be dead and not need him. Since Beth had deserted her she could take the blame. And feel guilty the rest of her life. The hell with the trip. The hell with the company. The hell with *everybody*!

IN her jewelry box Julie found the key. Bottle in one hand she unlocked the door with the other. And kicked the door opened. It banged against one of Vicki's chests. Julie stood at the doorway and let her eyes dart around the room. The silence became deafening. She began to feel the memories fill the room. The desk where Vicki had composed some of her novels. The bookcase protecting her favorite books. The table which had held refreshments for her famous guests. The chairs which held her favorite friends. The couch where she could have allowed her lovers to join her. Cringing, she knew what was going to happen. It had happened whenever she wanted to torture herself and opened the door. She would feel the frustration and anguish of knowing how popular her sister had been. Vicki always would be remembered at the height of her career.

Julie began to wail. "It isn't fair. She had everything. Even my husband. And I'm left with the pain and the aftermath. I wish I could let his goddamn company go down the drain." She leaned against the door jam and sobbed, "It isn't fair I have to suffer. Alone. Again."

Julie held the bottle to her lips and drank deep. She coughed, hiccupped and cried. Until her eyes suddenly focused on the envelopes which contained the love letters. Why didn't she burn them? Get them out of her life. Out of existence. Perhaps some of the hatred would go away. Beth said she should forgive. Forgive and forget. She was trying.

Until Beth told her she had a boyfriend.

And she learned who he was.

Another drink.   Another hard cough.   Beads of perspiration appeared on her forehead and upper lip.

She walked to the desk.   Hugging the manila envelope she hoarsely whispered into the stillness of the room,   "So what if I burn them?   I'll never forget.   And now, because I've lost her, I can't forgive.

"I hate you, Vicki. I hate you."

As though some unseen force pushed her, Julie sagged to the floor.

FORTY THREE

BETH STEPPED OFF the bus in Norfolk and began to look for a phone booth. She was going to call Julie but when she saw a telephone directory she looked for a Lester Smith. There was no such name on Park Street. Why didn't Evan have a lover boy in the Philadelphia Navy Base. She felt anxiety kick in and began to search in her handbag for the envelope. She had memorized the return address but she wanted to hold the envelope while she asked for directions. Hopefully from a policeman.

"Oh, that's on the other side of town," the short fat man in a police uniform told her. "You'll have to take a couple of busses to get there."

"Could you tell me which ones?" Beth held a pen ready to write on the envelope. "I'd like to go there now."

"You'd be better off if you'd go stay in that hotel." The policeman pointed to a building in the next block. "Park Street is in the old run down part of the city and I'd feel better if you'd wait until tomorrow."

BETH was determined to find Evan. After she stepped off the second bus at the corner of East Park and Herman Streets she realized the concern of the policeman. It was a helluva neighborhood to be walking around in.

Alone.

After dark.

Checking address numbers she noticed the overall appearance of the neighborhood. This could not be happening to her. Maybe she could wake up and escape from this nightmare. Not only was she fearful, she was having difficulty in believing this was where Evan was living.

She found the address on the shabby door of a three story gray stone building. She paused before the steep steps and dared to look around her. She caught sight of four men walking through the dimly lit park, across the street. She wouldn't have been afraid in Bridgeboro.

She opened the door and stepped into a vestibule with a bare yellow bulb hanging from the ceiling. Along the right wall were mailboxes. Pieces of paper with names and numbers, were taped or glued above each box. On the last one, bottom row, she saw the name **Rhodes, #5.** Beth opened the next door and walked into a hallway.

How unsafe the apartment house was compared to Geoff's. Funny, she should think of Geoff. No, nothing was funny.

The hall also was illuminated by one naked yellow bulb hanging from the ceiling. A stairway was on the right wall. A door with #1 was to her left.

Beth sneaked down the hall, past a #2 door. She came to a wider and longer hall, thankful there was another bulb to help her see six more doors. An open door revealed the contents of a bucket, a mop, a broom and a large trash can. She decided to turn left. The first door had a #3 on it. And next was #5! The door looked sinister in the amber glow. What was on the other side? What would she hear if she knocked? What would happen if it were opened?

Her heart beats boomed louder than her knock. There was no answer. She stepped below the yellow bulb to look at her watch. It was after one o'clock in the morning. Should she knock again and brave the angry words of an irate sister. Or maybe a man? Where would she stay? There was a light showing beneath the door. Beth knocked. Louder.

"Is somebody knocking?" an unfamiliar voice called out.

Her heart beats pounded against her eardrums as she thought, My god, Evan doesn't live here after all! She tapped again. Maybe the person could help her locate her sister? "Yes. I need help."

"Wait a minute." There was a sound of someone blowing their nose and footsteps. "Who is it?" a voice asked on the other side of the door. It sounded more familiar this time.

"Evan? It's Beth."

"Beth . . . Rhodes?"

"Yes. Come on . . . open..."

The door opened a few inches and eyes peered into the hall. The sisters stared at each other, in disbelief at what they saw. And relief they saw it.

"Oh my god," Evan gasped. She unfastened the safety chain and opened the door. Tears filled her red rimmed eyes. She threw open her arms as if to embrace Beth but she had to lean against the door jam.

"Evan!" Beth dropped everything to the floor and tried to support Evan's sagging body. She thought her sister was going to faint and she wanted to get her to the bed which she could see from the doorway. Evan was a dead weight. Beth struggled to keep her sister from sinking to the floor.

Because she knew it would be difficult to lift her pregnant body!

BETH helped Evan sit on the bed and studied her panting sister. "Are you okay?"

Evan hesitatingly touched Beth's hand. "Now I am. God, you're a sight for sore eyes." She laughed gently, as though it hurt to do so. Still clutching a tissue she blotted her face.

Beth felt touched. Evan was glad to see her. She was surprised at her sister's show of emotion. She remembered Evan as sarcastic and defiant. And so particular about her appearance. Evan's hair, never out of place, looked as though it had never been brushed. The ends still were blonde but from at least three inches from the roots it was several shades of orange and brown. Her face was void of make-up. She not only was unbecoming but almost a stranger.

Again Beth thought of Geoff. Wouldn't he be surprised. She could almost hear Liz say, "What did I tell you? She's a goddamn bum."

She put two pillows against the headboard. "Lean back so you'll feel better."

The old Evan appeared. "Shit. I don't feel any better down than sitting up." She frowned into Beth's face. "Are you planning on staying here?"

"Well, maybe overnight."

"Then you better get your handbag and suitcase. And make sure the door is locked."

Beth put her suitcase inside the door. Again Evan blew her nose. "Do you have a cold?"

"Yeah. We've been having a lot of rainy weather."

Beth smiled to herself as she remembered her sister never cried in front of anybody. At least not in front of their parents. "We've been having rain in Bridgeboro." Interesting, weather was already a topic for discussion.

Evan wiped her nose. "So how's the old town?"

Beth shrugged. "Trying to hide from developers." She watched Evan rest her hands on her large abdomen and decided to add, "A couple of big apartment houses have been built on Jacksonville Road. And a shopping center at the corner of County Line and The Pike."

Evan finally looked into Beth's eyes. "How about Taylor Park?" She forced a snicker. "Has it been condemned yet?"

"Not yet."

"When did you graduate?"

Beth frowned. When in the hell was it? "Thursday night."

Evan managed to rearrange herself against the pillows. She looked interested as she asked, "How'd ya make out? Any awards? She watched Beth nod and smile. As Beth said, "A National Honor Certificate and some service letters," she ran her eyes over Beth's clothes and hair and returned to her face. "How come you're here?"

"Since you included your address with the card I wanted to see how you're doing."

"I hope Liz doesn't know you were coming here."

"She's in Florida. On her honeymoon."

Evan couldn't hide her surprise. She had to sound sarcastic as she said, "So she got somebody to marry her?"

Beth was surprised how annoyed she felt. How dare Evan ridicule Liz! "Well, it wouldn't be a honeymoon if she hadn't gotten married. And it was a nice wedding."

"Who's the lucky guy?"

"Lou King."

"No shit. She still was working and bedding *him*?"

"Lou cares for her very much. And he paid big bucks to have the restaurant decorated. And have a big reception. And a good band."

"And you were invited."

Beth felt smug. What she was going to say would not hurt her sister but she was hoping it would have an impact. "I was her maid of honor." She watched Evan laugh and her protruding abdomen bounce up and down. "Don't bother to make any nasty remarks, Evan. You weren't there so you don't know how nice she looked. And how happy she is."

"Okay. I'll be a caring daughter and just ask, who all was there?"

Now they were moving up on the *Geoff* question? "Lou invited all the members of the Chamber of Commerce and Rotary. And lots of people you don't know. And . . . some you do . . . know."

"Okay. I know you're going to make me ask. Was the successful lawyer there?" After Beth nodded she asked, "Did you tell him I wrote to you?"

"Yeah. I told him. While we were dancing. But he doesn't know I decided to visit you." Beth forced a yawn. She looked at her watch. The name Brad jumped into her mind. Was he home? Had he recovered from the night before? Had he escaped from the wrath of his parents? How was she going to find out?

Beth watched her sister struggle to sit up. "How pregnant are you?"

"Very," Evan said standing before Beth.

"I can see that. How many months.?"

"I'm ready to pop. The baby is in position and . . . " she shrugged her shoulders, "maybe I'll know tomorrow. I'm going to the clinic in the morning. For a check-up."

"Where do you go?"

"Norfolk General."

"I thought you'd go to a government hospital?"

"Don't be a smart ass, Beth. You knew Les was married."

"Okay, I knew. So how long have you lived here?"

"About seven months."

Beth gave up. She was too tired to play the question and answer game. She glanced behind Evan at two doors. "Which one is your john?"

Evan turned and pointed. "That's my closet. That's the bathroom. It's only a toilet and basin. There's a tub and shower down the hall. But Old Mrs. Malone, the witch who owns this dump, insists I use her walk- in shower. In Number Three."

"Why is she a witch? She sounds like she's doing you a favor."

"She's creepy looking. In case you get to see her, she has a big scar on her face and neck. One of her kids, he's in jail right now, he threw some lye on her while they were having a fight. She's blind in that eye too." Evan gave a snort. "And her hair is even messier than mine. And most of her teeth are missing and on to a better subject, how's the Mawhorter gang?"

"Okay. They might move to Europe. Because of Alan's job with the Fischer Company."

"Peg still a sharp dresser?"

"Uh huh. But she'll be wearing maternity dresses soon."

"Oh boy. You know she's the only broad I know who isn't afraid to tell people how much she loves to screw. Were they invited to the wedding?"

"Of course. And Alan came to my graduation. Peg wasn't feeling too hot. They gave me matching luggage. But I left it home." Should she add, *for the trip? With Julie?* She must call Julie, as soon as she got up!

"Did you invite Geoff?" Again Beth nodded so she asked, "Did he give you something?"

"Expensive gold jewelry. I left it . . . home."

Evan studied Beth's face before she asked, "How about Liz?"

"She and Lou gave me money. We have a successful business man for a step-father."

"Shit. That's all we need. A step-father."

"Lou isn't going to interfere with our lives. And not only that," Beth yawned, "he's okay." She yawned again. "Hey, as long as I'm staying overnight let's go to bed. I'm dying."

After Evan shuffled into the john and closed the door, Beth reached into the bottom of her suitcase and removed a folded leather case. She opened it and smiled at the pictures of her father and Brad. She smiled back at them. *It's you and me, Daddy. Liz is a King. And I don't care who Evan is. And you, Bradford Livingston. You're the reason why I'm here. No matter who you are, I love you.*

The door to the bathroom opened. "Your turn."

Beth closed the leather case and slid it under her clothes. She pulled out her new pajamas, purchased for the upcoming trip.

"Do you have any tooth paste?" Evan asked. "I ran out. I'll buy more in the Clinic tomorrow." Evan took the tube Beth offered her and left the bathroom door opened. After she rinsed her mouth she waddled to the bed. "Do you have any jobs lined up?"

"I'm going to college."

Evan pulled down a thread-bare chenille spread and plopped on the bed. "How in the hell are you swinging that? Or is Lou paying for it?"

"I'm going to Penn State and work for a Professor Williams. And Mrs. Fischer is paying me to work for her."

"You mean old Julie Fischer?"

"I mean, Mrs. William Fischer." Beth's voice was strong. And defensive. "I moved out of Taylor Park and I'm living with her. And I work for her also."

"No shit? Sounds as though you're doing okay. Weren't her husband and sister killed in a fire?"

"Yes," Beth replied before she closed the bathroom door.

Evan was scratching her belly when Beth returned to the bedroom. "All ready?"

"Yep. Don't look so surprised. I have two maternity dresses." Evan nodded toward the closet door where a dress was hanging on a hanger. "That one is washed and ironed, waiting for my visit to the Clinic. So this is my nightgown before I wash it."

Beth sat on her side of the bed. She ran her eyes around the room. This time she noticed a small wooden table against the far wall. Under a high window. On the table was a small television set, a two burner hot plate and a toaster. Also a small fan which was circulating the hot air around the small room. Next to the table, in a corner was a metal cabinet which Beth imagined contained dishes, pots, maybe some canned goods and whatever. Pushed under the front of the table was a wooden chair with a matching one opposite the metal cabinet. Even their house in Taylor Park gave a better impression than this . . . dump.

Before she planned to say it, Beth blurted out, "Is Les the father?"

"Yes. And yes he has a wife and three kids and he isn't getting a divorce."

"Did you know all that when you went out with him?"

"You mean when I screwed around with him. I never thought he'd marry me. I just wanted to get away. I guess that's hard for you to understand."

"Not really. But how about the baby? Are you going to keep it?" She immediately thought of Brad. Could this be the story of his conception?

"I want to. Even though people at the Clinic want me to put her up for adoption."

Beth managed to smile. "Her, huh? You put your order in for a girl."

"I think it'll be easier if I have a girl. We could be closer. And all."

"But it could still be hard. For both of you. You'll need a job."

Evan smeared tears across her cheeks. "It couldn't be any worse than it's been so far. I'm going to keep the baby because old lady Malone said I can stay here and work for her. It might not be as nice as working for old lady Fischer but at least she gives me the room free and a little spending money. I can keep helping her around here until I find somebody and I can get away." Evan squinted at Beth. "So you told Geoff I sent you a card. Did he tell you anything about him and me?"

Beth frowned. "Like what?"

"Like the real story about us?" She watched Beth shrug. "Okay, so you're not going to talk. First of all, I truly loved him. Still do. Always will. Even after he told me the truth. He was using me as a cover-up. Because he's gay. Just let me finish. Of course I didn't believe him until I understood he was taking a big chance to spill his guts. He told me he cared about me but could never get serious. Did you know he's gay?"

Beth nodded. "He told Julie and me he's dating someone special. Of course we believed a female. Then at the wedding reception he told me the truth. He knows I'll never tell anybody. And he told me he'll always love you. You covered for him and pretended you broke up because of Les. And yes, Evan, I love him also. He's one of my special friends." *And, I am not going to tell you about being in bed with him.*

"Since he works for Julie, you get to see him?" She watched Beth smile and nod. She added, "He did do me one big favor. I told him he had to be the first guy to make love to me. He didn't want to because I was still a virgin . . . but it was great. I can always remember I had my first orgasm with him." She laughed. "Too bad you can't have a turn. He's a sexy lover."

"I'm going steady with Brad Livingston." She held out her arms. "He gave me *this* bracelet. And this watch."

"The son of the creep who owns the . . . newspaper? " She watched Beth nod. "My god, that's as bad as dating a gay."

Beth updated her sister about Brad then forced a yawn. "Now we have to go to sleep." She turned off the light and tried to settle on the lumpy mattress. She heard Evan blow her nose. It was Evan, wasn't it? Or was she dreaming? Was this reality? Why was she here? To escape? From Julie. She must call her! She must call Geoff. She must call Brad. She must remember they all were the real people in her life.

"Goodnight," whispered the stranger next to her.

"Goodnight," Beth whispered back. She slid her forefinger under the watch to feel the engraving - *Yours, til the end of time.*

FORTY FOUR

A LOUD TAPPING on the hall door disturbed Beth the next morning. There was enough light coming through the high window for her to see the ungodly time on her watch. Who in the hell was knocking and yelling through the door?

"Come on, Evan. It's time to get your big fat ass out of bed and get moving. Or you'll never get a seat in the Clinic."

"Okay. I hear you," Evan replied loudly.

"Who's that?" Beth asked. She sounded as annoyed as she felt.

"Old lady Malone."

"Are you alone?"

"No."

"Who's with you? You sure as hell ain't good for anything now."

"It so happens it's my sister."

"She's here from Pennsy?"

"She got here last night."

"Well open up. I want to meet her."

MRS. MALONE was an unpleasant sight. She stuck her hand out and introduced herself. "I guess Evan told you about my face?"

Beth did nod. "She said you had an accident." She backed up. Mrs. Malone's breath was unpleasant enough she did not to want to stand close to the short, thin lady with the scared face.

"Huh," Mrs. Malone grunted. "It was an accident all right. One of my big bad boys did it. He's serving time now. The judge said he wasn't crazy enough to put him in the nut house. He's twenty-two. And I got one twenty and one eighteen too. And a girl twelve and another one," she squinted her good eye, "Josie must be almost nine."

Beth frowned. "Do they live *here*?"

"Hell, no. This ain't no place for kids. I gave them away. They're in good homes, with lots of grass and sunshine. Nothing like that crap heap park. Across the street. Did Evan tell you what we call it?"

As she watched Beth shake her head she cackled. "Pervert Park. And we call this here street, Rape Row." Mrs. Malone's smile revealed empty gums. "I made Evan send you that card. She didn't want to. But I said to let 'em know where you are. Especially your mom. Moms like to know where their kids are."

After they dressed and had a quick breakfast in Mrs. Malone's apartment, Evan and Beth walked to the bus stop. She told Beth it cost her two dollars every time she went to the Clinic.

"Do you have enough money for cab fare when you're in labor?"

"I'll get a ride in a police car." Evan put a hand against her lower back. "And maybe they'll keep me today. I'm going to tell them about these lousy backaches."

SATURDAY MORNING in Bridgeboro was as humid and hot as it was in Norfolk.

Alan Mawhorter was wearing a pair of cutoff jeans with his fat bulging over the waistband. He was searching through the Chinese Red bookcase in the living room. "Peg. Where in the hell is the phone book?"

Peg was sitting on the steps of their small front porch watching Di and Millie enjoying their new sand box. She was thinking about her unborn child. It was a more active baby than either of the girls had been. And it was rapidly pushing her out of shape.

When she had made the announcement, everybody was pleased. The grandparents and neighbors and especially Gert. Millie and Di were so excited their frequent questions were becoming annoying.

"I'm out front." Peg's voice reflected her frustration.

Alan walked to the screen door. "Where in the hell is the phone book?"

"On the bottom shelf."

"Oh yeah? Well I can't find it."

Peg sighed. It was a challenge getting used to having her husband home again. As Alan held the screen open for her, she walked into the living room. She tried not to look disgusted as she caught sight of the unfastened buttons at the top of his shorts. Her shorts were unbuttoned also.

"I wish you'd keep the girls away from this book case. I've told you before, I don't appreciate their getting into my text books and journals."

"You lay down the law. I can't watch them every minute."

"They do have their own room and . . . "

"And, here's the phone book. God, if you felt like I do, you'd . . . "

"Drown myself. After two pregnancies already, why is it such a big thing? This time?"

"Because I'm older. Who are you looking for?"

He was running his forefinger down a page. "Geoff Greer."

"You mean the Geoff who used to be Evan's boyfriend?"

"I happen to think of him as the company's lawyer. I have something to discuss with him."

"About the company?"

"No. About the price of gasoline."

"Ha ha. You do remember it *is* Saturday."

"I want to talk with Beth. But no one answers at Mrs. Fischer's house."

"Maybe they're shopping. Why do you want to talk with Beth?"

"Because she knows a lot about the company now. And she knows how to handle Julie."

"Huh," Peg grunted. "Tell her I want to move a.s.a.p. Before I get too big."

"I told you I have a big job to finish up in the Accounting Department."

"All the time you put in you should be finished by now." As she returned to the porch, the door slammed behind her.

Alan put his finger on the name Geoffrey Greer and began to ponder. He wished he could make up his mind. He scowled as he thought, *I really want to tell Beth I was told Dick Livingston is becoming a little too interested in company business. I know it's only rumors, but ever since he came here and upset Beth, I hate his guts.*

He dialed Julie's number again. He was certain Beth could decide whether or not Julie should know. Again, no answer. He decided to call Howard Whiteside to ask if he heard about how many times Hank Orhle and Dick Livingston talked on the phone together? He did not want that s.o.b. Livingston getting his foot in the door. Everyone knew he disliked Mrs. Fischer. After ten rings, Alan dialed Geoff Greer's number. After ten rings he needed another can of beer. And more pretzels.

PERSPIRATION was beading on her brow and upper lip as Beth sat at the shaky table in an unstable chair. She was writing in her diary.

The new larger fan, which she had bought that afternoon, was stirring up the hot air a little faster than the smaller one had done.

343

Trying to ignore Evan's snoring, Beth was happy she had remembered her diary. Not only to make several entries but to read. And reminisce.

After she covered her graduation she had to add an additional piece of paper to cover her conversation with Julie, her trip to Norfolk and her opinion of Evan. She was up to the present time. The first sentence was the foremost thing on her mind.

Worried about Julie. Have called 5 x. I feel so far away. Wish Doc would come back early. Should I call Sam? She drank before we met but she didn't want me to leave. Should return. Tomorrow. Know Evan needs me. Cried in the store when I bought baby clothes and diapers. Doctor said she can deliver any day. Should I stay to go to the hospital with her? Meanwhile, what is Julie doing???

IN the master bathroom Richard was showering. Although they had window air conditioners, Bernice still was perspiring as she struggled into a new girdle. She would not concede to the realization the girdle could be the wrong size.

When Richard hurried into the bedroom, in his white cotton underwear, Bernice was seated in front of the triple mirror of her dressing table. Carefully applying foundation.

Richard made several glances at Bernice trying to determine what mood she was in. He knew she still was recovering from entertaining her sister and brother-in-law. And he couldn't tell her how happy he had been to see them drive away.

"Do I remember you were going to a new mall today?" Shopping always was a good subject. He watched her nod. "Were you looking for anything . . . special?"

"The new dress on the bed."

"Did Eunice tell you what your brother-in-law is giving her for her birthday?"

"A new car. Made in Italy. I forget the name of it, but Eliza has one. So Eunice wants one too."

"I'm sure you'd have lots of fun, whipping around Bucks County, in a sport's car."

Bernice stopped tracing her eyebrow and watched Richard tuck his starched white shirt into his black trousers. "Are you teasing me?"

Richard forced a laugh. "No. In a few months I'll be able to buy you one."

"We really could afford to buy one, right now. I know we have enough money."

The cuff link fell to the floor. "In a few months we could each have one." He prolonged the search for the cuff link. "Nothing like matching foreign sports cars."

Bernice sighed. "Please don't start beating around the bush. Especially when we're getting ready to go out. If you have something to tell me, then come out with it."

"It doesn't matter how I try to tell you something. You immediately take the defensive."

"I just don't feel like playing games. Are you working on another deal?"

Richard poked the cuff link into the two holes. "I resent your insinuation that everything I do is a deal. I'm working on an arrangement that should become quite lucrative. In time."

"And how much is this arrangement costing us?

"I'm going to borrow some of the college money."

"You're using Brad's college money! For what!"

"Shhh. Brad's still in his room. I'm investing in stocks. In the *Fischer Company*."

Bernice shook her head back and forth. "Dear god. I should have known. That's why you meet and talk with Hank Orehle so often. You've let him talk you into something stupid."

"He's giving me inside information. Just listen to what I'm going to do." He told her his plans. Then he smiled and said, "Would being president of the *Fischer Company* be stupid?"

"That's beyond being stupid. What makes you think you can prove Julie is unfit to run that company? And you don't even know if you'd be on the Board of Directors. We have so much. Why are you always dreaming of having more?"

"It's not enough for me. And if you were honest with yourself, you want more too. You should get a look at yourself when you talk about your sisters? Even about Lou Barnes."

"That's not true. Eunice is very impressed with my beautiful colonial home and expensive antiques. And I'm not envious of anyone in Bridgeboro."

"Well I'll admit I am. And, I aim to do something about it. I'm not going to be remembered as the son of printer, Paul Livingston, all my life."

"You're not using my money. I've promised Brad a trip to Europe and . . . "

"Oh, since Julie and that girl are going to Europe, you have to go too. Isn't that envy?"

"No. After all, my sister invited us to visit her. Plus Brad deserves the trip. After earning so many awards and for being so . . ." Bernice searched for the right word.

Richard interjected, "I can give him more than a trip. I can give us prestige and power."

Bernice did not reply. She turned to stare out a window. Inside she thought to herself, *If Richard only knew how I manage to tolerate and survive through this marriage. It's because I made my dream came true.* A smile formed on her mouth as she remembered making love with Bill Fischer. Suddenly, the cloud of reality passed through her mind and she frowned. She turned to the mirror and spoke to Richard from the reflection. "Besides your plans being asinine - they could be dangerous."

"You're still afraid of Julie? I'm going to move in on her before she can make a counter move." Richard walked to his tie rack. "I'm ready to buy as soon as she goes public."

Richard walked to the mirror and watched himself make a knot which pleased him. He stood tall and tried to look impressive. As though he really meant what he was explaining to Bernice. "This is a chance of a lifetime," he remarked to the man in the mirror.

"I've had my lifetime," Bernice whispered, inaudibly. She looked into the mirror and realized how much she disliked Richard. She marveled that he thought he was manly. If only he knew how unimpressed she was. In fact, she cared so little it wasn't worth the bother to confront him when she had learned he was having an affair. She felt sorry for him that he had to settle for a waitress. She had been worthy enough to attract Bill Fischer.

"Thanks for warning me. But I'm going to tell you this. I've been embarrassed and humiliated remembering above all that I am your wife. But if you fall flat on your ass from another greedy and ridiculous get-rich-scheme, I will leave you and Bridgeboro. And take my son with me."

BY Saturday evening Beth wanted to scream. She was beginning to envision the rooming house as a cell block and Evan's room as a holding cell. She had even taken a walk through the dust and litter of Pervert Park and to the corner mom and pop store to buy sandwiches and sodas and magazines. She had tried to call Julie many more times and each time she hung up the receiver she felt further away from Bridgeboro. As she slumped in the lumpy upholstered chair, Mrs. Malone had insisted they move into Evan's room, she was pretending she was reading a magazine. But her thoughts were miles away, wondering what was happening in Julie's house.

If anything happened to Julie it would be her fault. She shouldn't have gone away when Geoff and Doc were going to be out of town.

She glanced at her watch. If it was as hot in Bridgeboro as it was in Norfolk, Brad most likely was swimming in Barnes' pool. Of course there were thousands of people who could not be together. How many wives of sailors and Marines in Norfolk were missing husbands? And lovers? She just had to believe Brad loved her. And needed her. She needed to talk to him.

Beth held her change purse. "I'm going to make another phone call."

Evan lowered the magazine to her lump. "Again? You must really want to talk to her."

Beth nodded. "She's a very important person in my life." Quickly, she left the cell.

Beth stared at the pay phone. She weighed the pros and the cons of calling Brad. It could mean trouble for him. Again she dialed Geoff's number. Maybe if she talked to Geoff she wouldn't want to talk to Brad so badly. Geoff still did not answer. Damn. Beth decided to dial Brad's number. And worry later.

BRAD had stayed home Friday and Saturday. He had washed his car, cleaned out bureau drawers, burned throw away junk, reread Beth's notes and poems and tried to concentrate on watching television. Still no news about what happened to the missing submarine, THRESHER. So what, if President Kennedy and Jackie, were going to Berlin? Also Kennedy claimed segregation as immoral and there were no "colored" signs on foxholes. So Reverend King was out of jail but now Medgar Evers was shot.

Ha. Wait until he told Beth, illegitimate births among teenagers were up by one hundred and fifty percent. Thank god he had kept his dick in his pants and left Jeanne nude on her bed. He was happy she had another headache so he didn't have to be with her until Saturday night.

When the telephones rang in the Livingston house, Brad was in a hammock on the patio. After a restless night he was tired. Still he could not sleep because he had too much on his mind.

Since he left Beth standing in Julie's driveway he had been anticipating that every time the phones rang on Friday the caller would be Julie. He actually hoped it would be. Somebody had to start the ball rolling. Finally he believed Julie was not going to call. The ball was in his court.

As soon as the phone rang Brad hurried into the kitchen. "I've got it," he yelled.

"Hello," Beth said loudly. Over the sound of her heart beats. "Is this 346-1756?"

"Beth?"

"Yes. Are you alone? No one is on an extension?"

"I can talk. Where are you?"

"Just listen to me. I'm calling from Norfolk because Evan sent me a graduation card with her address. Julie and I had an argument on Friday and I decided to visit Evan. So Julie and I could cool off but I am going to come home tomorrow."

Beth knew she was rambling. She really wanted to hear how Brad was doing but she had so much to tell him. "Julie won't answer her phone. And Geoff went to the shore. Would you drive by her house, just to see if there are any lights on? And in Doc's house. At least call Geoff to tell him I'm not with Julie and he should go down to check on her."

Brad heard his mother coming down the stairs. "I have to hang up now."

"No." Beth cried out. "Tell me how you are. Did you get in trouble?"

"I'm working in my father's office." He placed his mouth right on the mouthpiece. "I love you. I'll do what I can."

After Bernice walked into the kitchen he said, "Hey, thanks for calling." He laughed. "You take care of yourself, ya heah?" After he hung up he closed his eyes. Now for the lies.

"Boy, is that girl a nut. Know where I met her?" He waited for his mother to shake her head. "*Pop McDevitt's Driving Range*. A couple of nights ago. She was with a bunch of girls. From some church.

They were on a crusade and just because I listened to her and I guess I told her my name. Anyway, she decided to find me. So she can convert me." Brad laughed. It was such a crazy story, why couldn't it be true?

Suddenly he did not even care if his mother believed him. All that mattered was that Beth had called him. And she still loved him.

He decided to say, "You look real nice for your date tonight."

"And you and Jeanne have fun at the cook-out."

SATURDAY evening, Beth made a decision. So had Brad. Each knew their decision could bring about an unforeseen outcome.

Beth told her sister, "I'm leaving tomorrow. I'm going to make bus reservations."

Evan had a look of desperation. "You mean go back home?"

Beth nodded. "I'm worried about Julie."

"I'm your sister. Aren't you worried about me?"

Beth forced a smile. "Of course. But Mrs. Malone will help you."

"Thanks a lot."

Beth felt confusion. Even guilt. "When I came here I didn't know you were pregnant. You might not deliver for another week or so. And I can't stay that long."

"I told you I feel lousy. My back is killing me." Evan hid her face behind a magazine.

Beth's confusion became frustration. "If you go into labor during the night then I'll stay. Otherwise, I'm leaving tomorrow morning."

BRAD had picked up Jeanne about an hour after he talked to Beth. Even before he talked with Beth he didn't want to go. The gatherings of his high school friends were not fun anymore. He had too much on his mind to be amused with corny jokes and loud music. Since Beth's call he had developed his plan. If she had to sacrifice and suffer, so would he.

Brad studied Jeanne eating a piece of cake. She *was* attractive. Her profile was perfect and her long hair was the color of corn silk. Who wouldn't be pleased to have her be his steady girl.

Brad wiped his mouth "Jeanne," he began. "I have something on my mind."

Jeanne frowned at him. "Well. Congratulations."

"Something pretty serious."

"Oh? More serious than I have to pay my parents for the booze and the damage from the bash? From which you managed to escape." She sounded annoyed.

"I told you I'm sorry. But I have to tell you I want to break off with you."

The sly smile disappeared from Jeanne's face. "Of course this is your sense of humor?"

"No. I'm telling you what I'm going to do."

Jeanne observed everyone on the patio. Her eyes paused on the broad shoulders of Jim Bender before she turned back to Brad. "You really know how to tease a girl."

"I'm not teasing. I've given it a lot of consideration and I think we're just hanging on.

Jeanne frowned. "Whatever gave you that idea?"

This was not the response he had expected. "Admit it. You won't hurt my feelings. We're just a habit with each other."

Jeanne squinted. "I still have fun with you."

"Wow. So it's fun to be with me with this crowd or our parents, but . . . "

Jeanne reached for his closest hand. "Is there somebody else?"

Brad forced a grin. "Shit. When do you think I'd find time to have another girl? Our parents are always thinking up something for us to do."

"So? What if they do? Now we can't go to the big bash at the Club   next   Saturday."

"I'll take the blame. They just have to realize, oh shit, Jeanne, why the tears?"

Jeanne sniffed. "How about the gang?"

"Nobody has to know right now. But I *am* telling my folks. Tomorrow." He watched tears trickle down her cheeks. He could not believe that Jeanne had any feelings for him. He could not believe he was hurting her.

"Are you mad because of what we did in the cabana?"

"Of course not. I was as much to blame."

"And you really mean what you just said. You really want to break off?"

Brad looked around the patio. Was anybody watching them? He nodded. "I'm for real."

Jeanne wiped her nose with her paper napkin. She looked forlorn. "I don't want to tell anybody we're not a pair anymore."

Brad's heart beats began to pound behind his ears. "I can't believe you're so upset."

"Why shouldn't I be upset? You've just devastated me." Jeanne threw her paper plate, with the unfinished cake on the patio. "And ruined my entire summer."

"Come on, Jeanne. Knock it off. "Let's leave and talk it over in the car." He picked up Jeanne's cake plate and fork and began to walk to a table. He hoped to thank the hostess and say a few "see you guys later" and "so long" statements, before Jeanne could make a scene.

He watched her talking to Jim Bender. After a few minutes, she ambled up to where he was waiting. Loudly she remarked, "Okay, let's leave. Because I don't feel like hanging around here."

Jeanne looked at Shirley Chappel and forced a laugh. She had an audience so she said, "Brad just told me a really funny story. I have to leave, before I . . . break up."

FORTY FIVE

BETH AWAKANED EARLY the next morning.   She wondered if she had been asleep at all? She could not remember Evan ever snoring as much while they shared the same bed, in Taylor Park. Nor could she remember any bed being as uncomfortable. She thought about being in bed with Geoff.

But then, so had Evan!

Beth studied Evan. Her pregnant sister was sleeping on her back. Her large lump loomed high. Evidently the baby had decided not to be born yet.

Beth stared at the cracks in the ceiling as her mind became caught in a mental whirlpool.   Should she return to Bridgeboro? Who was more important? Flesh and blood or someone who needed her? Of course, Evan needed her. If she returned, should she tell Geoff about Evan? Geoff, dear Geoff. Her skin tingled as she remembered. She imagined Evan laughing if she told her about sharing Geoff's bed.

Beth closed her eyes and continued to wonder. *Daddy. What would Brad say if he knew? I never should have learned about Jeanne and him. People should never tell other people what might hurt them. Julie found out and got hurt. But Vicki and Bill had to tell her. And she would have to know about Brad and me. Eventually.   Maybe she doesn't want to share me with him?   I read some people want a person all for themselves. I can't believe Brad's adopted. But I guess he is because Julie really went all out to hurt me. Maybe she already knows Geoff is gay? Stay tuned in Daddy.*

Beth tried to get out of the bed as quietly as she could.

Evan turned her head and moaned, "What time is it?"

Beth squinted at her watch. "Almost six-thirty."

"Are you just going to the bathroom?"

"I'm getting up. I have to call the bus company."

Evan forced a yawn.   "Why don't you call her again? I still think she went somewhere for the week-end."

As Beth walked into the bathroom she said, "I hope you're right. But I doubt it."

Before she closed the door, her sister called out sarcastically, "What a riot. You still have a soft spot for drunks."

After Beth walked back into the bedroom she noticed Evan was almost hiding in her closet while she asked, "Are you going to tell Liz?"

"Maybe that I visited with you." She watched Evan searching through a large box.

"So tell her I'm pregnant. Just don't give her my address."

Beth continued to dress. "Don't you want her to send you a baby present? I could tell her you need a crib and a high chair and . . . "she paused as soon as she realized Evan was crying. She led Evan back to the bed. She sat beside her and patted her shoulder. "I really am sorry, Evan. I'll even send you some money."

"Take me with you."

"You're too pregnant. The bus ride would be awful for you."

"It wouldn't be as bad as staying here. Please?" Evan watched Beth knowing she was doing some deep thinking. Finally she knew what to say, "I'll bet you'll want your babies born in Bridgeboro."

The only answer Beth could think of was, "The closest hospital is in Langhorne."

"I know. And I know what I'll be letting myself in for. But shit, it couldn't be much worse than living in this dump and having an old prostitute for a landlady who lets you clean toilets and hallways, for a place to stay." She searched her sister's face. "Can't you understand?" She grabbed Beth's hands. "I won't be afraid if I'm near you."

Beth knew Evan was flattering her, but it felt good. She managed a weak smile. "You don't have to be afraid. The doctor said you're doing okay." She allowed Evan to hold her hand. "And you should have an easy and quick delivery."

"Sometimes I'm afraid I'm going to be punished for all the bad things I've done. The people I've hurt. And I've even dreamed the baby dies."

"Stop it, Evan. You're just trying to upset yourself. And me. You better realize, even though we're both in Bridgeboro, I'll be living with Julie."

"I'll find a place. I just don't want my baby to grow up in the slums." Evan squeezed Beth's hand. "Please, take me back?"

"I wish I could get in touch with your doctor. I want to make sure the bus ride will be . . . "

"I feel okay," Evan blurted out. "My back doesn't even hurt this morning."

Beth knew Evan was lying. She was more than just concerned but she nodded. "Okay. Even though I know it's the wrong thing to do."

MRS. Malone tried to convince Evan the trip could be dangerous. For her and the baby. Next, she tried to convince Evan she needed her to help in the rooming house. She failed and turned nasty.

"Okay, girlie. In that case, you're going to owe me some money. You've been living here for I figured it up to be three weeks, without doing much more than washing toilets and mopping floors. So that'll be half rent. You owe me eighteen bucks."

Beth saw Evan's look of despair. Should she get involved?

"Of course," Mrs. Malone said, in a softer voice, "You could stay and work off your bill. After the baby is born. I told you before, I'd let you do that. But if you're going to shove off, then I want my money."

Evan reached into the pocket of her maternity dress and looked like the old defiant Evan as she held out five bills. "Here's the twenty-five dollars you've paid me. The extra can pay for the meals you gave me."

"I don't want no money for no meals. You'll need all the money you've saved, girlie."

"I don't have any ones," Evan said.

Without any hesitation, Beth said, "I have."

Mrs. Malone took the money. "I'll keep your room empty for a few days. When the bus driver takes a look at your big belly he may not let you on the bus. You just might be back."

Beth suddenly realized Mrs. Malone was not being sarcastic. Just hopeful. She remembered Julie trying to convince her to stay. Mrs. Malone needed Evan also.

"And look at your poor sister there. All of the things she has to carry. Just came here for a visit and here you are using her for a pack horse."

Beth forced a smile as she eyed the three suitcases and two large paper bags, tied with string to make handles. And her multi colored drawstring bag.

"I'll bet in all that stuff you don't have the things you'll really be needing. Like a pair of scissors and some pads." Mrs. Malone cackled at her own humor. "At least you got string."

Beth wanted to scream. She looked at her watch. "We better get started." She looked at Mrs. Malone. "Thanks for everything."

FROM his bed, Brad watched the sun come into view from behind Wilcke's house. They lived across the street from the Livingston's and every June and December the sun came up between the two chimneys.

Again, Brad had not slept well. First he felt excited. Then he felt fearful. At least, he felt relief that he had finally told Jeanne. The first act was over. Even though it had been an upsetting experience Brad was certain the second act was going to be more dramatic. He still had to tell his parents! They had not been home when he returned from taking Jeanne home. And he chickened out from staying up and waiting for them.

He knew his father would be angry. And, most likely his mother would cry. It could be a real headache scene. Maybe he could run away? Could he find Beth in Norfolk? Then they could run away, together. No. He'd find her and bring her back to Bridgeboro. And tell everybody. With her by his side, he would make an announcement. Maybe even posters? Better yet, put it in *The B.C.*. Bradford Livingston loves Elizabeth Rhodes!

Suddenly his mother called through the bedroom door. "Brad. You better get up. Your father wants to talk with you."

As soon as he entered the kitchen his father pointed to a chair and said, "Your mother and I are so upset we're going to skip church. We just got a phone call from Lou Barnes."

After he realized Brad was not going to respond, Richard almost shouted, "What in the hell did you do to Jeanne last night? Lou said she hasn't stopped crying since you took her home."

"I told her I want to break off. She must have told her parents. Before I had a chance to tell you."

"She's almost hysterical. Lou says she's going to have to call a doctor."

"I can't believe it. She's really playing it to the hilt." He rubbed his damp hands down his pants. "She just wants to play the martyr."

"She says she doesn't want to lose you. She loves you. And, your mother says you received a phone call from some girl last night. Have you become involved with another girl?"

"I already told Mom I haven't. When would I have time? And I'm sure Jeanne will calm down as soon as she stops getting so much attention. And consolation."

Suddenly Brad had enough courage to add, "I've been wanting to tell you and Mom how I've felt for months. Jeanne and I are tired of each other. I just couldn't go on. Pretending. Any longer."

"I don't understand why you'd have to pretend. Jeanne's one of the most popular, best catches, in town. I should think you'd feel lucky to go out with her."

"Well, I don't. It's been a drag for both of us. I really did both of us a favor."

"You certainly didn't do me one. Nor your poor mother. She's terribly upset."

"I'm sure you and the Barnes can still be friends. After all . . . ."

"After all," Richard interrupted, "The Barnes are powerful people in Bridgeboro."

"Are you afraid of them?"

Richard sat tall. He tried to appear confident. Why not blame Brad. "No. But I don't see why in the hell you couldn't have waited until after you went away to college. Now the whole summer is shot. And we had plans with Lou and Charles. We were going to Virginia Beach and . . ."

"You mean a trip to Virginia Beach is more important than the way I feel?"

"I mean what's a few months out of your life? Don't you know you have to sacrifice to get the things you want?" Richard pushed up his glasses. "You should have consulted me first."

"You didn't have to go out with her."

"Don't get mouthy with me. You've been very rash and thoughtless. You've hurt Jeanne and you've embarrassed your mother. And I'm disappointed in you. You must know it's advantageous to be on good terms with influential people. Especially, if you have a business which relies on their advertising. The paper is your business too. Everything with the Livingston name attached to it is yours." Richard paused to study his son's reactions.

With the pause at his advantage, Brad quickly asked, "Are you telling me what I did will affect the newspaper?"

Richard cleared his throat. "I'm suggesting that someday we will not have to give a damn about being on good terms with certain people. The Livingston name will be synonymous with success and . . ." Richard stopped as Bernice entered the kitchen. "But until I can trust your judgment I'm going to have to supervise your activities. Your mother and I cannot have you acting immature and insolent without a curbing of some kind."

Richard removed his glasses. He felt Brad watching him message his nose and use a clean handkerchief to wipe the lens. He knew Brad was waiting for his verdict.

"I've decided until this unpleasant situation with Lou and Charles can be straightened out you'll work in the office during the day and either stay home or go out with only your mother and me, in the evenings. And over the week-ends. You cannot cause us humiliation and then think you can have fun. While other people attempt to put the pieces back together."

After Brad left the kitchen Richard blotted his forehead. He had given Brad a stiff penalty for being honest. Brad had been brave to have the guts to live up to his convictions. But then, so was he. He had to be hard on the boy to prove to Charles he valued their friendship. He was out to please everyone. Even at the price of sacrificing his son. But he would wait until Monday to call Charlie to explain he was punishing Brad.

Someday he wouldn't have to kiss ass.

FORTY SIX

THE BUS DRIVER did frown when he first saw Evan. He even shook his head expressing more disbelief than concern as he took her ticket.

Beth waited behind Evan as she slowly climbed the narrow steep steps. She knew Evan felt miserable. It was obvious her back was hurting by the way she gently lowered herself into the seat. She knew Evan would not complain. Not even moan. She wanted to go home.

Beth packed the suitcases and bags on the rack above, under their seats and held some on her lap. She tried to give Evan as much room as she could.

Evan dozed for several hours as the bus traveled through Maryland. Beth had too much on her mind to be able to sleep.

Would she dare take Evan to Julie's? Or should she take her to a motel? Where would she have the baby? When would Geoff answer his phone? Should she tell Doc about Evan? Where was Brad right then? She glanced at her watch. Maybe still in bed? Had he driven past Julie's house? Had he made contact with Geoff? Beth felt a shiver as she envisioned Julie intoxicated. Maybe unconsciousness. Geoff, save Julie. Brad, save Beth. Beth save Evan. Shit! What a mess.

As soon as they arrived in the bus terminal in Philadelphia, Beth found a bench for Evan. "You watch our stuff. I have to find a taxi to take us to the other bus station."

Evan was perspiring profusely. She looked forlorn. Almost like a refugee. A forlorn refugee wearing a kerchief on a warm summer night. To hide her multicolored hair.

After a weary one hour delay the tired sisters, weighted down by their stuff, boarded a bus bound for Bridgeboro. It really was bound for Doylestown but it would stop at the second traffic light at the corner of Bridge Pike and Monument Avenue. Then Beth would have to find another cab to take them to Julie's house. That was where she decided to go. Evan be damned. She had to find out how Julie was.

Beth was exhausted. She knew Evan was running on fumes. They shared a bag of pretzels and a soda Beth bought from a machine. Beth could not remember feeling so grubby since she had gone camping with the Girl Scouts. She was sitting next to the window. Since it was dark outside she couldn't focus on anything but lights and traffic. She closed her eyes and leaned her head against the glass. It was cool. Almost soothing, except for the vibration. Suddenly she turned to look at Evan.

"I'm going to try to persuade the driver to let us off at the corner above Julie's house. There's only four other people in here and they shouldn't complain."

"I thought we were going to the *Fiesta Motel*? What if she says I can't stay with you? Then what will I do? " Evan had tears in her eyes.

"I think she'll say it's okay. Just for tonight." In fact, Beth believed Evan might be able to sneak into her bedroom. While she made sure Julie was all right.

The driver agreed. After Beth helped her sister down the steps and watched the bus drive away Evan held the paper bags and Beth picked up the suitcases. And her drawstring bag.

On the wrong shoulder of Bridge Pike, they walked toward Julie's house. When they reached the post which held the **WELCOME TO BRIDGEBOROUGH** sign, Evan leaned against it. "Wait a minute," she breathed.

Beth felt compassion for her sister. "You feel lousy don't you?"

"I'm just beat. I'll bet this baby weighs twenty pounds."

Beth looked up at the sign. In the glare of a street light she ran her eyes over the words. She knew the message by heart. She hoped the word WELCOME was meant for Evan and her also.

As quietly as they could, the girls walked across the flagstone path. As soon as Evan saw the patio furniture she moaned, "Oh thank god. A place for me to sit down."

Beth watched her sister gently lower her cumbersome body into a chair. She slowly opened the screen door. The brass knocker stared back at her as she remembered the first time she had used it. How could she ever have known how much her life would be changed, just because she had opened that door. She unlocked the door and took a deep breath.

As soon as she entered the foyer she discovered the mirror had been broken and she was standing on glass. She flipped on the hall light and the light in the hall bathroom. She went to the door of Julie's dark bedroom and whispered her name. She walked into the room and saw the empty bed. She turned on the lights and gasped.

The mirrors which had been behind the dressing table, the bureau and on the closet doors, were shattered. Mixed with the shards of glass on the floor were many pieces of Julie's jewelry which had been gifts from Bill Fischer.

Beth returned to the hall and called, "Julie. Where are you? Answer...." She noticed a light under the door of the room which contained Vicki's possessions. "Julie? Are you in here?"

There was no answer but Beth found the door unlocked. She opened it. The light was coming from a bare bulb of a lamp that was lying on the floor beside a book case. Julie was propped against the couch. She resembled a rag doll. Holding an empty Scotch bottle.

Beth stooped next to Julie, afraid to touch her. Would she be warm or... her chest was moving. "Julie. Wake up. It's Beth."

Julie opened one eye. She moved her head as though she was trying to focus on the face above her. Then she rolled her head away from Beth. "Go to hell."

Beth felt relief knowing Julie was alive. There were stains on her clothing, runners in her stockings but worst of all her arms and legs were covered with scratches and cuts. Some oozing blood. Beth believed all from broken glass.

Beth peered at the pages scattered around Julie. Julie must have tossed the love letters into a pile of confusion, as they had affected her life. Even with tears in her eyes Beth felt relief, noticing that Julie had not stained or torn any of the letters. Suddenly the letters were more important than Julie. Beth began to gather the pages.

She felt disbelief from the damage in the room and a strong dislike for the person who was responsible. Several lamps and shades had been broken. The contents of the desk drawers had been scattered and glass doors to a book case had been smashed. Beth knew she was viewing the results of an uncontrollable hatred. She had to check her own anger and tend to Julie. She shook the limp body. "Julie. Listen to me. I want to help you get into your bedroom."

Julie squinted at Beth. "Go to hell."

Beth began to slide her hands under Julie's arms. "You have to stand up and..."

Julie hit Beth with a fist. "Keep your crummy hands off me."

"I'm trying to help you. You can't stay here."

"I'll stay where I want to be. And I don't need you to help me." Julie coughed and almost gagged. "Especially since you've been contaminated." She spit on Beth.

Beth gasped. As she wiped the spittle off her arm she declared, "You are a hateful person. I should leave you here. To rot." She collected more love letters and held them to her chest. She felt a thud against her left shin. Julie had hit her with the bottle!

"You and your precious Vicki." Julie coughed out. "I took care of her. And you."

Beth finished gathering envelopes and letters to put into the manila envelopes and walked to the door. "One more time. Are you going to let me help you into bed?" After Julie said another "Go to hell," Beth said, "Call me, if you need me." She heard Julie yell, "I'll never need you again." before she closed the door.

She had to do some quick thinking. She'd bring Evan inside. And after she used the bathroom she would put her into her bed. Then she would try to help Julie again. She flipped on the wall switch in her bedroom and cried out, "Oh, no. Damn her!"

The mirrors had been smashed. The contents of her bureau and desk had been dumped on the floor. She had to sweep up the glass before she helped Evan inside. She hurried into the kitchen. Nothing had been broken but she noticed Gerry's aquarium upside down on a counter. Where was Gerry? She walked into the mud room and found a broom and dust pan.

Beth swept up glass, stuffed her clothes into drawers and hid the love letters on a shelf in her closet. She turned down the bedspread and looked around the room, wondering what else she should do before she helped Evan lay her sweaty swollen body in her clean bed.

After she swept the floor in the bathroom, she hurried into the dining room. The mirror that had been over the buffet no longer reflected her image. She hurried into the living room and cried out. "My god. She's smashed every mirror in the house. And even threw her brother's picture into the fireplace." Beth suddenly heard Evan calling her.

Beth hurried to the door. "Here I am. I was getting my bedroom ready for us."

"I thought I heard you talking to someone."

"Julie was awake but she's . . . "

"She's *what!*" a hoarse voice asked behind her.

Beth whirled around and saw Julie standing in the living room. She was leaning against a chair in front of the fireplace. She looked frightful. And sinister. She glared at Beth with a wild look in her red rimmed eyes. Slowly, she raised a knife. "Who's out there?"

Beth stared at the knife. She thought she had learned to understand this woman. But she was facing a stranger. She wanted to believe that alcohol was partially responsible but she also feared Julie's overkill hatred had caused her to lose control. Beth was unable to speak.

"*Who* is out there?"

"My sister," Beth managed to whisper.

"You brought her here for a free bed."

"I came here to find out how you were. I tried to . . ."

"Liar!" Julie yelled. "Your bed's turned down, so you were . . . "

"We don't have to stay." Beth yelled back. "We can go to a motel. I just stopped in, in case you needed me. Why didn't you answer your phone?"

Julie sneered at Beth. "Can't you see? I've been busy." She pointed the knife toward the front door. "Tell you sister to get in here."

"She doesn't have to come in. Now that I know you're alright we can go uptown."

Julie walked toward Beth. "You're not going anywhere."

Beth reached behind her for the handle to the screen door. "We have . . . reservations at the Fiesta Motel. Don't you dare touch me with that knife. Julie! Stop it, or I'll..."

Julie began to laugh. "You'll get cut, that's what. Now, you listen to me. Now that you have so thoughtfully returned, you stay here! You have a job here. And you're going to stay and do it." She coughed. Hard. "Do you understand me?" She watched Beth nod. "Good. Now, tell your sister to get the hell in here. So we can all go to bed."

As Beth opened the screen door Julie yelled, "Stop, right there. You stay inside and tell her to come in here."

Beth felt frightened. "Evan?"

"I heard her," Evan replied.

"You get your smart ass in here," Julie called out. And coughed.

"I can't," Evan said weakly.

Julie stepped to the door. Into the night, she yelled, "I said for you to get the hell in this house. I have a knife and I'll hurt your sister if you don't get in here. Now!"

"I can't move," Evan whined.

"She doesn't feel well. I promise I won't run away. Just let me help her."

Julie lifted the knife again. She looked pleased to have control. "If she could make it this far then she can get into the house. Come on you out there. Get a move on."

Beth watched Evan shuffle across the patio, whimpering until she reached the screen door. She waited for Beth to open it and as soon as she stepped into the foyer she grabbed at Beth. "Help me. I'm having a . . . pain."

"My god," Julie declared. "She finally got knocked up!"

"Just shut up," Beth dared to say to Julie. She looked at Evan. "Your dress is wet."

"I felt my water break. I can't move."

"You have to sit down." She began to lead her sister into the living room.

"She doesn't sit anywhere until you get some towels," Julie ordered.

Beth hurried into the bathroom and grabbed towels off the racks. She returned to the living room and placed one of them on a chair. Without any hesitation, she stuffed another one under Evan's dress, between her legs. "Everything is going to be okay, "she said. For Evan's benefit. And hers. "You sit down while I call the Rescue Squad."

Julie stood by the phone. "You're not going to call anybody."

"For heaven's sake, Julie, I have to. She's going to have a baby."

"She can have it here. Living room couch. Your bed. But she stays here."

"Julie. I'll do anything you want me to do but please, let Evan go to a hospital. This is her first baby. And she's scared."

"Ha!" Julie snorted. "She wasn't scared nine months ago. While she was screwing with her boyfriend." Julie looked as though she was enjoying her own humor.

Beth reached for the receiver.

Julie laid the knife on Beth's arm. "Don't make me hurt you."

"You mean you're going to make her have her baby, with no one to help her?"

Julie kept the knife against Beth's arm. "I'll help her."

"I don't want you near me. Beth will . . . " Evan winced. She was having another pain.

Julie watched Evan and cackled like the Wicked Witch of the East. It was obvious she was enjoying watching Evan suffer. "Hurts, doesn't it? Wait until later. It'll get better."

"And you're going to just let her suffer?" Beth cried out.

"Yep," Julie replied. She shuffled to the front door, closed and locked it.

Beth decided this was her chance to try to get some help. She picked up the receiver.

As soon as Julie observed Beth, she laughed. "It isn't working. I pulled out the wires."

Beth realized how helpless she was. "And I kept trying to call you. Because I was worried about you." She slammed down the receiver.

Keeping the knife in front of her, Julie walked closer to Beth. "Your calls annoyed me. I knew it was you and I didn't want to be disturbed. Help her to the bathroom. Then take her to your room."

After they walked from the bathroom, Julie followed the sisters into Beth's bedroom. "Here. Put this rubber sheet under her ass. And here's more towels and sheets and alcohol and peroxide. You have to wash her down and keep your hands clean. I'll be right back."

Beth helped Evan remove her wet dress. "Have you been timing your pains?"

"How can I do that? I don't have a….ohhh, here comes another one."

Julie returned to the room. With a bottle of Scotch.

"Where have you been hiding all that stuff?" Beth blurted out.

"Wouldn't you just love to know?" Julie pushed past Beth and settled into a chaise lounge. "This is the director's seat." She laughed and took a long gulp.

"Evan and I would really prefer you wouldn't stay here. I can take care of my sister."

Julie laughed. "Really? Okay, then I'll just watch."

"I read a Medical Book we had at home and . . . "

Julie interrupted. "Home? And just where is your home? For both of you tramps."

Evan grabbed Beth's arm. "Ohhh. Here comes another one."

Beth looked at her watch. "They're about six minutes apart. I'll time them better."

"Your watch is wrong," Julie declared.

Beth yelled back, "It is not!"

"Ha! I've known for weeks that watch was special to you. And that bracelet. Your lover boy gave them to you, didn't he?"

"Brad is not my lover boy. He's the boy I love. And you can never change that."

"Of course not. You're so stupid that you're beyond help. Only a fool would deliberately forfeit everything I've given her and what I can give her. Just for a bastard. Look at your sister, lying there in a pool of sweat, wanting to die because it hurts so much, just because . . . "

"Shut up," Evan yelled out. "I don't want to die." She squeezed Beth's arm. "Just don't let her hurt my baby." She winced as another pain ground away.

"Suffer. Whore. That's what all of you are who have little bastards." She leaned her head against the back of the lounge and closed her eyes. She appeared to be drifting off to sleep, but she murmured, "No matter if you insist it was love. You're all whores."

Beth could not stop herself from demanding, "And under what category do you come? You tricked Bill Fischer into believing you were pregnant."

Julie's eyes opened wide. She focused on Beth and smiled. "*Touché*. I never did have that baby, did I? All of those months of screwing around hoping I'd get pregnant. To keep him with me."

"What's she talking about?" Evan watched Beth put fingers to her mouth.

Julie rolled her head so she could look at Evan. "I'm talking about my husband and my sister." She smiled at Beth. "Tell her. And Dickie Livingston. Tell the whole damn world how my wonderful and famous sister screwed my husband. I don't care anymore."

She coughed and sighed deeply before she added, "That's why I broke the mirrors. Who wants to look at a zombie?" She took a quick drink and lowered the bottle to her lap. She seemed tired. Spent. She frowned at Beth and whispered, "You know I'm dead, don't you?"

"Not yet. But you will be if you don't stop drinking. You know what Doc said."

"The hell with Philip," Julie said loudly. "The hell with all of you." She seemed to have tapped into a new supply of energy. She leaned toward Evan. "Don't you think I look dead? They say I did it to myself. Because they don't want to take any of the blame. But they all killed me. They destroyed my very soul. And then Beth tells me I could help myself. Well, I was trying. She even said she was going to help me. But she joined my enemies."

Evan frowned at Beth. "What's she talking about?"

"She's just upset. Because I left."

"You're a liar! A liar and a cheat. Tell her the truth. I'm upset because you're in love with a bastard. And because you had the nerve to bring him…"

"Shut up!" Beth shouted. "Just shut up. Don't you dare call Brad a bastard. Just because he's adopted doesn't mean that his parents weren't married."

Julie coughed. Hard and long. "Sure. Just like your sister is." She slumped into the lounge, closed her eyes and appeared to be falling asleep.

Beth leaned close to Evan's face. "I'm going to try to get some help. Just lie still and try not to make any noise." She backed away from the bed. Just as she reached the doorway Julie lifted her head and smiled at Beth. "Where do you think you're going?"

Suddenly Beth felt defiant. "I'm going to find a neighbor who will let me use their telephone. Or stop a car." She took another step backwards. She was almost in the hall.

"Beth!" Evan yelled out. "She has a gun!"

FORTY SEVEN

BETH FROZE!

As Julie raised her right hand Beth's breath caught in her throat. From somewhere, Julie had magically produced a silver pistol. Large enough to look menacing. And she was pointing it at her! Her legs felt as though they were going to let her down.

"Now, my dear," Julie said slowly and emphatically. "One more foolish mistake and I shall be forced to hurt you. Am I getting through to you?" She watched a frightened Beth nod. "I hope so. For your sake and your sister's. You will do exactly as I tell you to do." She focused on Evan squirming on the bed, in her bra and pants. "It was more fun screwing, wasn't it?"

"Please let me give her a little Scotch." Beth pleaded.

"Nothing. Thousands of women have babies with nothing. She's lucky she's off the streets. If you do want to do something for her, make her some tugging straps. Tear a sheet into strips and tie them to the foot board. They'll come in handy when the pains get closer."

Tearing up a sheet, Beth watched Julie out of the corner of one eye. As the fearful woman held the gun in one hand she sipped from the bottle with the other. Beth hoped she would overload. And pass out.

"Now," Julie said. "Put some towels on top of that rubber sheet. To soak up the blood. Oops, wait a minute. She's having another jolt. Look at her suffer. My. My."

"Don't fight it, Evan. Try to relax. Let your muscles do the work. According to the Medical Book if you breathe in, long deep breaths, it doesn't hurt as much."

BETH stared at Julie. A stranger with soiled and stinking clothes, pointing a gun in her direction. She stared at Evan. Another stranger. Trying to be brave. She used to complain over the smallest abrasion or wail over her monthly cramps but here she was defying Julie and helping her stressed out sister. The lack of sleep plus the emotional strain of the preceding days and nights were taking effect. Or she was having a nightmare!

"You have to look at her crotch," Julie snapped out. "Why the look? She wasn't embarrassed with her lover boy. Loosen that sheet so you can keep looking." Julie held up her bottle and pretended to toast Evan. "Here's to you. Isn't this fun?"

"Leave her alone, Julie. Stop trying to upset her."

"Hey, think of the embarrassment I'm saving her. They'd ask her all kinds of questions in a hospital and this way she can have the little bastard and disappear into the night."

"You're not going to make her leave, are you?" Beth blurted out.

Julie took another swig. "No. She can stay. I wish the phones were working. I have a hankering to call Geoff and get him down here to watch this little scene."

"What are we going to do with the baby? I mean, we do have baby clothes and diapers. If you'll let me go to the patio to get them."

Julie coughed. "Don't be so concerned. Mary wrapped her babe in swaddling clothes."

"You're not funny." And before she could stop herself, she blurted out, "You're . . . a pathetic drunk." She wiped Evan's forehead. "Breathe. In. Out. Breathe with the pain."

"Sure, bring everything in." Julie lifted the gun. "But hurry back."

THE sisters watched Julie. Several times she laid her head back and appeared to be falling asleep. Beth was so tired she had to lie beside Evan. She even dozed off, in between feeling Evan use the tug straps while she was panting. Several hours dragged by.

Suddenly, Julie said loudly, "Why is it so quiet?" She leaned toward Evan. "Do think if you're quiet you'll be forgiven? You have to suffer."

"Don't pay any attention to her, "Beth whispered. "She's talking in her sleep."

"I am not. I have to be awake to deliver the . . . here it comes! Here comes the baby!" She cackled several times, held the bottle to her lips and then sagged against the chair. Eyes closed.

Quickly, Beth got off the bed. She lifted the sheet and looked at her sister.

"Am I all right?" Evan struggled to lean on her elbows.

"I think so. But something *is* happening."

"You're not kidding. Oh god. I feel . . . like . . . I'm breaking apart."

Beth carefully picked up the bottle from the side of the lounge. As she eyed the gun, still clutched in Julie's right hand she handed the bottle to her sister. "Just take a few sips. It might numb the pain. We have to be quiet and hope she is asleep." After Evan sipped Beth put the bottle on the bureau.

Evan pulled on the tug straps with her eyes squeezed shut. "Beth. Oh god, Beth. I think . . . oh, god."

Beth threw back the sheet and spread her sister's legs. "Just take it easy." She almost blurted out, Oh my god, I see hair . . . on a slimy head.

"Is she coming out?" After she watched Beth nod she said, almost in a prayer, "Please god, let her be all right."

"The baby is going to be fine. Just stay calm. And breathe deep."

Evan screwed up her face and panted. She tugged and tugged and finally moaned, "Oh, God. Did it hurt this much for Mary? Something's happening."

Beth tried to sound in control as she whispered, "It's the head. I can see . . . the . . . push, Evan. Push." Almost in a daze, Beth held a towel below her sister's fanny and watched a baby's head and trunk, slide into it. "Push. Push. Here . . . it . . . comes."

Beth gave a gentle tug and pulled out the baby's feet. She looked in wonderment at what she was holding. A slippery, mottled red, messy baby girl! Suddenly tears came to her eyes and with a quivering voice, she murmured, "You got your wish. You have a baby girl."

Evan moaned. After a struggle she managed to prop herself up on her elbows and peer between her legs. "I did it! I, no you and I, actually did it."

"Just lie still 'cause I have to cut the cord and hope I do everything . . . like I should. "

Beth had found scissors which she wiped with alcohol. And the string which Mrs. Malone said they would need. With shaking hands, she cut the cord and tied it at both ends.

Evan watched, then asked, "Shouldn't she cry?"

"Okay." Beth smacked her niece on the buttocks. The baby wailed! Evan cried out in delight.

Beth smiled broadly.

JULIE woke up! She yelled out, "The baby's here!"

She appeared to be dazed as she struggled to sit up. While doing so, she was unaware the gun fell from her lap and was hidden between the cushion and the side of the chair.

"The baby's here," she repeated. She struggled to stand next to the chair. She focused on Evan. She looked to Beth and then what she was holding in her arms. A squirming baby, wrapped in a bath towel.

Julie took two unsteady steps away from the chair and reached out. "Give me the baby."

"Beth. No!" Evan cried out. "Don't let her touch my baby."

Beth turned sideways to shield the baby from Julie.

Julie took several more unsteady steps, to the foot of the bed.

Beth began to back up. She thought she would have more of a chance to keep the baby from Julie if she stepped into the hall. During the few minutes, Julie lost her balance and fell. With a loud thud, her right temple hit the edge of the bureau. She crumpled to the floor. And . . . lay still.

"Oh my god," Beth breathed. She quickly gave the baby to Evan and knelt beside Julie. She shook her shoulder. "Julie. Can you hear me?"

"Is she still breathing?" Evan asked.

Beth felt Julie's wrist. "She still has a pulse. But I'm afraid she's really hurt."

"What are we going to do?"

"I have to go to a neighbor's house. And call for an ambulance."

"Not for me. Just for her. I'm staying here."

"No, you have to go too. I don't know what to do about the afterbirth. And I don't want you to have a problem."

"I don't want to go to any hospital. Pioneer women had babies without any doctors."

"They had mid-wives. I'll call Doc but if he isn't home I have to call for an ambulance."

"What time is it?"

Beth looked at her watch. "It's eight o-clock."

Beth returned to Julie's limp form and knelt beside her. Gently, she shook her. "Julie. It's Beth. Can you hear me?"

No reply.

"Okay, Evan. I'm going . . . what's the matter?"

"I think . . . I'm going to have another baby."

Beth quickly lifted the sheet. "No. But I think if I pull a little on the cord, then the placenta might . . . wait a minute . . . yes, here it comes. Ugh. What a mess. I'm just going to put it in this towel so Doc or somebody, can look at it. You need a pad between your legs."

"Now, I won't have to go to the hospital." Evan reached out and grabbed Beth's skirt. "Beth. Thank you. You were great." She managed to laugh. "But I can't name her Elizabeth."

Beth laughed. "Please don't. Just hold her."

Evan propped herself up on her elbows. "You're not going to leave her here, are you?"

"I'm just going to get a wash cloth. I want to dry the baby. And you."

"She might come to. And get up again." Then what will I do?"

"Okay. I'll get her into the hall. Maybe I can even get her into her room."

"And shut this door."

Beth slid her hands under Julie's armpits. She dragged the limp body out of the room. She decided she might as well continue through the hall to Julie's bedroom door. She was going to try to convince whoever came to the house that Julie had hit her head against the door jam. She put a pillow under Julie's head.

Evan and the baby were sleeping. She woke Evan up to put some pads between her legs and make sure the baby was breathing. She put a diaper on the baby and tucked her next to Evan.

She had to use the bathroom before she went to the neighbor's house. While she was taking one more look at Julie, she heard a knock on the mud room door. She looked at her watch.

Who? At this hour!

Through the door window, she saw who was knocking.

Beth let out a whimper of relief

FORTY EIGHT

"**OH THANK GOD** it's you," Beth cried out.

As soon as Geoff stepped into the house Beth threw herself against him.

Geoff pushed Beth away. He held her upper arms and looked into her face. "Why don't you answer the telephone?"

"It's not working."

"Why didn't you get it fixed? I tried to get in touch with you last night when I got home. And again this morning. You look awful. What the hell is going on down here?"

Beth bit her lower lip. She knew she was going to lie. "Julie fell and hit her head. I was just going to go next door. To call Doc. And you."

"Where is she?"

"In the hall. Maybe you can help me get her into bed."

Julie still was lying on the floor. Geoff knelt by Julie's side. He felt for a pulse in her neck. He opened one eye. It stared up at him but Julie did not react. He stood and glared at Beth. "When did she fall?"

"Just a little while ago. She hit her head." She pointed to the door-jam but did not put the lie into words. "And she's too heavy for me to lift, so . . . I had to leave her here."

Geoff carried Julie into her bedroom. Beth managed to hurry around Geoff, to the bed. She quickly pulled down the spread and top sheet. She waited for Geoff to ask why Julie had not slept in the bed. And why she had broken the mirrors.

Geoff removed Julie's shoes and pulled up the sheet.

Beth blurted out, "Would you go call Doc?" and turned to leave the bedroom.

Geoff was right behind her. "Just a minute. Before I go anywhere, I want to know what the hell happened? And who broke the mirrors?"

"She did. We had an argument."

"It looks like it was an intense fight to me. Was it over her drinking?"

"No. She must of started drinking, after I . . . left."

"Damn it, Beth. I know you're trying to avoid telling me something. But this is serious."

Beth nodded and then decided to use another way to avoid telling Geoff, everything. "Look, I promise. I will tell you what happened. But it's a long story and I think we should call Doc. Maybe he'll want her in a hospital."

"You're right. But I'm going to drive uptown and get him. I know he's home because I called him this morning to find out if he knew what was going on down here." Holding his car keys he began to walk toward the door. He turned around. "Don't touch anything. I want Doc to see this house, just the way it is."

Beth nodded, as she thought, *You haven't seen half of it, yourself.*

AS soon as Geoff closed the screen door behind him, Beth began to whimper. She found a box of cookies. She sniffed and wiped her nose and sniffed some more, while she ate two cookies. Suddenly she focused on Gerry's aquarium. Where was her dear little pet? She put some peanuts and sunflower seeds in his dish under the table. Evan could be hungry also. They had nothing to call a real meal since that hurried breakfast with Mrs. Malone. Only yesterday, but it seemed like last week. It *was* last week, when her life hit a detour.

Beth wiped her mouth on the dish towel. Not even Liz would do that. Why in the hell was she thinking of Liz? Because Evan had returned to Bridgeboro. Because Evan had just had a baby. Because she better stop thinking and do something! She washed her hands because anyone who handles a baby should have clean hands. And she was going to see how the mother and child were doing. After she checked on Julie.

Beth walked to the foot of Julie's bed. She sensed Julie had moved or she didn't remember in what position she and Geoff had left her. She stepped closer and rearranged the sheet. It was difficult to believe how much she really cared for this woman.

But now she also feared her. Why did they have to have such an unpleasant, even controversial relationship? Because she wanted to write an essay about Vicki Lynn? Or because of Brad Livingston?

She backed out of the room and walked to her bedroom. Evan and her daughter still were asleep. Should she wake Evan to ask how she felt? Was she hungry? Did she want some milk? In case, she was going to nurse the baby? Or just let her sleep? Until Doc arrived? She had to tell him. She and Evan had been lucky everything went so well.

Waiting in the kitchen, Beth felt relief when she heard two cars drive into the parking area. Doors slammed shut. Feet pounded across the patio. Carrying his black bag, Doc entered first. Geoff was right behind him.

Doc nodded as he muttered, "Young lady," to acknowledge her presence. He quickly slid out of a rumpled suit jacket and handed it to her. He hurried through the kitchen, the hall, into Julie's bedroom. Geoff and Beth followed and stood at the foot of the bed.

Doc put the black bag on the floor and sat on the side of the bed. He picked up a limp wrist and put fingers on her pulse. "Julie! Can you hear me?" He looked in her eyes. He examined the lump on her temple.

Julie gave no response.

Doc turned to Beth. "What made all these cuts?"

"I guess glass. She broke a lot of the mirrors."

Doc glanced toward the dressing table and bureau. "God damn it." He began to look at the numerous scratches and cuts on Julie's arms and legs. "The worst one is here, on her arm. It should have stitches. "Julie! Can you hear me?" Doc looked at Beth again. "How much did she have to drink?"

"I don't know." Suddenly she felt a different kind of fear. One kind was for how seriously Julie had been injured and the other fear was of Doc. And Geoff. She knew they were going to blame her. Maybe even hate her.

Doc looked at Geoff. In a loud voice he instructed, "Geoff, call the Rescue Squad. I'm going to have her admitted to the hospital."

They all waited.

Without opening her eyes, Julie murmured, "Try it."

Doc winked at Beth and Geoff. He turned back to Julie. "I knew if there was one ounce of consciousness in you that would do the trick." He took her hand in his. "Although I am sorry you are conscious because no matter what you say I am going to admit you."

"I'll sue you."

"You're in no condition to do much of anything. You're sick. Besides losing too much weight and looking like hell, you are a sick lady."

"I've been worse. Go away and leave me alone."

"I have no intention of leaving you. You need help. More than I can give you. Besides needing to be dried out you need a physical and some tests taken. I'll bet your liver is about to quit functioning."

Julie opened both eyes. "I don't give a damn about my liver. Just leave me alone,"

"I'm in charge here. And I say you're going to a hospital."

"Not as long as I can make my own decisions."

Doc stood and stepped away from the bed. "Okay. I'm leaving. I can't be responsible for what happens to you." He picked up his black bag.

"You never have been. Where the hell is Beth? Ask her who's to blame?"

Beth felt a wave of panic. She longed to back out of the room, then out of the house. And take off. She knew Julie was sneaking up on telling what had happened before she fell.

"She's right here. Worried about you. Just like Geoff is. You've got to stop blaming other people for your own behavior. Next thing you'll be blaming me, because I went fishing. Or Geoff because he had a date. I don't know what has happened between you two since last Thursday but from the looks of you and this house, I'd say you need a lot of help."

Julie changed her position. "My help comes in a bottle."

"So does embalming fluid." He stepped to the bed and put the bag down.

"Go away. All of you. It's my life." She turned her head away from Philip.

Doc turned to Beth and Geoff. "You're my witnesses. I tried." He finished saturating a large wad of cotton with alcohol and wiped the cuts on Julie's arms.

Julie grabbed his hand. "What in the hell are you doing?"

"Before I leave I'm going to stitch you up. Maybe even your mouth."

As Philip cleaned her cuts, Julie looked at Beth. "Have you told Geoff the good news?"

Beth felt as though her throat was closing up. She shook her head.

"Wish you didn't have to, don't you?"

Geoff stepped closer to Beth. "What's the good news?"

Beth felt Geoff studying her face. "Evan's here. Remember I told you she sent me a card? I went to Norfolk to visit her. Then when

Julie wouldn't answer the phone and I decided to come back, Evan came with me."

Doc turned sideways. "Why didn't you take Julie with you?"

"I wouldn't go anywhere with her. You haven't heard the whole story yet."

"I don't give a damn about a story. It's obvious you can't be left alone."

Geoff looked at his watch. He appeared to be nervous. "I have to go to the office."

Julie pushed herself up. "Beth has more to tell you. Tell them what happened last night."

Beth forced herself to look into Geoff's eyes. "Evan had a baby."

Geoff appeared to be searching for what to say but remained silent.

Beth laid a hand on Doc's closest shoulder. "That's why Julie fell. After the baby was born, she tried to take it away from me and she stumbled and fell. Against my bureau."

"She pushed me." Julie shouted. And coughed.

"You lost your balance."

Doc put up his hands. "I don't give a damn how Julie fell. I care about right now."

Finally Geoff did speak. "Thanks for the news update and I hope everybody will be okay. Expect somebody from the phone company because I called them from Doc's house. But I have to go."

Geoff pushed Beth out of the room. "Would you walk to the door with me?"

"Ask her why she decided to leave me. It wasn't just to see her sister," Julie called out after them. "And call Sam. Tell him to bring Ellie with him."

As soon as they walked into the kitchen Beth stopped by the refrigerator. "I need something to drink. Want something?"

Geoff nodded. "Some instant coffee. Use the high octane stuff. I need some caffeine. And I have something to tell *you*." He knew where the coffee mugs and spoons were located. He turned to Beth who was putting water in a tea kettle.

"Look, Beth. Right now, I don't care that you went to Norfolk. Or Evan came back with you. The most important thing is the phone call I got last night. From Alan Mawhorter."

"Oh my god. Is Peg okay?" Beth blurted out and then saw Geoff hold up his hand.

"Everybody is okay. Alan also tried to call you before he called me. Then I tried to call you. Anyway, he's very concerned. He thinks there may be something highly irregular going on in the office. He's worried there's too many phone calls and too many rumors."

Beth stood still, holding the jar of coffee and two napkins. "Meaning who?"

"Hank Orhle and Dick Livingston. They might be up to making trouble."

"Oh my god," Beth breathed. "What are you going to do?"

"For starters Alan wants to talk with you and me. He wants to explain why he's concerned." Geoff watched Beth pour hot water into his mug. He began to stir. "We may decide to meet with Howard Whiteside."

Geoff took a little sip of the hot liquid and winked at Beth. "Please don't take this personally but you do need to look a little more presentable. I know you must be beat. And I really hate to push you but I told Alan I'd call him *if* you and I could not meet him this AM."

Geoff reached out and patted Beth' left hand. "Hey. No tears. We can get emotional later. Everything is going to be okay."

Beth shook her head. "No, it isn't. It'll never be okay." She wiped her eyes with her napkin. "Betty will tell you I called your office on Friday and told her I was leaving. And I called you yesterday, hoping you might have come home early and . . . "

"It's okay. I believe you. But I also believe you didn't leave just to see Evan."

"She found out Brad Livingston is my boyfriend." She watched Geoff pucker his lips but he did not whistle. "He came here. Thursday night. After you left."

Beth told Geoff the entire story. About Brad upchucking. About Julie finding them in the laundry room. About finding Evan. Very pregnant. And she cried. So Beth felt sorry for her.

SHE stopped talking as they heard Doc clear his throat, in the doorway. He looked forlorn as he shuffled into the kitchen.

"How is she?" Beth asked.

"Mean and miserable."

"How about some coffee?"

"Later. I'd like to see your sister and the baby. If you can believe this, Julie is concerned about their wellbeing."

Beth felt as surprised as she looked, then asked, "Julie will be all right, won't she?"

"She should be in a hospital. Sure, I can take care of the cuts and bruises and a vial of blood . . . but I really would feel better if she would go through some tests. And some X-rays. I just have a feeling she feels worse than she wants us to believe. I even insisted on a round the clock private duty nurse, but she'll have no parts of the idea."

He looked at Beth. "She said you'll take care of her. It will be a penance."

"In other words," Beth said hesitantly, "she wants me to stay?"

Doc shrugged. "I didn't know she wanted you to leave."

"Hasn't she told you we had a fight? That's why I went to Virginia?"

"Ahhh." Doc sounded. "Not really. What was the fight about?"

Beth glanced at Geoff. "She found Brad Livingston in her laundry room. And I had to tell her he's my boyfriend."

"For god's sake," Doc almost shouted. Then he stared at Geoff. "And from what I gather, you and the girl who just had the baby, used to be soft on each other.

"Whooo," he blew out. "Why in the hell didn't I stay away a little longer?" Doc sat. "This is too much excitement for a man my age. I think I do need a cup of coffee. And I'll take a mug of tea in to Julie."

"Doc," Geoff began. "I have to tell you why I'm here. Is Julie well enough to hear any more bad news?" He watched Doc raise his eyebrows. "I got a phone call from one of the men at the company who has a feeling one of the new men is sharing inside information with Richard Livingston. And he may also be spreading rumors that Julie is taking the company public. Beth lived next door to Alan and he wants to tell us what he knows. As in, as soon as Beth changes."

"My god," Doc declared. "No wonder she drinks." He looked at Beth. "First, it's you and a Livingston and now it's the company and a Livingston. Seems as though they've been a curse on her since the day she became a Fischer." He stood and dunked a tea bag, with two scoops of sugar. "If this person does have important information then we'll decide what to do."

He nodded at Beth. "Meanwhile, congratulations on delivering a baby. I haven't done that for quite a few years. I'll give this tea to Julie and have my coffee later. I have a need to hold a new innocent baby."

WELCOME to BRIDGEBORO

E.J.B.B. BARDSLEY

FORTY NINE

WHILE ALAN MAWHORTER was in his office, anxiously waiting for Beth and Geoff to arrive, Richard Livingston was in his office having a telephone conversation with Elmer Hoxie.

"I got the information from a very reliable source. Everything is being set up for the initial public offering. As soon as she returns from Europe. So I would appreciate your keeping tuned in. And ready to buy for me."

There was a smug smile on his face. Not only was he gloating because Hank Ohrle had indicated the rumor was true but also he was preparing himself to make a quick move to alert everybody that Julie Fischer was not capable to be the controlling stockholder.

Preparing his qualifications he was bragging, but it all was true. He was a third generation and active resident of Bridgeboro. He was personally aware of the growth of the company, from a small machine shop where the career of his best friend had begun. And up until now the successful business that it was. He did consider himself as highly qualified and more than willing to donate his talent and time to observe carefully and constantly the management of the company, making certain those involved act with the utmost regard for the company's continued success and growth. For the benefit of all the investors.

Richard would stop typing and reread, to soak in the impact of the words. The letter had to be precisely worded. It had to be one of his best compositions. Several times he rubbed his hands together. Just like Ebenezer Scrooge after reaffirming his wealth.

He sighed deeply and realized he was becoming preoccupied with his dream of taking over the *Fischer Company*. Having a goal was one thing, but he wasn't sleeping well and . . . " he said out loud, "Maybe I'm becoming obsessive-compulsive? Maybe Bill is haunting me!"

He began to gather his notes and memos to put into his brief case. Soon the office force would begin wandering in. And Brad. To suffer. Work every day. Stay at home every night. But it had to be obvious he was punishing the boy. If only to show Lou and Charlie he had control over *his* child. He remembered how pleased he was Brad had not been at Barnes' when Lou and Charles returned home to find the mess from the party. Drunks. Nudes. Drugs.

380

He was certain Bernice had complimented Brad enough for both of them. He was glad he had not been around to hear her. Sometimes she made him want to upchuck. There was a time, he felt some jealousy. Now he just felt disgusted.

He wondered how Brad could stomach his mother's attention? Bernice was upset because she said Jeanne wasn't worth so much punishment for Brad. It was true but the boy could suffer, just a little longer. Their friends would be impressed. In fact all three of them could suffer until this great and glorious project materialized. Or was it a scheme? Whatever, the Livingston's would be the rightful first family of Bridgeboro. Maybe he *was* obsessed. But he had to be in control of his own destiny.

ALAN stood as his secretary brought Beth and Geoff into his office. There was an obvious look of relief in his eyes. He smiled broadly as he pumped Geoff's hand and kissed Beth.

"Sit down," he urged, pointing to chairs in front of his desk. After his secretary closed the door to the outer office of the Accounting Department he sat behind his desk.

Geoff quickly said, "I'm sorry we're late. I had to make several phone calls."

"I'm sorry for any inconvenience." He frowned at Beth. "You look tired."

Beth only shrugged but Geoff spoke up, "She's beat. Julie's been sick again. That's why we decided to listen to you first. Before we tell her anything."

Alan shook his head, sighing deeply. "I really hope I'm wrong. But my secretary and Oehrle's secretary believe something, they use the word *sneaky*, is happening. Oehrle was hired as Assistant Vice President only a few months ago and Betty Tolson, his secretary has become aware how many times he and Dick Livingston talk to each other. Also Oehrle invited Livingston to tour the plant and look behind the scenes because Dick Livingston wanted to give us a big write-up in *The B.C.*"

"Am I to believe only you and two women know about the phone calls?" Geoff asked.

Alan nodded. "As far as I know."

"I have to assume both of the women have overheard some of the conversations?"

Alan nodded again. "They're nervous about my telling you but they're both company girls. Oehrle is keeping Livingston updated on how Mrs. Fischer is going to pay for the new office building." He smiled at Beth. "I'm sure you know if anything has been settled. But Betty clearly heard Hank tell Livingston, Julie is getting geared up to file a registration statement with the Securities and Exchange Commission for a public offering. And we don't even have a Treasurer to head up the Financial Department."

Beth shook her head. "I don't think even Julie knows she's going to do that."

GEOFF decided Howard Whiteside should be updated. He invited them to his office.

After he heard Alan's concern he decided to excuse Alan and call Hank Oehrle to his office.

Within five minutes using his best lawyer's tactics Geoff had the Assistant Vice President's admission he had deliberately developed a behind- the- scenes relationship with Livingston because . . . and then he stopped and shrugged. He appeared embarrassed. He looked at Beth, then Geoff, before he remarked to his boss, "You want to know why?"

Beth and Geoff watched Howard nod. "It might help with your job evaluation."

"I've developed a deep dislike for the s.o.b. I knew when he buttered me up about making the company the first one for his big Public Relations Series he was full of . . . hot air. He's too obvious to ignore that he wants more than just stock. He believes because he and Bill Fischer were friends that he has a right to take over. He wants to be in control of Bill Fischer's company. And destroy Julie Fischer.

"My wife is a psychologist by profession. And from the first evening we met the Livingston's, she told me to be careful. She will not accept any of Bernice Livingston's invitations. To attend meetings and meet local women. Also we've turned down invitations to their house and will not invite them to ours."

He paused to shrug. "My loyalty always is with the company for which I work and even though what I have been doing may cost me my job, I've actually enjoyed misleading the s.o.b."

Howard laughed. Geoff joined in. Beth snickered but she kept thinking of Brad.

Howard was the first to make a comment. "You know what? I know just how you feel. I've lived in the County for many years and I don't know of anybody who likes the editor of *The B.C.* I will tell you it's because of two women and another man who also are loyal to this company that we learned about your relationship with Livingston. I'm sure I don't have to tell you to severe your connection with him. No more phone calls, either way." After everybody saw Hank nod Howard looked at Geoff. "Are you satisfied with that decision?"

Geoff looked at Beth. "We still have to tell Julie because she'll find out. In her mysterious way."

"She has to know," she whispered. "And Mr. Whiteside, I think we should get the two secretaries and Alan in here so we can all admit to each other how much this company means to us. And how we are going to save it. For Julie."

All those involved gathered in Mr. Whiteside's office. A review of the events and the mutual solution were agreed upon. It was apparent everybody was relieved and happy. There were handshakes and hugs. Before he said goodbye, Alan hugged and kissed both of Beth's cheeks.

DRIVING back to Julie's house Beth stared through the windshield. She believed Geoff had much to ponder. Finally he laid his right hand on top of her folded ones.

"We make a good team. But I'm not looking forward to telling Julie."

"I'm worried what if she decides to strike back?"

"What if the Livingston's decide to move? And take Brad with them?"

"He wouldn't go. He knows I love him. That's why he went to Julie's."

"I hope he knows how lucky he is. That you'll put up with Jeanne, still in his life."

They turned into Julie's driveway. After Geoff parked behind the garage Beth grabbed his arm. "Before we go inside. I want to tell you something about Brad. That Julie told me. At first, I didn't believe her but I don't think she'd make up such a big story . . . just to hurt me.

If she gets real mad at tricky Dickie as she calls him, over this stock business, she just might let them know she knows that Brad was adopted."

She took a deep breath. "They got him from the orphanage at *The Good Samaritan Church.* But they do have a real son who is retarded and lives in a private home. Somewhere in Virginia."

She waited. "Well? Had you heard about all of that story? Before?"

Geoff shook his head. "First time. And I'm sorry. For you. And for Brad." He leaned toward Beth and took her face in his hands. "But you and I have to keep our secret. From Evan and from Brad." He watched Beth smile.

"How about Terry? Does he know about you and Evan?"

Geoff nodded and whispered, "He knows about both of you. And he knows I really want to see her and . . . " after Beth whispered, "And give her a hug." he added, "and be happy the baby isn't mine."

He kissed her forehead. "So as of right now you and I and Evan know all about each other. I want to congratulate Brad about a special you in his life and you want to meet Terry and," he held Beth's face in his hands and kissed her mouth, "you and I have to bite the bullet and update Julie. Ready?"

DOC'S jacket was still draped around the back of a kitchen chair. Beth slowly walked past the office following the sound of a stern voice coming from Julie's bedroom.

"Drink it anyway," Doc was saying in a gruff voice.

Beth stood by Geoff and frowned. And made a face. Then slowly nodded.

She stepped into the room and declared in a cheerful voice, "Hi, you two. We're back." She walked to the foot of the bed. "Are you feeling better?"

Julie was propped against three pillows. "I'm feeling lousy. Thank you."

"I finally got her cleaned up and taped up." Doc sounded as though he was reporting for Beth's approval. "Now, I'm forcing some nourishment into her. I took some cereal and toast into your sister also. She and the baby are okay."

"Thanks Doc. I'll take the mug," Beth declared. "Geoff wants to talk with you."

Doc handed Beth a mug of noodle soup. He made Julie reach out to hold the crackers. He left the room.

Beth sat on the edge of the bed. All of a sudden she realized she was alone with Julie. She began to feel nervous. Tense. Worried. And exhausted.

"Where have you and Geoff been?" Julie demanded as she took the mug.

"Geoff will tell you. Would you like me to help you change into a clean nightgown?"

"I can dress myself, thank you. You'll have enough to do helping your sister take care of the . . . the baby. I guess you'll have to sleep on the couch. Until we get her out of here. Just remember, I'm not running a home for unwed mothers."

Beth felt spiteful. "Evan doesn't want to stay here. In fact if you can remember, she didn't intend on having the baby here."

Julie sipped from the mug. Squinting, she asked, "Why *did* you come back?"

"You didn't tell me not to. And after I called . . .too many times. Without an answer, I began to worry about you."

Julie laughed. "How thoughtful of you. Especially after what you . . . " She looked beyond Beth at Doc standing at her door.

Doc shuffled to the side of Julie's bed. Geoff entered the room and stood by Doc.

Julie eyed both of them. "Now what in the hell is wrong?"

"Geoff has some news I want him to discuss with you. About the company."

Julie's eyes opened wide. "What about the company?"

Geoff cleared his throat. "There's an unexpected situation you should know about."

Doc hiked up his trousers. "Ha! Geoff is being gentle. It could have been a catastrophe. And while you lie here, recovering from trying to kill yourself, these young people were trying to straighten it out. '

Julie struggled to sit higher. Doc reached for the mug and Beth rearranged the pillows.

Julie coughed, looked at Geoff and demanded, "What's happened with the company?"

"Dick Livingston is getting geared up to get his foot in the door."

The color drained from Julie's face. She looked at Philip. "What kind of a joke is he trying to tell me?"

"No joke, Julie," Doc mumbled. "No joke."

"Well, I wouldn't put anything past him." She glared at Beth. "Is this all news to you?"

Geoff spoke up. "Beth and I just found out this morning."

"Okay. Tell me everything."

GEOFF sat on the bench in front of the dressing table as he explained the details to Julie. Doc sat on her chaise lounge, took out a small pen knife and began to clean his nails. Beth was sitting on the end of the bed.

She wished she could leave the room. Even Bridgeboro. With Brad. Whatever Julie was thinking, it had to include hatred. Retaliation. Toward anyone with the name Livingston.

All at once, Julie began to laugh. She noticed the surprised reactions of the three people with her. "I'm laughing at what you just told me. The dumb shit head. Too greedy to enjoy what he has. Two times I've bid higher to keep him from using his extra money. I want him to keep Bernice happy. Although maybe she *should* move back to Virginia. And I want that boy to go to a good college. But Dickie keeps grasping. Ever since Bill died he's been obsessed with owning the Company." Julie laughed and coughed. "It's his quest for *The Impossible Dream*." She continued to cough.

Beth hurried into the bathroom to fill the mug with water.

After several sips of water, Julie whispered, hoarsely. "Geoff. Call the underwriters. Tell them we're going to put the brakes on our plans.

"Then call Howard Whiteside. Tell him he's running the show. If Oehrle wants to stay, okay. Just so he and everybody knows that Howard has my full permission to do whatever has to be done."

Doc looked up from his nails. "To save the boat from being shipwrecked. Again." He shook his head. "I hope someday Howard finds enough guts to tell you to go to hell. And he takes his patient family and moves. Far away from you."

"And I hope someday I get enough brains to get another doctor," Julie coughed. "Instead of sitting there criticizing me, you could buy some diapers and bottles and whatever that baby will need."

Doc stood and saluted. "Yes m'am! At your service, Mrs. Fischer! So glad there is something that can get you back on track."

Julie frowned at Geoff. "Did you call Sam? And Ellie." She watched him nod. "Thank god for Sam and his family." She watched Geoff nod. Again.

Beth waited. She felt Julie's eyes observing her. She hoped she did not look as frightened as she was. She knew her turn was next.

"And as for you, get the typewriter ready. I have some letters I want to send out."

DOC and Geoff said their good-byes and left the bedroom. Beth hurried after them. She wished she could make them stay. Or go with them.

She peeked into her bedroom. Mother and child were sleeping. Beth wandered into the dining room. She was hoping to avoid returning to Julie's bedroom so she found the dust pan and broom and began to collect pieces of glass from the carpet. Suddenly a stern voice startled her.

"What in the hell are you doing?" Julie demanded. "I've been waiting for you."

"I thought I should clean up. Before the telephone man arrives."

"The hell with the telephone man. Tell him we had a party." Julie pulled out a dining room chair and gently lowered her body into it. Even though she had changed into a new colorful caftan, that she had bought for their upcoming trip, she looked pathetic. Her hair was uncombed and her face was pale and puffy. It also was apparent she still was losing weight. After a deep sigh she declared, "Sam will clean up the mess."

"Aren't you ever afraid Sam might tell somebody about what goes on down here?"

"I can trust Sam. And all of his family. They all know I love them. He and his family began to work for Dad Fischer, then Bill and now me.

"Didn't you ever think I might have my own Detective Agency? Sam used to be one of my spies but he's beginning to slow down. He just keeps his relatives working for me." Julie paused to smile. "Everybody on Station Street are my friends. And confidants."

Beth grinned. "So, it's Ellie Carpenter who passes on what happens at Livingstons?"

Julie nodded. "And Tony Miles goes to Virginia to visit relatives and check up on what's going on with Bernice's family and friends.

He has a network with their maids and gardeners. And he has an *in* at the private Home, where the boy is living."

"Are you going to do anything about what Mr. Livingston tried to do?"

"I suppose you would like to know that, wouldn't you? And since it means so much to you, do you have any suggestions?"

"I couldn't possibly think of anything you haven't already considered. But," Beth raised her chin and stood tall, "whatever you might do to embarrass them, I'll always stand by Brad. If you make me choose, I'll take his side."

"Are you trying to upset me? Again."

"No. But I imagine you could throw them to the wolves. And throw me with them. Get rid of everybody who has upset your life. But Brad and I will have each other."

Julie looked into Beth's eyes. "Don't make me pity you. That boy will never marry you. Just as Bill never married Vicki. She died a Phipps. I'm the Fischer!" She had to pause to cough. "And you'll *never* be a Livingston."

"He loves me. And if what you told me about him is true then he'll need me."

"Keep saying it. Over and over." Julie struggled to get out of the chair. "Now I'm going back to my room."

Beth stepped forward. "Let me help you. You really do look tired. Maybe you should let Doc take you to the hospital for some tests?"

"I'll decide when I'm going to the hospital. I still have things to take care of." She let Beth support one of her arms as she walked into the hall. "But, I *am* too tired to do any letters."

Beth watched Julie struggle to settle into her bed. As she arranged the covers around Julie's arms she whispered, "We're all worried about you. We know you're pushing yourself. And for whatever reason. Let Howard take care of the Company. "

"You all can just mind your own business. Obviously I'm not upchucking and I don't have blurred vision so just get me some ginger ale. It's time to take one of Philip's pills."

When she handed Beth the empty glass Julie dismissed her by saying, "Now shut the door and leave me alone. I'll let you know . . . if I need you."

After Beth closed the door, Julie got out of bed and shuffled to her closet. She felt around behind the shoe rack, until she felt the bottle. After a long gulp she smiled.

The poor girl. The poor boy. They also had an impossible dream.

And she still had so much to tell the girl. No wonder she was so thirsty! She took another long gulp. Finally, she convinced herself to hide the bottle behind the shoes.

And escape, by sleeping.

FIFTY

BRAD LOOKED UP from his small cluttered desk as his father walked into the main office. He observed the smile on his father's face. He thought, Now, what has he been up to? He watched his father chat with the Sports Editor, laugh and even pat the man on his back. Then with a big smile on his face he looked around the office, winked at Brad and walked into the shop.

Thirty minutes later, Florence Mann, Richard's secretary hurried to catch up with him, before he closed the door to his office. After six years of working for him, she knew him well enough that during the present exhilarated mood he would shut the door. To gloat behind it. And her boss hated to have his gloating interrupted.

"Richard," Florence called. "May I have a few minutes?"

"Come on in, Flo. Have a chair. Lay it on me." Richard chuckled.

With a memo pad and an envelope, she followed Richard into his office. She waited until he loosened his tie. She agreed with him the weather was unseasonably warm and listened as he decided the office should be centrally air conditioned. He suddenly directed her to get prices for such a job.

"And now," Richard declared as he settled behind his impressive desk. "Just what is on your lovely mind?"

"Mr. Oehrle's secretary called. Mr. Oehrle is going away on company business, meaning he will not be able to take your phone calls. She even added, that he will not be making any calls to you.

"Also, Mr. Powell called. Only he said he'd try later. Here's the letter you asked me to type. And the two articles you asked me to look up."

"Good. Good." He almost grabbed the papers from the unattractive but extremely efficient woman. "Thank you, Flo. Please shut the door as you leave."

Alone, Richard pulled off his glasses and slapped them down on his desk. "Damn," he stated out loud. "Something must have happened inside the company. And Hank is giving me a warning."

The ringing of the telephone made Richard jump. He knew Flo would answer it. After she buzzed him he was going to tell her to take a message. But after Flo told him the caller was Elmer Hoxie, Richard knew he could not avoid taking the call.

"How are you, Elmer?"

"Do you really want to know?"

"Oh oh. Sounds as though you have a concern."

"What in the hell is going on up there in Bridgeboro? With the *Fischer Company*. We got word there will be no stock issue."

Richard felt a vise like grip around his chest. "Are you sure?" Maybe he was going to have a heart attack?

"I am now. Somebody in the Accounting Department told me to call the company attorney's office and I just talked to a Geoff Greer."

"You didn't tell him you knew me, did you?"

"Of course not. I just asked for a news update. There's been changes in top level management and it's not a good time. The Executive Vice president has just been promoted and the new VP of Finance has to get his feet wet.   And Mrs. Fischer will make an announcement as to what her intentions will be.   You know management changes can affect stock prices?"

Richard closed his eyes. If only he knew what was happening. Didn't this internal change in top management back up what he had explained in his letter? The *Fischer Company* was mismanaged!   It needed someone to take over the helm and steer it back onto course. Should he continue with his plan? Or should he be careful? That's what he should be. Careful! Now was the time to back off, lay low, just in case Julie had learned something.

Finally Richard almost whispered, "Whatever happens, count me out."

"You have to be kidding," Elmer responded. "This could be a perfect time to . . . "

"I discussed my plan with my wife. And," he forced a laugh, "and she convinced me we should go to Europe this summer. Obviously I'll need some extra money. To keep her happy."

Elmer suspected he was hearing a tall tale. "Okay, but I still think you could be missing a good opportunity. Call me, if you change your mind."

"If I change my mind," Richard whispered as he hung up the receiver. He had to think fast. He had to tell Bernice. Before he punched in their home number what in the hell was he going to say to her? Why not ask her out to lunch? Tell her his new plans. Over a martini. Good idea. They certainly would not argue in a restaurant. Just as he was dialing the numbers, there was a knock on the door. "Who is it?"

"Brad."

"Come on in." He hung up the receiver.

"Sorry to interrupt you," Brad said politely. "But my stomach says it's lunch time."

Richard checked his watch. Damn. He had forgotten he told Brad he was not to go to lunch without him. Unless he went directly home. It had been part of the punishment.

Richard pushed up his glasses. He smiled before he sounded, "Hmmm. And it just so happens I can't go with you today."

"Should I go home?"

"No. It would mess up my plans. I mean I'm taking your mother out. And if you went home she'd have to get your lunch first." He forced another smile. "I'll tell you what." Richard stood and pulled out his wallet. "Here's a fiver. Go to the Diner." He had to add something strong. "But as soon as you're finished come right back to the office."

Once again, Richard picked up the receiver. He noticed how damp his palms were. Was he that nervous? That tense? He was feeling trapped. With his back against a wall, surrounded by Whiteside, Oehrle, and Charlie. Then he heard Julie cackling.

He could even hear Bill laughing at him From the grave.

"Hello, Bernice."

"Richard?" Bernice asked into the kitchen phone.

"Of course. Does my voice sound different? What are you doing?"

"Making up a shopping list. For our Friday evening card party."

"Oh good. You're dressed to go out. I want to take you out for lunch. And you can't say no . . . because you're not dressed."

"You have something to tell me." She waited. "Why can't we eat and talk at home?

"No. Let's splurge. I'll pick you up in about . . . "

"No. I'll meet you. That way I'll have my car so I can go shopping. How about the *Hartsville Inn*?

"Sounds good to me." So she had deliberately picked an expensive restaurant. At least they wouldn't argue there. "I'll meet you in the lobby. In about forty-five minutes."

As soon as Richard heard Bernice hang up, he dialed "O". He asked for a phone number. Finally a male voice said, "Thank you for calling the *Hartsville Inn*. How may I help you?"

"This is Richard Livingston, the editor of *The Bridgeborough Courier*. I'd like to reserve a table for two, for lunch. My wife is impressed with your formal garden and I want our table to be in front of the picture window.

"And, of course . . . I'll mention the lovely view and delicious lunch. In tomorrow's paper."

EVAN was awake when Beth entered the bedroom. She was carrying a tray with a mug of soup, a sandwich and a glass of milk

"Hi. Hungry?" She set the tray on the bureau.

Evan grunted, "I think so," while she struggled to sit up. "God, I hurt."

Beth put more pillows behind her sister. "Doc said you took a shower."

"Yeah. I thought I'd die. Then he watched me wash the baby. I couldn't wait to get back to bed."

Beth placed the table tray in front of Evan. "He said you're doing just fine. And the baby too."

She stepped closer to look into a clothes basket which was next to the bed. With a smile on her face, she studied the baby for many seconds. "Have you thought up a name yet?" She waited, "How about Leslie?"

Evan frowned. "You have to be kidding?"

"Well, it is a pretty name. Hey, Doc said you're going to nurse her."

Evan looked annoyed. "I said I'll *try*."

"I think you should." She watched Evan's eyebrows raise as high as they could. "I read that it makes a mother feel closer to her baby."

"I thought you were going to say because I've got big udders."

Beth forced a laugh. Then she yawned. If only she could lie down. Anywhere.

"You look tired," Evan said between chewing a large bite of a peanut butter and jelly sandwich. After Beth nodded, she asked, "How's Annie Oakley Fischer? She sure was on tear. Thank God, our old man never got that bad."

"Doc told me you gave the gun to him. And told him Julie threatened to shoot me. Please, don't tell anybody else. She just wanted to scare me."

"Oh yeah. Well she could have fooled me. Are you going to keep living here?"

"Of course. And keep working for her."

"In other words she isn't pissed at you anymore." Evan drank some milk. "I mean, we had mentioned you and me getting an apartment, and . . . " she shrugged.

"Julie said you can stay until you feel okay. Then you can move into one of the apartments in The Greenbrier. She owns the building and she'll let you have it, rent free."

"You think she needs you and I think she needs a psychiatrist."

"She had too much to drink."

"Rather you than me. I've had my share of drunks. That's why I got out of Taylor Park."

Beth felt anger. "Don't you dare blame Daddy for what you did. You followed Les because you were a smart ass. You could have just broken off with Geoff and stayed in town."

"Sure. I was real smart." She ran her eyes around her sister's angry face. "You're the smart one. You have it made." She stuffed her mouth with another bite.

With sarcasm dripping from her words, Beth said, "Why don't you call Liz? After she gets past the crap she just might feel sorry for you. Especially since you can present her with her first granddaughter. And she is loaded now."

"I could care how loaded she is. In fact do me a favor and don't let her know I'm in town." She spooned noodles from the mug. "Does Geoff know?" After Beth nodded, she added, "What did he say?"

"He wanted to know you and the baby are okay."

"In other words he doesn't want to see me?" Evan finished the soup.

Beth stepped to the bed. "I didn't say that. Geoff will decide when."

"Could you do some shopping for me. Buy me some hair coloring. And make-up. And especially a girdle. I have to look nice So I can get a job."

"Make a list for me. I need to go to the store for some stuff that Julie wants."

Evan added   "Thanks. I'm good for it. As soon as I get some money."

Beth carried the tray to the door. She paused and said, "Believe me, I'll give you an itemized bill"

FIFTY ONE

AS SHE WALKED across the parking lot Bernice remembered the original name of the *Hartsville Inn* had been *The Sign of the Heart*. That was when it had been established in the eighteenth century by Colonel William Hart, a veteran of the Revolutionary War.

The current owners had changed the name and made the inn famous for an award winning English Garden. Many shrubs and bedding plants were in full bloom. Any knowing person, such as she who was the president of the *Bridgeboro Garden Club*, would realize the garden was so planned for it to be beautiful from early spring until late fall.

As soon as they were seated, their waiter asked if they would like to order a cocktail. Richard ordered a martini.

Bernice put up her hand. "None for me."

"Of course you want a drink," Richard insisted.

Bernice used her Southern drawl and said, "I've got to do some shoppin'."

"You can shop anytime. Live it up. After all, it's not too often I have the time to take you out for lunch." He winked at the waiter. "Two up, very dry, *Beefeaters*."

The waiter put a menu in front of each of them. And hurried away.

"Where's Brad?"

"Eating at the Diner. I told him he could go alone today."

"Why couldn't he eat with us?"

"I've decided to give him more freedom. What you said made me realize I am being awfully hard on him. And what happened wasn't his fault."

"I'm glad you realize you haven't been fair to him."

"And he's doing a great job at the office." Surely that would please her.

"Brad always does a good job." Bernice observed her husband. He was becoming anxious. She decided she would push him. "What do you really want to talk about?

"To talk about Brad," he insisted.

Bernice was about to respond when the waiter appeared, carrying a tray with two martinis. Richard actually reached for one. After his first sip he wondered what Bernice would say if he ordered another? He did anyway.

"Richard," Bernice said, sharply. "You'll fall asleep at your desk."

Richard took another sip and winked at the waiter. "We can go home and go to bed."

The waiter did smile. "I'll be right back with your drink, sir."

Bernice picked up her water glass. "And some cheese and crackers." She sipped from the glass and then almost demanded, "What do you want to discuss about Brad?"

"Well, I already told you I've decided not to be so tough on him. And this morning after I watched him working I got to thinking. You are right. He did exceptionally well in school. And here I am making him perform again. With no break between high school and college. So," Richard paused to quickly finish his first drink, "so I decided we should go to Europe. As soon as we can get his passport and make the reservations. We'll rent a car, visit your sister . . . and take a grand tour of Europe." Richard dared to look into Bernice's eyes. "How about that for an idea? Doesn't that make a luncheon date worthwhile?"

Bernice sipped more water before she smiled at her husband. She enjoyed seeing him suffer. "It sounds wonderful. And it would sound even better if I knew it were sincere."

"What do you mean by that?"

"I mean I know you well enough to know your sudden idea is a cover-up. Why do you want us to get away from Bridgeboro?"

"You and Brad deserve a trip. And it's obvious you've been dying to see your sister's palace, or whatever." The waiter arrived to replace his empty glass with a full one.

Bernice held up the menu. "I'd like to order the lobster salad and iced tea."

She watched Richard take a quick sip and nod. "Ahh, you can make that two" As soon as they were alone Bernice remarked, "I seem to remember you told me I wanted to go to Europe because Julie and that girl are going. I was the one who said Brad deserved the trip."

"I've changed my mind." Richard took a long sip.

"Something has gone wrong with your plans trying to get control of Bill's company. What's going to happen?"

"Just stay calm. It's nothing serious."

"But something has happened?" She pushed her martini to him.

Richard talked to the olives on the toothpick. "Only that I began to weigh the pros and the cons and suddenly it seemed wiser to change my mind."

"I'm happy to hear that. But my immediate concern is what might I be hearing that means all of a sudden we should go to Europe?"

He chewed on an olive. "You won't be hearing anything."

"In other words you haven't fallen completely flat on your face? Just tripped, huh? And how about Julie? We still have to wait for her to find out? About your brainstorm?"

Richard took a deep breath. "She already does."

Bernice sighed. She felt as though she had gone shopping, cleaned the house and weeded her garden. How could she feel so spent? "I could say how brazen you were to think you could pull something over on Julie Fischer. But this time I'm not going to bother."

Suddenly she saw the enthusiastic waiter approaching their table. Carrying a tray with their artistically arranged lunches on lovely china plates. Bernice declared in a cheerful voice, "Oh my. Doesn't that look just scrumptious? And I know the rolls are fresh baked."

Bernice finished several large bites of her salad before she spoke again, in a clear, crisp voice. "Richard, I do believe it's about time I take one of your asinine ideas, seriously. I'm really quite tired of listening about how you're going to become rich. And powerful. The biggest businessman in Bridgeboro."

As she buttered a piece of roll she continued. "You'll never be the biggest anything. Except the biggest fool. And since your memory is so good you remember it was I who said Brad deserved a trip. Then perhaps you'll also remember I said if you failed in one more of your greedy schemes, I was going to leave you and Bridgeboro. Do you remember that?"

"Bernice. Let's not spoil this nice lunch. We'll tell Brad he can go out tonight and we'll discuss it . . . " He stopped as soon as he saw Bernice shaking her head from side to side, making her fleshy jowl swing with her jaw.

"I'm tired of pretending."

"Pretending? About what?"

"About our marriage. Our entire relationship has been a sham."

Richard knew his face was becoming flushed. "That's because you've made it that way. With your god damn southern pompous attitude."

"Lower your voice. Or I shall leave. Right now."

"Okay. I'll whisper. I can prove to you . . . this is not as big a deal as you're making it."

Bernice drank iced tea then whispered, "And I suppose you'd tell Julie the same thing? And she'll smile and think how nice you are to believe so much in Bill's company. You fool. She's going to bare her claws and rip you wide open. And not just your guts will come pouring out. But my guts And Brad's guts. So thank you in behalf of Brad for offering us a trip to Europe. In fact, we might even stay there." She buttered her second roll.

"That's a good idea. We could sell the house, the business, everything, and move to Europe." He quickly smiled and tried to look knowledgeable. "Although I have read the ideal place to move for housing and business opportunities is Costa Rica.

"I'm not inviting you to move anywhere with us. I said Brad and I."

"Wellll. The change would do me as much good as it would you. I've been working damn hard lately. Under some great strain. And I'd like to get away, too."

"Fine. Go away. But you are not going with Brad and me."

"What would you tell Brad?"

Bernice thought fast. What *would* she tell Brad? His father was a moron! A wheeling dealing hateful, lying cheat. But she knew Richard could retaliate by telling Brad the story! Sitting taller in her Windsor chair, Bernice said strongly, "I'll tell him everything."

Richard smiled a cruel smile. "You're surprising me. I never knew you as a gambler."

Bernice finished her iced tea. "What's my alternative? Stay in Bridgeboro and know people are snickering behind my back? I can hear the whispering now at the luncheons and meetings of all the Boards and Committees I serve on. And don't say I could resign because then people will think I'm too embarrassed to appear in public. Lou would have a ball."

Richard pushed his salad plate away from him. Inside, he was gloating. He never dreamed this luncheon would turn out in his favor.

After the waiter refilled her glass with ice tea, Bernice gently dabbed at her mouth. "I will condescend to take time to rethink my priorities. While I'm in Europe. With Brad."

"Just remember I'm going with you."

Suddenly Bernice smiled and announced, "You win.   We'll tell Brad."

Richard felt deflated.   Just like that she agreed with him?   Could she be saying something he didn't understand?   "You haven't finished your salad."

"I'm full.   I shouldn't have eaten the roll.   Ask for the check." Bernice smiled another sweet smile.   "Do you prefer to go by plane? Or by cruise ship?"   She pushed her chair away from the table.

"I think we should fly."

"Since our passports are still valid I just have to take Brad to have his picture taken and apply for one.   And I must take him shopping for a suitable wardrobe."   She smiled another happy smile.   "I was going to need him anyway.   To shop for his college wardrobe. This way we can do both at the same time."   She raised her eyebrows.   "Shall I call the airlines for prices?"

"I will.   Just remember I will have to discuss the trip with Flo and George Clopper. And lay out their responsibilities."   He frowned at Bernice's grin.   "You must realize I just can't walk out.   All businessmen have to make arrangements. Especially for long trips."

"And I have to make arrangements also. With Ellie to check the house and for Tony to water my flower beds. I might even suggest Ellie just stay at the house."   She stood and began to walk away. From the table. And from Richard.

After Richard paid the bill he managed to catch up with her in the parking lot.   As she unlocked her car Bernice remarked, "Thank you for asking me out for such delightful lunch."

"My pleasure. And thank you for changing your mind. I promise we'll solve our problems and have a great time." Richard held the door of her car opened,   He watched Bernice settle behind the wheel before he added, "Don't be surprised if Brad and I come home early."

Richard watched Bernice drive out of the parking lot and turn south. He assumed she was going shopping. He knew he was going back to the office but wondered if he would be able to concentrate. As Bernice had predicted he did feel sluggish.   But he would call the airlines.

He did look forward to telling Brad about a pending trip. Until he recalled his ruined plan. His shattered dream. Damn Julie Fischer . . . again. He had an impulse to drive and drive, and drive . . . until Bernice and Julie and Bridgeboro were far removed from his life.

Richard drove his car toward the old building with the modern lobby which housed the glaring truth. Being the owner and editor of *The Bridgeborough Courier* was the only really logical, practical, but disheartening way of life for him. Not to succeed. To survive!

IN the restaurant Bernice had decided what she was going to do.

She drove home. She locked the mud room door and hurried into the den. She searched through a telephone directory and dialed a number she wanted. A cunning smile crept across her thick lips. Her heart was pounding in her ample chest and a tingle of excitement swept through her as she heard a male voice announce, "American Airways. How may I help you?"

"I need information on flights to . . . to Mexico City. For two."

FIFTY TWO

THE RINGING OF the telephone in the living room made Beth jump. She was lying on the couch, eyes closed but not asleep. She had been talking to her daddy. There were so many stories to sort out. So much to review about Brad. So much to worry about Julie. And the company. If her daddy were with her, they would have sorted it out. Together.

She quickly picked up the receiver. "Fischer's residence. How may I help you?"

"Guess who?" Geoff asked.

"Oh, hi. What a surprise." She wished she could sound more enthused.

"What's wrong? Are you okay?"

"I was sleeping."

"Damn. I'm sorry. I should have checked my watch. I see now it's nap time."

"Don't be funny. I'm trying to catch up for four nights sleep."

"Sorry. But I just had to call. I have a surprise to tell you."

"It'll take a miracle to make me forgive you."

"I have an exclusive miracle. I had lunch with Brad Livingston. We sat with each other at The Pike Diner. An hour ago."

"Oh my god. How is he? I mean, is he okay?"

"He looks tired. And frustrated. As soon as I saw him alone I decided it couldn't be a better time. Even though I was prepared to dislike him. But he's so damn good looking and likeable. I almost fell in love with him." Geoff paused while Beth laughed. "I had the guts to tell him I knew your secret. And he told me something you don't know. He broke off with Jeanne Barnes."

Hot tears filled her eyes. And began to overflow.

"Did you hear me?"

"Uh huh. I just can't believe he . . . he did it. Or that he told you."

"He not only did it, he's been grounded for doing it. He can only leave the house to go to the office. He's not allowed out at night or go anywhere, anytime, alone. He doesn't know why he was permitted to eat alone today."

"Did he tell you when he told Jeanne?"

"After you called from Norfolk. He thought you still were in Norfolk. I brought him up to date and I took it upon myself to tell him I know you l.o.v.e. him."

"Geoff! I don't know what I'm going to do with you. Or without you. You are a dear."

"A dear!" Geoff heard himself declare. "I'm d.u.m.b. Who else carries love messages for their favorite girl. And oh yeah, he gave me a note for you. He's afraid to call you. I can bring it down after work. Or do you want to drive up to my office?"

"I have to do some shopping for Evan and Julie. I'll pick it up. And give you a hug."

"Okay. But I do want to see Evan and her baby."

"She's sleeping right now. But I know she wants to see you." Inside she knew somehow, something had happened. There wasn't as much of a thrill talking with Geoff. Brad loved her. And now he was free. They could face any obstacles, together.

"Beth. Didn't you hear me?" Geoff used a strong voice. How is Julie?"

"Recovering and also sleeping. She did offer to give Evan an apartment. Rent free. In The Greenbrier. I'm going to move her up there this week-end."

"Does Liz know about Evan?"

"I promised Evan I won't tell her. If she calls to tell me she's home."

"Have you stopped to think how much has happened since you graduated."

Beth laughed. "Yeah. It's unbelievable. And scary."

"But you'll forgive me because I woke you up?"

"I'll forgive you because I still love you." But when she added, "Goodbye, Geoff," she felt as though she truly meant it.

FIFTY THREE

WHEN BETH GOT up on Thursday morning she felt frustrated. It was raining. Doc had said if it was a warm and sunny day they could take the baby outside because Evan had convinced him she had to see the apartment. Sam Carpenter and Ellie had put the house back in order, the mirrors had been replaced and Gerry had been found hiding in the laundry room. But even though their lives were on track, she wanted to get out.

Now they'd have to stay home which meant she would have to listen to Evan sigh and complain about how bored she was, how she didn't like the daytime shows on the "boob tube" and how she didn't feel like reading. Beth decided it could be an expected reaction of females who were not ready to have babies. But it still was damn annoying.

The only good thing was what she had tucked in her bra. Brad's note! Geoff had given it to her in his office. She slept with it under her pillow and now she was keeping it next to her heart. She and Brad belonged together. And right there, in his own handwriting he wrote Always and all ways. I loved you yesterday – I love you today – and I'll love you all of our tomorrows. I'm going to tell my folks about us tonight. Then I can call you. The next time Julie tried to convince her that Brad might just be saying he loved her, she would show it to her! Maybe?

PEG Mawhorter sighed loudly as soon as she saw the rain. It meant the girls would have to play indoors. She hoped she could tolerate their noise and bickering without scolding too much. Being in a bad mood had become a habit. Sometimes when she looked in a mirror, she was afraid at how much hatred she felt. All because of that one night when she had been so foolish.

WHEN Bernice Livingston looked out her bedroom window, she murmured, "Oh damn." How she detested shopping in the rain. Brad really did have enough clothes for a trip. To anywhere. So did she. But she didn't want Brad to go to the office. She wanted him to be with her. It had been so delightful the day before. She so enjoyed how many girls stared after him. Even some of the sales ladies. What a thrill to show him off. Let people know he was hers. And very soon he would be. All hers.

BETH stood in the living room and stared at the new mantle clock. When in the hell was Evan going to wake up?   Why should she be angry at Evan? She knew her sister had been up twice with the baby. And she had decided to ignore the baby's crying and Evan's shuffling around the house.

The first two nights Beth had struggled to get up and help Evan. But last night she had decided Evan might as well get used to being a single mother.

Beth surmised Julie would not be waking for several more hours. She knew Julie was drinking herself to sleep. Drinking and coughing. But Beth wasn't going to let her kill herself. She'd tell Doc today that Julie was drinking again.

Beth was in the kitchen when the wall phone rang. She quickly lifted the receiver before the phone could ring again.   "Hello. Fischer's residence. How may I help you?"

"Hello.   This is Peg Mawhorter and I'd like to talk with Beth Rhodes."

"This is Beth. What a nice surprise. Everything is okay, isn't it?"

"Oh yeah.   I just thought I'd give you a call on this ugh, rainy day."

"I can hear the girls. How are you all?"

"We're all okay. At the present time I could scream. Rainy days and kids don't go together. I miss you sitting with the girls. How are you doing?"

"I'm fine. But I am ..." Beth paused and thought, do *not* say you are tired. Then you'll have to explain why? "a little lost. I'm sure you can remember graduating from high school can make a big change in your life. It even feels different than a regular summer vacation."

"And you don't have a regular job. I mean you're working where you're living. How do like working for Julie?"

"I'm enjoying it."

"Of course you know Alan got a promotion? To Vice President of Finance."

"I've already called to congratulate him. He's not only ambitious and loyal, but very smart. He's going to need you to keep up with him."

Peg sighed, "I know." Then she quickly scolded, "Di, you better stop doing that or I'm going to send you to your room."

Beth ignored the outburst. "You do know Alan is the youngest man who ever has been the Treasurer of the Fischer Company?"

"Maybe he told you but just in case he didn't I might as well be honest with you. I haven't told anybody else but I'm disappointed because we aren't moving to Europe. He was supposed to be the Manager of Europe and England Companies. Or something like that. And I was really looking forward to getting out of here."

"You *are* going to move. Alan told me about your new house. I forget what it's called."

"It's called a saltbox. It's a two story colonial, four bedrooms, three baths and a fireplace in a big family room. And a two car garage."

"Wow. You sure will have plenty of room for three or more children." And then she blurted out, "How have you been feeling, Peg?"

"Pregnant. I'm already in maternity clothes and . . . I'm a sight."

"Come on. You always look sharp in anything you wear."

"Thanks. But right now I look like hell." Peg sighed loudly. "You must know I didn't want to get pregnant. At least not this year."

What could she say? She, who might know more about this baby than she should.

"I'll bet the girls are happy. I mean, you have told them . . . wait a minute, Peg." Beth had heard a knock on the mud room door.

Beth put down the receiver and hurried to the door. There was Doc peering at her through the locked screen door.

"Good morning, Doc," Beth said cheerfully. "Julie's still sleeping."

"Good morning, young lady. Thought I'd check on my patients. Sorry to have to knock. I should put the key on my key chain. " He walked into the kitchen. "Seems she's sleeping later and later. The baby okay?"

Beth nodded. She picked up the receiver and put her finger over the speaker. "I'm talking on the phone. But I want to talk to you before you see Julie."

Doc nodded. "Sure. I'll just make myself a cup of tea."

Beth removed her finger before Doc decided to add, "If it's Geoff, tell him I said 'Good morning'. Or, maybe it's that Livingston boy?" He chuckled as he put water in the tea kettle.

Oh God. How can he do this? First the baby, now Brad. She said into the receiver, "Peg, Doctor Rexinger just arrived. He wants a cup of...what? He didn't say anything about a baby. He calls me young lady." Beth smiled sweetly at Doc. "Doc and Julie are very good friends. He comes to visit us and..."

"Alan says she's sick again. That's why you had to cancel your trip to Europe. I'll bet you're as disappointed as I am? Di! Stop doing that. Right now!"

"Yeah. I was kinda disappointed. But, as soon as she's better, we're ..."

"Alan says she looked really great, the last time you and she met with the biggies."

"Yes. She did look great. But she ... "

"Alan says that Geoff Greer was with you. Are you two seeing each other? Besides on company time?"

Peg laughed. "Boy, I can't get over how he turned out. He's really sharp looking. And, I'll bet he's fun to be with. Huh?"

"Peg. Doc is waiting to talk to me. I'll call you back."

"Okay, but before you hang up. Have you heard from Liz?"

"The last card was from Key Largo."

"Ours was too. She sounds as though she's having a ball. Shouldn't she be home soon? After Beth said, "This week." she asked, "How about Evan?"

Beth looked at Doc and smiled. "Funny you should ask. I got a graduation card from her." At least Doc knew where everything was, for his cup of tea.

"No kidding. How is she?"

"She just wrote she was sorry she couldn't be with me on my big night."

"I'm awfully sorry I couldn't be there. But I felt lousy that night. I haven't been feeling too hot with this baby."

"I'm sorry about that. But listen, Peg. I really have to ... "

"You know Alan is rooting for a boy. But he really could care less about how I feel. I mean, he's so busy at work. He's hardly ever home. Oh, maybe on Sundays. But ... "

"Alan needs you to support him. He doesn't need..."

"I know. A nagging wife. But it isn't fair. I've got these two kids and I'm home all day, and, oh sure, he's getting a company car so I can use our car, but . . . " Peg sighed loudly.

"Start thinking about your new house. And how you're going to decorate it. You and Gert can start going to furniture stores."

"I'm too tired to care about the house."

"I'll come over and stay with the girls while you and Alan go shopping." She shrugged at Doc, who was sitting at the table. "Doc is waiting to talk with me. Thanks heaps for calling. Think house. And," she decided to give Peg some food for thought. She would either swallow it or spit it out "Remember, you're the wife of an executive now. Nice house, entertaining important people, nice clothes, devoted wife and loving mother. Keeping busy while father is making his first million." Beth forced a laugh. "Good talking with you. Call me again."

"Beth, come see me. Please?"

"I will. And you take care of yourself. Goodbye, Peg."

After Peg hung up she put her hand on her bulging abdomen. Within, several seconds, tears began to drip from her jaws and wet her bare arms. She whispered, "After all, you're the wife of an executive, so you have to start . . . acting like one." What a crock of shit!

BETH walked to the table and focused on Doc drinking his tea. Now, it was time to have another serious conversation.

Doc pointed to the chair opposite to his. "Sit down. No wonder you look so tired. Too much stress in your life."

Beth sat. "That was my next door neighbor in Taylor Park. You know her husband Alan works for the company. She's upset because he's in the office more than he's home."

"Huh! She should be married to a doctor." He finished his tea and stood. "I'm going to make another cup. Want one? After she nodded he asked, "Everybody okay in this house?"

He studied Beth's face and added, "Julie giving you too much to do?"

"Not really. Phone calls. Some letters. Shopping. She *is* drinking again. She has some bottles hidden somewhere. Because Sam says he's not buying anything for her."

"I thought I smelled what she calls her medicine. Yesterday. And you haven't been able to catch her?"

"She locks her door every evening and sleeps late the next day. She's been doing a lot of coughing. So she's tried to convince me coughing keeps her awake and she needs to sleep late. When I do go into her bedroom in the morning, the window is open and . . . " she shrugged.

"And she looks like hell." Doc put two cups of tea on the table.

"I know this set back really is my fault. I never should have left her." Beth willed herself not to cry so she quickly stood and said, "I need sugar."

"Her drinking is not your fault. After Bill died, Earle and I were busy keeping her away from the bottle. Earle tried to keep her involved helping him run the company but she'd fall apart every holiday or when something would remind her of Bill. She just couldn't put him out of her life. And now that Earle is gone . . . " Doc sighed deeply and shook his head. "Thank god for the dedicated and competent company men who keep it as successful as it is. I wish she could sell it. But I don't think that would stop the drinking binges."

"She has told me how much she loved Mr. Fischer," Beth almost whispered.

"She was crazy about him. But hell. Everybody was. He was all things to all people."

Beth looked into Doc's blue eyes. "Did you know him? Well?"

"Well enough to like him. And envy him. He had most of the men in Bridgeboro and a fifty mile radius, green with envy. And most of the women behaving like they were in heat. Just to get his attention. And Julie knew it. She worked hard to be a good wife for him."

"She told me she wanted a baby, very badly. She thought if . . . it would have made the marriage . . . I mean Mr. Fischer, very happy."

Doc frowned. "Huh. I didn't know she would open up with anyone. You keep her talking. That's better than my medicine."

"She opened up to me . . . until I told her about Brad and me. Besides the fact my confession upset her, I think she feels rotten."

Doc reached across the table and patted Beth's hand. "You did throw her a curve ball with your news. But she is pushing. As though she's on a collision course."

Beth felt hot tears welling up. "Do you think it would help any if I moved out? I mean, I could live with Evan."

"My god young lady, don't you even think of leaving. She may come across as mean, even unpredictable, but she needs you. And she loves you."

"I love her too. But I've brought her problems closer to her. I remind her of the things she wants to forget."

"You stay. Doctor's orders."

"But isn't there something you . . . we can do?"

"I should have her admitted to a hospital." He pushed back his chair and stood. "I'm concerned about the way she looks. And like you, afraid she's pretending she feels okay."

Beth focused on Doc's wrinkled face. He looked worried. "How about if you knock on her door. Like, right now?"

Doc stood and hiked up his trousers. "Okay. What have I got to lose? I'll wake up Julie and you tell your sister I want to see her and the baby."

Beth stood by Doc's side as he knocked on Julie's bedroom door. "Good morning, Mrs. Fischer. Time to rise and shine."

After no answer Doc wiggled the knob. "Come on, open up. It's time to get up."

"Go to hell." Julie replied in a husky voice. Then she coughed.

"Not before I see you." He wiggled the knob again. "Come on. Unlock this door."

"I'm not ready to get up. Come back later. I'll call you when."

"I'm not leaving until I see you. As your physician I'm here to make a house call."

Julie coughed, hard. "Who called you? Beth?"

"I decided all by myself. Unlock the door or I'll have to break it down."

"I'll call the police."

"I find that difficult to believe since you don't want me to see you. I'll bet you look like hell and your room stinks. Since I know what you've been doing, you might as well let me in."

AS soon as Beth heard the sound of movement from the room she hurried to her bedroom, opened the door and backed into the room.

From the bed, Evan mumbled, "What's going on out there?"

Beth opened the blinds. "Doc is trying to get Julie to unlock her door."

"Shit. I was sound asleep and then all of a sudden *bang bang*. He wants to catch her, huh?"

"How do you know?"

"Yesterday while you were doing errands, I saw Sam with an empty bottle. I guessed he was getting rid of it for her."

"Don't tell Doc. No use getting Sam in hot water. He does what Julie tells him to do."

Beth pictured Doc scaring away Sam and then Julie possibly losing her contact with what went on at the Livingston's. Right now, Beth wanted to know as much as Julie did. She smiled at Evan and announced, "Doc wants to see you and the baby. And you better hurry up and name her because he has to send the information into the Registration Office."

Evan yawned. "I know." She sat on the edge of the bed and yawned louder.

"I guess you don't like the idea of having to use your name on her Birth Certificate. But when you do get married your husband can adopt her and it'll be easy to change." She watched Evan frown. "Well you can't lie. And Doc knows everything."

"Even though you're buying the formula and diapers in the Mall, all of Bridgeboro will find out. I guess it's still raining? It was when I got up for her six o'clock bottle."

Beth nodded. "Yeah. Sorry."

"I'm going to tell Doc I have to get out. After all, you can carry an umbrella while we walk from the car to the lobby of the apartment house."

"I think Doc will say it should be a better day, for both of you to go out. Anyway, do whatever you have to do, before Doc is ready to see you."

AS Beth walked through the hall she heard Doc's voice through the closed bedroom door. "If you don't care about yourself, you could at least think about what you're doing to others."

"Oh? Such as?"

"That young lady cares about you. She cares very much. Have you looked at her lately? She looks terrible. Worried and beat. She's lost weight. She's depressed. And . . .

"Wait a minute," Julie said strongly. "I'm not to blame for the way *that* young lady looks. She's tired because she's up during the night to take care of *that* baby. I'll be damn glad when it's out of this house. It disturbs me. Every night.

"Disturbs your what? Not your sleep. Once you fall to sleep you probably wouldn't hear an accident, even if the cars came through your wall.

"Your damn pills don't help me so I'm using my way of getting a good night's sleep."

Beth hurried from the hall to the laundry room. She could sort clothes. And hide.

JULIE sat on the edge of the bed while Philip stood in front of her. "That girl blames herself. She thinks you're drinking again because of the fight you two had."

"Will you stop worrying about that girl! She not only has a roof over head but now she has her boyfriend."

"Don't spoil it for her. Let her and the boy love each other."

"If I was going to louse it up, don't you think I would have done it. By now?" Julie peered into Philip's eyes. "I'm actually trying to help her. I called Herb Gillon yesterday and got him to rewrite my will."

Julie paused, knowing she had Philip's attention. "Beth convinced me to give Vicki's manuscripts to the Library. So that gives his law office some extra paper work. And I decided the hell with The Church of The Whatever. They'll still get Earle's investments and insurance but I'm trying to leave this house to her. Meanwhile, I'm giving her a free apartment and some loose change to pay the taxes and whatever. And, I'm sure you knew I wasn't going to make her pay me back for the college bills." Julie had to grin at the expression on her friend's craggy face. "I can tell you're just as surprised as Herb was. No one thinks I have any kindness in me."

Philip patted Julie's bony shoulders. "I've always known you have a nice streak. Even though you try to hide it. I'm impressed with your generosity. For the girl's welfare."

"Welfare, hell. I'm just trying to make her as flush as I can. If it can't be Geoff, I've decided I want that boy to stay interested in her."

EVAN was miserable. Doc had told her not to take the baby outside. And Beth told her she could not drive Julie's automobile to the apartment. Damn both of them!

Hour after hour she had peered out the windows in the bedroom, stood in front of the French doors in the dining room, stared through the bay window in the kitchen, willing the rain to stop. Around noon time, it looked as though the rain clouds were disappearing so she got dressed, only to be disappointed when the weather man's prediction came true. A downpour.

Being dressed was another reason she was suffering, Her new girdle was pinching her and her feet didn't like her new shoes. But she wasn't about to complain about being uncomfortable because she was grateful to her sister for the new clothes. Beth had also bought her an attractive blonde shade of hair dye and make-up which was very becoming.

Even though she wished her feet didn't hurt, she felt good. She enjoyed a nap every afternoon determined to recover quickly from birthing. She didn't want Beth to think she was a wimp. And give Julie any more reason to criticize her. Besides Doc's and Beth's compliments, she was pleased with the results which she saw in a full length mirror.

Sitting at the kitchen table sipping a mug of tea, she tried to analyze her feelings. Sure, she got mad at Beth. It was because her sister was so lucky. Beth had a job. She had a place to live. She had a future. Okay, so she had had some kind of a blow-up with old Julie. Still she didn't have to move. Everything always seemed to turn out okay for Beth.

And Beth was smart. That was one reason why she got mad at her sister. Because she was so damned smart. But Beth *was* trying to help her. She had bought make-up and new clothes for her. And she had gotten Evan her very own apartment which she could move . . . What was that noise? A car door?

Was Doc returning? Maybe it was Sam Carpenter? She heard footsteps stop at the screen door. Someone tapped. She knew the door was locked. She could quickly leave the room and hide in the bedroom. Let Beth answer the door.

Except she was in the bathroom.

The person knocked harder. "Beth?" a male voice called out.

Evan closed her eyes as she supported herself against the sink.

It was Geoff!

Was she ready?

FIFTY FOUR

DRINKING A CUP of coffee at the kitchen table Bernice decided she would go shopping. Even if it was raining. She'd ask Brad to drive her to the Mall. Keep him out of the office, again. The day before she had given him permission to call his friends, even though most of them were either working or away.

In three days she and Brad would be leaving Bridgeboro. Without regret. True, she did consider Bridgeboro a lovely little historical village. She had even learned to disregard the damn Yankees. It just represented unpleasant memories, except for one glorious afternoon. But she could take that memory with her, anywhere. A glow appeared on her face. Eyes closed she peered inwardly. Bill Fischer was smiling at her. What a handsome face he had. What expressive eyes. What a distracting mouth. And his hands, so strong and yet so gentle. His manliness, so unyielding, except for those moments she had shared his passion.

Brad ambled into the kitchen and saw his mother with eyes closed and an unusual look on her fleshy face. Should he back out of the room? He was hungry so he cleared his throat. He really wanted to eat something quick and easy, so he could escape to the office. Working near his father was not enjoyable but he had had his fill of shopping with his mother. And now he was going to have to travel with both of them. For weeks! Out of touch with Beth!

"Ohh. Good morning, dear. I didn't hear you come downstairs. Your eggs and bacon are in the warming oven. Even though it's raining we'll go to Southampton Mall anyway. It'll give you a chance to wear your new raincoat."

"I was planning to go to the office." He took the plate to the table.

"I want to go back to Gamburg's. For those shoes I saw yesterday. Then we can drive to Market Street for a Philly cheese steak sandwich. Unless you want to drive up to New York?"

Brad frowned. "New York? Make a break, Mom."

Bernice felt alarm. She did not want to annoy Brad. "Louise and I have done it lots of times. And after we go shopping we could have a nice lunch in *The Tavern on the Green.*"

Brad wiped his mouth with a red napkin. The color matched the red geraniums on the table and window sill. "Have you seen Mrs. B. lately?"

"We attended the same meeting on Tuesday. I didn't ask about Jeanne. They'll be surprised when they hear about our trip."

Brad shrugged. "Most people know you want to see Aunt Liz's mansion in Italy."

"We'll go to Paris first. If they aren't there, then we'll go to Italy." She saw the confused look on Brad's face and heard him remark, loudly...

"We're just going to fly to Paris and if she isn't there, then look for her in Italy?"

"You don't have to be at Princeton until August."

"I thought we'd be gone for just a couple of weeks."

"Would you rather we go someplace else?"

"Yo, Mom. We're leaving in three days. We've stuffed our suitcases with new clothes and I've convinced myself I'm curious enough to want to see Aunt Liz's shacks."

Was now the time to tell him just the two of them were going to Mexico City, in two days? If she did she'd have to tell him she already had made arrangements to get a quick divorce. She'd also have to explain she was planning on moving her family's antiques and all of her favorite things to furnish the house she was going to rent, near his college. She would keep house for him so he wouldn't have to live in a shabby Frat House. Or with strangers. Just the two of them. And her memories.

Bernice patted Brad's hand. "We're going to have fun. While I stack the dishwasher, go put on a nicer shirt. And get your raincoat. We'll go to New York. I can look for shoes there."

Brad was in his room when the four telephones rang throughout the house. Let his mother answer. He didn't feel like talking to anybody.

Bernice had to struggle to keep the annoyance from her voice. "Good morning."

"Bernice." Richard's voice had an urgency in it.

"Of course. What do you want?"

"To tell you and Brad to stay put. I'm coming right home. To meet Charles and Lou. I can't take the time to tell you now. Just be ready for an important discussion. "

"Don't you remember I told you I'm going shopping? Brad and I are just about…"

"Just shut up and listen to what I'm telling you. Charles wants to see us, this morning."

"Don't you tell me to shut up. Why do you have to be so wishy washy with Charles? Just call him back and tell him it's inconvenient. Never mind. I'll do it myself."

"Don't call anyone. I'm coming home right now. I want to tell you the way I want this. . . this problem to be handled."

"Problem? I want to know what it is *now*, Richard."

Richard slammed the receiver down hoping Bernice still had hers against her ear. He pushed up his glasses.

EVAN couldn't make herself move. One hand was holding on to the edge of the sink and the other hand was spread across her chest. Her heart beats were pounding in her ears and her thoughts were colliding against each other. Why was she so nervous? She was dressed as nicely as he ever had seen her. And she did want to see him. But maybe she really meant uptown. In a store? Surrounded by people. Not in the kitchen! Alone!

Geoff knocked again. "Beth?"

She tugged at her girdle before she walked to the screen door. "Hello, Geoff." She opened the door. And stood back.

"Helloooo Evan," Geoff said. Then he followed her into the kitchen.

Evan returned to the sink. She washed and dried the mug and the spoon. She had to remain nonchalant.

Geoff stood in front of the refrigerator. He felt in his coat pocket for his keys. He needed something to hold and rub. "Long time no see. How the heck have you been?"

Evan nodded. "Okay. And you?"

Geoff shook his head up and down, too many times. "Also okay."

Evan clung to the towel. "You want me to find Beth? Or did you come to see Julie?"

"Both of them. But there's no hurry." He began to relax. "You look great, Evan."

"Thank you. You look great yourself." She managed a little laugh before she added, "Just as I pictured a successful lawyer should look."

"Beth did tell me you were here. But if I looked surprised I guess I didn't expect to see you looking so pretty and perky. I mean after having a baby and . . ." he grinned and shrugged.

Evan grinned back. "And she's adorable and I'll even let you hold her. Beth and I were going uptown to see my apartment. I guess you know Julie's letting me have a furnished one in *The Greenbrier*. But," she paused to sigh, "Doc said I shouldn't take the baby out in the rain. So I was having a cup of tea and deciding if I'll go by myself. By taxi."

"If you can wait for a few minutes, I can take you uptown."

"That would be great. I mean, if it won't be taking you out of your way."

"Of course not. And you can show me your apartment."

Unprepared for what she was about to blurt out, Evan said, "Maybe you could let me run into the library also? I want to get more books." Why in the hell would she say that? Except she was trying to brag. After a quick laugh, she added, "I want to stock up for the next couple of weeks. Or, until the baby is ready for a Day Care program."

"What have you been reading? Lately?"

She knew he was trying to trap her. She hadn't held a book since the telephone directory. "Would you believe Doctor Spock? The plot's terrific."

"I'll help you find something by Ayn Rand. She's one of my favorites." He stepped closer to her. "The hell with books." He wrapped his hands around her upper arms. "I want to hug you. You look good, you smell good," he pulled her against him, "and I still love you."

Evan slid her arms around his waist. "I said I never wanted to see you again but . . . I knew I was lying. I miss you. And I still love you." She raised her face and leaned into him. Their kiss meant more than just friends happy to be together again.

After many seconds of kissing and stroking, she pulled away. "Hi, Geoff. Want to see my baby?"

"I sure do. Now. Before I see Julie." He followed Evan through the hall. Into the bedroom.

Geoff played with the baby's fingers and stroked her cheek   He almost refused to hold her but wanted to please Evan.   Smiling he moved his gaze from the baby to Evan. He felt her looking into his soul. "She's adorable," he whispered before he kissed Evan's forehead.

"Good luck to you and the baby and I hope you'll be happy being a mother."

He gave the baby to Evan, to take out his wallet. He handed her his business card. "Evan, always remember, if you need anything or you just want to talk, find me."

Beth appeared at the door. They all looked at a loss of what to say so they just held their smiles until Beth blurted out, "Have you two been introduced?"

Geoff forced a chuckle. "We introduced ourselves. And I told her how great she looks." He reached into a pocket in his jacket. "And since I was coming here, I brought the note to you. Special delivery."

"Geoff's going to take me uptown. To the apartment. And to the library. I should have asked if you'd mind staying with the baby. Just for a little while?"

Beth took the baby. "Aunt Beth to the rescue. And you don't have to hurry back."

GEOFF had brought papers for Julie to sign and within fifteen minutes Geoff was holding an umbrella over Evan and helping her into his sports car. Beth had hoped they would see each other but now that it had happened, how did she feel? Sad? Jealous? Because she knew Evan had been closer with Geoff, than she had? Okay, so she was never going to have him make love to her. At least she had been in bed with him!

Holding Brad's note against her chest, Beth was dozing on the couch when she heard the baby begin to cry. She tucked the note inside her bra and hurried to her bedroom. She slid two fingers inside the baby's diaper and discovered what might be the problem. She changed the diaper, laid the baby on the bed and waited. Her niece began to cry again.

Beth looked at her watch. How many hours since Evan had fed her? In fact, how many hours had Evan been gone? She could call the manager of the apartment house and ask if Evan and Geoff were still there? Why should she care?

Carrying the baby into the kitchen she put a bottle of formula in a pan of water, turned on the stove and sat down. She patted the baby and rubbed her cheek against the baby's face. She pressed her lips to the downy head. Dear precious bastard. Was she feeling love for this helpless baby because she considered it her niece? Or was she feeling compassion?

While she held the bottle, Beth relaxed in the corner of the couch and studied the baby's face as she sucked on the nipple. She continued to imagine how a person might react when they discovered they were "illegitimate"? What would Brad do? Would he feel anger? Royals, show biz people, thousands were conceived from a relationship which made the word illegitimate the legal term which could be . . .

THE ringing of the telephone made Beth jump. The baby jumped. The telephone rang again before Beth could reach the receiver "Good afternoon, Mrs. Fischer's residence." It could be someone from the company. And she *was* Julie Fischer's secretary. "How may I help you?"

"Thank god! It's you!" Brad exclaimed.

"Brad! What's wrong? Where are you?"

"In my bedroom. And I've got to talk fast."

"What's wrong? Who's yelling?"

"My mother. At my father. They're having a high decibel fight. I have something rotten to tell you. They're going to make me marry Jeanne."

As she squeezed the receiver between her shoulder and neck, Beth gently laid the baby on the cushion next to her. She felt so lightheaded she was afraid she might drop her. "Say it again. They're going to make you do what?"

"Jeanne is pregnant. And she says I'm the father."

"Oh my god. Is it true?"

"No. I keep telling them, I'm not. I never did anything to her after that one time that you know about. If she won't get rid of it, I'm going to sneak out tonight and take off. I'll get in touch with you. Oh shit, Mom's yelling for me to come downstairs. I've gotta go."

"Brad! Don't run away. I love you."

"I'll get in touch as soon as I can. I love you back." She heard a click. And Brad was gone. Beth hoped not out of her life.

FINALLY Beth remembered to replace the receiver. She sobbed in her hands for several minutes until she heard someone clear their throat. With tears dripping off her chin, Beth looked up at Julie.

Julie pushed uncombed hair from her face before she said, hoarsely, "I heard you yell his name. And I thought he might be here."

After Beth cried out the story, Julie pulled her to stand before her. She patted her. Like Beth had patted the baby. "Calm down. Bradford Livingston is not going to marry Jeanne Barnes. Even if he did get her pregnant. I'll put an end to this nonsense."

Beth clung to Julie. She whispered into her old bathrobe, "I don't care what you have to do. I love him and he needs me."

Julie stroked Beth's hair. Damn the reason why they were embracing each other. Why couldn't Beth need *her*? She gave Beth a strong hug before she pushed her away.

"Then you and I will help him."

FIFTY FIVE

BETH WANTED TO leave Geoff's office. His secretary, Betty Chapman, would think she was going to the Rest Room. But she'd leave the building. And get in Julie's car and escape. But she knew Brad needed her.

"The meeting is in Mr. Gillon's office. Because it's larger than Geoff's," Betty had told her. So Beth was sitting. With hands firmly wrapped around the new shoulder bag, One which had been purchased for the trip.

She was waiting. To be called into Mr. Gillion's office. Where she imagined everybody was gathered. And where she could not cry.

SHE tried to remember what happened after Brad had made the hectic phone call. She had fought to stay calm as she finished feeding the baby. And managed to get her to burp.

"So how long has your sister been out?" Julie demanded.

"She wanted to show Geoff her new apartment. Ahh, she's really excited about living there. I can take care of the baby."

" I don't care about the baby. I'm interested in what you heard in the Girl's Room. You're sure it was Jeanne who wanted the money?" After she saw Beth nod, she directed, "Prop the baby in the corner and go make me some tea. I have to make a phone call."

She watched Julie transform from being pale and frail into an assertive business woman. "Find him, Betty. Call the manager, Manny Arthur. I need to talk to Geoff. He's to call me immediately."

"Why are you calling Geoff?"

"To tell him to call Brad and tell him he's his lawyer."

"Oh, thank you, Julie. I don't want him to run away. I want him cleared."

"You still love him even though you know he did screw her?" After Beth nodded she added, "I can hear you thinking that Bill screwed more women than I know about, and I still loved him." She watched Beth shrug. And you're right."

I'm going to tell Geoff you'll speak in Brad's defense."

Beth's eyes opened wide. "You mean I might have to tell what I heard! In the Girls' Room?"

"Yes. And, as soon as Geoff sets up the meeting, I'm sure the Charlie Barnes will get George Bailey to represent Jeanne."

Beth shook her head. "I could never tell what I heard. In front of … men."

"I thought you wanted to come to Brad's aid." Julie surprised herself how easily she said his name. "Sorry, but you have to reveal your beautiful love story."

She almost whispered, "You could even throw in what else you know about him." She watched Beth suffer. "So you're the one who tells everybody that he's adopted. Get it all out in the open."

"My god, Julie," Beth breathed. "You have to think how he'll feel."

Julie frowned her mean look and used her stern voice. "Don't blame me. For what's happening. I didn't screw around with Jeanne Barnes." She was happy when Beth began to cry. "I hear the tea pot whistling."

"Okay." Beth began to hurry toward the kitchen. "I'll say anything you want me to. In front of everybody."

Using forced sarcasm, Julie replied, "Atta girl. Devotion to the rescue. Now, we just have to discuss the soap opera with Geoff." Julie turned to look toward the hall. "Ahh, me thinks I hear a sister returning."

"Geoff. Geoff. If you're in the kitchen, I want to see you."

Evan walked to the doorway, holding two books. "He just dropped me off because he has to make some phone calls." Evan looked past Julie to see Beth crying. Next she saw the baby lying on the couch. She ran to her daughter and knelt by the couch. Realizing the baby was sleeping she peered into Beth's wet face. "What happened?"

Julie gave the answer. "Beth and I are happy Geoff took you to the apartment. And the library. But Beth and I have a problem. So please take your daughter into your bedroom and read a book, until I call you. Since you feel good enough to go uptown you can be the cook tonight."

Julie watched Evan carry the baby and books out of the living room. "Seeing her so happy, makes *me* want to cry," Julie murmured. "Although maybe I should be praying that Geoff is as smart as I think he is. He either ignores her or has a condom."

Finally the phone rang. With forced cheerfulness in her voice, Beth said, "Good afternoon. Mrs. Fischer's residence. How may I help you?...Oh hi, Geoff...I'm glad Betty told you. I think you better talk to Julie."

Julie took the receiver. "We all have a problem. Don't talk. Just listen to me."

After she gave Geoff her instructions Julie studied Beth's wet face. Words, comforting words, motherly words, dashed through her mind, but she said, "I want you to wear that khaki suit we bought in New York. With the navy blouse, shoes and handbag. You'll be the star of the meeting. Geoff will practice what to say with you. Now help me back to bed."

She let Beth take her arm to shuffle through the hall into her room. Standing by the bed she grasped Beth's hand. "You may find it difficult to believe, but I care about you. Both of you."

She was about to say, "Shut the door, please." when Beth wrapped her arms around her and whispered, "Thank you. I love you."

She gave the girl a quick hug and stepped to her bed. She hoped the girl did not see the tears.

Outside the door Beth smiled. Julie had hugged her. Julie cared about her.

NOW in Geoff's office Beth tried to relax in the large swivel chair. Behind the large cherry desk. It was obvious an organized person worked in that room. She smiled as she noticed the three monkeys with ears, eyes and mouth covered. She reached for a double frame. One picture was of Mr. and Mrs. Greer. In the other frame was Geoff's sister with her husband, in his officer's uniform. His sister most likely would be a caring sister-in-law . . . to Geoff's lover.

As soon as Beth thought the word *family*, tears filled her eyes. When Liz had called the evening before she had not told her mother any news update.   She just let Liz ramble about her honeymoon and how happy she was. Yeah, Liz.

That morning, when she had called out, "I'm leaving, Julie," Julie had not come out of her bedroom.   But she called through the door, "Stay strong,"

And that was *her* family.

Holding Geoff's letter opener, she *really* wanted her father to be with her. Sitting in that chair over there, smiling and giving her another wink.   Other people were counting on her but she was going to be Norman Rhodes' daughter, Elizabeth.   She would show them what a good job he had done, raising her.

Daddy. I hope you know where I am In Geoff's office. Thank God, for Geoff Greer. I know how lucky I am to know him. Even though I'm still having trouble believing that he's gay! And I know what gay guys do with . . . to each other. But I hope I can meet his friend, Terry. Daddy, please stay tuned in.

Finally Betty appeared at the doorway. "Geoff is ready for you to go in."

Beth followed Betty's wide hips to the end of a hallway.   Betty raised her hand to knock but turned to Beth and raised her eyebrows. They both listened as Richard Livingston demanded, "Just what in the hell is going on? Believe me, Charles, I didn't know anybody else would be here. In fact, if it weren't for Bernice, we wouldn't even be here."

"I agreed with Geoff," Bernice said in a thick southern drawl. "A lawyer's office is the best place to be."

Betty knocked. Loudly. The room became quiet.

Geoff was happy that Betty had placed herself in front of Beth. He excused himself and stepped into the hall. He hugged Beth to his chest. "Hang in there, kiddo. Don't let anybody know . . . that I love you.'"

Inside the room Beth became aware of the faces. All looking at her. And Mr. Livingston demanding, "What in the hell is she doing here?" She looked at Bernice as she asked, "Is *she* the girl who lives with Julie?" She looked at Brad sitting between his mother and Mr. Gillon's large desk. They all appeared memorized, although she knew Brad's sad eyes said *I love you.*

Geoff relocated an empty chair so that Beth would be seated on the opposite side of Mr. Gillon's desk. He stood behind her chair. "Mr.

Bailey and anyone else who may not know, this is Elizabeth Rhodes. She's agreed to testify in Brad's behalf." He sat behind the desk.

Charles Barnes looked at his lawyer and asked loudly, "Isn't this highly irregular?"

Mr. Bailey raised his eyebrows and shrugged, "The boy *is* trying to prove his innocence."

Beth sat tall and observed Jeanne, her mother and father and Mr. Bailey. Lou Barnes spoke. "I know Jeanne could get some classmates to testify for her too."

Beth noticed Lou's hair matched her gold sheath dress. There was a wide display of Jeanne's tanned legs between her knees and the hem of her white dress with canary yellow trim. Jeanne's hair matched the yellow.

She remembered to place the handbag next to the chair. Then fold her hands and cross her legs at the ankles. As Julie had told her to do. She looked at Geoff.

Geoff gave everyone a pleasant smile before he asked, "Mr. Bailey, may I have your permission to tape the following discussion?"

Mr. Bailey nodded and watched Geoff put a small recorder on the desk, test the volume and then position the recorder to face the gathered Earthlings. The four parents did not object.

Geoff began. "Would you tell us your name please?"

"Elizabeth Rhodes."

"Nickname, Beth?" After she agreed he asked, "Why have I asked you to attend this meeting?"

"To help clear Brad Livingston. Because . . . he," she saw Geoff raise his right hand.

"How long have you known Brad Livingston?"

"We went to Junior High and Senior High . . . together."

"I went to Elementary School with him too," Jeanne announced. "Even Kindergarten. And, oh yeah, Sunday School."

"Beth, tell us about your friendship with Bradford Livingston."

She had to glance at Brad. Her eyes asked him, *Are you ready?*

Beth's brief hesitation gave Brad the seconds he needed. "Geoff, excuse me. This isn't fair to Beth. Let me tell everybody that Beth and I have been meeting for months."

Bernice gasped. "Oh, dear me."

Richard declared, "This is ridiculous!"

Lou and Charles uttered, "What!"

Jeanne announced loudly, "You're full of shit!"

Richard glared at Brad. "If you think for one minute I'll believe you and this girl," he spoke to Bernice, "she's from Taylor Park." He watched tears fall on Bernice's bosom.

Geoff surprised himself by saying, "Regardless, where Beth is *from* should not enter into this discussion. And it just happens Beth and I were neighbors. In Taylor Park."

No one spoke for many seconds, all waiting for someone else to break the chilly silence. Finally Charles stared at Brad and asked loudly, "How in the hell could you possibly have the time to see this girl, when you're always with Jeanne?"

"Not always." Brad replied. "I'm sure you can remember when Jeanne claimed she wasn't feeling well. Or she had something to do with somebody else. Especially lately."

Jeanne spoke. "Tell the little machine how long you two have been doing your own thing? Behind my back!"

Brad almost smiled. "Since last November."

"What?" Richard yelled. "I've known where you've been and what you've been . . . "he paused as Brad shook his head from side to side.

"What a skunk," Jeanne announced. "All these months he's been telling me how much he loves me and wants to marry me." She turned to her mother. "I would never have gone all the way if I hadn't believed him."

Lou Barnes put an arm around Jeanne's shoulder. Charles Barnes patted her bare knee.

Brad leaned forward to glare at Jeanne. "You know you're lying. I haven't told you I loved you for months. And," he looked at the desk, "for the little machine, I've been going out with Jeanne because I'm a coward. I was too scared to rebel against my parents. And mess up their plans. A couple of days ago I got enough guts to tell Jeanne I didn't want to go steady anymore. And if she's honest, she'll admit the only reason she's been going out with me is because of *her* parents."

He decided to look at Mr. Bailey. "You must know what good friends our parents are. Always belonging to the same clubs and committees. Always planning parties and things to do together." He took a deep breath, "Now I'm lying. I was crazy about Jeanne. And I really did want to be with her. Then last summer I began to realize I was kidding myself." Brad looked at Beth, "And I began to pay attention to Beth. And I knew I really liked her."

Jeanne quickly yelled in Brad's direction, "You told me that you loved me."

"When was the last time I told you that?"

"The night we did it. In the cabana."

"What night in the cabana?' Lou asked Jeanne. "You led your father and me to believe you and Brad made love on the night of your graduation party."

"We did."

Mr. Bailey took off his glasses. He pulled a white handkerchief from his breast pocket and began to slowly clean his glasses. He gave Geoff a meaningful glance.

Geoff turned off the tape recorder and tapped his pen. "I realize this is an upsetting conversation. But please speak only when a question has been directed to you. And let's give Beth a chance to explain why she's here." He clicked the tape recorder on. Geoff turned to Beth and asked one of their preplanned questions. "Beth. How did you learn Brad needed your help?"

"He called me. From his . . . bedroom."

"In other words you and Brad keep in contact with each other?" He watched Beth nod. "And you see each other?" Again she nodded. "Did anyone else know about you and Brad?"

"Not until Julie . . . Mrs. Fischer found out. The night Brad went to her house. He was sick and he wanted me to help him."

A loud gasp escaped from Bernice. "You went to Julie's house?"

"This meeting is asinine," Richard announced loudly. "I do not believe any of what this girl is trying to make us swallow." He took off his glasses and rubbed the bridge of his nose.

Geoff continued as though there had been no interruptions. "What night did Brad go to Mrs. Fischer's house to see you?"

"The night of the graduation party. After he had been at Jeanne's house."

"Why he came right home. And went to bed."

"Be quiet, Bernice. I want to hear what Julie did after she found Brad in her house."

"Mrs. Fischer asked Brad to leave her house."

"I'm sure she did. If you think I'll believe my son would deliberately go to Julie Fischer's house to see you, you are more foolish than I thought you were."

Geoff ignored Richard. "How could you be sure Brad came directly from the party?"

"Because he was sick and started upchucking. He said the kids found the booze supply and practically everybody was drinking. And smoking pot."

Lou exclaimed, "Do we have to talk about that awful party? I just want to forget about it." She looked at Mr. Bailey as she added, "Except what happened to Jeanne."

Mr. Bailey responded. "Lou, I understand how frustrated you must feel but Geoff is trying to establish some facts. That is the night Jeanne accuses Brad of raping her."

"I didn't touch her," Brad yelled. "I went to see Beth."

Jeanne turned to Beth. "He stripped me and then after he was through with me, he just walked out. That's the kind of dog he is."

Charles looked at George Bailey. "I really believe he has been seeing this girl. I imagine she's quite flattered to have Brad pay attention to her. She's willing to back Brad that he left the party to see her but what she doesn't know is what he did before he left the party."

"Beth, just what *did* Brad tell you at Julie's house?" Geoff asked.

"At first he just puked. Outside and in the laundry tub. He asked me to make him some coffee. And yes, he told me he had been in Jeanne's bedroom. He said she was already nude and she tried to convince him to have sex with her."

After Jeanne yelled, "He's lying!" Geoff stood and asked Beth, "Why would Brad specifically tell you he had not done anything to Jeanne?"

"Because, I had found out that he had sex with her before that night."

"You bastard," Jeanne almost screamed.

Beth raised her voice to add, "That was the night in the cabana. Everybody was drinking pink champagne and he had too much and he confessed he . . . he got carried away."

"For god's sake," Louise said. "George is going to think all you do is drink at our house."

"And screw," Charles added.

"That night was the first and only time," Brad declared.

Mr. Bailey raised his right hand. The room became quiet. He turned to Geoff. "I would like to ask this young lady a few questions?"

After Geoff nodded he looked into Beth's eyes.

"Have you ever had intercourse with Brad Livingston?"

"No. I have not. I told him I want to wait. Even though I love him"

"And here she sits. Saint Beth. You're just trying to make me look like a bum." Jeanne glared at Mr. Bailey as he held up his hand again. "No, I will not shut up. Just because she's sitting there, so prim and proper in that outfit we all know Julie Fischer paid for, she's not any better than I am. Beth Rhodes will always be from Taylor Park. And besides being pathetic, she's a creep. Here I am, going around with . . . "she pointed to Brad," with him. Believing we're going to get married.

"Oh, don't look so surprised. I could get three girls who'd tell you they heard I was getting a ring for graduation. I agree with Daddy. I believe he *is* going out with her. And for the tape machine's sake, just how did you two get together before Thanksgiving?"

Brad spoke. "During the Class play."

"Did everybody hear that? I'm home with a fractured foot and he decides to have a ball with this hot number who probably was so thrilled the great Brad Livingston was paying attention to her she laid down every time he wiggled his finger."

Before Geoff could interrupt, Brad demanded, "Since you want to get real nasty, Jeanne, how about if I ask how come you weren't a virgin that night? I was. You even told me how awful I was. That's more than you can say."

Brad looked around the room as he quickly added, "And as for the rest of you, I don't care what you believe. But I don't want any of you to say another mean thing about Beth. I love her. And I am *not* marrying Jeanne. And no one is going to make me."

Richard cleared his throat before he loudly announced, "You'll do as you're told to do. If I say you'll marry Jeanne you'll marry her. Whether or not anybody believes what that girl is telling us does not matter. What does matter is that you live up to the standards by which I've raised you. You'll assume the duty of your mistake." He looked at Charles for approval.

"I am *not* the father of . . . " Brad stopped talking and frowned at the door to the hall. Everybody turned toward the door.

428

A noise on the other side had attracted their attention.
Transfixed, they waited.
All unprepared.

FIFTY SIX

GEOFF HURRIED TO the door. He was curious, but also worried.

A nervous Betty Chapman was standing on the other side of the door. A pale Julie Fischer was holding on to her arm. Betty forced a quick smile and whispered to Geoff, "I . . . I told her I didn't think she should interrupt the meeting."

Immediately Geoff felt panic. Was she intoxicated? Had she come to destroy what she had asked Beth and him to save?

Julie removed her arm from Betty's and grabbed Geoff's arm. She was trembling. She sensed Geoff was worried. He most likely was hoping he could convince her to go away. Holding his arm, she forced him to step back into the room.

Richard immediately stood. "What in the hell is she doing here?"

Bernice turned to Brad. "Did you ask *her* to come . . . too?"

Brad shook his head and watched Beth hurry across the room.

"I came to save the boy," Julie said strongly. "Put a chair next to Beth." Her face was ashen except for pink lipstick. Her hair was attractively combed and she was wearing a new dress she had purchased for their postponed trip. Beth wondered if Evan had helped Julie get dressed?   And how had she gotten there? After all, Beth had driven Julie's car.

GEORGE Bailey immediately stood and relocated a chair. Julie shook George's extended hand and told him, "I just couldn't sit in the house and wonder and wait. I had to make certain Brad gets a chance to prove his innocence."

She looked at a dumbfounded Brad and gave him a warm motherly smile. After she took time to position herself in the chair, knowing everybody was watching her, she patted the chair next to her. Indicating Beth was to sit down.

Geoff finally settled behind the desk.

Julie looked around the room. She nodded and said, "Lou. Charles." Finally she looked at Bernice. "How are you?" She shook her head after Bernice said, "I'm awful."

Julie decided to ignore Richard. "It's too bad you've all had to meet like this. All determined to save your own child. And you're all wondering why am I here?"

She reached out and put a hand on Beth's leg. "I'm here, because I consider Beth my own." She paused to let the words sink in. "And I happen to know how much Beth and Brad care for each other."

She decided to glance at Richard. "Has Beth told you Brad came down to my house the night of the party? The night Jeanne is accusing him of raping her?"

Geoff cleared his throat and said, "Yes. She has."

"Beth was trying to hush up Brad while he was puking in my laundry tub." She paused to smile. "I'll admit I did kind of sneak up and listen to them. Before I let them know I was in the kitchen. Mad as hell.

"Besides being sick Brad was upset. He was telling Beth how Jeanne had tried to seduce him. She had taken off her clothes and he covered her up and left. It was a miracle he could drive."

Lou announced. "When we got home, she was in her p.j.'s. Asleep."

"I'm glad to hear that," Julie said, smugly.

"And," Charles added, "Jeanne did not accuse Brad of raping her until she found out she was pregnant. So he didn't have to go running to your house. To cook up an alibi. Maybe you believe this girl but I happen to believe my *own* flesh and blood."

"Good for you," Julie said strongly. She turned and asked, "How about you, Bernice? Whom do you believe? Your own flesh and blood?" She watched Bernice suffer. "Well, I believe in Beth. And Beth believes in Brad. Now, how do we prove who is right?" Julie looked at George Bailey. "Evidently no one was paying attention to what Beth was saying."

Julie looked back at Bernice. "Can you believe she loves Brad so much that even *I* could not make her change her mind? For your sake and mine. As soon as I learned they were seeing each other, I told her she was crazy. Besides a few other choice words.

"Then guess what I did? I kicked her out." Julie smiled as soon as she got the reaction she wanted. She turned and looked at Geoff. "Geoff knows. I told her no companion of mine, no matter how much I needed her, could live in *my* house if she was going to be asinine enough to date a Livingston. So she moved out. She gave up the roof

431

over her head, the food, the money, the chance to go to college. Since she was cheated out of winning the essay contest. That's how much she loves him."

Everyone sat motionless, entranced with Julie's story. Finally she continued, "But, thank god she loves me also. She came back, because she was worried about me. But she told me she wouldn't stop seeing Brad. And I gave in and told her she could even invite him to my house."

Charles spoke next. "Julie, that's nice you believe Beth loves Brad. But just because he came to your house, do you know how Brad feels about Beth?"

"I take into account what he had to go through just to talk with her. To be with her. Did she tell you he gave her that watch? Did she tell you what the inscription says? Did she tell you what he gave her for graduation? Did she tell you how many notes they slipped to each other, in school? Why would he do all that? Because he's a risk taker? Why did he break off with Jeanne? Especially since we know she was handing out favors, as she claims Beth was? And his father saw fit to punish him for breaking up with Jeanne."

"How touching," Jeanne said. "I have lots of notes. And jewelry also."

Beth found the confidence to ask, "From Brad?"

"Of course Brad!" Jeanne snapped back.

Mr. Bailey spoke. Slowly. "I certainly can understand why these two young ladies want to believe this popular and good looking young man loves them. But it still has not been proven he is innocent. Of Jeanne's charges."

"I agree," Lou said. "As *I* see it, no matter what Julie has said, all we know is he's been cheating. Behind Jeanne's back."

Julie looked at Jeanne. "What do you want to happen as a result of this meeting?" She watched Jeanne squirm. She looked at Charles. "You want a wedding?" She looked at Lou. "Or do you just want a different last name for the baby?"

Charles remained silent. Lou shrugged. "We want Brad to admit he's the father."

"Yeah," Jeanne breathed. "I just want him to admit he made me pregnant."

"To save whom?" Julie asked Jeanne. She watched Jeanne place her hand on her abdomen and whispered, "My baby." Julie smiled and asked, "Are you going to keep it?"

"I . . . don't know," Jeanne whimpered. "I'm supposed to go to college."

Lou challenged, "I don't think this is any of your business, Julie. This is a difficult experience for all of us and we haven't made any definite plans. Yet. We just want Brad to know he has a responsibility."

Julie turned to Geoff. Beth saw the look. She understood what it meant. Julie was telling Geoff to begin the beginning. Of the end. Beth hoped she was ready.

Geoff cleared his throat. "I believe we should determine how pregnant is Jeanne?"

"Wait a minute, Lou said. "Just because she's missed only one period, I knew the next day I was pregnant. With both of our children." Lou gave Charles a quick smile before she added, "And one of my sister's girls thought she might be pregnant a few days after she and her husband had intercourse and the tests confirmed her suspicions, so you see . . . " her voice drifted away as she noticed Beth and Julie smile at each other.

Geoff looked at Brad. They had decided he would sound more convincing if he did not know about Jim Bender. He said, "Brad. I'd like to ask you the question one more time. Did you have sexual relations with Jeanne Barnes the night of her graduation party?" After Brad said "No." Geoff asked, "Jeanne. Would you care to reconsider your accusations?"

"No, she would not!" Lou blurted out.

Jeanne squirmed. "Well, I...ah . . . have to admit, I . . . had been drinking and maybe I . . . "

Charles put a hand on his daughter's knee. "Don't let anyone intimidate you, Jeanne. We all know you had been drinking but you still remembered Brad undressing you and . . . " Charles paused as he noticed the tears in his daughter's eyes. "You are telling us the truth?"

Jeanne squirmed closer to her mother. "Not really. I mean, I wanted to tell you that I was pregnant, before the party. I got pregnant the night we did it in the cabana."

Charles shook his head as Lou cried out, "Damn it, Jeanne. Why have you been hiding it from us? For all these weeks."

Geoff tapped his pen for attention. As soon as everyone became quiet, Geoff remarked, "Jeanne. "I don't know about the evening in the cabana, so would you fill us in?"

"That was the night of my birthday dinner. I was going to tell Brad but I kept putting it off because . . . well, I thought he was going to ask me to marry him. Then we could figure out what to do. But then when he told me he wanted to break off, well . . . " she looked to her mother.

Geoff continued. "I dislike having to discuss events of such a personal nature but I believe you had a period after you and Brad had sexual relations in the cabana."

Jeanne's eyes opened as wide as they could. "How in the hell could you know that?"

"You're damn right! This is becoming personal." Charles yelled. "What in the hell are you trying to prove?"

"I'm trying to prove Jeanne still is not admitting the complete truth." After Geoff knew Jeanne was not going to reply he added, "Does the name Jim Bender mean anything to you?"

Lou spoke up. "What does Jim Bender have to do . . . " slowly she stopped asking. She appeared to know the answer.

Jeanne stared at Geoff. "He went to school with all of us."

Charles looked at his wife. "Who are they talking about?

"That good looking blonde who works at the *Stop and Shop Foods Market*." Lou blurted out.

"Was he at the party?" Charles asked Jeanne.

"Yes." She stared at Beth. "Who in the hell told you?"

Geoff asked, "You've been going steady with Brad and cheating with Jim?"

Lou wiped away tears. "Jeanne Barnes. I can't believe you would do such a thing."

"And all the time she was criticizing Brad," Bernice blurted out.

"Like Brad said. You made us cheat. And sneak around. Because you were always on our backs. Manipulating our lives."

"I can't believe you're saying this," Charles declared. "After all we've done for you."

"That's just it. You made too damn many plans for us. Brad and I were tired of each other. So I had to go out with Jim, or . . . go crazy."

I guess you're telling us that Jim Bender is the father." Lou sobbed.

Jeanne smiled and announced, almost smugly, "It's Jim's baby."

Lou turned to Brad. "Forgive us, Brad. We knew not what we were doing."

"I can't believe this. What were you trying to do? Punish us?" Charles looked at George Bailey. "I suppose we'll have to go through this shit again. With Jim and his mother and father."

Charles turned to Richard. "We thought we had done such a damn good job. Then they pull the rug out from under you and let you fall on your ass."

Richard slowly shook his head. "Sorry, Charles, but I don't agree with you. I raised Brad as best I could. With discipline and good judgment."

"I don't doubt you did. But still you must admit you could have been too busy, too preoccupied, when he may have needed you." Suddenly Charles decided to add, "Otherwise, why did Brad turn to that girl?" He nodded toward Beth.

Julie coughed. She was getting ready to become involved. She did feel sorry for Beth. She did feel sorry for Brad. Beth was right. He really was, what did she call him? A handsome hunk. Julie even felt compassion for Bernice. She had done a good job. It was too bad she was going to be hurt. Julie opened her handbag and pulled out an envelope. She looked directly at Richard's flushed face. "I have a question for you. If you honestly believe you have done your best raising Brad, then why didn't *you* believe him?"

Richard looked at what Julie was holding. Was it an envelope he should recognize? He felt bile burn his throat. Why should he sit there and let her make him vulnerable? Helpless. He had to free himself of her bonds.

Now! Too loudly he announced, "I didn't rush to his defense because . . Charles defended his daughter because he believed her and look what happened. I used caution because I might be gambling. "

Bernice held up a hand. "Richard. Please," she blurted out.

Richard ignored Bernice. "Even though Brad was telling the truth, I still got hurt. I found out he betrayed me, by going to *your* house. And just to see a girl who . . . " he paused to weigh his words, "well, his choice of friends proves how untrustworthy he is." He pushed up his glasses. "But then why should I be disappointed? I had nothing to do with his heredity."

"Richard!" Bernice cried out. "Please." She looked around the room at everybody's face "Let's all forgive each other and leave now." She edged forward in her chair.

Julie leaned forward as though trying to stand. She heard Geoff push back his chair and felt him behind her. "I just want to give Richard this letter and then I agree we're finished here."

"*I'm* not through yet," Richard declared. "I have something to say to you, Julie Fischer."

Julie squinted. "Excuse me, Richard. I thought you were through when you heard you can't invest in Bill's company. Too bad you don't work for my company so you can take advantage of our newly offered employee stock options. My loyal employees want a bigger office building as badly as I do."

"You're not going to ridicule me any longer. I'm not a Geoff Greer. Or those wishy-washy company men who let you keep pulling their strings, expecting them to jump. The time has come for everybody to know why I've let you get away with making me look asinine. And sacrifice myself."

Richard pointed to Brad. "He knew it would hurt me yet he was ungrateful enough to go to *your* house. But then why not?" Richard paused to take a breath. "He isn't trustworthy because he isn't my own flesh and blood."

Bernice's hand covered her chest. "I wish I had a gun."

Charles Barnes began to wiggle toward the edge of the couch. "I have no idea what you're trying to tell us Dick but I do believe there has been enough hurt for today."

"Today for you," Richard shouted. "How would you like to be hurt for years? I'm tired of having my nose rubbed in shit just because I've been afraid of her," he pointed at Julie, "and what she might know. About our retarded son. And you know where I got this boy, don't you?"

Julie nodded. "And thank god Bernice and I have more compassion than you have. She looked at Bernice. "I'm sorry, Bernice. Let's just end the conversation." She watched Bernice nod.

Brad looked from his mother to Julie. Finally he looked at Beth. "Do you know what they're talking about?" He waited. "Beth! Tell me."

"Maybe she doesn't know," Richard said loudly. "But it's time for me to inform everybody you are not related to me. I picked you up at the church orphanage."

Bernice grabbed Brad's closest arm. "I've always loved you," she choked out. "Just as though you were my very own flesh and blood."

The members of the Barnes family were having difficulty in understanding the real live soap unfolding in front of them. Charles Barnes thought the embarrassment Jeanne had heaped on his good name was enough. Now, he was hearing something even more unbelievable.

GEORGE Bailey decided whatever was being indicated should concern Geoff Greer. He was sure Charles Barnes would call him later. He stood, picked up his brief case, nodded at Charles, Geoff and Julie, and before he quickly left the room, he did announce, "I believe this discussion is not why I am here. Good afternoon. Everybody."

Brad ignored Bernice's hold on his arm. He was staring at Beth. "Am I adopted?"

He watched her nod. "Did you know? That I didn't know?" he murmured.

Beth managed to whisper, "It was up to your mother and father to tell you."

Brad removed Bernice's hand. "So? Why didn't *you* tell me?" He watched Bernice shake her head.

"She couldn't," Julie said. She glared at Richard. "You should be ashamed of yourself."

As soon as Brad stood, Beth stood and spread her arms. She wrapped them around Brad's waist and whispered into his neck, "I love you. No matter what they tell you, I love you. And so does your mother." She was glad she could kiss him in front of Jeanne.

Julie made an effort to stand but knew she could not do it alone. No one must know how terrible she felt. She marveled how, even with the driver's help, she had been able to get in and out of the taxi. Looking at Geoff she let him know. She needed him to help her stand.

Beth whispered to Brad. "Go to your mother. She needs you."

She took one of Julie's arms. She felt her body trembling from the exertion. Julie moved in the direction of Bernice and Richard. Holding the envelope she stood in front of Bernice.

With tears rolling down her cheeks and dripping onto her dress, Bernice murmured, "Why did you have to come here? You've ruined . . . everything."

"My being here forced you to face the truth. No matter how much you dislike me, Bernice, I want to sincerely compliment you for being such a loving mother. You've done a fine job and you have a son you can be proud of. And I know he'll always care for you." She indicated she wanted to approach Richard.

Geoff put an arm around her waist. He was very concerned about her frail appearance. He looked at the envelope and wondered what she was going to do? Did Beth know?

Julie was able to keep the hatred from her eyes. She even sounded sympathetic as she said, "As for you Richard, I'm sorry I've made you suffer so long. But then you've made other people suffer also. Especially Bernice. Even Beth. I know about your visit to her house.

"And now Brad. A son you should be proud of. A son who certainly doesn't deserve the shock and embarrassment you just heaped on him. When all you had to do was tell him the truth when he was old enough to understand. You should be ashamed."

Richard glared directly into Julie's face. "I won't accept the blame. It was Bernice who didn't want to tell him. But you have something to be ashamed of. You made Bill and Vicki suffer."

He focused on the envelope. Why should he shut up? He wanted to tell everyone she killed her husband and sister. But if she hadn't, then . . . he would wait and listen to what she had to say.

"I think you better weigh your words. After all, there is a lawyer present to hear what you might blurt out." Julie handed Richard the envelope. "I want to be kind enough to return this letter to you. I'm sure you remember writing it. Right after I became a rich widow. You even personally delivered it."

Julie smiled one of her cruel smiles. "I'm glad I wasn't flattered by your offer. Since I've learned you want to own the *Fischer Company*, I realize it really was the company that was your main concern." She smiled at Richard and then Bernice. "Bill would have been pleased to know how much you two cared about my wellbeing."

Julie turned to Brad. "Brad. Please remember you are always welcome in my house. And I would like to know you better."

As though dismissing everyone, she announced, "And now, I'd like to talk with Geoff."

WELCOME to BRIDGEBORO

FIFTY SEVEN

AFTER THE BARNES left the office, Brad moved closer to Beth and took her hand. She sensed he wanted to remain with her but his sense of duty told him he should be with his mother. She whispered how much she loved him before he reluctantly followed his parents out of the office.

"I didn't want to say this in front of Bernice and Dick but," and then Julie instructed Geoff he must keep in touch with Brad. Just in case he needed, not only a male friend, but a lawyer who could answer any questions he might have. And he must keep her updated.

"And now you two, help me through the hall. I'm ready to leave." After they arrived in the Waiting Room, Julie indicated she had to sit down. "Get the car, Beth. I want to go home."

Geoff frowned at Beth. "I'm going to call Doc to meet you at the house."

Beth nodded in agreement. She too felt alarm over Julie's weakness and trembling.

After a hard cough, Julie replied, "Thanks for caring but don't bother. When I decide I need Philip, Beth will call him. You both did very well today." Julie nodded to Geoff and smiled at Beth. "We got a lot accomplished. Didn't we?"

Beth forced a weak smile. She wished she could feel more elation. After all, Brad had been saved. At least from Jeanne. But not from that hateful man he called Dad. Now what was going to happen in the Livingston house? She studied Julie's pale face. She should stop worrying about Brad and take care of Julie. It was obvious she did not feel well.

"I'll park her door next to the curb," she remarked to Geoff. She forced herself not to touch him. But her eyes told him how much she cared. "A big thank you from me."

He led her to the outside door. He wrapped his arms around her and held her close. She leaned into him and whispered, "I'll always love you. Don't walk out of my life."

"Never." He kissed her forehead, "And *you* better not forget *me*."

Beth peered deeply into Geoff's eyes as she said softly, "We'll get together soon. And Geoff, I want to meet Terry." She watched him nod and smile. Then she walked away from him.

To park in front of the office building with the passenger's side next to the curb meant the car was facing north. After Geoff helped Julie into the front seat Beth waved and slowly drove away.

"Do you want to go out for lunch? Or stop at the office?" After Julie replied, "I just want to go to Deer Lake Manor." Beth added, "Not today. I didn't even want to go out for lunch. Because I know you should be in bed."

"I'm dressed and there's not going to be too many more todays for me to go back . . . to my yesterdays."

Julie laid her head against the back of the seat and closed her eyes. She willed herself to have enough strength to walk around the house. One more time. Was the girl crying? She should be happy. After all, she helped to save Brad. She had been nice to Bernice. She had let Richard know he was despicable. She rolled her head. "Why tears?"

"I'm worried about how mixed up Brad must feel. And maybe you came to the meeting, not to save Brad but to embarrass . . . his father. In front of everybody who was there."

"Of course I took advantage of a golden opportunity to embarrass Dick. As for Brad, I've been waiting and hoping for years that Bernice would tell him the truth. He had to find out, sooner or later. So it was today." Julie snickered. "I was hoping Dick would shit himself."

"He sure was upset. At whatever was in that envelope." *Please tell me.*

Julie lifted her head to cough hard. She quickly got a handkerchief out of her handbag and spit into it. After she wiped her lips she murmured, "I'm sure you want to know."

"If you think he'll tell Brad, then I'd like to know."

"I don't know if he'll tell Brad. But I'm hoping Bernice insists she has to know." Julie managed to snicker. "It's a love letter. Dickie sent it to me right after Bill died. Handwritten and signed.

"Look at the road and stop staring at me! I know you're as surprised as I was, after I read it. You believed only Vicki got love letters. The fool tried to convince me he not only was at my beck and call but that he actually cared for me. I wonder how many times he could kick himself for being so reckless? And dumb." Julie coughed and wiped her mouth again.

"I guess he thought you . . . wouldn't save it. Mrs. Livingston may really kill him."

"Or just laugh in his face. It's always been obvious they just tolerate each other. For the sake of convenience. Dickie had the hots for Vicki. He was one of her ardent admirers. Obviously thrilled whenever she tossed crumbs his way. And I knew Bernice was always attracted to Bill. Someone should write a book about Bridgeboro. The whole town is a soap opera."

"I'm still worried about Brad. He's so confused. And hurt. I hope he'll be okay."

"He's strong. With you by his side, he'll be fine. Someday, it may be poor Beth." *Damn. Why did she have to say that?* "You can call him tonight.

"Right now, all I care about is returning to where I lived with the man I loved."

FIFTY EIGHT

AFTER TRAVELING ABOUT ten miles north on Bridge Pike, Julie ordered, "Slow down. You have to turn left at the next intersection. Warwick Road will take us to Manor Road."

"You have your own road?" Beth stopped, checked for traffic and turned left.

"Certainly. I told you it was a land grant from William Penn and it covered thousands of acres."

They passed miles of fields planted in corn, soybeans and alfalfa. "This is all yours?"

"Uh huh. I rent out the fields. The farmer who lives in the largest tenant house is using the dairy barn for a herd of Holsteins. Over on Cowpath Road." Julie leaned closer to the windshield. "Slow down. We're coming up on the little bridge that crosses Deer Creek. See that big oak tree? The lane is right past there. Turn here."

She leaned back against the seat. "Now, comes a long lane and then the gate house. I already called my caretaker, Al Wright. To tell him we're coming. Just slow down in front of their house and beep the horn so I can wave to him or his wife. And then keep on going. I don't feel up to talking to them today. Look for a fork in the road where you'll bear left. And take me home."

Beth realized she was becoming excited. She had never seen a picture of Deer Lake Manor but she knew it was going to be impressive. So much had taken place here. If someone did write a book about Bridgeboro and the lives and loves of the locals, they certainly should include Deer Lake Manor. Beth smiled. *This is where the action was!*

Beth was not prepared for the size, nor overwhelming first impression of the Manor House. *My god! I can imagine how many people were hoping to be invited to a dinner or a party. Mr. and Mrs. William Fischer request the honor of your presence at a reception for the President of Mexico . . . on whenever.*

"What a wedding present. You *should* want to live here. Please invite me too." Beth laughed, and added, "But I insist somebody else do the cleaning. And the garden work."

Julie forced a smile. "Al and his son and some college kids, work full time keeping the grounds picture perfect. Al Junior even got a degree in landscaping at Del Val College. Ruth oversees two ladies from their church, who do the cleaning. She does the fine tuning such as polishing and waxing. They more than love this place. It's their pride and joy. Pull up to the front door."

Beth parked the car on the cobble-stone driveway. As excited as she was, she began to worry if Julie was strong enough to get out of the car and walk across the brick path to the large maroon door. Not knowing what to say, she blurted out, "Do you have the key?"

"It's unlocked. I'm sure Ruth and Al have it all ready, waiting for me."

"Maybe I should find Al? To help you walk around?"

"Believe me. I'm going to find the strength to walk through every room. And if it's time for me to die, I'm going to die right here. With my memories."

With her handbag hanging from her left arm, Julie held tightly to Beth's arm. With pride in her voice, she murmured, "We're going to enter into what was the original house, built in 1782. This section is classified as a colonial farmhouse of that period. As we walk around I'll tell you about the additions. Bill and I added the last and largest one out to the back. I coaxed him into adding a solarium with a view of Deer Lake." She told Beth to open the front door and help her step inside. "The original house was just two rooms downstairs and that spiral stairway which goes to two rooms upstairs. How do you like the size of this walk-in fireplace?"

"I'm beyond impressed. I'm overwhelmed." After Julie coughed long and hard Beth added, "Julie. I want to see the rest of the house. But I think we should go home."

"Not yet. I want to show off the kitchen and keeping room. With the impressive island in the middle. I'll rest in my favorite rocker in front of another walk-in fireplace and Dutch oven, while you wander around the library, solarium, bathroom and mudroom. Take your time in the living room and dining room. They're *my* pride and joy."

After Beth reappeared in the keeping room and admired the large hooked oval rug, Julie had to indicate she needed assistance to stand. "We're going to use the stairway in the living room. And no advice, please. I have to go upstairs. For very personal reasons."

Julie sat in a window seat in a wide hallway, watching Beth wander in and out of the four bedrooms, each with its own small bathroom which Julie explained had been cleverly added.

She shuffled to the end of the long hall and sensed Beth was interested as they stood in front of a closed door. She took a collection of keys from her jacket pocket. "Only Ruth has another key. No one was or is allowed in this wing. It's *our* bedroom. Bill's and mine. Plus a few surprises." She opened the door and stepped inside.

EVEN though Beth had just seen room after room decorated with the most beautiful furniture she had seen only in magazines, she was unprepared for the large room ahead of her. She whispered, "Oh, Julie, this is . . . unreal. I mean, I thought the rest of the rooms and the antiques look like a museum, but this is the most beautiful room I've ever seen."

Julie leaned against a highboy and forced a smile on her pale face. Not because the room was praiseworthy. The smile was the expression of a response, From within her soul.

Beth began to wander and inspect the contents of the bedroom and the master bathroom, while Julie shuffled around the spacious room, allowing her eyes to caress the chairs, the highboy, the bureaus, the cherry blanket chest, the expansive fireplace with a raised hearth from which a cheerful fire could be enjoyed from the bed. She studied the wide window sills, the frames around special pictures and photographs and all of wood trim throughout the room. She remembered how many hours she and Bill had discussed whether they should paint the woodwork Wedgwood Blue, the color they had agreed to use in the other bedrooms and hall, or the dark brown, which Bill liked?

She stood by the side of the extra wide cherry canopy bed. Lovingly, she rubbed her hands over the handmade quilt as she told Beth she had paid the prize winning quilters at the Deep Run Mennonite Meeting House to design and make it for her. She ran her eyes over the random width pine floor boards, and the Oriental scatter rugs. Tears rolled down her cheeks. "Oh god, how I loved being in this room. With him."

Beth smiled as she envisioned a glowing fire and cuddling with Brad. On the bed or on the rug. Suddenly she let her imagination think about Julie and Bill making love in this room. She remained quiet because she wanted the woman to reminisce.

Julie sighed, deeply. "My love for him was beyond description." She peered into Beth's eyes. "Remember the day you were interviewing me when you told me how much you and your daddy enjoyed poems by Edna S. Vincent Millay?" She watched Beth frown and nod, "I have a favorite which you have to read at my funeral."

Beth squinted into Julie's eyes. "You have to be kidding."

Julie shook her head from side to side. "Herb Gillon has a copy of it. With my new Will." She forced a laugh. "Tell me the truth. Have you made love with Brad?"

Beth shook her head. "Why are you asking me again?"

"I was hoping you finally did. I want you to know what it's like to feel him enter your body . . . overpower your soul and fill you with more emotion than you knew you could hold. You'll want him to drive his energy and love into you as deeply as he can. Sometimes I thought I was going to explode. Or maybe faint from such an exciting and overcoming experience. It's like an everything extravaganza."

Beth tried to appear unruffled. *This is a Julie nobody knows. What a guy he must have been.* Quietly she said, "Don't forget Mr. Fischer was more experienced and Brad . . ."

"Will get better and better. Just you remember he's going away to college and . . . oh hell, you do it your way." She backed herself to lean against the bed. "I'm just happy I did it my way and got Bill to marry me. Get a bath towel. I don't want to soil my quilt."

After Beth spread a towel Julie struggled onto the bed. She allowed Beth to position a pillow under her neck and head. As she eyed the white plaster ceiling, she could not remember ever looking beyond Bill's handsome face above her, to notice it before. "I can remember the times I laid here on fire with passion, before or after he had made love to me and I still was afraid that I couldn't keep him." She rolled her head to look at Beth. She patted the bed and waited for the girl to sit beside her. "At least I had more than some women dream of having."

"And more than any other woman *ever* had. You have his name."

"Sure. I'm Mrs. William Frederick Fischer." She clasped one of Beth's hands. "Bear with me, while I take you down memory lane." She pointed. "See that chest on chest over there? It still has his clothes in it. Many afternoons after he came home from the office I'd be lying here, all but my shoes and dress, to go somewhere and I'd wait for him to get a shower. With just a towel wrapped around him, he'd come back in here. With wet mussed hair and…"

"What color?" Beth blurted out.

"Dark brown. Everywhere. Arms, legs, chest. And he'd go over there to get his shorts and undershirt and a dress shirt and all the while he'd be driving me crazy. Then he'd put on his trousers and tuck in the shirt. Next, he'd pick out a tie and I'd remind him about the tie clip, because he always forgot. The first day I met him, his tie was flapping around like a big loose tongue. I can almost smell the soap and the after shave cologne. He smelled so vigorous. And desirable." She slowly rubbed her hand over the quilt. "Down in Earle's house, I can only remember what I used to do in this bed."

Beth laid a hand on Julie's hot bony hand. "Move back. This is where your heart and soul are. Put Earle's house up for sale."

"I tried to change his will and give it to you. But it has to go to the church."

Beth felt a rush of excitement. "I don't want Earle's house."

"SINCE today is the day for secrets, I'll tell you I'm giving you an apartment. In the elegant Warrington Estates. I even added more than enough money to buy your choice of furniture, cover taxes and six years in college. I'm expecting you to make me proud of you, young lady."

"My god. I never expected you to give me any more than a job and a bed." Should she kiss the woman? At least, give her a hug. What in the hell would Liz say when she found out? "It'll take me awhile to believe what you just told me, but thank you. Very much."

Julie nodded and began to cough. She pointed toward the bathroom and croaked, "I need water." After Beth hurried into the bathroom Julie found a wad of tissues. She spit into them and then looked at the blood. After Beth returned, she took a long drink of water she laid her head back on the pillow and closed her eyes.

Beth noticed the perspiration on Julie's upper lip and brow. She decided she didn't want to be alone with Julie. "Do the telephones work?" After Julie replied, "Everything works. I want to keep this house alive." Beth insisted, "Let me call Doc. I'll take off your shoes and help you under the covers. You sound as though you might be getting another cold."

Julie rolled her head from side to side. "I'm all right. I'm just tired. No Philip. Right now I want to finish my story. See those two doors? I want you to open the door on the right." She watched Beth try to open the door. "Huh. I guess Ruth still keeps them locked.

"When I rented this house to Commander Bittner, it was with the understanding no one could ever come into this part of the house. This suite of rooms was off limits. That door is to our private sitting room and office. You can see that later." She leaned on an elbow. "I left the keys in the door. You can figure out which one will open the other door. To my big surprise."

Beth felt uneasy as she opened the door wide enough to peer inside. She froze! She was viewing a nursery. Crib, changing table, chest, rocking chair. Even a diaper pail. She turned to look at Julie. "This was for the baby you . . . lost?"

Julie sighed. "I never could get pregnant. That's for the baby we were going to adopt."

Even though during the night she had reviewed her speech she realized she still was unprepared to share the truth with Beth. But now that Earle was gone she had to tell someone! She patted the bed. After Beth sat she began. "Before Bernice and Dick adopted Brad he was supposed to be ours." Then she coughed into the wad of tissues. And waited.

Finally Beth murmured, "I do believe you faked being pregnant and that Brad really is adopted but I cannot believe that he could have been your son."

"SO listen to my story. But do not interrupt me. I hope you never know what it's like to want to have a baby so badly that you not only pray but you beg and try to bribe God. And you let too many damn doctors make you spread your legs, and peer and probe. And take tests and finally when they tell you there's nothing wrong with your husband, you die a little, because it's your fault.

"Oh sure, I was enjoying trying to make a baby and it did keep Bill busy, but every month I went through hell, waiting and wondering and then . . .damn, another period. I wanted to scream today, realizing Jeanne Barnes does not want to have a baby and remembering how badly I wanted Bill's child. We decided to adopt. Obviously we had an *in* with the Home with Earle being so involved at the church. But still there was no bribing or favoritism. We had to put our name on the waiting list."

"I'll bet Mr. and Mrs. Livingston wanted a baby just as much as you and Mr. Fischer. Especially after everybody knew she had a baby in Virginia."

"They didn't know we were ahead of them on the list. The Home was waiting for two teenagers and a married woman who had fun while her husband was away, to give up their babies for adoption.

"Yes, I can relate to how anxious Bernice must have been because Bill and I were ecstatic when the Director of the Home called Bill to tell him a baby boy had been left on the porch."

"You mean someone just left a baby. Outside! That's awful."

Julie squinted at Beth. "It's a covered porch and obviously you don't know how many babies are found in train stations and school bathrooms. There still are lots of women who have to hide their identity with an illegitimate baby. Or do you think your sister thinks of her baby as a love child? .

"Now, don't interrupt me. The Director told Bill that after the necessary examinations and paper work to make it a legal adoption, then Baby Bill could be ours. But . . . " Damn. Hot tears were rolling into her ears.

Beth patted Julie's hand. "Why was he named Baby Bill?"

"For the sake of identification. Before he was adopted."

"You were going to name him William Frederick Fischer?" Beth watched Julie blot tears. "And you didn't adopt him because . . ." She paused, to wait. For the answer. To what she wanted to know.

"Bill died." Julie blew her nose. "I wanted to adopt him but Earle and the Director, even the Minister or Brother, whoever, damn him, said I was too unstable. So, for Baby Bill's sake I had to let someone else adopt him. I was heartbroken when I agreed to let them contact Richard because Bernice wanted a baby so badly."

"After she found out her own baby had Down's Syndrome?" Beth commented. She watched Julie nod.

"Give me my handbag." Julie said. She was going to go for broke. She held an envelope. "After I returned Richard's letter I was going to give this one to Bernice. But then I decided why destroy her? She had been hurt enough by her despicable husband. I found this letter among Bill's papers. I am going to destroy it because Bernice can't pretend any longer. What I'm telling you is Bernice tried to convince Bill that her baby was his."

She held up a hand to stop Beth from making a comment. "I always knew Bill could have any woman he wanted. I can't believe he considered screwing Bernice any more than a conquest . . . or that he did her a favor. Don't look so surprised. Brad's mother, to put it in nice terms, made love with my husband. Then she tried to convince him she was pregnant with his child. And the poor thing must have assumed Bill believed her. Because after she had the handicapped child and her family convinced her the baby should be put away, she wanted a son to show Bill. In fact I heard she almost flipped out until the director of the Home called Richard to tell him he had a baby boy for them. Alias Baby Bill." She smiled and whispered, "Quite a story, isn't it?"

"So that letter is from Mr. Fischer to Bernice telling her he knows her blood relation baby was not his?"

Julie nodded. "And Bill never knew she ended up with the baby that was supposed to be ours. And neither did Bernice. And hateful Dick. Although I'm sure they worried and wondered if Earle might have told me."

"That's why you dislike the Livingston's? Because they got Brad, instead of you?"

"I suppose that enters into it. Although I never really liked them. They're both phonies. But yes, I suppose I've been jealous. I know I shouldn't have disliked Brad. Except I wanted him to be a Fischer. Not a Livingston." Julie paused to cough and spit into the tissues.

"How did Mr. Fischer know Bernice's baby wasn't his?"

"Our spy network. Somebody in Sam's family convinced somebody at the private home, to share the lab work up on Richie, which is what they call him. There were too many medical findings that didn't match Bill's genetic make-up plus Bernice agreeing with her family that Richard had fathered a defective child. I know they never wanted her to marry the damn Yankee in the first place. But Bernice insisted she have a baby boy to show off in Bridgeboro. After you read Bill's letter you'll understand how devastated she would be if I had given it to her." Julie tried to roll toward the side of the bed. "Help me up so I can . . ."

"No, Julie," Beth said loudly. "You're going to stay right here. You're pooped. I'm going to call Evan to tell her where we are and then call Doc and ask him to drive up and make you . . ." She watched Julie sit up.

"I said before, 'No Philip'! You can call Evan so she knows where we are. Because I have more to tell you."

"Stop being so stubborn. If you ever fell what would I do? You said you wanted to stay here. So we will. Why do you want . . . "

Julie managed to put her legs over the side of the bed. "Just be quiet and help me into the bathroom. Then we're going to the car. I'm sure you want to see where Vicki Lynn died."

Beth felt a shiver of excitement from head to toe. "You mean the cabin?"

Julie nodded. She realized how much energy it was going to take to finish the story but she said, "Don't you think *love nest* sounds more romantic?"

"Of course you know I want to see it but it can wait until tomorrow. I'd feel better if Doc were here to help us."

"Philip couldn't go there with us. Now I need to go to the bathroom."

Beth could not stop disagreeing. "Julie. Please. You know it's going to upset you."

"I said, *be quiet!*"

WHILE Julie was in the bathroom, Beth used the phone. "Evan, just listen. We're up at Deer Lake Manor. Do *not*, I repeat do not tell anyone Julie and I went to a meeting about Brad... Yes, he is *not* the father but listen, I could get a call from Peg or even Liz." Beth smiled as she heard Evan inhale loudly. After she heard her mother's name. "Just tell anybody who calls . . . he has?... when?...two times?...well, if he calls again, tell him I'll call him as soon as I can. And I love him....If Jill calls again, tell her I'll get back to her. And the same thing to Danny. And listen," Beth lowered her voice, "Call Doc and tell him I'm going to call him as soon as I get her home. Gotta go."

After Beth managed to help Julie into the car she followed Julie's instructions of . . . "Drive slowly until you get to the road again. Okay, now turn right and drive past the Spring House and then . . . now turn out that lane. See, if I had been able to walk, we would have gone out the mud room or the solarium and walked across the path. Slow down! Pull up to that clearing and closer to that cement slab . . . good, good."

Julie leaned her head back closed her eyes and whispered, "Well, you're here. Where it all happened."

FIFTY NINE

BETH TURNED OFF the engine. Looking from Julie's face to the view through the windshield she tuned in to her reaction.   She knew she was concerned about Julie but she also was aware of overwhelming excitement.   The pictures of the fire engines, the ambulance, the police, the funerals, the magazine articles and Vicki's books had traveled around the world.   Beth remembered the stories her father told her of the shock wave that ran through Bridgeboro, the *Fischer Company*, and the literary world.

Now, she was where the story had happened.   She was hearing more than most knew.   Yet some suspected.   About a love affair.   She was going to wait until the widow told her what to do next.

"Open my door. You're going to have to help me get out so I can show you the rooms. Then you can pay your respect."

"Julie. Why can't I just walk around by myself and know I was here. We can come back another day. When you feel better."

"Because it's more than your *just* being here. I'll let you be alone. But I want to tell you where the rooms were. And what happened. Open my door and help me out."

Beth obeyed because she did not want to upset Julie. She believed Julie was making this sojourn because she wanted her to know where Vicki Lynn had died! The unwritten last page of her losing essay, *Victoria Lynn, Noted American Writer of the Twentieth Century.*

She tried not to remember why Dick Livingston had made the visit to her house! Indicating he knew the truth!   Or was Julie forcing herself to retrace her life with Bill for a purpose unknown to Beth? Surely Julie wasn't sick enough she was making her last pilgrimage?

Julie leaned heavily on Beth's arm as she shuffled across the cracked flagstone patio and stepped across a door sill to a large charred cement slab. What had been the front wall and the wall along the right side of the cabin had been removed. Remaining of the building were two partially destroyed walls that still formed the far left corner of the building. In height they could be measured from shoulder down to knee high. Visible across the damaged slab were broken plumbing and sewage pipes.

"This was the living room. And what's left of the fireplace. And . . . this was the kitchen. And next to it was the bathroom."

"I can see where the pipes were." Beth allowed Julie to push her forward.

Finally Julie stopped and leaned against Beth. "This was the bedroom. Take me over there. I want to sit on that wall."

"I don't think we should stay. I want to take you back home."

"I want to sit," Julie demanded.

"I wish you would stop pushing yourself. You don't have to do this for me."

Sitting on the wall Julie coughed and wiped her mouth. She wondered if her dress was becoming stained because she did not want Beth to know she was bleeding. She whispered, "I'm okay. I'll try to be quiet while you pay your respects."

Beth slowly walked across the broken slab until she paused by the front door sill. Where they entered. Their love nest. Their place of broken dreams. She became unaware of Julie. She began to focus on the weeds growing through the cracks of the foundation.

No! Not weeds. They were wild flowers, making a statement that here, Victoria Lynn Phipps had lived. And loved. *Daddy, I hope you know where I am. Where Vicki wrote some of the books you and I read. And where she died! I know I shouldn't cry but I'm so sad. For all of them. Vicki and Bill and Julie. Maybe mostly for Julie. I better perk up because I don't want Julie to get upset with me.*

Beth tuned into the sound of a small plane flying overhead. Then she became aware of birds. Chirping. Even insects. Buzzing and flying around her. She reminded herself there was a reality filled with thousands of people going about their business while she was at a special place she never imagined she would ever be. The sound of Julie's coughing penetrated her concentration. She was interrupting Beth's meditation. Quickly Beth wiped away the tears and wandered back. To sit by Julie.

"Why don't you just have all of this bull dozed and covered with sod? Bury it and your memories and free yourself . . . of what happened here." *Jeez. She's holding another envelope.*

"I don't consider this hallowed ground. Although I have thought about putting a marker or a granite slab here. Yes, I stayed away from Deer Lake Manor for years. Until Earle convinced me I should let somebody enjoy the place. So I rented the house. And I still suffered in Earle's house.

"I brought you here to tell you what I wanted you to write in your essay." Again, she had a hard coughing spell, but she raised her hand to signal Beth to remain quiet. She offered the envelope to the girl. "You have to know the end of the story. Maybe you'll decide to write a biography about Vicki. Although Bill deserves a biography also."

Carefully, Beth removed a picture. She studied the face of a handsome young man who was smiling directly into her eyes. He was wearing an officer's uniform of the United States Navy. He had dark brown eyes and dark brown hair and a wide handsome face. Suddenly Beth felt a shock jolt through her. She looked at Julie and breathed, "I've never seen a picture of him but I'll guess it's Mr. Fischer." She watched Julie nod.

Beth dared to stare at the picture again. She closed her eyes. *No. It can't be. No. It can't be . . .* screamed inside her mind. She looked into Julie's pale face. "I want to be wrong."

"I'm sure you're right," Julie whispered. "He's Brad's real father. "Brad was born right here. In this bedroom."

Beth was able to add, "And Vicki Lynn . . . is his mother. Now I know why you almost freaked out when Evan had her baby. You helped deliver him, didn't you?" Beth watched Julie nod. "But why didn't Vicki keep him?"

"Because of me. Way back then, it wouldn't have been as acceptable for an unwed Vicki Lynn to have an illegitimate child. Remember how many movie stars went into hiding and never revealed they had had a baby? And, I wouldn't agree to a divorce, until . . . Until the night they both died."

Julie held up her hand. "Please. I have to tell you. Not even Earle knew everything. Oh, he knew Brad was their baby. And Brad will find out when it's time to read the wills. But before I die, I want him to know who he really is. And now that he knows he's adopted, let's let Bernice and Dick find out whose son they raised!" Before she could cover her mouth with the tissues, Julie coughed. Observing Beth's expression she knew Beth saw some blood on her lips.

"You're bleeding! I need to call Doc."

Julie grabbed Beth's closest hand and squeezed it tightly enough to make Beth wince. "Later. I know I'm bleeding but I have to finish my story." She handed Beth two legal size envelopes. "Read these out loud. I want to hear the truth. Again."

As Beth unfolded a single sheet of white stationary she noticed her hands were shaking. Slowly she began to read a letter which she realized Vicki had written to Bill.

Dearest Darling, Why play around with words when my heart is bursting to tell you what I just discovered to be absolutely true! I'm pregnant! When I first suspected, I was just plain scared. I thought, it couldn't be true. We've been so careful, until that unforgettable night under the full moon. When I was certain I wondered what in the hell shall I do now? Shall I try to get rid of it? Shall I go to Europe and hide? Shall I kill myself? But now, as I write this, I'm not afraid. I'm going to have your baby. Our baby. Wherever you want me to be. My only desire is you shall be with me."

Beth held the letter in two moist hands and realized what she was learning. Incredible! Her hands were shaking so badly she could barely hold the letter from Mr. Fischer.

Vicki darling, My god! My hands still are trembling and my heart still is doing double time. I just finished reading your letter again and am answering it as best I can.

At first, I was furious! I accused you of being brazen, myself for being foolish and the two of us for being idiotic! Now, even though I am mindful of the problems we shall have to face, I am deliriously happy. Please, for God's sake and my sake and your sake and our baby's sake, take care of yourself.

So often we have wished for something, shall I call it tangible for the want of a better word, which could result from our love. What could be better than a child? It shall not suffer because we will not let it. And when it is old enough we shall explain it was conceived from pure and adoring love. And before it is old enough to know, let us hope we shall be husband and wife.

Beth folded the letters and returned them to the envelopes. She stared at Julie. She looked at the blood on Julie's lips but she didn't even care. "Why didn't you let them get married?"

"I wanted to be the only Mrs. William Fischer. My rational was she would have his child and I would have his name."

"And they agreed?"

"They had to. I made ugly threats. I was going to tell everybody. Especially Dad Fischer. He was in very poor health around that time. Remember I told you he had a heart attack. Bill loved his dad and Vicki just gave in. So we decided she would go into hiding. Here.

Under the pretense of writing another novel. Which she really did begin. You can see the manuscript.

"Vicki was to have the baby here and then Bill and I would adopt it. Only Earle and Alice knew what our plans were because he agreed to take the baby to the Home, make sure it was found and convince the director and medical team to let us adopt it. Earle and Alice took the secret to their graves. We told Dad he was a grandfather but he never saw the baby. He died after Earle had taken Baby Bill, alias William Frederick Fischer, to *The Home For Lost Lambs*. Vicki decided since Dad couldn't be hurt, the hell with everybody else, she wanted *her* baby back. And she meant it! I had become a real lush but in a lucid span of time I decided the name was not worth the aggravation and why kid myself? She would always have more and be better than I am. She had fame. And fortune. But more than that, she had the man, Bill Fischer. And his baby. Why pretend I was the mother of what was *her* love child. Why spoil an innocent baby's life?"

Julie used the tissues to wipe her eyes. Barely audible she murmured, "I knew he would live up to his promise to look after my wellbeing. So I decided to give Bill a divorce."

Beth leaned closer to Julie and wrapped an arm around her slouching body. She was fearful Julie might fall off the wall. "Julie. Please let me help you back to the car."

"Not yet. I have to finish the story. Brad won't learn any of this until maybe he's twenty-one, or when Herb Gillon knows it's time to read Bill's will. Before Bill died, he had prepared a will naming Baby Bill to be his heir."

"And he died before you could adopt his real son . . . so he became a Livingston."

"I changed Bill's will, to give Bradford Livingston the Fischer estate. Believe me Herb Gillon's partner, who fortunately has died also, was as surprised as you are when I explained my rationale was because Bill had already chosen Baby Bill to be his heir." She coughed and smiled. "Since Brad knows he's adopted why wait until the wills become known? He loves you and you can soften the shock. Just remember he's also the son of Vicki Lynn."

"You're telling me, he's . . . going to inherit her estate also?"

Julie nodded. "Fairy tales do come true. Vicki had decided to do what Bill was doing. Baby Bill, alias Brad, will inherit her entire estate, minus a few thousand dollars which she willed to some charities." She put up her right hand so Beth would not interrupt her. "I'm almost finished."

She coughed, gagged, coughed, wiped her mouth and leaned against Beth. "Bill and I helped Vicki have her baby. Then we washed and dressed him and put him in a basket. And Earle put him on the church porch. He made a phone call to the orphanage and hid until someone took in the basket. The next day the Director called to tell Bill the good news. An unexpected baby had arrived! And after it was decided he was healthy and the necessary paperwork was completed, he could be ours. We decided only Earle and Alice would know until we made an announcement. But we did tell Dad the happy news before he died. I managed to look presentable to attend Dad's funeral. I could have won an Oscar. Being a loving wife. But I truly was a forlorn daughter-in-law.

"After the wake Bill came here, where Vicki was waiting for him. He said she was very depressed. Thank god she was as healthy as your sister, meaning she was recovering physically but she was full of remorse from giving away her baby. You asked why didn't I stay friends with Bernice and Dick so I could have watched Brad grow up? Imagine what it would have been like for Vicki? Watching me raise her love child.

"After the wake, I went to bed. I'm telling you this because I want you to know I was cold sober when I decided it was time for me to convince myself that Vicki had had his baby, let her have his name. And make the baby legitimate. Don't ask me why, because I don't know why, but I got out of bed but did not get dressed. I decided to put on Bill's long raincoat over my nightgown. I remember it was a chilly night but I decided to walk, from the mud room to here."

She shook her hand in front of Beth, signifying she wanted her to be quiet. "I walked up to the living room window and watched them. Bill was holding Vicki in his arms. She was crying. Sobbing. There was a bottle of wine and two glasses on the coffee table. I remember wondering how much they had to drink? I watched them. For a long time. Until I knocked on the door. Bill opened it and because he was always polite and knew it was chilly outside, he asked me in. That's when I . . . I smelled gas." Julie began to cry.

"Oh my god. Don't tell me anymore," Beth whispered. "I can imagine the rest." She felt bile come up from her stomach. Now was not the time to throw up.

"No, you can't. You weren't here. And I can't live with my lies any longer. No one knows the truth, except me. Not even Earle knew everything that happened. I immediately suspected the heater had not been completely repaired. I told myself it was just a little leak. And Bill would smell it when he returned to the cabin and walked inside, out of the fresh air. Before he started a fire in the fireplace. I should have suggested they both come to stay at the big house. Instead, I told them I had decided to give him a divorce. She could have her baby. And his father."

Julie sobbed and coughed. "Vicki cried tears of joy before she poured herself a glass of wine and drank all of it. I began to cry. I thought since I made them both happy why shouldn't I ask Bill to walk me back to the big house? Just as we were ready to leave, I mentioned how chilly it was outside. She wanted Bill to put on a jacket which I'm glad he didn't do. He gave her an afghan and said he'd start a fire when he returned. Vicki poured another glass of wine, held up the glass and thanked me. I never even said goodbye to her. I told the truth when I said she must have decided to start a fire. We had reached the mud room when . . . the cabin exploded."

Leaning against Beth, Julie coughed and sobbed.

"My god! Mr. Livingston was right! You . . .could have saved them. You . . . did kill them!"

As though she didn't hear Beth's accusation Julie whispered, "Bill began to run back to the cabin. I began to scream. And run after him. I actually hoped Vicki would be dead and he would belong to me. Of course, Ruth and Al heard the explosion. And my screaming. And they saw us running from the house . . . to the cabin.

"They knew Vicki was here, working on another book. And why would he have taken time to put on a jacket? I guess they thought I had grabbed a coat to cover my nightgown. I kept screaming for Bill to stay away from the fire. But he did, come back . . . inside. I heard him calling her name but evidently he couldn't get to her. I screamed for him to come outside. His clothes were smoldering. Al told everybody he saw me wrapping the coat around Bill and sitting on the ground and holding him and rocking back and forth. In my nightgown. Now I want to stand up and show you one more thing."

"Then you'll get in the car?" Beth asked, innocently, because she knew as soon as she had Julie in the car she was going to drive directly to the hospital. After Julie nodded she asked, "Where are we going?"

"I'll steer you there. Help me up." She stood and clung to Beth's right arm.

Beth gasped as she saw a wash cloth fall to the ground, at Julie's feet. It was heavy with blood. "My god, Julie. You're bleeding! You have to get in the car! Now!"

"Just take me to that big oak tree. Where I sat on the ground and held Bill in my arms and told him how much I loved him. And yes, I did realize what I had done." Julie swayed to the ground.

Beth sat on the ground and held Julie to her. She stared at Julie's stained dress as she heard Julie ask, "You know what he said to me?"

Beth shook her head from side. She was half listening to Julie and wondering what she should do? Just let Julie lie on the ground while she ran into the house to use the telephone or . . . she tuned into what Julie was telling her. While she was sobbing and coughing.

"I'll always remember him . . . looking into my eyes . . . deep . . . inside my soul... as he breathed, "You . . . must tell my son. Who his mother . . . is.""

"Oh god," Beth murmured. "Well, you'll have to do that."

"I'm telling you."

"*You* promised his father."

Julie shook her head from side to side. "You love Vicki Lynn's son. You tell him. Here. Tell him everything. I did what I did . . . because I loved his father. But I never got him back. He went to be . . . .with her. And I've had to live with my lie. And hate myself. And I hope to die."

Julie gagged. She turned her head away from Beth and threw up. It appeared as though she was hemorrhaging to . . . death. Then her head fell against Beth's chest.

Beth began to tremble. "Julie. Julie. Can you hear me? I'm going to leave you here . . . just for a minute, while I . . . I find somebody to help me." Gently she lowered Julie to the ground and ran to the car.

She sounded the horn for what seemed too long. No one was coming to where they were. She began to scream as she ran toward the path to the gate house.

"Help! Somebody, help me!"

SIXTY

AS RUTH AND AL knelt on the ground, they all decided not to move Julie. Beth sat on the ground with Julie's head in her lap, while Ruth hurried to their house for a blanket and towels. Al would make the telephone call to demand an ambulance be sent immediately.

Mrs. William Fischer was very sick!

As the gurney was locked into place, inside the ambulance and one of the attendants was holding the oxygen cone over Julie's face, Beth declared she was going to stay with Julie. She ran to the car for her handbag, Julie's handbag and the car keys. She asked Al to call Doc to meet her at the hospital. And she would come back for the car.

After she was settled in the front seat, she clutched the manila envelopes and handbags against her abdomen, which was hurting from the worst gut pain she could ever remember. *Daddy. Help. Julie really did kill Vicki. At least let her die. But . . . I really don't want Julie to die.*

Doc was waiting in Emergency in the Bucks County Hospital when they arrived. He allowed Beth to hug him and cry into his shoulder before he saw Julie being whisked away from him. He began to run after her.

Beth decided to call Evan. She strongly emphasized that Evan was not to tell *anyone* Julie was in the hospital. Evan told her Brad had called again. Beth knew Brad needed her. She called Geoff because she needed him. After Geoff said he'd leave the office immediately, Beth allowed herself to cry. She knew some tears were for Julie. Some were for Brad. And for herself. She was even crying for Vicki Lynn. And Bill Fischer.

She didn't call Brad. She wasn't ready to talk with him.

IN the waiting room Geoff sat next to Beth and held her hand. Beth tried to make small talk about Deer Lake Manor. They even reviewed the meeting in Mr. Gillon's office. She told Geoff that Evan told her how many times Brad had called. She was happy when Geoff told her she must call him. Whatever Geoff said was what she had to do. She was counting change for the phone call when Doc shuffled into the Waiting Room. Immediately they blurted out, "How is she?"

Doc closed his eyes and shook his head. "It will be a miracle if she makes it. And I let her kill herself." He wiped tears from his cheeks.

Beth wrapped her arms around Doc and whispered, "I took her to Deer Lake Manor. Because she said that's where she wanted to die. But believe me, I didn't know she was bleeding until I saw the blood on her mouth." Beth began to cry.

Geoff gave Beth his folded handkerchief. "We all have a piece of the guilt. We just let her do. . . what she wanted to do. She shouldn't have come to the office today. After the meeting, the two of us should have insisted she return to Earle's house."

Doc said he had to sit down. Geoff helped him to a black plastic couch and moved two chairs closer. "Tell us what to expect."

"She's still unconscious. In Intensive Care. And a pitiful sight. A small balloon has been inserted into her esophagus and inflated. This should collapse the leaking veins against the wall of her esophagus and encourage clotting. Which of course should stop the bleeding."

"While we were in the bedroom, I told her to get into the bed. And I was going to call you. But she insisted she had to take me out to where the fire was. I didn't know she had stuffed a wash cloth in . . . her pants."

"She's getting a transfusion now. God only knows how many she'll need. That's in one hand. The other hand has a needle connected to more tubes. She's getting intravenous nourishment and blood clotting agents. They had to tap into her abdominal cavity to drain out the fluid accumulation. And, of course, she's hooked up to a urine catheter. If she knew what's happening to her, she'd fight like hell. We all agreed to keep her sedated."

Beth wiped her eyes with Geoff's handkerchief. "She wouldn't let me call you. She just kept talking until she upchucked. Lots of blood. And then she fainted."

Doc patted Beth's hand. "It would look like a lot because it was thinned with stomach acids. I don't know whether or not Julie was checking her stool because that would have indicated she had internal bleeding. Regardless, we all have to hope the balloon and the clotting agents will stop the bleeding."

"I imagine her liver is just about shot?" Geoff made it sound like a question but he really was making a statement.

"She was warned last year. Even though her diet improved after Beth moved in, her liver still could not recover because she kept drinking. She knew she had cirrhosis from a needle biopsy last year. And we all know she looked tired. Even weak. Cirrhosis causes bleeding from the varicose veins of the stomach and esophagus. And it's the seventh cause of death by disease."

"I'll give blood," Beth blurted out.

Geoff patted Beth's knee. "We'll find enough donors. It's just what are the odds?"

Doc sighed, deeply. "And of course if she does recover, will she begin drinking again?"

"I won't let her. Even if I have to forget about going to college. And we can get someone in Sam's family to help me and . . . " she stopped as she realized Doc was not agreeing with her.

"Right now, we have to stop the bleeding."

"Can I see her?" Beth asked.

"Not yet. They're still cleaning her up."

More tears ran down Beth's face. "I promised the people who take care of Deer Lake Manor I'd call them. What shall I tell them?"

Doc gave Beth the answer. "Just tell them that Julie is resting comfortably and we won't know anything until the doctors make some decisions."

Geoff took one of Beth's hands and stood. He urged her to stand. "Doc, when was the last time you had something to eat? Beth can make her phone calls and then we'll eat and wait."

Doc shook his head *no*. "You two go. Wherever. I can get something from the machines."

Beth laid a hand on Doc's slumped shoulder. "We want to feel as though we're taking care of you. We want to buy you a gourmet dinner from," she looked at Geoff. "McDonalds?"

"Why not. Fast and simple. So, how about a cheeseburger, fries and what kind of shake?" Geoff waited.

Doc shrugged. "A vanilla shake would be fine. A small one. And no fries for me." He watched them walk out of the room. Holding hands.

AS soon as she saw a pay phone Beth let go of Geoff's hand. "After I call Al, I'm going to call Brad. And invite him to join us." Inside she thought, That way I won't be alone with him, because I know I'm nervous about being with him. I need to have time to decide how and where to tell him. And how much!

Geoff decided he must call Mr. Gillon to alert him about Julie's condition.   He was certain Herbert Gillon would prepare an announcement, alert Howard Whiteside and . . . give orders to the hospital personnel that Mrs. William Fischer was to have complete privacy! No one was to give any information to the media!

BERNICE was lying on her bed when the telephone rang. She had told Brad if anyone called, he had to answer it. She was not going to talk to *anyone*. Of course, she would want to know who called. She hoped it would not be Richard. As soon as they had returned from that horrible meeting, he had thrown his razor and toothbrush and some things she didn't see, into his briefcase and said he was going to the office. And he did not know when he would return. Bernice felt great relief to have him out of the house.

Brad answered the phone in the kitchen.

"Hi, babe," Beth said softly.

"Thank god. I've been hoping you'd call. Did Evan tell you, I've been calling. "

"Hush up and just listen. I'm at a pay phone in the hospital, and . . . yes, Julie is in here. And everything is not all right. But I can't talk now. Geoff and I are going to McDonald's and we want you join us. Then I'll fill you in.

"Brad, *do not* tell your mom and dad she's in the hospital because we don't want anybody to know yet. Just meet us at the McDonalds at Monument and County Line. Okay?"

BRAD felt a surge of happiness. He knew his mother would cry again if he told her he was going out, but he convinced himself he couldn't do anything to help her.

And why shouldn't he be able to do what he wanted to do.   His father didn't care. And she was not incapacitated. Just too damn many tranquilizers.   No matter how many years she had fed him, he was not going to get her dinner. He was going to take the coward's way out by writing a note. He was meeting Beth. Even though Geoff would be with them.   He liked Geoff.   He knew Beth liked, maybe even loved Geoff, but he also knew he needed to be with her.   She was his lifeline.

As soon as Beth saw Brad she got out of Geoff's car. She wrapped him in her arms and whispered, "I love you."

Geoff suggested Beth and Brad eat in the restaurant. He would eat with Doc in the hospital. Brad insisted they return to the hospital also. He knew how much Julie meant to Beth and he did not want her to miss what might happen. Carrying the bags of food, Beth headed to Brad's car. Geoff would follow them.

Doc was in the Waiting Room. "How is she?" they all asked him.

"Thank god, she's in a hospital. We know what's wrong and we're doing all that can be done. Which includes waiting.

Doc nodded to Brad and added, "Beth told me what your parents told you today. My brother and I were adopted. Our parents died in a car accident. But we were lucky because we were told as soon as our aunt and uncle thought we should know. Just try to understand and forgive them for not telling you sooner."

"Thank you, Doctor Rexinger. If it weren't for Beth and Geoff, I probably would be more upset. And I do understand my mom just couldn't tell me."

"Now we should all try to be strong." Doc looked at Geoff. "Mr. Gillon returned your call and talked to me. He's coming here, as soon as he can wrap up a dinner meeting. And, I've made arrangements for round the clock nurses. But I'm going stay with her tonight."

"When can I see her?" Beth asked before she put catsup on some limp French fries.

"Not yet. I did tell Doctor Dillingham you're to have visitation rights as soon as he decides when. Right now the room is so full of people there isn't room for anyone to visit."

Finally, Mr. Gillon arrived. Beth and Brad stood to indicate their respect. Beth was flattered when he extended his small hand to her and put a wide smile on his troll like face. "Julie has told me how fond she is of you. In fact, we've had many conversations about you." He raised his eyebrows. "You and I should talk. Soon." He watched Beth frown and nod.

Mr. Gillon offered his hand to Brad. "Brad. It's about time we met each other. I'm sorry you had such an unpleasant meeting in my office." He patted Brad's hand.

Mr. Gillon, Geoff and Doc had a conversation while Beth and Brad finished their shakes. Finally, Mr. Gillon commented he was going to ask for a meeting with Doctor Dillingham.

A short, bald younger man invited everyone to gather in a private office. Doc introduced Irvin Dillingham as the Internist who had taken charge of the medical procedures to Mrs. Fischer.

"Mrs. Fischer is not responding as well as we had hoped she would. But it still is early to make any predictions. He looked at Beth and gave a slight smile. "I know you'll feel a little better if you see where she is and what is happening. Just remember we're doing everything we can and you will not see the Mrs. Fischer you care about. Also, after your visit I want you to go home. It's surprising how much better one feels . . . after a shower and being away from this place. I know Doctor Rexinger will call you if he believes it's necessary." He patted Beth's shoulder. "Now, let me take you upstairs. For a quick visit."

Help Daddy! I need you. No matter what she's told me, I have to tell her I love her. Daddy. Stay with me. I need you!

SIXTY ONE

BETH KNEW BRAD wanted her to ask him inside Julie's house. With more wisdom than she knew she had, she told him, "I can't let you come in. Because I wouldn't let you leave. We're both too vulnerable right now. Besides I have a sister living with me."

As soon as Brad took her face in his hands and began to kiss her, Beth knew how emotional she was. They both had been drained of feelings and now he wanted her to refill his well. And she wanted to. "Brad. I love you and I know how much you love me. But we're not thinking about what's best for us to do. We're going to kiss goodbye, I'm getting out of the car and I'll see you tomorrow. I'm tired and . . . why are you laughing?"

"Next you'll be telling me you have a headache." He kissed her nose. "Okay. Although I hate it when you're so damn smart. I'm beat too. This has been one of the worst days of my life."

"I know. And we still have lots ahead of us. Brad? Are you still going to Princeton?"

"Nobody has said I can't. Although Mom informed me not to tell anybody but she wants me to go to Mexico with her. She already has plane tickets and reservations because she's decided to get a divorce Even before what my dad did today." After Beth whispered, "And what did you say?" he added, "I told her I won't go. I understand why she wants a divorce and I know she has bunches of money but I couldn't believe she wants to leave our house . . . until she told me she wants to move from Bridgeboro and the two of us to live together. In Princeton! Because she loves me so much!" He covered his face with his hands.

Observing Brad's emotional outburst Beth's heart was aching for his plight. It was unfair he had to suffer so much. Just because he had been adopted. It was unfair she had to suffer so much. Just because he had been adopted. *Damn you, Julie!* she yelled out inside. *Why should I have to tell him he should have been William Fischer!*

Beth lowered Brad's hands and wiped away some tears. "You've been her life line. Who else does she have? Just be kind and gentle to her. Now according to this watch that a very special someone gave me, it is l.a.t.e. And as Scarlet O'Hara would say, 'tomorrow is another day', so let's try to get some sleep and don't you dare leave Bridgeboro."

"How about your car?"

"You mean Julie's car. It's at Deer Lake Manor."

"Tomorrow, after we find out Julie is okay, I'll drive you there to get it."

Double damn. He knew she needed the car. He would be hurt if she said Geoff would take her. Was this a twist of fate? Was she ready to return to Deer Lake Manor? With the son of Bill Fischer. And, Vicki Lynn?

EVAN was awake when Beth walked into the house. She got out of bed and walked into the hall, wearing a shortie nightgown. "Beth? I have something to tell you."

Beth did not feel like having a conversation with her sister. But she knew she had to. "Let's go sit on the bed."

"How's Julie?? After she heard the details Evan asked, "And Brad? I mean, I guess he's kinda stressed out. Huh?"

"Of course he's upset. He's coming to pick me up tomorrow morning. Julie's car is still at Deer Lake Manor."

"Maybe I can meet him? Okay?" After Beth whispered, "Sure. Why not?" Evan added, "Danny Friedman is going on his trip to Israel and he really wants you to call him. And . . . Liz called. You said she might. So now she knows I'm here. Isn't that a bitch?"

Beth stared at her sister. "What did you tell her?"

"I told her you were out with Julie."

"I mean, *why* you're in Bridgeboro?" Beth studied Evan's face. "Hey. Don't expect *me* to tell her she's a grandmother. What you should do is take the baby . . . you have to name your daughter pretty soon, and surprise Liz. I'll take you." Beth watched Evan thinking.

"I'll let you know. And I do have a name. How about Vicki Lynn? I know that's a special name for you. Or would that upset Julie too much?"

Beth yawned. "I'll have to think about it. Right now, I'm ready to crash. I'm going to sleep in Julie's bed." Funny, how she hadn't even thought about Julie's room, until she had heard herself say it. She got her p.j.'s and walked to the hall. "When will my niece want her next bottle?"

Evan sighed. "I hope not until five or six."

"Good. Brad's going to call before he comes down. So I'll answer the phone."

"Beth. Thanks a lot for all you've done for me. I really do appreciate it."

"You're welcome. That's what sisters are for. Goodnight."

"Goodnight, Beth."

AS soon as Beth awakened she called Doc. He had gone home. To take a shower. And change his clothes.

The good news was the balloon was reducing the hemorrhaging. Julie still was being transfused and sedated. Doc told Beth he was returning to the hospital. Even though Beth would have loved to hear Geoff's soothing voice she knew Doc would give Julie's lawyers a progress report. A little voice told her she should save her emotions for Brad.

An hour later, smiling at Brad on the other side of the screen door, she felt her heart begin to pound out of synch. He was so damn handsome. He was so damned innocent. She had stayed awake pondering how she was going to tell him. Who he was.

In the kitchen they hugged. And kissed. And hugged until Beth stepped back, smiled into his tired looking eyes and suggested he have some coffee. While she was filling two mugs, she told him Evan wanted to meet him, so just relax while she went to see if her sister was dressed.

As Evan walked into the kitchen Brad politely stood. He felt her eyes roaming around his face, down his shirt and all over his jeans. He gave her one of his sexy smiles, extended his right hand, and told her he was happy to meet her.

Beth invited Evan to have some toast and cold cereal with them. Evan accepted, surprised that Beth really wanted her to stay in the kitchen. Hell, why wouldn't she want to? She wanted to observe the handsome and popular son of the snobs, Bernice and Richard Livingston. Get a feel for what her sister had managed to snare. Study this guy who had been found on the porch of an orphanage.

While they were having a pleasant conversation, the cries of a baby crept into the kitchen. Beth smiled. "Good. Now Brad can meet my niece."

While Evan was in the bedroom Brad asked, "Does Geoff know Evan is here?"

"Yeah. But no matter. He already has someone else in his life. I'm going to move mother and child into the apartment Julie has given Evan. Up in Greenbrier. And babe I might as well tell you, Julie is giving me an apartment to call my own, in Warrington Estates." She waited for his response.

"Why are you moving out of here?"

"Because Julie wants to move back to Deer Lake Manor. And she wants me to live with her. This was Earle's house and it's included in his estate, meaning it goes to *The Church of The Good Samaritan.*"

"My mom told me I came from the church orphanage."

Beth nodded. Good. We're talking about the story. How much does he know? She decided to ask, "Has your mother told you, you have a brother?"

"Yeah. He's living in Virginia. In a home. She insists he's not a retard. She keeps saying, 'Richie has Down's Syndrome'. Now it makes sense why she's always been involved with the *Bucks County Association for Retarded Children.*" Brad raised his eyebrows and looked beyond Beth to observe Evan, holding her baby.

"Here's my big production," Evan remarked with pride in her voice. "Did Aunt Beth tell you she delivered her?"

Brad looked at Beth. "Let me guess. It was an according- to - what -I -read experience."

Beth had to laugh. "Yep. And thank god I read the last chapter." She took the squirming baby and walked to Brad. "Isn't she adorable? Here. Take her."

"No way. I've never held a baby and she's too little. Cute but too little. I don't know anything about babies and thank god, I don't have to. I wonder if Mr. B. got in touch with the Benders yet. Personally, I think Jeanne should have an abortion. It could be a vacation trip."

"But me thinks they wanted Bradford Livingston for a son-in-law." Beth gave the baby to Evan. "If she doesn't happen to have a miscarriage, her baby should be a real winner. Mom and dad sure are lookers." She kissed Brad's cheek. "But your kids will be lookers also. When it's the right time."

BETH and Brad promised Evan they would buy formula and diapers. And of course, some magazines and ice cream. And if Jill or Peg called, tell them she'd call back. Beth watched her sister cringe as she said Peg and she knew Evan dreaded talking to Peg as much as to Liz.

IN the hospital they asked the volunteer at the Reception Desk to please page Doctor Rexinger. Doc met them in the Waiting Room. Beth could see her as soon as the nurses finished bathing her.

Beth smiled but inside she yelled, *If anyone should be able to visit her, it's her nephew! As soon as he knows who he is. And guess who tells him!*

Thirty minutes later Beth did hold Julie's hand as she kissed her closest cheek.

"Good morning, Julie. Doc told me you're doing much better." She studied Julie's face. "I'm going to Deer Lake Manor, to get your car. Is there anything you'd like me to get for you? Like something that belonged to Mr. Fischer?" She watched Julie's face. "How about his picture on the night table, where you can see it?" Beth's heart skipped several beats. She was certain she felt Julie squeeze her hand! She leaned to Julie's ear. "I love you. Please get better. For you. For me. For Doc. He loves you too. And for Brad. So he can get to know his Aunt Julie."

Julie's eyelids fluttered Beth wanted to believe she was looking at her. Beth felt elation. She took Julie's hand to her mouth and kissed it. "Thank you for letting me know you hear me. I want to tell Doc, but . . ." She knew Julie was trying to roll her head, "You don't want me to?"

She caressed Julie's forehead. "You just keep hanging in, so we can talk." Beth heard Doc clear his throat. She knew he was alerting her she should leave. Again, Beth kissed Julie's cheek. "Goodbye for now. But I'll be back." As she walked away from the bed, she wondered if she should tell Doc that Julie gave her a sign? No. She wanted it to be their secret.

In the hall, she hugged Doc. "I know she's going to get better."

Doc shrugged. "As long as they keep pumping blood into her, she'll hang in. But, we don't know about later."

"I want *you* to take it easy. I know you love her but you have to think of yourself. And I love you." She kissed her make believe grandfather on the cheek. "We're driving to Deer Lake Manor to get Julie's car."

"I'm going to stop in with the Birth Certificate, to force your sister to name the baby."

"Hey, good idea. I don't know if she was serious but she said maybe Vicki Lynn."

AS Beth and Brad walked past a public phone, Beth suggested Brad call his mom. "Just to tell her Julie is in the hospital. After all, Mr. Gillon is going to call your dad, to have a medical report put in *The B.C.*

After eight rings Bernice answered the telephone. She sounded annoyed. "Hello." As soon as she heard Brad's voice, she said, "I'm so glad you called me. I'm sorry I didn't come out of my bedroom, but . . . I didn't want you to see how awful I look. I need to talk with you. Are you with *that* girl?"

Brad looked at Beth and nodded. "Yes, I'm with Beth. And Doctor Rexinger. We're all at the hospital. Visiting Julie…Yeah. She really was sick yesterday….She fainted later. They're preparing an announcement for *The B.C.* and . . . .as soon as I hang up I'm taking Beth to Deer Lake Manor…..We have to get Julie's car. They had gone there to look around and… I'll keep in touch with you….Yeah. I know you're upset but I can't stay home and….I know, you'd take care of me. Did Dad come home? Okay, so you don't care. Well, just remember I am not going to Mexico, with you….You do what you want to do…. I have to sign off… I love you too. You take care of yourself. Bye."

Brad frowned at Beth. "At least I called her and…damn. What a bummer. She's sure trying to make me feel guilty, when it was her and my dad, who hurt me."

Beth took Brad's hand. "She must be very upset. I know, so are you. But you have me." Beth kissed the back of Brad's hand. "And now, I better call Ruth and Al."

Beth informed the caretakers she was coming for the car. She gave them a medical update on Julie's condition, thanked them again for their assistance, quickly added she had Julie's house keys and might be driving up now and then. If Mrs. Fischer requested her to get anything out of the house. There, that would give her an out, in case of.what? In case she couldn't tell Brad today? And they would have to return.

AS soon as they drove away from the hospital, Beth snuggled up to Brad and laid her head on his shoulder. She would pretend she was tired. She needed time to think. Here she was, allowed to be seen publicly with Bradford Livingston. Let everybody know they loved each other. And yet she was so nervous she was trembling inside.

Daddy. If ever I've needed you, it's like right now. Don't let me mess this up. Send me a sign. Send me something.

Not having come up with any preset plan, Beth directed Brad to park in front of the big house. Brad ooohed and aaahed, just as she had done. Was it just the day before?

"If *you're* impressed, you can imagine how I felt. I was even impressed with how many acres go with the house. And isn't this house right out of *House Beautiful?* Julie had told me all about the history of Manor Houses and . . . " Beth tried not to laugh as she thought, *Your mom is going to wet her pants when she finds out it all belongs to you.* "Let's go inside."

As they ambled across the brick walkway, Beth realized what she was going to do. Telling Brad to wait, she unlocked the door and stepped inside.

She turned to face him and declared, "Welcome to Deer Lake Manor. I'm very happy I can be the one to show you around." After he stepped inside, she closed the door and added, "I hope you like it, as much as Mr. Fischer did. You know he bought this for Julie. For her wedding present."

Brad looked around the living room. He walked to the fireplace and studied the depth and the length before he remarked, "I'll bet my mom was green with envy she didn't have a walk-in fireplace like this one." He walked into the large dining room. "No wonder Mr. B wants to buy this place. To make it into a Bed and Breakfast. If he advertised what happened here, it would be a terrific money maker."

"Let's not talk about selling or buying. I told you Julie is going to move back here. Now let me show you around. And there's a room upstairs, I want to show you." *My god, why did I say that?*

Even though she suspected Brad was not interested in her newly acquired knowledge of periods and woods and designers of furniture, Beth had a need to prolong the tour of the first floor. She forced Brad to observe the views from each room and lingered too long in the solarium.

All too soon, it was time to go up the grand staircase. Slowly, she took him in and out of the bedrooms and bathrooms, until she ran out of rooms. She led him to the wing, behind the locked door and held keys in her hand. Her heartbeats were pounding in her chest. She began to feel quivers of excitement. Or was it fright?

Damn*! Why did Julie have to tell me? And, insist I tell Brad. Talk about cowards. First his mom and dad won't tell him he's adopted. And then Julie won't tell him who he really is. Now, I have to show him the nursery.*

Beth opened the door and stepped into the large bedroom. "No one is allowed in here because this was Julie and Mr. Fischer's bedroom. And that's the huge bathroom. She waited while Brad looked around the room. "That towel is on top of the quilt because that's where Julie was lying down, while I looked around the room. Another nice fireplace, huh? And that's the door to their sitting room and . . ."

Damn. It was now . . . or never. She had to tell him! She walked to the door to the nursery. She unlocked the door and waited for Brad to look at her. "I have something to show you. Really, I *have* to show you something."

Brad frowned and walked to Beth's side. "Is this where the skeletons are?"

"I guess, kinda. Come on in and . . . " she remembered how shocked she had been when she first peered inside the room, so she studied Brad's face as he took his first look. "And . . . surprise!" She forced a laugh. For Brad. For herself.

"Yeah. Surprise. How . . . about . . . that? The gossip was right. Julie pretended she was pregnant. Or, she lost it. After they got married."

"Well, that's almost the truth. What everybody doesn't know is Julie and Mr. Fischer decided to *adopt* a baby. Just like your mom and dad did. Why don't you sit down in the rocking chair, and I'll tell you a nursery story."

Beth waited for Brad to settle in the rocker before she sat on the floor and leaned against a bureau. If she was going to faint she wouldn't have far to fall.

Smiling into his squinting eyes, Beth heard herself begin. Slowly. Carefully. "The plot is, Julie and Mr. Fischer really did want a baby. Just like your mom and dad. Of course your mom did have a baby but

Julie never could get pregnant. So she and Bill decided to put their name on the waiting list at the Home." Beth ran out of words. *Ask me some questions. Help me!*

"You're telling me they got this room ready for a baby, they were going to adopt?" He watched Beth smile and nod. "And? So? What happened?" He began to rock. .

"Mr. Fischer died. Before the adoption went through."

"So? I know you're trying to tell me something. But I'm not catching on. Right?"

Beth reminded herself to breathe. She kept willing she could find the words she needed. *Damn Julie. Damn Vicki. Damn Bill Fischer.*

Brad studied Beth's upturned face. "After somebody left me at the Home, I…was the baby they were supposed to adopt?"

"Right! You were supposed to be a Fischer, instead of a Livingston." There, she had said it. Now how much more was she going to tell him?

Brad's face became flushed from anger. "How in the hell do you know so damn much?" After Beth replied, "Julie told me. Yesterday." he added, "So? Maybe she was . . . lying to you?"

"Brad. We both know how she forced herself to go to your defense yesterday. She cares about you and she wanted to save you from Jeanne. And why did she insist I had to bring her up here? She wanted me to see the nursery and tell me her heartbreaking story. Believe me, she and Mr. Fischer really wanted you to be their son."

Brad shook his head. "You know it's a shitty story because it stinks. I can't believe that Mr. Fischer, as you call him, could have raised me. And" he declared loudly, "I'd be calling Julie, Mom. Sorry, but it sounds too unreal."

"I told Julie I didn't want to be the person to tell you but she said since you found out you were adopted, then you might as well know. All of the story. Like she and Mr. Fischer had even decided to name you William Frederick Fischer." *Now, shut up! Let him talk.*

"*That's* why she hates my mom and dad! They got me, instead of her." Brad wiped some tears on the sleeve of his shirt.

"Julie and Mr. Fischer honestly believed you were going to be their son. So much so, that's why this room is . . . was all ready for you."

Brad slid off the rocking chair and sat on the floor. "I'm so damned mad. I'm even mad at you for knowing more about me than I do. But, I'm glad you did tell me 'cause I wouldn't want anybody else to tell me." Slowly he crawled to Beth.

Beth reached into the pocket of her skirt and gave Brad a tissue. "I'm glad you're crying. I've read crying is like medicine."

Brad wrapped his arms around Beth's waist. "Even though you know so damn much, I love you." More tears and a big sob.

Beth snuggled Brad closer. "I know you do. That's why I'm telling you." She kissed his tears away. "And you know how much I love you. And need you. And . . . " she thought about saying, "and want you," but she decided to just say, "and I'm with you- all the way." After many minutes, Beth felt Brad begin to relax.

She smiled as she realized he was asleep. What else did she have to do, but hold Vicki Lynn's son and let her eyes caress his handsome face. Inside she thought, *Daddy. I know you had something to do with what's happening. I just couldn't decide to write an essay about Vicki Lynn and then end up in love with her son. I have to tell him. He deserves to know. Vicki and Bill should be recognized, no, honored, as his rightful parents. Daddy, is it true, what she told me? About the explosion? You got me into this mess. Now you get me out of it.*

Even though her back began to hurt, leaning against the unyielding piece of furniture and she felt cramps in her legs, Beth sat as still as she could. She leaned her head against the bureau and even dozed herself. It was when her mouth dropped opened and her throat became dry enough to cause her to cough that she disturbed Brad enough to awaken him.

Brad returned Beth's smile. "I guess I fell asleep." He sat up and stretched.

"So did I. Me thinks we might not have had a good night's sleep, huh?" Beth was so stiff she had to move slowly. She looked at her watch "Yikes. Can you believe we've been asleep for almost an hour."

Brad looked around the room, shook his head from side to side and murmured, "In my nursery." He stood and walked to the crib. He picked up a teddy bear, snuggled it against his chest and asked, "Do you think I should tell my mom? That I almost wasn't hers?"

Beth stood. She hunched her shoulders. "That's up to you. You have to decide just how much you can heap on her plate." *Like I have*

475

to heap on yours. "Hey, I have to make a visit. To the you know what. And then we better lock up and get Julie's car."

"Maybe I might want to come back? Do you think that would be okay with Julie?"

"Julie would love it. You have to know, she's *never* disliked you. She's even been saving your pictures, in *The B.C.* I thought she knew we were cheating behind Jeanne's back, but now it makes sense. Hey, gotta go. I'll meet you downstairs."

"I'll make a visit downstairs and wait at the front door."

BEFORE Beth walked out of Julie and Bill's bedroom, she walked to the chest on chest and opened the top drawer. There were *his* handkerchiefs. She decided to take one to Julie. She decided to take one for herself. She smiled as she thought she would keep it with Geoff's and Mr. Stookey's.

She examined the collection of name tags. *Bill Fischer. William Fischer.* She fingered some of the assorted loose keys. And a leather key case. Beth closed that drawer and opened the next one.

Socks and underwear. She had to touch them. My god, her heart was pounding in her ears. Should she call Brad? This would be one way to tell him. See these clothes? They belonged to your father. Your *real* father! Julie's husband. Vicki's lover. In fact, I think I've fallen in love with him too.

After closing the second drawer, Beth approached the bed. Carefully, she folded the towel. Slowly, she smoothed the quilt. She locked the door to the nursery and walked out of the bedroom. She locked the door to the hall and descended the staircase.

Standing inside the foyer she stated to Brad, "I'm going to call the hospital. To find out how Julie is. Before we decide if we'll go somewhere for lunch."

"Good idea. I don't want to eat in that hospital cafeteria."

"Wait in your car. We'll drive back to where I left Julie's car."

She put the handkerchiefs in her handbag and tucked the towel under her arm. Then she made the telephone call.

SIXTY TWO

DOC GAVE BETH an updated report.

The bleeding was under control and the medical team had decided to decrease the sedation.

Geoff had stopped in. Evan had not answered the telephone, which reminded her to write herself a note on the tablet next to the phone, *formula, diapers, ice cream.* And Doc added that if Julie came to, he'd tell her Beth was coming to visit. Nothing to worry about regarding Julie so she should concentrate on being with that forlorn Livingston boy. Why not the two of them have a nice lunch together.

Holding the folded towel under her arm, Beth locked the front door and got into Brad's car. As she gave Brad directions, she smiled to herself. She remembered Julie doing the same thing, just the day before.

Brad parked his car in front of Julie's car. With the motor running he remained behind the wheel.

Daddy. He thinks we're going to leave right away. He doesn't care where we are. You have to help me . . . tell him. Beth opened the car door. "Don't you want to know why the car's parked here?"

"Because this is where Julie fainted."

"But why were we here?"

Brad shrugged. "Well, from the looks of the place I have to guess this is where the fire was. Where Mr. Fischer died. And she wanted to see it and torture herself again." He watched Beth nod and ask, "And?" Brad sighed and said, "You want me to say this is where Vicki Lynn died. Julie thought you'd want to pay your respects and add the last paragraph to your essay."

"You're almost right. Let's look around."

"Why? My mom showed me pictures one time. I think they were in *Time* or *Life*. After all, Mr. Fischer and Vicki Lynn were big names. Personally, I think Julie should get rid of what's left. It's not good to keep a place where you can keep reliving sad memories."

"Maybe she will. But walk around with me. Please." She left the towel and her handbag on the seat. She felt in her skirt pocket to touch the picture and letters which she had transferred from her handbag before she began to amble toward the scarred patio. Making certain Brad was following.

Behind her Brad remarked, "I feel as though I'm visiting a . . . shrine."

Why did she think he would be interested in visiting this place? Because this was where the popular and powerful Bill Fischer had died? That's what his mom had called him. He couldn't remember what his dad had called him. He had a feeling his dad had been jealous of Bill Fischer. But definitely was an admirer of Vicki Lynn. Just as he was certain his mom had the hots for Bill and was jealous of Vicki.

As they stood on the cracked slab which had been a floor, he asked, "What do you want to show me? I can see that's what's left of the fireplace. And over there, some of the walls. I seem to remember reading or having my mom tell me that the caretakers backed up Julie's story. About an explosion?"

Beth nodded. "Caused by a gas leak. From a tank to an inside heater."

"In other words, my dad's story is not true. Julie did not start the fire."

"She did not start the fire." Quickly she pointed. "Look over there and you can tell from the pipes and outline of the walls that was the bathroom. And the kitchen was in that corner." *And why can't I breathe? Can he hear my heart pounding? Because now I know that Julie could have saved them. Maybe that's why she drinks. It helps her to escape. From the guilt. From remembering. Or . . . it's a way to self-destruct."*

"Brad. I have to sit down. I feel . . . lightheaded. I want to sit on the wall."

"You've let yourself become too involved in Vicki Lynn's life. And this place is upsetting you. First Julie, and now you. Let's go back to the car."

Beth closed her eyes. She really did feel funny. If *she* was feeling weak and woozy, how was Brad going to react? Maybe they *should* just drive away!

Brad slid an arm around Beth's shoulders. "Are you okay?"

Beth inhaled, deeply. "I have to be. I have to drive the car."

"We can leave it here. And come back tomorrow." He heard Beth say, "I promised something to Julie." so he replied, "You've been upset ever since you met Julie. What in the hell is she doing to you?"

"She's telling me stories. That I have to tell you." She decided she would tell Brad in the sequence Julie had told her. "First of all, I have to tell you that during the interviews, Julie confessed she knew Mr. Fischer and Vicki fell in love with each other. It was more than one of their casual affairs. And they used this place as their love nest."

"So my dad *was* right that Mr. Fischer had another woman in his life! After Beth said, "Please don't tell him." Brad added, "I don't expect to tell him a damn thing. I just might hope I never see him again." He squinted at Beth and added, "So Vicki had an affair with Julie's husband. And they used to meet. Here. While she thought Vicki was writing and her husband was at a meeting. Right?"

Beth felt annoyed. Damn him for making it sound so . . . simple. "Yo, Brad. This isn't easy for me. Now I know that they sent love letters to each other. Because Julie gave me all of the letters. Not only to read. But to decide what to do with them. Even the last two they each wrote to each other."

"Wow! Julie really went all out for the interview. Too bad you didn't include that info in your essay. My dad would have gone wild and even paid you out of his own check book."

Beth closed her eyes. *Double damn him. Which do I show him first? The picture? Or the letters?* "Would you like to read them?"

"I'm getting really hungry. How about I read them during lunch?" Brad watched Beth pull two envelopes from the pocket of her skirt.

"I think you should read them . . . *now.*"

Brad shrugged. "Okay. I'll read them *now*. To myself? Or out loud?"

"Why not out loud?" She checked the addresses. "This one first."

Brad began, slowly. Dramatically. *Dearest Darling, Why play around with words when my heart is bursting to tell you what I just discovered to be absolutely . . . true! I'm pregnant!*

Brad stopped reading out loud. He looked up at Beth and frowned. Then slowly, he continued to softly read and absorb each word. After he finished reading Vicki's letter he handed it to Beth. He stared into her eyes, waiting for her to say something. Finally she handed him the second letter.

As though he was unsure if he should, he slowly unfolded it. Whispering, he began to read, *"Vicki darling, My god! My hands still are trembling and my heart still is doing double time."* ...Brad continued just mouthing the words until he came to, *What could be better than a child? It shall not suffer because we will not let it. And when it is old enough, we shall tell it, that it was conceived from pure*

479

and adoring love. And, before it is old enough to be told, let us hope we shall be husband and wife.

He had to avoid Beth's eyes so he stared at her mole. "So? Vicki Lynn got pregnant . . . but even though it sounds as though Mr. Fischer wanted the baby, she decided she wouldn't keep the baby." He swallowed hard. And waited. "Well? Is that the story? She didn't want a baby. Because she didn't want to get married?"

"She couldn't. Because Julie wouldn't give up Mr. Fischer. But Vicki did decide if she let Julie raise her son she could watch him grow up. Just as Julie did, letting your mother and father raise you."

"The hell with Julie." He squinted at Beth and added, "And you too. Because I understand that you're trying to make me believe that I was Vicki's baby.

"Well, I don't believe you! And I'll bet Vicki didn't really want a baby. Because it would interfere with her career."

"Not true. Julie admits it was her fault because she wouldn't give Mr. Fischer a divorce. Because she loved him and didn't want to lose him." Her heart was aching as she watched Brad begin to weep. Still she decided not to touch him.

"Listen to me, Brad. You also have to know that Julie did change her mind. And she told Vicki and Mr. Fischer she *would* give him a divorce. So they could get married and keep you. She told them, before the fire."

"Oh sure. So she says. I can't believe you'd swallow this . . . crap. Except it does sound like a best seller love story. Like something Vicki Lynn would write. Plus the fact, you believe *every*thing Julie tells you."

Brad thrust the letter at Beth. "So they loved each other. And Vicki had a baby. It still doesn't mean that - just where did she have their love child?"

"Right here. In what was the bedroom. Mr. Fischer and Julie delivered the baby. Just like I delivered Evan's baby."

"So Vicki had a baby," Brad repeated, as though trying to convince himself. "Right here. And Bill and Julie were going to adopt . . . the baby." He frowned as Beth offered him a picture. "What's this? Brad allowed himself to study the face. His nostrils flared and there was anger in his eyes as he demanded, "Who's this?"

"Your father. He was an officer in the Navy. In his early twenties. It could be your picture, couldn't it?" She watched Brad's hand begin to tremble. She laid a hand on his closest leg. "He *really* is your father."

Brad managed to whisper, "And . . .she's . . . my . . . mother?"

She nodded. But now was not the time to tell him - everything. Now was not the time to say, *let's go get something to eat.* What was it time for? It still was not the time to hug him. Even though she wanted to wrap her arms around him.

After she watched him suffer, too long, Beth whispered, "Brad, I really am sorry. I was afraid you'd be upset. But I promised Julie I'd tell you. Just as she promised . . . "

"Don't tell me another god damn thing! It's nothing but a shitty story about two people who . . . who didn't stop to think about what might happen after they fucked under a full moon and now, here I am. Without them. And . . ." Brad began to stumble away from Beth. "I don't belong to anybody."

Beth hurried after him and grabbed one of his arms. "Brad! You belong to me." She stepped in front of him and peered into his eyes. "I want to belong to you. We need each other."

Brad's eyes were filled with confusion. Suddenly he wrapped his arms around her and crushed her to him. "Oh shit. I've never felt so damn mixed up. Just let me hold onto you. So I don't feel so alone."

Beth hugged him as firmly as she could wrap her arms around his tense body. "Please don't hate me, Brad. I never realized it would be so awful for you. I thought you'd be happy to find out who your parents were. And . . ." Brad covered her mouth with his and began to kiss her. Forcefully. Desperately.

With a hand on each cheek, he held her face and searched into her eyes. Looking for the comfort he needed. "I could never hate you. It's just that I wasn't ready. It's too much. All at once." He held her to his chest and kissed her hair, "Don't ever leave me. You're the only person I have left."

With her face pressing against his damp shirt, Beth murmured, "Just remember we're in this together. I belong to you and you belong to me."

Slowly, Brad pushed her away as he whispered, "I want to make you belong to me."

"Now?"

"Here. Where my father fucked my mother and . . . "

"Brad! Stop saying that! He loved her. Just as I love you."

"Then show me how much you love me."

Beth's mind raced with words, which became ideas, which she finally blurted out, "But I don't want to . . . get pregnant."

Brad smiled into her frightened eyes. "I'll be smarter than my old man. I have another rubber in my wallet."

"Then it could be okay. But I think the cement will be too hard." She began to quickly search around them and heard herself blurt out, "How about under that tree? Over there?"

Brad crushed her to him again. In her hair he murmured, "You pick the spot. Because we'll always remember where . . . we first did it."

Fighting to keep her emotions under control, Beth whispered, "Is it okay if I want to remember it's where we first made love. With each other."

"I'm sorry. I'm just so mixed up. Jeez, babe, did I upset you so much you have to cry?"

After Beth murmured, "I'm scared," Brad picked her up and carried her to the tree. "So am I. I don't want to hurt you." He lowered her on the ground. He sat beside her. "I want the first time to be good for you." He wanted her to belong to him. Everything that belonged to her. He had been starving for this moment.

He slowly pushed her to lie on the ground and leaned over her. He unbuttoned the top buttons of her blouse and pushed her bra straps down so that he could gently caress and kiss her breasts.

Beth pulled his shirt high enough that she could rub her face against the hair on his chest and kiss his nipples. She looked into his eyes as his hand pushed up her skirt and pressed between her legs. He looked sincere. And caring. She knew he wanted her. Because he loved her.

Cool air rushed around her thighs as he slid down her pants. Then she felt him begin to massage her. She knew she wanted this to happen.

Brad felt Beth trying to unfasten his belt. "Wait, babe. Before I have to hobble with my pants around my ankles, let me get that towel to put under you." He tried to roll away from her, but Beth held onto him.

Beth reached to the front of Brad's jeans and felt the bulge in his jeans. "You just want to put the rubber on. Where I can't see you. But I want to watch you do it."

After Brad returned he helped Beth strategically place the towel. Then he opened his wallet and found what he was looking for. He knelt alongside of her and began to unfasten his belt, all the while studying her face. "While we're still rational, are you sure?"

"I've never been more sure. I've wanted you inside of me for too long." She pulled down his zipper and helped him push down his jeans and jockies. She leaned on an elbow and watched him.

Brad hoped Beth did not know how nervous he was as he decided it was time to slowly enter her. He had to make her feel good. Should he use a finger to cause the discomfort? He did not want to louse up the experience.

Mixed in with the passion Beth did feel pain. But she welcomed it. She assured Brad she was okay and not to stop what he was doing. She wrapped her arms around him. She knew words were not needed. She couldn't think of any to say anyway. As she watched the expression on Brad's face change from tenderness to ecstasy, she knew her body was enough for him. She could tell he had been satisfied.

Brad leaned on his elbows to remain above her. He studied her face and then kissed her lips. "It wasn't as great for you, was it?"

"Next time. After all, experience is the best teacher."

"You know what your problem is?"

"I didn't know I have a problem."

"You keep your eyes open."

"I enjoyed watching you."

"That keeps you from concentrating." He kissed her eyes closed. "Now keep them closed. And just concentrate on what I'm doing."

Beth felt Brad lower himself until his mouth was between her legs. She struggled to raise herself on her elbows only to be held down by Brad's hands. "I want to watch what . . ."

He held her down.

Beth heard herself gasp. She squeezed her eyes shut and envisioned what he was doing to her. *Damn. How can I be so embarrassed . . .and have it feel so good. I never knew it could . . .oh,* "Oh god, Brad. I think I'm going to . . .Why did you stop?"

Brad moved up. He pushed her legs wider apart until he could slide into her. "Keep your eyes closed."

Finally he heard Beth's gasping become a cry of ecstasy. He made two more deep thrusts and then felt the surge of rapture fill his own groins.

He smiled as he saw that Beth's eyes still were closed. He studied her pretty face and freckles while feelings of happiness and pride filled his mind. Finally, they had made love. And he made her have an orgasm. Now they did belong to each other.

Brad kissed Beth's eyes. "You can open them now."

"I don't want to. I'm afraid it was a dream. And I don't want to wake up." Beth opened her eyes and glanced them around Brad's face. She touched his scar as she murmured, "I think I could become addicted. Thank you . . . for making it special."

"Thank god this rubber stayed on. As soon as I buy more, watch out babe."

Beth sat up. "Let's uncover him and . . . " Beth pulled out a corner of the towel and began to wipe. "Should I just use the word *him*? I mean I remember I said I didn't like the word *dick* and so you called him . . . your member?" She watched Brad nod. "Member? Or him? Yes, for him?" She laughed. "Okay. Is it safe to let him know what a great job he did?"

Brad laughed. "Hey, remember he does what *I* tell him to do."

"And I did what you told me to do and now, you and him and her and I means all four of us happy."

"Hey girl, as much as I love what you're doing, I think we better remember I don't have any more rubbers. And we *should* go to the hospital."

SIXTY THREE

MIXED IN WITH the tingling feeling left over from making love with Beth. But as he was driving away from Deer Lake Manor, Brad also still was feeling nervous. Even downright afraid. He allowed his thoughts to stray from sex to *the story*.

Those were the words which came to his mind when he remembered what Beth had told him. As they sat amid the ruins. Where he had been born. Somewhere, even conceived, if that was where his parents had used the light of a full moon to . . . Brad smiled as he thought of the word *howl*. Yeah, they had howled alright. But then so had he and Beth.

If he and Beth believed they were in love, then why couldn't Vicki and Bill also? Would that make it alright? Make him feel any less angry?

What if they had made a declaration to the world! We have a son! Before they had died. He still would be an orphan. And there would still be an Aunt Julie in his life.

And now he was going to visit her.

Beth looked into the rear view mirror and waved to Brad several times. He had to know how happy she was. She whispered, *Daddy. Were you there? Should I be embarrassed? You saw me bare assed, letting Brad do the same thing to me that Evan let Les do to her. Only I'm not going to get pregnant. And she even let Geoff do it to her!*

So, I want to yell out the window I just made love with Brad Livingston. How can I be so happy for one thing and feel so worried about what's going to happen to him? Keep tuned in. In case I need you. Earth to Vicki Lynn? And Bill Fischer. Your son knows who he is and he's going to need you guys to help him. And Julie is very sick. If she doesn't make it, please forgive her. P.S. your son is a great lover!

She laughed as she thought, *What am I going to write in my diary?*

BETH and Brad washed their hands and combed their hair and made certain they looked neat and innocent, while they shared a package of cheese and crackers and a soda before they got on the elevator to go to Julie's room.

They found Doc dozing in a chair, unmindful of the sun shining on his face. The private duty nurse was reading a book. She looked up and smiled. Julie was propped into a sitting position. Pillows were tucked behind her head and shoulders. She also appeared to be asleep.

Brad stood by the door while Beth walked to the bed. She studied the tubes and the needles going in and out of Julie and wondered when the doctors were going to decide Julie did not need to be hooked up to all of those things? Hopefully, soon.

She took Julie's closest hand in hers. "Julie?" She waited. "July Phipps Fischer. Time to wake up." Did Julie move her fingers?

Doc opened his eyes and yawned, loudly

Quickly, Beth put her mouth near Julie's closest ear. "Julie. If you can hear me, Brad is with me." Julie did squeeze her fingers! "I'm going to let him hold you hand."

Beth reached out and motioned for Brad to come to the bed. She took one of his hands and put it under Julie's closest hand. Beth again whispered in Julie's ear, "Now it's the four of us, holding hands. I can tell you. Brad knows. I told him most of the story. I did what his father wanted *you* to do."

Doc stood and stretched. "Do you think she can hear you?" He walked to the bed. "Even though she keeps her eyes closed I think she's aware of voices. Herb Whiteside and Harold Gillon stopped in and, even though we spoke softly, at the doorway, I swear she was listening."

Beth nodded. "Doctor Rexinger. And Mrs. Samson? Can we be alone?

"Sure", Doc declared. "I need to take a walk anyway. I'll wait out at the Nurses' Station." Doc looked at Brad as though he expected him to follow him.

"Brad's going to stay with me."

Doc shrugged and left the room.

Nurse Samson followed. With her book.

"If you hear me, squeeze Brad's hand. Once for yes and two for no. Did you hear me tell you that I told Brad?" She watched Brad open his eyes wide and nod.

"Julie, we went to get your car and I showed him your house and then I took him where you and I were. When you told me. Understand?"

Beth watched Brad nod and then she mouthed to Brad, "Call her Aunt Julie."

"Aunt Julie. It's Brad. I just want to say hello. And I'm glad I can call you Aunt Julie."

Beth smiled at Brad and whispered, "I'm going to tell her a secret." She caressed Julie's forehead and pushed the hair away from her ear before she put her lips next to it. "Julie. We . . . did it. Under the tree, where you told Mr. Fischer how much you loved him. I have to believe his son is as great a lover as his father was. Understand?"

Julie's lips pulled at the tape and a weak smile wrinkled her lower face. She squeezed Brad's hand.

Brad looked at Beth and whispered, "What did you tell her?"

"That I'm glad your father didn't wear a condom."

She was happy to watch Brad laugh.

Brad said, "Goodbye, Aunt Julie. I hope to meet you soon. So get well." Beth kissed Julie and told her she loved her and they would return to see her the next day.

They met Doc at the Nurse's Station. He told them the latest medical update was encouraging news. Julie would still receive several more liters of blood but the medical team believed the bleeding had stopped. And Julie was showing signs of stabilization. He and Doctor Dillingham had decided they would consider removing the balloon.

Beth kissed Doc's cheek and Brad shook his hand.

"We're going to get something to eat. I'll be back this evening."

"No need to. Enjoy yourselves. I'm going to stay until the shifts change. And you know I'll call you if I get a phone call. By the way, I never did get your sister on the phone. So I still haven't seen her since the first visit. You tell her I'm stopping in tomorrow. Before I come here."

BETH and Brad wanted Chinese food. They chose a new restaurant in the Northampton Shopping Mall. They ordered and whispered and laughed. Then they ate and laughed. They kicked each other under the table and ate and laughed. For over an hour.

Finally, Beth's eyes focused across the parking lot at a Quick Shop store. "I almost forgot I have to buy formula and diapers."

"Let's go to the Top Foods Market. So we can be seen together."

"My goodness, Brad Livingston Fischer, you sure are the sly one. Was it just yesterday it was decided that you are not going to be a father! And it was that Jim Bender did not wear a condom? Pay the bill because it's your treat and let's go."

In the Top Foods Market they looked up and down the row of cash registers. Neither of them could see Jim Bender. After they got the attention of Ed Gotzi, another Hi School classmate, they decided to get into Ed's line. Beth held the bar of the shopping cart, with Brad standing behind her. His hands were on either side of hers. Brad worried he might get a hard on.

"Hi, Eddie," Beth said. "No Jim today?"

"He called in sick. So I'm in charge of padding your bill."

"What's wrong with the lover boy of the checkout department?" Brad asked.

Ed shrugged as he wondered why in the hell would Beth or Brad be buying formula and diapers? Besides two pints of ice cream, orange juice, bread and four magazines."

Brad had teased Beth by telling her if they sold condoms in the store, he would put a couple dozen in the basket. He wanted to give Ed lots to talk about.

"Will that be all?" Ed asked automatically. He refused to fall into a trap.

Brad counted his paper money. "I guess so. Unless you want to hear some gossip?"

Ed grinned. "According to how many people I can tell." He counted the bills.

"Everybody. Jeanne finally confessed she's been having fun with Jim while I've been dying to tell the world I'm in love with Beth."

"I kinda thought you two hadn't just met each other. And it's none of my business but somebody had a baby?" Ed handed Brad the change.

Beth snickered. "Yeah. My sister. I am now known as Aunt Beth." She picked up the bag with the diapers, bread and magazines. Brad picked up the bag with the rest of the order. Before he stepped away from the counter he decided to hastily add, "And oh yeah, if you hear any rumors about me, they're most likely true. I also found out I was adopted."

Ed frowned. "This is some kind of a joke, isn't it?"

"No joke. I even know who my real mother and father are and it's going to be a big surprise." He wrapped an arm around Beth.

Beth put an arm about Brad's waist. "Just remember, Beth Rhodes loves Brad Livingston, no matter who he is. So long, Eddie. See you around."

Brad put the groceries in Julie's car before he kissed Beth, long and hard. "Where are you going now?" Beth asked.

"To a Drug Store where nobody knows me. To buy a case of condoms."

"Only that many?"

"I'd have to go home, to get more money. Can't you hear me asking my mom for some money. So I can buy condoms? Then after she comes to, I'll add, 'Oh yeah, I found out Bill Fischer is my father. Aren't you thrilled you got to raise his son?'"

Beth added, "And then, after she comes to again, you can tell her the rest of the story. Hey, babe, I'm glad you can joke about it. When will I see you again?"

"You tell me. If Evan wasn't in the house, I'd ask if I could come down. And share your bedroom."

Beth got into the front seat. "And now that I know what a lover you are, I'd never let you go home. Until I wore you out. Call me as soon as you get home. Which I better do, so I can get the ice cream in the freezer." She lifted her face so that Brad could kiss her again, before he closed the door. Through the window, she mouthed *I love you.*

They watched each other drive out of the parking lot.

AS Beth drove into the driveway she noticed there were no lights on. After she parked in front of a garage door, she hurried to the screen door in the mud room. It was unlocked but the inside door was locked. Beth hurried into the kitchen and flipped a wall switch. "Evan, I'm home. Want some ice cream?" She felt anxiety kick in.

Beth put the ice cream in the freezer and the orange juice in the refrigerator. The anxiety increased to panic.

She flipped on the hall light. "Yo, Evan. Wherever you are." She wanted to hear the baby cry.

She hurried to her bedroom and stared at the smooth bedspread. She hurried around the bed and saw the basket was gone. Where was her niece? Damn that sister of hers.

Beth ran into the living room. She turned on table lamps and stood in the middle of the room. Tears began to roll down her cheeks. Was she angry or scared? Well, she had told Doc and Brad that Evan probably was up in the apartment house. How could she get in touch with her? Drive up? No, call Geoff.

After four rings, Beth heard Geoff's smooth deep voice say, "Hello. Greer here."

"Hi. Beth here."

"I hope you're not calling about Julie."

"Julie's okay. But, I'm not. Would you happen to know where Evan might be? I know it's none of my business, but I . . ."

"Wait a minute. Just slow down and let me tell you, no, I do not know where Evan is. And wherever she is, it's none of my business."

"Doc said he called her several times to tell her he was coming down with a Birth Certificate and she didn't answer. And she's not here."

"Well, believe me, she's not here."

"Honest to god, Geoff, I'm sorry I called you. I just wanted to know she's okay. No, I really wanted to know the baby is okay. Maybe she did go to see Liz?" Beth sank into the closest chair and continued. "Yesterday, she told me Liz called. I told her now Liz knows she's in Bridgeboro she should make a surprise visit. There's nothing like a baby to help people make up."

"Let me know if you can't find her."

They both hung up their receivers and stared at their telephones.

THE telephone rang four times before Liz picked up the receiver. "Good evening. King's Restaurant. How may I help you?"

"Hi. Lou has you back in the salt mine, huh?"

"Oh, hi. I was hoping you'd call. I want to invite you and Geoff to have dinner with us. And then Lou and me can show you the pictures from our honeymoon."

"Do you know where Evan is?"

"No. And I don't really care. I couldn't believe it when she answered the phone. She had a helluva lot of nerve coming back to Bridgeboro. I told her so."

"I brought her back. To have her baby here."

"She never told me she has a baby. She told me she was just . . . passing through."

"I don't care what she told you. She has an adorable daughter and..."

Disregarding what Beth was telling her, Liz yelled into the phone, "What kind of fool are you? Get rid of her. She'll only mess up things between you and . . ."

"Liz, just give up," Beth yelled back. "Geoff and I are nothing more than good friends. I have to find out where she is."

"I hope she left town. Like I told her to do. Is Les the father?"

"It doesn't matter. I have to hang up. I have to find her."

"Wait a minute. I told you I want you and Geoff to come for dinner."

"You're not hearing me. Geoff and I are just friends. And if you said anything that made Evan leave Bridgeboro, then you've lost two daughters. Hello to Lou. And goodbye."

Beth heard herself scream. *Damn. Damn. Damn. Where is she?*

Geoff answered his telephone immediately.

"Liz sent her away. She still thinks you and I could be more than friends. And of course Evan would not tell Liz anything about *your* secret. But I can't believe she would even listen to Liz. Other times she'd tell her to go to hell. Why not now?"

"Because Evan wants to go back to Norfolk? Or to California? Can't you find a note?"

"I've looked all over my bedroom. And the living room. Even in the kitchen and . . . everywhere." Her voice trailed off.

Geoff laughed. "How about the bathroom?"

"Okay. Hang on." A minute later Beth reported. "Nothing. Tell me what to do?"

"Since it's closer for me, I'll drive up to the apartment house. Then I'll call you back."

Geoff did not call Beth. Instead he drove to the house to tell her Evan was not in the apartment house. The manager told Geoff he had not seen Evan all day. Beth told Geoff all of Evan's clothes and the baby's clothes were gone. Evan had moved them both. Out of the house. As they looked at each other they each knew the other also believed, out of Bridgeboro.

WHILE they were discussing Julie's condition, a knock sounded on the front door. Beth hurried to the door. As she and Brad both saw the surprise on the face of the other, he blurted out, "Why is Geoff here? I was driving back from a drug store in Willow Grove and his car is in the driveway."

"I called him because Evan has left. With the baby."

"Oh. Well I wanted to know. Because. I'm sorry. I was thinking maybe you two . . . but then I forgot that Evan and the baby should be here."

"Come on in. We'll all so upset we're thinking dumb things."

In the living room, Geoff patted the couch. "Hello, Brad. Sit down. I'm sorry seeing my car upset you. We're trying to decide where Evan might be."

Brad sat at the opposite end from where Geoff was sitting. Beth returned to rock in her favorite chair. Brad faced Geoff and said, "I'm sorry I suspected that you and Beth might be . . . you know . . . my brain has been overcharged." He frowned at Beth. "Does Geoff know about me? I mean more than I was adopted?"

Beth shook her head from side to side and rocked a little faster.

"So just you and Julie know?" After she nodded he turned to Geoff and said, "Beth told me who my real mother and father are. While we up at Deer Lake Manor. Getting Julie's car."

After Geoff sounded, "Ohh?" Brad added, "Julie told her. Before she fainted." He watched Geoff raise his eyebrows. "Bill Fischer and Vicki Lynn are my parents. I'm still in shock."

"Yesss sireee. I guess it would take a while for that kind of a surprise to sink in." Geoff gave Beth a questioning look. "Sorry but I have to ask. What kind of proof does Julie have?"

"Hand written love letters. And copies of wills. In your office safe. And she and Mr. Fischer delivered Brad. In the cabin."

Geoff shook his head from side to side, blew out his pursed lips and finally asked Brad, "So, now you actually know who you really are."

"Yeah. And I guess I believe it because I called Julie, Aunt Julie. Now, I'm wondering when to tell my mom." He looked at Beth. "I was thinking, maybe you'd be with me, when I do?"

Beth hunched her shoulders. "Oh? I'll have to think about that." She directed her concern to Geoff. Maybe *he* would add some words of wisdom?

Geoff forced a laugh. "I don't know if I should say congratulations? I never expected anyone to tell me they're the son of the famous Bill Fischer and Vicki Lynn. My unasked for advice is, just be careful. I'll even add, remember not to say anything to anybody, that you might regret later.

"In fact, you might want to ask Mr. Gillon for his advice? Even I have to digest what you told me and my god, can you imagine how everybody in Bridgeboro and the literary world will react? I hope your mother can handle the news."

"She told me she's going to get a divorce. And my dad didn't come home last night." He looked embarrassed as he added, "I really am sorry I suspected nasty things about you and Beth."

He stopped as Geoff raised a hand and said, "Since this seems to be tell - the – truth - time, let me tell you in person, I love Beth Rhodes. But you do not have to suspect that she and I are doing what obviously your mother and father did. Behind Julie's back.

"So now I know who you *really* are I shall tell you what I *really* am. I'm gay. And I have a special companion in my life. Only Evan, Beth and Mr. Gillon and my family know that fact."

He stood. "Since I can't be of any immediate assistance, I shall return to my abode." He paused to smile. "If I can help either of you in any way, just get in touch."

Beth stood and stepped up to Geoff. "Promise. If Evan gets in touch, you'll call." After Geoff nodded she added, "And if you see Liz, give her a kick in the ass for me. The only consolation is, she's going to miss holding her granddaughter."

After Geoff kissed Beth on her forehead he extended his hand to Brad. Brad quickly stood and during the hand shake he pulled Brad into his arms, patted him on the back and said, "I don't know what to say except, good luck. I hope you have an easy and happy future." He winked." And I trust you."

"And you know your secret is safe with me." Brad looked at Beth. "I wish I could help you find your sister but I don't know her well enough to know what she might do. And I better go home and . . . see my mom."

The three of them walked to the screen door, said sincere farewells again, and Beth and Brad watched Geoff walk to his car.

Beth turned to Brad. "As much as I want you to stay, I know you should make sure your mom is okay. If she's still there. If I hear any news about Julie or about Evan, I'll call you. Otherwise, we'll talk tomorrow."

They hugged and kissed and hugged and said "I love you" before they parted.

SIXTY FOUR

FOR BETH, WHAT to do happened within the next thirty minutes. As she took a shower in Julie's bathroom, she convinced herself it was best she had told Brad to go home. Would she ever let him spend the night with her? In which bed? Hers? Or Julie's? In Julie's bedroom she began to turn down the spread. On the closest pillow was a note.

Dear Beth, I decided to hide the note in Julie's bed, hoping you would not find it until I got far away from Bridgeboro. I guess I always knew I wouldn't stay in Bridgeboro and then after I talked to Liz, I knew I had to leave. But don't blame her. Even though she hates me and told me to leave, I knew she was right.

I do not have the baby with me. I kept hoping I wouldn't have to name her because I never was really sure I was going to keep her. And when you name something, you generally end up keeping it. This morning after I met Brad I knew I had to give her up. So I'm taking her to the orphanage. I hope the church is open because I want to sneak her in there. If my baby gets the breaks Brad did, then she'll be better off without me trying to raise her as a single parent and who is going nowhere FAST!

It really made me feel good that Geoff was nice to me. I'm smart enough to know even though he and I can never get married, I still love him and don't want to cause him any kind of a problem by staying in Bridgeboro. And in case he doesn't tell you, he gave me some money. Lots. I used some to lease a car.

Maybe I'll let you know where I end up? I feel happy we were getting along real good. And thank you for all you did for me and my baby. Please tell Julie I appreciate all she did for me. The visit to Bridgeboro and being with you really did me good. And of all places in the world, it's where I want my baby to grow up.

I love you. Evan.

Beth began to tremble as she read the letter the second time. Each word, more carefully. Did she hope she had not understood it the first time? Did she think some of the words would change? Tears filled her eyes and curses filled her mind. Damn Liz. Damn Evan. Now what was she going to do?

Without looking at the clock, Beth grabbed the receiver and dialed Geoff's number.

The telephone rang five times before he said, "Hello? Greer here."

"I found a note. Evan wrote it." After Geoff asked, "Where was it?" she began to cry. "I decided to sleep in Julie's room and it was under the bedspread. Because she hoped I wouldn't find it until she's far away. Somewhere."

"Slow down. Take it slow and easy."

"I can't! She took my niece to the orphanage. And I'm going to go get her."

"You stay right where you are. I'm going to get dressed and come right down. Don't you dare go anywhere. You understand me?"

"I want the baby. I don't want her . . . to be like Brad."

"You do not need a baby in your life. She'll be better off if she is adopted. Just stay right there. Turn the lights on and I have a key."

IT took Geoff several hours to calm Beth down. And to convince her she was not going to drive to *The Home for Lost Lambs*. What he did do was to call The Home, identify himself and ask if a baby girl had been delivered there? Within the past twenty-four hours? The person who answered the telephone refused to give him any information. He told Beth he would ask Doc to call the next day. He was certain a doctor would be given updated information.

Finally Beth cried herself to sleep on the davenport. Geoff covered her with the afghan and decided he should stay with her. He left a table lamp on and managed to doze off, in the new reclining chair.

THE shrill ringing of the telephone in the living room jolted Beth and Geoff out of their shallow slumber. Geoff finally remembered where the telephone was. Suddenly he realized he should not be answering the telephone in Julie's house. He handed the receiver to Beth.

A weary Beth looked at her watch and whispered, "It's only four o'clock." She felt lightheaded. And scared.

"Hello?....Yes, Doc. This is Beth." She stared at Geoff's pale face as she listened to the unexpected story Doc was telling her.

Beth heard herself yell, "She did what!" She lowered the receiver and declared loudly, "Doc's trying to tell me . . . Julie . . . managed to

495

pull the needles out of her. . . hands." She allowed Geoff to take the receiver from her hand.

"Doc. This is Geoff. I'm here because Evan took the baby to the orphanage and Beth is upset. Tell me what happened?"

Geoff listened as Doc explained after checking the flow from each hanging bag and knowing the balloon still was in place, the private duty nurse went to the Nurse's Station. She wanted to refill her mug with coffee and stayed to chat. Just long enough for Julie to tear off the tape, pull out the needles and the balloon. After the nurse returned she became hysterical. And all hell broke loose.

Geoff hung up the receiver and said, "Julie is hemorrhaging again. And things are not good. We should go to the hospital. Right away."

Beth nodded. "I have to tell her I love her."

SIXTY FIVE

THE MEMORIAL SERVICE for Mrs. William Fischer was held a week after she died.

The first day afterwards Beth, Brad, Geoff, Mr. Gillon, Herb Whiteside, Brother Coleman from *The Church of the Good Samaritan* and Mr. Felty had met in the *Felty Funeral Home.* Julie's instructions became plans for the funeral service.   Finally, everything necessary was finalized.

As per Julie's instructions, there would be no viewing.   There would be a closed casket Memorial Service, followed by burying Julie in a Fischer plot. Next to her husband, William, who had been buried next to his father. Mrs. Fischer and the unnamed "Infant Girl" had been buried on the other side of Dad Fischer.   After a lengthy discussion which included a concern for enough parking spaces, it was decided to have a buffet lunch served in the cafeteria of the Fischer Company office building. For family, friends and employees.

The largest chapel in the Felty Funeral Home could not hold any more chairs. Sliding walls opened the additional two chapels into the largest chapel. The walls were lined with standing people.   Beth remembered attending the Memorial Service for Norman Rhodes, approximately two years before. A much smaller chapel had been used. Because so few family and friends attended.

BETH sat between the two people she loved most. How could she feel worried, even anxious, with Brad on one side and Geoff on the other. Not only was Geoff her dear friend, but he had the responsibility of being the corporate attorney of the *Fischer Company.* Next to Geoff sat Howard Whiteside, the recognized CEO of the company. Next to him was Herbert Gillon who had the responsibility of the Trusts and Guardianship and Wills of Vicki Lynn Phipps, and William and July Fischer.

Next to Brad was Doctor Philip Rexinger. Everyone knew how faithful he had been in his care of Julie. Across the aisle in the front row, was where Brother Coleman from the *Church of the Good Samaritan* had sat. With Julie's living brothers, Edward and Elwood Phipps and their wives.

After they had arrived from New York, the day before, Mr. Gillon had met and taken them to reserved rooms at The Fiesta Motel. Which their sister had owned. They were told they should plan to meet in the conference room of Gillon and Greer after the reception.

Sam Carpenter, and his entire family, were sitting in the rows behind Beth. She insisted they sit there. To denote their importance in the lives of Mr. and Mrs. Fischer.

Everybody present were facing the podium, while listening to Brother Coleman. He had to mention that two years before he had conducted the service for Earle Phipps, in the church. And before that, the service for Earle's sister, Victoria Lynn Phipps and his brother-in-law, the famous, William Fischer.

He read excerpts from *The Holy Bible* and finally looked up, smiled at everyone and said, "We brought nothing into this world, and it is certain we can carry nothing out. The Lord gave, and the Lord hath taken away. Blessed be the name of the Lord. The Lord be with you. Let us pray."

After the prayer he began praising Julie for her charitable contributions. He was certain most citizens of Bridgeboro knew of her support for the Bucks County Hospital and her donation for the building of the new wing of the Bridgeborough Library. Her most recent gift to the lib   rary was loaning manuscripts and important letters from the estate of her sister, Vicki Lynn. He smiled at Beth as he added that for safe keeping, she was loaning her gift from Julie, of the first editions of all of the famous author's books. He also revealed that Julie had donated the cost of a new building and new equipment to the Day Care Center in Taylor Park. Also, to the Orphanage, next to the Church of the Good Samaritan.

Beth's thoughts kept drifting. So much had happened within the previous two weeks! As she fingered the unfamiliar ring on her right ring finger she allowed herself to tune out what Sam Carpenter was saying. He wanted everybody to know how good Mr. and Mrs. Fischer had been to his family.

Daddy. I hope you're here. So you can see how many people are paying their respects to Julie. I heard there's a crowd outside too, waiting to go to the cemetery with us.

Mr. Whiteside closed the company so lots of the people are from the company. Alan and Peg have matching tummies. I wonder who is the father of her baby? I saw Mr. and Mrs. Barnes. Brad heard Jim is going to marry Jeanne and move in with the Barnes. He lucked out with a good catch.

Geoff told Doc what Evan had done and Doc went to the Home and found out Evan's baby is there. The director wanted to know if Doc could give them any information about the baby's identity? Doc told them the mother had been in good health and it was her desire her baby be adopted. He and I are going to meet with the Director in a couple of days. She is your granddaughter, so look after her!

Have you seen Liz and Lou? She noticed the ring on my right hand and had to ask me where I got it? I told her it was Julie's engagement ring. Julie left it to me in her new will. It makes me feel close to her. I told Liz I'm moving into Warrington Estates. Brad thinks he may rent Deer Lake Manor again and he and I will live together in the apartment. Until we finish college.

Also he's going to have the ruins from the fire removed. But he is going to have a marker placed under our tree, with the names of his mother and father and their birth and death dates. The Church is going to take Earle's house as soon as Brad and I finish moving all of Julie's belongings to Deer Lake Manor. And Vicki's, I mean his mother's. So far we've made three trips and made love in the master bedroom. Brad thinks of it as his father's room and I keep remembering it as Julie's bedroom. Brad.is wearing protection. We are not going to mess up our plans.

Daddy, I still believe you got me involved in this unbelievable story. When I decided to interview Julie, because she was Vicki Lynn's sister, how could I ever have dreamed I'd be in love with her son? His other parents, Bernice and Richard Livingston are somewhere behind us. Mr. Gillon and Brad and I are going to meet with them before he makes the announcement to the media. They have to be told their adopted son is the sole heir to William Fischer and Victoria Lynn's estates. Brad is worried about when his mom and dad find out whose son they raised. We all wonder if Mr. Livingston is going to leave The B.C. to Brad? If just the Livingston's had him in their wills he'd be rich. And will they stay in Bridgeboro?

Julie. Are you here? I should be talking to you instead of my daddy. Did you see your picture on the front page of The B.C.? Trickie Dickie went all out to give recognition and praise to Mrs. William Fischer, For all she has done for Bridgeboro. And the community.

Julie, I hope you know how much I loved you. Remember that day I shook your hand and said, 'How do you do, Mrs. Fischer. I'm happy to meet you'? And even though you've burdened me with your confession, thank you for letting me be part of your exciting life.

In fact I like your idea that someone should write a story about Bridgeborough. Including Victoria Lynn and William Fischer. I'm going to ask Professor Williams to help me write it. Of course, July Phipps Fischer is going to be the main character. And what a character you were!

Oh oh, Brother Coleman is looking at me. He's going to introduce me. It's my turn.

WHEN Mr. Gillon told Beth that Julie had decided she should have a turn in the sun, in front of the rich and famous in Bridgeboro and Bucks County, she tried to beg off. But after she learned what Julie had planned she do, she looked forward to Julie's request.

Looking pleased and proud, Beth stood tall behind the podium. She thanked Brother Coleman for announcing the well-known and the little known accomplishments which Julie had made during her life in Bridgeboro. However, a very important one was missing. The gift of the now recognized County Park which she and Julie had suggested be named, not Fischer Park, but Lenni Lenape Park. It would be so named in recognition of the Native Americans who had lived and loved in that local community. And all of Bucks County. After the Parking areas, the Restrooms and Picnic Pavilions, which would be named after the three tribes of the Lenni Lenape, and whatever additional facilities might be necessary, according to the local and County laws, there would be a grand opening of Lenni Lenape Park.

Holding a piece of paper in both hands Beth smiled and announced, "It is an honor and a privilege for me to be standing here. All because I decided to be brave enough to write a letter to Mrs. William Fischer, asking if I could interview her. I needed information about her sister, Victoria Lynn Phipps, pen name, Vicki Lynn, to enter an annual essay contest. To hopefully win money, which I needed in order to attend college.

As many of you know, I was not chosen to win the contest. Instead, my reward was far greater than I ever could imagine. I was given the opportunity to become a friend and a companion, of Julie Fischer. I had the privilege to live with and work with her."

Beth paused to look at Doc and Geoff. She smiled at them. Then Brad. Then slowly she ran her eyes around the rows of serious faces.

"I believe I earned equivalent to a Master's Degree in Business Administration, Committee Meetings, Assertiveness, Shopping, Meal Planning and Entertaining, Gardening, Ornithology, Researching, American History, American Antiques and Decorating, just to name the highlights of what I learned about and to appreciate, while living with the famous lady, July Fischer.

"I also learned about the true meaning of caring and sharing of one's wealth, and one's self. Instead of a chore, even a curse, living with Julie taught me, being wealthy could be a daily challenge and present lessons to be learned. And lived. Together, she and I learned not only to communicate and to cooperate but also to enjoy . . . knowing each other. And for me, the privilege of learning to love a wonderful person. I shall miss her. Forever."

AND so Beth shared the thrill of becoming a part of the life of Julie Fischer. And that she learned how much Julie Fischer loved William Fischer.

"As many of you who are attending this Memorial Service, I never had the privilege of knowing William Fischer." She paused to slowly look at the Friedmans, the Barnes, the Livingstons, and Doc. She also smiled at the Officers of the company. Then many of the employees she had met. And finally she smiled at Brad.

"Many of you not only went to high school with him or worked with him, but also knew him well enough to either envy him . . . or to love him.

I can only know him through memos and instructions. And from letters he wrote and received. And from Julie's memories. How proud she was that she alone had been his wife, Mrs. William Fischer. In tribute of her love, I am going to read a poem. Which Julie requested be read. It was one of her favorites, written by Edna St. Vincent Millay.

Time does not bring relief: you all have lied
Who told me time would ease me of my pain
I miss him in the weeping of the rain;

I want him at the shrinking of the tide;
  The old snows melt from every mountain-side,
  And last year's bitter loving must remain
  Heaped on my heart, and my old thoughts abide.
  There are a hundred places where I fear
  To go, - so with his memories they brim.
  And entering with relief some quiet place
  Where never fell his foot or shone his face
  I say, "There is no memory of him here?"
  And so stand stricken, so remembering him.

Again Beth smiled at Brad before she said, "And now let us sing *Amazing Grace* as Julie's brothers, Elwood and Edward Phipps, Doctor Rexinger, Geoff Greer, Howard Whiteside and Samuel Carpenter wheel the casket outside.

You all are invited to go to the grave site with us.""

And Brad and I will follow.   Holding hands.   It's time for us to appear together. Watch out everybody. Here we come!

Through us, you all will remember Victoria Lynn Phipps, William Fischer and July Fischer.   Forever!

THE END

www.ingramcontent.com/pod-product-compliance
Lightning Source LLC
Chambersburg PA
CBHW020246030726
47499CB00001B/74